The Lost Father

The
Lost Father

MONA SIMPSON

ALFRED A. KNOPF

New York

1992

THIS IS A BORZOI BOOK
PUBLISHED BY ALFRED A. KNOPF, INC.

Copyright © 1991 by Mona Simpson

A section of this novel, entitled "Ramadan," appeared in *Granta*.

Library of Congress Cataloging-in-Publication Data
Simpson, Mona.
The lost father / Mona Simpson.
p.   cm.
ISBN 0-394-58916-5
I. Title
PS3569.I5117L   1991   91-52715
813'.54—dc20   CIP

Manufactured in the United States of America

FIRST EDITION

For Richard Appel

"If it is miracles you are after, you must know how to wait."

—Oskar, *The Tim Drum*

The Lost Father

Prologue

WE BELIEVED. All our lives we believed, all our separate lives.

My grandmother never did. She died old, never believing, and she was the only one of us who went to regular church, with a pocketbook to match the season, at the nine o'clock mass every Sunday. She had never been a Christian until her husband died. Then she capitulated, gracefully, ending the one battle that had lasted them all his life. It was then that she began to buy hats.

There were two of us who were his. My mother and me. My grandmother respected our feelings although she had never liked my father. She made my cousin give me the cowboy suit just because I didn't have enough myself from him. My cousin didn't see the point. "Your dad's an Indian giver."

"Shht. Now do like I tell you," my grandmother finished our fight. She could be unfair and we would obey her, because she cared for our comforts. She was good to us. We trusted her.

My mother is fifty-six years old and in a way she still believes. She would say she does not but she has saved herself for him, saved herself beyond saving, to a spoiled bitter that expects only the worst. But in her private soul she is a child holding an empty glass jar waiting for the sky to fill it, for him to return and restore to us our lives. To me, my childhood; to her, the marriage she once had and threw away and will now cherish forever as some unreachable crystal heaven. It is he, she believes, who stole her glitter and throne, her money, her wings, which after all are only petals of the years.

My grandmother was always on the other side. She used herself and whatever she had for her life. Her husband was dead and to her, so was my father. There was no Head of Household. But at the age of fifty, she learned to pay taxes and to drive. She spent. We, even in our extravagance, were always saving.

Now, I can tell in children, who has that hole that is belief and which children will be children of this world. You can see it in a class of first-graders. You can recognize in a group of eleven-year-olds, the children who lose their rings and their gloves, their keys, the same children who themselves get lost in department stores, on the way to the library or to school. They are the children who are waiting, in their hectic way, for something. You can read from the small things that collect and disappear around them, the quality not of their order or disorder, but of their aspect to it. Any stranger could have seen it in me.

It depended on how quick you had an answer. I was too quick on the top but really I was infinitely slow. Our patience was tragic. We were people who could spend our lives loving one person who never cared for us.

I grew up without a father, but those years while it was happening, I never understood that it would always be that way. We expected him to come back. Any day. And then, when he didn't, my mother thought she would marry someone else and he would be the father. "He'll buy you things," she said. "You just wait and see."

I waited. There was nothing else I could do.

My mother was a young woman then; she was waiting, also, for her life.

From place to place we moved an embroidered sampler. *Row Row Row Your Boat, Gently Down the Stream, Merrily, Merrily, Merrily, Merrily, Life Is But a Dream.* She always hung it in the kitchen, usually near the sink. Sometimes she looked at it and sighed.

Once she did marry someone else. But he never seemed to either of us like a father.

ABSENCE HAS QUALITIES, properties all its own, but no voice. The colors of his absence were the blue and white of a Wisconsin sky, a black like telephone poles and lines falsely on the distance, or a tossed spray of crows. The brown of a man's old suit, bagging pants and worn leather shoes; there were traveling men, hoboes, those days, and every time we saw one across a field it was him. The yellow of a moth, the gray of sheer mountain rock in Colorado, even the dusk smell of a summer field. He was the forced empty clean of those cheap mints from taverns, green in the middle of white. That taste meant empty, like the tiled tavern my mother and I went in once during the daytime to use the phone and buy gum.

He would never know. He wasn't watching us. Days went by and years. We understood we'd never remember all we had to tell. It was just now—the elapsing of our time and lives. Nothing much. We would have left it for an afternoon with him.

There were two times. Wisconsin time and his. Everything in the Midwest was patient and had to do with seasons. Everything seemed too easy for us there. Nothing was hard. In school, for me, everything was beside the point.

I never found the faith I wanted and all along I had it. It just wasn't colored and fleshed the way I'd imagined. It was like the time my class was taken to hear a symphony orchestra. The children around me were playing hang-the-man, passing paper and pencil back and forth. They offered me a place in their game but I refused. I was following the program intently. It said two things and then *Hansel and Gretel.*

I imagined sets and capes and pink ballerinas. Choral opera vaulting into the sky.

Then the concert ended and there was an encore and people stood and left their programs on their seats. I never saw the pageant I expected.

Faith was that way. Thinner, abstract. Only music.

We wanted too much from this world.

WE BELIEVED in an altogether different life than the one we had, my mother and I. We wanted brightness. We believed in heaven. We thought a man would show us there. First it was my father. We believed he would come back and make me a daughter again, make my mother a wife. My grandmother did not like him, but I prayed for her anyway. If he came, we didn't want her to be left behind.

My mother never lost her faith in men, but after years, it became more general. She believed a man would come and be my father, some man. It didn't have to be our original one, the one we'd prayed to first as one and only. Any man with certain assets would do.

In this we disagreed, but quietly. I was becoming a fanatic.

We moved to California. I thought maybe if he saw my face on TV. That is the way I was with men. I wanted love but a high far kind that made my breath hard as if it wouldn't last.

I was ashamed of my wishes as if there were inherent wrong in them that showed and if I told anyone they would see it was my own fault I would never be happy. I wanted too much. Foolish things. But I wanted them anyway. I couldn't stop my longings. I could only keep them to myself.

It is pathetic now to remember. They were ordinary girlish toys, full of netting and spotlights, sugar and ballet. I wanted wands, wings, glittery slippers from my father. I wanted to dance while someone watched me.

"Look at me," I dared.

"Shht," my grandmother used to say. "Keep still." She settled my arms against my sides. "There now, that's better. What have you got you think is so special, huh?"

"I don't know," I said. That was the answer to everything in childhood. "Nothing" and "I don't know."

My grandmother didn't care about brightness in any of its forms. She didn't care about fancy, shining things, she had all the money she needed. She didn't care about intelligence or newness. My mother understood too that these qualities weren't any closer to God. But God would always be there like the stones in the road, there was all the time in the world for God, we could go back and pick God up, after we were young. But when a person bad-off slanted across the street, when my mother helped someone old, she would remember. You could see it in her eyes.

FOR YEARS my mother and I waited together. We had been together my whole life. Other people had come into our family, but only she and I stayed. The hardest thing I ever did was leave my mother.

The spring before I first went away, to college, we drove out to get ice cream cones at night.

I told her she might still get married. "But he won't be my father," I said. Our time for that had passed.

My mother had tried substituting once before, in Wisconsin, with Ted Stevenson the ice-skating pro, but she thought it would be different here in California, the man would be rich, someone who could give us life.

"Well sure he will. You'll see. Just wait and see."

I had waited already a long time.

"I don't need a father anymore. You don't need a father when you're twenty, Mom."

"Sure you do. Just wait'll you come home from college and want to bring the boys and your friends to a place that'll impress them a little. That's when you'll really need a father. And he'll buy you things maybe, and make a nice place for you to bring kids home to and see. Just wait. You can't know how you'll feel then. You'll see." That was her way of getting off a subject when she had to.

"I already had a father and he wasn't there."

"He wasn't there for me either," she said.

"I don't want one anymore."

Then, later, she began to expect him too, but in a bad way, as a danger that could drive me from her.

MY MOTHER had always talked to me about marriage. It was her great subject because it was what she never really had. She felt she had missed the boat, so she advised me, starting when I was very young, too young to do anything about her suggestions. College, she said, college was the promising time and place. When I was a child in Wisconsin, I already knew I'd go to college. From the way she talked it was a large green summer camp where everyone wore beautiful clothes. Hundreds of good young men just walked around waiting to be picked. When I wanted things in high school, the same as what she bought for herself, she'd scream at me, you, you don't really need the clothes now, I need them, I'm the one who has to catch a man, you won't marry any of these boys you know now. You think it's important because you're in it, but it's really not. High school doesn't matter. Unh-uh. She was angry at me. I still had it ahead of me—college—she was way past that. When you'll really need the clothes and the house and the car and the everything is in college, and then maybe, if I get someone now, I'll have it all to give you.

"Marry someone in college," she said, "that's when you meet the really great kids. Find him there."

But then when I was in college, she didn't like who I found. I didn't want to marry him anyway. I used to say that I couldn't imagine a wedding because I had no one to walk me down the aisle. But it was worse than just my father. We were a carnival freak show, us. And I didn't like other people's better families adopting me either. They seemed as bad, only with money. And not mine.

I always knew I wouldn't do it my mother's way. That seemed like an old-fashioned wish. When I went to my first wedding I was twenty-two and I kept thinking that they were too young. Their faces looked round and liquid the same as always and they looked funny in their clothes. I was a bridesmaid in a mint green chiffon dress. All the rest of us were still just graduate students, or kids with promising stupid jobs. I didn't envy the bride and groom at all. I thought I'd get married late. Well, I thought I knew exactly when. I thought twenty-seven. By then, I wanted to be rich and have the Beatles play at my wedding. That was already impossible. The Beatles had been apart for years. But I still thought about it. Poor people always want things like that.

You will, my mother whispered once. I didn't really expect the things she promised anymore, but I didn't disbelieve her yet either. She always told me we were royalty really. People didn't know it, but we were. It was something we whispered about. I wasn't supposed to tell.

I always wanted to marry an architect, even when I was a little girl. It was the first idea I had about who I wanted to marry. I thought I'd be a ballerina. And the only reason I'd thought of being a ballerina was our fifth-grade teacher was trying to teach us about money. We had to make a budget. First, he wanted us to choose a profession and ask for a particular salary. He let everyone be what they said and gave them the salary they had asked for. Mine was the most in the class. I'd asked for three hundred and fifty dollars a week. "Performers make a lot of money," my mother had told me. "Go ahead and ask."

"You have to ask for what you want in the world," the teacher said. "Put a high price on yourselves and the world will probably be fool enough to pay it." He was using me as a positive point, this teacher, to teach us all to feel entitled to more than we had. But I could tell in a way he hated me. He was like the others himself. Three hundred and fifty dollars a week was more than he or any of our parents earned in Wisconsin.

Even then I didn't really want to be a ballerina. You would have to go somewhere like New York City to do that and I didn't want to go. I didn't even like practicing that much. My mother and Ted the ice-skating pro had never gotten around to putting up a barre for me in the basement. Dance was just the only thing I did then besides school. And what I was good at and cared about—marbles it used to be, and then cartwheels, a perfect, light, high cartwheel, hands sequential like the two parts of a footstep—everyone knew you couldn't ask a weekly salary for that.

An architect was a funny thing to think of, where we lived. The houses were small tract, prefabs, most of them, with aluminum siding that, if you looked from a ways away, seemed like painted wood. People from the top part of town hired architects, but anyway most of those houses were just copies from other houses in slightly bigger, more glamorous places. The people had seen what they wanted in Minneapolis, say, or Milwaukee, and then had paid to have it built with its same columns along our smaller lake here.

I didn't take ballet much longer after that year we made our budgets. When I was twelve, my mother and I moved to California so I could be on television. Even in California, my mother still never made three hundred and fifty dollars a week and I saw the world in a way much closer to my fifth-grade teacher's than he could have imagined. Still, he shouldn't have hated me. He didn't know the half of it. My mom and I ate dinner on top of sealed-up cardboard boxes every night.

Is it a fortunate or an unfortunate thing, to own a life that makes you believe in the invisible? I still don't know. Faith can come to a person slowly, like a gradual climb up a long stairs, or it can be heady and dizzying. Or it can be strong as an iron banister, never reached for or thought of at all. But the propensity for faith is inherent, like an organ or a sexual inclination. I always possessed the place for religion, but faith was unsteady in me, flitting. I didn't always believe my father existed. The sacred had no voice for me, I was sure of it. I had been listening all my life. And whose faith was more true, those who searched for it, working and strained, or those who had never thought of it at all?

WHEN I WAS EIGHTEEN I left. It is a different thing to wait with another person than it is to wait alone. But I still believed.

I believed without knowing I believed and then, the year I was twenty-eight, I stopped. When that happened I did not know if I could continue. I had lived that way, trying, for so long.

Then the world was stiller, less light. Spirit was not everywhere but a common, transient thing.

All my life I had been looking for my father. It had been my own shame. Then, the year I was twenty-eight, I found him. And everything changed.

1

I LIVED in a small, low-ceilinged apartment beneath an old man. He was cane walking, stooped and Chinese. In the elevator he stood just to my eyebrows. He seemed to be completely alone. I weighed those factors at midnight, again, as I sat by the spray of lamplight over my textbook, while the vague, indoor noises of his television fell down through my ceiling. Outside my one window, another brick building rose, like a piece of dark paper.

I was twenty-seven and in medical school. The only reason I was in the East was to read these pages. I scratched out a note to the man above. "Dear Sir, Could you please turn down your television?" I balled it up. I had no garbage can. That was another thing. To Do.

And so I went to bed. I loved sleep. I was new in New York City, new in medical school, sleep was my voluptuous sanctuary. I slept in linen closets, on cots, floors, in waiting rooms on foam-covered chairs. I slept, and could sleep, anywhere. Under a sheet, my limbs would move in the thick pleasure of being unseen. I could sleep most times, especially if I had something warm. I dressed in layers of cotton and would leave some piece, a sweatshirt or a T-shirt, on top of a radiator. Then I took the warm thing and hugged it in my arms by my face and before the heat drained out of it I was fast asleep. I did that in boys' apartments to help assuage the strangeness. I always woke up first, in the morning. I hated mornings there. They seemed so ordinary and industrial, machinery of the material world gearing up in hitches noisy outside. This life was approximate, I knew, standing at the window, whether or not there were any others.

I wanted to be a country doctor. I knew what I wanted my office to look like. It would be a room at the end of an orchard, with wooden bureaus and shelves, magnifying glasses, bird skeletons, nests, butterflies behind glass, a live parrot in a cage, an examining table with a clean roll of white paper. I would treat whole families, the migrant cherry pickers, Gypsies who came to the Wisconsin peninsula every year, and I would keep their histories in an even penmanship in lined notebooks. There would be a small laboratory at the back. I was specializing in internal medicine, but I did not want to get too far away from home. Most people in the world suffered common, eternal diseases.

I'd picked New York because I had a vision of myself wearing white bucks and a pink cable-knit sweater, holding the silver subway pole.

I lived there, but I never had a strong sense of place. I was always standing at a window, looking at the buildings and a small portion of the sky. Even when I walked in the park by the river, the trees never seemed beholden to that place. They were trees that could have been anywhere, just trees. I'd come to get my training. I wanted to use the place, not the other way around, and I approached with a kind of wariness.

My first day of college chemistry, a Nobel Prize winner who'd discovered an element, now colored on the periodic table, said into the microphone, "Look to your left and look to your right. Because two of you won't get in." He didn't even have to say get in what. We knew. That was Brown. The tall, off-handed man wasn't even a doctor. He was a scientist. The distinction hardly mattered to me then. I found my pencil in my mouth. Two others waited, sharpened, in a clear case. I had a good seat, because I'd come twenty minutes early, but for those in back, video monitors on the ceilings played the lecture. And that was the last joke he told all semester, if you can call it a joke.

One out of three wasn't bad odds. Four kids from West Racine's two-hundred-and-eighty-nine-person class went to college. Any college. And they were teachers' children. I came from a high school in California where all the mothers cared about was colleges and straight teeth. Pencils grated around me. Brown seemed full of valedictorians.

But that time I didn't last in the East. I transferred, the next year, to Wisconsin, after my grandmother's third stroke. Then, only once, she came to visit me in my dormitory room in Madison. I'd encouraged the trip. I thought she would be proud of me, on campus, and that she would enjoy the idea of a scholarly life. And she would have, but she was just too old. I saw when she stepped off the bus. She held the metal bar with two hands and her feet went off parallel, stiff coming down. She pointed to a green tin box on the curb. When my mother had tried college, she'd sent her sorority clothes home to be laundered every other week and my grandmother had sent them back in this same box, all washed and pressed. Now she wanted to do the same for me. We walked a little through campus and she nodded solemnly with a downward frown. She gripped my arm too hard and I felt glad and relieved to get her into the dormitory. I had a good room and my roommate was gone for the weekend. At the hall kitchenette, I made my grandmother the Sanka that she liked. I'd bought powdered Cremora so it would be just like at home. When I walked back balancing the cup, I found she'd lowered herself to her knees. She had her hands on the top of the bed for balance. My mattress lay on an eighteen-inch platform that somebody's boyfriend had built.

"You know what I'd do," my grandmother whispered, the skin around her mouth gathering, "I'd get a saw and two such hinges"— she spanned her thumb and first finger to show me the size—"and build a door in here." Her hand traced on the wood of the platform. "Then, if you hear anything trying to get in, you just crawl under and shut the door. They'll never even know you're here."

She worried about the window. My roommate, Emily, and I lived in two rooms. The front one had a nice window with a tree outside. Other windows in the building had security bars but I didn't want them because of the tree. I'd pushed my desk there and I scattered birdseed on the wood to lure birds: bluejays, robins and once a cardinal, skitting the meal over my papers as I worked.

I borrowed a car and drove my grandmother home. By the time we turned onto the old small roads outside Racine, she began to forget me. She could still take care of herself, alone in the house, but that was all. She was glad enough to let me go. At home, I undressed her and she went right to sleep, on her back, her nose the highest place on her.

LIVING IN NEW YORK, in the apartment with one window and the man who watched TV upstairs, I had no tree. I turned the light on first thing in the morning. But the brick wall outside, the hot plate on the floor in the closet, even the ticking pattern of cockroaches, made me know what I was there for. I felt a weakness in my neck. The book lay open to page 485. I stayed up later than I could, marking with yellow highlights, slowly and more slowly turning the pages. Getting in turned out to be the least of it.

I had nine thousand dollars in the bank. My inheritance. The

money represented a third of the proceeds from a gasoline station
my grandmother had owned. For twenty-four years after her husband died, my grandmother had dutifully driven out to the Mohawk
Gasoline Station every month to collect the rent. I had often gone
along and waited in the car. When we drove up slowly, the car coast-
ing into a slot by the high red and white pumps, the manager would
run out, fill up our tank and hand my grandmother an envelope.
Sometimes he had a bottle of chocolate milk for me and a straw. She
always paid him for the gasoline and she tried to pay him for the milk,
too. My cousins and I often collected gifts we didn't deserve because
we were the owner's children.

I kept the money in the Racine National Savings and Loan Bank. I
owned a small cardboard accordion file, where I slotted the dark
green passbook under S, for security. I kept all my valuables in that
file, my grandfather's watch and my mother's costume jewelry from
her college years. I hadn't touched the money yet and I felt some satisfaction, knowing I had more than the numbers printed in blue,
because there would be interest. Sometimes, I took the book out and
just held it.

I'd managed major expenditures without touching that. It had
been a question, when I moved, whether to come lightly and buy a
futon in New York or to truck the family furniture, my desk and the
old gray couch from the living room, the bed and green-and-white-
striped bedspreads. If I didn't keep the stuff, nobody else would. I
saved the money from my job after college at the Wildlife Sanctuary.
The salary had been small but I had no expenses. After my grandmother's fourth stroke, my senior year, I'd moved back into the
house on Guns Road.

It seemed an odd thing to do, moving half a houseful of furniture
across the country, worrying over trucks, examining the arrived
familiar things for nicks and scratches. That is the middle class: paying thousands of dollars trucking pieces of junk from one state to
another. These were not antiques or anything. But I was from the
West. I hadn't planned on my New York apartment being so small. I
was embarrassed and I didn't want people to know I'd moved all
these chairs here. There was something not young about me when I
was young. I lived in an overfull room, hitting my hipbones on table
corners.

Once when I was asleep, I heard a thump against my door just before it was light. The sky was streaked with gray and blue and a strange pale cream. I hadn't locked the door. I just forgot. That was another thing I couldn't get in the habit of doing right. I never locked doors. I reached down the side of my platform, touched the rough wood I'd shipped from Wisconsin. I thought of the hinged door. There was no hinged door. It was my own fault and now I waited on my back in bed. My mother had always been terrified and locked everything six times, even car doors. I hated that. I wanted to feel careless. I tried to be.

Later, the upstairs neighbor's water rushing thoroughly in the walls, I turned on the light and opened the door. A new phone book, the yellow pages, slumped against the wood. This seemed hilariously funny. Once before, in Madison, I'd been in bed and I heard something alive land through the window. It turned out to be a twelve-pound cat. So far in my life, for me, nothing that followed was as bad as that first gasp.

It was just morning. Nothing had happened. The old man upstairs had on his TV already and I forgave him. I even liked it. I made a strong cup of coffee and began flipping through the yellow pages. I turned to the D's. *Detective Svce* wedged between *Dentists* and *Dia-monds*. "*See* Investigators—Private," the book said. I almost didn't, but I did. All the boxed entries advertised MISSING PERSONS. After MATRIMONIAL, they seemed to be the main attraction. Some firms bragged about the numbers of unmarked cars, others claimed international service. A lot of them seemed to be run by ex–police lieutenants and ex–district attorneys. One ad said UNUSUAL CASES! DIFFICULT PROBLEMS and I turned the corner of the page back, thinking that was me, until I realized, with a funny feeling, that missing persons did not seem to be unusual.

Right then I started calling agencies. I didn't really mean to. It was an odd thing to do when I was always behind with work and sleep stole my time. A luxury meant caramel flan and café con leche at the green-lit Cuban-Chinese diner on Amsterdam. That morning, spatters of unremitting rain ticked on the window. There is glamorous and dull rain. This was dull rain.

The first detective put me on hold. He transferred me to Missing Persons. When I told Missing Persons what I knew, a sure-sounding guy said he'd be wasting my time. "You just don't have enough. It's a big country," he said.

The next one was a young woman. "Wait a minute, wait a minute," she said while I told my story. I didn't like talking about him. It reminded me of being a girl, standing still while the interrogation slanted down on me. *Have you heard anything from your dad? Do you miss him?* I felt sullen. But of course, I'd called her. Still, I said as little as possible. I answered her questions with yeses and nos. Mostly nos.

"Twenty-five hundred," she said. "That's ballpark, you understand."

The next place I called transferred me three times before anyone would listen. But then, the man seemed kind. He said hmmm, thoughtfully and somehow impersonal in a way I liked, as if this weren't my life we were talking about, but something general. "Why don't we schedule a meeting just so I can hear all the facts."

I had to ask him first, how much that would cost.

"Oh, nothing yet," he said.

He actually came to my apartment. I suppose his seeing where I lived helped me with the price. Hard as it might have been for other people to believe, I felt sort of proud of my apartment. It was the first place I'd had on my own. Sometimes I missed that: the refrigerator door yawning open in the other room, Emily clomping in, a cat draping silkily around my legs. Here, no matter how poor I was, I had furniture. I felt proud and ashamed of that, depending on how the other person seemed.

I don't even remember the detective's name. This bothers me, but when I think about him, even hard, I know I don't know it. I'm pretty sure I never even received a report from him, anything in writing. It's all vague to me, the way a casual affair might be. That's what I did instead of casual affairs my first year in the East.

I offered the detective tea and he accepted, then seemed to regret it as I clanged about my closet kitchen, bumping my hot plate on the floor, extracting two cups from their unlikely situation in the half-size refrigerator. "No storage," I apologized. The apartment building had once been a hotel and the kitchen, a linen closet. Racine's old downtown had this kind of brick building. Downtown and this kind of place meant squalor there, old single men with strange-smelling habits. The detective sat in my grandmother's coil rocker. When I gave him his tea, there was nowhere for him to put it, so he held it in his open palm on his thigh. With his other hand, he took notes on what I told him about my father. He didn't ask much. We settled on a price of fifteen hundred. Seven hundred and fifty then, the subsequent seven hundred fifty upon location. C.O.D., so to speak. I wrote out the check. I hadn't budgeted the money and I didn't want to take it out of the bank. I didn't want to use my grandmother's gas station money to do this. I just wanted to do it. Sort of on the side.

That night I balanced my checkbook. I determined to stop buying Cuban coffee from the cart outside school. I had a predilection for little luxuries. They reminded me of my mother. Gish, the only one of my grandmother's friends still alive in Racine, used to scold me for this. I should be saving my money for a house. "I myself buy Sealtest," she said. "And, I'll have you know, it's very tasty. Plenty tasty." I knew I'd never have a house.

After I'd subtracted the seven hundred and fifty dollars, I had forty left. Okay, so I wouldn't go home for Christmas. I'd stay here and work. I'd been given to understand, by the detective, that this fee represented a reduction from his ordinary schedule and also, that mine was not a job he approached with any great optimism. What little information I owned was scarce. The last place I'd seen my father was California. I didn't know if he'd held down any kind of job out there.

"It would really help if you could get that social security number," the detective said. I shook my head. I had no way of getting it. My mother said she didn't have it and she didn't want me to find him anyway. Not just for myself, the way it was by then.

The detective wore a large, square ring on his middle finger, and I wanted it. Sometimes I used to get like that with a thing. I'd never owned a ring. His would have been too big, I'd have had to wind yarn around the bottom the way I did as a child with rings from my grandmother's top dresser drawer. I'd fill my hands with family jewels and ask where each one came from, lifting them to the light by the kitchen windows. "Ugh, I don't know. I don't know where I got all such junk," my grandmother said.

The detective didn't particularly look like a detective. He wore thick-soled, tie-up shoes, the comfortable kind you often saw on college professors and legal aid lawyers. I rode down the elevator with him and walked him to the outer door. He told me when he was my age, he had lived in Queens and written a detective novel. A company called Endicott had offered to publish it. But the advance had seemed insultingly small and he had said no. That seemed to be all there was to it. "Probably my big mistake," he said.

I asked him where he lived now. Outside it was raining, silver falling in the darkness.

"Queens," he said. At the revolving doors, he put on his hat and buttoned his coat.

He remained a polite man. All that September, he returned my phone calls but initiated only two. In October, he picked up a shred of a trail in Washington State, but after a few weeks, that seemed to go nowhere. I stayed over Christmas and I guess I left a lot of messages for him then. By the third week in January, I had to withdraw money from my inheritance. Four hundred dollars. I told myself that this was only the interest. That I still had what she left me. But by then I needed food. It wasn't a choice anymore. It was erosion, life costing and wearing me back to nothing. That is the way I always was. With my mother and me, poverty was never far away. College seemed a lighter world. The other kids talked about money, even bounced checks, but none of it was real.

It took a day getting the money to where I was. I'd started too late, when my checking account was already down below zero, so I had to call the Wisconsin bank long distance and ask them to wire it to me. All the people at that bank knew my grandmother and they didn't like to hear that I needed money fast. That was like my mother.

Finally, it was all done. I walked home with a bag of groceries, a hot barbecued chicken releasing its moisture up towards my face in the cold air. It made me think of sex with a woman. I clutched the bag tighter to me. At least I had the chicken. It would last that night and tomorrow. So tomorrow wouldn't cost any money. Spent money was like that.

By February, the detective sounded unhappy to hear from me. "Yes," he said when I said who I was. He was like someone I'd slept with once. I called him on a Wednesday and then again on a Friday. He had that pause-then-all-right hello. It was dumb to call him when he didn't want to hear from me, I knew it, but I had to. I couldn't help it. Then, after, I felt worse.

When I called again the first Monday in March, he asked if I'd like a refund and he would just quit. I felt sort of stung; my hand lifted up in front of my face. Had I been that bad? Fumbling, I said that was okay, and he turned all business, getting my address again and the zip code. It wasn't the first time I'd heard someone giving up on me.

And sure enough, four days later, his check arrived, the whole seven hundred and fifty dollars. In a way I was glad to have my money again. That was something.

I WAS ALWAYS trying to find my father except when I was in love. And not too long after the detective whose name I've forgotten sent back my money, I met Bud Edison. His real name was Guy and he seemed enough. That was a year and then some time after.

I'd had boyfriends, I guess the same amount of all that as anybody, but I was never partial to the ones who were there, the ones who fixed my car and noticed my haircuts and went with me to see afternoon movies. They seemed only the people who had picked me. I wanted to pick. And the men I picked were hard to know. I understood the pain of that, I recognized it in the first froth of attraction. I knew this was how it was with my father, but then a lot of girls were the same way and they had fathers and everything.

I was twenty-seven and Bud Edison was, in a way, my first date. In the West, we didn't do that. We'd go out with a bunch of friends or sort of hang out at someone's house and then you'd get together and that was it. But Bud Edison was definitely a date. When we came out from the movie, a blind man asked us to walk him to the bus stop. We each took one of his arms. He tested the pavement in front of him with a nimble white cane. We weren't looking at each other but we were there, holding him up on both sides. Once he almost slipped and I felt Bud Edison's arm, on the other side, lifting him back up, as I did the same thing, and it was true, we were falling in love, as we waited for the bus.

When the lighted bus swam away into the dark, Bud leaned against an old brick wall and pulled me to him by my two lapels. It was very cold, night clouds held still in the sky and we felt bulky in our coats and gloves. He wore a particular kind of woolen hat pulled down and in it he looked bald and like idiot boys I'd seen on the bus to special school in Wisconsin. Just then I understood for the first time: you can love an idiot, a blind man or an ugly woman as deep as you can love anyone. He pushed me against the wall then and kissed me, his eyes closed so he reached for me by feel as a young animal would.

I was afraid to do anything wrong, so I never called him. I just waited. I counted the days between and each more day seemed like saved money. When I saw him, we did things that made New York seem like a place. I was still new and I'd stand on a street I'd never seen before and look up at the tall buildings and then back at myself. I didn't know how I could keep him.

He'd told me, "There are better-looking women than you, but no one smarter." He had said he wanted us to have children, see our mix in them. The same day, he'd looked at me and said, "That's really your best thing. The black. And those earrings." The earrings were from my grandmother's drawer, made of paste.

There are few people whose presence can equal or even contain their absence, who can maintain a daily density. But when you meet them, the music starts and you go, oh, God. It is not a matter of decision. You are along for the ride as long as it lasts. I always knew that for me falling in love would mean being toppled over, darkened out completely. There was nothing else anymore I really wanted.

By THE SUMMER, I called him all the time, late at night and said, in a weak voice, "I don't know." I was the one who always wanted more. Once, he came to my apartment in a taxi and we walked to Grant's Tomb. It was hours before light and I had just a jacket on over my nightgown. The trees swayed above us, ferny, mysterious, and it was a summer sky with full night clouds and the river. Kissing him, I could never quite get where I wanted. We knew we were young and this was the last of it.

There were problems. I cried a lot. Even when we laughed and smiled there was a trace of sadness in it. He often took a deep breath and ran the pad of one finger over my face as if soon he would have to be remembering.

I didn't really blame him for leaving me. "I want to see you laugh again," he said. After we stopped talking, I began writing him letters I didn't send. I thought if I kept my vigil, I could give them all to him someday and then he would understand.

"I'm on a plane to Wisconsin. One of my worse recurring fears, driving, flying—I even wear my seat belt now—is that I will die and no one will know—really how much I have loved you. You will sort of know but maybe doubt in time. I have loved you to the bottom of myself. It is the most valuable thing I ever had to give on this earth. Please value it."

Other letters had less sky in them. Some were pretty mean. I felt everything for him, the whole carousel of mouthing color. There were forty-three letters in all. Then I stopped writing, not because my feelings changed, but because I decided to do something else. I decided again to find my father. I had not seen my father for thirteen maybe fourteen years. Something like that. And even before, I did not know him really. I didn't know what he was like, what kind of man he was. I had never seen him as much as I wanted.

Then finally, when I was twenty-eight, I put the letters and everything I had from Bud away. I tied the papers with a ribbon in a cigar box from Boss's Tobacco and Magazine Shop. I had packages like this, offerings to my father, all over my apartment. He was why I saved things. An envelope contained two butterflies and four dried flowers with their stems from the Glacier Trail. Paintbrush, black-eyed Susan, juniper and thimbleberry. My father would have been fifty-five this year, or fifty-six. I knew because my mother always told me that they were the same age. That seemed romantic to me, like a couple of equal height dancing.

I was starting up again with my father because I wanted to end something. Sometimes I lost interest for a while, but it always came back. In a way I had been looking for my father all my life. But what I'd called looking had really been something else. I made substitutes. My efforts were superstitious. They were things I did to myself, for him. Many times I'd followed a man walking down a street until I could see his face. Then I just stopped, still.

I had to stop dabbling and wondering, scribbling on stray envelopes, and admit how little I had. I would have to take actions in the physical world. I had not really been looking for him there.

For a long time, I'd wanted to get into medical school more than everything—I believed that would be the rest. And here I was, in with hundreds of others. It didn't seem like such a big deal.

There are different ways to end a long passion. One is to find the thing you always wanted, even if you cannot hold it, to touch it once. Another is just to forget. Another, I suppose, is revenge. I never wanted revenge, for Bud Edison or for my father. I always wanted people back.

LOOKING BACK NOW, I would say, for me, growing up without a father meant a sense of extraordinarily open geographic possibility. I would look at a map of the fifty states. At school, I volunteered to clean the blackboards so I could stay after and pull down the huge maps. I imagined my father and me on a long afternoon in the thin blue air of the Rockies, a yellow butterfly drifting before my eyes, nothing else but fields and line-stemmed flowers and sheer gray rock. Our shoes sank in the loamy mountain soil, my blue sneakers with white rubber rims and white laces and his man's shoes, oblong, serious. Time hung as the butterfly, without moving at all, an arm's length from us on the weightless air.

I would spin the globe hard, all the oceans and countries streaking by in vivid school colors. I knew my father was not anyplace there.

From the way I grew up, unattended much of the time, and in the country, I had a sense of vast space, slow open land and late afternoon diminishment and stillness. When we all lived together in my grandmother's house, I would set the table, she'd peel her apron off and take my cousin Ben and me on a walk before we ate. That was like my grandmother. She always finished everything early. The walk was for my mother, too. She always looked rinsed and the two sides of her face seemed more even after we'd left her alone. My mother had changed rooms in the house since my father left. She stayed in the upstairs room she'd had as a child and she didn't like us to go in. "Knock," she used to say.

We learned proportion from walking as the light left. We circled our old grandmother, who never once inquired how we were doing in school. The brick school stood in town, far away from where we lived. It was something we did by ourselves and seemed to hold no interest for our elders. We went off in the morning carrying lunch pails. It was like having a tiny job.

From school, though, we had become regular children after all. We ran in the same kind of shoes the other kids had and we believed, as they did, in progress and all the things we could expect. Every afternoon, we rode the school bus home. I looked out the window and saw workmen high on poles, yellow helmets on their heads. I tried to believe that all the open land would eventually be strapped and bound by the nicked wooden poles and looping black telephone wires, so that someone anywhere could be found.

For me, the telephone held magic. When I lived with my grandmother, my father came alive only through the old heavy black plastic receiver. He could be anyplace and I always sat in the corner of the kitchen in the chair with the luffed stuffing coming out of a cracked

T in the vinyl. He called seven times over those years—I kept count: from Montana, Wyoming, Nevada twice, California, Arizona and Texas.

I learned how to use the phone when I was very young, soon after I learned to walk and talk. It was a secret thing I did. I told nobody. Not even my grandmother or my best friend, later, when I had one. This didn't fall within friendship. It was something else altogether. I always had a deep sense of the private.

Through all the school field trips of fun, there would be a moment I'd slip away from the bus and the chain of singsong voices; I'd walk until I found a phone book in a dusty store in Michigan, say, under the ice cooler full of pop, and I'd look up my father's name. Atassi. He could be there. Names were printed alphabetically. Other A's. I couldn't picture him though, in May, on this quiet main street, red wheelbarrows out the window already marked half-price. My father had always been different. The way he stood up straight. And then there were the letters before and the letters after. He wasn't there.

Then I changed a little. This was one more place he wasn't: Flint, Michigan. Now I could enjoy it, see it, just Flint, a place somewhere, like so many others. My day didn't matter so much anymore. The country seemed big, big. And what was I doing standing with a phone book in a store, only one dime in my pocket? Someone might notice me. I took my time walking back to the game. I saw the yellow bus perched in the distance, I heard my classmates' voices like one village on a hill, far away. Old cherry trees blossomed on the green hillside of Flint, Michigan, and fog glaciered in, surrounding the trucks to their knees. I stopped and touched the frail, cool blossoms. I didn't run. I knew I could bear whatever I was missing. I didn't want excitement then. I was saving it. For later.

Eventually I learned about 411. "Information," they'd say, or "Directory assistance." Telephones then, like cars at first, came only black and heavy. On mouthpieces you could taste other people's breath, get the shine of their chins, smell the ends of their perfume. I held the receiver in my right hand a little away from my face. I lived with a grandmother very much afraid of germs. She'd taught me, when I was little, how to go to the bathroom in gas stations and how to use public telephones. In gas stations, it depended on whether it was the kind of bathroom with only one toilet or the type that had stalls. If there was only one, you locked the door. Otherwise you left the outer door open a little, so somebody nearby could hear if you screamed. One thing my mother and grandmother agreed on was the protection of my body from men. They made me practice scream. I felt embarrassed, standing on our own back porch, no one around us but trees. Across the street Paddy Winkler cut his lawn with a hand mower. He was blind but not deaf. I sent off weak sounds that flew and landed quickly. That was the thing about there, it stayed so quiet. My grandmother stood, her hands working together on the front of her dress, mouth different with worry, whispering, "Come on now, I can't hardly hear you. Really scream so someone will come and save you. You never know who'll be in there."

I was to take toilet paper squares and overlap them on the seat, using enough so that none of the porcelain showed. Chances were, the toilet paper dispenser would be empty and so I was supposed to carry, at all times, a packet of Kleenex for the purpose. Then, under-wear down around knees, skirt held up, I was trained to balance care-fully. The full weight of my bottom should hang a good two inches above the buffered toilet seat throughout the whole operation. My grandmother had demonstrated at home. After all this, of course, I was supposed to clean up for the next person. The main thing was, I should wash my hands. No matter what, I had to wash my hands, and good. This was a time before public awareness of the deforestation of our region in North America or the conservation of paper were much considered. In fact, our small city made paper: toilet paper, paper towels and all manner of industrial paper. I still see the name of our paper mill raised up in relief on the tin toilet-paper dispensers all over the country: Fort Howard. That is the only public reminder of my hometown. I once pulled Bud Edison, dazed, into a Ladies' Room stall to see. "That's where I'm from." Racine is not a place that has produced that many movie stars or politicians.

As for the pay phones, they formed another station where my Kleenex would come in handy. I could wet one with my mouth and rub it on the plastic. But even so, I was to keep the whole instrument a few inches from my head. This became such a habit with my grand-mother that she did it even at home, holding her own, daily-wiped receiver far out from her face. This accounted for her shouting, and for her frantic "What? What did you say, I can't hear you," when she was never even the slightest bit deaf. She looked at the instrument with such expressive suspicion, it seemed she expected the plastic to respond.

I don't mean my grandmother was ridiculous. She was asked to raise children at a time when she was already old and beginning to find trouble with the simple acts of reaching and bending. She felt she had to teach me and Ben about everything impending while she still could. She fashioned the kind of cautious childhood, though, that made me seek out danger.

Over the years of my grammar school education, I called information, gave a hundred women with mother-cool voices the spelling of my father's name. They never found him. Not even the wrong one. It is not a common name. It was because he was Arab. Egyptian. I understood that Egyptian was more foreign than German or even Swedish or Polish. I knew that my hair and skin came from Egypt, but the rest of me was American. "You look like a regular enough kid to me," my grandmother said, frowning, after I'd pestered her.

Later, the phone company started charging for information. I've spent hundreds of dollars on those charges, maybe into the thousands. It was something I did absentmindedly, the way some people eat. This held an edge of risk but it was not risk. You could always hang up.

I always knew my father gambled. Twice, he had been in Nevada when we talked to him. He'd been married there, to a woman named Uta. Once, my mother and I flew out to visit him when he was a waiter in Las Vegas. The second time I saw him, we went to Disneyland with Uta and Uta's granddaughter. You might think we would have kept addresses and phone numbers, but none of that worked for us. My father disappeared without a trace. Other people, like my grandmother, deeply trusted the mails and used the telephone with determination. But we knew none of those systems bound. They broke. People could go absolutely lost. As a child I never owned stamps or an address book. I didn't write thank-you notes or anything. My mother meant to teach me these things, but there was never time. We were always so behind.

I worked in a hospital ward for money. It was a job I found through school; I was supposed to assist a man named Dr. Chase, but he was busy with his research; he studied the masoteric response of cats in different stages of sleep, spent as little time with his human patients as possible, and so I hardly ever saw him. Usually, he left me a pile of charts and I did the rounds, taking temperatures and pulses. Sometimes I drew blood and elicited urine samples. When I walked in, in the afternoon, and put on my white coat, it felt like I was entering the slow TV time of children in pajamas having sick days at home.

Once, two men in bathrobes were dealing cards at a low table in the recreation room, and that made me think again of Nevada. I didn't remember if I'd ever called directory assistance in Reno or Las Vegas and if I had, it was a long time ago.

I ran down the three empty flights of hospital stairs and heard my steps behind me like a summer school, empty and echoing. I wiped the pay phone receiver on my shirt. It was oily from use and slightly antiseptic. People had urgent pale conversations from hospital booths. First I had to call the operator for the area code of Nevada. 702. Even these numbers made me feel warmer. I dialed and then heard a metallic sound. "I'm sorry. All circuits are busy now." It was a recorded voice—you couldn't talk back. I dialed again. Same thing. My childhood wish had been satisfied. You could dial anywhere in the world quickly. But even in this country, a person could still go unlisted if he wanted to.

I gave up and did my rounds. They were all routine except the old woman from Michigan who felt pain in her chest and the girl with hepatitis, who whimpered while I took her blood. She had deep veins, hard to get in. I kept Emory's room for last. In the corridor, I took two trays from the dinner cart. I hadn't eaten for a long time, it seemed like. I knocked twice, Emory didn't answer, and so I turned the knob and set the door opening. Nothing was locked here, except supply closets. Patients weren't allowed locks. I shut the door behind me and took a sharp breath. I'd forgot how cold Emory's room always was. His desk was completely covered with toothpick boxes, paper and glue, as was the small medicine table. Emory sat at his desk holding together a new joint in his conservatorium. I swung out the tray from the metal arm of the hospital bed, set both our dinners there, and slid on top of the sheets. The bed felt good. My legs, on their own, fanned a little.

Emory was ten years older and my favorite. I always had a favorite and that was who made me like my job enough. He was an artist and a thief. He had a record. He was losing hair and graying at the same time and he had overlapping front teeth. His features seemed fastened, close together in the middle of his face. The skin was loose and blotchy, his features uneven, but he could cast a look of intent insulted torment that made him almost beautiful. He spent the day in his hospital room working, making miniature buildings of toothpicks and Elmer's glue. He was in for nine weeks, the time the state insurance for indigents allowed for his diagnosis, which was periocarditis, water around the lining of the heart. His buildings were all civic centers or temples, places of worship and imaginary factories and bridges. He called them models. His life in the hospital, he said, was not much different than outside except that here he did not have to worry about making a living. He had another six weeks.

I lifted the cover from one dinner. Steam rose with the smell of overboiled peas. It was stew.

"You always start with the dessert, that's your problem," Emory said. And he was right, I was already eating the pudding. One thing I'd discovered from years of institutional food was that a certain kind of custard survived the huge kitchens, even flourished there. The little odd square dessert in TV dinners; the airplane cobbler; I still remembered a butterscotch pudding from a dormitory cafeteria. And it was impossible to resist a dessert when I hadn't had enough sleep. This was warm custard with berries. The rest of the meal, the overcooked unapparent greens, looked bad.

"Can I have yours then?"

Emory still sat holding his toothpick joint. Then he leaned his face close and blew on it. Gently, his hands opened out and he slid the white enamel chair back. It worked. The joint held. In this small room, Emory's sketches, made with pencil on brown grocery bag paper, were taped on every wall. His own toothpick structures stood on all surfaces and on the floor.

"Take it. I, as you know, cannot stand the sweet."

"That's your problem."

"Yes." Emory twirled the flat dark-green strands of vegetable on his fork as if they were pasta. Emory was a vegetarian and he ate slowly around the meat.

I shifted a little and felt something hard underneath me. I reached and found an empty spool.

"That's mine," Emory said, grabbing it from my hand.

"I wasn't going to take it from you."

"I'm sorry," he said, already shaking his head, "but I need that."

Emory's room worked this way. Papers and objects teetered on every surface, thrilled by breeze. Needed things rose and Emory pocketed them, saved them to lose them again. As an absolute rule, he threw nothing out. Order was not natural to Emory. He accepted this. He lived in a filled world and feathers appeared in his hands, spools survived, you could see the shadows of his toothpick structures, with the air inside them. The only living thing in his room was a red full rose.

When he finished eating, I tied the rubber band around his arm and asked him to make a fist. He looked away while I took blood.

"I decided something, Emory."

"I knew she was gonna do this. I asked you just last week and you said no."

"I'm not leaving, Emory."

"Oh. So, what you saying?"

"I don't think I ever talked to you about my father. But I haven't seen him since I was a child."

"Good riddance, probably."

A knock at the door stopped me. It was a clean, hard knock, even like a woodpecker. "That's Lynn the candy striper. I like her, let her in," Emory said.

I was sitting, my legs M'ed on the bed, changing the full tube for an empty, and I thought of standing up, but Emory, I could see, was observing me and I decided to stay where I was.

Lynn pecked in on her hard high heels, hitched for a moment, seeing us on the bed, then decided, apparently, to go on as usual. "Medicine time, Mr. Sparn."

She held a paper cup of water and two pills. She was a nurse, in a white uniform. He grabbed them, swallowed quickly, and then she reversed herself, left.

"Anyway, I decided I'm going to find my father. I don't know how yet, but I'm going to really try."

"What for? Hardly nobody I know got a dad, 's a white girl hang-up. Most of them aren't worth having once you've got them anyway. Mine was nothing. Junk."

"But just to know him, to see." I shrugged. It wasn't worth arguing. "Okay, now close your arm. There. Hold it."

Emory, who was capable of great economy of movement, true stillness, began jiggling his left knee. He did that when he wanted time to go faster. That was how I could tell he wanted me to take my tubes and leave.

By then it was three-twenty. Circuits rang free. I told the operator that I didn't know if it was Las Vegas or Reno that I was looking for. I gave her the name. Residence, I said.

"I have no listing for a residence in either Reno or Las Vegas," she said.

"Okay, business," I said.

"Just one moment," she said. "I show no listing under business either."

"Are you sure?"

"Yes, ma'am."

"Spell it back to me, please?"

"A-T-A-S-S-I. Atassi," she said. "We have nothing."

The thing about doing that was, when it's over, it was still me in the hospital, hearing the same light rumble I didn't notice for a moment. It was only my life.

THE LAST PLACE I saw my father was California. My mother and I lived in a rented room with rented furniture, the two of us. We'd left my mother's husband, Ted Stevenson the ice-skating pro. My grandmother was in her house alone again. I'd wanted to go to California, even though it hurt like a shock whenever I remembered her. But then in Los Angeles, my father turned up. I'm not sure if my mother knew he would be there or not. Nobody told me much. Just one Saturday, he came over and kind of sat there, acting something like a divorced dad. We knew he was married and living with Uta in Pasadena, but he didn't bring her along that day.

My mom was getting dressed. She was still putting on makeup when he arrived. He slumped in the corner chair wearing tennis clothes, cream-colored and clean. I remember the cloth looked light against his skin. His racket was propped against his knee and he seemed comfortable on our furniture. He thought nothing of taking the best chair. He'd allegedly come to see me, but I guess I was still an age that required translation. My mother, I suppose, was easier to talk to.

We heard her knocking over brushes, things breaking in the little bathroom, which was sectioned off from the rest with a beaded curtain. "Damn," we heard and a jar cracked. My mother had a lot of sounds.

My father shouted questions to her about my progress in school.

She lied, making me sound better than I was. It wasn't just that she lied. A lot of the answers she really didn't know. I tried to make jokes, get them to fuss, prolong this rare concern. I liked being the kid of parents.

"Well, so, what's what?" my mother said, stepping out, posing, one leg bent, hands on hips.

"Why don't you let me take your daughter out to dinner? Would you like that, Mayan?" He stood up and took my hand.

I curtseyed, imitating royalty. That was something we did together, my father and me. "Do oy know yow?" I said.

She looked over me right at him. "Well, I thought we'd all go, if that's okay?"

He raised his eyebrows, then did his part. "Do I know you?" He didn't have to exaggerate. He already had an accent.

We drove in his car, me in the backseat. I was still at an age when my parents looked so big to me. As big and regular-profiled as people on billboards. Nobody else that we grew up around, even my grand-mother or the Briggses, who owned the department store, looked like that. But they did. My parents seemed glamorous, if only to me. They knew how large they loomed to me and I think they found that consoling.

"They're thinking of skipping her," my mother said, "but I don't know if that's such a good idea."

"Yes but her name is really Atassi. Do you understand that, Mayan?" My father looked over his shoulder at me. Then he steered over to the side of the road and stopped the car. "Your name is not Stevenson. Your name is Mayan Atassi. I am your father," he told me. "No one else can be that."

My name in school, on the right-hand corner of every page, was Mayan Stevenson. "Okay," I told him, with my head down so my mother couldn't see my eyes.

We ate dinner but we couldn't have dessert because my father had his tennis game at eight.

THE LAST PLACE I saw him was a Los Angeles restaurant that same year. It was the Hamburger Hamlet and I'm embarrassed, even now, that it wasn't someplace better. I've heard of divorced dads who took their daughters for hundred-dollar days. The daughter could pick out anything she wanted up to a hundred dollars. I would have wanted to eat in a ballroom with a quartet, but I never would have said so. I imagined waiters who would bring silver dishes they opened with a flourish at the end, their hands in gloves. Me in an ice-blue gown and long white gloves. I wanted my father to give me a velvet box, with a ring inside. I thought that would make me feel like his daughter.

I was never a fancy child. I didn't have velvet slippers and sequiny things. I didn't put my hair up different ways. I was always too embarrassed to be that. I wanted to be but I thought if people looked at me that way they'd laugh. It seemed like they had laughed at my mother once long ago before I was born, and that was when she sealed up herself and learned to shrug and just say, they don't know, they don't know at all, these people around here, what I have in me.

It was only a weekday morning and I was sick. So far in California, my mother had left me alone when I was sick. She had to. She had to go to work. But now, since we'd seen my father that one time, she wanted to call him.

"Don't," I said. I really didn't want her to. I didn't know him that well. He seemed like too much work.

"If he wants to be your father, let him do what fathers do for a change."

"Don't. Please."

But then she called and he was coming and I had to get dressed. I already understood that you had to look nice for men. Any time. It wasn't like being at home with women. I fought on tights and shoes. Standing up, I looked normal but I felt sick at the back of my neck.

It was a weekday morning and so I guess he wasn't working. He hadn't really told us. My mother figured Uta was supporting him. "Are you kidding, why else do you think he's with her?" I waited, dressed up in my best dress, collapsed in our corner chair. I felt like being in bed, not hot and dressed up, the comb pressed through my limp, sick-day hair. But also, I knew I'd better not miss a chance with my father. I couldn't tell how many more chances I would get.

My mother was gone by the time he arrived. I unlocked the door and let him in. "Hungry?" he said, standing there. His keys dangled off the end of his right hand.

We drove to the Hamburger Hamlet my mother and I went to all the time for dinner. It was an odd time of day, though. And my father asked the hostess to give us a booth in the bar. I'd never sat in the bar part before. TV voices were mumbling in the background and we sat in the dark. I kept an empty place on my left side. I didn't know where to put my hands, with my father. They seemed wrong everywhere. I sat on them.

"Coffee black," he ordered like my mother always did. They said it with a kind of air. Coffee with milk was tawdry, something housewives drank.

Now that I am grown up, I understand how hard it is to talk to children. Sometimes you just want relief. But he and I, we didn't light up once that day. I was too tired to help him much. Usually I helped. Then he drove me home and left, telling me to lock the door from the inside. I heard his shuffling footsteps on the landing, then his car, and I took my good clothes off, not hanging them up, leaving them like petals just where they dropped, and fell nude and slender and hot under the quilt and slept. It was a quilt my grandmother had made on her gray living-room carpet. I'd helped her measure with my hands and tied the yarns.

That was the last time I saw my father. It was a weekday in 1970, in Los Angeles. It took me a while to understand that that was the last time I would see him. I don't think he knew this at the time either.

Three weeks later, we hadn't heard from him and so my mother called the number in Pasadena he had written down. The operator told us it had been disconnected and there was no new number. I called 411 for every city and town in southern California. None of them found him either.

I decided if I ever saw him again he would not be my father, but just a man.

AFTER THAT ONCE, it went back to the way it had always been. He lived everywhere and nowhere. He could come back, any day, so we had to be ready all the time. We lived like that, jangled, for years, looking over our shoulders, feeling nervous and watched, expecting. We tried to have everything about us look nice always but we got tired. It took too much effort. When he came, we knew, we had to be there and open the door. We would not get a second chance. And on that day, he would look at us and judge. It was like a surprise inspection. My father was like God. He seemed always to be watching. You'd think it would have made us neat and proper, organized, prepared. But we felt defeated. We were only ashamed.

I did certain things for him. And I guess they had to do with pain. I was afraid I would forget. Especially when our life looked normal. Once before, my mother married a man and we lived in a house on a road with other low houses, Carriage Court. I stood outside and the sky was immense and our garbage cans stood dented by the garage, our lawn tools, like other people's. That was when it was hard to believe. So I touched my tooth in a certain way. I bit my inside cheek so it bled.

I felt an attraction to fire. Always. I took matches from anywhere that offered them. And then I'd go outside alone and light them one by one. I tried to make them burn down as far as I could, so there was nothing left when they went out. For no reason. I came close to burning my fingernails but I never felt it. A lot of the days and nights of my childhood were spent that way, doing tiny things that I couldn't really explain to anybody else. I'd stop when I heard the train go by, its rush of air like wings.

I used to burn food. I started that in the far yard by my grandmother's house when I was a child and I did it, even in California. I liked the way different things burned. Once, at my grandmother's I burned a Rock Cornish hen over a garbage tank. We had a fire and other people were roasting hens and corn on the cob to eat. Everyone had been out for hours raking leaves and now there was the burn. I watched until I was alone and then held my hen on the stick over the fire. I did what the others had but I never took it out. First it just went orange and slick, then it turned dark like caramel but still shiny and that was when it was smelling in a curl high up to heaven, but then it got harder and tight, the skin close to the bones like an old face. Finally it flamed. All the while a transparent banner was lifting, the odor, I felt I was feeding the sky. Once it was pure flame it cracked and popped, a shot of liquid struck out and singed the metal, and it burned itself out, still the same shape and I saw it, like a skeleton, the same thing, but like the ribs of a house, no walls, and then the carbon collapsed and one round ash rose into the air. There was nothing like the smell of burning meat in the night country air. It seemed to feed something invisible and high.

I had rare capacities for concentration, but always for the wrong thing. In school, I couldn't really pay attention. All our exercises seemed small, everything on paper made up. I think they thought of me then as a normal kid. They didn't know. I fasted. I was the first anorexic in America. I made it up myself. All my girlfriends dieted too but I possessed more discipline. It entered me like the spine that had always been missing. I was growing up without order. We had no rules. My mother meant to, but we were always too far behind. So when I made the promise to myself I kept it, absolutely. I'd burn a whole meal and smelling it disappear into the sky was almost the same as eating. I could step into a bakery and distinguish the chocolate and the glazed caramel, the soft bland sweetness of the buns. That was enough.

Once, I went to a fund-raising benefit for the Racine Public Library's refurbishment. Marion Werth, our librarian, held the sides of the podium and read a speech about the history of Racine, the French fur traders and Menomenee Indians coloring the clear river waters with war paint and open blood. It was my fifth day of eating only lettuce and raw cow corn. My mother would cut a head of tight iceberg into four. We'd sprinkle red wine vinegar and salt on it and stand there eating in the bare kitchen. She was always dieting too. It was May and on the way home from school, I just walked through the cornfields, picked the small fresh cobs and stood there eating them. I was ten. Nobody watched those fields.

Each plate at the benefit was supposed to cost a hundred dollars. But nobody had paid for me. Our eight-plate table had nine people. The Briggses bought a whole table for the department store, and at the last minute they invited me. Emily and I were supposed to share a plate. A Black Forest Torte, intricately layered, waited at the center of the table for Marion Werth to finish. We knew it was a Black Forest Torte because there was a little cream-colored card propped there, calligraphed in brown-gold, that said so. Everyone said Marion Werth wrote only with fountain pens and brown ink. Uniformed Catholic High boys, holding polished silver cake servers, stood stationed by each table. The one by ours slipped his into his pants pocket. The fancy end stuck out. Emily Briggs at that time had a weight problem. She was short-legged: "long-waisted," she herself called it. She was wearing a blue party dress, and her graduated pearl necklace. Finally the audience was applauding, Marion Werth ducked into something half a curtsy, half a bow and then Catholic High boys bent over tables to cut the fancy cakes. "Two please," I heard Emily ask for. Then our small plate was jammed with two large slabs of the thing, one with a huge pink frosting rose. Our plate was so full a side of one piece went over the end of the china. You could see the layers—the middle one seemed to be cream with whole cherries suspended in it. I bent down close to it. I tried to get the smell. There was some bitter chocolate, a high shrill cooling scent like mint.

I promised myself I wouldn't eat it, but I'd never seen a cake this fancy. My grandmother was a baker, but you needed contraptions to make a cake look like this. It was the kind of cake I'd imagined I'd eat at the big city restaurants I'd go to with my father. I wanted to take the piece home to my mother, to somehow save it. But they had cloth napkins and Emily already had ours on her lap. I didn't have a purse.

Emily took a bite and then another. She looked around and then whispered to me, "I got two pieces, one for you and one for me, so eat some, okay?"

I picked up a dry fork and fingered it down to the prongs, but I didn't touch the cake.

"If you don't eat this, it'll look like I took two just for me." There was horror in her voice. She was begging. She wiggled on her seat, shifting weight from one buttock to the other. She squirmed in pinned misery. Emily felt watched, too, not by one high being but by everyone low and close, the teenage boys at every table.

She kept eating and pleading. "They'll think I'm a pig!" She looked near crying. Her urgent whispers didn't stop. Neither did her fork. I guess she thought however much she ate would look like less on our plate. I wanted to help her. My fork scrolled the air, my wrist shook, my mouth filled with spit that felt sweet and fattening itself. But I couldn't. She was temptation. You couldn't listen to other people. If you did you would get lost in the world. You had to keep the promise. The bad changed itself into pleading faces and good reasons, but as soon as you bent to them, they disappeared, forgetting, and you would lose your course forever. Eating was eating, no matter why. I wanted the cake so water rose from my throat and fell back again in poignant trickles like nostalgia. But I felt commanded not to eat and I didn't, as if a bar of metal lay in my mouth.

She had gone through a piece and a half and was still working.

My cousin Hal was one of the servers. He bent down behind us, looked at our plate, moved a hand across each of our backs—that stopped Emily, fork partway to her mouth with a whole cherry on it—

and said, "Oink, oink," and then she did start crying and it was too late, there was no explaining and she would never forgive me.

At my least I was sixty-seven pounds. I went into Bellin Hospital first and then they put me in Brown County. But my mother encouraged me, sort of. She wanted me to be thin.

I was ruined before I ever had my chance. And blame is everywhere and nowhere, pollen in the wind. I was dry now. My period was never much. The doctors said they didn't know; it may come again, it may not.

And Emily Briggs turned out beautiful, tall and long-legged.

WHEN I WENT to work in the hospital at night, I bought something to eat on the way. I liked kimchee. It was strange-smelling and hot and it felt like the kind of food that cleaned you out and burned more calories than it was. I got a pound of it at the Korean market across the street from the hospital. I ran streaking across then, it was almost dark, and I felt the water-swelled air in the loose arms of my hospital coat and all the lights—the green traffic lights, the gel of fuzzy deep yellow taxi beams, blue-spilling store signs, red brake signals— seemed to acquire weight and substance jingling on my wrists like transitory jewels.

I was becoming a doctor because going to the doctor's office as a child meant going downtown, to the city part of where we lived. There, on Monroe Street, the office held a kind of clean peace. Music came out of the walls, we waited in rooms full of shiny, expensive new magazines. We felt rich and clean. Our grandmother had scrubbed us carefully beforehand, using the rough corner of a washcloth for our ears. She seemed timid, holding her purse, facing the doctor.

"What do you hear from Adele?" the doctor asked. My mother was gone a lot then. Before we moved, she'd take off for California by herself and leave me with my grandmother.

"Nothing, why?" My grandmother looked up at him, curious, but curious the way someone is, prepared for pain.

"Just wondered. Great girl, Adele. Spunky."

"Not a thing, I heard. I haven't heard a thing."

Doctors' offices seemed to make even my mother feel she had to behave like other people. Later, when we lived in Los Angeles, it was the one place I could count on her kindness. Sometimes I would get candy, a slow lollipop that lasted hours until the white string came out bare and stained with color.

The hospital I worked in felt so different from those clean offices.

Now, my mother tells me, I wouldn't recognize her anymore. I have lots of gray now in my hair, she said, with a little falling laugh. I've stopped taking it out, you know, dyeing it.

I try to imagine it hanging, pewter-colored, the same hair, just the same.

I want my mother to have whatever limited happiness she can still find on the earth.

We had been through something amazing together. Our drive west, our life alone, without other people. We had been to such heights maybe nothing in either of our lives again would equal. A violent intimacy full of animal sweetness, rage, diamonds of light raw sun, blooded fur, a mixing of spit and tongue.

We have been, ever since, too dull. As if our life then spent the most of us.

BEFORE I LEFT the hospital for the night, I walked to Emory's door. I turned the knob, heard the thick metal apparatus crunching and stepped in the cold gray room. He was on his belly on the bed, clutching his pillow the way he did when things were worst. The room smelled wet and dim. The blinds weren't drawn and light from outside cornered in.

"Do you want company?"

He waited a moment before answering, as if reviewing hope. "No."

"Can I get you anything?"

"I should be alone."

"Have you taken your medicine?"

"No."

"Should I make you, Emory?"

"Not now, Doc. Just leave me be."

Other people would have made him, doctors, the candy striper Lynn would, I probably should have, but I left Emory as he was and stepped out, leaving him to one of his nights. The days after gave his best hours of work. I knew this cycle, instinctively, from my childhood with my mother. I could remember the watery, just-born cast of the world, as if it were always Sunday morning, with new irises, sharp-pointed, deep purple and frail papery yellow, after one of those nights. Then, the same red terror ran in both of our veins and we were on the long bad ride together.

I left with my carton of kimchee, eating the end of it. Outside it was warm. The dark seemed to carry water sounds. Okay, I'm out, I'm done, I thought, and the moisture lipped my skin. A streak of fear ran through me as I bent down to unlock my bike, already thinking of being home in my apartment, whom I'd call, what if Emory woke up bad and I'm not there.

All you have to do to become somebody's God is disappear.

2

I CALLED THE FBI.

First I'd started a letter to Marion Werth, who worked at the Racine Public Library. All my life, she had stood behind the main desk and stamped my books every Tuesday afternoon, small-eyed, quick-fingered, interested. She was a tall woman with red curly hair and freckles, who wore a suit each day in a different color. She wore primary colors, no prints, and each with matching earrings and accessories. She had six in all. I'd counted. She was the aunt type. She took an interest in every kid's personal life and she tried to instruct us with books. I knew her because she had taught me how to pin and label my butterfly collection. She felt glad I read—not that many children in Racine did—but she didn't trust me, because I wouldn't sit on the chairs.

For all her size, she moved with a dainty grace. I would have bet anything that she had never, even at ten years old, been a tomboy. Nothing I could do with my legs felt right. So I crouched in the stacks, leaning against walls, dustying my school uniform on the floor. My grandmother didn't mind. It gave her something to do. Keeping me clean.

Every Tuesday night, Marion Werth led a group of Racine women in a club to build their family trees, placing names and pictures in little oval circles of cardboard cutouts. One of the women embroidered hers. Each of them did it her own way, some with felt and sequins and all manner of millinery ornament, others with colored construction paper and scraps and scissors. One nun I knew—Sister Mary Bede—meticulously scripted hers in tiny letters on a single piece of eight-by-eleven paper. It was just like her. Tidy, not wasting. My grandmother's friend Jen represented each relative with a different dried flower. The men got spikier plants, mostly thistles and cacti. She pressed them all behind glass, the flowers and names and labels—birth dates, death dates and some handwritten descriptions, like "such bright red hair they all said" or "never married. Funny" or "he drank and the wife ran around, it wasn't so good." She pestered my grandmother to join, but my grandmother wouldn't budge. "Uchh, I know who they are already. There's no one fancy. What do you think, you're going to find a queen or a duke in there, Jen?" My grandmother sat down at the kitchen table every night for an hour and answered letters from her relatives, but in a different way. The club women each wanted something. My grandmother's letters mostly contained Wisconsin weather. Sometimes she would mention the name of a bird she'd seen.

The club women traced and traced, through the mail. They all hoped for some tie to the Revolution or at least to some great family, with a coat of arms or its own tartan plaid. So far, none of them had found much. When I flew home last time, my second Christmas in medical school, I saw posters stapled on the nicked old telephone poles announcing a public library exhibit of the Family-Trees-In-Progress.

I'd never liked Marion Werth that much—she didn't like me—but I'd always respected her. She was famous in Racine for her organization and her cheerfulness. Her plump hands and long freckled fingers and always elegantly filed and polished nails. Her fingers, in particular, expressed an exquisite febrile sensibility. They were creamy-colored and very nimble. She was our career woman. In a town that size, people were famous for preposterous things. Everyone knew about Katie Maguire's jelly donuts. Or Dolly Henahan's handmade silk felt on Styrofoam Christmas tree balls. If you were fat and neat you would be known for that, but not if you were just neat or just fat.

I stopped halfway through my letter. I never thought much of the mail. It seemed to take too long and I didn't have the patience. I was like that then. I couldn't wait the normal time and then I ended up waiting forever.

There had to be a better way, I figured. Faster. And so I called an old boyfriend. I was still young enough that, when in doubt, I'd call an old boyfriend. My mother used to tell me how someday we'd own a house. We'd buy it for almost nothing, she said, because it would be a fixer-upper, and all her admirers would come around, and when I was a little older, my boyfriends too, and instead of taking us out to fattening meals, they'd drop over and do something useful, like paint a wall or fix wiring.

This was the guy I'd been with in college. I used to call him The Prosecution. He worked for the Justice Department now. I always thought if I were a lawyer I'd be defense. I feel too guilty myself to be that sure.

"I don't have much access," Paul said. "He wouldn't show up on my file unless he had a federal felony conviction." That seemed above even my father's abilities. But he typed the name in anyway, while I waited. I was kind of surprised he remembered it without my saying.

"Nope," he said.

"Good."

"You're right, good."

"I guess good."

"You're still nuts." Then he suggested the FBI.

I didn't want to call then. Not right away. I am not exactly an unarrested person. I have a record somewhere, they pressed my thumbs in ink, marked them on a paper form, took my unhappy picture. And this was not for anything hip, like drugs or a protest march either. It's something old I'm not proud of. That's when you're glad how big and sloppy a country this is. When you are part of the mess. When it is you wrong, you want history to lose its beads and forget. And you can calm some knowing it will. My record is in some colorless file cabinet somewhere. It might be as hard to find as my father.

And from what little I knew about him, I didn't guess my father would be pleased to see FBI men at his door either. He could've been a petty criminal, something of a gigolo. My mother once said he'd run off with a department head's wife. Or was it the daughter? He might have been almost anything then. Not good, I thought. But not unforgivable either.

I didn't want to call, but it came down to boredom and studying one day and there I was still safe at my desk, the book glaring, picking off a dry geranium opening the whole astringent garden of smell. I was supposed to go to a party later and I didn't really want to and I shouldn't have, I was so behind, but I thought I really had to, I said I would, people would be mad if I didn't. It would be all the same people. In classes, we hated each other, every day. But then at parties everybody got drunk and told all kinds of things. At the last party, a forty-year-old woman came up to the guy I was standing next to and said, "I really have problems with you, and now I'm going to tell you why." The parties began in one apartment and then rumors started that everyone was going to another apartment on the East Side. And from there the party would divide and congregate again downtown. I never made it past the second move. I probably didn't stay long enough.

I left before midnight so I could take the subway. I only had two real friends in New York, Timothy and Emily, and neither was from school. Emily was from before. She'd moved to New York after I did and she'd just started working at the Metropolitan Museum. Her father knew somebody there.

Three afternoons a week, I worked at the hospital, for Dr. Chase. Mornings I had classes and the rest of the time I studied or meant to. Memorized. Did you ever want a letter in the mail or a phone call or a stranger at the door, anonymous flowers—some touch from the outside to change your life? If you haven't, try reading Robbins's *Pathology*.

I called information.

"What city, please?" the operator said.

I didn't know where the FBI was. Everywhere you didn't want them. "Washington, D.C.," I said.

"We have a local listing, ma'am."

I got a nice-sounding woman and I told her what I knew.

"You don't know me but I'm looking for my father who's been sort of missing for a long time. The last time I saw him was 1970. You probably can't help me but I wanted to call because I hoped at least you might be able to tell me what to try."

She laughed a laugh, not funny. "I'm the wrong person to talk to. I looked for my father for five years and even with my job I couldn't find him. I gave up. But usually, we usually tell people to call the Salvation Army."

"The Salvation Army? Why? What do they do?"

"They run shelters all over the country. Lot of men on their own end up there."

In college, I'd bought a desk from the Salvation Army. It had cost ninety dollars and was the nicest thing I owned. Three men worked tying it down to the top of my car. When they were through, I had to climb in the open window. They'd roped the doors shut. I remembered their faces, nude, capped with wool hats. A roundness poured into their features when they realized the mistake. Their noses seemed too big then. They looked to their hands. They seemed used to trying and getting it wrong. I bellied in as fast as I could to show them it was okay. No problem.

"I don't think my father would be there," I said. "He was a college professor and kind of a gigolo. He did things like run off with the department head's wife or something, but I can't see him that down and out."

"No, doesn't seem likely, huh? I don't know what to tell you."

She talked more. She had never seen her father. He'd left when she was six months old.

"Did you look in phone books for him?" I'd never said that I'd done that, to anybody.

This woman could snort without its being derisive. "That's the first thing you do." Everything about her voice was soft.

"Oh." I thought of sights: the Grand Canyon, monuments, space. I'd never seen those places. I pictured Mount Rushmore, a handkerchief of moths turning around Lincoln's sandstone face. A person could be anywhere in this country. A nation full of privacies, jangling.

"I tried everything. And with my job you know, even then, I couldn't. But my father wasn't born here."

"Mine either," I said.

"I didn't have much to go on."

"Where's yours from?"

"He's from Jamaica. Negril Beach." She said that as if it were a sorrow. "But he left my mother when I was six months old. He worked for the railroad then, I don't know, maybe he was a porter or something. Once I even called the railroad union but they didn't have anything."

"No?"

"No."

"That's the kind of job I guess you might not keep forever." I was just talking. I talked too much then. I guess I'd meant how the railroad lines dwindled in our lifetimes from something that started grand, with tablecloths and chandeliers, observation cars for the night sky. Now the trains went practically like buses. It was less an idea than just something to say.

"He's Jamaican," she repeated, as if that explained something. "I imagine he was a porter or a conductor. Or maybe a cook."

I thought of the white gloves and brass shined buttons and I knew she had pictured them too until it was worn out for her, and she could get no more from it. "Are you married?"

"I'm a widow."

"Do you have any kids?"

She paused as if I were asking too much and I was, I knew I was, but then she said, "One son. I have one son. Look, I'd like to find him too because my mother's dead and there's nobody else there, but, I've been through a lot of therapy and after that it doesn't seem so important anymore. When somebody does that to you, it makes you feel worthless. When they leave you. And when you understand that you're not worthless, then it doesn't matter so much anymore."

"I know," I said and I sort of did know too. "I mean our fathers are probably not swell guys."

"No, I don't think so. They're not." Her voice lifted a little.

I took the phone and moved off my chair. I sat on the floor. That felt better, my back against the heater.

"I don't know what to tell you. It's hard to find somebody. I even called people with his same name in the phone book."

I stopped. That had never happened to me. I never found the same name.

"Did you learn anything?"

"Nothing. I don't know what to tell you. I suggest you go to a therapist. I gave up. But it took me five years. And a lot of therapy. Lot of hard work with a therapist."

"Is it an unusual name?"

"No, it's a common name."

She told me. Though I'd given her no reason to, not really. Her name was Venise King. She didn't ask me my name at all, and I hadn't told her, so even calling the FBI there would be no record, unless they kept track through the phones. And I doubted that. To do that would cost too much money.

She was black. Her father had been a porter or a conductor or maybe a cook. He'd worked on the trains. Was I somehow pulling rank when I said I didn't think mine would end up at the Salvation Army? Or did she pity me my scrap of vanity?

But mine was not a common name. I felt guilty and relieved, as if we'd both opened our folded lottery papers at the same time and hers was the one with the X.

HER FATHER might have had reasons. My family was not even disadvantaged. My mother's family was regular middle class, upright, self-supporting, with savings in the bank and a cellar full of canned goods. She grew up with matching sweater sets and a red ukulele. I'd always been told my father's family was royal over there, one of the nine richest in Egypt. I was poor but that was because my mother bought too many dresses.

My father had never been in any war, either ours or over there. According to the encyclopedia, they had military coups every couple of years during the fifties and sixties. But none of the upheavals seemed to deprive my father of anything but money or even once, that we knew of, to see him into uniform. We escaped the world's public trouble. But then, far away from everything in Wisconsin, we made our own.

Once I met a man who was Indian and had grown up in boarding schools. People were too busy to raise their own children, he said. They were building the new nation. But I doubted that my father saw himself as any part of the New Egypt.

And my mother paid no attention to public life whatsoever. She had never even learned to read the newspaper, except for her horoscope. It was a habit she could not sustain like so many others. We felt far away from the people sitting at the table making up rules.

My grandmother had a working sense of community. The way she saw it, we made the fabric of the many. "Just be glad you aren't—" my grandmother used to say, filling in the blank to give the necessary relief, the way she'd match a purse to a dress.

There were fathers and daughters whose separation meant honest tragedy. For a long time I tried to believe we were that. But we were not. "He walked out on his own two feet," my grandmother used to say.

· · ·

THAT SAME WEEK I had to fly home to see my mother. I was really mad. I hadn't been speaking to her exactly and then she called and said that word. Cancer. It wasn't the first time. Of course she was crying. It took nothing to set my mother crying. Crying was nearer her natural state than repose. Something had to trigger her to stop.

She'd called me late on Wednesday and it was a holiday weekend, so the flight cost a fortune. Nine hundred dollars. I was mad at myself for minding but I couldn't help remembering all those other times flights were in the paper, a hundred and thirty-nine dollars each way. Poverty doesn't make squalor but it does let you see it in yourself.

She was going to have to have her insides cut out and she wouldn't get her period anymore. "They say after, your hair goes gray and I don't know, you just age," she said. She was going to need chemotherapy and radiation, she told me. That sounded really bad. A full hysterectomy. "I just don't want it," she said. "I don't know if I'll even feel like a woman anymore, honey."

All this time, I had been trying to get away from her, but it chased me, something, I couldn't get free. For one thing, she was in trouble. The convalescent hospital she'd been working for had been closed. There was some kind of investigation. I didn't think she was working and I couldn't see how she would be able to afford her life. She didn't tell me much, she just hinted. I hated thinking about it, I was afraid to let myself imagine what would happen. This had been going on for a while now and it would probably go on a long time.

That Thursday I left the hospital early. I forgot about finding my father. My mother had already stopped it so many times in my life and now this. But she didn't even know. All she knew was she was getting her femininity cut out.

It was a wind-bright autumn day, changing, and I needed to get home and pack. Four o'clock light gilded the city behind me, all points and towers. My block still seemed a quiet forgotten neighborhood subject to a different lower light. At the corner, a wrought-iron fence protected one small churchyard and a poor row of flowers. The walls of the stucco church curved out convexly and all the windows were boarded with green shutters. The stucco took on a violet hue. I didn't want to go. But I never liked to leave anywhere.

I packed and dressed and carried my old suitcase with me. In the elevator my upstairs neighbor stood with his cane. It was reddish wood, silver-handled. At the ground floor, I offered to help him with my arm.

"I don't need," he said. We walked together outside. "Cane just for looks. New York everybody push and shove, steal my taxi. I use cane, the people they just look and say oh-oh old man, and they very nice. Keep away."

A film was running at the Pleiades Palace, where I stopped on my way, and I pushed the heavy velvet curtains aside to get to Timothy, sitting on a high stool by the ticket booth. He had a tiny light there. He wasn't watching, he was reading a big-print book.

"So it's cancer again?" he said, looking up.

We just stood there a minute, the words and pictures moving below us like an outside rain.

I COULD IMAGINE her doing absolutely anything anywhere. It seemed to me on the plane that day that whatever you imagined was true when you knew someone deeply enough. You can see them many ways they will never be and still, you are right—it is true. When I was young I used to mimic people, but that is not what I mean. I am not talking about imitating a tic or a limp or a way of talking. When you know a person to the bottom, nothing they do can ever sur-prise you.

Your understanding of them is not bound by the limits of time or geography or circumstance or luck. I know my mother in prison, if she is never in trouble, never caught, I know her in bed, though I have never seen her with a man that way and what I know is not what she has told me. I know her married safe with money, though that will not happen to her anymore in her life, it could have, and I know the generous luncheon parties she would have given, frantic with flowers.

We all own many existences besides the material one we are occu-pying now. But what I am talking about is not reincarnation. Because each version of ourselves, each possible manifestation, lives around us, like a circle of our own children, apparent to those who know us best.

You can probably know a person like that once or twice in a life-time. I hope it will happen to me again, with a man. I've sometimes, for a few moments, thought I was close. It seemed different, then, with a man, the way I love. But now I think that silvery quality to it, that solitary gasp, is not knowing a person. And that the way I know my mother is deeper than gender.

Perhaps families of six or eight children get more. Or maybe my mother and I had something wholly extraordinary between us, with our clairvoyance. But I could stun my mother. She never knew me the way I did her.

I wanted to picture my father those ways. I tried to. Because my father still could have been anything. I tried to see him rich, in a suit, showing me down the machine aisles of a factory he owned. I have been in factories and office buildings, but I couldn't see him there. I could see other people I'd met before in the world. I tried to picture him a bum. I couldn't really do that either. My mother and other people too had always told me he was a man with women. I tried to see that. Him in bed with a woman, lifting up under her hair, his ministrations. But I couldn't. What I saw wasn't him. All I could do was substitute other men, men I'd known.

I tried teacher, doctor, politician, traveling salesman, driving. Nothing would come. All I could sense was a presence stationary in a chair, me stamping around the room in white, accusing, his face a still draped rag, showing no movement as I accused without time. He would never be as real on this earth as she was, even if I did find him alive.

In six hours I was at the place where my mother was. LA. Somewhere I couldn't save her. It was hot. Overpopulated. You knew just as you stepped off the plane. A kind of soot seemed dispersed in the air. I came out and looked over the expectant crowd of faces like so many balloons. Always, walking out of an airplane even if I knew no one was waiting for me, I couldn't help but look.

She wasn't there so I kept walking with the line that seemed to know where it was going. Maybe she was at the luggage conveyor. I'd brought only carry-on. But she wouldn't assume that. She always came to see me with two huge perfect suitcases too big to carry.

When she wasn't there at baggage claim, I ran to a phone booth, paged her, all the while looking around, worrying I was in the wrong place and wanting to get out. Then I just gave up and didn't care anymore, like dropping a piece of paper. I was going to be in the airport for a while.

It was a freak show, LAX. People looked like demons in their clothes and their hard hair.

I stood at one of the doors, just outside. My mother was getting her femininity cut out. The palm leaves, high above, moved just a little, up and down in the sooted heat. In the distance I could see metal fences, random concrete, long lots of cars with strings of little plastic flags and the curved big freeway on-ramps.

Finally, the white Mercedes screeched to a stop. She didn't see me yet. She was all out in one jerk, standing with her hands angry on hips, surveying the world. She looked the same, straight up and down, with sunglasses. I took my time, my jacket looped from the peg hook on a finger behind me.

FIRST SHE TOOK me on an errand. Something about the car. She left me sitting in an auto shop forty-five minutes while she was outside, standing by the open hood, pointing, talking to the submerged mechanic, riding him it looked like. This was just like my mother. I was used to it in a way. Even though I hadn't seen her for two years. The couch where I was sitting was greasy and taped. There was nothing to read. One *TV Guide* with the cover partly ripped off. A girl calendar on the wall. There was time like this, just time.

"Well say something," she said later, driving the way she drove, full of gasps and skids and halts. "Ooh, watch out, I didn't see that."

I didn't say anything. I fingered the window well.

"I had to do that," she said.

"Where are we going?" I said.

"Well, to the doctor, what did you think?"

It was a small square building, a kind of feminist women's practice, a place I was surprised to see my mother, and the doctor looked gay but I guess she wasn't, she had pictures of a man with kids. And when we went in it wasn't cancer at all but precancerous cells, she didn't need chemotherapy or even a hysterectomy, just her cervix scraped the way my friend Mai linn already had, when she was twenty-five.

We were sitting in the doctor's office.

"I thought you said you had to have radiation," I said to my mother.

"I didn't say that." She shook her head. "Boy, you sure imagine things, brother."

She had to go into the hospital the next day. Sunday morning, she could go home. I already didn't want to be there. I felt tricked. All I could do was count off hours.

We had brilliant fights, with an arc of night. I kept wanting to go home. "Take a taxi," she screamed, from the backhouse, where I heard things fall crashing around her, "damnit, damn you!"

I was sitting out in the little garden, on my mother's furniture. It seemed flimsy now, all her attempts. There was a ceramic rabbit sitting at the edge of the rose bed, a smaller one just next to it. A reclining concrete cat curled on the table with the umbrella. None of it was hers really. She bought these little ornaments, but she didn't own anything. Not the land.

I kept thinking of calling a taxi, but I didn't want to go inside. My hands lay fallow and useless the way they always did here. Here with her, I was a bomb, always ticking and waiting. I told myself a taxi from where she lived in Beverly Hills to the airport would cost a hundred dollars or even more. We both used money that way, always as the excuse to be stuck together. We couldn't admit any love.

The next day she packed her suitcase with all hard steps and jabbing elbows. She got up to do this at five o'clock.

"Come on, get up, I've got things to do." She shook my shoulder.

"I don't, so let me sleep."

"Hunh-ah, come on, get going. I want to straighten up here before I leave." There was metal in her voice.

So I sat there and watched her and listened to her for four hours.

Then oddly, at the end, in a strange voice, she said she would take me to the airport. "What are you talking about?" I said. "Well," she said with a high laugh, "to tell the truth, I don't really want you to stay here, tonight when I'm not here."

"Why?"

"Well, I know you. You'll take things. I never say anything, but I notice after you go, certain things are missing. I know you have my father's ring and other little things. Choice things that are mine."

"You don't trust me to stay in your house?"

"No, I really don't," she said.

That was just part of the long movement. Of course she didn't drive me to the airport. I waited at the hospital. One of her friends, Audrey, a woman who had once been a starlet and still received fan mail from the third world, came to visit my mother in pigtails and a pink gingham blouse all kindness and child-voiced concern. I left them and wandered to the hospital cafeteria. Outside were bushes with flat waxy green leaves. Everything in LA seemed almost still.

The next day she was like something hard cracked open so all the sweetness came out. She was soft and quiet and older and grateful. She begged me to stay longer. She thanked me for coming. To all of it I said no.

I slouched in the space between her bed and the table, talking on the phone to New York. I was telling Emily she had to meet me for dinner the night I got back.

My mother tried one more thing. She said she felt too weak to take me to the airport, but she could in the morning, once she got back her strength. I said no and that time I did start dialing a taxi. She got dressed then and drove me.

I had taken something from her apartment. It was a pin like a bobby pin with an enamel picture of a dog's head on it. I'd found it in a little dish with buttons and pennies.

"Well, honey, I was scared. It's very frightening. You know your hormones get funny. You're not as much a woman anymore."

She taught me, during our years alone, to forgive her absolutely anything.

When I got back, I took out my textbooks. I wanted to get down to business. I'd brought them along, but I hadn't opened them. Every time I meant to and didn't.

My mother once told me something, I could still repeat the grim dreamy smile, an I'll-get-you smile, of complete power and its satisfaction, the smile a parent has banding back the pleasure his face can barely contain when he says to his child, "Take your pants down and go to your room," before a spanking. But I was a girl. You cannot mark a girl's soul just through her body. Girls' bodies are used so much anyway. Girls, more than boys, learn to unhinge the two.

The thing my mother said to me that lasted was "You're an overachiever. You're not really that smart. I am, but you're not as high. My IQ is much better than yours, yours is just a little over average, really. You do well because you work hard."

I believed her that day and nothing exactly changed. She watched, waiting. I willed myself absolutely still but what had been natural I now forced from memory. This foot before that foot was walking. I kept myself the same. I didn't cry. Her eyes searched, her lips nervous with hunger. I don't think I gave her anything. I cannot be sure. Her message, though, left me still on the outside, but fell deep and stayed. I learned that I would always have to work harder. This came to feel like something I could accept.

I liked school and I began to find interest in it, to get something from it for myself. I ended up a college student who needed vast hours to draw plans on paper. I drew buildings and cities, highway ramps, roads around mountains. I drew while I tinkered in the lab, waiting for results. My mind spread and serened with the ticking of that soft pencil on paper the way another person's might among the constant wood sound of prayer beads.

I was behind now, though, with my books. I settled down and made coffee and just decided I was up for the night. Sounds filtered down through the ceiling from the man upstairs, his TV.

I'd never used my own good habits to find my father. He was something else altogether. He was not school. He lived in a universe away from my cup of strong coffee and list of things to do. I never believed he was a regular man.

I had a matchbox, painted, full with faint papery violets, picked perfect, wild in the back fields when I was eight years old. I had used hours that way, picking the frail stems one by one. I had fasts written down, a line for each day on the cardboard insides of school notebooks. But superstition, deep as it ran, hadn't gotten me any closer to him. And time was falling, falling. My father now would have been almost sixty.

I determined to try. I'd bought a black notebook, the kind students used as sketchpads. I liked that. I think every doctor or lawyer would kind of like to be an architect or an art student with a new clean sketchpad, beginning. I wrote down Venise King's name. The Salvation Army. See a therapist. My mother had always told me I had two uncles in the United Nations. They never contacted me, never sent a card. I was always promised things like that—a rich family somewhere else, royalty, uncles in the UN—as if any of these people could have helped us, where we were, in Wisconsin. Once from California we wrote them a letter asking for money. I hardly believed they existed.

But Tuesday, the next day, I took off early from the hospital, well, at six o'clock. I suppose that's a normal time to leave most occupations behind in buildings and to step outside. Not medicine. Leaving medicine at six o'clock felt like ditching school at noon, stepping into that bright flat dangerous quiet midday sun. It was October.

On the East Side, men carried light coats over their arms, women rubbed the skin of their elbows, their bare shoulders. I marveled at the colors. Orange seemed to be fashion this year. Orange and a kind of greenish turquoise.

I regretted my own clothes. I felt all covered up, square, not anything. I forgot, living near school and in the hospital, responding to its schedules, its food, its noises as to an enormous mother, I forgot how there were other worlds, simultaneous and brilliant. These women outside, my same age, looked made of entirely different things. Their hair benefited from effort, their arms stretched thin and bejeweled, legs bare, dark and hairless, thighs shyly touching soft fabrics. The tendon behind the knee of one woman was as delicate and taut with skin as a bird's wing. I stopped in front of the United Nations buildings, by a fountain. My parents had been in New York for a while when they were first married, and one of the things my mother always talked about was the United Nations. I didn't know for sure if they'd really lived here or only visited, she was pretty vague, but when she was here she would have been like these women, not like me. She would have known about dresses and parties, different kinds of shoes. She wouldn't have been studying something off in a quiet place for years and years. The United Nations reminded me of the New York City in movies. I didn't expect to see anyone I knew over here. Women in sling-back shoes rushed up the stairs, the white flash of their heels eager—but for what? I felt overbundled in my jeans and running shoes and like a man in a regular button-down white shirt. I rolled up the sleeves of my lab coat. A little spray from the fountain moistened the inside of my arm and I remembered sex. This was a time of day, early evening, I hardly ever saw outside.

I forged up the white steps and pushed inside. A round information desk stood with a glass vase of tall, branchy flowers. Things like that intimidated me, I don't know. Anything could make me feel not good enough then. The place reminded me of fancy things or Beverly Hills. For a long time, I'd worked in public service where rooms were plain and bare. Luxuries like those flowers seemed almost immoral. A twenty-eight-year-old woman who felt insulted by papery red-orange poppies and waxy lilies, tissue-thin irises that would be gone tomorrow—I was in trouble. I didn't really want happiness at that time. It was hard to imagine the man who could love me.

I thought I would forget today. It seemed flimsy and pretty. I didn't really think an agency could help a person like me.

The woman behind the desk had a mole on her cheek. This had been a sign of beauty when I was a child. We marked our lower cheeks with our mother's makeup pencils and debated the difference between a freckle and a mole. I hadn't seen one for years. Mary, her name tag read.

"Yes?" she said in a foreign voice. Something settled in me right. I asked her if an Atassi was listed.

"What do they do? You know what department?"

"No, I don't. I think maybe he's my uncle," I said. I felt the black book in my lab coat pocket. I began to doubt that an uncle even existed.

Her eyebrows worked down. "Yes? Oh, okay." I love the way foreigners say okay. "I have a Salimiddin Atassi." She told me how to get to him. He worked, apparently, in the horizontal building closer to the water. So I would really see an Atassi. I thanked the woman, whose gold buttons marched equally in two lines on her wool red jacket. Halfway across the lobby, I turned back to her. She was talking lushly on the phone now, her voice hilting and skidding.

"What nationality are you?"

She saw me and stopped, covering the receiver with a hand. I noticed that her hand was plump and also carried two moles in the fleshy part between thumb and first finger.

"Excuse me?" she said, eyebrows moving.

"Where are you from?"

"Oh me?" she said. "I am from Poland."

Moving down the stone steps in a crowd, the small, hard clicks of high heels echoing around me, I thought of going home to change. But it was a long way, it was late, I was here. Tomorrow I had a test.

I would meet this Atassi. The adrenaline in me rose a little. I felt a certain excited elation whenever something my mother told me turned out to be really true. It made the world seem magically alive. The names of those Uncles in the UN had hovered and chimed around my childhood, like dark moths. One was Atassi, one was something else. Allam, I thought. Or maybe that was a first name. My mother had an ability to imbue the things we had with value. Our bracelets were museum pieces, we ourselves, no one was supposed to know, were royalty.

These buildings, with their tiara of rushing fountains, made somber by flags, my mother loved them. They would make her inhale with an upwards shudder, basking in their intended posture of importance. Her profile would lift a little higher in front of the rushing water. I didn't like them much. They could have been simple and great. Le Corbusier had wanted to build them. They would have been the monument of his life. He got killed by a committee. Somebody thought the architect should be American. I knew a little about architecture. Pat Briggs got me interested in Le Corbusier and Mies van der Rohe when I was a child. He lent me books. No one else, Merl or Emily cared a hoot. Then, later, I majored in it.

I followed numbers down an upstairs corridor. I tried to remember what my mother had told me about the Uncles. "Let's see." Her voice went low and authoritative. "The younger one is short—I'm pretty sure he got married. A Yugoslav, I think. Yah, uh-hum. I'm sure of it. And the older one, the older one is a ladies' man. He'll never marry. Huh-uh." I could see her in her bathrobe, pink or peach, and her hair up in a ponytail, with a rubber band. Her hair now took her hours to prepare and she would be just home, in her big room. Nothing to dress all up for.

Then her voice went queer, whenever I asked her too much about anything near my father. "You're not trying to look around for him, are you? Because if you are just tell me."

"Why?" I said.

"Well because. I might just have to make some decisions of my own, if after all these years you decide to find him, sure you go on ahead after I've drudged and worked and—"

"I'm *not*, okay? Don't even think about it."

I'd always pictured the UN a huge oblong mahogany table with men around it, clean good hands on the surface. Different colors but all regular faces. Now I wondered which one I'd find, the ladies' man or the husband, and how I would tell the difference. Even when I thought my mother was lying, I believed her.

I'd always assumed weird people traced family trees—unfortunates, spinsters who saved their money for a bus trip to Maryland to meet children who could not have cared less that they were so-and-so's second cousin and distantly related. Relative seekers always seemed to me the unendowed, the ugly, tirelessly searching for superior cousins and aunts and nieces to prove that traces of beauty lived hidden in their bloodlines. And why? So what? What good did it do them? Better to spend the time and work on yourself. But here I was.

I knocked on the door and a man answered, his hand on the wood. "Yes?"

I explained my father's name and that seemed to mollify him some. "Come in, then. Come in."

He stood rubbing his hands together. "Well," he said, in his office. He was an older man than I'd expected. "So you are an Atassi. How is your father?"

"Well, I don't know," I said. "That's what I came to ask you."

Then we were a man and a woman, descending the steps in the light. I looked at him when I could without being too obvious. This was the first relative of my father I'd ever met. He seemed a well-fed man, his bald spot stretched and gleamed, his skin evenly dark: you could see he was sort of handsome. This is my uncle, I thought. It seemed easy. I still didn't know if this was the playboy or the husband.

He nudged me into a restaurant, where, it seemed, everyone I'd noticed on the street was also dining. There was the orange dress, there the turquoise chiffon scarf, there the red sling-back shoes, one white fleshy foot escaped and up on the seat, in hand. I'd been slipped into a corner chair, with the uncle at an angle to me. I switched so the place at my left was empty. I could never sit with someone on my left. "Claustrophobic," I explained.

His hands worked at the backs of chairs, lifting your coat right off your neck. He was probably the playboy. Just then, the Polish woman with the mole, Mary, entered the restaurant, her face moving as she looked for someone. I felt surprised: standing, she was no taller than a child.

"So you're my father's . . . brother or cousin?" I said.

"It's not that close," Salimiddin Atassi said. "In Egypt, you know, we all have very big families. You know there are a lot of Atassis in Egypt. Like your Smith or Jones. But he is Atassi and I am Atassi. And you are Atassi. And all the Atassis are somehow related. Way back. Your father's family I think is from Alexandria. Or is he Luxor? I don't know. My family is in Cairo. I don't know the Alexandrine side. I've been here twenty-three years." He smiled saying this and I saw gold fillings which seemed just right with the rest of him. He had a thick voice, with the soft clicks of an accent, maintained like a fine car.

So he wasn't really an uncle after all. But still a relative. I looked at his face for some resemblance to me. He had a gourd-shaped head, full and round at the bottom, narrower at the top. Maybe that was Egyptian.

"Do you know my father?"

But before he answered the waiter arrived. This restaurant embarrassed me because it pleased me so much. I ordered salmon and felt grateful with anticipation. I couldn't afford meals like this. I was still paying off student loans from college at the same time I was taking more. I couldn't really afford anything. Even necessities, like socks, seemed extravagant. And I was like my mother. Once in a while I'd buy something like a hundred-dollar blouse and then I wouldn't eat for three days.

The Uncle sat heavily, but in the extremely smooth tapered way of a seal. Somebody once told me that swimming caused your body to form an even top layer of fat. "Of course, I knew your father. Momo, we called your father, Momo. Your father when he first came here, he was a student at Columbia."

He started asking me if I spoke any Arabic.

I didn't.

Then he asked me if I'd been to the Middle East.

I said no, but I'd like to.

"You know French, though?" he asked.

I almost lied but I thought he might test me. "No." I shrugged.

"Oh, that's too bad. Too bad because I don't think your relatives there would speak English, you know. The women, especially." He believed my grandparents were dead, but there might be sisters, who would be my aunts.

We worked our way down to food. Did I like Middle Eastern food?

"Yes!" There for the first time I could say yes.

"Good," he said, patting my hand. " 'Tis in the blood."

I tried to ask him about my father but he was unable to tell me much. "I just don't know where Momo would be now. He married your mother and then he moved away, west."

"He studied politics," I said. "Political philosophy?"

"Political philosophy, yes," he said.

I found out Salimiddin Atassi was not an ambassador but had worked for twenty-two years in the Public Relations office of the UN. His smooth dark hands moved bare of rings. "Are you married?" I asked.

"No, I am a bachelor."

"How come?"

He smiled and I noticed hair-thin spaces between his teeth. "I haven't met the right girl, yet," he said. "But," he said, first finger lifted, eyebrows pressed into a severe V, "I am always looking."

He was kind to me, he paid for my supper as he told me he had no idea where my father was. He shook his head as we walked outside, fitting my collar back onto me. "I wonder where he could be."

The air outside still felt warm and material. It would have been good to be wearing lighter clothes.

"Oh, he must have been nineteen or twenty when he was here. And he worked, I suppose part time, in a tie shop."

I imagined my father a young man in New York City. I saw him in a hat and a suit, hard shoes, maybe even a cane. It would have been a different kind of life.

I stood waiting, the high lit flags important and foolish behind running water. Egypt might have felt less foreign to me than these three blocks on the East Side.

"Oh, they were very good ties," he assured me, features pressed together in the middle of his face for emphasis. "Silk. The best."

He told me he was about to leave on a trip to the Middle East and that he would make inquiries there. I asked him to call me if he heard anything and please call collect.

"No, no, no. No, don't think of it."

I said, "Yes, please." I was pretty lame. He said, no, no, no. I said, really yes. This was dumb. We both knew he wouldn't call me.

"We should talk after the new year," he said. "I'll be home and have a chance to unpack." It was now October. That was too long.

My most urgent question was the last trivial item on someone else's scribbled to-do list. And that seemed always the case. It had been that way growing up, living with my mother. Even my lunch money, that was not high in her mind. I grew up having no rights. That was how I learned to pester. I knew to ask for things more than once if I really needed them.

"Do you know the other uncle who worked at the UN?"

"There is no other Atassi."

"Allam?"

"Azzam? Oh, Azzam hasn't been here for years, no."

I told myself to remember to mark my calendar, Call Salimiddin Atassi, even though he'd said he would get in touch with me. I already felt a grim determination. I knew that I'd be doing all the work. I tried not to take it personally. Before we parted, he asked how my mother was doing.

I shrugged. "The same." Wind from the other river, the East, seemed to blow a mouthful of rivertaste into me, dirty and with a back gag in it. I pulled my coat collar closed with one hand.

"I always liked your mother. Very beautiful woman."

I nodded my head. "She's nice," I said.

"Tall, no?" he said, his eyebrows asking.

"No," I said. Then I thought he didn't really remember her, beautiful was just something he said about women.

As I left, I turned to tell him where I lived. He hadn't asked. "I live up near Columbia," I said. "When you get back from your trip maybe you can come up there and I'll make you some dinner." He's family, I was thinking.

He agreed, though not enthusiastically. "Good, Columbia, good," he said.

That was okay. I'd made my decision. I would take what I could get.

Later, on the way to the bus, I kicked a garbage can. I heard a person's footsteps behind me. I waited for the man to pass and then I kicked it again. I was glad to be wearing my old shoes. I should have pressed for his number in Egypt. He may not have wanted to give it to me. But formal considerations would have prevented him from saying no.

I was a realist. I was not above getting what I needed even from people who didn't especially care for me. I grew up poor. I could never afford to be proud. My mother had a flashy pride anyway, and I saw where that had gotten her. This man himself wasn't really the point anyway. I could do that, sometimes, put away the normal prides like little glass bottles, each holding a different color, separate on a shelf.

WHEN I FINALLY stepped off the bus, fliers and old leaves blew up around my ankles and touched through my socks. It felt good to be back where I knew. Everything here hovered lower to the ground. I passed the slice-of-pizza store with its high good tremolo oregano smell, the open fruit market where an immigrant stood hosing vegetables in the dark. Suddenly, lit in the window of the shoe store, I saw them: golden shoes. High-heeled, curved like swan's necks. I wanted them. All of a sudden. They were not the kind of thing I would usually ever buy. I stopped, took a pen out and wrote on my hand, *golden shoes.*

Back in the apartment, I called California to tell Stevie Howard about the Uncle. Stevie Howard was a boy from home in Wisconsin, the one I should have slept with first. I lay on my floor with my legs up crossed on the wall. I told him the Uncle had no idea where my father was.

"And you believe him?" Stevie said. That stopped me a minute. I hadn't wondered that exactly.

"Sure I believe him. Why would he lie?"

"I wouldn't be sure I believed him."

I heard wind, that gathering sound of leaves. "You outside?"

"Yup. Sweeping." I liked to know where Stevie was when I talked to him. He never sat anywhere normal, at a desk say, when he talked on the phone. He owned the kind of phone you could carry around. I could see him now, in the backyard of the Berkeley house, sweeping the sidewalk by his garden, eucalyptus rattling like so many years, dropping more buttons for him to clear. We had grown up across the road from each other. I knew how he was.

"I should have asked him for more. Like did he have names and phone numbers of my relatives in Egypt."

"That doesn't sound like you. Why didn't you ask?" Stevie said.

I sighed. Partly I hadn't because of his accent. His speech took on a high grand tone, full of velvet curtains and stages, well-being, power. "I will." Like so many times, I knew what to say after.

"So you really want to start this whole thing again," he said.

"I guess so," I said.

"I'd set a definite limit this time," he said. "Like you'll spend just so many days and then give up."

The rasping sound of Stevie's rake stopped and I knew what it could feel like to stand in that backyard, just leaning your chin on the old wooden end of a tool, watching the sky and waiting for all you didn't know to begin.

So I CALLED the relative back. The phone clicked onto an answering machine, his thick, accented voice saying, "I yam not home as you can tell."

I asked him to call me. At the end I paused. I didn't want to say my name. I'd let him think it was Atassi. He wouldn't connect at all to Stevenson. Still, it seemed like a lie. My mailbox and my phone bills and everything said Stevenson. Then I just said Atassi and hung up.

I ripped through the phone book checking for Azzam. One was listed, an A. Azzam. I called and got another machine, a high musical girl's voice saying, "Hey, it's Aleya and I'm not home right now . . ." I thought she was maybe married to the other Uncle. Or his daughter.

I said I was Mayan Atassi to her machine too. The second time, a lie is always easier.

THAT NIGHT I looked around the walls of my apartment. They made me tired. They were bare and cracked but alive with sound from pipes and from my neighbor's television above. I felt too much myself. Like the yellowish color of these old walls, that came from a day of strangers and then just talking on the phone.

In bed holding my pillow, I tried to think of my father in a Salvation Army shelter. Black men, white men, bald men, all men and my father. His chin would go a certain way for being there. He wouldn't like it. Who would? I suppose, who does? But if you're used to it, my grandmother would say. That was true. And he wouldn't be used to it. After years of fine restaurants, wine, silk ties, this? But there must have been so many moments of such questions already in his life. They would settle in a certain way of his lips, lines crossed there, a folded mouth. No, he wouldn't like it, but he would be doing it anyway, standing in line, quietly, straightening the soles of his good shoes. Eventually, another man might make a joke and my father's held expression would break, his short upper lip sassy, a big-shot smile. He would have a buddy. They'd make a plan. They would shuffle up to the soup ladle together and sneer at the food. But he would eat.

That was something I'd done all my life: held my pillow in my arms at night and closed my eyes and tried to see my father. I had nothing really, not even pictures. My mother had burned every trace of him when he'd left that first time. She'd thrown her ring over the Brooklyn Bridge when she went on the honeymoon with Ted Stevenson. She did that even though I'd told her I wanted it for me someday. "No, that you can't have, honey, that's mine to do with what I want to." I sometimes pictured it—the spindly cabled Brooklyn Bridge, glazed yellow car lights at night, choppy green-gray water and her slender ring with its small diamond, never large, slipping in, slanting down, finally lodging in the far bottom sand, among big rusty metal parts of machines. From some low place, all the things of the world must have seemed debris, junk after the circus left the town.

My mother bought a huge expensive scrapbook for me when I was born. In it was a small bouquet of tiny yellow roses, my birth certificate with my inked baby footprints and a jar with my fallen-out first teeth, and the plastic strip of her hospital identification bracelet, for when she checked in Bellin to deliver me. Then she had a few things, a crayon drawing of a tree and a sheet of paper I'd printed full of A's. But most of the book was empty. She kept it in the attic near a suitcase full of stuff she meant to put in it someday. Nothing she did for me like that was ever finished.

I fell asleep at night trying to imagine my father different ways. He could have been anywhere, in jungles, hotels, alleys, casinos, on stage somewhere, and even when I saw the president with his children on television, it seemed easy to blur and forget and feel happy in my chest for a moment like a dissolving taste, that it was him. It was easy to slip when someone was not there. I never did that with anyone else. I never pictured a different grandmother or a different cousin, even, a different mother. I always knew, with a sinking claim, she was mine.

Just talking to the FBI had done something. I'd started to finish this. Now I was really looking for my father and I would not stop until the end. I'd marked the date in my book, wrote down Venise King's name. I really did mean to call her again if I ever found him.

The strangest thing was having said out loud what had been my secret. And then hearing Venise King recognize it and find me familiar. He had always seemed to me truly different from other people missing in the world. My mother had told me how lucky I was to be one of our family and not other people. And I'd believed her. In a way I'd always believed we were better than other families.

3

I WAS ALWAYS doing things over again in my life. I lost things, replaced them, bought things twice. Nothing around me was well ordered. I was getting a detective again. I had done this before. But I knew I hadn't really done it right the first time. The first detective was nothing like me. I'd picked him because he was the cheapest. I found him when things were terrible and I was alone. No boyfriend in the picture and the old one didn't want to talk to me. Now it seemed to me that it hadn't been true what I'd always thought. That I let things stop my course. Maybe my efforts had failed and there was nothing I could do about it. This wasn't just now. It was all my life. I was going to find out if it was possible.

This was the last time.

"I WANT A LOCATE," I said, to the girl who answered the phone.

"You'd like him to find somebody?" she asked.

"My father."

"Uh-huh," she said.

This didn't seem to surprise anybody. There were a lot of missing dads. I wondered if anything betrayed that; if you could see it in a man, a gesture of his wrist, maybe, or the way his chin was near a school playground.

When the detective came on the line, I pushed the record button on my answering machine. I hadn't done that before. I just felt like it. A slight, strange mechanical sound beeped every minute or so.

"Wynne here," he said. His name was Jim Wynne.

I told him what I wanted. "I've tried a number of things and been unsuccessful," I said. Yes. That was true.

"What have you tried?"

"Well, um . . ." I felt guilty then. I couldn't really say. I'd not stepped on cracks in sidewalks, I'd torn flowers, saved butterflies. I'd burned food. I had shrines all over my apartment but nothing I could tell him. "I hired a detective once before, and I just try to review a lot of phone books, um . . ."

"What did this detective do?"

"I think he did a lot but he didn't come up with anything."

"What's his name?"

"I don't know. I could maybe look it up."

"Do you have your father's full name?"

"Yeah, sure."

"Date of birth?"

"Yeah."

"Okay, sweetheart, listen to me. My suggestion to you is you get some, do you have a file or anything together? Get all the information you have together—"

I interrupted. "There's very little information."

"Do you have a report from the other investigator?"

"No, I mean I might have it, but I don't know if I can even find it. I don't think he even gave me one. I haven't been very organized about this and all of a sudden I want to get organized and do it, but I've been sort of haphazard."

"What's his last name?"

"Atassi?" Hearing myself say it felt strange. I said it again, spelling it out.

"Well, if he's still using that name, that, you know, that in itself is helpful, 'cause that's not a very popular name, is—"

"No, very unpopular name. I'll tell you, there's never any listing in the phone book for it."

"All right. Well then, why don't you come to the office?" He gave me the address. It was somewhere I'd never heard of. "That's at Cadman Plaza," he said. "Cross the street from Brooklyn Criminal Court Building."

"What do you think we can do?"

"We can try and find him."

"How would we do that though?"

"Aw, there's many ways. Computers. Ah, with credit, with—"

"That's a good idea." I was easy to please. I felt held in his confidence. Emily's father's lawyer had recommended him. I knew he was famous in a local way, like Sal and Carmine's, the pizza place near Columbia. I was that much like everybody else.

"All right. Bring everything you can. All the information you have."

My voice fell into a soft wail. "I've got like everything in my head. I don't really have any information, I'm sorry, I wish I had more, believe me."

"I'm gonna give you a flat rate so you won't get—"

"Could you tell me what it is so I can . . . afford it."

He laughed. This was wonderful. "Eleven fifty including expenses."

"Eleven hundred fifty dollars?" I wanted to make sure. This guy was supposed to be famous. I didn't want him to be talking thousands.

"That's to you. I charge fifteen hundred, that's what I normally charge." My grandmother would never have fallen for an old pitch like that but I did. Why me? she would've said, why are you doing me favors? You don't even know me.

"What would expenses . . ."

"No, no, no, no. That *includes* expenses."

"Oh, okay. Sure. That's great." I was remembering the first detective. Maybe if I'd paid more, his interest in me might have lasted.

"Awright, come on in tomorrow. Just call Tina before you leave and make sure. Oh, by the way, you want to tape conversations on the phone there's a way to do it without the beep. You have to buy a gizmo at the Radio Shack. See, it's illegal so all the regular machines have that noise now. 'S'annoying."

THE DETECTIVE DAY was Wednesday. I thought of canceling. I had a party that night and then a date to something else.

This wasn't really my life. I wanted to cancel.

In bed, I made a list. If I went, as soon as I left the apartment, I'd be gone, there'd be no time to come back and change, so I'd have to be dressed for the night and bring along everything I needed. I sort of had a date. I didn't know if it was a date. He was an older guy, a professor. Gastroenterology. I hated this. Dressing up and doing all that. I was back in bed, shower-wet, still planning. I'd have to put on my black velvet dress and wear that on the subway to Brooklyn. The dress was my aunt's from before she was married. It was definitely the only thing I had. The dress. I wore it a lot.

Wednesday was my one day off. I felt like staying home. But I always did. I was two vertebrae systems behind in anatomy. I thought of my grandmother looking down at me, saying, yah yah, you're like me, aren't you? My grandmother always did stay home. I thought of her now, maybe for the first time ever, as a woman of my own age. She never went anywhere. So much of my life was making myself. She lived a life without dread. She was alone in the country and raked leaves in men's heavy clothes, hauling them into three or four huge piles and then setting them on fire herself. She stood by, watching, tall, with white hair. She wore a lumberjack plaid red cap. She made a peculiar sight. Even then, I'd never wanted to go to school in the morning, never wanted to leave that house or the warm car. She had an automatic garage door and something in my chest pressed like a clamshell being forced open, as the wall lifted and exposed us and we rolled going backwards over gravel.

But I'd canceled the detective last Wednesday. I had to go if I was ever going to go.

So I went, in my black velvet dress and sneakers, old pumps knocking in my backpack. I'd bought the golden shoes. I just charged them. They were expensive, so much I didn't put them on to wear. I carried them home dry and clean in the tissued box. That night I'd tried them. What I didn't realize until just then, seeing them in the mirror under the whitened, crenellated bottoms of my jeans, was I really had nothing to go with them. I put them in my closet. I knew I'd find use for them later. I believed, absolutely, in that other higher life. I almost brought them with me for tonight but they were still too new. I wanted to save them. Tonight wasn't enough.

I was on the subway at noon. I couldn't stand to put on makeup, especially in the morning, so that was in the pack too, in a Ziploc baggie. Getting off at Borough Hall I came out at a wire-fenced segment of what seemed to be a freeway. Cars zoomed by feet away from me. I didn't know where I was. They kept telling me on the phone it was right across from the court building. This was a busy intersection, ramps and construction. I didn't see any court building. No columns, anyway. I expected all courts to look Greek. They did at home in Racine.

I tapped the shoulder of a large-backed man at a pay phone, who turned away. I waited until he hung up. "What do you want?" he said.

"Do you know where the court building is?"

"That depends. Criminal or civil? Depends on what you done." He looked me over, slowly, deciding. My black dress seemed flimsy here, too long, eveningish. There was no good way to explain.

"I'm not going to court. I'm going across the street to 67-42 Tillary Avenue."

"Oh." He stared again, trying to decide whether to believe me. Then he just pointed. I passed a laundry with a clock. I was still early. This neighborhood reminded me of the old industrial Midwest. Poor but white. Less than urban. I turned and walked through a market. For no reason. I hadn't eaten anything but I felt queasy. I'd always liked to just walk through markets and look at food. When I was new here, some nights, I'd go to the bright stores and walk through the aisles. This market had little bananas from the islands. They were dry and sweet. I'd never seen those in the West. I thought of getting some now, but my throat closed. In the market's refrigerator section, they had the same fancy kinds of pasta and expensive ready sauces posed on the shelves. In poor neighborhoods everything—even the canned soft drinks—had different names. Inca Cola.

I passed a shoe repair store, with a display in its small window—
two foot-shaped pieces, one on the right smoothed with a sheet of
rubber. The other had the kind of hole that's bad to look at, a deep
hole, layered and ragged at the edges. A hand-printed sign on brown
cardboard, pointed BEFORE SOLE FIX.

Jim Wynne's address turned out to be a high-rise building. Names,
most of them attorneys, appeared on the listing board. Handy by the
courts, I supposed. I was alone in the elevator and glad of it. My
hands touched my two earrings. Still in my ears.

I'd imagined a low building, two or four stories, square. I pictured
thick Venetian blinds, plain metal file cabinets. A trenchcoat on a
wooden peg. No clutter. I wanted an office from the forties showing
spare male taste, like a nun's cell.

This detective's office was male, but a different way. You could
smell him. I didn't like it. The room had shag carpet and fake wood
paneling. Another vague smell of food tinged the air, but I couldn't
place what it was. On a center island, Tina wiggled in her chair, surrounded by necessary machinery. She leaned forward, hair spilling,
free to swivel on the four feet of plastic covering the carpet like a
nylon stocking over a hairy leg. Her breasts looked like they were
made of pure soft fat.

"You Maya?" She seemed very friendly, and like many friendly
people she had extraordinarily large teeth. She yanked up a ringing
phone.

A floor-length dirty curtain hid most of the one window, but a
painted brick wall outside said: SHORT STAY RATES. Radio dispatches
crackled up from the desk. "Following her from the garage on Lex-
ington and Eighty-one. Entering building on northwest corner."

Then he stood there. The detective. He was older than he'd
sounded on the phone, about—I didn't know—father age. He
showed me into his office and slid behind a desk. He had light hair
and freckles on top of a tan. I didn't think any of the wood in there
was real. Clutter balanced on tabletops, bookshelves and the window
ledge. An old newspaper page on the bulletin board had a picture of
my detective with the caption THE BOGART OF BROOKLYN. The kidney-
shaped coffee table held stacks of legal-looking papers. I sat on the
edge of an orange couch.

He leaned back in his chair and stretched his arms up to touch the
wall behind him, one fist knocking the plaster. "So what have we
got?"

In the newspaper picture he was young, full-lipped, leaning against a lamppost in a sloppy trench coat. It amazed me to see young men, men I could fall in love with, in pictures and then meet them the way they were now. He was still kind of handsome.

"Not much," I said.

"How old a man would your father be now?"

"Fifty-five."

"You got a date of birth?"

"I have a year, but not a day." I didn't ever think of it until just then, that I didn't know my father's birthday. "He's the same age as my mother. So that's what, 1931."

"You have a social security number?"

"No. He's been immigrated, I mean, my father's Egyptian, he became a citizen sometime when I was a child, I don't remember when."

"'31. Awright. We'll have to yank a date of birth and a social."

Then he picked up the phone. "Listen, I'm looking for a guy with a very unusual name. I'd like you to run him through computers in several states, uh—" He looked up.

I whispered, "Wisconsin, Colorado, California."

He said, "Wisconsin, Colorado, California, Illinois and Arizona."

"And Nevada," I said. "He's kind of a gambler."

"And give me Nevada too. I really got to get this guy." He was bouncing now on his chair. "So I want you to do everything you can, okay, don't embarrass me, awright. I want you to pull up a birth date and a social. Hit the gambling areas in particular. The guy's a gambler so you want to ask around the casinos for debts. I gotta find this guy. So hit the computers and hit the DMVs. Tell you what, you get this for me, I'll buy you a steak dinner, not that it's any pleasure to watch you eat. Awright, T-bone at Calabresi's. What's this gonna cost me? Ouch. Wait a second." He palmed the telephone. "Sweetheart, you sure you're gonna retain us 'cause this's expensive."

I waved my arm. "Sure."

"Awright, can you bring that down a little because you're cutting way into my profits. Get me a date of birth and grab the social. How long will it take you to hit those computers? Awright, awright. Now the name is—sweetheart, you're gonna have to spell this . . ."

I started. He repeated after me into the phone. "M like mountain, O like orchard . . ."

"Uh-oh. I'm not sure if it's one or two M's." Mohammed. I knew this looked bad, not knowing how to spell my father's name, but if I was spending all this money, I was going to be honest. I wasn't going to lose him because of an M.

"Awright, that could be one M or two M's and the last name is—" And here he glanced at me again. "This you got to be right on."

It was my name too for so long.

I said the name and he repeated it and then he hung up the phone. He rubbed the back of his neck. "Dealing with that guy will give you a headache."

"Sometimes he went by the name of John," I said. "Over here, I mean."

"John," he said. "Awright. John."

"So what are you going to do?"

"Oh, there's lots of ways. First I'm gonna see if he'll get us a birth date and when I've got a birth date I can run him through DMV. I found somebody in an hour once with DMV."

"Really? How'd you do that?"

"Oh, a woman walked in here one day, she'd put up a boy for adoption, long time ago, sixteen years ago. And she knew the birth date and she knew the state he was in and I thought, the kid turns sixteen, what's the first thing he's gonna do, he's gonna take his driver's test, get a license." He punched the wall behind him. "Had him in an hour."

"Then what?"

"Oh, I don't know. I don't get involved in that. There's so many people. I handle hundreds of cases, thousands over the years. 'S up to them what they do with it." That made me a little sad. My heel hit something granular, like a paper-covered ant hill: Sweet 'n Low packets, one punctured, on the carpet, next to a book called *B Is for Burglar*.

"See if he has Blue Cross Blue Shield. There's many ways, all right? Many ways."

I doubted that my father had Blue Cross Blue Shield. Three things my family never has used: umbrellas, sunglasses and medical insurance. We never did. Any of us. We lived streaking lives, unsheltered.

"But I don't think he's going to have any insurance."

"How old's your father, '31, let's see, you're telling me a fifty-five-year-old man doesn't have health insurance, and a guy who's taught college, a lot of jobs he had, it just comes with them."

"I know, but he didn't keep jobs for long. He was more the type to run off with a student or marry a rich older woman, that kind of thing."

"Kind of a con artist, you're saying."

"Yeah, maybe. I don't know. I just don't think he'll have health insurance."

"Awright, well, we'll go another way then. Do you know if he ever had any health problems?"

"He had liver problems, I think. He'd had hepatitis once and sometimes his liver swelled. He couldn't eat fat, I remember." In Los Angeles, that last breakfast, he'd ordered coffee black and a glass of grapefruit juice.

"That's good. Hepatitis is good. See, he checks into a hospital, there'd be a record there. Do you know if he has any credit? Bank loan, credit cards, anything like that? You say he's a gambler. Well, a lot of gamblers are gonna have credit lines around the gambling areas."

"Bad credit probably. I doubt he has any cards."

He slapped the wall again, this time with an open hand. "Good. Debts are good! Bad credit is good! Now tell me a place I can start, somewhere he actually worked and was employed."

"University of Wisconsin at Madison."

"Now, you're sure of that."

"Absolutely sure. He met my mom there."

"Good, I'll start there then."

"And what do you do?"

"Oh, we have ways, we can do a lot of different things, but I'll call the college and feel around, try and get somebody to cooperate with me, see. I don't do anything illegal, mind you. What's your father's field, his specialty?"

"Political philosophy, I think."

"So I might say I'm looking for him to contribute to a magazine I'm doing on Egyptian political philosophy, say. I lie. I call it pretexting but I lie. What we really do is lie. You develop your ways. Technique. I've been doing this a long time, my intuition and timing, they're refined. When I started I had talent but I tried a lot of things that didn't work. There aren't two people in the country doing what I'm doing, with the sophistication, you know? You're getting the benefit of experience."

"Do you think you can find him?"

"I can find him if anybody can. You ask a lot of questions. I like that because I'm good. I've been doin' this for thirty-some-odd years now." He stood up then, shouting, "Tina, gimme a contract for Ms. Stevenson here, would ya?"

I noticed the holster dropping on his hip, a handgun. He had slim hips. He never asked me how it was I didn't have my father's name. I suppose he could have assumed I was married.

He arched back in his chair, arms crossed over his head. I'd always associated arched backs with sex.

"How'd you start in this line of work?" I still had to wait for the contract, I figured I could stay awhile. I wasn't bothering anybody.

"I was an actor. Trying to be. I auditioned for a part in *O Mistress Mine,* and I got the part. I was Montgomery Clift's brother, but he cracked up and so they didn't shoot the movie. I started this business out of a phone booth. Found I was pretty good at it. I'd sleep in cars, benches, anywhere. I used to be a severe workaholic. Been in it thirty years now."

That sounded like fun, being a young actor and sleeping in cars and everything. Romance could be urban I guess: ducking under a marquee, staring through big windows into a ballroom, dancing on the pavement outside, pulling up cloth coat collars, sharing a joint or cigarette pulled from a trench-coat pocket inside city rain. Bud Edison and I had been like that—young and in a place. I didn't have enough of that.

I mostly stayed in my apartment at the desk with my book open under the lamplight. I drank coffee, bit the ends of my hair, memorizing bones. I tried to plan rewards that would not involve calories. Everywhere outside, parties lit windows in tall grim buildings one by one like so many fireflies on a bush.

"YOU MARRIED?" I said.

"Married sixteen years. Divorced eight."

"What happened there?"

"Aw, I don't know." He held his fingernails up towards his face. "My wife called and said, let's go out for dinner tonight and see a show, and I took her to dinner and I said, I want a divorce. Just like that. I worked all the time those years, I never came home, slept on benches, in cars, whatever. I'm talkin' severe workaholic."

"And you're not anymore?"

"I'm a little better now."

Tina tilted in. Her shoes, her skirt, everything on the bottom was tight. She handed him the freshly typed sheet of paper.

"Awright," he said, "here's your contract. Eleven hundred fifty, plus eight and a quarter state tax, there's nothing I can do about that. How would you like to pay me?"

"I could give you a check, but can you not cash it for a few days? I have to put money in."

"No problem."

I wrote out the check, then I walked over to hand it to him.

The meeting seemed over but I didn't feel like leaving. The detective was kind of handsome.

As I walked out, I looked over his desk and found a girl in a framed picture. She stood wearing a bikini with her hair frilly in the wind and then I saw it, it was Tina and all of a sudden I understood, oh, okay. People were living all that right now, here it was rushing by. Then, I noticed an open blue box of graham crackers on the plastic bank under her chair. That was it, the smell, graham crackers. That was a disappointment, a small one.

EVERYTHING I'D DONE before had been secret. At night I kept a kind of record. I had hair from when I was a child. I'd kept all kinds of things like that. In case he wanted to see.

I fasted. In all my fasts, I learned, my body stayed the same shape, translucently thin but the same, girllike. The curves and outlines shrank but didn't change. And that was what I had wanted to eradicate. That shape was what I hated and tried to starve out. But even bodies seemed to have a soul. Something given, what you cannot alter.

At times, I abandoned sacrifice. When I lived with my mother in California, we went to sleep hungry some nights. I'd lie in my bed imagining food, tender pork chops, mashed potatoes. You'd think that time with not enough we would have wasted thin. But I didn't. That was the fattest I ever was. I couldn't stop myself. Our poverty was not starving, it was eating the box of old saltines for dinner because you were alone in the apartment and that's all that there was and not feeling bad about it, really, it was just a night, a nothing night in a million nights. All our time together was like that. It never had any height for her. She never felt that I was the life she was supposed to be living. And after we waited two hours sitting on the hard plastic chairs in the Western Union office and the wire finally came in from Wisconsin and we had some money, we drove to a restaurant and we stuffed.

I baby-sat for the food. There in California, the neighbors got to know me. When the kids went to bed, I'd open all the cupboard doors and leave them hanging on their hinges, and look for a long time at the food. I tried to figure out what I could eat without them seeing. I took one or two things out of a box or a jar. One pickle. A cinnamon Pop-Tart. After the first few times, one wife left notes about what might be good. "There's leftover brisket and a strawberry compote. Help yourself," she wrote. That house always lay open, strewn and messy, the kitchen cleaned only on the top layer, but there was something about the wife. When she smiled, there was something sad in it, wise and sad. She motioned to her husband with her eyebrows to give me the dollar more. While they were gone, I looked in her closet at the glittery purses, the delicate gold-colored shoes with worn places from her heels and each of her toes.

I could only fast at my grandmother's house where there was always plenty. My father then lived far away. I kept a kind of vigil and twice, I became thin in a terrible way. I got so I couldn't stop losing. But my father never saw me that way.

I did things to myself for him, but that wasn't the only part of my life. It didn't take time exactly. It wasn't even the main thing. It had about the same relation to my life as buying a lottery ticket might. You'd see it in your wallet a few times a day, you'd remember it, but it was not really anything. Still, if you took it away, your life would be different.

EVEN THOUGH I was always looking, sometimes I didn't want to find him. It was the way you touched a sore. It depended. Some days I was too tired and solace mattered more. Solace was women, kind hands on foreheads, my grandmother. Once, when I was a child raking leaves in old loose clothes with my grandmother, the autumn gathering its huge skirts of wind, fall dark threatening, the window lights in houses blurring deeper orange, I saw a man in a shiny dark suit walking, turning in our drive. I couldn't tell if his suit was green or black. He walked with a slight drag on the left. At that moment, I didn't want him to be my father.

The man was a knife sharpener. My grandmother had a whetstone in the kitchen. We sent him away.

Other days I had surges of animal strength and longed for the circus, whatever the end. Those were the days I did things to myself. I learned about pain from teeth. I pulled at the loose ones, I tested pain.

Sometimes it went gentler. I collected things from outside to save, to show him what he'd missed while he was gone. I had a wasp's nest from Wisconsin I'd moved with me everyplace I'd lived, I still had it, and my butterflies in cigar boxes, all my saved things.

My grandmother called me outside—this was always—and said, come here, lookit see. She'd whisper if it was a bird or an insect or cat babies, something animal and skittish. But she'd point at the shape of a flower, slight as a lily of the valley or as large as the oak. Even a cloud. She took a walk every day.

"I'm glad you saw that," she said after, as if there were some positive good in just seeing.

We were different. I had to take everything and keep it, so it meant something. I wanted him to see it too. I liked to own. I filled my pockets with stones and acorns. My grandmother just left it all where it was. While she watched, her mouth grew nervous with the tension of someone frightened while receiving a pleasure, frightened that she would move or do something to make it stop and go away. If she ever had sex, she'd have been like that too, I know that. She'd have kept still until it was over and only then could she laugh and spill over relief that she hadn't spoilt it somehow. By doing something herself, something that she'd thought of on her own. You understand that about people you know from every day. How they'd be in love at night or anywhere. She felt ashamed of herself. She most often wanted to make herself invisible.

I hope she had real love. There's no way to find out such things. It is a constant and sad thing to love a person whose lifetime only barely intersects your own.

She was best later, smiling with that after gasp of "I'm glad you got to see that too."

But what is it if a person sees the change of seasons all her life, studies the progress of flowers, wonders at the sky. What do they leave? They leave no record.

Maybe though there was more to it than I understood. Maybe she was trying to show me religion. My own attempts now seemed to me just superstition, a thousand teeth and dry leaves and acorns and nests. But even my father, whom they were all meant for, he would not know picking up a nest, what I had felt when I ran with it to the house. If he is only a man.

Maybe she tried to teach me to see a part and get something from the symmetry that would change me, and then, it would not be from her to me, personal, but from me to something bigger, her taking my child's hand and touching it to the wide flat cloud thin eternal so I could feel the glacial weightlessness fill inside.

Where did the day go? My grandmother always asked that at dusk. Whatever she was doing, wherever she was in the house, she'd step out on the porch and lean her chin on the broom top, and hold each of her elbows with the other hand and say, "Where did the day go?"

BACK IN MANHATTAN, as I walked up from the subway, the sky was already feathering, coming to dark. At a cash machine, I took out my last forty dollars. I'd have to call the bank at home again in the morning. Now the street was falling under the spell of late afternoon, silence and ending. Beyond this block, the space between trees filled gray-blue, and a dark haze smudged the tips of bushes.

I was walking to the Pleiades Palace. I thought of Venise King, her "see a therapist." Timothy was not exactly a therapist, he was a movie usher, but we were trying. He was trying to analyze me.

I believed it was my father. I didn't love right. Sometimes it seemed I only loved people who would be better off without me.

I'd always had a type. But the type changed. At one time, they were all very stumbling-young blonds, fair-haired. Virgins. The sort of boy you found yourself baking cookies with. Then for a long time they had to be dark. Dark skin, dark hair, dark eyes—everything a certain way.

Timothy—it wasn't my first time at this either. It seemed I had already tried and failed at everything. In college once, I went to a therapist. He was cheap almost to the point of free. It was probably my mistake. I had gone to the Community Counseling Center, because they had sliding fee scales, but then I demanded a man. I wanted an MD and a man. That was the way I was then. The woman I said this to frowned. Apparently the vast majority of Community Counseling Center therapists were women. UnMDed. "Are you sure?" she asked.

"I know," I said. "I need a man."

And so they found me Garth. I told Garth I was there because I kept ending up with guys who weren't my type, and then, when I was with them, I fell for other ones who were. Garth nodded too sympathetically. The next week he had a whole theory worked out about my father and my stepfather and their hair colors. Except he got Ted's hair wrong.

I stopped going. Garth wrote me two notes and then called me on the phone once to ask why. I never could give him an answer.

On Amsterdam Avenue I passed Haitian shops that sold love potions and hexes, either one the same price, five dollars.

Timothy and I had started six months ago. This was our experiment. For five years, he had been teaching himself to be an analyst, with books, and so he was ready to try. And I needed help. I figured we had as good a chance as anybody.

He hadn't finished college. He didn't like school. That was something I never really understood. Teachers to me always seemed slow and kind. School was outside and apart from the dangers in the world. For me it was always so much simpler than home. Once out, Timothy felt disinclined to go back for so long that it became a decision made in sleep—that his education would be private, unwatched and tested only by life.

I met Timothy at the Pleiades Palace. Nights when I was lonely I either went to the Piggly Wiggly and walked down the bright aisles looking at food or I went to the Pleiades Palace. All I needed was the darkness and close other bodies and the tick of reel-to-reel film. I liked to let my head sink back while the big pictures overwhelmed me. Timothy managed the theater, sometimes he ran the projector, and every month he programmed and ordered the films. He had a taste for dark glamorous movies, with an undercurrent of violence. He had a long black ponytail which pendulumed on his back. He always wore the same brown bomber jacket and boxy shirts. He moved with grace. All over the neighborhood, people knew Timothy as the charity usher. When he collected tickets, a minute before the film started, if there were seats left, he'd let in anybody who wanted from the street; there were regulars, a woman who was suing the government and carried her voluminous documents everywhere, a woman who lived in her car. Most of the homeless in our neighborhood were women.

I met Timothy there my first year in New York when I applied for a job as an usher. I lasted three weeks. I couldn't keep with the hours. But it was a nice place to work. You picked up your schedule for the week every Sunday night. If you wanted to change shifts, you asked someone else to switch or just cover for you. And this was the thing: everybody always said yes. Timothy never said no and so everyone else kind of followed the example. And then, because you knew whoever you asked would say yes, even at a cost, you tried not to ask. The bakeries nearby and one cheese shop sometimes brought us leftover food at closing time.

Timothy was always studying some hard-bound, large-printed book. He didn't read randomly, the way I did, according to craving or whim, but methodically. When he read an author he worked through the novels, the letters and the diaries concurrently. His life was the opposite of most people's college, where students immersed themselves in desperate scholarship, frenzied before tests, they would never again equal in their lives. Timothy's education started once he'd left the university classroom, moved in a slow, thorough manner and showed no signs of ever stopping.

Timothy had read every book of Freud's, most more than once—he'd learned German at night from send-away books and tapes and from Fassbinder movies—and many of the subsequent textbooks of psychoanalysis. He came to his belief in it slowly and, I think, profoundly, and if anyone owned the gift of reception, he did. He was a listener, and his remarks were scarce but dense. You always stopped and listened to what he said. Even at the Pleiades people did. The woman who screamed all day about the government spying on her through her blender raved to him in a lower voice. With him, she was almost talking.

He had a natural authority. My grandmother was like that. Still, but with a dignity so we hung on to whatever little she said. And we fought over her bitterly. We all wanted her preference and no one seemed to have it. She loved us all, we knew, but she could be truly impartial. That made her unlike the rest of us.

You instinctively looked to Timothy when you wanted a referee. He could be easily fair. Something like goodness seemed to hold him the way he was, the same as my grandmother. My grandmother or Timothy if they had a plan with a friend, any friend, and something else came up, some sweet, high temptation, they would right away say no, it wouldn't even make them waver. It was as if they decided on rules to govern themselves long ago. I will never be like that. Conduct, in that way, is not determined by the depth or nature of your attachment to other people. It has to do with your fundamental notion of yourself. The way a certain man knows himself would make it almost impossible to endure a secret love affair. It would destroy his own and deepest familiarities to the world. Both my grandmother and Timothy were loners. And they held a certain mystery, a rectitude. Those of us who didn't have that, and there were so many, sensed this and felt the lure of it, despite any apparent advantages we may have had. Timothy was a person you went to for absolution because there was something contained and steady about his life. I had so many ragged edges, so many desires.

But what could Timothy do? His talent was invisible and would never be recognized by the psychoanalytic channels which were as elaborate as the Ivy League college system with its specific initiation rites and requirements.

Whenever possible he hired graduate students in clinical psych to usher at the Pleiades. There was the tall girl who was doing her dissertation on anorexia. She wore flower pins and long skirts, blouses with pleats in them. You could see she ran herself thin over selfish, too handsome men. In this group, everyone was too much what happened to them. The girl who had been raped in a fraternity at college I associate with long curly hair and something uneven about the lip. There was a shy tall man, just venturing, it seemed, into the world of friends. He was apparently some kind of star at school. The ones who seemed like they'd be the best therapists were also the ones blocked on their dissertations.

Timothy and I decided to go ahead and try analysis. Why not? We had to believe in a way outside the regular. I couldn't afford the regular. He didn't qualify. Not to believe in each other was not to trust ourselves. But there are a lot of people like that, who, the first moment they can, abandon their whole past for better names.

Emily Briggs taxied across the park to see an analyst five times a week. His name was Dr. Bach. She told me she was always late. She left from the Met or from her apartment a few minutes late, but that didn't stop her from running into a place for a four-dollar cappuccino to go. For two years I heard about it, how unfair it was that he wouldn't let her take her beverage inside. This is not a restaurant, he'd said. But recently they had a breakthrough. She'd discovered a type of spill-proof top and once she had demonstrated its infallibility, he allowed her to enter with her drink. It's not even like he had any great rugs or anything, she said. Every time I'd seen Emily in New York, she'd been wearing a different hat. I imagined those hats waiting on a hatstand, in an empty room.

I walked into Timothy's apartment, which had once been a garage. There were two small rooms with high ceilings, first a kitchen which always looked neat and dry, clear-surfaced, the mugs with their railroad line logo hanging on hooks over the sink. The second room was bigger and beautiful. Light slanted down from the high garage windows. Books lined the walls. He had an old leather and wicker chaise longue and he showed me to it that day. He pulled a small footstool out from under his desk, setting his sneakered feet upon it, the way he always did. I'd seen a wedge of his closet once—white sneakers, many times washed, and three pairs of loafers, worn to the shape of his feet, unmistakably polished.

Once we'd arranged ourselves, a still, hushed quality held the room. I felt apart from the world and for a moment I just stared at the most peculiar life in the room. On the opposite wall, tropical fish moved in a large tank. Since the room held a dim diffused light, the visceral equivalent of air kept in a jar, as if all time were old, caught and held here, the bright fish with their occasional, accusing flashes and tail turns worked as clocks, reminding that colors lived, there was light, other places than here, there was a now. But no matter how propulsive the turn, they only hit the other glass wall, they hung in a futile drama of motion.

"So hi," I said. "I went to the detective today. That's all I did. All day. But this morning before I got up, I had a dream. First there was this square of cement with a handprint on it, a man's handprint. And then a stern woman in glasses led me up some official stairs. And we walked down corridors and corridors, first her footsteps and then mine. Finally she opened a door and we were in one brown room. The walls were corrugated like the inside of a lung. I guess a bad lung. There was a food line but it wasn't moving. 'There,' the woman pointed. And I saw my father, he was near the front, thin still, good in clothes. He's talking to another guy, looking down at his shoes. I didn't want to bother him. I sucked in my breath. It was hard to move, I had on a suit, not anything I really have, but a tight suit, with shoulders and a double row of gold buttons, a short skirt. And I had on silk stockings. Do they even still make silk stockings? I never owned a suit like that. For that matter, I've never owned a body like that either, but I walked with a kind of purpose and padding over to where he was. I threw my shoulders back, it didn't work, I felt like an idiot, I looked down at the flecked linoleum floor and the corners of the tiles were curling up like the toes of old shoes. 'I'm your daughter,' I said to him. 'I know who you are,' he said, as if nothing were even strange. 'Can I talk to you?' I said. And then his voice went a way I knew the answer. 'Well, this is not a good time right now, Mayan, I'm in the middle of a meeting with Mr. Harold here and it's very important.' I said, 'Oh, okay.' 'Be good, Mayan,' he said, with his smile flashing. I kind of remember his smile. Not the way it looks really, but I'd recognize it. I turned around. I had to walk a long length of gym to the door with the feel of all those brown eyes following me. Then he called my name, it hooked in over my shoulder. And I got really excited. The rest I'd been prepared for. But now I let go and I turned around and said, 'Yes, Dad? I'm still here.' And he shouted, 'Are you first in your class at school?'"

"Mmm," Timothy said. But he didn't say much in regular life either. I was supposed to say what I thought about the parts of the dream, whatever it was—that was a rule from one of the old books.

"I don't know what the handprint means, or the suit. The suit I guess makes me think of Emily. I'm going to a party tonight for them. Some friend of her dad's is giving them an engagement party in the Met. The Egyptian Wing. Like they have any connection to Egypt. I just feel funny at those things. I feel like I look wrong. I don't even feel like a grown-up. Tad, that guy she's marrying, you know, he never even looks at me. I don't mean looks at me like flirts with me, I mean, literally, he never looks at me."

I was propped up on an arm and I twisted around to look at Timothy. I saw his profile and each time I did that I was surprised how close up he was.

"I guess I'm just jealous of them. She says Tad cuts out of work sometimes in the middle of the afternoon and they have sex with the windows open. And after, they get up and put new clothes on and go and eat in restaurants. Did I tell you she has an antique beaded dress collection? Well she does. From the twenties. And what am I doing? I'm taking the subway to Brooklyn and spending my last money on a detective to find my father. I should be falling in love and having sex and buying clothes."

There was fight in the air and the fish turned and jetted forward like fists in the lighted green aquarium.

I really was too alone. I said those things but I was even worse than I knew. And I blamed it all on money. I thought money was why I didn't feel yet like an adult, money was why I didn't fall in love right.

But other people my age with no more were helping each other, living together in their lives. None of them had any money, really, just Emily. Some people were even married. On the other side of my building a guy hung out of his window at seven o'clock every Friday night, waiting for his wife, who commuted. She'd pull the car in front and toot and then he ran down and she'd slide over and he drove until they found a parking place. My other friend from childhood, Mai linn, was in music school in Philadelphia, and she was just figuring out she was gay. That was something definite, a permanence.

I didn't know if I should be finding my father or making a life with other people, going to parties, spreading out and feeling the medium of being young.

"But you're not wasting your time. You've said often that finding your father would be very important to you. Would help you."

"Yeah, I know. It is. But I'm tired of it being so hard. I hate that I have to do it."

"Well, I know," he said. We let that settle a minute. "I think the dream is also about being a woman."

I turned my head to the side and so my long cheek was against the smooth leather, the way some people go to sleep.

"What do you make of the stockings?" Timothy said.

"I don't know, I hate stockings, I'm so bad at all that. I mean, I never paid enough attention when it was the time you were supposed to learn those things. I thought I could save it for later. I remember saying once to Mai linn, while all these girls are fussing around with eye shadow we'll learn things and then later when we're grown up we can go to some department store like Briggs's and pay an expert a hundred dollars and they'll teach us everything in one day. I felt sorry for the girls with their makeup sessions and hair problems and dress catastrophes. It seemed so futile. All that time wasted. That's why I think of Emily I guess, too, because she has men, she's living a life in the physical world, and the truth is she's smart. She's just as smart as I am. She doesn't get credit because of the way she looks. Mai linn doesn't dress up either. She doesn't shave. She hasn't put on finger-nail polish in her life." I remembered Mai linn's hands and feet. She has Asian skin and fingernails that looked a certain way over skin, like a washed-out white transparent shell. "We both have to wear this bridesmaid's dress for Emily's wedding."

"What's it like?"

"I haven't seen it yet but all I know is it's knee length and pink. And I have to wear it with green shoes."

Timothy just muttered.

"'Like a flower,' she says, you know, stem and petals. She's going to have pink tulip centerpieces. I hate wearing short dresses. I don't look right in them. And pink, too."

"What comes to mind?"

"I just don't want to look like a fool at Emily's wedding."

"You seem to feel Emily is a woman in a way you're not," Timothy said.

"She is."

"Well, what about your mother?"

I readjusted on the couch and thought I hadn't talked to her once since I was back. This father business, I was getting behind with every-one. Emily wasn't looking for anybody. And people lived around her every day. When we were roommates, we planned we'd work together in the end. We'd be architects or something. I'd design the buildings and she'd decorate them.

"My mother. Oh, well, she's glamorous all right. She did that, she spent her life chasing dresses and little purses and manicures. All that money."

What is being a woman anyway? Buying dresses and making par-ties, I thought. Not being president. The way a foot curves in a formal shoe, tucked up on a chair.

Timothy and I kept tinkering in the intricate, remote way you do when you're playing but playing seriously, using what we knew from the old books when it worked. In the stillness, the dim soft light punctured with the flashing tail-socked turn of a striped fish, I imagined us shipwrecked on a Pacific island with only our broken boat, a trunk of books.

"Maybe that's why I think of Mai linn. 'Cause she's not like that. She doesn't worry about clothes and hair and all that stuff."

"Mai linn is from a very different background." That was true. Mai linn was an orphan. But her parents had been intellectuals. Her mother was a pianist. She remembered her parents sitting, thigh to thigh, on the balcony of their apartment at night, their gray-white heads together, two cigarettes ribboning smoke up from an ashtray. They would talk on and on, in French, until Mai linn and her sister fell asleep, a smell of burnt sugar in the air.

"I guess I was always a tomboy. I never liked the girl stuff. I always thought it was less. And it seemed like a waste of time. I never felt I had the time. Emily Briggs would sit around spending all Saturday hovering over her toes. She'd polish them three layers of pink and then she'd take that off and start over and do four layers of peach and then take that off and finally end up with pearl. And that would be her day.

"'You can be both!' my mother would tell me. But what was she? She wasn't both. Neither was anybody else I saw around. She was always trying to deny the limits of time and space."

Timothy told me it was time to stop and I felt startled. I stood up, brushed off the front of my dress and moved back into the kitchen room. I felt strange, a little embarrassed, something ended. I brushed my hands against each other a way my grandmother did after she wiped down the table.

"I wish it was over and I'd already found him and now I was just living my life."

"What is the feeling that you can't wait?"

"I've been waiting all my life. Too long."

The displaced gorgeous fish moved now in a kind of jagged stunted fury for spending their youth in this unobserved dim country, and then exhausted, they hung in place fanning their delicate, extravagantly colored fins, like tissued jewel.

I didn't pay Timothy. Emily's analyst thought payment was impor-

tant for the patient's recovery, so just to be safe I usually brought
Timothy a little food. But that day I had nothing.

I STILL HAD THREE places to go before home. I went to a flower store
that smelled like rain, dirt and moss. They had lilies of the valley, tiny
roses, old lady flowers I hadn't seen for years. I wouldn't have been
surprised to find dandelions. Flower deliveries were a thing like written invitations, something I didn't grow up around. They didn't really
have all that in Racine. Few children were even taught to write thank-
you notes. They seemed to me like something from an old book. My
mother always meant to send me to charm school. Marion Werth
headed that program downtown at the YWCA once a week. We never
managed to get organized enough for that, but we carried a battered
book from move to move, called *White Gloves and Party Manners*. I
read it again and again, just for solace, at night in my bed, listening
to the trains moan by outside in the cold dark. It was all about whose
name you say first when you are introducing someone royal. Which
fork to use for shrimp and what to do if you are a guest and you break
a vase. When we lived in California in empty apartments, with just our
boxes, I used to lie sometimes on the carpet, late afternoons, for
hours I just sat in the lightless dusk reading, waiting for the sound of
my mother's tires outside.
    In the flower store, I picked two champagne roses which were a
color like what pink is dipped in tea. My mother once showed me how
to make the new ivory beads Merl Briggs brought from her travels in
the Orient seem dimmer, old with value. We gently dipped the
strand, string and all, in tea. These roses had very long stems and the
blooms felt disproportionately heavy. Their color concentrated and
waned like color in a cheek or a lip.
    Tonight I wished I were home in my bed, eating take-out Chinese
food from the carton. Still, the dark shook glamorous wings with new
lights. The white tissue for the flowers rustled like party slips. I
stopped a taxi, slid in and we swam in the just lit public world. I pulled
out my better shoes from the backpack, traded them for bad, tried to
put on lipstick by touch, brushed my hair. I should learn to carry a
mirror, I thought. Another thing to get. How many times had I
brushed my hair in the back of a taxi or walking up from the subway,
sucked in breath as I went to the door of a party that could, maybe

would, just might . . . but then never did change my life. At a stop-
light, I asked the driver, "Could I come up front and use your mirror?" So we rode together, he somehow dodging cars without the
rearview, which I used to draw on my eye makeup. I looked like an
owl. I never did learn how to do makeup right.

I always thought I'd want to go to parties like this, but now I wasn't
in the mood. Still, Emily was engaged. I had to go for a while even if
Tad wouldn't look at me. I felt the fragile light bundle of flowers in
my arms. Good.

I knew what a father was from what Emily had. I had a little of Doc
Briggs too. He liked me. I knew I reminded him of himself. He'd married late and everyone always said he'd been kind of weird before
that. I'd ask them what they meant, and they'd all shrug or shake their
heads, like my grandmother, and say, "I don't know, just funny." He
had lived all that time, even being a doctor, with his mother. After six
or seven years, he decided he didn't like medicine and he opened a
gift shop. A year later, he was running his father's store, Briggs's.

At Racine parties, when I was a child, we'd end up sitting at right
angles to each other and having a real talk. He asked me what I
thought about kids getting allowances, whether they should get paid
for chores or just be given money every week. We were always, by the
end, talking about death. He was the only person my whole childhood
who asked if I thought my father was alive. "I know he is," I said. It
wasn't that often I saw him but I liked our talks. He knew who I was.
He'd taught me, when I was ten, to play chess. We played chess and
we talked about things from school and eventually, death. Those were
the years my grandmother's aunts were dying. There were seven sisters in all, counting her mother, and they all died within five years.
My cousin Ben and I were taken to every funeral. Doc Briggs's
brother was an undertaker so he and I discussed the comparative
merits of each laying out, each embalmment. Two of the great-grand-
aunts I saw for the first time at their funerals.

But here was the thing. I'd be myself, in my jeans and hands in
jacket pockets, and we'd be talking, looking not at each other at all
but far off in the field say, back of their house, and then Emily would
prance in and she was completely something else, and she would
come over and climb on him or lean her hands just on the back of his
shoulders and we would be talking about something still and true and
she would come and frill and natter about dresses and parties and

buying things and what she didn't have that someone else had and could she, Dad, could she please? And they were connected, with something that was as visceral and repellent to me as the slime of snails, its oozing glitter. That was them. He loved her like that.

No one ever loved me that way. No one at all. Not my stepfather. Not the men I made my fathers. They cared for me in a stiller way, standing up and looking in the distance. They acknowledged more who I was, like a vertical pole, something they might have respected, but nothing that melted them down. I never knew if my real father would have either. I didn't think so. I didn't remember him being that way.

And Emily and I were such different children. We played dress-up and I would usually be the man. She was always being a princess. Or a fairy. Something that had a cape or evanescent wings. And she leapt and jumped, she was always wearing pink and silk net tutus.

Now, Emily tended to get what she wanted from the world. Except my cousin Ben. She probably would have gotten him too eventually. But he died first, when he was too young to see what she could've given him, and that—his death—was the most solemn bead in her. I could feel where that was in her, always. But she worked now to the top of her abilities, while Mai linn stood blowing them away, her advantages, talents, like a puff of dandelion wish in the vague indiscriminate wind. A girl with a father and a girl without.

I was jealous of Emily, sure. But one thing that kept me from being too jealous, or confident either, was that I was never sure of what seemed true. I believed, in a way, that Emily was smart but not that smart and that she was beautiful, and that I was smart enough but only borderline good-looking. But I was never sure. Sometimes I thought Emily only seemed that way to me because I wanted her to and then, in certain glances from certain mirrors, I maybe thought I could have been beautiful too.

At the museum entrance, a man asked if I'd like to check my bag. I said no. I never checked my bag. I needed my things too much. Once I was with Bud Edison at the beach in January and he wanted to walk on the sand in the snow. I made him wait while I went back to the car so I could change out of my boots to old sneakers. I lived that winter with the cushion of my one coat padding my chair in restaurants, I knew the fall of it over my knees at the movies. My hands grew used to touching the things I owned. Checking.

I had this one pair of earrings I wore always. I bought them when I finished college. Graduating college was no big deal, my mother wasn't around, and I missed her getting me a present. My grandmother did. She sent me a check to buy myself something. I used to always save her checks, never to buy anything, and she'd always scold me to go out and spend.

"Take the two of yourselves to a nice dinner or go to a show. Get out and have a ball."

"I don't even know if he's the one, Gramma," I'd said. Everything always seemed to me so dire.

"Well, go ahead and have a nice time anyway. Buy yourself a new dress."

But she never taught me to wear clothes, to use things the way she had. But this one time I did go out to the best jewelry store in Madison, LaVakes, and I bought earrings.

I touched them, left ear, right. Still there. One thing I should have been was more careless.

THE CEILING of the ancient wing was as high as any church I'd been in. I guess I was early. Emily wasn't there yet. I sat on a stone ruin to get myself together. I rummaged in my bag for paste pins. Emily had called yesterday needing to borrow a pin. Pins, like linens, were things I was rich in from my grandmother's drawers. I'd thrown a handful into my backpack. They were dreamy things. Bits of glass, cherries, nursery rhyme flowers. One was a picture made of shimmery butterfly wings. The backs were stained a dry hard clear color from the safety pin being glued on more than once.

Heels made a certain sound in this huge room. Emily had told me about the museum. They had an endowment, from the *Reader's Digest* heiress, to replace the huge extravagant flowers every other day. The blossoms were everywhere, the best of the season. In spring they had had cherry blossoms. Now there were branches of bittersweet. Huge tulips—things impossible in nature, but this wasn't nature, this was New York. I watched the kid caterers nail atmosphere together piece by piece. Dressed in twenty-two-year-olds' clothes—black things from thrift stores and running shoes, Chinese slippers—they curved over every table lighting candles, the girls' long hair falling, just as the buildings out the window lit from within, so they loomed closer, silver and gold. I'd always wondered, in my grandmother's house and in all those empty rented places with my mother, if people felt different when they had a dining room. At my grandmother's, we ate in the kitchen with the sound of the highway running outside.

Emily told me after the second day all those thousands of dollars' worth of flowers were heaped like rot in big metal garbage bins in the back.

That would never happen in Wisconsin. A thing like that would just never happen.

"I'd go take 'em," I said.

When we talked to each other, our Midwest accents fell back into our voices like the heels of boots.

"I tried one day right at the beginning, there were these enormous branches of forsythia—it was perfectly fresh and I was carrying them home. I'd worked late. And I ran into a curator I knew from upstairs. They talked to me the next day."

"I'd just do it anyway."

"No you wouldn't. People would think you were funny."

"I don care."

"Yah you do."

I sighed, waiting for her. Where was she? I lay down on the alabaster slab, the little run of fountains gurgling below me. It was interesting that they used the ruins this way. For a party. In an hour the room would be full of flimsy silly dresses, food and evanescent life. You could see the people in the close corner stepping in, down, taking drinks from a waiter's tray. All presided by the stone ruins which were outside once, subject to the sun and wind. I slipped behind a temple arch. I wanted to be hidden just then. My family had never given parties. It wasn't just that we had had so little but that we hadn't used what we had. We'd lived in places and left them, afraid of ruining the walls, the floor. We'd never hosted meals, friends, the disorganized mess of life. And this temple had. There were just stone walls now and cut places for windows but you could still feel how it must have been used. By people no more serious, no less petty and jingling than tonight's. I watched a woman walk in a diagonal across the room: she was wearing a blouse with shells tied to the bottom hem; their noise carried up and then hung a certain distance above our heads, like a canopy. I thought of a book I'd read about Katsura, rich and empty with the lives it had housed. The moon-watching parties on the lake, the tea ceremonies. Sometimes I've thought that everyone wants parties, even scholars. So many of us read history because we are afraid to inhabit our own youth.

I was still standing behind a wall, looking through the thick window. I was dressed up too. This was public time. Passions ran and had always run deep under all the walls and monuments, under the silver and gold of New York City, unaltered even by the moon. I thought of my father still free somewhere in the dark northwest, altitudinous, windy black pines. Passions were by nature secret, and tonight I felt closer to that hidden life. I had my own mission, too.

Then I saw Emily and I stepped down and around. I followed her to the ladies' room, where a window opened, screenless, to the near lit buzzing city towers. I fished the pins out of my backpack, held them all in one palm, their candy innocence.

"Tell me which one," she said.

I picked and she stood carefully still while I pinned it on her collar. She looked at herself in the mirror a moment. She really did turn out beautiful. Once in a while, I thought, she wanted me to be her sister. She had better pins than I did, ones with real jewels, and she knew enough to tell the difference. The door was open. Outside, people moved tenderly, holding thick glasses with drinks. Far away I saw a guy I always flirted with at Emily's parties by talking about my ineptness. He always laughed and seemed to like it. I gave her the roses. We had been so different growing up but now we were both just young women living alone. We both lived primarily on muffins. They were good and comforting and they didn't get you fat. We talked on the phone while we baked. We didn't use sugar or even honey. We sweetened with just banana.

"Have you seen Tad?" she said as we stood near the wall, before really entering the crowd.

"No, not yet, was he looking for me?"

She turned to me blank.

Tad never made it to the party, but when he arrived home from London, after midnight, he had a strand of pink pearls with a butterfly Romanov clasp.

I TOUCHED MY EARRINGS, both still there, and lay my head back on the seat while the cabdriver took up my panic, plotting through the streets recklessly and fast. I was late. Really late. I kept waiting for Tad to get there before I left. Finally we approached the quiet school gates. My date, the gastroenterologist, stood outside, hair blowing in the wet wind, arms crossed. I didn't know about him. He was divorced.

"Don't run," he shouted as I slanted over the brick sidewalk.

"I'm sorry." Having rushed and skidded like that, it was a funny thing then stopping, straightening my scarf, to wade into the slow, well-lighted plan of a reception hall. It had seemed to matter so much getting here before too late and now it was nothing at all. "Will they be sitting down?"

"No, I don't think so, and if they are, then it will be a dramatic entrance."

They were sitting down. A salad and a cup of soup were waiting at my place. I tried to land gracefully in the chair held out for me. From here on, it would be soft and slow now. All I had to do was eat. It would be easy here to be kind.

The night peeled away evenly. There was nothing more I had to do.

I sipped. I leaned in to hear my table partner's story, folding my hands under my chin a way I'd watched my mother once hold her arms long ago. I was the youngest person at the table. It was easy to get the men to look at me. I hardly had to do anything at all. I was glad for the feel of silk velvet and its folds in candlelight. For a moment, while my date was talking, I thought what my family would have been like if we'd had money. This was a weak thing to do. But I did it anyway, alone, just seconds at a time. I imagined my mother in a kind institution, a place with three-tiered lawns rippling down. And every day she rested. She was saving up for me. For the energy I would take. Then, once in a while, maybe twice a year, we would have our night, beginning early, with the sky darkening but still a blue. If you looked at us, we would seem normal, but a little softer. We'd go to a restaurant, a quiet place with candles, and we'd enjoy the food, her especially, we'd be clean and dressed nice, we'd ask each other questions, she would touch my face like a mother . . .

My mother, one thing about her, sometimes she appreciated a thing so much, a petal of the world, like a meal or a pair of shoes.

A man across the table was asking me where I came from. "Wisconsin? I lived a lot of places, but mainly a small city in Wisconsin. Racine." Sometimes when people asked I just said California. It depended. I was the only nonwife at the table. All I had to do was answer simply and smile. The older women had to work harder. I didn't feel bad about that at all. It just felt like something I had. In me. Particularly.

The women must have watched with a curl of rue in their laughs. They recognized my vulnerability more than I did.

After, we stood outside the school gates, a wife and a different husband holding bowls of flowers that had been the centerpieces to take home. Standing, talking, touching each other's wrists and coat shoulders, we moved frugally, all university people, enchanted by the winter flowers. The first cab came, a couple folded in, and I jumped in too, they were going in my direction. From inside I saw my date stand there hands in his coat pockets, his thin hair in the front moving in the wind and then in a few minutes I was home.

My apartment was a ravage around me; I just added to the mess. I untwined scarves, slipped off shoes, rolled down tights. I took the earrings out and set them on a table. Pretty soon I was in my slip, fabrics draped over every chair and doorknob. I felt loose at last. It came from a country childhood, I always took my good clothes off when I got home. I grabbed a bill envelope and pushed the button to play my phone messages.

"'S Wynne, I've got quite a bit of information already about your father. Date of birth and I've got up to where he's been, I tracked his life up to the seventies. I think I'm gonna get him soon, I think so. I think I'm gonna get him. Get back to me, make sure you get back to me tomorrow afternoon but it looks encouraging."

What was so strange then was time. I'd been looking for my father, always, forever, but now it seemed, it only began yesterday and a night was already too long to wait. Absolutely too many hours. Before I could have gone on waiting without end.

Now I could begin to imagine an after.

And when I found him, would I wait, lose eleven pounds, get in shape, go shopping? Would I charge a new suit to wear to meet him and worry about it later? Or would I just jump on a plane and go?

I HAD TO GET OUT. I put on jeans and grabbed my jacket. I had to get out. I never felt this. Ever. Usually I was housebound. I liked to stay home. But tonight I had to go outside.

I went to Tacita de Oro, the corner place, and sat on the first counter stool. The inside of the neon sign spurted fretfully; green letters and a perfect yellow cup and saucer. Chinese and Spanish food. Order to take out.

They had cigars, flan. "I Left My Heart in San Francisco" played from a little radio.

Why was their coffee so good? The same guys as always worked behind the counter, the one I liked with no chin and glasses, neat, and the other better-looking one, not my favorite.

When I come home to you, San Francisco . . .

It was one of those nights where everything seemed meant for me. Near my shoulder, a girl whispered, "Can you lend me five dollars?" I shook my head no. "Ya sure?" she said.

I thought of my mother laughing and crying entirely without me.

I felt the way I did when I knew a few days before I officially heard that I'd get into medical school, I just knew, and that it would change my life.

I kept buying coffees for a dollar.

The man with no chin and glasses was now eating his dinner. He sat at a table, his ankles nicely crossed, hands on the cloth. A plate of rice and one of stew. He stared at the food, mixed it and lifted the spoon to his mouth very slowly. Everything seemed beautiful and mine. I felt I was going to lose this life. I would lose it because I would want to. How could I stop? There was once before Mai linn went away, when she still lived in Racine. She and Ben were in their days. I said, I was afraid if I went with my mother to California, we'd forget about each other. Mai linn knew already that she was going to move and Ben would be far away.

Mai linn was already unsentimental. "It seems sad to you now because now you don't want to lose us. But it won't be sad then. You'll keep knowing the people you bother to."

That has not always been true. We have all lost, Mai linn the most. But it was mainly that: mainly our own desire that left.

I came here alone. I counted: the butter on the counter, hot sauce, soy sauce, ketchup, sugar, salt, pepper, oil, vinegar, toothpicks, cigars, flan. I wanted to remember it all.

FOR ONCE, I really couldn't sleep. It was one o'clock, then two. It went on and on. This was really a disaster. I had class all morning. Then work. Emory. The TV noise drizzled down from upstairs. I got mad and madder. Didn't he ever stop? I suppose for him night was noth-ing, he didn't have to get up in the morning, he didn't have to mem-orize femurs, he didn't have to worry about flunking out. Finally, I pulled jeans on from the floor, stamped upstairs and got ready to knock. The noise spread out of the apartment, leaking. It was defi-nitely him.

He opened the door, first giving me a hard blank look, then remembering, and said, "Come in, come in." What could I do? He ushered me into his apartment. He wrung his hands in front of his pants. "I make tea," he said as if this were the middle of the after-noon. His pants were some shiny fabric. Old men's pants.

On a small table covered with faded fabric, the TV. As I'd sus-pected, this was right over my desk. It was positioned at the far end of the room, all the furniture facing it. On the same little table sat a bouquet of false flowers and a stick of incense, like a sad altar. It looked like an old movie running, black and white, with rounded cars and cops. Up here, it didn't seem so loud. When he brought tea out on a tray, he stopped and snapped the thing off.

"Oh, you don't have to do that," I said. What was my problem?

"Company," he mumbled and his lips spread. Some teeth were missing.

He rubbed his hands together, then sat down across from me, pick-ing up his teacup in both hands.

The tea was bitter and dry and tasted something like cherries.

"Did you use to work for Columbia?"

"Used to be professor," he said. "Mathematics."

"Were you married?"

"I never marry. No," he said.

And then I knew I couldn't say it. I just couldn't. Now I tried to think of some excuse. For being here.

"Oh, there are your canes," I said. You couldn't miss them. There they were. Three, all wood, each a little different, hanging on a hatrack on the wall.

"I collect," he said. He went up to touch the one on the far right. It had a silver handle, tarnished. "Present," he said, "my niece in California."

"Oh," I said. "Nice."

He rubbed his hands again. "I show you something," he said. He was relishing this visit. Now I had to find a way to get out. The apartment looked like a cave. It was bare and dimly lit and the walls seemed streaked and browned. I couldn't make out any bed. Maybe the couch I was sitting on was where he slept. If he ever slept. He made noises in the closet, and I thought of slipping out, but then he emerged with something wrapped in layers of yellowed tissue paper. He unwrapped and unwrapped, smoothing each wrinkled sheet of tissue out with his creased palm on the table. Finally, he lifted a cane up in both hands. The whole top half gleamed bone.

"My father's," he said. "You collect?"

That stopped me a moment. It was a question I hadn't been asked for years. Where I was from, in Wisconsin, everyone collected. Paddy Winkler collected guns. People collected stamps, souvenir spoons, different teacups. Merl Briggs collected ormolu, Majolica china and this year's shoes from her twice-a-season shopping trips to Chicago.

Women collected Hummel figures, antique doilies, all manner of colored glass bottles. It was odd not to own a collection. Teachers regularly expected children to tote something to school and elucidate for Show and Tell. Many of the more prosperous families collected religious tokens, such as rosaries blessed personally by the pope or relics: splinters cased in oval glass and worn around the neck, supposedly from the wood of His cross; pieces of certain saints' hair, packaged in little boxes, with glass open sides, the hair, laid on velvet, translucent, no larger than a capillary or a nerve. For some reason, the saints seemed always to be blond. Once, for a while, I kept asking my mother if she had one of my father's hairs.

"No," she said. I remember her shaking down a pillow into a clean white case.

"But you must have one somewhere." I could get like that.

She laughed, a little distracted. "Well, I don't know where."

"I collect butterflies," I told the man.

"Butterfly!" he said.

Last year, I spent so many nights in the hospital. A wooden drawer with its silver handle intact stood upended at the nurses' desk, butterflies pinned behind glass. It had been left there by the first patient I knew who died. No one else seemed to like it much. One day the head nurse touched each of her elbows and said it gave her the creeps. Then it was turned to the wall, finally an aide moved it to the closet. I almost asked if I could take it right then, but I decided no, this job was something I really wanted to be good at, I wanted to do it right. If I did really well there, I promised myself, on the last day, I would take it or, if I felt I deserved it, I'd summon the nerve to ask.

It was odd, though, wanting to take something out of a place that had so little. But I did. Mai linn said a psychologist told her that when people treat kids who were sexually abused, the shrinks can't help imagining the crime and wanting to touch the girls, too. "It's a turn-on, a little," she said. "I mean they don't do anything, that's just one of the things they fight." She sighed. "Everyone in this culture wants to touch girls."

By the end of the year, I deserved the butterflies. I knew that, but then I didn't really care anymore. I asked anyway, the day before the new shifts.

"You can keep 'em," the head nurse said. "You're the only one around here who liked 'em anyway. You like 'em, Druse?" she asked the orderly.

He shook his head, wheeling the squeaking intravenous cart down the hall.

I touched the drawer of butterflies with its rough silver handle.

"Do you think the father would want them back?" I said.

The nurse shook her head no, she didn't think so.

A father from Illinois had brought the butterflies to his son. I remember the father's hands, huge, callused, embarrassed of their size, soft and helpless in his lap. He sat beside his son's bed, wishing for another form, those butterfly tentacles, with their capacity for reception. I never saw a mother.

The son died while it was still snowing. We were the same age then, twenty-seven. He was an architect. Jack. When he first came to the hospital, he spent his hours drawing his ideal chair. "For a competition," he said. One day he finished, and I took the drawing and the written forms and mailed them for him, Federal Express. I never heard if he won or not. Later that day, I lifted his gold wire glasses off his face once and rubbed his skin with a cool washcloth, touched with witch hazel. I brought my own witch hazel from the health food store and carried it around in my white hospital jacket pocket. People liked it. The glasses stayed like that, notched, one leg over the other, in a triangle, on the bedside table.

"Butterfly." The old man's fingers made a gesture. "Up your ceiling? Or in cage?"

Then I thought what he saw. Butterflies aloft everywhere in my warm small room. Spots of beating color on the ceiling. Or maybe an elaborate bamboo cage.

"Oh, no. No. Dead. Dead butterflies. Pinned."

"Ah, yes," he said and looked down at his hands.

"You should come down and see them some time," I said, nodding, standing up. "But now I have to get home. Sleep," I said, too loudly, the way I couldn't help talking to old people.

I went back down. My door was open again. I just could never get in the habit of locking.

He didn't turn his TV on. Still, I couldn't sleep anyway. I got up and stared at my textbook, until I caught myself reading the same paragraph three times. Then I hit the bed. I must have fallen asleep eventually because the ringing phone in the morning woke me up.

It was my mother. "I have something to ask you, honey, and I want you to tell me the truth."

"Go ahead. Ask."

"Don't be afraid to tell me. Ann, are you on drugs?"

"No, Mother. Is that all? What got you started on that?" I had this bad tendency to laugh whenever she accused me of anything. I always laughed, whether or not I'd done it. And she took that as a sign of guilt. She always had.

"Well, how are you going through all this money then? Merl Briggs wrote me that they called her from the bank. They're worried about you."

Goddamn small-town bank, goddamn Merl Briggs. "Mom, life is expensive in New York, okay? I don't spend a lot of money."

"Well, be careful, because Gramma left you ten thousand—"

"Nine!"

"That's nine more than I was left. That's a lot of money, nine. That's more than I have and when that's gone, there'll be nothing, do you understand? I can't give you anything!"

4

Today I:

left my card in the cash machine.

broke two glasses, washing the dishes. That's out of three that I had.

flunked a test. Anatomy. Bad.

tore the apartment apart looking for my butterfly-wing pin. It was a scene of a boat on a river, made out of butterfly wings. I pulled every pocket inside out. I didn't find it. It was lost. Really gone. I hate that, it starts me going.

Then I got a ticket for riding my bike through a red light. The cop had a helmet that fastened under his chin. He just wrote, his profile stern. I wondered about his hair. He might have been younger than I was.

The worst thing was I broke one of Emory's towers. I knocked it with my leg and a rampart of glued toothpicks separated and fell.

I was nervous. I guess that was it. Or maybe I was always like this. I looked at my hands with wonder. They looked big. Maybe I was always this bad.

I rolled my bike to the Pleiades Palace. I didn't want to ride anymore. It was a rainy Tuesday afternoon. I didn't have an umbrella or a hat so my hair was flat strands on my forehead and over my ears by the time I got there. Elementary school kids in bright-colored hooded slickers fidgeted in a long line. You could hear the zup of their rubbery sleeves and boots, making squeaking noises. Timothy ushered them in the way he ushered anyone, bending down to take tickets, making conversation. The kids settled in the movie seats, unbuckling galoshes, dropping coats.

We stood behind the velvet curtain listening to their swaying voices. "It's all happening so fast," I whispered. "I wanted to find him all these years and now this really might be it. And I don't know if it's even a good time. What about Emory? He expects everyone to leave him. And school."

"The projectionist'll close up," Timothy said. "We can go."

He took his jacket off the peg and opened a black umbrella over us as we walked outside. We headed down towards the river, trees tenting over us, the choral rain echoing on all sides. "And I don't know," I said, "lately I've been liking my life here."

"What makes you think it's going to happen so fast?"

"This detective sounds like it might. Yesterday they were checking computers in five states. He said it could be any day now." He'd called again today, panting on the phone. "I'm gonna get him, I can feel it, I'm gonna get him soon"—his breath going almost creepy. "Oh, by the way, you said to hold your check for a few days and it's been three, so I'm gonna go ahead and put it through, awright?" The money had come from the Racine National Savings and Loan, with a note from the president saying *Prudence! When this goes, that's all there is.* I knew him. He was my grandmother's friend Jen's brother-in-law, Homer Hollander. The bank building had white pillars and the names of the virtues carved at the top in stone. Constance, Prudence, Charity, Pride, Honor and Hope. Good families in Racine named their daughters these things. Their sons they called Lewis and Donald. It seemed I was giving away my share of the bank at home, and what would I get for it?

"Even if he shows up on a computer," Timothy said, "that's not necessarily going to be his current address, they're going to have to cross-check, send somebody there or call . . ."

"I don't know. I'm afraid. Tonight I'm not even sure I want it."

He put a hand under his ponytail, pulled the rubber band out and swung the hair free on his back. He kept the plain liver-colored rubber band on his wrist. His wrist was wide, the bones round. His cuff touched my cheek. The old suede chafed rough on my skin like a man's face, this time of day. "You know, you don't have to see your father when you find him. You'll have all the information. You can wait. It might be enough just to know."

"Yup." I guessed that was the advantage of me finding him, that I could take my time. But even there, he had me. "He seems like such a wily guy, though. What if I paid all my good money and found where he was and then, by the time I was ready to go, he'd've moved again. Then I'd have to start all over."

It had stopped raining. Timothy took the umbrella down. And the sky thickened to that liquid deep blue it did just before it was really dark and lights came on, the bridge lamps and strings of lanterns across the river making the buildings over there look like a small carnival. I still wasn't used to eastern light and weather.

"Will you go alone?"

I shook my head, sending water flying. "Who would I take?"

"You could bring a friend. Stevie. Or Emily."

"Naa. I'd have to bring my mom or somebody who knew him. And she's not into it."

"No."

"I kind of want to go alone." I'd have rather had someone. A brother or a sister. The way it was, my family things were an embarrassment. After all this time it was still hard to be different. And the being different didn't go away ever. But that was my life: alone. There was a spare thrill to that, too.

"I wonder where he'll be."

"The West somewhere." I shrugged. "Some people you just know aren't in the South. And I can't see him in the Middle either." I knew a lot of places. I'd had years of driving. Now I was settled down to my dark apartment and quiet books. "He tried Wisconsin. And Michigan. Like it won't be Arkansas or Texas or Georgia. Not the plains. He'd never be in Boston. I haven't seen him in so many years but I still have all these ideas. Maybe he's nothing like I think. Maybe he's right over there in New Jersey." We stood looking at New Jersey a moment, the green banks, rich from rain.

The sky and water were hardening into their colors, their edges making one sharp line.

But I knew he wasn't in New Jersey. I absolutely knew.

I'D LEFT my door open again.

I rolled my bike in, pitched it against a wall. I walked around in the dark and just touched things, all my old furniture. I had the feeling you might get knowing you were about to receive a summons to pack up your belongings. My breath came from the top of me, a high, almost giddy kind of waiting. I squeezed the shoulder of my grandmother's couch the way I would a person. Maybe I could have liked this life. I was leaving before I really got to know it.

What had been abstract, diffuse, so one night it was the spell of a vast deep sky, the touch of a stranger's two fingers on my neck, could become everyday and of this world. I'd need to buy a plane ticket. I'd have to travel, maybe stay in a hotel, rent a car. What would I bring?

Would I even take my life here into consideration? Wait till it was a good time to leave school, get someone to fill in for me at the hospital? I should really get a haircut, lose six pounds, get my clothes in order, pay my bills. Once I went over to Stevie Howard's apartment in Madison when he was packing, the bed was a ravage of clothes and dry-cleaner cellophane. A huge suitcase was half full on the sheets. Talcum was spilled on the floor and the open bathroom yawned male smells. His apartment was no better than mine. He'd gone shopping that day. We were still the age when we bought our new clothes for going home. Or everybody else did. Not me. My mother was different. When I went to see her I'd see just her. There weren't friends and parties, none of that. There wasn't even a house. She lived in a rented backhouse she couldn't afford and still, there was no room for me.

My father, I couldn't see staying the same place long. I'd paid the detective my money, I'd better jump on a plane and do what I needed to, before he disappeared again.

It would be his time, not mine. All these years, he lived everywhere, the eye in the seed, pollen in the wind. That was different and maybe easier. Now, if he was going to be a man, just wearing brown clothes, living in some city, then it seemed things should be fair. My turn and then his turn. But we never would be fair.

I held on to the back of my rocker. I didn't want to go. Anywhere. I loved my small life, unwatched and unbothered, just as it was, one more night. I loved it for all I hadn't given it.

I collapsed on the gray couch, one hand on my belly. I hadn't had sex for more than a year now. I had never been pregnant. And I hadn't been perfect either. It was weird. I always felt proud of that—no abortions. It was another kind of virginity. But now I was twenty-eight, and it was something I worried over a little. Why hadn't I ever been pregnant? Most of my friends had. I'd wanted to, deep at the center of a few nights.

Stevie had had two girlfriends who got pregnant. When Mai linn was seventeen, the artist in San Francisco used to cry out, "Ooch, I want to make you pregnant." Once she brought up the subject the next morning while he sat cross-legged on the bedspread unballing a pair of socks. He made his bed every morning and then ironed the shirt he was going to wear that day. He patted her belly and said, "It's enough just to think it." She told Stevie and me that she wanted his baby. Stevie looked at her like being pregnant with that asshole's child would ruin her. His name was Kevin June. I believe in naming the names of assholes.

Bud Edison asked me once, "Are you preggy?" I'd never heard that word before. I thought he'd made it up. He'd thought up the idea of me being pregnant because of what I was eating. Then he said, "You can't imagine any circumstances so that you'd be married in the next year?" His voice worked like a knob turning the whole room forty-five degrees more still and permanent.

"No-oh," I said, like of course not.

I hurled onto his lap, my socked feet on his knees. I was like that with him. We'd be in his apartment, allegedly working, books open, and I kept looming across the room falling on him. It wasn't desire exactly, it wasn't that. I imagined large twelve-year-olds throwing themselves on their fathers, all girl.

I pulled at his sweater. It was an odd blue. "Can I have this?"

"I can't give that to you. It was Asia's father's." He'd had a real girlfriend before me. She'd gone to Reed College and her name was Asia. She'd left him. It bugged me, her power.

"Was her father dead?"

"No."

"So why was she giving away his clothes?"

"She just gave it to me," he said, picking at a thread. "It was nice."

Once, later, we really thought I was. He called every morning to check. I hadn't told him about my fasting and my insides. Most of my friends had had abortions already. We didn't talk about what we'd do. I suppose that was what my parents did. They never planned their lives. I didn't want to have a life like theirs, but I didn't want to be one of those sensible people from good schools either, planning every test of their lives as if there were nothing higher. It depressed me to think—this was all there was.

I PUSHED UP OFF THE COUCH. I slid in the gloom around tables and then dialed the detective, standing in the dark, undressing. First I rubbed off running shoes with my heels, then peeled down socks, shirt, jeans, underwear. It was still ringing. I looked at the underwear. The elastic was frilled from so many washings. I was getting to an age where I wanted better. Young and poor was invisibly changing to just poor.

"Yeah," he answered on the fifth ring, and then waited, like I had something to tell him.

"I'm just calling to see if you found out anything?"

"We're working on it, you gotta be patient, these things take time. And so far he's not coming up in any of the states we're checking for license or DMV. He's just not there."

"Oh, okay."

I angled my hipbones past the corner of our old Formica kitchen table. I knew how to move through the tunnels of my apartment, without hitting myself on edges. I collapsed again on the couch. It was the same furniture, the same darkness, the same lights and moving-wind string instrument noise outside. A siren coasted down from the neighbor's TV upstairs. I jammed open the window.

Everything was different.

I LEFT THE LIBRARY at midnight, riding my bike in the dark, wind separating my clothes from me a hand's width like a knife under the peel of a fruit. I would pay the bike ticket. I'd call the bank about my card tomorrow. Replace the water glasses. I had a jar. I could drink out of that, I didn't care. I'd talk to the anatomy teacher. Go back to work in the morning even though it wasn't my day and see if Emory'd repaired his tower. I'd try this life a little longer. I'd try and forget the butterfly pin because I'd have so much else to do. I hauled the bike in, took my earnings out, put them on the table. But I really did think I'd lost the butterfly pin. It was gone.

This was tedious. He was locatable. It would take time and patience.

But I was not as near as I'd thought. Maybe I was no closer than I ever was.

And then I had that feeling again of when the first blood comes. You'd call him on the telephone—he's relieved too, you talk soft child-voiced awhile, sweetakins, words you never use, then you sigh and hang up. It is evening, night. Outside, you hear the glass edges of screams, the gay lift of a teenage crowd. You tell yourself, actually say the words, you did not want to be. Not now, anyway. Honey, we really couldn't have handled it now, you know that, he said.

I know.

The apartment feels close. You open a window. Air is anyone's. You are a woman in rooms which have been other, strangers' rooms. Paint is such a thin light way we make ourselves feel clean. Like skin, you can scratch right through it with a fingernail.

You lie down fully clothed on the made bed, your high heels falling off onto the floor.

When. When will your life begin?

. . .

MY DAYS IN NEW YORK numbered. A month ended, six weeks. Jim Wynne seemed to dwindle. He had that oh-it's-you in his voice when I called. All the money I had didn't seem enough to keep up a man's interest long. By week four I told him I wanted to see him. He said there was nothing to talk about. "These things take time," he said.

I tried then to go back to my life. How many times had we come back? After the promise and glitter of tiara and throne. Twice, when we lived in Wisconsin, my father called and my mother and I got on planes and visited him in the West. And then we had to go back, to her work and my school, after our slight wingbrush of glamour. Or just when we called in sick and spent the day dressing up and getting ready and waiting, and then he didn't come. Our regular life looked different after we'd left even for a day. Walls grew up around it. Even daily life requires our allegiance in order to include us.

And everything else I did, every subject in school, anything I concentrated on, that became a way to know him. This is a quality of discipline—it will subject any practice to its rules and turn them into prayer.

I was still in medical school, but barely. I went to classes, I tried to memorize. But I was behind. I didn't go to my study groups, didn't do anything.

I had this secret life about to begin—and I was happy. That is the only way I'd ever lived. I'd never been so what I did every day was the point. People like that with their normal ambitions seemed so plain to me, like drills. Jobs, school . . . I was drawn to people who did them but always gave their best to something else hidden and invisible.

I suppose that is what my parents did. My mother's jobs were never really jobs, they were what she clunked out to do every day for a paycheck, skimping out early afternoons, the files settled in her cradled arms, guilt's assuagement, the paycheck a means to dinners, running butter and sour cream on potatoes, and dresses like dream, filmy things we wanted and couldn't afford that wouldn't last anyway but we couldn't get out of our minds until we possessed them.

BY WEEK FIVE I said I needed to go over everything we knew and didn't know.

"Mayan, for what we're paying these guys they're gonna do the checks on their own sweet time. I'll call you the minute I know anything. Period."

Meanwhile, things were going on at school that I should have been doing. There was a party at somebody's house, after midterms. I stayed until eleven-thirty. The next day when I came home, a guy called me and said, "Hi, this is Jordan David. Remember me? I was wondering if you'd like to have dinner some night."

It was a big party. I didn't know which one he was.

At work in the hospital and in my apartment, I grabbed the phone after the first ring. I always expected it to be the detective, with news. So far the answer to everything was Nope.

I hated phones. They were one of the things like airplanes I was convinced were ruining life. They were made to save time and cure distance but did the opposite, only teasing, the way the mirage of food and water must be in the desert.

And I spent too many of my nights on the phone. Most of my friends were far away. I still didn't really feel like I lived in the East. I said, all the time, that after this was done I'd move back. I promised that on the telephone to people at two o'clock, three o'clock in the morning, the TV sounds from my upstairs neighbor filtering down. Now I wonder what I could have done in my life then if I'd only been paying attention.

I walked to school, dumb and used in the morning from too little, vivid sleep. All my dreams happened in dark red. A flier rasped at my feet. I passed an empty school yard, then just a lot; even here there was unused land, you felt the value drop in Harlem from the peace of the sky, the feel of the side streets. If you are here you will stay slowly. Time is not for you until the end.

THE DETECTIVE had definitely become like a lover. He was sick of me. I begged. I called him from a pay phone at the library. I cared and he didn't. He hadn't returned my messages for days.

Then one night taking an old woman's pulse, counting, they paged me and it was him, excited again, pleased with himself. He had that bouncing-on-his-chair sound. "Listen, we got a lot of stuff on your father. We're typing up a report right now, I'm gonna send it to you." My heart stilled when I heard that and then it started again fast and regular like a small bird just held in the palm, after hysterical flight.

"Send me a report? Forget it! I want to see you today. How about dinner?"

"Wha, tonight? I dunno if I can do it."

I had plans that night too. I had a date with the guy from the party, whoever he was. But I knew if I let the detective off the phone without a promise, I might never get him again.

"Listen, Jim, I just want to sit down with you and hear what you've found and that way I can ask questions if I have them and we won't waste a week in the back and forth."

"Hold on a second, lemme see where I am." I held on. He was gone a long time. Two orderlies passed, pushing IVs, in the slow, regular pace of early evening. Hospital time. "Awright, well, I gotta be in Manhattan for a seven o'clock meeting, that'll go on, I don't know two hours, maybe longer. So it's gotta be late, you see what I'm sayin'?"

"Fine."

I knew I should have named a place, but I really couldn't think of one. My insisting was just bluster. I would have perfectly accepted a no. It's what I expected really. "Where do you want to meet? I should know a good place, but I'm in the library all the time, I don't even . . ."

I was working through my closet. I tended to keep an outfit four or five years and just wear it every time I needed dressy. But he'd already seen the one. "The dress," a guy at school had said, lifting my sleeve between his fingers. I'd been surprised to hear it cast in a dowdy way. It had been fine just a year ago. It was the same. Nothing about it had changed.

My mother once shook her head badly and screamed, "How can you do this to me! I only see you once a year, can't you just look nice once and let me be proud of you?"

That time I'd wheeled back on her and yelled. "You bought this for me! You bought this for me three years ago and you loved it then!"

"Then! Honey, that was three years ago. And you're not twenty-five anymore."

"LEMME SEE," Jim Wynne was saying, "I'm gonna be midtown, meet me at a place called Polanciani's—on, what's, damnit all. Tina," he screamed, "where's the Italian place with the red booths that I like? Awright. Forty-five, between Seventh and Eighth, you got that? Nine o'clock."

The two plastic trays on the cart outside Emory's room were luke-warm now. I lifted one. The potato dish with bits of hamburger cling-ing. Thursday. I felt bad for letting them cool and hurried to Emory's room. I still took both trays. If I didn't eat, it'd be a change for us. I could skip food tomorrow. I had to call that guy too and cancel our date. If I even had his number. But not now.

The toothpick factory rose under the window. He'd rebuilt and changed the place I'd bumped. Cardboard boxes lined the room, a pile of newspapers stacked next to the door. Emory had to move. A diagnosis of periocarditis allowed nine weeks in the hospital. He had been there eight. After that, they decided Emory was okay. Or okay enough to let out. We'd prescribe prednisone for when he got out. It cost too much money to keep a person here.

I kept imagining a safe place, one room, a small bed in the corner, regular meals on a plain wood table and Emory left free to work and roam the grounds, grounds like the ones at the Belgian monastery back home in Racine. The monastery had tiny rooms, just a bed and a dresser. It had rolls of land, going from the top of the hill down to the river. They had lawns and gardens and a vineyard. It all had that quiet static feel of private, almost unoccupied land. The place was nearly empty now. There were old men and a few young boys who were studying to enter the order. There were more flat white stones in the graveyard under the ash trees. They rented out rooms to peo-ple like me for seventeen dollars a night.

That was the kind of place I'd always wished for for my mother. A place in the country, almost anywhere, it didn't have to be beautiful in a spectacular way. Let the rich keep the beaches, this could be plain land, glory would come not from heights or size or jagged contrast but just the sky. Trees would grow there, an uneven orchard, land bound in beyond sight with a solid wood fence and old gates. Insti-tutions exist to give adults childhoods, the ones who needed them now. Everyone would have a clean room where they were allowed their own few things. A chair brought from home, a few pictures on the wall, my mother's hairbrush, Emory's shirt that he works in hang-ing on a peg, an old backpack sagging against the corner. And food served by an ample older woman with a regular eye towards kindness, who refused any seasonings even with the good kitchen garden just outside, and went by the day and recipe so that nothing was ever unknown and new except the sky.

Emory's foot was tapping. "Makin' me leave. To stay, I gotta do something else. Find something bad enough to get in somewhere for a while, but nothing so that I'll suffer. No place low."

"No."

"I've got a record, couldn't get worse."

"Sure could."

I was sitting on the bed, he was at his desk, twining string around his hands. This was more my life than the date I was supposed to be having. Dating never seemed true. I mean I wanted it, but I never had the right kind of time. Either I fell in love and that was enough to darken out everything else or I felt like I was lying. I always had something big in the front of my life that I couldn't tell the guy. Those nights when he told you his interests and you told him yours, they made me feel less where I was than just staying at my job or going home. Or calling a friend far away. And there was always the movies.

"There is no nice place to go, Emory. And then you'd lose all control."

"I know."

Emory had two arrests, on five counts, but no convictions. His crimes were simple thefts. He'd once worked in a large art supply store where he'd been caught stealing. When he was a school janitor, he was arrested for taking items, not of material but sentimental, even intimate, value from teachers' and administrators' desks and, in a few cases, students' lockers. The largest object stolen was a child's rain slicker and black buckle-up galoshes. A letter was removed from a teacher's desk, a small mirror from the principal's secretary, drawings were ripped out of students' notebooks. In both cases, the judge dropped the charges.

In Emory's room, amidst the clutter, both of us picking at food on the trays, we were used to each other. It was like setting out for a long walk, the same road every time, familiar gravel, the path winding to dirt under a lane of trees. The sun set at different times, the sky lifted and fell, weather changed. I took out the needle and vials for blood, the stethoscope, his chart. We knew each other now. I no longer felt frightened before I went in to see Emory that nothing would start, it was as if we both knew our time and meeting place by the rusty gate, we swung the heavy thing open and with our hands clumsy in our pockets we just went.

I ate both our desserts. The trays were empty when I carried them out again. Then I ran to the fifth-floor bathroom. It was a room where only one light worked, I didn't know how long the other'd been broken, a mirror hung over the old porcelain sink that had the bulbous lines and taperings of my grandmother's kitchen mangle. I looked in the mirror. Oh. Mirrors always disappointed me in myself. Tonight, again, I wasn't going to look very good. I didn't have time to go home and try to change myself. I didn't have the right things anyway. Just the one pair of golden shoes. I always had one element but that was never enough to do much.

I used to think I'd always lose. Anywhere with other women. So I'd not try. That way it might seem like I didn't care. And that, maybe, if I had tried, just maybe, I could have shined too.

But in other people, in Emory, the thing I could love was only their effort, the visible hub of want. Those toothpick structures. The awkward, the failed, the overardent.

Once in college, Stevie Howard and I went to dinner at the Moonie House. After supper, we sat in a room with folding chairs. Everybody there did something. Three girls with thin long hair played guitar and sang. Somebody read a poem. All the others told them how good they were. People clapped, whistled, honked. We decided on the walk home that was the worst way to control someone. Was to make them confident in virtues they didn't have because then they always had to come back to you.

I was sure—with looks—I'd be the fool.

JIM WYNNE'S RESTAURANT felt right, high red leather booths stained with use, cracked so the cushion enclosed you when you sat down on it. The place smelled of oil. The menu, written in tiny fancy script, plotted on for two feet. I'd been on time, my hair fixed up the best it would, lipstick, mascara and eye shadow. A touch of perfume from a sampler. Once, Emily Briggs led Mai linn and me through a Chicago department store and we stopped at the ground floor counters and asked for samplers of their best perfume. Emily knew all this stuff from Briggs's, the department store her family owned in Racine. Mai linn still hit Philadelphia department stores twice a year. "Student budget," she said.

He was still not there and it was nine-thirty. I looked at the name I'd written down on my hand and it was there, the same as on the menu. I had a premonition he wasn't going to come. I always felt like that. And then he was slipping in the booth, no apology, saying, "That guy will give you one headache, 'sa maniac. Waiter, we've gotta order in a hurry, I need a drink, you want anything? I'll have Scotch, better make it double, and a plate of your pasta, whad'ya have tonight?"

"How about the Matriciana?"

"Fine. Make it wet."

"I'll have the same thing, please. And a vodka."

A little candle flame wavered on the table and the waiter produced bread and our drinks, and this was pretty much the way I'd imagined, dark, like a date. The liquor helped. It seemed easier to smile.

"We made a lot a progress here," he said, opening the briefcase on his lap and taking out a manila file. "There was a woman who really dug for us out there at Wisconsin, she was just great, she remembered your father and she really went way out, a woman called, what's her name, a Dorothy Widmer."

I had to rummage in my backpack for a pen, thinking W-I-D-M-E-R. I wrote this name down on the scallop-edged paper place mat. I thought it might be important to me. Later.

"Awright, there's a solid record of him in Wisconsin. He was at the university, there in Madison, in the early fifties, first as a student, and then he taught. In December '59, he got offers from BU and MIT and Michigan State. And he took the job at Michigan State. And we got a birthdate. May 21, 1931."

I wrote that down, all of it exactly. That was my money's worth. May 21, 1931. A trinket. My father's birthday.

"Oh, his grade point average, by the way, was 3.9." The detective's voice swelled brass with the good news. Fluttering began in me, wings beating in a shoebox.

So those were the glory days of my father's life—a 3.9 average, job offers.

"East Lansing was the training ground for Harvard, they used to say," my mother repeated through my childhood. "Who used to say?" I wanted to know. "And who-oo-oo cares?" My cousin Ben would chorus with me. Benny had a family, he didn't have to sift through sands to find respectability, to weigh one grain against another, the glass, the stone, the lime. My mother had always been a great believer in education. Now, she kept talking about Columbia Medical School as if it were some great national monument.

"The training ground for Harvard," I'd heard my mother say that, perfectly earnest, head held high, in front of a dozen Racine ladies at Emily's yellow eighth-birthday lunch. I guess the Racine women were too polite to contradict. Or maybe they just didn't know. "That's what they all say," she'd capped it, though no one had whispered one word of dissent. Then she sighed. My mother had, apparently, for a while those years, tried to rally. She'd sucked in her breath, stood straight, hair coiled on top of her head, the pretty wife and young mother. Waiting for her husband to return. These duties proved truly beyond her and like any of us when we are ill, they shined for her with a hard semiprecious metal brilliance, just because they eluded her honest grasp. For a woman capable of making a home, preparing the dinners, maintaining the constancy necessary for the life my mother imagined, the work of it may have become boring. But my mother was never steady enough to be bored. The same was true of me. "You never sit still," my grandmother had said. I felt too, I don't know, almost grateful. And gratitude made me restless.

"Jim, I have a question for you."

"Shoot."

"You've found other people's fathers, right? What happened to them after? Do you know any?"

"Like I said before when you asked, what they do with it is their business. Sometimes I find out something, but just by chance, you see what I'm saying. There was one guy, kind of famous guy, worked in movies. Never called. He just waited for the report. I billed him monthly and his accountant paid, always on time and always by check, I remember. The guy had gold checks. And then I finally did find the father. Podiatrist. Lived somewhere in the suburbs. Outside Chicago. Then, my client wanted me to interview the neighbors, put together a kind of profile on the guy. I ran into him year or two later. He said he never went and met him. Didn't want to anymore. His business. He paid the bills, it's his business."

I nodded my head yes. That was right.

He turned to the file. "And after the job at Michigan State, he went back to work in Egypt. And this Dorothy Widmer got a Christmas card from him there. She's a saver. She went way back in the files and found it. So we have a return address."

This had the ping of a pinball hit. It was something.

Dorothy Widmer received a Christmas card addressed to her at the Alumni Association from my father in Egypt where he was, apparently, working in a refinery. Those must have been optimistic times. Times for keeping up contacts, including a return address on the card's upper left-hand corner. That was something I never received from my father. A return address. I don't think I ever got a letter.

Twenty-nine years later, Dorothy Widmer still had it. Who was this Dorothy Widmer? Who were these Dorothy Widmers, these Marion Werths, and would I rather be them, files fattened with stray Christmas cards from men you never saw again or a being like my father who traveled, dark, fleet, singular. Later, I believed, trails of him would be picked up in Arizona, Nevada, Oregon. Other places he'd called from. But they would seem inadvertent, probably less optimistic. Already then, batting around the West on his small wings, my father had begun his fall.

Just then a waiter in a maroon jacket wheeled a cart to our booth and served us with fancy old-fashioned silver implements. It was wet, good pasta.

Jim Wynne twirled the noodles around his fork, then cut the stray ends with a knife. "Now I'll tell you what I wantcha to do," he said. "Listen to me. I want you"—and he said this word-for-word slow, as if he were giving out the instructions for an important mission—"I want you to write a letter to this address in Egypt. It's the Refinery, in Luxor. And his home address when he applied to the university is listed as 34 Sharia Miramar. Now you write to them and you tell them who you are and that you're his daughter and do they have any information as to where he is or as to who might know anything about him, you understand?"

I wrote the address down. Besides these names and dates, I'd been doodling with the pen, so I'd moved the place mat when the food came. Practically the whole paper was full. "Yeah, I guess, but remember, everybody always said he was here."

"I think he's in Egypt," Jim Wynne said. "And I'll tell you why. That's what Dorothy Widmer thought, by the way, because after that postcard, everything on him stops. I've pulled credit, I've pulled DMV, I've pulled insurance and it all stops. And the postcard says he's glad to be home."

Maybe I'll just go there, I thought. I gulped a sip of vodka like water and felt the shock in my teeth. Maybe tonight I'd sleep with this man twice as old as I was and then I'd get on a plane and just go.

"What kind of a refinery?"

"Oil. And that's what she thinks he did. Otherwise, she thinks he would have kept up with her and the Alumni Association. She woulda heard something."

Who cared what she thought? She thought if he didn't keep up with his child he was going to keep up with the Alumni Association? It sounded too much like the detective'd had one conversation with this Dorothy Widmer and that was all.

"We're trying to track down the wife now. You know he got married?"

He got married. That stopped me. I put the pen down on the place mat. Married. Oh, okay.

"He got married. And her mother died."

That her mother died somehow made her blond. A blond child-faced woman with an upturned nose, proper, curly-haired, named Maryanne. The kind of girl who was pretty in a newly pulled way and whose liquid face would soon harden like candlewax. My breath tucked up under one rib bone, caught there. "Which time?"

"Wha?"

"Which wife?" I'd met one other. Uta. She was older.

"I got her name here. Lemme see and she went over with him to Egypt. And her mother died. An Adele August of Rural Route #3, Guns Road—"

"That's my mother!" I said. Some lid snapped shut. Now I was mad. "And they went to Egypt and they came back! And you're drawing all kinds of conclusions from someone who hasn't seen him since 1959. He lived here all through the sixties. I know that. I saw him. You've managed to trace him to 1959! I saw him in 1970! I told you that. He lived in Pasadena. That's something I'm sure of. You're telling me stuff I already know. I don't need you to tell me he went to Madison and married my mother. I know that."

"Listen, Mayan, I'm tellin' you, after that everything stops."

"It's a hard case. I said that. That's why I need a detective. I paid you to figure out what happened after 1970. Before that I know. I was there. Remember?" I could flash out with lights and fire.

"You're telling me that I've wasted three long days of work?"

"Yes!"

"Listen, we can close this case. Don't tell me that. I'm saying to you as an informed opinion that he's in Egypt. Nothing's coming up on him here."

A moment later, I thought, he is saying this because he means he could quit working and take my money, he's already cashed the check, he knows I can't stop him, I have no power, he's used to this, his contracts, his forms, he prevented my recourse the moment I signed my name. He does this for money every day and knows the laws and how they're worded and protects himself completely so that I am at his mercy and there is nothing a small person can do. I am so at his mercy that only my kindness would inspire him to work, my fucking womanly flirtation, submission and gratitude. That is a way I'd felt in the end all my life. My mother was right about the damn world. At first I would try the other, justice, but that ran out early. So I did what she would do. I put my chin in my hands and looked up at him. Smiled.

"Nothing anywhere here's coming up. Nothing at all. There's no trace of the guy." He shrugged. "Nada."

Fine. That didn't work. I folded up the white place mat and put it in my pocket. I just walked out, to his saying, "Hey. Hey!" A waiter stopped, two silver spoons in the air. A couple guys at the bar stared. I felt my skirt touch my leg. Okay, maybe I was becoming that kind of woman after all. I liked my back. Bud Edison used to run the side of his hand over it and say, this is my favorite part of your body. Backs always seemed to me the material aspect of desire. At least I felt victorious, leaving him with the supper bill.

Unfortunately for me, that walk-out satisfaction never lasted. I should have known.

I'd never been able to leave. I tried.

I'd walked away from boyfriends too but never really. With my mother, I pretended to run away. Then I always came back crying and shivering, a raw mess, too desperate for principles, only needing food and things—wanting my bed for sleep and to forget. I knew at the core that I was not the one who could leave and never come back. The other could do that. Not me. That was a right someone had taken away from me, just by doing it first.

That night I walked. With a guy like this detective, he just didn't care. He'd shrug and throw down his cigarette. That was all. Then he'd go back to his pasta. That was just how it was. I felt further away than ever from finding him. And that was almost fine. It was a cold moist night and there were a few dim stars. The buildings loomed tall and hard except for one thin-lit skyscraper that seemed diaphanous, filmy. It made me want to be a politician, run the world. Oh, I believed in power the way poor people do. My mother and I had been small people. We believed power worked, even to find the powerless. The powerful could locate the powerless, but not the other way around. The powerful could keep themselves invisible, if they chose, while the rest of us lived waiting to be conjured or not at somebody else's will and time.

When I got home, a guy was leaning against the wall in my lobby. The date. I'd forgotten to call him. Damn. I'd meant to. He was mad now, it was after ten o'clock.

"What happened?" he said.

I brushed my arm like I'd never be able to explain it's so much. "You got me at a bad time," I said.

"Why?"

"Oh, God, I don't even know you, but I'm sorry, I should have called."

"Yeah. You should have."

"Listen, things happen in people's lives, okay? So just forget about it."

"All right," he said. He was carrying something like a briefcase and he sort of swung it as he headed out the door. He wasn't bad-looking, I saw in that instant—the profile.

"Wait a minute," I said. I touched his arm, the layers of cloth. "This sounds weird, but I haven't seen my father since I was twelve and I'm looking for him. I hired a detective and the detective called tonight and I thought we were getting close but it turned out to be nothing. I'm sorry."

"Oh," he said and his briefcase was just hanging and his face went soft. This guy is going to be easy, I was thinking. Then right away I wanted him to leave. He shrugged. "You want to get something to eat?"

I knew I should but I didn't want to then. I promised him later.

I STILL THOUGHT of Bud Edison all the time. It was too long, I knew I shouldn't have. But I probably remembered something about him once a day. There was always a man I was suffering over. I had an unrequited crush even when I had boyfriends. I needed one to think about to get to sleep at night. Sometimes I lost one and I had to start another before that night's sleep. I was never without one. Not one day of my life. It may sound like something hurtful. And I suppose it was. But it also allowed the hope of perfection.

THAT NIGHT, Aleya Azzam called. "Hi, I'm not sure who you are, but you've left a lot of messages on my machine."

I startled right up in bed. "Hi. Thanks for calling me back. I was looking for an Azzam who might be my uncle. And he used to work for the United Nations. Do you know him?"

"No, I don't think so."

"Oh, I thought maybe you were his wife. But your name is Azzam?" I'd left maybe twenty or thirty messages on her machine.

"Yes, Azzam." Her voice built a little. She seemed eager too.

"But you're not Egyptian or anything?"

"Yes, I am Egyptian."

There was something about the first yes. The luck of it—not a common name.

"Do you know any Atassis?"

"My family's cousins are Atassis."

"I'm an Atassi. My father's name is Mohammed Atassi. He's from Alexandria. Do you know him?"

We were both getting excited now. "Yes. I'm from Cairo, but some of my family is from Alexandria. They always say the Atassis and the Azzams are cousins. Who is this other Azzam?"

"He used to work for the United Nations," I said.

"Yes, my father said there was an Azzam who worked for the United Nations."

"I'd love to meet you sometime, to talk about Egypt. I'm planning a trip there in the spring."

"Yes. I would too. Are you here for long?"

I smiled in the dark apartment—the foreign student's question. "Mmhm, I'm in medical school. What do you do here?"

"Civil engineering. I plan bridges."

"Oh, that's great. How old are you?"

"I'm thirty. But you know, um, this month is bad because we have a deadline." A thirty-year-old Egyptian woman building bridges! Good for her, was my first thought.

"Good for her," I said, after hanging up.

I marked down *Call Aleya* three weeks later in my calendar. Call Aleya.

AFTER CLASSES ONE FRIDAY, I went out drinking with some other students, new friends maybe. They went to a dark narrow place where a middle-aged woman was the bartender. She had long black hair she kept in a ponytail. We were the only people there. Regular living-room furniture crowded the room and in the back corner, on a gray large chair, sat an old old woman, watching television. She had long hair too, just growing down plain, a yellowish gray. There was a huge separation between the women that age who did their hair and the women who didn't. No matter what they talked about together, that would be more. I thought I'd be the type who didn't do it. In the Midwest, you could almost tell a woman's age by her hair. There was the hair of childhood, the long plain hair of the best years for a girl, the twenties' bangs and wings and upcurls, then the above-shoulder still-with-bangs cut of the thirties, beginning to be set in rollers, sprayed, the forties' style, definitely done. The stages here in the East looked more expensive but just as set. But some women everywhere stepped out of the procession.

Everyone was drinking drinks. I'd asked for coffee and the woman behind the bar, moving loosely, made me instant in a glass. I listened to everyone, spoke when I could. But it was hard. And when they were getting up for their second drinks, I left. I was supposed to be living this life. I tried but I was still never in it. As the time ticked thick and slow while they were drinking and spaces hung between what anybody said, I always knew I should have been doing something else. I wanted to go home and call my old friends far away. I noticed the sign outside as I walked away: THE BLUE ROSE. I passed a sedan jacked up on cement blocks in an empty car lot. That looked like so much unused land in the West.

THEN CAME the frustration days. Three weeks passed and I left more messages on Aleya's machine and she didn't answer them. I thought the detective was going on nothing, theories of some alumni bureaucrat who last saw him in 1959. Still, I started to wonder if maybe they were right. Maybe he was in Egypt. I thought of a toss of stars like dice on a pure black sky. What did I know of Egypt?

Well, okay, I decided, so maybe I'd just go. That had always been the wild card. After such an extravagance, something would have to change. Egypt would probably cost the rest of my money. I called the Egyptian Consulate and the Egyptian Embassy in Washington. I said I was looking for someone, anyone named Atassi. All I did was annoy them. But I asked them to send me a visa application. The piece of paper arrived a few weeks later in the mail. It was thin, blue-lined, made with an old-fashioned mimeograph machine, like the exercise sheets passed out years ago in grammar school. It looked crude compared to anything official and American.

I'd never asked anyone really how much it cost to go there, even though I'd heard the word all my childhood. Some things seemed possible in this life and some didn't. I was always drawn to those that hovered at the border. In childhood the moon was not possible. It was a thing of far beauty, a cool light on our everyday hands. Now, NASA kept a waiting list of civilians who wanted to go. Tad Alto, Emily's fiancé, he'd signed up. The going was such a different enterprise than gazing at the moon, your chin propped on a shovel handle. And so many things had felt impossible anyway in childhood, maybe to me more than to other kids. A lot of the big optimistic opportunities didn't reach the country in Wisconsin. And the systems priding America, we didn't believe they would work for us. I never felt surprised when a letter came back marked ADDRESSEE UNKNOWN RETURN TO SENDER, if a package never showed, if a telephone did not ring. I felt confirmed in what we already knew was the truth. Things didn't work. He couldn't get through to us. Our prayers fell down space and time, shreds like sound from the man upstairs and his TV, so you could make out noise and shuffle and static, a word now and then, but never a sentence that meant anything.

I couldn't even draw the shape of Egypt. Wisconsin was like a hand.

I went to a small travel agency near school. I'd heard about this guy; he was a dharma bum, ex-hippie, who would cheat on airline tickets, sticker them so you got the lowest available price no matter what. So much of what determined what was life and what dream was still only money.

The way the rich lived in movies when we were children was like New York City. It almost equaled the moon. But things went strange on us. If that first day the detective had said nine thousand dollars, I wouldn't have felt surprised. I probably would have given him all my money. Detectives, for me, came from movies anyway and could have been like the rich and the moon. I only knew Egypt from my father and the movies. When my grandmother was away and my mother wanted to go out, she'd drop me and my cousin Ben off at the Coliseum Cinema in our pajamas. She'd come late, late at night to pick us up and we'd be half asleep on the velvet benches in the lobby while the girl behind the candy counter vacuumed the star-flecked carpet and my grandmother's friend, Gish, tallied the ticket stubs from the red and silver wooden box, painted with stars.

Egypt could cost anything.

The travel agent worked out of his apartment. He was a large-featured man over forty with a goofy laugh that lurched towards the personal. "That'll be seventeen hundred sixty dollars, round trip, with two weeks advance purchase, open as far as return. That's the best I can do."

That was way too much money to make sense in my budget, budget who was I kidding, what budget? Too much money but it was not . . . impossible. I still had six thousand dollars left. I could do it. Or I could charge it and pay it off month by month.

I asked the travel agent if any courier services went to Egypt. Mai linn always signed up to be a courier and once they bumped her onto the Concorde.

"To Egypt, no, I don't think any legal ones." He loosened a crescendo of giggles. "For under a thousand I can get you to Thailand. Bangkok. That's a great trip. I was just there."

"Is there a way to get a ticket refunded once you buy it?"

"You gotta have a doctor's note. I guess that's no problem for you."

Money. Once in California, with Stevie Howard, we ate a tart made of golden raspberries, in a restaurant. He didn't particularly like it. "Fancy," he said, in his way. Stevie was a gardener, but to eat, he preferred plain things. But I remembered for a long time and the next winter I tried to find a bush of them to buy for my grandmother. She loved things like albino squirrels or berries of a different color. Those were the wonders of the world for her. I troubled over her presents. She didn't want enough. I finally called Marion Werth at the Racine Public Library long distance. She wrote a letter for me to the Brown County Horticultural Society, which tracked down the golden raspberry to a nursery in Nebraska. When I called, the woman on the telephone said the bushes were two-ninety-eight for three. That was more than I'd expected. I'd expected a golden raspberry bush to cost a hundred dollars, but I'd thought I could just buy one. My grandmother wouldn't need the harvest, she'd want to stand and marvel, the watery berry heavy-coned in her hand, still attached to the bush, soft against her soft palm. I told the Nebraska woman about being a student on financial aid and could I order just one bush for my grandmother. The woman sounded perplexed. "Do you understand I'm saying two dollars and ninety-eight cents?"

I bought twenty-four. They were still growing along the east side of the garage, next to the rhubarb patch. But other people lived there now.

"Whadaya say? Should I book it?"

I rested my hand lightly on the travel agent's desk, which was covered with layers and layers of paper, a real mess, but still, his room looked provisional somehow, scarcely inhabited. I was superstitious with money. I wanted to keep it tightly, a dark seed in me, but I also wanted to spend it all, like blowing a feathered dandelion, as if then, lightened, something would have to happen. My mother was that same way. She'd spend all our money on dresses and jackets as if she were threatening life and time. *Now what,* she seemed to dare the sky. I know what she wanted: a man with numberless money, to take us into his mansion. But what always happened was, we cried long distance on the telephone and wheedled just a little more money out of my grandmother.

"Not yet," I told the travel agent. "I need to think."

"I'm going to Nepal in three weeks. Now, that's a trip. Why don't you come along?"

I WAS DIFFERENT AT WORK. I tried to look at everything small. When I held a person's wrist I tried to see only her skin, the tiny hexagonals, and hear the vein ticking, watch just the patch of linoleum on that floor where her feet planted, tentative in large slippers. I did what I was supposed to do and marked the charts. Every old woman was to me my grandmother and so I was careful to be kind.

I watched Emory pack his boxes. Emory had found a job.

"Janiting," he said, "for a school at night. The school at night." He started howling. One thing Emory could mimic exactly was animal calls.

"When are you going?"

"Tomorrow." He nodded his head, mouth closed, up and down and up again, three times, like someone taking medicine they didn't like the taste of.

We sealed the boxes with packing tape, loaded them on a cart with wheels. "Tell me about the apartment," I said. "You haven't said anything about it."

"I think I might get a dog."

I joined him on the floor now, balling newspaper. "What does it look like?"

"There's one window with a windowsill really wide that I'm going to paint yellow. The floor slants. When you walk up the outside stairs, it turns and there's crack vials all over. Inside the ceiling slopes and it's light in front and dark in back."

I nodded. Being a doctor would always be this way. You released people to an unsafe world, partly well, with some of themselves intact.

"You'll paint and make it a home. And get a strong lock, too, Emory." I should talk.

"Maybe a Dalmatian. And not a puppy. I'm going to get me a dog. I remember I used to have these days, man, I'd just lie on my stomach, face mashed down on my bed, the sheet would look yellow, it would be tinged, even if it was white, tinged and I'd shake and sweat and I'd drool and the drool would make a circle and the circle had a smell like a bad coin."

He just stopped and so I asked, "And then what happened?"

"I would stay like that for a long time. Whole afternoons, evening, I don't think it was more than a day. And then I'd get up. I'd be tired, real tired. It was like I'd been on this circus ride all day long. Screamed my insides out. I got a new body and I'd walk around and touch things that were mine. Just my comb, chair, cereal bowl. They felt new. They didn't have me in 'em anymore. That used to happen a lot but it doesn't happen as much now. First thing I'm gonna get me a dog. In a week it'll be me and the dog."

"Do you know, when it gets like that, if there's anything you can do to make it less?"

"I learned about that, yeah. I figured out if I got myself up and went and saw somebody, even live people in a movie, it'd go away and I'd be better, I could chase it that way, but I don't know. I think it's better for me to stay in those hours and it's like on a ride, being spun all around so you hurl against walls and you shake so hard that when it's done with you're really through. When I get up, the world is straight. Like hundred years ago. I leaned up from my bed once and saw this black sky with silver clouds out the window, collected around the moon. And it stays small for a while like a kid's room, everything smooth and tiny under your hands. I think it's better for my work if I stay. Better for me. Plus I'll have the dog. Either a Dalmatian or a Lab. No terriers. I hate terriers. Never going to have a terrier again.''

I was propped against the wall, a ball of newspaper in my hands. "Does it scare you, that those spells may come back?"

"Oh, it'll come back all right. They'll probably come back my whole life. Like a full moon. *Rahr,*'' he growled. "Sometimes they're worse. When I was younger and stupid, almost every time I used to think, how can I go on after that and live, these hours I'm falling through, how could I ever tell another person. I thought I didn't want them knowing I've been made so low, been done that to. It's like being fucked, I guess.''

I leaned towards him, I didn't think about it or consider, this was fast, if I'd waited I would have known it was a bad idea, I guess I pure meant it and so it went exactly right, my hand took his and we gripped like a tight shake or arm wrestle and our faces found each other and we kissed and then drew back our eyes in a straight line.

"It's always that high wire, for each of us, one day to the next," I said.

"Yeah. There's good things too. Like, I was never a dumb fuck. Back in the days when my father and I had our fights, man, that was violence, I mean you could taste the metal in the air and you felt it in your mouth and then it went yellow. And I always believed it was pretty probable I would die. And then, after there was this green thin air. Peace. Could eat it.''

"Yes.'' If I were God, I'd have given the fourteen-year-old Emory some days of swagger and frivolity. But that is all just nothing. Wishing. I suppose most everybody, even the dumb and the mean, would not leave this world, with its beauties, as it is. Perhaps my grandmother would. Maybe that was what it was to believe.

"What about this?'' We'd boxed almost everything, but the factory stood unwrapped, just as it was. "We don't have a box big enough.'' The dried glue in the joints had turned a darker color, like sheer caramel.

"You want it? Take it. I was going to burn it."

"Oh no, you've got to bring it with you."

"Never find a box big enough and even in a box it'd probably break."

This confounded me. "Don't burn it, whatever you do, don't burn it."

"Well, you want it?"

"I'd love to have it, but you should keep it."

He said he'd leave it for me. That made me uneasy, but I couldn't think of anything. I wanted the factory but it seemed wrong. He shouldn't give it away. "Don't forget a lock," I said.

"Hey," he called out into the hall, "don't you forget Vanessa what's-her-name. He's probably not a swell guy." He fell to mumbling. "But I'll have to walk the dog. Every day I'll walk the dog."

"King. I'll remember. Not a swell guy." I had to turn. In my chest, a high trapeze swing of happiness.

5

I NEVER WANTED to be a girl.

I wanted to be president or something. Mai linn and Emily and I were three little girls squatting in the dirt hitting rocks on the ground. Promising each other. Never to be mothers. I was the leader. I wasn't going to be stopped from anything because I was a girl, I decided, and my playmates echoed me, the dust settling on our flimsy cotton dresses. This was our vow to ourselves when we were nine, that strange afternoon time of childhood when Mai linn and I sat cross-legged on Emily's pavement in her long-decaying garden, hitting rocks on the hard surface for no purpose, promising hard. We had to repeat the words, because we already knew our lives would be littered with temptation. Look at our mothers.

My mother worried about my appearance. She didn't think I made the most of myself. She knew I didn't pay enough attention. She claimed concern about my personal habits. I wasn't showing the usual signs. "Boy I don't know who's gonna want to sleep with you, all over the bed. Like this, this is what you look like." She made an ugly position with her arms and then her face like that. She was standing above me when I woke up one morning. "Do you have to sprawl over the bed?"

"That's the way I sleep," I said.

"Well, boy I'd change that if I were you. And fast."

My mother was young and full of vim. She didn't worry really at all about my grades. She would have been happier with another daughter altogether. If my mother thought about it now, she would not want a daughter like me. She would have wanted a young woman more like her own self: enthusiastic, spirited, pretty, full of life for the game.

She would not have wanted to make a child like me, even as she was doing so.

Emily's mother was different but also unhappy. She had the things my mother wanted, but she couldn't use them right. Emily's mother had no better life than we did. My mother always sighed when she picked me up. "What I could do with that house. And with her clothes."

"You could've married 'im," I said.

She sighed again. "I know. And don't think I don't think about it."

Mai linn had no mother.

We worried about Emily, losing her. Emily was beginning to have the kind of looks impossible to miss. She had ankles that dipped before long thin feet, and majestic features, the nose and overfull lips of a Greek statue. Plus she had blond, good hair. Only she was a little chubby.

We kept Emily on our side a little while longer due to a critical mistake she made in the shower one evening in August of our fourth-grade year. She mistook the depilatory bottle for shampoo and was bald the rest of elementary school. That and nothing else safeguarded her virginity. Emily had no will. She had been the kind of child her doctor father could pull up on his lap and arrange her flat-boned legs, putting them on one side of his knee or another. She mostly went along with what we said. But baldness became a mark of identity for Emily. First we all went shopping for a wig for her. Then, her family and I and Mai linn were supposed to be the only ones who knew. The wig shop was serious; it was a large warehouse with wigs and toupees on only one back aisle, the rest of the merchandise was prosthetics, wheelchairs and crutches. There were racks of nurses' uniforms in the front. We touched the hairs and said, this one seems pretty natural. I understood that day, you really are alone in life. Because just watching Mai linn try on the blond wig and feel the side of it and look around the store at the strange old ladies who worked there, I knew she was feeling what I was: this is Emily and not me. But somehow the word got around and my cousin Ben pulled the wig off Emily's head in American history and she cried and ran out of the classroom and everyone had seen and so the whole school knew. I think that was what started the long music of Emily's fall into love with Ben.

Emily rose to baldness. You could see her article "Baldness Is Freedom" in the January 1969 issue of *Seventeen* magazine. She stopped wearing the wig and her new appearance yielded a kind of dignity and status. She really did look good bald. She had a pretty-shaped head, all the knobs and bumps were in the right places, the two strings of her neck rising up gracefully like stems. She ran for vice president that spring and won. By then she was shaving her head to keep it bald and wearing long very thin earrings her father bought for her in New York City.

The three of us had vowed not to spend any time on the dumb girl things in life. We tried not to want to be queen. Years later we each, separately, set our alarms to get up at four and six o'clock—Pacific and Central time—to watch Princess Diana getting married on television. Jackie Kennedy didn't help but the others did. With the other presidents you'd rather be them than their wives.

We cautioned each other away from clothes and makeup, the charms that attracted boys, parties, homecoming queen nominations, jangles on one chain. Why? I believed we couldn't afford that. "While they're learning eye shadow," Mai linn said, "we can learn Latin." And we did, Emily straggling in late and drowsing through Cicero, but passing anyway. Even the old nun who taught Latin couldn't quite keep immune from our fervor.

With Emily it was only a matter of time. Her father owned Briggs's, Racine's largest department store, which supplied the high school girls with all the tools for their ascensions. He opened a boutique, on the second floor for mod, far-out teenage clothes, called The Id.

"We can go when we're twenty to a department store and buy all the clothes we need then," I said. It was amazing to me, the stupidity of girls. We marveled over them, girls who spent their afternoons lolling by pools, pulling the elastic of their bathing suit legs out to check color, their nights talking on Princess telephones about dresses and mascara and shoes, their only progress measured by getting their braces off. These afternoons we were studying our Latin, reading it aloud, declining.

Why? Because Mai linn was an undersized Vietnamese girl in Racine, Wisconsin, in the late nineteen sixties, and with me it was because of my mother. All she did was her looks. While she was married to Ted, she spent hours plucking and preening for Tom Sklarr, who I already knew wouldn't marry her years before she found the chest of letters from other women in the bar where he stored wine on his boat. I knew he wouldn't be any good for a father anyway. When my bike was stolen right in front of my own house he didn't even think of buying me a new one even though he had all that money. He just said it was too bad.

We promised ourselves not to try anything for men, never to go out of our way at all. No makeup, fancy clothes, anything. We each cheated a little and tried not to tell the others. At home, my mother whispered to me that I would be a movie star. Mai linn and I caught Emily once with an ankle bracelet.

Of the three of us Mai linn was the least. But she was an orphan. She had no money.

She came and sat on my bed one day after school, we were studying at my house. She hugged me and said if she were ever to want anything with a girl it would be me.

"No, Mai," I said. Emily and I and Ben were the only ones who called her her real name. At school, the nuns all said it was too hard to pronounce. They said her American name was Lynn.

She got up and went to the other bed across the room. "Okay," she said.

A year or two later, Emily confessed that she'd let Mai linn do it to her five or six times.

"You're one too then!" I said.

"I really only liked the back rubs."

"Why'd you do it, then?" I said. I hated that they did that together. That way.

She just shrugged. Emily was that way with boys too, later, even more so. We'd lost her for good by high school, but by then Mai linn and I had both moved anyway.

When my mom and I moved to California, I found another girl to boss. Calla and I were the first feminists in Los Angeles. We hadn't heard of it from anyone. We came to conclusions by ourselves. It wasn't hard. All you had to do was look.

"I'm never going to cook for a man," Calla declared one day in her empty kitchen. We were standing around there after school. Nobody cooked in that kitchen. Rosario, a small, frightened Mexican maid who seemed to speak utterly no English, came every day and cleaned, but she darted out whenever we marauded through and the only thing I ever saw her cook was a soft-boiled egg for herself.

I wasn't so sure about not cooking. I thought it was fine, all this learning in school now. But I did want to get married. "Well, what are you going to eat?"

"He'll have to be satisfied eating yogurt for dinner like I am."

I didn't say anything. Who wanted to eat yogurt for dinner? At least my mother and I ate a real supper when we went out at night. Ted would have never put up with yogurt. Yogurt's fine, he'd say, but what's for dinner?

Calla's mother was pretty too or at least my mother thought so. She was tall and bird-faced and she floated in her thirty-four-room house like a ghost, often in a bathrobe and puffed slippers. The house held silent as a convent, but dressed up in striped flowered wallpapers and matching elaborate skirted furniture. The living room and game room and den were huge done-up alleys no one used. Calla's mother lived stringently, treading a line only from her bedroom to the bird-print-walled dining room where she ate her silent pilgrim's breakfast of eggs and toast with coffee in a decent china cup and saucer and sat looking over bills, for the electricity or phone. Bills seemed to be her most important business with the world. Those were the two signs of life Janine Canter exhibited. She either sat in the dining room doing bills, dressed up in her prim lady's clothes, or she mooned through the cluttered dim space in slippers. She was a first wife.

Calla's mother complained in a tiny bitter voice about how evil people were and she was just seeing it now since the divorce. And it did seem unfair. Membership on all the charity boards where she'd worked hard volunteering, baking tea coffeecakes, hostessing cocktail parties, had somehow been mysteriously revoked, and next thing she heard, the new wife, a Swedish model, had been asked to join. What she did outside the house was shop. She had walls of boxes for three-hundred-dollar shoes she kept in her bedroom, RED

SATIN PUMPS, MEDIUM HEEL, she'd Magic-Marker on the outside card-board. She wouldn't let us borrow them even to dress up in just around the house. "Because they're too good for kids your age," she said.

Calla's mother every once in a while would consternate for a morning over the UCLA extension catalog, deliberating whether she shouldn't try to take a course. These mornings her toast would lie ravaged as she sat at the dining room table with a huge heated pot of coffee next to her. Her hair stuck out from her pulling it from the pins. "Go ahead, Mom," Calla would urge. "Sign up for something." It was hard to see what Mrs. Canter did all day.

She always studied the catalog, deliberated hard and then decided against. "It's too late for me to have a career," she said to us, "I would have had to start earlier."

She was thirty-six years old.

I ran for school president there my sophomore year. I tied with a boy. We each got three hundred forty-eight votes. The history teacher settled it by flipping a coin. I picked tails and he won.

"You're gonna let a coin decide?" I cried. The history teacher shrugged. "We can't have two."

That day the president—a guy named Ronnie—followed me home and asked me out. After that I worked on guys' campaigns.

I DIDN'T WANT to waste my life on frippery and look at me now. Better to have bought bras. I'd watched all those girls giving their lives up to men, spending days in preparation, painting toenails, brushing on powder, opening the flower. That was for men who were there. Men who stroked them and gave them things. I was worse.

I was like a nun, making my whole life for a man who wasn't even there.

AND OUTSIDE, on the street, after class, I saw men again everywhere, one in a phone booth, hand spread and plastered against the glass wall, his breath steaming a patch around him so I couldn't make out his face. They were young. I saw it in the tight stretch of skin from the tendon connecting head to shoulder. And so was I.

THE PHONE RANG at eight in the morning. An assured female voice said, "Shawn Timmelund has to cancel his appointment today. His elbow is sore." This was the guy who cut my hair and made me look better than I did.

I asked if I could reschedule. "You'll have to call back later in the week," she said. "Shawn makes all his own appointments."

It seemed I had to chase everyone. Even paying them didn't help.

The detective petered out. He hadn't called at all since I'd left him in the restaurant with the bill. So I began to do more myself. It was hard for me now not to.

But I'd flunked anatomy. The professor asked the three people to stay after class and he told us we would have to take it again next semester. I guessed that was all right.

When I did things to find my father I knew I should really be studying. But I felt like, if I could just get this one thing done, then I could concentrate on everything else, patiently, for the rest of my life.

I WALKED UP the United Nations steps again, the near echo of many heels louder than the steady roar of water splashing the somber Las Vegasy fountains. I'd dressed up. Some. Still, as I stood for a moment at the top, before going in, I saw all that made the place feel important and it was nothing—empty flags, towered rows of high straight loud water rushing. But the buildings and their plazas made no monument, nothing really, that would last. No pyramids. Just another committee's work.

The same Polish receptionist, who showed no flicker of remembering me, looked up Azzam's name on a computer printout. "Uh, Said Azzam is not here in New York. He's stationed at the Geneva Mission."

She gave me the number in Switzerland. There was nothing to do but hoop my purse over my shoulder, turn around and start back to school. It was embarrassing, what happened next. I spent the afternoon in my same wooden library phone booth. I felt like carving my initials into the already scarred-up wall. I'd found a maze and I couldn't get out or stop. So much of my life has been waste.

The Geneva Mission seemed to have heard of Said Azzam but he wasn't there.

They gave me another number in Geneva.

The other number in Geneva said he had gone to Vienna and they gave me a number in Vienna.

The Vienna number didn't answer.

I tried again eighteen times and when it finally did, they said he had gone back to New York.

I called the UN switchboard again. Forty-one rings. Then they said they didn't know, on their listing he was still in Geneva.

Okay. All these phone calls I'd charged to my calling card number. Just wait till that bill came. I'd developed a kind of shudder in my back, just below the right shoulder.

Said Azzam, whoever he was, had vanished. It was as if my father taught his magic to everyone with a trace to him.

A day like today. "What points do you get in heaven for hours of this total waste?"

Stevie Howard laughed into the telephone. He was in his Berkeley backyard. I heard his kid screeching behind him, the trees beyond. It was a cool day there and windy. "None. I don't think. I don't think you get a single point, Mayan."

"Great," I said.

"You've got to think, how long are you willing to do this and have days like this before you just give up and decide that even if you could find him, what you'd lose wouldn't be worth it."

How many people would have turned back there? I knew girls like that. Girls who would measure, weigh, play the odds. Not a swell guy. And they were right, the smart ones. It is not hard as some people think to admit the mistakes of your life. The real ones that cost years and loosen the cohesion of your only heart. It is easy. The waste is irredeemable, the devastation absolute. I am not afraid to say it— what's lost is already permanently gone.

I TOLD THE DATE guy anything because I didn't care. But half the time when I picked up the phone it was him or I'd come home and he'd be leaning against the building wall.

I'd told him silly things. I said I thought men only looked good in jeans and white shirts and knit ties—I talked like that about nothing, just from the top of myself, because he was listening and I wanted to sound absolute somehow—and then there he was with that on, the wind blowing his shirt out from his chest a little, his mouth in that way that was embarrassed of what it showed.

Jordan. His name was Jordan. He was some kind of lawyer.

THE PHONE RANG in the middle of the night. It was the international operator.

Calling Egypt was incredibly hard if what you were calling was information. You called the international operator and she worked on it and said she'd call you back in a few hours when she had someone on the line who could help. So she was getting back to me now at four in the morning. I woke up right away. I was glad. This was more like love than love.

My bedroom shades were up and the moon hung about a foot over the top rail of the building next door. The water tower etched plain and drawn on the night and spires impinged on silver clouds. My bare feet touched the ground. What a sky. I paced, nude. The old man's TV was running upstairs, dropping shreds of noise through my ceiling. I didn't even mind. Tonight it sounded like comfort.

I heard the international operator, somebody in Cairo, a translator and all our echoes. I pictured three people standing in a line.

"Atassi in Alexandria." I heard myself shouting into the phone like my grandmother.

My words were repeated three times, twice spelled in the other language.

Finally, the answer came back. "What is the first name?"

"I don't know. Any Atassi will do."

That went back again and then rumbled.

"They can't do it without a first name," the international operator finally said. "There are more than a hundred Atassis."

More than a hundred Atassis. I thought of an old monument standing in the dark on a hill, more than a hundred pillars, slanted moonlight, crumbling stone. "Okay, Mohammed," I said. My father's name. I didn't think he was there, but I only had a few chances. The whole relay wouldn't stay up all night while I guessed. I wished I had a little book of Mohammedan names. Then I remembered I did. The Bible. Where was it? Damn. I pulled the phone cord as far as it would go. My bookshelf had *Anatomy, Organic Chemistry, Histology*. That architecture book.

"You're going to have to spell that," the international operator said. Even she sounded very far away.

We spelled the alphabet letters slowly and I heard the far ripple of translation. But then after all that, they had no listing. Later I learned that Mohammed and Abdullah are like John and David, the most common names.

Even so far away, it was the same. So that was done. Egypt ended like any other place.

ONE TIME Bud Edison had woken up and walked with his arms out to where I was naked, crouched over the phone on his desk. I felt caught. It was hard to explain. I'd been calling information in Montana. "That was directory assistance. I was trying to see—"

He didn't even ask what. We had a moment of blunt hug, bones meeting at knee and elbow, awkward, dry, adult. We went back to the bed and lay in the dark looking outside at the night alive and I told him some more about my father. I guess I'd always used men for that. To talk about him.

"It bothers me that he didn't know me when I was a baby. My mother told me he was back in Egypt then," I said.

Bud kept looking at me, squinting. He wanted to minister and did, dabbing the edge of my eye with a piece of sheet, but he also looked a little scared. That blue cold night, clouds hung silver-edged, majestic, spread and stretched by wind, a taut wingspan. It felt like a privilege to be awake then, as if all the nights when we slept we were missing this.

We began again, me in his arms, and I was almost asleep when I startled and shocked rigid and then it was over in a minute. That scared him.

The next morning, pulling on his jeans, he said, "You were talking last night in your sleep."

"What did I say?"

"I'm not sure. I think you said, 'Say my name.'"

That was nicer than the truth. What I really said was just what I said all my life, in that time just before sleep. I didn't tell him.

I STOPPED AT the office to pay my rent the next morning. My landlord was occupied with a massive suspendered man, who held the thin shoulder of a girl curled over the desk filling out a rental application. "Take good care of her, my daughter here. And the bills come to me, you understand? I don't want you touching her money."

The girl's hair half-obscured her face, but her profile was slight and pretty. Thin gold chains hung from her ears and on both wrists. Tiny even pearls like teeth lay on her delicate breastbone.

"She's gonna be a surgeon, my girl. Columbia Medical School. Top school. Top top school. Sure I'm proud."

I had to turn the other way. I left my yellow check on the edge of the desk. I didn't want them to see me. I had this odd feeling, of, oh that's right, that's the way it should be, I'll leave and she'll take my place. Those are the people who should be doctors. The fathered.

Walking down the street, I pulled my sweatshirt hood up. That was familiar, seeing girls with fathers. It bothered me. I tried to picture mine. I tried to think of him leading me through someplace big that was his. I worked to imagine a factory that made some American product, rows and rows of beige blenders on a conveyor belt, but I couldn't hold it. All I could picture was the night sky between empty beams like Emory's toothpick factory. Empty and abandoned in a high field.

If there was money it would be bad money. I believed that, I didn't know quite why. I could almost get a casino: imagine my high heels on the hard polished stone floor and him taking me through Atassi's Palace, gold-plate endless fountains and tiled pools of water and slot machines jingling and, above, rapturous Persian shapes, an atrium with blue and green tropical birds, but still it was all his and I was the boss's daughter.

Maybe he was a terrorist. Yasser Arafat was at least compelling. I thought of the man telling me that in India parents had more important things to do than raise their children. Maybe an idea could be that. Not money.

"He doesn't sound reliable enough to be a terrorist," Timothy had said. "Or committed enough."

Why you are unwanted: that is the endless, secret question, asked over again and again.

I wanted to have been given up for something that was beautiful, even once.

. . .

I SAW ANOTHER guy in a phone booth, his knee up pushing against the glass. Eagerness, it looked like.

That did it. I veered into a lingerie store. I'd never been inside one. They'd always given me the creeps. But this one looked sort of athletic. There's athletic and there's intimate. It's a distinction. You get to be an age, I guess, when you want good underwear. I used to never think about it. Then the last time I'd visited my friend Stevie Howard in Berkeley I was really shocked because on his comforter was a pair of black lace underwear. I asked. I couldn't believe his wife didn't wear regular underwear. Helen was a botanist. He was a tree pathologist. They were both, most of the day, in dirt.

We were sitting at Stevie's little kitchen table drinking herb tea and he was looking all over away from me. The stove pipe. The corner. Baskets above the refrigerator where they kept the napkins and bananas.

"What do you mean regular?" he'd said then.

"You know."

"Well, I guess she doesn't."

I'd always thought he would marry someone like me. "What do you mean, you mean bikini or you mean not cotton?"

"I don't know, I guess sort of both."

"I can't believe this. You mean like fancy lacy stuff?"

"Well, it's very tasteful."

"Silk?"

"I don't know but I guess so, kind of silky."

"Lace?"

"I suppose some lace."

"What color?"

At that point he stopped me. He'd lost interest. I wanted to see. We actually had an arm fight over her dresser drawer. She was gone to work at the lab.

I was twenty-eight. I'd never had anything but plain cotton underwear. I had poor people's underwear. Some of it not even mine. My own closet and dresser were filled with clothes I didn't buy. When I was young, Mrs. Briggs used to send over her old clothes, maid-laundered, after she'd cleaned out her closets. But she kept things so long, they were years out of style and hardly ever worn by the time I got them. My mother did that now. She hated throwing things out so she sent them to me, but even her old clothes were never gifts. She was letting me use them, she would say. Any time she could decide she wanted one piece back and she'd call me, demanding I send it overnight mail. Once I was wearing her eight-year-old flowered skirt that she'd said came from Paris and I was ducking through a metal fence in college and I tore it. I freaked out, shuddering and crying, Stevie Howard stood with me as I begged and tormented a Chinese tailor at the dry cleaners because it was my mother's and expensive and it was from years ago and I could never find one like it and she would kill me, kill me when she saw. "I don't know why you wear that thing," Stevie had said, "you have a lot of your own clothes that're nicer."

Most of mine were old and grayed and some of the elastic frilled from so many times washing. Years ago, when Stevie and I had lived together in Madison, he used to do our laundry in one big scramble and when I ran out of mine, I'd just wear his. Mai linn quit wearing underwear altogether. She just wore jeans. "Except with skirts," she said. "I don't like the feel. Actually it's a really sexy feeling to wear a dress without any."

Emily had a boyfriend once in college who used to buy her stuff like that. She never wore it. You wouldn't guess from knowing him that he'd have ever been the type either. It was supposed to be knitted silk or something. Then one day she came home and he was in their futon with the covers pulled up to his chin. He had on all of the stuff he'd given her, layer over layer.

But now, I was in this store fingering panties and bras and one-piece things. All of a sudden these skimpy soft things didn't scare me anymore. When I first saw them, they seemed almost dirty. But the fragile fabrics felt good against your skin. I was embarrassed, though, about the salesgirls. They didn't hover. They looked distracted, following the traffic outside. It was a job, I supposed. I'd worked in stores. This time of day especially was slow.

I didn't think about my body much. But when I did I knew I didn't have a body like other people. It didn't have what it was supposed to. Clothes didn't go right on me. My mother talked about it like a deformed thing. A year ago, I was home and she shook her head and said, "We look better in pants. I do too, so don't feel bad. That's why I'm telling you, it's not morality, if you're one of these big models or starlets with the long long legs, sure, go ahead and sleep with him the first night. But with legs like ours, they're better off seeing you dressed up in great pants until they're really in love. Then, when they're hooked, you can take it off and it's no big deal.''

It was true: I only wore pants. The one dress I had went down below my knees. Still, people wanted to use my body, just as it was. My mother and grandmother made me feel that. I had to be careful. Maybe even my stepfather. Men would always try and have you. When I was growing up, we all heard the story about them using Netty Griling, men who worked for the place where she was. Netty was a retarded girl who'd lived down the road from my grandmother. They took her away to a place they had for them a long time before we left, when she was nine or ten.

I often thought of the men with Netty Griling, in a field maybe, the weeds over the height of her face, and what they did. She would look down with her mouth open a little as if she were watching something far away. And who knew what would register on her and stay inside, there would be something, a cramp or a slight twitch. Nothing she could ever know or say.

Even though I thought all these things I knew I was better off too. I wasn't fat and I wasn't ugly. I'd had boyfriends all along who told me that, told me I was better-looking than my mother. So I believed and I didn't believe. I guess I was that way with many things. But that day in the store, I was just beginning to try to build myself up a little. I thought I'd just buy one thing and then leave. I felt guilty even before. Here I was buying something nobody would see.

And that was only the beginning.

I didn't know what I wanted. Some were sort of like light fancy shorts, some the regular shape I'd worn all my life, made out of different fabrics with lace insets, and some skimpier, bikini-ish and even some high-waisted like my grandmother wore over her girdle, but bedecked. There were many colors and degrees of lace. I eliminated red. Did I want white or black or some kind of mute rosy silk or blue? I didn't think too much lace. I supposed like with any kind of clothes, some shapes were best for different bodies.

I picked out a few. I liked an ivory-colored one-piece thing but it cost a hundred dollars and that just was definitely way too much so I let the price tag drop back on the silk. And what about bras? I didn't own a bra. I hadn't had one for years. I picked a few simple ones. Matching? Matching.

Then I braved a salesgirl. "Excuse me, can I try these on please?"

"We can let you try on the bras, but it's illegal to try on underwear."

"Oh, okay." I thought she could probably see right through to the shabby stuff I lived my life in. I owned two weeks' worth before I had to do laundry again and this was near the end.

I tried the bras. That wasn't too bad because I kind of liked my breasts. They weren't big or anything, but nothing was wrong with them. All the bras looked pretty good. The underwear would be a different story. Hips were what I'd wanted to get rid of when I fasted. And they shrunk but the proportion never changed. By now I understood that it was me.

I went back to the counter to buy one bra. I had the underwear in my hand.

"How do you know which fits?" I asked.

I seemed to be the only customer buying. Another woman dallied in the corner where the fragile night things hung.

"I guess it's okay if you try 'em on over your panties."

I was glad I asked. "You're a small," she said. She gave me petites and smalls, but they felt like strings on me, nothing. So I went out and got mediums and larges. Better. I liked baggy underwear.

I bought five pairs and a matching bra. One black, two white, one pale blue and one a beigey pink. All larges. I hoped they were sexy enough this way, loose. I didn't know. How did people learn these things?

I gave the girl my credit card. One more thing. Now that I'd blown half my savings it seemed even easier to spend. My life was definitely moving like some momentous train gathering speed, dark trees pressing and then falling away at the oval windows. A woman in a cap carrying the bags she lived out of drifted by the luminous glass front wall of the store. This was one time in my life I felt completely severed from everyone. My family seemed to have forgotten about me. My grandmother used to send me packages of new socks and underwear, nothing like this, just from the Kmart. And my first fall here, Stevie and Helen had sent me a coat. He was rich then, with his first degree job, or he felt rich. That wouldn't last, either. But we didn't know that then.

Learning femininity, I felt like I was guessing piece by piece. Women just with each other became different, I supposed. Like a solitary herd. I never really grew up girl enough.

With my mother, somebody had to put gas in the car. I became strong and silent, stealthy, like her dream of a son.

A woman rushed in from outside wearing a raincoat. Her face was urgent, checked. She stood next to me at the counter and extracted a long beige thing from her bag. She showed the girl where a thin rolled strap was broken and a panel of lace ripped. "A successful honeymoon," she said. Then she slid on glasses and bent over closer. "Can it be fixed, you think?"

Spending all this money made me think of Jack's chair. I had seen one like his drawing in a store. I'd tried to save for it so many times and now I was doing what I said I'd never do, I was spending all my money from my grandmother, and I wouldn't even have the chair when it was done. I might have nothing. I walked towards the showroom, my eighty dollars transformed into a light tiny bag holding fragile delicacy. I passed men slumped against the walls, asking for money mostly just with their eyes.

I understood: I would never own a house. I would never have the chair. Even if someday I had my inheritance money back again, and that would never happen, I could not spend so much on a chair anymore. That made me want to see Jack's drawing again. I wished I hadn't sent it away. And I wanted something too. I wanted a box.

I passed an open empty garage, its dark tunnels stained on the walls.

The showroom door was open and I walked to the back. I went through a swinging gate I wasn't supposed to pass. A young man was there, lugging something out of a huge crate. I liked watching him work, his back an artistic thing, and then the thunder of the emergence, the chair over his head like a man bringing forth what he'd wanted out of stone. He set the chair down in what little there was of room. Sawdust scattered on the backroom floor. He hadn't even seen I was there but then he did. He stood heaving, blood slowing in his veins. He had on a tight green T-shirt. We both looked down at the chair awhile. It was perfect. It caught the light in its leather folds like a hand would or a jewel, as unalike as those things are.

"May I have the box?"

"Sure." He lifted the cardboard box out of the crate and tipped it upside down. White nugget-shaped Styrofoam fillers showered out, but I touched him.

"No, I need that. It's to move something fragile." The skin of his arm had been warm.

"Take it," he said.

It wasn't heavy carrying it, just awkward, like dancing with an inanimate thing. I knocked on Emory's door. There was no answer. I left it in the hall with a note to the janitor—DO NOT TAKE—and one to Emory, "For safe passage of factory to Brooklyn."

WHEN I CAME home from school, I put them away in a drawer, the new underwear and bras wrapped flat in white tissue from the store. I was just studying tonight. No one would see me. These, too, I was saving for the other life, with the golden shoes.

I never understood about fashion. Why you can't put a thing away for years until later when you've finally assembled all the pieces one by one. But a real piece of fashion is perishable, subject to time, like life itself.

Emily could buy something and she'd wear it home that day.

MY GRANDMOTHER owned her own house in Wisconsin. The other places we lived were always rented. My mother left Racine and sometimes took me with her, but my grandmother's house was the only place we always returned to. There was one clock in the house. When we came inside, we all took our watches off and when we needed the time, we walked into the kitchen where it was.

I had to be told how old I was when my father left. Nobody remembered exactly. It seemed he left more than once. But they thought three. The last time he left I was three.

For many years I didn't remember. I thought he left in our sleep. But then the day of my grandmother's funeral, it came back to me. Because he left on a day when we had relatives in the house for a family party. And the only family parties we had tended to be funerals. My cousin Ben and I were taken to eleven funerals before we were ten years old. We became experts in the conversation. Who looked nice and who didn't look anything like herself. She would have been glad, somebody usually said and sighed. We came to like the activity of after, the bratwurst. It usually meant a calm outside afternoon and then a barbecue. We drank out of the dead woman's cups. It was always a woman. The men all seemed to have died before we were born. We were introduced early and death didn't seem so bad.

Most of them were for my grandmother's aunts, who lived in Bay

City and Sheboygan. But this party was at our house and I can't think who could have died. But the day he left we were not alone. Ben and I moved at the fringes of the family house, filled with people. We were not easy to see, among cousins, alighting and then running, folding between the bushes and the house. My father called me, from the intimacy of hiding, where I smelled the dirt and felt the raw, reddish new branches of bushes on my bare legs, and I ran out to him over the long yard. Ben skidded up after me. My father stood by the open door of his car, just at the point the driveway met the real road.

He was a tall man with good posture and I had often been told to stand like him.

"Can you manage by yourself?" he said.

"Yes."

Ben's leg swung from the knee because we were talking without him.

"Where are you going?"

"I have to leave, Mayan, but I'll come back." Then he bent and pulled up each of my socks as far as they would go on my shins. He tied one of my shoes—I remembered the strict upward pull of the bow-knot thrilling like all rectitude. He straightened my collar, lay his palm over my neck, as if that were where the heartbeat felt. He touched the serrated edges of my two new front teeth, growing in.

"Don't forget I am your father. Nobody else can ever be that." Those were his last words to me. Then he walked around to his car door, rolled each of the front windows down an equal inch so he could taste the swelled summer farm air, and began to drive.

There is Wisconsin light and Wisconsin color. It is like Dutch but poor; a kind of pale, live blue sky, with clouds and the color black, superimposed; the humming telephone wires, crows.

"I won't, I won't," I yelled to his windows a second too late, running by the car as long as I could keep up. Ben touched the tail fin just before he fell gasping in the soft ditch, his legs mildly scraped by the sharp, high grass. Heaving, we watched there like posts, even though our cousins' high voices ribboned the air, calling.

My father that day was thirty years old, a young man, but to me he was already eternal. He must have known, already then, about my mother: what was curled in her, one tight paisley that would grow as it escaped, like fire. But he left me to her anyway for our lives. Perhaps he trusted the house, its sturdy trees like old women's legs, the honor of decent relatives. All of those proud structures changed as I grew up inside them. And I did not understand for a long long time what was wrong with my mother.

I ALWAYS SAVED a place for my father. That is what waiting is. I still kept something, one scratched light, the secret. If I'd let that fall, like a held candy dirtied on the ground, I would have made a different life. I sometimes wish I had grown up to be more ruthless. Mai linn, for that quality, sometimes awes me.

The first instance was my fifth birthday. We all thought he would come home for that. Ben and I stood scrubbed, pink and red, wearing our best clothes as the other children arrived. We set his place for him at the table, with his glass for ice water and his cup and saucer for coffee. His coffee had to be scalding hot. Playing pin-the-tail-on-the-donkey, blindfolded, when some hands clutched and turned me from the waist, each time I thought the stranger was him.

We waited and waited, stalling an hour and an hour to cut the cake. Finally, high afternoon passed, the youngest guests cried with the exasperation of exhaustion and other children's mothers arrived to take them home. Then when they were all gone, we ate the cake greedily, with our hands. Our grandmother, who cared deeply about nutrition, said nothing.

We found out later that for months, even years, we had been talked about, famous for our cake inhospitality. "And there they sat with the cake perfect on the cake plate for everybody to see. They'd invited us for strawberry cake and vanilla ice cream and we sat and we sat and they never offered us a thing. Finally we left. It was suppertime!" Stevie Howard from across the street told me that years later when we were together in the barn.

I learned to wait with no end. After the birthday passed, we began to understand that all clocks were not the same. It did not matter to him how old we turned. We could not accurately predict or expect. Waiting became our deepest habit, my mother's and mine. We did not need to remember.

For a long time, I set an extra place for every supper. An extra knife, an extra glass, an extra fork. A cup and a saucer. He had always had both coffee and ice water. He and my mother relished their liquids.

Then, one evening, my grandmother asked me to stop. I obeyed immediately and without a fuss. Of course, what she said made sense, but at that time, I changed my chair at the table and wouldn't sit with anyone on my left. That was where he sat. At the long school cafeteria, I had to have a chair open on my left side. I couldn't explain. I didn't use my left hand as much anymore. I was saving it.

I wouldn't wear rings, after a while I forgot how it started. Even now I didn't like jewelry. All aesthetics trace to superstition. Taste is the deepest strand in us, holding all our time.

People assumed I kept my hands bare for hospital work. Some young women doctors took off all their rings and bracelets, one by one, before an operation, slowly pulled on the gloves. After, they put each metal thing on again. I admired them this, it seemed a deep and secret feminine prayer, as long-known as my own, other ways.

After three years, we had ceased to expect him back to such an extent, it embarrassed me to say the words "Our Father." The Lord's Prayer, mumbled every day in school, made me think people were staring. Still, we waited for something to happen to us. We expected a great event. I would never have said, "I hope my father comes home." My father, by that time, seemed vague and large as the sky. If the man we'd once believed in did materialize, in a car say, turning down our long driveway, we would not have felt ready. All our daily rituals of preparation were so deeply assimilated, we knew them only as the way we lived. They no longer had anything to do with him. I probably wouldn't have let him sit on my left side at the table, either.

If someone asked me, when I was a child, what it was like to be growing up without a father, I only shrugged and said, "Nothing." I didn't want to talk more. I didn't understand questions that went, what is it like. I didn't know any different. It seemed I had a life the same as anybody.

My mother had given me a sentence to say when people asked if I missed him. "No, because I didn't really know him." That was not true. But truth was not what I needed. Truth hurtled small and dense, an object, like a tiny building loose, turning in the sky. I hated pity and just wanted to ward it away. "Say you're very close to your mother," my mother said.

"We did know him though," I told my grandmother after I'd lied the first time. Amber Felchner had been asking me. I wanted things straight with my grandmother anyhow.

"Ugh, no you didn't. None of us did. If you think you know him so well, then tell me where he is now."

She had me there.

TIMOTHY AND I watched movies at the Pleiades and he told me what was wrong with each of the leading men.

Jimmy Dean was a masochist, Alan Ladd was really short and Errol Flynn was everything.

Emily and Mai linn and I used to lie around the Briggses' house in the summer when we started really reading and pick apart the books for which ones we could marry. "Darcy," I decided. They turned over like bugs on their backs shrieking and then told me everything the matter with him.

On the chaise longue, I told Timothy what was wrong with Jordan. "Do you think I'm nuts?" I said.

"No. I don't think you're nuts. If you don't like the guy you don't like him. You've got to like him."

I STOOD IN Emory's empty room, back to its institutional plainness, waiting for the janitor's sopping to make it thoroughly anonymous again. I just stood there for a while with the windows open to feel his absence.

I put my hand on the back rung of Emory's old chair and thought, let's get money straight for a moment. It was just going. Fast. My inheritance from my grandmother was almost half gone. When the phone bills came in, and everything I'd been charging, it would be down to five thousand, maybe less. I stood for a moment looking out at the blind snow, the city stunned to softness. One year for Christmas I told my mother I wanted nothing but to be on a TV show called "Shenanigans." "Shenanigans" was a kids' game show that was kind of an obstacle course, and at every corner you got something big, a TV or a dirt bike or a thousand dollars' worth of clothes or money and it seemed by the end of the hour you had everything imaginable, so that there was nothing more—not one thing—to want. My mom was with Ted then and they tried to get me on the show. They wrote to the network and everything. I think my mother called long distance. We stopped in New York City on the way to visit Ted's parents in the Catskills and we got a tour of the studio where they filmed "Captain Kangaroo" and the people in black clothes referred to me as the girl who wanted to be on "Shenanigans." I was embarrassed. That was the last time it was like that. That I wanted just one thing to end all wanting.

Or maybe looking for my father was just the same.

My eyes stung a moment in the odd dim light like a woman just now realizing she was grown-up, at, say, a supermarket, where she must continue to reach and bend filling her metal basket to prepare dinner for a family—but she just this moment understood her parents were dead and in their graves and that she would never be cared for that way again.

This was taking over my life. And I was close, real close, to trouble.

THE MEDICAL SCHOOL gang—drinkers—had another party. It was a benefit, kind of, at the Blue Rose Bar. The bartender's mother needed an operation, kidneys, so they invited everyone for the night and drinks were double price. We played music on the jukebox and some people danced.

I wore my new things, all of them, the pink underwear and matching bra and the golden shoes, with my jeans. I decided to try my best with the here and now.

I kind of danced but mostly I sat and talked to people. All the people I knew from the last time had new boyfriends. It was amazing. A girl I'd had a long conversation with once after class about Bud Edison and her boyfriend, who'd left her, she was with someone new, a pale, heavy guy whose features looked tiny in the globe of his face. But he laughed nicely and said kind, short things. He was always looking at her.

I left early, the jukebox music following me a little ways down the street. At home I sat on my grandmother's big gray sofa and unbuckled the straps of my shoes. I put them back in the box in the closet. Then I decided to call Jordan. I was going over the other people's boyfriends and girlfriends. He's as good as that, I thought.

"WE'LL JUST FORGET that you didn't call me for six weeks," he said with a nervous laugh, opening the door.

We were going out to a restaurant. I was wearing my normal clothes. I didn't have on the golden shoes or anything. I didn't think this was dire enough for all that. I wasn't too nervous. But I sort of noticed him every few minutes, like as he told the girl his name and said we had reservations, he was as cute as anybody else's.

Sitting across from him it still seemed like it would be easy. He was watching me. I put my arms like my mother would. He had that neat collar look, his teeth all even and eagerness. He had a simple niceness.

"So," I said. He seemed ready and easy to laugh.

"We won't talk about the obvious," he said softly.

"What do you even do," I said. "I know you're a lawyer. What do lawyers do all day?"

I thought it was probably something like business but he told me he was a Public Defender. He worked downtown in those court buildings by the Brooklyn Bridge.

He asked me what was going on with the detective and my father, so I told him more. I told him my name. He was one of those people who'd met me as just Ann.

"My—what?" he was saying. His brow set a certain way. He didn't ask me in a pitying voice the way the women had, pulling me against aproned fat all my childhood. I lived in a house with no time.

"Mayan. Like the ruins," I said. "M-A-Y-A-N." If I had to spell that, I was thinking . . .

"What kind of name is that?"

I sighed. "Egyptian. I'm half Arab. My father's Egyptian." The guy was definitely Jewish. I shook my head, twirled the wine in the glass. I was beginning to have trouble looking at him.

"Egyptian?" Jordan looked blank. His face was completely open. "The one you haven't seen? Oh, well, I guess there is only one. You grew up with your mother?"

"Yes."

"Do you have brothers and sisters?"

"No, it was just me and my mom."

"And that whole time, you didn't know where he even was?"

"Nope."

I felt kind of bad admitting that. But it felt clean too. My hand stayed around the wineglass. I hoped this wasn't one of those times I'd wish later I'd said much less.

"So why are you so normal?" he said and then he closed his mouth and his lips looked too big. That startled me because it was the first thing really wrong with him.

He asks that just hearing about my father, I thought. Wait'll he gets the rest.

A minute later, his mouth was beautiful.

I shrugged. "Everybody in America grew up without a father even if they had one. It was the fifties. They were working."

He touched my nose. "You didn't grow up in the fifties."

"Sixties, but not *our* sixties."

He laughed. He had a nice laugh. "Good answer. True."

He picked up his fork and moved it around, looking at it. "But it must be hard not having one at all," he said.

"I never knew enough to miss it."

"You're not mad at him?"

"I love my father." I couldn't believe I was saying that to this guy.

"How do you know?"

What a question. "Here," I said, tapping my shirt pocket. There was paper inside. It crackled.

"Do you think that could change?"

I didn't know what he was getting at for a minute and then it occurred to me that Jordan was one of these guys who are afraid to use the word love. "Change from what?"

"If you met him or I don't know, even found out something about him."

Somebody had once told me a story of an adopted girl, my age, who'd gone to look for her real mother. I remembered all the stories people told about children looking for their parents. I don't think she had a detective, she had aunts who helped and she got to a certain point and the person telling me raised her hand like a stop sign and said, they told her, stop don't go any further. And she stopped. I'd thought about that a lot of times. I didn't think anything could make me stop.

"No, I've thought of everything possible bad. Nothing nicks it. That much I know." I just blurted things out to Jordan. He had something about him, so I told him the truth even when it made me look bad. Which it mostly did.

There was something light about the guy like Fred Astaire in a movie. He paid for supper with a laugh to it. In my family, money was never funny. At my door he kind of twirled around and made some joke about the days when women invited men up to their apartments.

That made me, I had to smile. I was inventorying my apartment and smarting at everything I remembered, the running shoes and dirty running socks just where you came in on the floor, the newspaper fanned out in front of the bathtub, my bed unmade.

"Where'd you get Stevenson? Were you ever married?"

Oh God, I'm old enough that the guy thinks I could have been married. "Stepfather." I shook my head and got out my keys. Now he followed me.

I talked too much all the way upstairs, lying but dumbly. I told him I had house guests for a long time, they'd just left and they were really messy. That's why the place was so bad.

I opened the door and it was worse than I thought. The shadowing room looked like an antique store, one of those dim places where a heavy-sounding cat bounds down, shocking you, from some unapparent shelf.

He looked at me now like I might be seriously crazy.

I excused myself to the bedroom, leaving him in the dark, and kicked all the clothes from the floor under the bed.

"What time is it?" He probably wanted to get out. "I have to get up early for work tomorrow."

"Time, I don't know." I lived in a house the way my mother did, with clocks all over the place, unwound. Watches busted on me. I lived in a house without time.

Later, on the gray couch, I told him, "I'm not really normal."

"I know."

"I cry almost every day."

"You're kidding. Over what?"

I shrugged. "Just a few minutes, usually."

"That's not normal," he said.

SO THERE I WAS trying something with a random guy in the city. He left in the deep middle of the night. After he did and I heard the elevator, I got up myself and sat on the window ledge. I shoved open the back window, expecting a wind and it was there.

At work the next day, Jim Wynne showed up. He was standing at the nurse's station with an envelope, when I came back from my rounds. "Ya left in a bit of a rush the other night. Didn't take our report. I was in the neighborhood so I brought it by."

"Oh, good. Anything new?"

"We got the guy checking passports. We should hear in from him, I don't know, couple a days. For sure before Christmas."

MY MOTHER WENT AWAY and came back a hundred times during my childhood. She never had the courage just to leave. And every time, she was different for a while when she returned. My grandmother and I understood that we had to let her be alone. She seemed to make many trips west, to California, but she also went north to Alberta, Canada, and sometimes just to Iron Mountain. When I was first in school she went away for a long time, months, and when she came back it felt like something was over. My mother seemed nervous during that time, preoccupied and perhaps sad. She always wore a certain long raincoat, a bluish-gray color, belted loose like a bathrobe. She didn't work. She lived with us in the house and spent most of her time with me. She seemed to have decided that: she would spend time with her child. But she did not seem to know what to do with me. She'd stand outside the school, against the brick wall, and always look a little surprised to see me when I filed out in the line of children. She'd take me to a restaurant then and she'd sit by the window with an end of her hair in her mouth. I'd tasted her hair too. It was like a pill or like metal.

We had no rules. She'd order tea and keep getting more hot water from the old waitress and I'd have to remind her that I needed to do my homework.

"Oh, okay," she'd say and move the white scalloped place mat to make room for me.

I tried to arrange my workbooks on the surface of the wooden booth. There wasn't enough room.

"I need light," I'd say. My pencil had to be sharpened. My grandmother did that with a knife, over a brown paper bag.

"Oh, I see." My mother sighed.

She would have let me order anything, even a hot fudge sundae or a lemon cake, but I didn't want to.

I had to remind her what time dinner was.

"Dinner'll wait," she said, "it's only us. She won't start before we get there."

Dinner had always seemed fixed, dinner. This view made my grandmother look small to me. She was waiting too but only for us. Time for both my parents was a private thing they carried with them in hidden pockets.

ON ONE OF HER TRIPS, my mother bought fancy sailor suits, one for Ben and one for me. Mine was a dress and his was shorts, both were shiny white-and-blue material with satin ribbons. We wore them with new socks and white shoes, first at Easter and then again one Saturday morning in April. She took us to Boss's Tobacco and Magazine Shop. The square store felt strange and downtown. It was a glass cube with nickel metal over the doors and windows. The glass looked greenish from the outside, where everything told spring, the blossoms heavy, vibrating their stiff branches, clouds moving in the sky. Inside, it smelled old from tobacco and heating oil. This was the most male place I knew. A machine revolved, displaying pipes and lighters and cigarette holders and cases that never ceased to draw our hands to the glass. Our close breath clouded it, obscuring the very things we wanted to see. The man behind the counter gave us pipe cleaners to amuse ourselves. We sat on stools at his counter, eating pie and fooling, making figures with the colored pipe cleaners. My mother stood in her raincoat by the magazine rack and browsed.

That was when she met Mrs. Briggs. The way we always heard the story later, Mrs. Briggs saw us in our sailor suits, just children fidgeting on the stools, and she took out a crumpled handkerchief and started crying. And this pealing of female tears changed Boss's. She had just been to the doctor's office and found out she couldn't have more children. Emily would never have any brother or sister.

Bald Bruce Nadel moved briskly behind the counter, wiping. My mother approached Mrs. Briggs and they talked. The Briggses were people we would not ordinarily know. They were rich; everything kept them separate. They owned thick-walled cars, they lived on a hill in a big house architects had come from Chicago to build, they looked neat and quiet and normally there was no excuse to get near them. I had seen them before in clothes like you only saw in movies: long dresses and fur stoles. Doc Briggs owned the largest department store in Racine, called Briggs's.

"You could give them so many advantages that I can't," my mother remembered saying.

"I need some time to straighten myself out and get *me* better" is what Mrs. Briggs repeated to Emily, years later, what she never forgot my mother saying.

We still knew nothing. The lady stopped her crying and dabbed at her face with a striped handkerchief. We toyed with our pie crusts; the banana cream insides all eaten, we pushed against the counter wall with our feet, making our stool tops spin.

"Kids, sit still," my mother said and I remember how piercing sharp the order.

She must have worried that we'd change the Briggses' minds.

Later, when we were alone, my mother told me I would move in with the Briggses.

"For how long?" I asked.

"Just for now," she said. "I've got to get away for a little and then I'll come back for you and we'll move somewhere else and find a house for the two of us. But for a while, instead of just living with Gramma, who's getting old and can't do so much anymore, you can stay at the Briggses'. And they'll give you a nice bedroom with a canopy bed, would you like that?"

I nodded yes I would like that.

She continued. "And they'll get you nice clothes from their store and they have a piano, I bet if you ask her someday, just say I'd love to learn how to play, they'd arrange piano lessons. You wait and see. Really, they can give you anything you want, honey. Just think, you won't have to pay for things in Briggs's."

I was supposed to get to know Emily so my mother could be friends with the parents. I knew that. And I would try. Things like that did seem easier for me. My mother always told me it was because I was a kid.

In school, I wandered during lunch to the orchestra room, slipped around black music stands to the piano. When I looked at a piano, so ordered and tensely ready, it seemed it would just play. It was a shock—those first few sounds. I didn't know how, I really didn't. Notes from my random fingers plinked thin and odd in corners of the room. I lifted my hands up, thinking I'd start again, this time some music would just . . . go. Footsteps voiced into the room. I stilled, caught. Eli Timber, the district music teacher, slid down on the bench next to me. Uh-oh. Now I'd be in trouble.

"So you've discovered a musical calling?" He talked like that.

"No," I said. I was shy then when men talked to me. "I don't know."

"But would you like to learn anyway?"

I nodded yes that I would. I couldn't think of what to say.

"Do you have a piano at home to practice on?"

"No, but I might have soon."

He put my hands on top of his hands the way my father, when I was a little girl, danced with my feet on top of his feet. He'd pull me by the arms so I went generally in the right direction. My hands over his like that, Eli Timber began to play something I remember and have been looking for ever since.

"So you and your mom might move and then she might buy a piano? You can rent one, you know."

"No."

He kept playing. It was faint, like people going away through a woods of all birches rising from a single plane. "No? So. How does moving help the practice problem? Because, Ann, in music, practice is everything." Then he ran a flourish up the keys, leaving my hands behind.

"I mean, I might move. Not my whole family."

"By yourself?"

I nodded. "And where I'll move they already have a piano. I'm probably going to live with the Briggses." As soon as I said that I thought I shouldn't have, I was telling a secret. "But I'm not supposed to tell."

Everyone knew who Briggses were.

"Well, and is that good, moving in with the Briggses?"

"Yes," I said. But it made me nervous that he asked. He should know. "I'll get my own canopy bed."

For three months I went to the orchestra room during lunchtime and afternoon recess. Eli taught me scales.

When he wasn't there, I made up a song of my own. My father had wanted to be a songwriter. It galled my mother. She wanted him to be world famous or at least make money.

My song went, When you are/All alone/And you're so unhap-py/ You just sing this lit-tle song/And try and make it snappy.

But it turned out the Briggses wanted a boy. They wanted Ben, not me. And when my mother mentioned the idea to her sister, Carol of course said no and started another family fight and the Briggses just left it that we kids should all be friends. That was how Emily and I first got to know each other. Years later, Emily fell in love with Ben with a straight, steady concentration no one had ever seen before in her.

It didn't turn out so bad after all, my mother said. "You're getting in good with Emily, she can introduce you to a lot of the nicest kids, you just watch, when you're older they'll probably get you invited to Cotillion." We'd read about Cotillion in *White Gloves and Party Manners*. Marion Werth directed the Racine Cotillion, with Eli Timber, in the old Elks Club the first Friday of every month. The girls wore fancy dresses and gloves and there were little pretty refreshments the boys delivered to you on a napkin. Sounded good to me.

OUR TRIANGLE OF friendship broke up after Emily grew her hair back in. She wanted to be a girl again. After I talked her into refusing for three years, she finally said yes to Cotillion. She wanted my cousin Ben to go too. She felt all she'd ever known for him. Even now, I don't understand why he didn't like her. Ben never cared about rich girls. I felt faintly responsible, though I know that was not exactly right either. But if he'd been able to bring more good out of himself for her, some allowance, it would have made all our lives better—his, mine and Mai linn's too. Emily's parents watched her with a long love bent for protection. All of their consternation settled on the simple fact that the one thing they could not do was to make Ben look at her and act towards her the way she wanted. This was only a sixth-grade crush. But Mrs. Briggs called my aunt Carol and when Carol apologetically told her she didn't know what she could do and invited Mrs. Briggs to her bridge club, Mrs. Briggs resorted to my mother. My mother talked to Ben. That only made it worse. Then Emily begged her parents, sobbing face down, slanted on her bed one Saturday afternoon, legs swim-kicking the pillows, to leave him alone. Helpless, they instead yielded to her greedy wish to remove every obstacle in her way. First and most difficult, there was me. But the Briggses shied around me, always. I was Ben's cousin, I could see him whenever I wanted. The only thing they took away from me that I knew of was that piano practice. That and I didn't get invited to Cotillion. Mai linn proved to be an easier problem. Mai linn was just a stem-thin girl, the first one Ben ever wanted to touch. When she found out they were going together, Emily went to bed for five days.

I spent time in the house on the hill but the Briggses never felt to me like family. Mai linn came closer to that than Emily. Mai linn lived next door to us with my aunt and uncle when she was eleven. She'd been with another family in Racine and before that, the orphanage. The trouble was she came with a saxophone. My aunt Carol, try as she did, could not bear her practicing. We tried setting her up in the barn, and a few nights, I took her out there with the flashlight and she played under the one bare bulb and the sheets of moon through splinters in the old wood, but she felt afraid of mice and just empty darkness and so she left us.

But finally, it was Ben's desire that delivered Mai linn to the Greyhound bus that took her to the foster home where she was never cared for. The Briggses saw Mai linn as the fever infecting their sturdy blond girl. And then Mrs. Briggs found out what Mai linn had made Emily do. Practicing for boys, Emily told her mother. We'll never know but we all felt sure that Mrs. Briggs made scarved missionary visits to all the prospective good houses in Racine and warned the mothers, begging them, for her child's sake, not to take in the Asian orphan. So by the time Eli Timber, in his odd straight jeans and small-collared shirt and wrong tie, knocked to implore the women, they stood warned and implacable.

They found her a foster home in Hebron, North Dakota. Eli Timber acted as her sponsor with the church. He tried to place her with a musical family in Racine first; he asked the Briggses, the way he'd tried, on my behalf, to convince them to let me come practice on their Düsseldorf grand piano every day after school, and both times they refused because of Emily.

We didn't say anything, my grandmother and I. In a way it was always simple when people left. The night after Mai linn left, we were sitting at the kitchen table in our pajamas, spooning the rough ice cream from a square box, and my grandmother said, "I suppose sometimes you wish you were over there in that fancy house on the hill too."

"No I don't, Gramma," I said. I never did.

· · ·

EMILY TRIED to take solace from the future. She was sobbing on her bed, and my mother and her mother sat down over her. "You watch," my mother told her, "he likes her now, but when he's older he'll go for girls more your type. You wait and see."

I was sitting in a chair in the corner. My mother was doing this to get in good with the Briggses. I just waited, my hands on the chair arms. "She's a real cute child, sure, but she won't grow. She'll be short when she's an adult and that little face will just get rounder. And once you cut that hair off, she'd be nothing. A little chipmunk. Really, you're much prettier, Emily Ann."

"Yes, look at how pretty you were even without the hair." Mrs. Briggs ran a finger along her daughter's widow's peak. She was glad the hair was back.

Emily stilled on the bed. She rubbed her eyes and tried to think of Mai linn as a dull college student, maybe not even a college student because she was an orphan and who would pay? Even then Emily knew to take for granted that her father owned shares of the *Press Gazette* and the Fort Howard Paper Mill. She bittered her life for what she didn't have but she already believed to the bottom of herself that she deserved all she had been randomly born with. She tried to picture Mai linn older: round-faced, four-eyed, unpopular. Average.

A new gale of sobs winded Emily. "It's good to be short, all the popular girls are short!"

"Now it is, but it won't always be," Mrs. Briggs promised, glancing down the length of her own leg. This exasperated her. She had always been long-boned, light-skinned. That was how she'd become Mrs. Briggs.

"You don't know anything, Mom."

"No, honey, really," my mother said, pushing herself in. But no matter how hard she tried, Emily never liked her.

Mr. Briggs stood at the bottom of the stairs yelling. "Emily. Get down here this minute. Emily, come here."

"I don't want to," Emily mumbled.

"Emily Mae, I'm going to count to ten. One, two, three—"

She ran down with a huff and Mr. Briggs took her off in the car to buy her the ruby and pearl ring she still has.

My mother and Mrs. Briggs ought to have taken a different course in consoling her. There were better things to teach a child than to wait. Because the envied never go away. They only change faces and bodies, names, fan into multiples, so the future becomes an ever expanding staircase of them. You can wait your whole life for someone to come and for the others to go away.

Emily didn't quiet down until after Mai linn and I had both left. Then, inexplicably, she missed us.

Ben and I had always been close but we had been rivals too, over my grandmother. "You gave her the hand without the purse." My mother tried to console me. "She likes you better. I can just tell," she said. My aunt Carol would never have done that.

"I like you both the same," our grandmother always said, like she was slicing a loaf of her bread open with a knife, into even parts.

AND WHAT MADE Mai linn a compelling child was never a matter of size, hair, or face shape anyway. Of anything material. She was a child with an already clear character.

She was able to give things away. She did her homework, all of it, lying on the floor, the hour she came home from school. She always had a sense of order. Even young, Mai Linn lived a way we somehow knew would be permanent and irrevocable. She had almost nothing. She shed things, keeping her life portable. Her rooms all felt the same. She'd paint them white, hang a bamboo shade and put sisal on the floor, and she'd lay a futon in the corner, maybe one slim black modern lamp, a few books.

Once I had the two of them over to my dorm room and we went through my closets. "Throw," Mai linn said, "throw." Her arm would bend in a perfect right angle. Emily watched in horror. She was a saver and unlike me, she never worried about it. After Mai linn left, Emily and I snuck things back from the garbage.

Mai linn always surprised me with her ruthlessness. She seemed to have no regrets.

I understood I wanted to know her always, to stand over a sink rinsing vegetables together at the end of life and learn age from her, from the sharpness of her slightly bitter belly laugh. She would lose nothing to time.

Neither of us talked too much about our parents. Little had changed since our childhoods; there was still almost nothing to say. But they were a fact in us, like a number.

. . .

MAI LINN WAS MOLESTED by her foster father every Sunday in the basement room until she ran away forever, at sixteen. To other people, she was many other things first. But to Mai linn that was what she was first.

Eli Timber had assented to the man because the social workers had said he directed the Hebron High School Marching Band.

She never told me what he looked like or smelled like, anything physical. He had built her the basement room himself, battening it with insulation for sound. They said they put her in the basement so she could practice her saxophone. But even with the soundproofing, her scales drifted into the ceiling around insulation padding up through the floors to where the foster family slept on double beds. But Mai linn never stopped. She said after he left her Sunday nights, ascending the slow stairs back to the kitchen, she played in the dark, from memory. Above her, she heard him turn on the faucet for a glass of water. He drank it, set the glass down in the sink. She saw it there every Monday morning, empty. She'd made transcriptions, borrowing from the violin and the viola repertoire and, especially, from the cello. For a year, she played one long Bach solo cello sonata, before bed every night, like a prayer. Sometimes this was ten o'clock, sometimes this was midnight, sometimes later. Mai linn never thought anything of transcription. She was no purist in that way.

Practicing, Mai linn told me much later, was the way she ensured that she would have the hours she needed alone every day. She needed time and a room alone to feel right. "Like being inside a clean lung," she said.

She wrote letters to Eli Timber, but they were almost all about music. For a while, she kept in touch with Ben too. They had a system with pay phones. I saw him running in a diagonal up the junior high school lawn once, with a tearing violence I'd never seen in him. Drugs, I thought. We had read about drugs. Ben told me later a blue uniformed cop had just stood up out of a car. If they'd tied that one call to all the other calls, our grandmother would have had to pay. His parents were like mine. They had no savings.

But Ben couldn't give Mai linn a place to live. I'm not sure he ever saw how much she really needed. A house, clothes, dinner every night, all those days and years. Eventually, his helplessness dried up her romance. She felt ashamed for the size of her need. She ran away to San Francisco and lived with a guy there. The asshole artist named Kevin June.

She was known for carefulness. In college, she'd taken science for two years and she'd won a big prize in biology. They told her she had good hands. But then she quit. For a long time, Mai linn didn't talk about the North Dakota foster family. Klicka, their name was. Then she did in a torrent and all the bad came out. For a while she went to a group. Secrets weigh, she said now.

The worst thing was the secret. But if we are lucky, secrets end. You turn adult in a world of people holding your same shame.

I'D ALWAYS BEEN ASHAMED. My father left. What did that make me?

I began to tell people about the detective. The guy, Jordan, and other people too. Mai linn knew and Emily and of course Timothy and Stevie Howard. And that made me closer to my friends. I thought of Mai linn with her secret, which was, in a way, the opposite of mine. When we were young, we were sure no one else could understand. But everything that happened to us had happened before. Most of my friends knew my mother from a long time ago. Mai linn's real parents were saints like on wood or in lockets.

Mai linn owned two pairs of shoe trees. Beautiful old ones, wooden. For a long time, I thought maybe they'd been her mother's and she'd carried them all the way from Asia the way refugees grabbed the family silver candlesticks. But when I did ask I found out she came with absolutely nothing. A car slowed at her school one day, a long black limousine, and picked her up and took her to an airplane and that was the last she saw of anything. She bought the shoe trees here in an antique store. And she never owned more than two pairs of shoes, not counting sneakers.

She was good at all the possible things you could be good at without doing yourself any lasting advantage. In childhood, they were jacks, marbles, cartwheels, singing, dancing, carrying a tune.

She could have been a scientist. She got A pluses at Berkeley and a scholarship for her last two years. Then she quit to play jazz.

She shrugged, saying, I don't want to succeed.

She had boys' dead-end interests too. Pool, cars, baseball. Mai linn was the only girl I ever knew who truly cared about baseball, not to fit in with men. She liked it because it was without general time. It had time subject only to itself.

. . .

I TOOK OUT MY SAVINGS BOOK from the accordion file every night and just looked at the numbers. I knew I was going to withdraw more. By the end, it would probably cost all of it. But I still hadn't called Homer Hollander in the bank at home. I just looked at the printed numbers.

I was always bad with money. I'd never gotten money right. Some people did. Timothy didn't own a wallet. Crinkled bills stretched the pockets of his leather jacket. We were always somewhere outside and it was cold then, we were in some line for a first-run movie, or in some little side restaurant and he'd reach in the deep pockets of his jacket, greenish from age, getting dollars and fives, tens, with his square fingers, counting them out, paying for me for some small reason and we'd file into the movie, the waiter would hand us our drinks in glasses, like everybody else.

I kept calling the Uncle and getting his machine. I left messages with my number and each time a different request. This was my tenth or eleventh message and he still hadn't called me back. After a while if someone didn't call you back it became easier and easier to pester them. I called the Azzam woman with the pretty voice too. I was up to about seven on her machine. This seemed time most likely wasted. Calling people who might have no relation whatsoever. I felt I was way in now, looking for my father. But so far, all I'd really done was talk on the phone.

MAI LINN LEFT RACINE in 1969. I moved with my mother to California in 1970. Emily was left alone then, her friends safely gone, but Ben was still never more than decent to her, in his regular way. That, perhaps, was bearable until he met Susie—a girl none of us had ever thought about before or known. That was in the high school. He was with Susie until he died, in the car accident, three years later.

When we were children, I loved games where you sat in a circle cross-legged and closed your eyes and someone else came around and touched the top of your head. Duck duck goose. But this was what I imagined: one day my hair would be touched and he would be there and that would be the signal and he would take me out of my life, out of my first-row desk, out of the classroom where the nun would still be teaching the parts of the plant and photosynthesis.

Later I hoped it would be the Hollywood agent in a long coat who would be in the cafeteria and see my good table manners and pick me.

I always knew I would have to leave the circle of game.

I don't know. We were children. We had that too. We had the other but we had that too. I put on my red cowboy boots with my cousin and Mai linn and we danced hoedown to country western music. We ran silently, like the truest stealth of light and shadow through tall fields of wheat and corn where no one minded us, we made ourselves invisible to no one looking. Mai linn grew up in a small North Dakota town, climbing hedges, making holes, yelling for other children to follow her and they did. There were moments, sure, for each of us when we stood still and fixed on a thing, a car on the highway, the moon in the sky and thought of our parents, who they were and what their absence made us. But that too was not all. There were other children, songs. Other children lured us back into the game, at least I sat in the circle, my hands in their hands, even if in my spirit, I was chasing other far things. And both of us had, most of the time, turned our backs on that truer self, and gone running, arms open, to join in the game.

6

IT WAS AN ORDINARY Wednesday morning, but I woke up wanting to be pretty. I stood in front of the mirror. I didn't know, really, what I looked like. It started out when you were a girl staring in the mirror and seeing your face. You recognized yourself but didn't know what that was, if that was good or not. The way you learned was only people telling you.

Emily had said once, "Someone in love with you could really find you beautiful." She said that like she'd discovered something where everyone else had looked. I had been trying on one of her hats.

Once, when I'd cried in a whole loop to my boyfriend, Paul, about everything, he'd said, "Oh, come on. You have a lot going for you." People agreed too readily when I told them I felt bad about my looks. They quickly mentioned other things that were good about me.

The last time I saw Merl Briggs, she'd said, "You look glamorous. You didn't use to think of yourself as glamorous but I guess you do now." Her voice was wistful, as if all that had been good in me was gone.

I don't know why I was thinking about this just then. Maybe I wanted to be presentable to my father.

It was something I never talked about long with anyone but my mother. I was embarrassed when other people mentioned my appearance. I thought I was plain, but not completely. And like with her paste jewelry, my mother could make me valuable, but she could take it away again. Most things my mother said, I'd stopped believing years before, discarded. Almost everything she said, except about my body. And that was bad. I had legs I couldn't show and a neck that wasn't as good as anybody else's, but sometimes, when she was happy and we were alone in a way that made the room small, she could look at me and say, *oh you're beautiful,* with awe in her voice.

I didn't want to give up the chance of that.

IT WASN'T too many times I'd had said to me the word beautiful in my life, and it never really rested still. It had the tentative quality of a butterfly's landing, or the hurried tripping whisper people get when they lie. Bud Edison told me I was beautiful, and my mother. Two people. Even Stevie Howard, who'd said he loved me, never did that. I tried to warn Bud Edison, when he told me he loved me. "You see, you're only the second person who's said that to me in my life. I'm not somebody who a lot of people say that to." It made an impression on me.

Most people, even liars, want to be telling the truth. I'd met few men in my life who could look in an ugly woman's eyes and tell her she is beautiful. But my father might have been that kind of man.

FIRST THING in the morning, I went and knocked on Timothy's door. We didn't have an appointment, but I brought food. A wooden box of winter clementines.

He let me in and showed me to the couch. He was holding a white mug of coffee.

"Do you think I'm pretty?" I asked.

He was quiet before he said anything. And then I could hear, it was a question he didn't like to answer. It was going to be bad. I knew the second before he started talking.

"In the conventional sense, no. But—"

I began a spiraling fall. I'd always thought really I was somehow.

"But when you're relaxed you can look very attractive."

"Attractive is a euphemism."

"Well I didn't mean it that way."

Sometimes it is almost a relief to hear the truth is what you most feared. Because though everyone else had lied and flattered, their flattery was never truly consoling. Even in those committed to kindness, there is a vague sabotaging wish for the truth.

I thought: maybe I am not more than this. Than what I am. Maybe this is all.

I RAN OUT and it was a slow morning. A woman pushed a supermarket cart filled solid with belongings, she herself was wearing two layers of coat with the double hem of a frilly cotton dress below. Her legs were bare and had sores. Her face, though, could have had a kind of beauty. It was twisted too hard around the mouth and there was an unevenness, but the cheekbones were right, the placement of the eyes, light gray and shot with unattached rage.

In a clothing store on the corner, I saw a short-haired woman sitting on a stool. She was overweight, eating a bagel.

Two young men walked by, hands in coat pockets.

Not everybody else around was so damn gorgeous either.

I needed a haircut.

Call Shawn, I wrote on my list, after my class notes of all I had to study. Shawn was a genius. He cut my hair a certain way so I looked better than I was. He'd touch the shape of your head and he didn't make me feel embarrassed. He worked in a place with a waterfall and marble floors. Once, my first month here, I saw a woman on a bus with a brown bag of groceries, the ferny tops of carrots sticking out, she was dressed well with hair something like mine and I just asked her and she told me this man at that place. Shawn looked like an apostle. His blond hair fell almost to his shoulders and he was always changing it. He'd say, I liked Madonna's hair in the play last night so I did mine that way. Or he'd watch an old movie and be impressed by some actress's long bangs. And he stood, snipping, telling me to lift my chin or drop it, he made my hair so it would be good even if I didn't do anything to it. He showed me how to pin the front back, told me where to put one hot roller before I tied it in a ponytail.

Tricks like that. I needed this kind of help. But I still hadn't gotten around to buying hot rollers.

"You're getting so expensive, Shawn," a woman in the chair was saying, the last time I'd gone in. I always stood like a goon, waiting. I knew how I compared. I'd put my smock on right away and then I stood unevenly not knowing where to go. One look at the lady in the chair, you knew she could afford it no matter how expensive Shawn got. Those were the people who joked about money. I looked at the floor where curls of hair settled like leaves under a tree. The lady in the chair bent down writing her check. An assistant in soft shoes so they made no footsteps delivered cappuccino to my hands. This was such luxury for me. The air in the place pressed so warm you could wear nothing, it would force open budded flowers. It reminded me of doctors' offices when I was a child. All clean, chemical and astringent. And since I'd moved East I'd never gone in to a doctor. I tried to look up whatever I had in my own books. I figured I was spending my health care money on hair. I needed this more.

"You're costing me more than the shrink!" the lady said, handing Shawn the check.

"Mmhm," Shawn said, "but this is your head *and* it shows."

The lady in the chair was my age. I didn't see that until she stood up. It dismayed me, the rings on her hand. It was easier to be poor when you were young. Pretty soon I'd have to begin to say never.

I studied for once. All morning. I got through two systems. Respiratory and blood. And when I called the hair place a girl told me Shawn Timmelund was on a shoot in Hawaii.

Could she make an appointment?

Oh no, she said. Not without Shawn.

Then Emily Briggs came over at her lunch break and we ran. It was cold, clouds banking the sky in pale ridges over the Hudson. The pines shook with a hint of water.

She was on this thing about how her mother wasn't very smart but her father was really brilliant. Even if he wasn't a lot of other things, she was lucky to have been, well, like him, or did it always go like that when smart men married, well, you know, not dumb but lesser women. Lesser, she said again.

And I was thinking, but Emily you're not *that* smart.

Now she was listing all the couples in Racine, whose wives were smart and whose were lesser. I didn't like to talk while I ran anyway.

Then she got to my parents and was going on about what my father would be like, how he had to be smart because I was and I got what she was saying and I stopped running.

"Oh. But my mother's not dumb," I said.

"I didn't say *dumb*," she said, "just less—"

"Oh but she is," I said. "She's really smart." She was. My mother was crazy. That was the problem. She wasn't stupid.

We started up again. "I'm smart," my mother told me once, "and so was your father. We had good genes. And you got them from me. Not your grandmother."

Emily sighed, which isn't the easiest thing to do running. And then she said, "It's scary when you think how many men did that, men we grew up around. I mean, married down." It took her a while but then she continued because I didn't take it up. "I'm still going to be really curious to see what your dad's like. You sure you want to do this?" she said, her voice thin from breath. "What if you don't like what you find?"

You don't have to answer things running.

"Aren't you afraid?" she said. Easy for her to say. She had her father. She had everything from him and that was a lot.

This was not a new question, anyway. People'd warned me all my life. *You might not like what you find.*

I shrugged. There was a gesture I had as a child: a series of shrugs, meaning, *don't ask me.* Emily, when I first met her, was a sturdy, two-parent girl, ribboned at the ends of her braids, coming up to me, while I dance-stepped down the pavement. I didn't walk at that age. I shuffled and two-stepped, waltzed, arms doing something showy and reaching.

"What are you doing?" she'd said. There was a hill in her voice. She was the voice of second-grade convention. And the genius of Emily is that she's perfectly conventional without ever copying. The standard came to her absolutely naturally. She could have been great in advertising.

I'd shrugged and then she started copying me, marching, arms out, down the uneven squares of pavement. Emily had never particularly moved well. But if I didn't think I was anything special, she'd go along with it.

I tried now to think of the worst thing my father could be. What was the worst I could find.

It lay there, metal in my mouth, one word, it always had been there: prison. Federal prison. Everyone believed in you being your father's child and paying for his sins. It was old as the Bible, the good families spreading out, sons of sons of sons punished.

There was still a chance, just a flint chance, he was a great man and then we all were too. Good, I meant.

We ran down by the boat basin. It was very still at the river, no wind, the sky blue and gray. The banks of the Jersey shore across the water were a mossy, inner-lit green. A couple leaned on the rail and kissed. They were not particularly young. But they meant it, you could tell. We passed them loudly, the way you can't help running. I had gotten to a point where it was hard to see lovers. I didn't have enough fun.

With the people she had always known, my grandmother moved a certain way. She'd laugh and say, "Those were the days, huh. We had our fun." She didn't mean much. She meant just her friends, cards with the girls or dinner out with the mink people.

When would be my days? I looked over at Emily. She really was beautiful. And she wasn't happy either. I couldn't talk to her about Tad. Maybe I was just jealous. She would think I was anyway. He was supposed to be the best in the world at this particular kind of deal. She thought together they were this glamorous couple.

On the way back, we passed a group of kids nine or ten years younger than we were, getting out from school. The girls walked, heads back, laughing, in short frilly skirts that looked like paper, the thin ones, the husky-legged girls too. There was a boy in among them and one or two were flirting with him, but you could tell all the references were back to themselves, the girls between one another. In Wisconsin, husky legs were like a tragedy. My cousin Hal's wife had had them. My aunt always mentioned her husky legs and the bad street she was from as reasons he should have never married her. A girl who her whole life would never be seen in a short skirt. Here they just pulled on black tights and went outside.

Running past the green-shuttered church near where I lived, I thought of Bud Edison. I thought of him whenever I passed a place we'd kissed. We kissed and pushed our hands against each other's thick winter coats in apartment house doorways, on stoops, against that wrought-iron fence around this old church. It was that kind of romance, jewels spaced on a chain. His stare went intent and steady, his lips groping the air for me the way a puppy does before it has eyes, and I pulled on his collar, tilting on my heels.

I looked at Emily, running next to me, her hair in an arched pony-tail. She was running in pearls. They tapped up and down on her blue T-shirt.

I said, "You forgot to take them off," and touched my hand to my collarbone.

"Oh, it's good for them to be on your skin. It keeps them nice." She caught her breath, slipped them under her collar. "They're these South Sea pearls. My father's trip to Japan."

"What's the difference," I said.

"I don't know exactly. Just bigger, I guess."

I looked again. They were.

On the corner, we stopped. That was our four miles. We stood panting a minute, we always did. I watched, entranced by a boy in a phone booth, fingers stretching, pushing out, the cold making the glass seem wavery. When would be my turn?

I knew Emily was wondering something about Tad, and even walking next to each other, our shoulders touching, we couldn't either of us say it. When we passed, the guy shifted his position in the phone booth, pressing a knee up against the glass.

INSTEAD OF GOING BACK to the library, I got a manicure. There were Korean nail shops on almost every block now. They were all new this year.

"You have boyfriend?" the woman asked, pushing my hand down into a bowl of viscous water.

"Sort of." Jordan had called. He'd left a message and then he'd called again. His voice was too fast and enthusiastic. People like that lacked stillness, I thought. A capacity for wonder.

"You must not be from around here," I'd said to him.

"Why do you say that?"

"Because a New Yorker, if they'd already left a message and the person hadn't returned it, wouldn't call again."

He'd laughed. "Well, in fact I'm from Michigan."

With a person like that, I thought I'd always feel like I'd gone home from school and found myself in the wrong house.

There were times in my life, only once or twice a year, when I felt like some door was opened and everything in the world was sexual and I was part of it too. It was there, underlining everything, like unheard music you can sometimes sense the ends of, even if you were taking the pulse of an overweight old man who smelled of urine.

I was wearing the new underwear and wind entered my blouse from the neckline. Falling in love, really falling in love, must be like this. It is there all the time, in the kitchen, drawing itself beneath and around all the everyday fixtures of life, sinks, toilets, dishwashing machines, the music is there, the silent music. If I can keep that door forced open somehow, I was thinking, keep my ear to the right pitch, maybe . . .

My daughter is waiting for me to die, my mother was telling her manicurist in Los Angeles, so she can inherit my clothes. But I am planning to fool them all.

My mother has many treasures. She knew how to make an ordinary small thing cherished, the way her own mother could make a jewel nothing, a dull stone of the world. Here take it, she would say, at the end of her life, I don't care. What am *I* going to do with it? She had given things up one by one. Finally, she lay in the hospital calling only my mother's name.

But things of the world had not disappointed her daughter. Materials hadn't proved themselves empty to her. My mother knew her pine chests and the riding bench and the metal bed, her purse made of silver and a seashell. She had intimacies with her clothes, her jackets and each of her blouses. They were loyal to her. They were still. And there was the constant drama of fear and recovery: the button lost that she talked a salesgirl on Camden Drive into matching for her, snipping one off the racks of hanging new clothes for sale, for the cost of a lunch; the belt lost but found just in the nick of time; the satin flower from the garment district at one tenth of the price. And now, the last half of her life, my mother became the anxious reverent custodian of her things.

When she broke a nail, she recovered the piece from the floor and dashed over to Melrose to have the girl repair it with a fine silk that kept the alive and the dead together. With polish over it, you could never tell the difference. My mother's manicurist herself drove a Mercedes. She kept it parked outside her shop, and whenever anyone else parallel-parked, she ran out, hands on hips, watching.

THE WOMAN TOOK my two hands flat on the palms of hers and said, "Oh, you very bad. No good. You bite. You must to quit. I do what I can do but this no good."

I needed some self-improvement. I knew it. This was just another thing.

My grandmother had had a little zippered red case she kept in the medicine cabinet that contained her manicuring tools. All the silver implements and files and clippers had their own slots and built-in straps. There was a compartment for cotton balls. She took the whole business out and gave herself a manicure every week at the kitchen table. She gave me one too when I was a very little girl. "That's about as good as it's going to get," she said at the end. My nails were always bitten.

MY GRANDMOTHER stood between me and the orphanage. For my mother, she became less a person than a place she could bus me off to when I got to be too much for her. And a place to call for money, to be wired into the Western Union office.

In Racine at least we always knew where the orphanage was. We drove by the dark red building and peered over the long, hilled lawn. It was on Hennigan Drive on the east side, just across the road from the coal yards and the river. You drove past Heritage Park and the prison and the abbey; its small lights winked out like lights on a boat at sea. They were too far back from the road. You could never see anything inside. Even when we drove up the long drive, all you could tell was shadows, a suggestion of motion.

In Los Angeles, who knew where orphans went, or runaways. It seemed abstract and more violating. Worse. Like you'd fall away into a black number.

My grandmother was mysterious and kind. Her husband died when she was only in her fifties and she'd never remarried. That didn't seem strange to me until I was grown up myself and by then she was dead. There were so many things I never asked her. She lived alone, had few friends, worked diligently and carefully raising her children, and then again raising me. I like to imagine secret pockets of grandeur in her life. I tried to think of her happiness without me. As in her death, there were so many places I couldn't follow. It was a certain kind of love, with no trace elements of passion. A clean love. I wanted her to take pleasures without me. I wanted her even to forget me. It was a love that had nothing to do with possession or jealousy, a love only half in this world. My own mother sometimes called me now from far away and espoused ideas like this on my answering machine. "You're sounding better on the tape," she said the last time, although I hadn't changed my message. "I want you to find joy in whatever you're doing, to become your own self and at peace with that. Whether or not I'm in your life, I want that independence for you." But her words gave me no solace. I hardly believed her. She seemed to learn the words from cheap poetry, the kind of thing printed in greeting cards. Sentiments blew through her from the television and she voiced them and then they left. Her own feelings were unhinged and terrible, tufts of wind, and they too inhabited my mother and then left, just as completely, sweeping her empty and clean as new paper. My mother was ill. I accepted that, in some final way, long ago.

Time with my grandmother was cooler. I always felt a little shy when I came back to Racine, right before I saw her. Nothing was the same as my mother. I'd never lived so much with anybody. Everyone else was another person.

"The house stayed so clean without you. I had nothing to do," my grandmother said, every time. When I came back, it was hard at first to think of things to say, we had to get used to each other again. We sat at the kitchen table with the night quiet and the highway outside and my own thoughts running their course and my grandmother's hands and eyes busy at work shucking hickory nuts.

And my grandmother sewed. She washed and ironed endlessly, though it seemed effortless, the running of the house, and hours always hung long to fill, more than enough time and too few imperatives. Our clothes stayed clean and pressed, my tights with a hole mended, socks darned, elbows patched neat and tastefully—an orange rectangle on a blue shirt. The patch would be sewn with yellow yarn.

Ribbons and ironed bows clasped the ends of my braids. The kitchen curtains stayed fresh and white and billowy, the heavy floor-length gray drapes in the living room went twice a year to the cleaners downtown. All this felt managed, regular.

"How do you do it?" I called once from college, standing in a scrambled mess on the floor—papers, books, shirts, socks, rubbers, pens, a borrowed stethoscope on my bare chest, a box of graham crackers open.

"Shucks," she said. "It stays clean. I don't do much. I played cards all morning."

Upstairs there were five bureaus and twenty-one drawers built into the wall. They were packed with ironed, folded, bleached white cotton sheets and pillow slips, each embroidered by her hand in a standard form of lace. Tablecloths and napkins waited there too, maybe a hundred doilies and handkerchiefs. Many she'd embroidered or edged but all with a pattern I could find named somewhere in a book.

My grandmother left nothing fanciful, no mistakes and nothing extra, nothing she'd made up in bold color just for the afternoon's flare of it.

It was maddening in a way, to love someone so plain.

My grandmother, in living and in dying, left no clues.

THAT WAS A REFRAIN from my childhood with her. "Sit still awhile, why don't you?" I always did, when she asked me, but I didn't need to rest so much. It was then that I wished I were back with my mother who was young.

In us each, there was a quality of being oddly marooned together. We looked at each other with depths of patience. We knew we were both working to make the best of it. But she was old. And I held still, containing all my vim and greed to yell and run and kick and boss. I did that at school. I became the rule maker who ran the long field, head down-pointed, marking the boundary line, shouting instructions.

At home I sealed up, mindful.

It was a different kind of bond. I observed children with their parents. Their touch held noise and color—they could kick each other and then fall together, bodies tangling. They were lovers, their bond physical, meant and necessary, with gold flashes of hate, the underside of ardor. They never doubted that they belonged together.

We did not have that. Or we did a little. But it seemed a fainter trace, her in me. We often mentioned when we found something in common. Our hands were the same, we discovered, the way our third nails grew faintly ridged. My mother and I, we never bothered with any of that. Sometimes other people would say the two of us looked alike or didn't, we shrugged and couldn't care. She was my mother. That was absolute. We didn't need to seem it.

I was a passenger, hand quiet on the seat beside me, in the car my grandmother steadily drove, taking me where I needed to go, picking up, the car idling, waiting, while I made my last glorious loud run on the play field. Every Tuesday in winter, after school, she drove me downtown to the big public library. I bounded down the steps, onto the dirty, slushy, crusted downtown snow and into the familiar-smelling heated car.

Now when I tried to remember the smell of the car, I thought only—it was women. It was a woman's car. It smelt of women. I own that car now.

What did women smell like? Like clear transparent things, see-through plastic umbrellas, like rain itself, which though it falls in its numerous choral broken lines, also implies a rising, a coherent belly rising like yeast. They smell like watery pink, like plain new floor, like camphor.

Korean music came from speakers on the ceiling and my manicurist sang along, her head swaying. She poked my cuticles back with a little wooden stick. She executed the job much more harshly than my grandmother had. My grandmother held you always so careful.

"Cut or push back?" the woman asked.

"Always push the cuticle back," my grandmother had said. It was one of those things you did by family, like toothpaste.

"Push back," I said.

She started but then shook her head. "You need cut," she said. Then she began going at me with a clipper. She skidded on my third finger and the blood came a pure ruby drop against my hand, drained white from soaking.

MY GRANDMOTHER had three friends and they made a regular foursome. They called each other "the girls" and had been doing so since they were. The other girls were Rene and Gish and Jen.

They played cards together once a month. This was a formal affair. The card table and folding chairs were extracted from the still, cool, male-smelling front closet, a cloth was borrowed from the cabinets upstairs, and though it had been pressed before its placement in the drawer, now it was ironed again. And there was time. Eclair puffs were baked, cooled, cream was whipped, the tin of strawberries thawed the night before in the sink was poured into a bowl and still there was time. We waited. We sat in the living room pulling back the heavy gray floor-length drapes to watch for cars to come. We never started eating or drinking anything ourselves. We didn't sneak, the way my mother would.

Exactly on time then they arrived. In Racine, Wisconsin, there was no fashionably late. Except my mother. I'm sure she thought she started that. These were close varieties of white women, all in their sixties and seventies, all widowed except Gish, who had never married. Jen was the small one, Rene the emoter. Gish, the oldest and the only working woman, complained of her health.

I sat in a chair, content, my hands on the armrests. I liked watching. It was the big activity in the house. My grandmother's head rose a little higher, her face more colored and filled. I taught myself bridge just watching. I began to see the cards on the table and make answers.

One night in October, when they were dividing up their pennies, finished, I hauled out my new Ouija board and made them all play. I'd bought it with allowance. My grandmother, when I lived there, gave me chore money. I loved games of prescience—wishes you made and didn't tell, the envelope of silence around the question I'd imagined over the whispery Ouija, moved it seemed by breath.

"Ugh, I don't believe in such stuff," my grandmother complained, but she played anyway that night for hours. She didn't seem to mind. She said the same thing about church. She'd go anyway, putting on a good knit dress with a belt and taking out the matching hat and handbag.

That night, the girls asked question after question about Hans, the guide they'd had in Europe. Twice, the girls had gone together on a European tour. They'd come back with dolls from every country for me. The dolls were all dressed as if for royal balls. I'd only seen Hans's picture. He wasn't my type. He had long fingers, a soft whiskery face. But the girls always went for a different sort than I did. They liked young men with exquisite manners and all the sex drained out of them. Even then, at eleven, that wasn't what I wanted.

"Is our dear Hans happy over there?" Jen started.

"And is his little *girl* well?"

"And the wife, don't forget the wife, even if we don't *personally* like her style of clothing."

"Or of the hygiene either."

"Well, she's got a lot to do too, I suppose, but that house. And the diapers everywhere! Right by with the food!"

"I don't know how he can concentrate on his schooling with all that going on."

"I don't know either. That's why you keep a house nice and orderly. So he can do what he's supposed to do."

"I always thought so."

"Of course you did. And you kept a real nice house, Jen."

"Just beautiful. I still remember your orange cakes."

"That I can't do anymore. My eyes aren't what they were."

"Well no, that's a lot of work. Too much work. For just us alone."

"But you did it for Alfred."

"And he appreciated it."

"I hope he did."

"Why sure he did."

"I know he did."

"He'd've been a fool if he didn't." That was Gish. Gish had always thought Alfred was a fool and rarely resisted an opportunity to suggest it. Gish was sly and large and caused trouble.

"Why, I'll tell you, he sure ate a lot of them for somebody who didn't!"

"But do you think that wife with the hair all over sprouting from her, do you think she's grating orange rinds for his cake? Why, she can't even wash the diapers."

"Lord knows what else would fall into her cake. That house was not clean."

"I know it." My grandmother pursed her lips.

By the time all this narrowed to a question, it was: "Well tell us, why don't you, if you know all the answers, you Ouija you, is she still letting that grow under her arms?"

The plastic heart lurched and skidded. The answer told a sudden yes. They giggled, climbing the steps of an octave—thrilled.

My questions I kept private. The Ouija skated as answers fluidly uncurled themselves in a script written with rapid jags between the numbers and letters. The answers never seemed to quite fit my questions, but I couldn't complain because I didn't want to tell them what I'd asked.

To "Will I see my father again?" it said ytab784.

"Will I be rich?" spun the heart waltzing to NO, then YES, then 59.

"Will I ever live with my father?" clearly, evenly spelled out the word DOG.

And "Is my father alive?" made the Ouija heart skitter off the board quickly, exiting straight through GOODBYE.

"No fair, you're pushing," my grandmother called in excitement years ago, as the heart flew, warm all over the board.

"No, I'm not, I'm not. Look," I shouted, and she half-believed, her cheeks flushed and mouth tense, as we felt the mysterious drag us in its trail. She looked up from the board and out the dark window. The lights were on inside so we could see nothing of the sky.

I didn't remember what all I asked anymore.

Will I be happy?

Does he remember me?

Even after, I never told. She didn't press. I was preparing for sleep when my grandmother clapped my board into its box, saying, "Well, that was fun, wasn't it. We all had a good laugh from it."

But the next time, the girls wouldn't touch the Ouija. They were afraid of it. They relented, though, and agreed to a game of Monopoly after bridge. I always won at board games. I cleaned them out that night. They all saved. They felt afraid to buy. Meanwhile I spent my money every chance I got and at the end, emptied them out from hotel rents. They counted their toy bills carefully.

"Well at least we *can* pay, I'm glad of that," my grandmother said, counting out nine hundred and fifty dollars when she landed on my hotel on St. James Place.

I was always trying to lure them into playing for money. Sometimes they would and I'd collect little piles of pennies and dimes. She worried that I might become a gambler like my dad. At home alone, my grandmother wouldn't use cash but she'd gamble hankies. She lost those too. I kept them in a gold cigar box from Boss's.

WE HAD TWO BOOKS: one old Bible and the *American Heritage Dictionary* from 1957. Stacks of yellow *National Geographic*s and *Reader's Digest*s filled the rest of the one bookshelf in the den. I never saw my grandmother read. But she looked at the pictures in the *National Geographic* and she used the heavy Bible to dry fall leaves.

After my grandmother died, I owned her furniture and her clothes. Other relatives and I inherited her money. But none of that seemed personal. I wondered a long time what she left that was her.

People were supposed to tell stories. Secrets. She didn't do that. People sometimes made a thing that showed themselves. Like my mother's needlepoint, a gorgeous thing, all her winding chemical rages refined to the points of a picture, frenetic in bright colors. Goldfish dashed maniacally at the center. But my mother couldn't finish things. She still had a little sweater she'd started knitting me when I was four, it was half finished in a basket, red, one-sleeved.

My grandmother fixed and mended, darned. Her handiwork was fine, but her efforts all attempted the standard. Her homemade things copied the storebought done on machines. Her stitches got that small. That was her goal, so you couldn't see the difference. You really couldn't tell her hand.

I don't have her signature. I have only copies, legal things, deeds, the Xerox of her will.

On letters she just signed Gram, not her name. But when I could have asked for it I was busy chasing other, more elusive things.

Most people tried to make something different, something only them, some proof like a document forever saying, I felt these wide bright things, I used my time on the earth. Most people wanted to leave a scratch of themselves behind here. She just left, giving all her things away before.

But for all the batter of my mother's madness, the shrill air of the Briggses' money, what colored my temperament was just the shadow of my grandmother's hand over me, not even touching, only shading me.

She sought not to alter anything, not to express, only to leave the world just as she found it, as if she had never been here. I kept looking for anything she might have left behind. I wanted that. But she'd taken herself out of the things she used long before she left us. The last few years she was alive, she kept giving away her things. She wanted to give everything away.

When my father left, he took things with him. From him, I wanted my own back. When I tried to imagine him, I thought of caves.

THE WOMAN LEFT ME, my nails suffered to evenness. I felt creased lines in the place where nail, which was really bone, met skin. She returned wheeling a cart of colored polishes.

"So now, what you want?"

Pictures of done hands superimposed on Asian temples hung all over on the walls. All of a sudden I felt shy. I did know what I wanted but I felt afraid to ask. I'd seen it in magazines.

"I'd like it clear but with the white underneath?"

"French. You want Fench manicure. The white under nail. But no can't have that. No nail. You let grow first, then I do. Now pick color."

MY GRANDMOTHER'S COLORS were winter in the place she lived. Her hair was white but the clean shock of real white, no yellow or blue in it. Her skin tinted softer, a pink beige, her teeth the patina of yellowed ivory.

I thought of her pearls, no long, flapper pearls, but pearls around her neck like two hands clasped, that kind of pearls. Of course they were never real. Nobody we knew had real, except the Briggses. My grandmother could have been a flapper. She was the right age during the twenties. But those city ways would have dismayed and even frightened her. Self-attending, that kind of flair, even just an open shout for joy, went all against her nature. That quality of suppression turned my own mother against her and sent us to Los Angeles chasing beautiful clothes and suntans, every form of immediate pleasure in this world.

My grandmother never changed friends, all her life. She stuck with her regular foursome. Gish was Jen's sister; her real name was Francesca but she'd never been called that since she turned nine and tried to mimic a movie star. Because of that, she had always been known as wild. The girls were deeply, habitually loyal, even to a common name.

I knew these were good qualities. But after a whole night of their trilled conversations, more repetitive than the most conventional fugue, I felt so alone.

Marion Werth had given me a book about Madame Curie. She died of her work, eventually, leukemia. She was an early widow, like my grandmother, and like my grandmother she never remarried. But she was a woman of science.

At the time of their lives when Marie Curie was traveling the world for science with her daughter—who also died of her work, leukemia, again from radium—my grandmother and the girls toured Europe, sightseeing and playing cards.

I was a teenager by then and I lived with my mother in apartment after apartment, all furnished or empty, in California.

Why did the girls go to Europe? They missed dancing. Their husbands had died early. All their lives, before and through the wars, the fun they knew best was dancing. But there was nowhere in Wisconsin that they could dance. Maybe a niece's or a nephew's wedding if one of the young men was courteous enough to ask them. And even then they'd only get the one dance. Jen had seven children and so one of the grandsons always seemed to be having a wedding. But the girls didn't like the music they played by then anyway.

"I can't pick up a beat," my grandmother said, whispering *one* two three, *one* two three.

My grandmother resorted to me, when I was there, on the carpeted living room floor. First she'd try to find a song with the right beat on the radio, but failing that, she'd hum, *ta da* deedum, *ta da* deedum, *de* de dah, teaching me the two-step and waltz. We practiced that way, there on the floor, and I did all the time, on the lawn, on the frozen-over driveway, I waltzed to the mailbox, polkaed to the school bus.

But in the European hotels where each of the girls had her own room, they danced. They came home with pictures of their guides. The guides were young men who took them climbing in the Alps, made sure they saw museums and choir boys in the city, and sat and joked with them in the good Swiss coffee houses.

In the old, grand hotel, the guide would take turns and dance with them each, gliding the women over the floor, their mouths held careful, their feet knowing the steps for years.

My grandmother packed good dresses to dance in, both times she went. And the first time she took her jewelry, her watch and pearls.

On the first trip, their guide was Hans. He accompanied them through Greece, Rome, Germany, Switzerland and Austria, finally parting from them in Vienna, putting them on the train to Paris. He was their favorite guide, then and always. They had taken that first trip when the last of the husbands died. That had been Jen's Alfred. Gish planned a month off from her job at the Coliseum Theater. She worked as hostess there, which meant she took the tickets in a long formal dress every evening. She'd had the idea to go abroad and they all agreed, the trip did them a lot of good. When they went back for the second time, they tried to arrange, through the travel agent, to tour with Hans again. Naturally, this posed difficulties to the agent, who told them flat out that finding and retaining a guide from five years earlier would be near impossible. Guides tended to be young. They took time off from their studies or went into businesses. It was hard and aimless work, abounding in flattery and remembrances, but leading nowhere. "You wouldn't want to be a guide when you're fifty," the agent said.

This was a new thought for the girls. They worried. They each privately wrote Hans long letters about his future prospects, and my grandmother considered the merits of sending along a check. They didn't tell each other. However, they assured the travel agent, there would be no problem locating Hans. They each possessed his full address and that of his mother in Bremen. They'd received Christmas cards from him just this last year. That had been the day. The girls on the phone like teenagers. Gish's was held up in the mail over the weekend, desperate thirty-six hours of wondering, had she done something wrong? She went to church Saturday morning before the matinee for an extra confession.

I think they really returned to Europe just to see Hans again. Word came through their travel agent at last, six weeks before their departure. Hans would not be their guide. Hans had married and had a child and there was some rumor of illness in the family. Hans wasn't working as a tour guide anymore.

They went anyway, secretly, conspiratorially, planning to make a visit to Hans themselves while there. They didn't reveal their plans but took off on the departing day full of exhilarated gigglings, carrying suitcases heavy with dresses and dancing shoes and suits and the machinery of undergarments, boxes of Kleenex, first-aid equipment, cough drops and Handi Wipes.

Hans—in the picture I still have of him—didn't look like a Hans. He looked like a George or a Scott. He was clean-cut, soft-haired, with a long nose, but his smile was slack and seemed to bespeak a love of pleasure. His lower lip drooped on the left.

I found out later about their pilgrimage to him. Apparently, Europe had less to see this time and they came home with colds and indigestion, complaining of the prices and telephones and toilet plumbing. They knew when they settled home that they would not go back for a very long time. My grandmother understood that she would never return. Never. She felt perfectly comfortable with notions of mortality of that kind.

I was not. I felt I'd missed too much already and I was missing things every day. Things I should have been learning, experiences. I didn't know how to keep up with my homework or make money or forget about my mother blowing up at me or how to stop being in trouble all the time. I didn't even know how to stop biting my nails.

I wanted to be whole, what I would have been. And I knew that wasn't going to be now. I couldn't live with the idea that what was supposed to be a gorgeous part of life was already over.

APPARENTLY, it was the last week in Europe when my grandmother and the girls found Hans. This new guide—the Swiss, they called him—couldn't understand why they so wished to see Bremen. "It is"—he shrugged—"what you call, university town. College only." But that last week, they broke away. They were already tired, Rene and Jen were sick, Gish had lost her best shirt in a Hamburg dry cleaner.

They hadn't danced as much on this trip. In fact, I had a feeling they hadn't danced at all. Who knows what they thought they'd find when they traced the streets to Hans's address and turned up at his door. Maybe they had lingering hopes, like the aftertaste and dissolve of a lunch sugar mint, for dancing there. They didn't know. Perhaps he'd come into money and lived in an old mansion with twenty-foot ceilings and velvet curtains and marble floors and an entryway and a balcony and . . .

But they were sensible women who lived ordinary lives back in Wisconsin. I suspect they already knew. They turned the corner to a house that was gray and run-down. The yard was small and mean, poor shoots of grass grew like a few hairs on the side of a bald man's head. Mostly, it was worn down to smooth, packed dirt. Things from inside spilled to the three bare stairs, a child's truck, a rubber ball, a bone, an old platform shoe.

Of course, they knew then. And the good religious women that they were, they felt no flashing urge to walk on—the way I would have—find an intersection, hail an anonymous taxi.

I wish they had. I wish they'd turned and gone, run helter-skelter, fast as they could in their pumps with their little purses hanging off their hands, asked the taxi for the best hotel in Bremen, gone there and sat in a wood-paneled room, listening to a string quartet, taking tea.

What they found was not so much worse than what they knew at home, in the bad parts of Racine, in their own parish, during some patchy years of their own children's lives. With my mother, my grandmother had known even worse.

Apparently, Hans's living room had been small and held the shrill reek of diapers somewhere nearby. He was there and the wife too, him hapless, holding the baby in just its rubber pants. It was the white and brown of winter then, the same time of year they'd come before when it was the red and white, the ermine and red velvet of a king's coat and outside the planted rows of pale, match-colored bare trees . . . The wife had heavy, messy hair and didn't shave under her arms.

"I did notice that," Jen said later.

"I did too," my grandmother confirmed.

Hans seemed downcast to them and older. A few attempts at beard wisped on his cheeks.

"Unsuccessful," Gish said. "Like a fool."

He was studying at the university now, he told them, engineering. This made him look sad.

"Oh, but that's good," Jen said.

"Good for you."

"You regularly read that there's lots of work for engineers."

"And always the building, more building, they're building, building, out by me even, too, way over there."

"Where I am too. Ugh, the noise." That was Gish.

"But it must be lucrative."

"Oh, yes, gracious, I should think so."

Downcast. The wife seemed cold at first. "Well, I suppose so, four women coming to their door in the middle of the day, what is she supposed to think!" But then she thawed a little. By the end she was running back and forth from the small kitchen to the living room, delivering coffee and little ham salad sandwiches.

They got to almost like her.

"Oh, but did it smell down in there. I didn't want to eat with that either, but here she brings it out and it's just us there and so I nibbled at one."

" 'Course I suppose she's got her studies too, they're both in school. It can't be easy," my grandmother said.

Before they left he apparently put a tape into a tiny player and danced a turn around the small living room with each of the women.

My grandmother didn't like it. I don't suppose the others did either. She said the room was so small and cluttered they bumped into furniture and the baby cried. Nobody probably much wanted to be dancing.

As they left the ladies fumbled awkwardly with their purse clasps. They gave him a little something for the child. They walked all the way back to their hotel and found themselves depressed. Instead of staying on as they'd planned, they took the train to Frankfurt that same night, spent a lackluster day there shopping and then came home.

So that was that for Europe. The girls had had enough of it. If you asked my grandmother, she'd say, "I'd just as soon stay home."

BUT THAT FIRST TIME—we can only imagine its opulence. There must have been palatial hotels kept up for the business of visiting old women and foreign bankers. Places with plush ballrooms where old women could dance under chandelier light with handsome strangers. I imagined my grandmother's face open in a surprised smile. After a day of sightseeing, even in gondolas, on a mountain, Hans had herded them back to their rooms in plenty of time to dress for dinner.

Gish had asked him, "Is it casual more or just a nice dress or sort of formal?"

He knew what they wanted. "Formal," he said, lips severe. "Do you have anything long? Floor length?"

They assured him. "Oh, yah yah, sure."

"Do it your best, ladies," he said, "tonight's the night."

And they'd scurried up to the private rooms and begun bathing and powdering and putting on their makeup. They called each other in to zip up the long back zippers and to fasten the clasps on the good watches and bracelets because they couldn't see them so well anymore. Out came the cuticle oils and dabs of perfume. The mink stoles, all first bought from my grandfather's pelts, musty from not being worn these twenty years and lingering in stale closets. My grandmother hadn't worn hers since her husband had been alive to lift it off her shoulders.

She wore pearls, which now held a patina of worth, from being touched.

They pushed on elbow-length gloves. These were dresses and

accessories they wouldn't have dared buy now or anytime in the last fifteen years but which they'd kept, carefully tended in their closets, on the chance that they might need them, once more.

And here they were, wrapping themselves in those taffetas and silks and satins, marveling that they still fit and at how good these soft and shiny fabrics felt against their skin, remembering, with a shiver, what bareness meant to an arm and then fur, lush and hot, on the outside shoulders.

They descended the stairs, heads high as they'd tried to keep them fifty years ago. This was the generation of girls whose mothers made them parade around the house, balancing Polish and German and Czech Bibles and heavy bilingual dictionaries on their heads. Their mothers had grown up in Europe. They had learned how to clasp and unclasp the small pearl buttons on gloves, they had learned how to waltz.

But the girls grew up in Wisconsin, where there was no need for ballroom manners and few opportunities for grand entrance until now, when, over sixty, they descended more glamorous than they had ever been, one by one, down the stairs.

I picture them as butterflies. Rene first, a painted lady in her thistle-colored plaid; Jen in orange and black with ruffles, a monarch; my grandmother, a Question Mark, the largest angel wing, in a straight dress of pure melon; and Gish, a swallowtail in an all-black sheath. My grandmother was tucked in the middle, second to last.

They ate at a round table, the five of them, tasting the herrings and foreign cheese, drinking champagne. Hans was adept at keeping the champagne moving from the silver ice bucket into their glasses. He wore a tuxedo, fashionable that year. He relished these touches. He, like they, had a predilection for the fancy.

There is a certain kind of man who understands older women. Hans loved the fruff of it all, the ruffles settling, fastidious care. This sort of man serves as the ideal host amongst finery. He immediately recognizes talent in a first-rate waiter. Usually, he is a man who is not paying.

It was funny to think that my father was a little bit like Hans.

MY GRANDMOTHER SIPPED her champagne and began to feel herself rise. Her body seemed to swell with lightness from the lower sides of her back through her shoulder blades, as if wings were pushing through her skin, beginning to extend.

At home, she made her own farm of liquor in the basement cellar, which was still cluttered with her husband's tools and saws and wood slabs and, on the other side, his Polynesian bar. Occasionally, in the winter, she crept down with a flashlight and liberated a bottle. Cherry bounce. She'd have a little glassful and then she'd climb down again, holding the banister, and put the bottle back.

She drank and her mouth opened to show more teeth in a wordless smile. The others were talking, a steady, above-water melody of how good everything was, how tasty that, did you get some of this, yes, I had a bite.

Drinking . . . all this was new and not new. My grandmother sat there still and rising, her cheeks full and embarrassed in the pleasure of someone giving her something.

She had dined out, years ago, with Art. Then it was always four, them with another couple. Rene and George. Jen and Alfred. Just now it occurred to my grandmother how Gish must have felt then, during those couple years. "Aw, shucks, I've got to work at the Coliseum anyway," Gish had said at the time and no one had pushed her because no one knew quite what to do with an extra woman. At a holiday yes, of course, sure, but not an ordinary Saturday night out. In the flush of inclusion, after so many years alone, in her delicate, hesitant appreciation, my grandmother remembered Gish and only then understood the randomness of fortune. Years before I was born, Alfred had asked Gish first and she had said no.

Everything had been built lower then. The glasses were not these tall flutes, but low wide cups, with not clear pink bubbles rising, but a heavy amber liquid. The table was low, as was the ceiling, the area they sat in was banked by a waist-high wall of polished mahogany. She had dressed up then too, but differently. Then she'd worn woolen suits, straight skirts and matching jackets, only a collar of fur, coordinated bags and heels. They'd had to be sophisticated women then.

Now, these were the dresses of childhood dolls and Hollywood movies. Their husbands would have frowned—they wanted their wives in neutrals. These were candy colors, the long gloves of ocean-liner pomp, royalty and Europe. And here they were ascending. The ceilings vaulted up towards the light of clouds.

Everyone seemed dressed in what would have seemed to us costumes. I saw that in New York sometimes. Yale girls in gem-colored dresses spilling out of unmarked doors, standing on the lit porch of the Plaza, tilting a little from their toe to heel, waiting, the wind dallying in their sleeves, their dresses without them in the dark windows of all of those little stores on Madison Avenue, deserted at midnight. Teatime at certain hotels you saw them, in hats and gloves, where all the doormen wore livery and braids. When I remembered my grandmother's Europe, I blamed less. If you love a person once, it changes everything.

Strings of the orchestra sawed as the meal thinned to desserts which came, first elaborately, in spun sugar baskets nesting ice cream, then in smaller and smaller tarts and petits fours. With the champagne still pouring, Hans took each of them for a perfect swooning dance around the floor.

First Rene, then Jen, my grandmother tucked in the middle, beautiful, but never knowing that and not calling attention. The man is supposed to lead: *The man is supposed to lead,* people had been telling me all my life. "A-hem," I'd been told again and again, gliding across the floor with the boy who was my partner. I supposed learning with my grandmother, I became the man.

They danced and danced. It felt good and in the dizzy swirl of lift, my grandmother thought she saw her own face reflected like a shine of cloud in the polished high boots of many men, men in military regalia, stars on the ceiling, ta da deedum, dada da da.

Later that night, he came to each of their rooms, in the same order. Rene, then Jen, my grandmother neither first nor last, nor assuming, then Gish.

He bent over my grandmother's bed and lifted her soft hand and kissed it. He asked if he could have some little thing to remember her by. She gave him the pearls. She didn't know what else to do. And on the plane home, each of the girls confessed that they left things—a string of pearls, a fox stole, a watch and a garnet ring—in Europe, at that last hotel. None of them seemed too upset.

AT MY DOOR, a brown paper bag, many times wrinkled, waited on the ground. In it was a little box, cotton-battened, glass-fronted, with two butterflies inside. "To your collection," neat printing on a piece of lined paper said. The man upstairs. I took it in, I'd left the door unlocked again, and I knew just where I had a nail. Stevie Howard had visited once and done two days of home repair. When he left, he bought me a toolbox with things like nails.

I put the butterflies up on the wall next to the cement print. One thing I did have of my grandmother was a rough cement square, boxed in a cedar frame I built crookedly when I was ten. It hung on my wall, over the desk.

When I was ten, I read books we called how-to, about animal tracks and electronics. I wanted to build a ham radio. I loved the idea of contact with the greater nighttime world far away, the voices of truck drivers. Nights I tinkered at the kitchen table making a battery from a book and lead and zinc I'd bought from the hobby shop. That you could make a thing like that way out where we were in the country— that seemed amazing. These were my own inquiries that my grandmother supported but didn't follow me on.

But I also liked the animal-following solitary crafts of the snowbound forgotten country where I lived. Those days they'd graduated me to the second floor of the library, which was the young adult division. Sometimes I strayed to the full-adult sections, like natural history. There was a hanging constellation of the Milky Way galaxy there, planets made from painted Styrofoam balls. I wanted any of the sciences then. They seemed new. And I lived among everything old. That was my school life, downtown.

I was still younger at home. I made animal tracks with cement. I woke up early one January Saturday morning and the sun beat hard on the snow so a little deep dirt and mud showed, the trees shuddering, and the cedar needles glittered, shrugging off loads of snow and the new and the old seemed the same again. I trooped out before eight o'clock in her clothes and mine, sealing, warm, loose. I tracked the fields where the drifts still came deep and took imprints of rabbit and deer prints. I got a rabbit, a deer, a squirrel and what might have been a fox. It kept me all morning. When I came back in, she had her back to me by the stove. I had the idea then in the kitchen. I didn't ask her, I told her. "Gramma, I'm going to take your handprint."

"Ugh, why do you want a thing like that? You'll just throw it out."

"No I won't."

"Oh, it'll end up in the basement."

"Gramma, I need it."

"Well, all right if you say so but hurry up about it then or your breakfast'll get cold."

I made her grease her hand with Crisco and then Vaseline. She didn't like this. You made a plaster cast first and then reversed it. She took her ring off and, palm smeared with Vaseline, she had to press down in the plaster.

"Ugh, such a mess," she said. "Well, what we wouldn't do for science, huh? That's my contribution to the world of learning." Later that night, she gave herself another manicure, to get off all the little bits of plaster.

Now I was glad I had that. It was her right hand. Right hand and your left, what you are and what you were supposed to be.

I stood up and set my own hand into her imprint, matching. My fingers were thinner and a little longer. But it almost fit.

It was the end of the day again. I was spending the last of my grandmother's money to find my father. She would not have wanted this. "Ugh, shucks, throw your money away why don't you," she would have said. "We worked hard for our money and here you're going to get rid of it chasing him and what does he care for you?"

She would have rather talked about my boyfriends. "So now you have Paul and Stevie," she said once when I was in college, "what are you going to do? Which one do you like better?"

I asked her about her husband, how she knew.

"Knew what?" she said. "I knew him from just around where I lived. He raked the leaves for my dad."

"But you must have fallen in love with him."

"Yah yah and I fell in love with him, oh yah sure, that too I suppose."

She wanted me to buy hair ribbons, dresses, rings, manicures, to take my friends to a show, to go out, have some fun while you're young . . .

I would not be doing this if she were alive.

That was the truth.

And it was too late to stop.

7

I REALLY HAD NOWHERE to go for Christmas and that was fine with me.

There was no place I could go that was home. My mother's apartment she had just how she wanted it. There was no room for me. And to go to Racine, I had to stay with someone else or be in a hotel.

Nobody I was related to owned anything anymore. Not in Wisconsin or anyplace.

When my grandmother died and we sold the house, none of us owned any part of the continent. We all just rented.

I'd dropped out for a while from my life. I was getting out of touch. I knew worlds; everybody does. I had Briggses in the Midwest, Stevie Howard and Helen and Jane in California, this friend, that friend. And I didn't want any of them now.

I was sick and tired of being the honorary aunt. The single adult following along at Christmas and New Year's, helping where I could, pleased, grateful—I'd had it. Always wondering, if I was sitting by the fire with a book, shouldn't I be chopping something? That came of having it never be your house. I guess my mother had probably felt that all her life.

I was ready for an island, sex in the water with dark-speaking teen-age boys.

Or maybe I'd stay here and study. I'd study until the day and then volunteer at a soup kitchen. There was a lot to do in hospitals on holidays. People need more.

I CALLED THE GUY, Jordan, and asked him if he wanted to go to some island. I hadn't returned his calls for a while. I'd been bad about that.

He was a little surprised to hear from me but kind of pleased. I thought he was playing with the phone cord, I don't know why. "Well, maybe," he said, "that's a definite possibility."

I never wanted to do the ordinary things until I was twenty-five and since then they sounded great. A thin lap of water, the rustle of dry yellow palm. The loll. I wanted to look as standard as possible, a body like an instrument, in a bronze bathing suit, laid out right.

He had a light laugh like froth, soon dissolving.

Then, the next night, we were sitting at a square table with a starched white tablecloth. We had travel brochures spread out—he'd brought them, the Caribbean, Mexico, the Amazon.

We studied them all and decided the Amazon. Maybe Peru.

"You keep disappearing," he said later.

I winced. I hated being accused. "I don't know," I said, "you're too normal."

He nodded. He seemed to accept that right away as if it were some kind of answer.

Normal. That was another thing I was and wasn't. I'd always tried to isolate him, the absence, and make it the only thing. The rest of my life was normal. I'd stood on wooden outside steps watching the highway. But I stepped off that porch, too, onto damp cool evening lawns with a lit birthday cake in my hands, fireflies daunting the night. I ran home on the gravel road, a report card in my fist, kicking up dust, and pulled up my socks inside the slow kitchen as my grandmother lifted a tray of cookies out of the oven.

But none of that was only that.

Not one room was untouched. I was not the same.

I FINALLY TOLD my mother I was looking for him. I don't know why I did that. I just did. She never wanted me to, I understood that.

And she started again. "Well why? Why do you want to find him?"

"Just to know."

"Know what?"

"You knew *your* father. I just want to know who he is."

"I can tell you who he is. He's a goddamn bum and a crook, that's who he is. Who took from me and took what would have been yours, too. Don't you think you could have had the dresses and the—"

I stopped her. "I didn't ask you."

She hung up on me. We'd done that for years, but every time I sort of sat there. I bit my lip. I always felt stunned, as if a bee stung me. There's the pain but also pure surprise.

She called back a couple hours later, in the middle of the night. "Have you ever talked to Pat Briggs about this?" she said. Not even, This is your mother. She expected me to know all that, and of course I did.

"No. Why?"

"'Cause he may have some information." She said that like she knew something she wasn't telling me. But half the time she sounded like that. Sometimes she did know more and a lot of times she just implied.

"Why would *Pat Briggs* have information about him?"

"Oh, there's a lot of things you don't know. And Gramma looked for him once."

"When?" When was that? Why didn't I know? This was outrageous. I wasn't sure yet that it was true but I believed her.

"I guess she knew you always wanted to find him."

"And what happened?" This had all gone on, in my family, without me.

"I think they found some pretty bad things and then they stopped. I think she felt it would be best to just drop it. But there was a box in the basement, if I remember, with all the files in it and I think Carol said when she went to Florida she drove it over to the Briggses'."

The box. It began to turn and glitter for me, like a geometric drawing or a cut jewel. It existed, hard and permanent, home, like a pearl.

My mother was going on. Her voice lowered and she laughed a little as if she were telling something that she did wrong but that was really kind of adorable. "I remember once I called her and I was going to send you back there and she wanted to find him, I think she thought in case she died or something. You should know where he was.

"I guess I really did want to send you back. That once. It was right around your eighth-grade graduation. Remember you had that beautiful dress that I couldn't afford that you *had* to have."

"No." I didn't remember it that way.

"Oh come on, you remember the dress Paulette made."

"I remember the dress."

"Well. I still have the bills." She laughed again.

I did remember the dress. I remembered her threats. I remembered the rest all different.

My mother always meant to leave. In Wisconsin she meant to but she didn't have the courage to do it alone. So she took me along. She needed someone to talk to and blame it on. Someone she could believe she was doing it all for. Once we were in California, where she'd wanted, it still wouldn't open for her and so what she wanted then was to be there alone. She thought men didn't want a woman with a child they'd have to support. She wanted to send me away. Back to Gramma. Or just leave me. Something. She thought maybe alone they would want her.

And she should have left. We both knew. I believed it too.

I thought of running away, a lot of times during all those years in California. I'd stand outside our apartment door and look at the block with its strange buildings and that blank sky. But I was too scared to do it, that was the thing. When she wanted me there, when she came back around her cycle and wanted me to stay with her forever, she told me I could not live without her. Nobody else would want me. The way I was. The ugly way I slept. The way I breathed.

It was bad around the time of my eighth-grade graduation, because she was going out with the orthodontist and he was dropping her.

For graduation, all the girls in my school had to have white dresses. You had to put them on twice, once for the graduation and once a month before, when they took the class picture. At first all that was okay. Because my mom found me a cute dress at Saks with a shirred waist that was cheap too, only forty-two dollars. But then when she came to pick me up from the pictures she saw that two other girls in my class had my same dress.

"Oh, will you look at that. Damn," my mother said. "Hmph."

Some of the girls who had been going to this school forever, they knew in advance about the white dress. There were girls who bought their white dresses in New York and in Paris the summer before.

I pouted a little about that but not really. I just liked to complain. There was so much I didn't have. But I didn't really care that other girls had my same dress. One of them was kind of popular. Actually it made me feel better.

But my mother got it in her mind that we had to have a better dress. *We'd show them.* A dress no one else would have. Now I wonder if it had anything to do with the orthodontist. She knew we would see him at the graduation. He had a daughter in my grade. And the ex-wife would be there, too. So I suppose she wanted us both to look good.

My mother found a French seamstress named Paulette and they became friends. Paulette was married but to a man who was a disappointment. He was bald and slope-bellied and he lay around in his socks watching sports games on TV. We hired Paulette to make a dress for me and we started driving to where she lived in West Hollywood several nights a week for fittings.

They worked and worked, Paulette and my mother, designing and sewing and redoing and shifting. They studied the magazines, the French and American *Vogue*s. My mother would come in with sketches of the dress on her manila school folders. All my life, she'd drawn clothes and I'd drawn buildings. We were both doodlers, so no paper we had in the house was ever clean.

It was a thick rare cream-colored silk. The dress went to my ankles. There was one band for a neck and a ruffle and one band too at the bottom. The sleeves were full, with a row of covered buttons. But the real glory was the belt, it was made out of eighteen different-colored satin ribbons. They got tied in three separate bows and hung down long in the front, like a maypole.

It was costing us a fortune, this dress.

My mother's temper was short and I could always ignite it, just by being the way I was.

We were driving home on Sunset Boulevard from Paulette's one night and I did it just by looking the way I did. I mean my face. I had some expression.

"That does it," she said, swerving the car. "You're going back to Wisconsin. You can live with Gramma. I can't take you anymore. But I'll give you a last big bang with that dress, boy, that's some dress they can all see you in, so you'll go out with a bang."

The dress was our apotheosis. It was perfect. I only wore it that once.

That day, seeing her daughter in the dress and new white shoes, on the velvet-thick lawn of El Rodeo School under a shimmering high light Los Angeles sky, a day clear enough you could feel the sharp top edges of the San Gabriel Mountains in the distance, if I'd risen up into the sky in that dress, the ribbons fluttering like the ends of a balloon touching the rough middle stalks of the palms, my mother would have felt a dissolving happy ending to her motherhood, she would have rubbed the stinging edges in her eyes, held her elbows in her hands a way she knew she looked good and that would have been her life's satisfaction. As it was there was me again on other days in worse clothes, bumping into her, getting in her way.

I think she really imagined it might work with the orthodontist— him seeing how good we looked at graduation and then I'd be gone and they could start over again and be young. She herself had a new yellow-and-white two-piece long suit she wore to the ceremony.

I had the best dress in the three-hundred-and-forty-person class and I was probably the poorest girl. "We showed them," my mother whispered. "Boy, I'll tell you." A tear gelled in her eye, she was so proud of herself. And it was hard for her, this life. No one will ever know.

That was on the lawn, her heels sinking in the grass. That was when she still had hopes. He was standing over with his son, by the empty basketball court. The orthodontist was muscular and tan, not a tall man.

My grandmother had not even been invited. "She'd never come," my mother said, bitter, but with a young breeze of snobbery, too. "She never goes anywhere. She could come and visit. I'm her daughter, you know. But no. She just stays in her house, in her own little yard. She's really a loner. When you're grown up I won't be that way. I'll come visit and see you with your children, wherever you are."

The orthodontist said hello to us, but mostly he stood with his ex-wife and his children. They all went out someplace to eat after. We were invited to a party and my mother decided we might as well go. Maybe he'd come later and anyway, what else were we going to do? We didn't say it but we were both thinking at least we didn't have to pay to go somewhere to eat. We weren't even hungry, but every-one else was going someplace planned so we felt like we wanted something.

A good deal of our gratitude fell that day on the family who had the party at their house. My mother kept showing me nice little ways the wife made her home attractive. Odd stone urns in the bathroom held fragile flowers that wouldn't live more than the day. My mother kept knuckling my back and whispering, Say thank you. I didn't want to. It was a party. It was no big deal. At home, we had our own back-yard and if you had a party you didn't expect to be thanked for every little thing. I knew all the kids but my mother didn't know their par-ents and not many of them talked to her. She said mostly they stuck together, the couples. And some of them seemed to be friends from before.

I no longer even remember any of their names.

By the end of the party my mother blamed money. It was money all the other women her age had.

"Did you see how they all had the pearls?" We were walking out to our car. We'd stayed till the end but then people were going with their families out to dinner.

I hadn't even noticed. I didn't notice what mothers wore, and always, my mother was the prettiest one. Other people told me that and I always said what they said to her. "Did they really say that, Annie-honey, really?" But she was alone in her glory. She shook her hair and looked at her profile lining up the car mirror.

Later that day it was the shoes. She decided the orthodontist had left her because she was wearing a yellow-and-white dress with black shoes. "I knew I shouldn't have. Damnit. But no. You had to have your dress and I didn't have the money to buy myself one pair of decent shoes for spring. He probably looked at my feet and said, no, I don't want a poor little chitty like that who can't even buy herself one elegant thing. Why should he? He can have any of those. Any one of them. I saw how they were looking at him."

"Most of them are married," I volunteered.

My mother turned her ankle in and out, surveying. Yes. She was deeply disappointed in the shoes.

I HAD ANOTHER PARTY that night but it was only for kids.

"Go on and go," she said. "Go ahead. I want to get home and out of these shoes."

And when I came in later with my key, I thought my mother was dead.

It was a strange haze light that came into that small apartment from the street lamp. There was only the one room.

She was just on the bed then and still, even when I shook her.

"Mom, come on, wake up," I said when I roughed her shoulder.

Then I just stopped and sat down on the chair and waited. I would die then too. I still had on the fragile party dress. I had played outside. There had been a pool. I distantly remembered the soft music of splashes. They seemed nothing now, foam on the top of the sea. A frill of breeze in the palms high above the people's pool.

I did not believe I could survive her. I still do not know.

I took the dress off first and set it on the back of a chair. It seemed thin now, almost transparent, a sunny white. It moved a little on its own. It was still perfect. I had been careful not to eat anything so there wouldn't be a stain.

A dress was always the end of the world for us, distillation of beauty.

I sat in that chair for a time I will never be able to determine or measure. Then, later, far later, she turned in her sleep. That was all. She turned to the other side.

I'll ship you off to your father and he can have you.

Go find your father and see how you like that.

I will. These were all things we had said before.

That's fine. You go ahead. Just go and see how you like that.

That next morning was our worst. The gunpowder violence was gone, my night of terror, rolling on the hard floor, but it had lasted. Usually our mornings were a sea wind, blue and yellow. That evil metal taste from the night vanished. But that morning it was still there.

It was day and we were almost standing tall.

"If you need to go, go then," I said biting my lip and tasting the faint salt of blood. "Or send me back to Gramma." As soon as I said that a flag rose. I saw something. I saw that I would respect her if she left me. Walking away was the right thing for her to do, the strong thing in her life. For her she should have left but not for me.

We stayed together like that. For five more years. Our biggest triumph would have been one for us strong enough to go off and try for a life on her own.

She never did really. Even now.

And I grew up able to love people without much relation to me. I could love the nuance of their lives and the drama of their other attachments. With my mother, I was never first. I am unusual in that I can love people for themselves.

That dress is one of the few things from my childhood we still have. It hangs in her closet, covered in plastic from the best dry cleaner in Los Angeles. Waiting.

"WHY DON'T YOU get Carol to send that box and we'll look through together at Christmas?" My mother's voice on the answering machine.

I STILL KEPT PLANNING for the island. Jordan brought more brochures. I wanted coconuts and little monkeys. One of the pictures had hand-sized monkeys scampering on the counter of a tiny wooden store, near fishnets and ships in a bottle. Through my childhood in Wisconsin we all wanted monkeys. Little squirrel monkeys for pets. We wanted different things each year but a monkey was the one that lasted. Every year we all asked for a monkey for Christmas. Emily Briggs was the only person who ever got one. But she turned out to be allergic so they put it in the new teen section of Briggs's called The Id. The next winter, it died, in its cage, of pneumonia.

I pictured brown water and palms above us like ceiling fans. We calculated money. My voice sank when Jordan called one day and said he'd bought us both panama hats at a store named Worth and Worth. He'd invested money. That seemed too far.

And with him, I still felt like I'd walked home from school one day and come into the wrong house. It might be a quiet house, a good house, they might sit around a clean round table, but it was still the wrong house.

In bed he didn't giggle. He was silent. And then he had a deep full laugh like a bell and it rang into the air as if just released, unfolding, rejoicing to be free.

BUT STEVIE HOWARD was going home for Christmas, back to Racine. I had a picture of Stevie still, when he was twelve, barefoot, sitting on a stone fence playing the banjo. No boy was as beautiful as Stevie was when he was twelve. But he didn't look like that anymore.

He called me and I could hear he was outside. The hot tub. I could hear the water loshing and above the spread of eucalyptus in the wind.

"I wasn't going to go home for Christmas," I told him. "I was thinking of flying to Egypt."

"To Egypt?" His voice sharpened. The loshing stopped. I guess he stood still in the water. He lowered his voice and went slow like he did when he thought I was crazy. "For Christmas? It's not a really great time to go there now. In terms of safety. You should look through that box first and see what they found."

"That Uncle's supposed to get back, I think, middle of January. Maybe he'll hear something over there."

"He says he has no idea where he is?"

"Yeah."

"Do you believe him?"

"Yeah. I told you before. Why would he lie?"

"I don't know, Mayan. People lie. And I think it's about time to start thinking about giving up altogether."

"Cutting my losses."

"Before this takes over your life. Quit while you still have plenty else. Nothing's worth this much. Think of what could justify all this time and, I don't know, absorption, at the end of it. What's he going to do? What's he going to be? Really."

I TOLD THE DETECTIVE about the box. I couldn't help it. I was so excited. A box, when I thought of it, held a kind of perfection.

. . .

I DIDN'T GET TO ANY ISLAND.

Jordan when I told him didn't say anything. He closed his mouth like he was taking back a breath. His head tilted down a little forward. He was usually such a confident guy. He had a beautiful back of the neck, I saw then. He had a regular man's haircut, short in back with the hair cut to a V. And his neck was long and thin, a cup between tendons. I was truly sorry. But all I could do was shake my head.

I always had the Oldsmobile key on my keychain. I owned it. My cousin Hal used it in Racine. He left it in the airport parking lot when he went to Florida so I could just get off the plane and walk out and find it. I didn't want to see anybody waiting for me by the luggage rack and there was no one.

The weather hung low and gray and snow fell small, closely spaced, in thread lines. It was snow in the air and wet on the tar parking lot and it was still afternoon. It smelled different here. I just stood by the car and looked around.

I started driving. I considered checking into a hotel. But the money. I didn't feel up to the Briggses yet. And that's where I had to go. It was Christmas Eve. Emily was already there. She had flown out five days before. It was still new to be going up the hill, to the Briggses' house. Where my grandmother had lived was in the other direction from the airport. I drove out on Allouez and all of a sudden I was at the cemetery.

The cemetery was fairly vast, you noticed only after you'd passed through the gate and driven in. It covered a wide strip of land along-side Mason Street and then continued down the hill to the river, so that where I was you could see out to the dark smokestacks across the water. The paper mills now sent plumes of smoke into the gray sky and they held like clouds. A timid, tender break of white and silver caught between the smokestack chimneys. The mounds of coal and sulfur down the river were lightly dusted with snow.

I didn't know if it was the first or the second road to the right. But the car drove itself, I followed under the thick trees and then I got a funny, itching sensation on my throat when I recognized the names.

Christiansen. When I saw that stone with the two urns on either side, lilies engraved, I stopped and I got out. Christiansen was always the one behind. With my finger, I scraped off hardened bird shit from the marble. A few plots away, a man in black sat crouched over on a low stone writing something. He wore mean black boots, high up for a man on his leg, a thick black coat, no hat. Bits of snow caught momentarily in his yellowish hair. He bent over, gripping the pen hard.

I walked back to the car and opened my suitcase. I wanted to change. I still had on the dress I'd worn on the plane. I slipped the good shoes off now, already snow-stained, and rubbed sneakers on over my heels. Behind the car seat, I took off the dress, put on a sweatshirt and yanked up jeans. Then just as I was zipping I heard footsteps.

"I know you," a voice dropped close.

A head popped over the open car door and it was Danny Felchner, Amber's boy. He'd lived on the end of Guns Road. Jim the Carpenter was his father and he'd been a momma's boy, always inside. When we were children, I saw him once, in his house, in an apricot-colored dress on backwards. He was four or five years older than me. I hadn't seen him for more than a decade. His family had moved away.

"Hi, Danny." I read over the stones. I didn't see any Felchners. "Do you know somebody around this part?"

He shrugged. "I come to get names."

He showed me the book he was writing in. It had a black-and-white-marbled cover. In it he had a vertical row of names. We were there. My grandmother and my grandfather, my cousin. That felt strange, on my neck.

"What for?" But then a long yellow car stopped a few yards away. A woman slammed the door and walked out. She made her way to a stone and stood there. She had something in her gloved hands. It looked like a washed-out jar.

Danny and I both watched. The woman faced the river and we saw her back and the live factories beyond. A barge moved slowly down the water. She stood so she was shaded by one large chestnut and a fir, the stone before her was rounded black granite. Her coat was car length, her boots and pants modest. She had the coin-sized curls all the women there wore. They went to the beauty shop once they'd turned twenty-nine or when they'd had a child, whichever came first, and gave their hair over to permanence.

Then another car came from far away, turning in the road by the river. That car was brown and inched on slowly. It looked like it would stop a long ways from us, on the lower part of the slope. But it was impossible that time of day not to watch. The snow swirled and ticked, fizzy around us, but there was no real movement. The barge hardly advanced on the gray-brown river. Finally the new car slowed and bobbed, lights flashing in front of the yellow sedan. The woman ran over, her boots ankle high just shirring the snow. The driver of the new car stood out and went around to open her door. She looked behind her shoulder, then tucked into the dark car. The yellow car sat, less yellow in time dimmed with snow.

"You know who that is?" Danny Felchner said.

"No."

"Pud Hollander, from the bank. I don't know the woman. Probably somebody from the west side."

"What are you doing here anyway, Danny? You're living around here? Writing down names in the cemetery?"

"I'll put you in," he said, tilting the left half of his face up towards me with a crooked smile, "but you're not Atassi are you, anymore, or August? You're what, Stevens, right?"

"Stevenson."

"Here." He passed me the book and the pen. But I just didn't feel like it. I didn't want to.

"I don't like to write my name," I said, handing him back his book and his pen.

"I've been living here for five years now. You heard of the Black Shutter?" I said I hadn't. "Well, it's my store. I own it."

"What kind of store?"

"Anti-Qs," he said. "Junk."

I wanted to ask him what he was doing in the cemetery writing down names but I could tell he would be mysterious. And I didn't want to be all day. "Can I give you a lift anywhere, Danny?"

He smiled in an odd way. He frightened me a little, but then I'd look again and he'd only be Danny Felchner, whom I'd always known. "You can give me a ride," he said.

I looked around, I kind of expected him to have a car there. An old battered truck or something. I remembered his dad's carpenter truck, a round-nosed thing, with yellow and green paint chipping off like a toy left outside. His father built my mother and me a kitchen table once. She was never satisfied with it. It always wobbled and we were forever sticking things underneath. Jim the Carpenter claimed it was our floor.

I tossed him the keys. "Warm it up a sec, okay?" I didn't have gloves on, so I brushed off the markers on the ground, first my cousin, then her, just with the side of my hand. I could read them, their full names. I heard the car idling behind me. I stood there a minute, just trying to feel right to her. It was hard with someone watching. Then I turned away and got in the car.

"So where shall I take you?"

He shrugged. "Where you going?" He'd opened his coat and he'd crossed his arms, like a pretzel in a black sweater. His big boots crept up on the carpeted walls of my grandmother's car.

I didn't exactly know. At the cemetery gate I turned left, towards town. I had no place to be really either. I didn't want to go to the Briggses' yet. It was still early. I flicked my hands up off the steering wheel. "Downtown?"

He smiled, head forward, purring. "What, you want to look at the Christmas windows at Briggs's?"

"No, not Briggs's," I said.

"We could go to the church bazaar in your old school basement."

"Saint Agnes?"

"Mmhm."

"Oh, let's do that." My fingers lifted straight back. "Where?"

"Follow the two steeples and then left."

Everything here was easy to see. The steeples exceeded everything but the smokestacks in the sky. Danny's pale fingers fluttered around my grandmother's car radio. It had hardly ever been used. We should have sold the car, but I just never did. My aunt advertised it once in the paper for me but the best offer we got was four hundred and fifty. That just didn't seem worth it.

"There's no music," Danny said.

And then I realized how still it was here. Everything seemed muffled and colored. The beginning of sunset streaked now between the steel bridges and the smokestacks and paper-mill workings across the Fox River. The clouds bottomed with strokes of pink and a lit orange that wouldn't last.

"Your radio's broken."

"Oh, that. Is it?" There were things about growing up without brothers and sisters. And my grandmother was old. She kept a radio in the kitchen, but she mostly listened to the weather or the talk news or WBAY, looking for a waltz. And with my mother she never let me play rock 'n' roll in the car. I couldn't have told you what it was to begin to hear music.

"It's my grandmother's car."

He nodded. "Your grandmother was a nice lady."

I coasted to an easy parking place and we walked down into the church basement. Women at a card table handed us white Styrofoam cups of hot chocolate with miniature marshmallows on top. We passed booths of felt sunbursts, painted yardsticks, complete with sewn yardstick jackets, mod woven potholders, family tree kits, child-made multicolored candles, embroidered calendars of the liturgical year, women in bright smocks selling all of it, along with powdered sugar twists, dark ginger cookies and endless crinkly home-baked pies.

"All I do here is eat," Danny said.

A few card tables looked almost like antique stalls in city flea markets. These were less antiques than stuff from the basement and attic, but at one, Danny found his prize. A tablecloth of names. There it was: a round, standard tablecloth, the borders factory-printed with maroon and brown, green-leaved, unpretty flowers. But a woman must have had all her guests from 1941 on sign the tablecloth. You could see the dull gray lead signatures under embroidery yarn. They spanned the forties though the sixties. Then she'd embroidered each signature a different color.

A tablecloth of handwritten names, colored as a circus poster. I looked it over. I recognized some families I knew, but none of the girls was there.

"And her children are selling it," he whispered to me. "Twenty dollars. Why would you sell a thing like that?"

I saw a cane. I'd never noticed canes until the man upstairs but this was a pretty one, light wood—all his had been dark—rustic but perfectly smooth, with some gnarls and raised joints of branch intact. The more I looked, it went beautiful. "How much is this?"

"I'll take three," the man said, slot-mouthed. He wore a T-shirt, arms crossed in front, muscles pressing everywhere.

I bought it for the man upstairs and then walked with it myself down the aisles. It felt good in the hand. I liked it. I hoped I'd really give it to the old man. My mother did that. Whenever my mother bought a present for anybody she got one for herself too, and she kept the one with the better color or without the scratch. It was so hard for her give away anything. She always felt like she had so little herself.

Danny had spread his tablecloth out across the worn knees of his black jeans. "I wonder who made it. You think their mother? Must be the mother."

I pulled him back through the crowded aisle. Danny's mother, Amber Felchner, was the fattest woman we knew growing up. She was a good cook. The other women on Guns Road were always borrowing her recipes. They usually had some chicken or meat in them and a Campbell's cream soup and biscuits baked on top of it all. But Jim, her husband, and her two boys, they never got fat. Danny and I then were sharing a paper plate of sticky rice crispy and marshmallow squares. You had to grow up in the Midwest not to find these things disgusting, but if you did grow up here there was something indoors about them. All walls and ceilings and safety and rain.

"Excuse me, he just bought this from you. Do you know who made it?"

An older woman with an ample face, vastly freckled, waited before us, her square hands useless, lifted. "Oh, why sure, my mother made that. She did it for their twenty-fifth anniversary. Never used it. 'S never been used. I found it upstairs in a drawer wrapped in brown tissue."

"You don't want it yourself? You sure you want to sell it?" Danny held it out as a kind of accusation. He couldn't help himself. It occurred to me then how he had loved his mother and that, by now, she might be dead. Fat people died. "She's gonna die soon," my mom had said about Amber Felchner, thirty years ago. She's gonna die soon. Every time you mentioned Amber Felchner, that was her refrain. My grandmother would shake her head, saying, "Such a pretty, pretty face."

The woman shriveled, somehow folding the many freckles. "Shucks no, I've got so much of such stuff around the house. You take it. Take it if you think you'll use it." The woman picked up the tiny white price tag affixed with white string to the corner, professionally, as if this were a store. "Twenty. I put on twenty." She reached into the glass mason jar and picked out a ten, moved to give it back. "That was high. Here. Take this."

Danny backed off, mouth open, jawy. "No, are you kidding? It's a great price, do you know what I'd pay for this in Chicago?" He pressed it, folded, to his chest. "I love it."

"Enjoy it, I'll be glad if you get some use out of it," she said. "And remember it all goes to Saint Agnes. New altar boys' robes and choir books.''

"What a trip," he said, walking out to the car. Now we were eating Mexican vertical donuts, hot and melting with powdered sugar. International sophistication in Racine seemed to exist mainly in baked goods. Sweets from many countries. I'd been there under a day and I could feel I'd already gained.

"I should really go back and give her another twenty. Can you be-*lieve* she sold this?"

I could believe. No problem. I'd known houses choked with hand-touched things. One tablecloth wouldn't be this mother's only legacy. People repeated themselves. There were few true quirks in character. This solid freckled woman, a daughter still at fifty, had probably always lived cluttered and impeded by meant mementos from her mother. Children like that don't need to save.

I tried to remember Danny better from when we were little. His brother was normal, but I don't think Danny had many friends. He was always at home with his mother.

I thought of the freckled woman, her red, preparatory hands. Her mother every day gave her what we looked for at flea markets. I remembered Emily's monument of a birthday cake, built and worked over with butter cream. I could see the little glass cups of food coloring, tinting the white frosting, the metal fluting frosting gun, their maid did most of the work but Merl signed her name, in frosting, at the end, on the right-hand bottom corner. It had a flourish to it. People who expressed themselves expressed everyplace, signing even things they barely touched. People like my grandmother kept on hiding over and over again, every day of their lives until the end when they finally disappeared, once and for all, leaving behind not even a signature.

I looked over at Danny. "You remember my mom?"

His head went down so it shook parallel to the ground. "Your grandma was such a nice person," he said. "Yeah, she was a great woman. I remember kids laughing at me over something and your grandma saying, 'Ugh, don't you care what they say, you just go about your own business, let 'em laugh, they'll get tired of it pretty soon and pick on someone else.' "

The funny thing was my grandmother was as bad as the others about Amber's Danny, behind his back. She blamed Amber for it.

"Where to now?" He put his boot on the dashboard. I must have looked at it funny because he said sorry and pulled his leg back, both arms around the knee. I'd never seen a boot on that dashboard before. My grandmother always kept her car perfect.

"I don't know," I said. "Do you have to be somewhere?"

He shrugged. Bells began to peal from churches. It must have been five o'clock.

I said, "I kind of don't want to go where I'm supposed to."

"Well, let's go downtown then."

Nothing here was far from anything else. I parked halfway down the block on Main Street. The library was one way, Boss's the other. "Where to?" I said. We just sat.

"I can buy some tobacco at Boss's. Check out the magazines."

I ran first to the library. It was still early but already darkening, winter. People rushed by carrying packages in both hands. I was thinking, I didn't even know what the country looked like: Egypt. I wanted to see and for some reason I wanted to know now, before I had to face the Briggses. I shuffled up the white long steps to the big doors. The Racine Public Library and Museum were attached, in this old building with the columns. At the main desk, under a huge wreath, I asked for Marion Werth. She had an office upstairs in a cage but I expected she would be walking through some part of the library now. Maybe they had their own Christmas party. I looked forward to her right then, her round face and red fringe of bangs. I wondered if it would be a red dress or a green dress. Her earrings would definitely have a Christmas theme: wreaths or trees or sleighbells that jingled.

"Up, they're gonna say, whatever happened to the girl that jingled," Eli Timber teased her one year. Stevie Howard was there too. All the teenage guys noticed what she wore and flirted with her. It was like practice.

"The girl *who* jingled? That was me!" she said, stamping a bookleaf. She had a cheerfulness, something proper you found only in the Midwest.

"She's not here anymore," the kid behind the desk said. I looked at him. He was someone I didn't know.

"Will she be in next week?" I thought vacation. Maybe she even found some relative on the family tree and took the train to meet him. Despite myself, I got excited about that.

"She doesn't work here anymore."

"Since when?"

"August."

I asked him where she worked now and his lips went tight and his chin crumbled the way some people's do. "I can't say that, ma'am, only that she is no longer employed by the Racine Public Library."

The kid was what, no more than eighteen or nineteen. Stern. I wanted to slap his chin for daring to imply anything less than right in Marion Werth's conduct. He bothered me so much I forgot what I was there for. Then I turned around and saw into the big reading room, the library tabletops under the slow shower of electric light: a father stood behind two children; leaning over them, pointing to things in a big book. A black teenaged boy stood gazing at the standing globe, his fingertips all on the surface of one yellow continent. An old woman sat in the corner by a swan's-neck lamp, the newspaper stretched taut between two gloved hands. The pads of her glove fingers were black. Kids browsed, slouching, at the new arrivals rack. A deep bright blue pressed against the long windows. It was quarter after five, the big clock on the north wall said. I went to the world atlas and found it: Egypt. It looked pretty large. I drew the shape in pencil on my checkbook. I decided I'd learn it the way I could anytime draw Wisconsin.

Wind skeeted down the empty main street, newspapers caught on alley garbage cans. I pulled up my collar. This was what it was like here. Sunset, brown-red and a sorrowing pink under looming purple clouds, stretched between the smokestacks across the river. The brick paper mill's windows lit yellow-orange.

I stopped at a phone booth on Main Street and called the detective long distance. I couldn't stay mad at anyone long. I had too many of my own problems. And with Jim Wynne, it was just like making up after any fight. We both sounded subdued, lower now. I put my hand on the glass, pressing to stretch, and for one moment, I looked down and saw myself in my jeans and thought, someone across the street could be glancing at me right now the way I'd watched people in phone booths, and I must—from this far away—assume some mystery, too.

We decided. I'd open the box and then he'd start work on whatever leads I found from that. So I'd have to get through Christmas alone.

"And what about the passport guy?" I said. "You were going to check on that." I'd gotten to feel that I had to keep the lists and remind him. That was a bad feeling, but if it was true, it was true. He'd never surprised me with anything good. Not since the very beginning, before the check was cashed. Still, I didn't think he was a bad man. I guessed it was normal to be lazy.

"Yeah, he's workin' on it, you know for what I paid him he's not gonna rush, but he'll, he's a good guy, he'll do it. I should be getting something from him any day now."

I tried to force him into a dinner when I got back.

"I'll have whatever's in the box then, we can just go over it together. I've got my calendar," I said. I already owned a calendar for the new year. I balanced the thing on my bent leg in the phone booth. January 5. I dallied a moment, writing his name down.

"Awright," he said in an upsigh way that made me know he was going to cancel. "Do you have those two addresses in Egypt, the Shahira Miramar and the Refinery? From that report I gave you?"

It was snowing outside, the street already furred with gray slush.

"Yeah," I said. That reminded me of when my mother wanted me to write to the United Arab Republic to ask where my trust fund money was. She told me all my life, I had a trust fund for college. Then the summer before I was supposed to go she said she was worried because nothing had come for me in the mail. Who was supposed to send it, I said. Well the Arabs, she said. You don't have a name or documents? Did you have the name of the lawyer or anything? No, but it was said that it would be done. It was promised me. When? Well, when you were born.

That summer when I was still hoping stupidly and watching the mail just because the other side was shell after shell of horror, I drafted a letter to my father's family. My mother went to dinner once in a while with a fat dark-skinned man named Fiaz. He was some kind of Arab but he'd said once to me that he didn't know my father or my father's family. He was from a different country altogether. I don't remember anymore which one. But my mother said he could take my letter to the family.

I wrote, "My mother has told me that you made arrangements for my college education at the time of my birth. As I am going to college in September, I need to know as soon as possible whether this is true."

She rewrote the letter for me with her friend Audrey. Audrey, she said, knows what men over there are like. These Arabs.

"Dear Relatives" (they wrote), "I have not seen my daddy for years and years," it began. "And now I am a straight A student in Beverly Hills High School hoping to go to college and study medicine. My mother works hard but she is all alone. Men ask her out on dates but she is too worried about me and my education. I have nowhere to turn for help."

It went on like that, all begging.

I refused. She could write it if she wanted but not like that in my name.

"Okay, it's your life," my mother said. "But I know these men. I know what they're like. They don't want you to just be so blunt. And tough."

Later she said my trust fund was her jewels.

JIM WYNNE TOLD ME the Miramar address had been on my father's record when he first came to the University of Wisconsin. It was that old. I supposed it was probably his home. I couldn't believe it would be there anymore.

Dorothy Widmer, that dust-file angel, had located it. I wasn't that far from Dorothy Widmer right now. Powell Street went along the river a ways and then veered up into the highway. Madison was what, less than a half day's drive away. I thought, maybe I should meet her. But no, why. The feather had touched her once but never again. Maybe she'd been his lover. I thought a lot of women probably were. Still. I fingered the travel agent's card in my wallet. On the back, I had the numbers written for the flights to Egypt. I imagined Dorothy Widmer egg-shaped, yearning. Egypt was my last resort. Secret. If I went there, I had to find him. I didn't tell the detective. I didn't want him thinking I had any more money.

"Do that," he said. "Write to them."

"I did already."

"Oh. Good," he said. That surprised him. "See, we're gettin' someplace now. See now you're catching on. Your attitude's better. We're makin' a lot of progress."

We hung up, together. Except I'd lied. That was my first lie to him. I didn't feel like writing to those thirty-year-old addresses without zip codes. I just didn't do it. I never trusted much good coming from the mail. Those systems broke. Or they worked but for other purposes, to relay the mundane tops of things. My grandmother's letters, sent and received, all recounted what was that day cooked and eaten. What parts of the body ached how and which ointments were tried as new relief. Those letters arrived. The ten-cent stamp could carry them. Once, absolutely alone with my mother in Los Angeles, I escaped out of the apartment and ran. After a while I just walked. Nobody was following me. She'd wait mad for me to come back in. I passed mansions with vast lawns and saw no people. Just for nothing I opened a mailbox and spread wide a fan of cobwebs.

No one in Los Angeles bothered with letters. It was too long and simple a wait. And people other places were too far away.

Danny Felchner was smoking a hand-rolled cigarette at the counter of Boss's. Piped Christmas music came in from an old radio on the top shelf. I didn't want it to be Christmas. I wanted just any other ordinary day. I slid onto the stool beside him.

"Who'd you call?" he said.

"Secret."

"Try these then," he said, and slipped a pair of sunglasses over my eyes.

With his finger, he revolved a circular wire rack of sunglasses. Next to it was a standing head mirror. The glasses were tinted silver. I looked criminal and mean. "Nope," I said.

He spun the rack harder, then lifted off another pair. "These are better." He fitted them over my ears. This pair was delicate, bookish. I liked them. I'd always believed people looked more intelligent in glasses.

Danny took them off my eyes and put them in my coat pocket. "Here," he said, patting the pocket. At first I flushed embarrassed, pleased. That he was going to buy me something. I liked it so much when someone did something for me I didn't know how to be. It pleased me too much just when someone liked me.

"Come on," he said, a hand under my elbow. Then I understood. He wasn't going to buy them for me. We were going to steal the sunglasses from Boss's. Then I felt ashamed for being so happy.

I was scared, real scared but with a sharp edge of thrill too, walking out as if something electric and loud, a buzzing, might start when I passed under the nickel plate door and my whole body felt different that second, but then we were out going to the car and his hand was still on my elbow and I shrugged it off. I wanted to be alone and all of a sudden it seemed late, night was blowing over the river, silver clouds, and the joy ride felt done.

Sunglasses. Now I'd have them. I already did have health insurance from school. Two out of three. But I didn't like stealing from Boss's.

It seemed to end our aimlessness. "I better get there," I said, my foot on the car floor. "Where should I bring you?"

He shrugged. "I'm parked by Price's," he said. "You can leave me anywhere."

"What are you doing? Are you going to your parents tonight?"

"No," he said.

I all of a sudden wanted to invite him with me. But it was the Briggses' and I couldn't really. I mean I could but it was a statement. But then I got mad.

Emily could always do anything and it was just because it was never my house. So I did invite him. He wanted to go and change first and come up later. I dropped him off at his car, an old car like mine. I wondered if it had been Amber's.

The Briggses lived on the Hill, a little out of town. Just driving there, I tried to subdue my excitement over the snow, lines and lines, curves overlapping, like stilled waves on the far distant ridges of old Italian paintings, the fields in their blue cartilage of snow, going on and on far enough to see stands of trees and beyond them, nothing; the dusk settling. Black stark twigs, the dried earth poking out at ditches, the lowness and closeness. I knew it wasn't so much. Everybody feels that way about the place they grew up.

AN EVENT YOU DREAD enough is always a relief when you arrive. Parties. Briggses' were always so much bigger on the way.

I parked about twenty feet down the hill and sat in the dark quiet car. The house was already lit. The made-to-look-old gas lanterns lining the drive from here really did seem tonight like torch flames. They had a gate, swung open now. The house, set halfway up old Baird's Hill, was pink brick in the shape of the White House. It was higher in the middle and that part had white pillars. There were two fancy neighborhoods in Racine, the old one along the Fox River and this. Pat Briggs's father and his grandfather both owned huge old houses in town on Mason Street. His Swiss grandfather had built an all-stone house there and he'd built his own church, of the same stone. Otto Kapp. He'd started Kapp's, a German restaurant and bakery on Main Street. Otto's wife was dead now for a long time, but he was still alive and so was his sister Clara, who'd never weighed more than about eighty pounds and who had seemed attached by wires to the cash register in the middle of the candy and cookie counter where you went in and out of Kapp's. People said that's why they got so rich, because either Otto or Clara was always at that register. "They never let anyone else get near it." I'd heard that all my youth. If someone got rich in Racine you could bet it was from some character defect.

Otto had been some kind of actor and singer when he was young and he spent his money building the church so he could start a boys' bell choir.

His only daughter had married Seamus Briggs and Seamus Briggs had started Briggs's. According to everyone alive to remember, that was some wedding in Otto's church. They still had the dress in a vault at Briggs's. It was supposed to have cost a thousand dollars then in the Depression. When Pat married Merl, he'd wanted to start a new neighborhood and they bought up Baird's Hill. They'd brought architects from Spring Green and from Chicago—in medical school in the East, Pat had followed the fashions—but the architects had begun excavating and planning something with local wood and clay and stones they just found in fields outside town and cement, all things which seemed to Merl dirty. She had wanted something fancy. The only person Merl really got along with during that period of construction was Scully, the stonemason for the cemetery. He and she were finally left together planning the house after everyone else went away. She'd wanted something grand. She'd always imagined columns and huge velvet stage curtains, that sort of thing. And she'd gotten it. There were bay windows with windowseats and a lot of statues. In the backyard, down the hill a ways, were the carved-out foundations the old architects had made, before they left in their muddy boots and yellow slickers. "Dirty men," Merl said whenever they were mentioned in the newspaper. We used to play there as children, we used it as an amphitheater.

Years later, Frank Lloyd Wright came to the public library and gave a speech. The Better Homes and Gardens Society had brought him up and they'd driven him around and asked him to pick the best house in town, from the architecture point of view. Marion Werth had introduced him at the podium. That was her first month at the library. He said in his speech that he could not select a winner because after a day tour he had not seen one example of architecture in Racine. All we had, he'd said, was building. He'd criticized the whole town as they sat below in their best clothes from Briggs's, and they all clapped politely when he was done talking.

I took a hard breath. I had to go in. I went around to the trunk and got out my backpack. I always felt sloppy and like a student when I walked into Briggses'. Sometimes I was fine about that. I thought it was good for them to just see how normal people lived when they were doing something serious. Tonight, though, I felt pretty shabby.

I expected Dorothy to be somewhere near the door. They had a maid and that was just natural to them. I can't quite explain the way that seemed to me. I was disappointed. It wasn't all neat and ordered, it didn't have that air of in-control comfort maids brought in the movies. It was just one other thing that couldn't touch the real mess of life.

The tall front door hung open a little, supporting an elaborate wreath, excrescent with dried flowers and miniature fruit. Inside, Emily waved at me. She was on the phone, stretching the cord the length of the circular marble foyer. "Tad," she mouthed. She always looked different at home, a way she didn't anywhere else. It was as if other places when she was sitting or standing, she was folded into too little space. Tonight, her feet pawed the pink stone floor and stretched. Her toenails were polished under the nylon.

She finished with Tad and then immediately began dialing again. "I'm trying to get this jacket before it's all sold out everywhere," she told me, phone tucked between her ear and shoulder. She showed me a page ripped out of a magazine. She'd always been a cutter-outer. Collage maker. The jacket was black with gold chains and spangles. I guessed it was nice.

"Aren't they closed?"

"Pacific time," she said. "Dad gave me a list of buyers." The Briggses shopped the way other people worked. Grimly. As if it made a difference. Gish had told me that when Mr. and Mrs. Briggs first married, he'd wanted her to throw out all she had, come to Briggs's and let him give her everything new, from the top lines. In Briggs's the top lines were all on the top floor. It went down that way to the bargain basement. But Merl hadn't liked much and when she did take to a sweater or a coat or pair of gloves, she insisted on buying duplicates. Closets filled with unused triplicates of four years ago's sweater. Mr. Briggs, a retailer, tried endlessly to explain to his wife about fashion, that it didn't last. But he never could teach her frivolity. For her it was all effort and no joy. She worried about waste. She could never see clothes as dispensable, understand that there would always be new and more.

Pat's wisdom worked on Emily, though. She really was his daughter. When she'd first moved to New York, I found her cross-legged on the floor of her empty apartment, having spent two hours calling Neiman Marcuses across America because she'd seen a dress in a magazine that seemed to her the dress Isabelle Archer had worn the day she landed in England. When the dress finally arrived, it didn't looked right on her. "Not enough butt," she'd decided, patting herself. A month after that, I got it. But she got sick of seeing her old things on me, so now she gives them to her cleaning woman.

"Hello. Size eight, but I could even take a six or a ten," she was saying, her voice loud on the phone.

"Can you do that?" I whispered.

She covered the mouthpiece. "Sure. Dressmaker."

"Oh," I nodded. I should know these things. Why didn't I?

She minced around the foyer, almost dancing, phone between cheek and breastbone, wearing just a pale peach slip and nylons. Her hair lifted way out crinkly the way it got when she braided it wet into a hundred tiny braids. The bottom almost reached her waist. She lifted some and pushed it back lightly. She was someone whose hair had always been brushed by another person. She treated it like a major personality.

"Got to get dressed," she breathed. "What are you gonna be?"

I'd let the backpack slide down off my shoulder.

"Huh?"

"What're you going to be tonight?"

Then I remembered. Of course. Merl had written me. I was supposed to bring a costume. This was a dress-up party.

"Um, surprise," I said.

"Yes, would you please check?" she was saying louder on the phone. "I'll wait."

"Emily, what are you going to be?"

"Angel," she said, then looked back down to the phone, where apparently some voice in California had returned to help her get the one more thing she momentarily wanted absolutely. "Yes, could I please speak to the manager."

THE WHOLE HOUSE had been done once by a decorator in 1963 and it was still that way. The dining room was cabana style with wide black and white stripes and the living room was a kind of fancy I couldn't identify. The windows all had floor-length drapes coming out from behind valances with scalloped edges. What was I going to be, I wondered, walking through the house. A fire shifted and broke in the fireplace and candles in silver and glass containers burned. No one was in the room. On tables at the ends of couches slipcovered with pictures of dogs hunting in cattail marshes were cut-glass bowls of miniature apples. Coming to this house, all I'd thought of was the box. I'd drawn it in margins of patient charts, then erasing again. It looked like this: a plain brown cardboard box, corrugated, the kind one uses moving. Just that there was, somewhere, a box with attempts like mine.

I'd always been so certain I was the only one in the world looking for him.

I passed the den and saw Pat Briggs at the far end crouched by the fireplace, moving logs. He was wearing a football player's outfit he was too thin for.

I found Dorothy in the kitchen, with about twenty colored tin trays of food. She snorted. "Here, try." She handed me a tiny Italian tomato half with something white on it and a snipping of basil, pressing it between her blunt fingers as if it was hard to keep a hold of something so tiny. Merl had always loved miniatures. When Emily was a child, Merl collected dollhouse furniture, and now the house was full of bonsai and miniature fruit.

Dorothy stood by the sink with a stream of water running. She spread a net of tiny grapes open between her fingers, delicately, as if she were opening a part of the body.

I hugged her and closed my eyes against her back. She smelled faintly of sugar.

"I better clean up and get my stuff upstairs." I took two bunches of island bananas, each no bigger than fingers, from my backpack. "I brought these for Merl." I wasn't big on presents but I'd hoped she hadn't discovered these yet. I'd never seen them in the Midwest. One bunch was red, one yellow.

"Oh, that she will like."

The room I was staying in was shoe box–shaped with one high window, which I closed. I opened my pack on the bed and took out the dress. It was wrinkled. I set the shower running and hung it up to steam. Then I lay down on the bed.

I was staring at the pinwheeling patch of uneven paint on the ceiling thinking that I'd been a tomboy and now it was getting late. I hadn't learned the other yet. My time with my mother was remote and wasted, we had loved things, and people, but it was only ours. Like Emily's life, you could tell about it. Here in the house, there were framed pictures all over the walls. They slanted on crooked nails in the hallways, they hung everywhere, on little draped tables they were propped in silver frames. At what age she did what. Guys who fell in love with her would want to see them. I could imagine Tad in a wool vest, picking up the picture of her bald in a lace dress on a horse. He would look at her lips and perfect head, wondering what it meant, her blank, clear expression. It meant nothing, I mouthed to no one, absolutely nothing. She had always had costume parties and she was always something like a princess or a fairy or a mermaid. When she was eight they'd had a dress-up party in Briggs's. They'd closed up, let the little girls rampage and then had them photographed in the store windows like mannequins. I'd been there. I was a pirate, with scarves tied on my pantlegs. There's one great picture of Mai linn and Emily and me in the window, the year Emily was bald, our limbs posed jerkily as if we were really made of materials.

But my years with my mother weren't like that. The two of us standing like bowling pins different places on a blacktop gas station lot, hands on hips, looking at the sky. My T-shirt sleeves rolled up on my arms, my nails bitten, my arms strong and a man's hands. I learned how to self-serve and fill it up. My mother didn't want to gas up her clothes. "I hate the smell," she'd said. "Pyew. I can't stand it. It makes me dizzy." She lifted her groomed hands to her nose and sniffed.

I was never so faint.

THE DOORBELL CHIMED and I heard footsteps. I thought of the box again. I had to say something right away tonight, I decided. I pushed my shoes off. The bed felt good, the little chenille bumps. I didn't want to go down yet. The sky was pretty with gray clouds from the small window up here, divided by a near black bare branch, ticking against the glass.

I came here my first Christmas in the East and that was my first time away from Bud Edison. I discovered then that you really fall in love with people during the time they're not there. You do it all by yourself.

We'd strategized at the supper table. Emily and I decided the coolest thing was to send him a postcard with nothing on the back but just my name. I sent him one with a picture of the paper-mill works. He'd hated it but not really. It made an impression for so long I felt guilty it wasn't really my idea.

It wasn't the same with Jordan. But I remembered little things I liked. One time in bed when I was on my back and he verged up like a sail.

I opened the bathroom door to check on the dress. Steam ghosted in, filming the window. Then Pat Briggs was at my door in a new costume. He was wearing some kind of muslin gown and sandals.

"What's going on in here?"

"I'm unwrinkling a dress." I peeled off my sweatshirt in the bathroom and pulled the dress on. It felt clammy, especially where it touched the back of my neck.

"Ever heard of hired help?"

"I thought you were going to say an iron."

"I have your Christmas present from your mother. She sent it here, care of the store."

"Oh." I sat on the bed and held my hands together. I began to see him more as the steam thinned.

"How is she?" He looked at me from an angle, keen.

I shrugged. "The same."

"I don't expect any of us really change." He wrung his hands. "But that's a hard life out there. Hard place."

I opened the high window and we heard a rise of laughter. People were walking down the drive. We heard the gravel move, women wobbling on high heels, grabbing their escorts' elbows, saying whew. My mother would have loved these parties. All my life, I'd been invited and she hadn't. In California, too. We'd sat on the bed of the small hotel when we first moved there and she'd said, "See, it's easier for you to get in with the kids 'cause you're young and you have school." I'd nodded. It was true. It was easier for me.

"What are you supposed to be?" I said.

"Jesus." He shrugged. "Merl made it up. I just have to put on something she got for around my neck. She couldn't decide between that and Bart Starr."

"You want me to lipstick on some stigmata?"

"Here, open it," he said, shoving the box closer to me. "She sent us something too. Some peanut brittle. Was pretty good. We managed to finish it."

The ribbon was a satin tartan plaid. I didn't really like doing this in front of him, opening my mother's present. It was a private thing. And I knew to him whatever it would be was small. Christmas was a big production for her. The paper was a ribbed pale brown. A piece of mistletoe was tied in with the bow. She'd always taken a real pride in wrappings.

I held the contents, a jar of something, up to the light. "Jam," I said. I opened the little card. "This is currant jam I made myself," it read. "I'm still making you the bigger present, but it's not finished yet. I did another inch of sky today on it!"

I kept the bow intact and smoothed the paper out, refolding it.

PAT BRIGGS LOOKED at my dress. "You want to hit my closet, kid?"

That was almost a joke. So many times my mother had brought me to a party without a costume and the Briggses had let me rifle through Pat's stuff. So I always ended up a man.

Pat Briggs had three closets, three stages of new. I found a tuxedo and began opening his drawers looking for socks. I stuffed toilet paper in the tips of Pat Briggs's shoes. I went into the bathroom, slicked back my hair.

"Very convincing," Pat said when I walked out.

He opened the top drawer of his desk and took out a stapler. "Give me your arms."

"Won't it ruin it?"

"Don't worry. It's on the way to Goodwill."

He stapled my cuffs together, put on his rosary and he stood in front of the mirror a moment and rubbed his palm over his head, where it would have been hair. That was something he did. He did it fast in a flickering way like he hoped people wouldn't see it. He had that and his tick.

EVERY PARTY at the Briggses' really centered around Tom Harris, the dog. When guests arrived, they would be led, either by Emily or Merl, one or two at a time, to pay homage. Pat wasn't any better. He would shrug his shoulders and nod at the procession over to Tom Harris, but he watched too closely to really mind it. Tonight Tom Harris was stationed in a new red plaid–lined basket in front of the fireplace. Merl Briggs had added straw to make it look like a manger. On either side of him were new statues of dog angels. Tom Harris himself was dressed in a handknit red sweater. He was an old dog now, fourteen (in human years), and his eyes were yellowed and immobile. On one side his fur was scratched down to just pinkish skin. I watched Emily haul Homer Hollander, from the bank, and his wife, Eileen, over and make them kneel down as she rolled her face against the dog's side. You could tell who was courting the Briggses' favor. Everyone else got up and away from there as quickly as possible. The dog smelled.

The most ingratiating, and some old indulgent friends of the family, brought little gifts for Tom Harris. A limp raw bone, barbelled, lay with a big green ribbon near his head. Tom Harris seemed disinterested, a being half in the next world.

The black-and-white dining room was filled with Academy nuns. They always stood around the food, because they were shy.

I found Pat in the foyer with an older woman who was famous for having been writing a novel for the last twenty-two years. Estella Clerf. No one had ever read it, but it was supposed to be about a farm in Illinois. It was said to exceed eleven hundred pages at present. She was a woman who stood out at these gatherings, because, although she was married to the owner of the newspaper and they had plenty of money, she was the only woman of her age in the room who didn't do her hair. It hung the way mine did, just down, and it was dark streaked with a crinkly, silvery white. She had little wire-rimmed glasses and teeth the size of corn kernels. Her voice was tiny like a little girl's. I'd always liked her. She was part of the book group Marion Werth led the first Monday of every month. One year they'd read *War and Peace,* the next year it was the Greeks, the year after that Proust and *Menus from the White House.* They'd made the dinners, at a different house every month.

She was asking Pat Briggs why the fifth floor of Briggs's showed furs.

"People want 'em." He shrugged.

The woman said it wasn't true that shearling coats didn't really hurt the sheep.

"Ann here's grandparents were mink people," Mr. Briggs said, winking at me.

"I know that," she said. "I know Ann."

Pat Briggs turned to a couple who had just walked in and stood, pulling off their gloves, finger by finger.

Merl joined us and began to talk about the book she and Emily were writing about Tom Harris. They had been talking about this for years. They were compiling an anthology of recollections of his exploits and Emily was going to do illustrations. They were asking all their friends to contribute. Merl brought this up because she was talking to the woman writer.

Behind her through the living room, I saw Emily kneeling on the floor again in front of the dog, whispering to him, the wings of her dress on the floor. As much as she worried about acquiring clothes, once she had something on, she didn't care.

The religious crowd had now gathered by the tree. They were delicately hanging ornaments and then standing back to gauge their perspectival effect. Others sat on the large stuffed chairs stringing popcorn. Several of those women were recipe editors. The church, every year, put out a local cookbook for fund-raising.

"Udgy budgy udgy budgy woodgy cudgy," Emily said.

I was waiting to get one of the Briggses alone. I had to ask about the box. The whole Tom Harris business bothered me. It wasn't the dog. It was them. They invited a hundred people over for food but mainly to follow them around and watch them in their mumming attentions to this private dog. My family had never been like that. We didn't invite people to come and watch us live our lives. We didn't really have lives that way, things we did every day the same. When we got dressed up it was for guests. We were there for the other people.

I touched Mr. Briggs's shoulder. It was funny to see him in this costume. A bald Jesus and too old.

He did his wince and tick. I looked down to the marble floor. People always looked away when he did that. Everyone except Emily. She would just look straight at him.

I told him what my mother had said about the box and that I was looking for my father. His features lined into an expression of intentness. He was completely, smoothly bald so that his whole head seemed cleanly nude, like a foot. The top of his skull ridged slightly. He rubbed his hand again, from the forehead back, where the hair would have been.

"Mmmm," he said, inhaling and closing his eyes. He had a certain style. For as long as I'd known him, he always wore thick black round glasses. I found out later that he'd copied them from Mies van der Rohe. He got me interested in Mies van der Rohe and Le Corbusier. He gave me books. No one else, Merl or Emily, cared a hoot.

"I hope we can round that up for you, Mayan. I have a vague recollection of it all. The box has got to be here somewhere, God knows Merl doesn't throw a thing out, but where—"

Just then, Danny stood there, his fingers in his jean belt loops, looking down. He was just wearing black clothes, I couldn't see that he'd changed at all. I felt bad for not telling him this was costume. Behind him stood another guy I knew—Eli Timber. He was carrying some kind of instrument in a case and he was dressed in an old-fashioned black suit and twenties tie.

A girl I didn't know, in an elf uniform, stood offering us miniature hot shepherd's pies from a tray. They probably hired her from Saint Joseph's Academy. That's where everyone got girls for parties. Danny looked around and then whispered to me, loudly, "Jeesh, I'll be right back, I'm gonna go outside and take a piss."

Merl tilted her cheek for Eli Timber to kiss. Her hair had been done so it was curled, not in ringlets but in long S's, and only starting about a foot down from her head. She had on white striped tights, a short dress and shoes like little girls' Mary Janes.

"Who was that?" Merl said. I started to explain. "He's from here?" She shook her head. "No. Felchner, I've never heard it. You can tell him we have indoor plumbing."

"And who are you?" Eli Timber asked.

"Guess," she said, holding her hands out. "I'm Alice. Alice in Wonderland."

When Danny returned, Merl looked up and said, "Have you met Tom Harris?"

"Uh, no, I don't think so," he said, hands in black belt loops.

"Oh, well, you boys are in for a treat. You, too, Eli. Come on."

THE PARTY WAS IN FULL FORM. The tree quivered, brimming with laden ornaments, and the chandelier had been dimmed twice now to allow for the effect of candles and the bulbed strings of lights. Just then Otto Kapp walked in. Otto Kapp looked like Mahatma Gandhi and at every one of the Briggses' costume parties he came as Mahatma Gandhi. He had his arm under his sister's elbow while Pat Briggs helped her fight off her coat. Underneath, Clara was dressed as some kind of wood sprite and looked almost dead. Her hair was light as cloud and pure white, and she had a head wreath of twigs and leaves and dry berries that looked like thorns. She wore a loose gown but what you saw in her was just skeleton: bones and teeth. Her hips were the size of a toaster. She advanced slowly towards the living room, her head bobbing in different directions, greedy. Her gaze went right over me.

They were the royalty in this room, because of their age and what they'd built. Money. Kapp's was closed and sold by then, the dark wood carved booths and cuckoo clocks auctioned off to collectors in Milwaukee, but a group of five of the old waitresses, each over eighty and European, met once a month for a kind of club. The recipe nuns were negotiating with them for a special cookbook but it seemed that none of the amounts or ingredients had ever been written down.

Emily sprang off the chair she was sitting in and the white wings of her dress wisped behind her. She went and curtseyed, kissing Clara's hand. Otto kept looking around the room. As Gandhi, he was part naked and extremely fit and tight for a man of his age. Slowly Emily led Otto and Clara over to Tom Harris and this was the sacred moment of the party—as when the hostess lifts her first spoonful to her mouth and, with everyone watching, lolls her tongue in a pantomime of savored communion—and now, tilting after, the party could really begin.

There were two types of religious. There were the artistic families—where the women went barefoot and cooked with gin and juniper berries and made tissue paper flowers in colors like deep red and purple and grouped them together on top of a grand piano. They were paid-up members of Saint Peter and Paul's, but they were known to drive out to the university for Saturday night guitar masses. They bought attractive Lenten wreaths and ceramic crèches made in third world countries and attended seminars and lectures at Saint Aubergine's Bookstore and Saint Norbert's College. The younger nuns wore regular clothes and had hair and worked for the poor and took a lot of trips to Latin America. They were the hip religious.

They had been my mother's friends. Among them, my mother was considered the one who had discovered white. The all-white apartment. In our family, we all sort of believed in each other's virtues, even when we hated each other. My grandmother or aunt would never have denied my mother's talents, or the quality of my grandmother's pies or kindness. There were limits, even in our jealousies.

And there were the old nuns. They mixed in the corners of the dining room or around the tree. You always found one or two of them in the kitchen getting in the way trying to help.

I sat down with the hip religious. There was an older couple I vaguely recognized, dressed as a Joker and a Dunce. There were other cards around us too. A Queen of Spades and of Diamonds. A King of Clubs.

Letitia Skees, the laywoman who owned Saint Aubergine's Bookstore, was talking about a trip a group of them had recently taken to Europe. They'd managed to spend under a thousand dollars each because they'd stayed in old Benedictine abbeys and they'd eaten with the monks. We heard about the meal in every abbey.

Someone lifted a needle onto a phonograph and the room began to sing. Emily and her mother, released by the ceremonial act of Otto Kapp and Clara greeting Tom Harris, began pushing the old couches and chairs against the wall, Emily's slippered feet kicking up dancily behind her as she skated with a slipcovered armchair. A tall woman dressed as a fish began to dance with a man in brown terry cloth meant to be, it seemed, a reindeer.

"I do hate decision, decision, don't you?" Viola Pride was asking at the puzzle table. Viola was known for having been, in her time, president of every women's club in Racine. I asked her what they all were. "Well, Rockland Art, Saint Fiacra Garden Club, Avila Book Club, Bread and Book, that's where we read and eat, Christian Women's, Bridge Clubs, Lawyers' Wives."

The room began to waltz. Mr. Briggs began with his wife, and several other costumed people rose and lurched and swayed. The Briggses were right about one thing. People danced with more abandon when you couldn't tell who they were. Several of the habited nuns clasped their hands together in front of them helpless and a little humiliated just where they stood. One of the younger nuns, Sister Peg, who'd just returned from Honduras, started to dance a hip-loose swing with a twelve-year-old child.

Danny sidled up to me and whispered, "You want to?"

"Somebody should ask the nuns," I said.

He went into the dining room and asked the first one against the wall. I watched her pantomime of no.

Mr. Briggs stopped and asked his daughter to dance and as her arms lifted and fit on his shoulders, I could imagine her wedding. Mr. and Mrs. Briggs had always said they wanted waltzes at Emily's wedding. I wasn't the least bit surprised Tad wasn't there. Tad was always late, if he showed up at all.

Otto Kapp moved onto the floor with Clara. He swayed and shuffled his feet in time and she barely moved. You could see her fingertips just touch his shoulders. For years she'd lived in a one-bedroom apartment they'd built her over the store.

"And then in Paris," Letitia Skees was saying behind me. I watched Danny through the arch as he asked the next nun against the wall. She shrank further, the small of her back pressing the way I did sometimes in an exercise for my stomach.

"That was our last stop. And we had to wash our clothes. We had loads of dirty clothes. You know those abbeys don't have washer-dryers. They did their wash by hand. And Paris was the only place we didn't stay in an abbey."

"We had a hotel there," the Dunce said.

"A nice hotel," added the Joker.

"Oh, very nice."

"And so we went out and found, you know, a laundromat. And there was an American girl, from Iowa, and she was working over there as a model and an actress. And she was wearing a black sweatshirt and jeans and tennis shoes. And she put all her clothes in the washmachine and then she took off her sweatshirt and she threw that in too and then she took off her bra and in that went and then, we're sort of looking and sort of not looking, we're wondering just how far this can go and so now she's not wearing anything on top and she unzips the jeans and they go and the panties and then she takes off the sneakers and she just sits like that and waits there until it's done."

"She had a magazine."

"I thought it was just great," said the Joker.

"I did too," said Letitia Skees. "To be a young actress living in Paris." She turned her large face up and sniffed, as if she were taking in free ocean air.

THEN ELI TIMBER came up and bowed and we danced. His arms and shoulders felt hard inside his shirt. I was thinking that small men look different when they're young. For a long time they look like boys but then all of a sudden they don't. It's as if they skip middle age.

Across the room, Danny was going around the walls. He implored the second-to-last nun in a full habit and she refused him. Emily sprawled in an upholstered chair, talking to an older couple I vaguely recognized. Her wings hung pleated over the arm of the chair. The man of the couple must have said something funny because Emily flattened a hand on the belly of her angel gown and bent laughing, but her drink spilled on the King of Club's sleeve. He stood up violently brushing at it.

"Mmwhy," I heard someone say as we danced past.

Eli Timber was a graceful dancer. He had long thin legs and they moved as if they were light and controlled from above by strings. I knew how to waltz too, not from Cotillion but my grandmother, but I found myself always counting and humming, in her voice, as I went along.

From a far corner of the room, we heard, "And who are you?" and gasps of delight as a mask was raised.

And then the music changed and we stopped waltzing. There was something underwater free about moving your hands and body and knowing you were being watched but not recognized.

THE MUSIC KEPT ON but I wanted to go outside. I moved to the edge of the room, by all the crowded furniture. On the mantel, I noticed a silver wire basket with my bananas in it. Good. The Briggses were fruit connoisseurs. They had things shipped especially to them from Florida and California, big boxes of pink grapefruits and kiwi and majool dates.

Dorothy walked across the room with a tray of soufflés in tiny ramikins. I took two and napkins and spoons.

It was strange being in Racine staying with the Briggses, my grandmother's house sold and gone. The French door sighed a little when I opened it. Outside was cold. Danny sat on the cement wall, next to a dry fountain. His cigarette was the only light, that and the small many stars.

My hands cupped my elbows.

"Want my jacket?" He didn't wait for me, but settled it on my shoulders, patting it down. "What a trip," he said.

"I'm sorry," I said. "Do you know anybody here?"

"A few."

"That's more than me. I don't know any of them." It was peaceful here. The weeds were familiar and the outside sounds. Mrs. Briggs's old fountains and sculptures were chipped and speckled. They looked like ruins. The moonlight made it all seem equal.

"I'm sorry," I said again.

"I like this. I'm having a good time."

"Outside?"

"I'm overhearing things. That's what I like to do at parties. I like to stand somewhere and listen. I know everybody's gossip by the end of the night."

Mrs. Briggs's copied *Winged Victory* had leaves caught between the right wing and shoulder. The moon lit half of her. I said, "Like your names at the cemetery." Venus de Milo was down about four feet. David was here, too.

"Should be the fucking Burghers of Calais," he said, flicking his ashes onto the old stone terrace.

I sighed. "I better go back in." I'd vowed tonight, I'd talk to every Briggs about the box. Parties were always that for me. Duties. It seemed I'd never gone for no reason. I usually had something else to do besides fun.

I found Merl sitting on a sofa with a group of people ringed around her. The more I looked, she did seem like Alice in Wonderland. It was the forehead.

"A hat shop," Merl repeated, when I stood next to her. "Millinery. Hat and Glove Heaven, it's called." On the coffee table, a tray of vegetables petaled around a dip: miniature carrots, baby corn cobs, tiny asparagus, small eggplant.

"That's what they told me," said Estella Clerf.

"From the center of the library and the Charity Benefit Committee to this?" That was the Queen of Hearts.

"And what did he want to do out there?" Merl spoke slowly as always.

"He wanted to be some kind of farmer. I guess he grew up on a farm." That was a man who was dressed in a toga and a holly wreath on his balding head.

"And here we fixed her up with everyone we knew. And I mean doctors and lawyers, she met at our house. We had everything for her. And she didn't want a one of them. We always thought she was married to her work."

Dorothy passed a tray of cheese with tiny red and yellow apples, mandarin oranges and bunches of the miniature grapes. The girl in the elf costume followed behind with pigs in a blanket.

"Italian sausage," Merl said.

Emily appeared behind her mother. She did almost look like an angel. In the low light and candle glow, her hair seemed to hold fire like a wick.

"He's a short little poop," Letitia Skees was saying.

"How old was she?" Emily said.

"And so," I felt like saying. All my life I'd fundamentally misunderstood social life. My mother had taught me to take it far too seriously. As if more could be gotten out of it than a raw good time. I wasn't even drinking. I wanted to stay alert. For the box.

Emily had asked the right question. The Joker's face opened with yawning delight. As she talked her jaw and painted eyebrows moved up and down as if her whole face were diamonds chewing. "Well that's the interesting thing. Nobody really knows. You know, we never asked. But now we're all thinking that she must've been a lot younger than anyone ever suspected."

"You are right, I think. And I always thought Marion was middle-aged. You know, you didn't expect her to change much."

Then of course I knew they were talking about Marion Werth. I'd wondered a second when they said Hat and Glove Heaven. Marion Werth had run the Saturday afternoon charm school. The Joker stopped for a moment, reached down for a miniature carrot. Her nails were long and bright red. I was noticing nails now, since the manicure. Mine were still good but I'd bitten on the plane. On the ends, I'd bitten the polish off.

"Well everybody got to figuring," the Joker went on, "and we realized that she was probably just out of college when she started here. It's true she was ensconced but she was only here what, fifteen,

twenty years tops, she just got involved. She really rose in the library.
She had couple of promotions first year so by the time we really knew
about her she was prettinear running the whole thing, but she could
have still been not too far past forty."

"Callie Hanson his name was," the Greek man said. "I offered to
have him checked out, see if he was just a ragtag person."

"Who?"

"Him."

Merl Briggs lifted one of the cherry tomatoes to her mouth and
snuck it in with a kind of hurry. She felt shy eating her own food, like
it wasn't for her too. Marriage to the richest man in Racine had never
really rinsed away that.

So Marion Werth had run off with a guy. Good for her, I thought,
good for her. Callie Hanson.

"How did they meet, anyway?" I said.

They all looked at me. I shrugged. Two people started to tell me at
once, and then Letitia Skees stopped talking, out of deference to the
superior wealth and status of the Joker. "Well, you know they had a
program with the monastery. Bookmobile. And she went in once,
twice a month to bring them the books. And I guess they all said he
sought her out to find out about his family tree. He was adopted, see,
and he wanted to find out who his real mother was. And I guess he
was a reader too like she was always and pretty soon they started reading the same book every week and talking about it I suppose and
before anyone knew it, he quits the seminary and they run off to California. I guess he inherited some money from a grandmother or
somebody, and they went out there to buy a farm. Turns out he had
always wanted to be a farmer. She called in from Santa Rosa to the
library on a Monday to say she wouldn't be in. Ever. They were going
to raise dates!"

"Had to terminate her insurance and benefits and all without her
signature even," the Greek man said. He had leaned forward, toga
taut between his knees.

"And I don't know if they ever did really find his mother," Letitia
Skees said now, glancing from face to face. "I never heard a thing
about that."

"A date farm, I think it is," the Joker said. "Different kinds of
dates. Everything I've heard leads me to believe it's a pretty small
enterprise."

"Can you just see her on a farm? Ugh," Letitia said.

"And with her nice suits and shoes."

"We worry about her," Merl said, "I really do. You know, a lot of times, we thought of getting together a collection pool and just sending her on a cruise somewhere to meet somebody nice. And now I wish we had done it. But you know it wasn't the money, we just didn't know how we'd bring it up."

"And she seemed to have a full schedule." That was Letitia Skees, sitting on the edge of her chair, her plump knees trembling with life. A shock of gray hair made a point on her forehead.

"Why sure."

"Are they," Emily said, pausing and then with difficulty, "they're really in love you think?"

"Certainly *they* think they are," the Joker said, crossing her diamond-tighted legs, pulling up closer to the edge of the couch. "But I wouldn't call that love." That was clearly one of her favorite subjects.

"No," the Greek man said. "Hormones."

"Merl?" I whispered. "Can I ask you something?"

"She just threw it all away," I heard someone say as we stood up and walked away.

In the kitchen Dorothy was preparing the last two phases of the party. Coffee percolated in huge silver serving urns and electric mixers went on their own, one beating whipped cream, the other egg whites. She was lifting tarts, made of wild strawberries and the tiniest raspberries I'd ever seen, onto doily-lined maroon tin platters.

I told Merl about the detective and the box. When I finished, she sighed. "Now where could that be now."

"Anywhere," Dorothy said from the other side of the counter. She'd been listening too. "Anywhere on this earth." To emphasize, she bumped the swinging door with her ass, backing out with the tray of tarts.

Merl Briggs's head flicked up sharply as a horse's. "Dottie, no, not yet. People are still eating real food. Wait a half hour to start dessert. Wait till after Tad's here. His plane should be landing any minute now." Then she turned back to me, with the air of finishing off something unpleasant but necessary. "Well, this'll be just the push I need to start organizing." She laughed, an upreaching helpless sound.

Dorothy mixed the egg whites and whipped cream in a bowl. She left the kitchen first, carrying a new cut-glass tureen of eggnog, then Mrs. Briggs followed, with more grapes and miniature pears, sliced

in half with almonds and crème fraîche. I just stayed, by the open
back door. It was nice to be alone a minute.

The Briggses always held one odd advantage; just their presence
made me listen for the wind and feel the rich seduction of my mother.
They made me almost love her. No matter what, no matter what.
Proximity to the Briggses seemed so random.

I heard Renaissance music start up in the other room. I still didn't
want to go back in.

"That's what I heard anyway," the urgent voice of the Joker carried clearly. "That's what they told me."

I fixed on the tray of perfect, broochlike tarts. I wanted one but
didn't want to be seen. Nobody would have minded, but still. I just
didn't want them to see me eat here in the kitchen, by myself. Then
Emily came in through the swinging doors.

She grabbed a tart, popped it her mouth. She took two more then
and looked at them on her palm while she chewed.

Dorothy returned with trays of ravaged food. Emily, with three
more tarts in her hand, opened the refrigerator. Two tarts dropped
on the floor, face down.

"She paid a lot for those little strawberries," Dorothy said, used to
it all, "this time of year."

Emily didn't answer, she just backed away from the refrigerator,
took two more tarts from the tray and put them over each of her eyes.
She reached her arms behind her head and began contorting towards
the floor in a backbend.

"Spoilt child." Dorothy bent down the usual way, picking up the
ruined tarts. She did what I'd do. She ate one.

Emily was still twisting and coiling, her hands reached the floor, the
tarts quivering, unsteady on her eyes.

Dorothy just sighed a sigh that was years long and bumped out of
the room carrying a tray of small silver sherbet stems with balls
of lime green sherbet. Sherbet to clear the palate was always one of
Merl's touches. You got the feeling she stayed in bed some bad days
watching old movies and then styled their household life after them.

"Emily," I said. She was walking on her hands and legs, hump-
bellied, the dress dragging on the floor. "Can you help me find that
box with stuff about my father?"

She sprang up, lifting the tarts off her eyes. "Ask my parents," she
said.

She gave that shrug I used to make. She was at home here. She could do anything.

I slipped outside, holding the tuxedo jacket closed in front of me. What a place, I was thinking, and what people to have to need something from. Pat Briggs was a good fifteen years older than his wife. Merl had been the pretty Swedish girl who'd grown up not even in Racine, but in the mud-poor outskirt you could barely call a town, which had a name and little else, Suamico. My mother bought gas there when she'd taught at the out-of-town school she'd had to go to after the Racine School District wouldn't take her anymore for missing so many class days. Pat had been thirty-two. My mother could have had him. Twice she could have. Most of the prettier girls in Racine could have married Pat. Even rich, he had trouble getting a wife. He had the twitch. Every few minutes his face winced up to the left. And he was bald young, just out of college. Once he came to my grandmother's house when we were living there and he ate cinnamon toast with us all. After he left, my aunt went around the whole day twitching her face and laughing. My grandmother tried not to smile when she saw Carol's face. She said, "Shush now, I don't like to see that." They said Merl was seventeen when she married Pat, but there was a lot of talk that she was younger even than that. It was all too apparent even for gossip.

"I wonder what she sees in him," Jen and the girls had said at the time.

"Oh yeah I wonder all right," Gish said. But even that wasn't much of a joke. ·

Pat and Merl provided better jokes in the years to come. The architects. She chased them away back where they came from with her drawn-from-crayon-on-grocery-bag plans of fountains and pillars, the atrium bird room in the foyer, the gilt and gold and torched entry. The architects left on a stormy Tuesday, sitting in the airport in one line with galoshes up to their knees. The rumor was that she told them all to just get out and never would they see a cent more of her husband's money, but her husband, hearing the story by telephone from Dorothy, had driven out himself to the airport and paid them each double, and in cash, and put them on the plane. Merl got her fountains. Oh, they were still there, I saw them as I turned the corner, dry in the moonlight, and the atrium, birdless now, it turned out Emily was allergic to all feathers. The skeletons of grandeur still lurked, isolate, crumbling, commissioned and made by Scully the stonemason, whose only work before and since Merl Briggs's statuary was gravestones, enough to keep him in business, but not for the flush of prosperity he'd felt the year her construction first surged and allowed him to double the stone yard and build a new storehouse.

Merl had the big house and she began, sometime in the middle of Emily's childhood, to fill it. She couldn't throw away. So the two-car garage now housed no cars. It was a filled rectangular vessel, packed densely from floor to ceiling, side to side. In the back den two decades of empty egg cartons nested inside one another neatly in columns connecting floor to roof. In everything, Merl favored columns. Merl was, in her own way, neat. In the Midwest, I'd known messes. Matzgees on our old road lived in nested filth. But Merl was a collector. She didn't just let things accrue and grow and mold and clutter. She tended them. She managed. She worked as custodian of a huge museum of worthless everyday things. I liked Merl, really. The empty tin cans she saved she soaked labels off, washed and scrubbed. A long string of maids had left the Briggses. Dorothy still came up the hill Monday through Thursdays, and for parties, but most of the real work, Mrs. Briggs did herself, because no one else, she found, acted with the same care. I'm sure that was true.

As I rounded the corner of the house, I saw a crowd out there in the moonlight, on the stone patio, by the statuary. They were watching something—I couldn't see what. They looked odd from here, the empty terraced gardens, the cracked stone, the little circle of costumed people. There was the Clown, the Dunce, the Joker, the Queen of Hearts, the Wraith. Someone was juggling white balls, so they gleamed in the dark.

I went back a little so they couldn't see me and just leaned against the house. Down the hill you could see Racine and its few lights, the dark outlines of buildings along the river, the sinister night lights and smoke of the paper mills. I took a breath and made myself join the crowd. Why, I was wondering, why was that always so hard? I grew up private. We didn't mix in close with big groups.

It was a man running on a wagon wheel, lit to fire on each end, and himself eating flames. Inside, the old music lifted on. The circle around the fire eater murmured loudly. The moon was full and close-seeming, veined with a crooked line of blue-gray like a map. People's feet were stamping, they started to clap.

A cute guy in medieval clothes I didn't know was saying to someone else in a low voice, "The Briggses'll accept any eccentricity except pretension. As long as you're yourself."

That was enough. I climbed the steps back inside. People felt obliged to compliment the Briggses. And it was money. That's what it was, just money.

I found a phone in the empty den and closed the door to call Stevie Howard. His mother, June, answered and told me the plane was grounded in Chicago, in a blizzard. She was calling the airport every half hour and they still hoped Stevie and Helen and Jane would get in tonight. She apologized again for not having room for me. I told her once more it was no problem, not to worry, and then I hung up and sat in the scratchy plaid chair a moment. I liked being alone during a party. I was thinking how strange it was to be closer to the Howards but stay here, because they didn't have room. And it didn't take being that close to the Briggses to stay here. This place was sort of like a compound.

When I went back, I found three old women bent cooing over the puzzle table. "When I was young I was a fancy worker," Viola Pride was saying. "There's only so much bridge you can play." Viola now taught bridge Tuesday and Thursday afternoons.

The puzzle they had spread out before them was of the Grand Canyon in lurid colored detail.

Near them Letitia Skees was talking to an old nun, whose chin was kept bound by her white habit, and to the Joker. "I think a man alone is very sad," she was saying. "A woman is different."

The nun didn't seem to be able to hear. Her head nodded along amiably to everything.

"People ask me," Letitia continued, "if I go out on dates. And the answer is yes and no. I decided a long time ago I didn't want to be married. But I still need touching and hugging like every person does. So I have friendships which give me the hugging and touching I need. I have a friend, we go for breakfast once a week at the bay shore at seven-thirty in the morning and we take a thermos of coffee and we just have breakfast and we sit on a blanket and watch the sun come up."

"How about you?" I asked the nun. I meant about friendship.

"Oh, me?" she said. "I don't know."

"What about you, Sister Maren?" Letitia said. "The girl is asking do you need loving and hugging too?"

"I like to know who's going up with who," she said.

The Joker had joined the older women at the puzzle table. They were talking about the chef of the fanciest restaurant in town, La Nuit. "Of course she wants everybody to think she's French," the Joker was saying, "but we all know she's from Belgium."

Belgian restaurants were a new trend in New York City. I hadn't been to any but you just could tell from people talking and articles in the newspaper.

Emily stood eating one of my small red bananas. Dorothy was now passing out the raspberry and strawberry gemlike tarts.

Pat Briggs and the woman novelist stood by the mantel over Tom Harris talking to the man in the reindeer outfit, with two pine cones attached to his forehead as antlers.

"You've got to let her drive, Mack," Pat was saying.

Behind me I heard Otto Kapp say clearly, "I am not. I am not afraid of it. Pff. Not at all."

A group of young boys in white choir robes pushed out from the kitchen then, red turtlenecks poking up to their chins. They formed a triangle on the left of the fireplace, opposite the Christmas tree. The room stilled. They each held one gold bell lifted, shoulder high. The only light in the room was from candles and the fire and the chandelier. Otto Kapp, sandaled and robed as Gandhi, stood before them, arms lifted, and for a long moment drew out the room's silence like a perfectly rosined violin bow on string.

Tad arrived. Merl and Emily rushed over to him and helped him off with his coat. He rubbed a hand on his stomach and whispered something to Merl and then they all went to the kitchen, where he stayed a long time, eating. When Emily came back out, she was holding a child's satin kimono from Tokyo for Tom Harris.

AFTER THE CONCERT, the room moved more loosely. Pat stood talking to his father's longtime rival, Frank Umberhum, who ran Shauer and Schumaker. Up until recently in the Midwest, the same people owned furniture stores and funeral parlors. The merchandise lines were shown together at the big buying shows, made by the same manufacturers. Pat's father had had the largest furniture collection in town, at Briggs's. Now in Racine, there were two large funeral families who also owned furniture stores. Shauer and Schumaker and Van Zieden Grieden. Whether you went to one or the other depended entirely on your family. It was like which brand of toothpaste you used.

"Remember 'Fish or Factories,'" Pat was saying and nodding.

"I sure do. We gave 'em a fight."

Pat stopped to explain to Tad how he and Frank had lobbied forty years ago to ban PCBs from the Fox River. The paper mills had mounted an advertising campaign in the *Press Gazette* with full-page ads that said FISH OR JOBS.

"Hey, want to do the Ouija board over by the fire?" Eli Timber asked. "Emily and Danny and a couple of us are going to set the thing up by the dog."

They were already opening the board in front of Tom Harris's crèche.

Pat Briggs was lifting a cloth coat onto the woman novelist's shoulder.

"I'm driving," the Reindeer was saying, wobbly, one of his pine cone antlers awry.

"No you are not," she said in her tiny voice. Keys threatened in her hand.

"Ann," Pat said, "Toddy Sullivan wanted to say good-bye to you."

The Queen of Hearts stood over me with the Dunce. "Excuse me but I just realized who your mother is. And I have a message to you from Ted Stevenson. He says hello and that he's so proud of you being in medical school and all. He said he was going to write you a letter one of these days."

"Where is he now?" I asked. "Minnesota still?"

"Oh no, he moved from there some time ago. He's a professor now in Nebraska. What is it, Edward, is it Wayne State?"

"They said it was Wayne State. That's what they said."

"Professor of what?"

"Well, of ice skating, I suppose."

AT THE OUIJA BOARD, Eli went first. He closed his eyes for a too-long time while all our fingers were cramping on the heart. It's like fingers poised over a piano, not the most comfortable position. He got a grin as the heart skated over the board. "A love-of-my-life question," he said. The thing landed on YES but then it moved, clunking off the board at the bottom. He shrugged. "Guess nothing lasts forever."

"Not of yours," Emily said.

I told Emily I liked her dress and asked her if it was from Briggs's. She thanked me and said no, it was couture.

Then I felt like a dummy. "What's that?"

"It's the top line a designer makes, so there's only a few. They only make a couple and they sell out right away." She was saying all that as simply as she could. For a second, I hated her.

"Oh." I didn't know these things. And I should have. There was so much.

We stopped talking because the heart was looping raucously around the board, we all bent over swaying with it. We must have looked like something religious. I thought of a glass of water.

"What'd you ask now, Eli?" Danny said.

It was sort of thrilling to be pulled like this, the thing really did seem to own a life. "I asked about Mai linn," he said. And that stilled it. It answered these letters: WATAD.

"I'm next," Emily said, and then Pat Briggs came and asked her to come say good-bye to someone. Danny was talking to Eli so I turned to Otto Kapp.

"What aren't you afraid of?" I asked. As soon as I said that, I heard how it sounded. Emily gave me a look from under her hair. I'd just been trying to make conversation. This is why I was such a hit at parties. Poise was not a word people would have used to describe me.

"I'm not afraid of death because I have already seen it. I went to the Black Forest in 1969. One year after my wife died." His mouth puckered and he said, "Fef." He had many lines on his face but his skin was dark enough and his bones clear enough that it looked good. "I saw my wife there for a moment, she just came like on an errand to tell me something. And she said, 'It's all right Otto, don't worry.' Her voice—it was her voice, I was married to her thirty-two years— came down from the trees. And so I don't worry anymore."

He looked away and after a while I turned to Danny. "So what do you think of Tad?"

He smiled. "Tad is a tad Tad," he said, smiling.

Then Emily returned and we did her question. The heart was sluggish. All our fingers waited, light, but the plastic stayed where it was.

"Come on, Emily, out with it," Danny said.

"No can do," she said.

It had to be about Mai linn, I decided. Or Tad. Or even me. Then the thing began to move in infinitesimal circles, it cranked and looped its way slowly and stalled on YES.

"Oh good," Emily said, with a certain kind of smile I recognized on her and then I understood that the question wasn't people at all but was about the jacket she'd been calling all over the continent for. Yes, she would get her coat.

Then it was my turn. I asked about the box. Would I find the box this week? By that time in my life I knew better than to ask a question without deadlines. The heart felt dizzy and warm but random. It spelled W then MAYBE then IS then T.

"We still haven't done Danny-my-man," Eli said.

"Or Otto," I said.

"Not me," Otto said, "I have no question."

I had another question. I asked if I would have a long life. The thing moved off the top of the board, over the round face of the moon. All those years of "Does he love me?" and now my question was "Would I live long enough?" I was old enough to know that you can outlive love and that, eventually, you will want to.

Danny closed his eyes a second then opened them. "Okay, I've got mine." The thing went in fits and starts, jagged, and only stopping on the beige blank places of the board where nothing was printed. Finally it ended, clear on NO.

That was it. We all took our hands off. Merl came and squatted down, asking Emily and me to help Dorothy with something in the kitchen, and the two of us staggered up.

We found her bent over four trays of meringue mounds, lighting them with a cigarette lighter. They flamed blue. The girl dressed as an elf carried the first, Emily the second, I was third and Dorothy last.

"What is this?" I whispered over my shoulder.

"Hmph," Dorothy snorted. "Baked Alaska."

It was dark in the room and murmuring ohs for the flaming desserts mixed with a thinning applause from outside, here and there I saw a flame reflected in a bell set on a table or on the mantelpiece, one still in a boy's hand.

I looked back at Dorothy. "Don't you mean miniature Baked Alaska, more like Baked Delaware?" and then as I turned I was falling, I saw Emily in front of me and her hair and the long gown and flames were sliding, I managed to right the tray on the ground but there was a lot of commotion, I started to apologize and almost cry but a crowd had gathered not by me but to my left a little and then I saw them swatting at Emily's hair. A bad metal taste rose. From somewhere else, the real lights flicked on. Then it was simple. I'd tripped on Emily's gown. Dorothy and I cleaned up, took the tray to the kitchen, and by the time we returned Emily looked fine, people stood awkwardly eating their desserts in the light. I heard footsteps in the foyer. I'd ruined the party. Ended the mood. People were beginning to get their coats.

Emily yawned. She lifted the piece of her hair that had burned up to her face. "Smell," she said.

Just then we began to hear the music, a flute, from the stone garden in back. Merl Briggs clapped her hands over her head. "Circle, everybody," she yelled. "Join up in the circle."

The awkward line of held hands drew us all outside and there, on the stone terrace, was a small stand of women playing wind instruments and three folk dancers who joined in among us and led the widening circle in a simple vine step. Everyone joined: the choir boys, the habited nuns, Tad, the hip religious, what was left of the costumed revelers. And then it struck me as I watched one of the nuns in habit, face down, following a dancer's feet on the stone ground, her soft chin and cheeks falling out of the stiff white ramikin—it wasn't that the nuns couldn't dance. They just didn't know how to waltz.

8

I HEARD THE VACUUM going somewhere in the house. Merl probably.

All the guests were gone. The paper sounds of their last good nights, called from outside, had fallen and settled long ago. It was late. Emily's door was open and she was snoring in a curl on her bed, the dress a tangled mess on the floor, Tom Harris enrapt inside it, his tail beating a steady knocking rhythm. I'd come upstairs to change. I had a thing about dressing up. As soon as the party was over, I put on my jeans and big socks and a loose shirt. I couldn't lounge around in a tuxedo, even one Pat was going to throw out the next day. I went downstairs and found Dorothy sitting, hat and scarf and coat and gloves on, at the edge of the piano bench, waiting for Pat Briggs to drive her home. We heard his footsteps overhead.

The vacuum kept going in a far distant corner of the house.

"I'll take you, Dorothy," I said.

"He's comin'." She nodded.

"But when?"

"Isn't that the truth."

"Why don't you just let me." I stood up to look for paper. "We can write a note."

"He's the boss," she said, still on the bench, her gloved hands folded. She made no moves, her body or her face.

"Yeah." Tomorrow and the next day he would be and all the days. My finger tinkled on the keys. I couldn't help it.

It was a German piano, supposedly the best in the world, and they'd had it here in this house for more than twenty years. No one touched it. I tried a little, from the scales Eli Timber had taught me years ago. It sounded horrible, but it was fun, anyway, trying to put the notes together from memory like a puzzle.

Once I'd slept over, in childhood, and I was the first one up. I walked down the stairs and saw Dorothy testing the keys, she could really play, but when she noticed me, she stood up and pretended to be cleaning it. She didn't even have a rag with her so she went at it with the hem of her dress. It amazed me then that I could scare someone. I was never a boss.

A clock chimed dumbly on the wall. Two a.m.

"Be right down," Pat shouted down the stairs.

I heard him step on the scale. The Briggs house had a scale in every bathroom. Those they used. I'd already gained four pounds. I knew it even without the scale. I know myself at a hundred fourteen. Racine bakery.

Dorothy gathered up her things. We both moved to wait by the car. The sky outside swung low and stars swirled close so my balance wavered, my stomach warm and funny. My feet trudged into the firm crusted snow and I felt the first rush of icy water soak through my shoes to touch skin. For some reason that first flush of wet always for an instant felt warm and then you woke up in it. Around us, the sky loomed and hazed, the stars glittered down to bushes, pine trees shed bulks of water whispering, the world turned live and spawning, warm and shocking cold at the same time.

We stood out there on the white gravel driveway. I looked back at the solid house. "Don't you sometimes wish you lived here too?"

Her shoulders lurched up further and she adjusted the hat on her head. "I live in my own house. With my mamma. Like you lived a lot of time with your granmama."

"I don't know. Sometimes I wonder if I would have loved anyone I grew up with."

"Your granmama gave you a lot."

"I know she did, Dorothy." I would never deny that. I didn't want to talk ungratefully about her.

Mr. Briggs stepped out of the house in clean, warm clothes, carrying cash in his left hand. Dorothy stood still and he went around and opened her door for her. She got in holding her purse on her lap with both hands and the car went slowly down the hill. And I followed, just walking. I heard snow melting all around, invisible as huge dry owls in the trees and tunneling insects and rodents underground working at their instinctive system of hydrology. I got as far as the highway I would have to cross or hitch at, it was still far to our road, but the highway spread wide and dirty and fenced and semis thundered by cracking wind as if it were wet sheets and leaving no sympathy for straight lines, no wrapping of me in their headlights and the dawn began somewhere else too I could feel it I knew the sky and the moisture of air so well here. I almost started back, but then I ran across. That was a long band of time like a tunnel or a scream.

And then I was in the soft ditchy ground, sinking, over the sewer pipe for the two little rental houses that had been in back with the butter barn. They looked dark and empty now like old jack-o'-lanterns. I walked the small gravel road that in summer would be cricket loud and bright, alive with wind this time of night. It was still and cold, as if the sky itself were cracked frozen. The bare trees and their branches, thinning to a notched delicacy, were very high and taut and everywhere there was the luminous blue sky over the tiny structures, dark with sleep.

At the end there was Stevie Howard's little brick house, small and low as a matchbox in the distance, completely outscaled by the land here and the trees and, like a mercy, that old soft yellow light was on in the kitchen and that was when I wondered if I'd died and so it had all come back.

But the cinching red wet pain at my ankles was real.

June and Chummy Howard were dark half silhouettes like schoolroom statues in the kitchen window. There was a pot of coffee on the table and three cups. Stevie's head was there too and his wife, Helen, and his daughter, Jane.

Everything was so much the same it seemed time only happened to me. But once I walked up the one cement step into the kitchen, differences were fluent in the light. Chummy and June sat, their arms propping their faces, not even older but old. And Stevie Howard was here married, his wife's fingernails hard and long and crimson like beads on the old gray-flecked linoleum table. Stevie and Helen and Jane had just come from the airport. Their plane had been seven hours late.

Helen was making good conversation, asking us questions, including me. Stevie got up and went back down the low hall to his little bedroom to put Jane to sleep. He came back in a T-shirt, with his suit pants and socks.

IN A WAY I didn't marry Stevie because of his feet. They were white and dry yellow, blue-veined.

I couldn't love him because I knew him so well. And I was still looking for something new and outside. I looked at the dark window, where the trees and clouds were only indistinct moving shapes, alive.

One thing about people on earth: you know their sounds and body pains. The irritation of their wombs, their feet's thud, the plink of their parings, the pain of bunions. Especially in houses the size of this. I could have drawn you my grandmother's feet. She was a majestic-faced woman, easily beautiful, but she did not have good feet. Her feet were the feet of a woman over sixty who had worked all her life in the country and who had not thought too much of herself. Her metatarsus protruded so that the insides of her foot formed a point, the kind of excrescence women of another place and culture would have saved from pain by cutting holes out of cloth slippers. Her toes too bore shapes made by time and the constrictions of hard shoes, and were festooned with bunions and corns. Looked at plainly and together, her feet were strong the way a pair of workman's hands are at the end of his life.

If I had penciled my grandmother's two feet, I would not have rendered them staunch pedestals, though they were that too, but never bare, when she stood sturdily working in the kitchen, they were modestly encapped with solid shoes and even stockings. I couldn't believe one foot of hers ever, even as a girl, demurely scratched an itch, the toes on the ankle or arch of the other. No, my grandmother was too embarrassed of herself. She was never coy. I think of them roughly parallel, resting on the floor, tilted to each other at the tips slightly, like hands veering but not daring yet to pray. They rested that way when she sat in a chair at night watching her variety show on the old TV.

My mother too, a glorious and vain woman, who hated herself first and then the world, felt tormented by her feet, which were mis-shapen, different, and, it seems, in several directions. She too had bad feet. Her toes, she blamed to no avail, again and again, crimped up in a curve permanently from wearing shoes too small that her parents made her walk too many miles in. A driven woman, she spent years of pedicures trying to shallow the rises of bumps and bunions and to candy up the effect anyway, with colored polishes on the nails.

It was not only women. To understand class in America, all you had to do was make everyone in the room take off his shoes. All of us sit for hours with a baby picking up his foot and marveling, taking pictures knowing, it'll never be this perfect again.

Everyone was a child once with unbent feet. My grandmother always told me about coming to a small rented place I lived with my mother and dad and finding me in winter with no shoes. My mother had defended herself. "Momo says babies don't need shoes!" My grandmother winced telling the story, how she took me into town to Briggs's and bought five pairs of socks and shoes. "Over there I bet they don't *get* any shoes."

Once when I was young, just before my father went away, he had traced my foot to buy me a pair of shoes from Beirut. I wanted pink slippers or golden. Or mint green. It was plain lined paper, a pencil drawing. He labeled it *my daughter's foot,* folded it and put it in his pocket. But the shoes never came.

For a long time, Stevie wouldn't let anyone see his feet. He and Helen made love twice a day for the first year, but always in his socks. He told her his feet were damaged. "High school football," he said, "my brother's shoes." But Jane had seen his feet. "They're ug-ly," she said in her shrieky voice. "One thing about kids," Stevie told me. "They tell the truth. If something's ugly to them, they'll say it. They don't know there's anything wrong."

Emily Briggs had the kind of straight long slender foot you could lay on a pure china plate. She took a strange pride in her feet. Even in one potato, two potato, the game children played with their feet in a circle, one child chanting and counting with a hand, seeing on whose foot the rhyme came out, I remembered her once saying, as if it were the most incredible thing, "Some people are ashamed of their feet."

"I'll take you home," Stevie said. "We've got to go to sleep."

Chummy and June were apologizing that there was no place for me to stay, they had grown children in every small room. In summer they used a tent outside for the young ones. "And that they like," Chummy said, "oh sure."

Helen said she was tired. She'd stay with Jane. His wife was like a picture of a wife, her face an oval emblem. Sitting in a chair.

Outside, the wind came up around us like stiff scarves. But I wanted to walk over and look at my grandmother's house. We walked a little ways up the driveway, under the trees. Shades in all the upstairs windows were pulled down.

"I wonder who lives there now."

"My dad's talked to them. The man is a manager at Shopko and I think his wife works there too, in the pet section. They were from somewhere else. I don't think they have children."

The house looked still and asleep. We kept walking, trying to be quiet. I opened the garage door. Different shapes loomed than we had had. When I pressed up against the kitchen windows, standing on the flimsy tin drainpipe, I saw they had changed it all, everything. There was plaid wallpaper and a sofa where there used to be the one table we ate on for every meal.

Even the dark trees in the yard looked older and vast. "Do trees live forever?" I asked Stevie. "Or do they die? I mean, if nobody cuts them, would they keep growing?"

"For thousands and thousands of years. They don't die of old age. But something will eventually get them."

I TOOK MY SHOES OFF outside the Briggses' back door and carried them up the stairs. I kissed Stevie good night. "Tomorrow I have to deal with the box," I whispered.

I WAS THE FIRST ONE UP. Then Emily stumbled in too, her nightgown frilled from washing, her triangular-shaped long legs seeming uninflected. Emily, what was it about her beauty—it seemed her soul hadn't inhabited her body yet. She was a body waiting, flexing, living in itself. Her body seemed general somehow, new. I used to think that meant she was a virgin. She really had been a virgin with an unconscious awkward spring in her legs. When she was excited she would stand in one place and jump up and down. But she was still that way now. I thought some man would fall ravishingly in love with her for that, exactly that. It would madden him that he could look and look and never find her. That wasn't Tad, though. He didn't seem to find her mysterious at all.

She sat down on the living room carpet, pitched on her hands. "It's so early," she said.

She did headstands, awkward attempts that spurted her bare ankles and feet up into the air. She'd always been a little bit an acrobat.

She did a back roll, tucking her head under. Her face flushed when she came up, her foot bumping on the washstand where they put their keys and mail. From what I understood, that washstand came from Merl's grandmother and she'd had to argue bitterly with her family to attain it. It was the only thing Mrs. Briggs had from her family.

"You know when Mai linn was away in North Dakota, once I got this letter. We'd been getting all her mail, your aunt brought it over—anyway, she got this letter from Interlochen which is this music camp my grandfather's on the board of that's a school too, and they said she could come and audition for a scholarship and it was like a form she had to fill out and when I put it down it dropped behind that thing, and I could never get it. I tried a bunch of times with a knife or a fork or something. I kept thinking tomorrow I'll get that out and send it to her. But I always felt bad because Mai linn might have had some kind of scholarship but she didn't even know."

"You never told her?"

"No, I felt so bad."

"You should, Emily."

"Not now," she said. And then she shot up, she had the longest ankles and they seemed to contain great springs of power, like a kangaroo's. "Want some coffee?" I heard her banging around in the kitchen.

I stayed on the living room floor, where the furniture loomed rounder and more oddly proportioned from my vantage, and vast spangles of light spurted and broke on the white walls. I did not believe in accidents. I based my life on that, it was the only way I knew how to bear it. I'd always told myself that tiny misunderstandings did not matter. There were always more chances.

In books, I hated things like that. The one letter that could have made a difference. I thought if I opened that as possible, I couldn't have lived with the regret.

But maybe it was true anyway. Mai linn could have gone to that school.

Emily called me into the kitchen. The room amazed with light. She hurried around the stove, opening the door, turning the gas off under a kettle. Her bones hit the floor hard and erratic. Maybe it wasn't accident in the world I feared, but malice. But Emily could not be evil. I knew Emily. She was an unlived girl here alone in a white kitchen, elbows and heels, the stove door banging. Still, Mai linn had already had so much taken from her. My mother had hated me sharply, not always, but sometimes with real point and glitter. The moments she came after me rang with terror. I lived with the shards of them. I tried to believe something else was true, but they were there in me, crystallized forever like shrapnel. Emily took a new pan of muffins out of the oven. "No sugar. I used your little bananas."

We sat at the white enamel table, rimmed with a red line, that was where Dorothy worked and sometimes sat at a forty-five-degree angle, looking slant out the window, eating her soup for lunch.

Emily took out her mother's Spode cups and slammed them on the tabletop, without saucers, as if they were any college mugs. Aw, I thought, that was what this marriage was for. So Merl and Pat Briggs could have a daughter and raise her to be this careless.

The snow sun glazed in off the walls, rebounding. Emily poured from the pot, then took the carton from the refrigerator, milk blooming slowly in the coffee.

For no reason right then I thought of my grandmother's hall closet, by the one bathroom. My grandmother's hall closet was a symphony of smells, eucalyptus, medicinal, with all manner of suppositories and foot remedy. Still, it was so clean. I don't know how you keep the house so clean, people would say. She shrugged. Uch, it doesn't get dirty.

I probably wasn't enough of a child. I supposed at one time the house had gone dirty when my mother was growing up, loudly, with violence, the way she would. I supposed those were my grandmother's real years of parenting. Maybe she missed that. I was something else.

Now Emily banged around the kitchen with new cooking gear.

There were copper bowls and trump pans and flutes. And it made me think of my grandmother's bad tin pie pans, their berry stain marks, how she'd make a pie in a square casserole dish, anything. Once you knew how you didn't bother with upgrading the equipment. Summer was berries and crust, cherries, grassy herbs. Winter was nuts ground in buttery cookie batter. It had nothing to do with the pans.

STEVIE AND HELEN and I ate. I got like that there. There was nothing else to do. You began to start looking for something to take home with you. Every day I asked about the box.

We drove to one place for breakfast cinnamon rolls. Baked goods in Racine seemed extraordinary. World class. Then, a little more than an hour later, we drove to the diner downtown for chili and pie. At night we met at Kroll's, the deco hamburger place all our parents had gone as teenagers for burgers and malteds. I'd been there four days and nothing had happened about the box. And I'd gained six pounds.

The diner itself was a monument. It was downtown, across Mason from Boss's, the inner-illuminated green glass cube surrounded by taller old brick buildings. The tan brick Odd Fellows Home, the charcoal brick Elks, and the YMCA, bricks the color of dried blood, towered over Boss's with their tiny shaded windows. Inside the diner, silver-pedestaled black scuffed leather stools stood on worn linoleum. The china was white with a rim of black and the glasses were very thick. All painting of downtowns seemed allusions, references to this. Men. We sat at the counter and I looked out at Boss's Tobacco and Magazine Shop, where the Briggses had first seen my cousin and me in our sailor suits and wanted us. The Briggses then had been different, tall, befurred, movie stars to my mother.

The chili was perfect.

All this was new to Helen and she had the goodness to like it. We drove, full, to the Wildlife Sanctuary, where I used to work. Ducks and geese sat ovally, tucked into themselves on the blue ice. In small wire cages, raccoons rattled. When Jane stuck her finger in, the one winged bald eagle jumped and rustled on his tree. Across the way, the Bay Beach Amusement Park Ferris wheel and train tracks looked toy and forgotten in the snow. We bought bags of corn kernels for ten cents to feed the birds. That was the price it had always been. Everything was the same as when I'd worked there. We tossed the stuff, throwing it everywhere, disturbing the fowl but not feeding them. We kept on and on until we saw, on the drained glass, the frozen pond, the mud, scattered corn. The ducks and geese were full too. They roosted where they were like eggs, indifferent. A sunset began, glorious pollution colors over the still winter bay, the paper-mill waterworks in the distance intricate and deep blue.

FOUR DAYS PASSED. Six. Then it was day seven. I'd gained nine pounds and no box. I snooped around the house. There was so much. My box could have been anywhere. I had a mission here and small talk was keeping me from it. Small talk and food. And damn Christmas.

Pat Briggs brought home a Swedish Ring Cake in a tall pink box, tied with string. Emily, Tad and I lay on the den floor, watching *The Wizard of Oz*. Emily and I broke off a ring at a time and let the flaky almond layers melt in our mouths. It is a strange thing to keep eating when you are already very full. My stomach protruded like a taut convex drum. The den was still fairly normal, Merl's filling kept to bureaus lining the walls. Pat shouted for her to come sit with us and watch the movie. We heard her tunneling, working, somewhere in the house.

I asked Pat about the box. We were all facing the screen. Dorothy had just met the Tin Man. Pat was leaning back in the brown-and-yellow-striped recliner. Tom Harris sprawled in a leather bean bag close to the screen. Tad was reading the *New York Times*. He and Emily had driven out first thing in the morning to find the paper, but they had to wait for Boss's to open at ten to ten.

"Oh, all right. We'll search it out tomorrow, how's that."

"Fine," I said. "Great." As soon as I said that I winced for being so grateful. My mother was that way. She felt so frightened and weak. Peeled. She taught me to try—at all times—to keep on everybody's good side, even more than that, on their list of favorites. We believed we needed people for protection.

Just then Merl appeared in her work clothes. Dirt marked her cheeks and one streak of hair escaped the rubber band. She wore a grayed white shirt and old pants, patched at the knee, pointed sneakers with a fur of dust. She was carrying file cards and a rag.

Pat looked at her and sank back into the recliner, compressing.

"Merl, get in the shower and put on that new silk robe I brought home for you and come and watch the movie with your daughter and her friends.''

"I can't," she said, holding her rag and cards stiffly in a panic of being caught. "I have to work."

"Merl, it's a classic, for God's sake. Everybody in the world but you's seen *The Wizard of Oz.*"

Her bottom teeth showed and her eyes darted. "I've got so much to do," she said and disappeared backwards.

Pat slid to the floor and Emily moved to the recliner above him. She had on jodhpurs that ended halfway up her calf and regular white socks. Then, she cast her right leg over her father's shoulder. He grabbed the white ankle and slowly peeled the cotton off. He looked at her toes, touching each one separately. "This little piggy," he said, in a voice I'd never heard from him. He looked at the bottom of her clean foot with such amazement.

He found every little part of her so perfect.

THERE WERE ONLY two days left before Emily, Tad and I went home. I couldn't think of anything else. I didn't even step on the scale. I was sick with food.

There are things worth more than money, all money, valueless things. The box. I thought of it with its secrets. To sit on the floor in my old clothes and have its contents spread out between my legs, would be almost more than meeting my father.

I began to understand obsession. There was this box. I drew it on every piece of paper I had a pencil near. I believed I could recognize it if I saw it. Even when I was talking about different things, it was always right there.

The guy Jordan called from New York and I could barely even talk to him. It was too long to explain. Somewhere in this house there was my box. There was no assuaging me for it. Even love—I needed the box more. But life at the Briggses' went on, food- and phone-call-filled as usual.

I began to understand about power. If you are powerless, then what is essential, central for you, is always peripheral, minor for someone else. You curtsy like my mother and ask your favor and then scurry into a bowing retreat. I knew how a poor person would feel observing Congress. And if you were powerful, you could delegate your most whimsical concerns to become the mission of another person's whole life. I had no doubt that if the box were for Emily, the Briggses could have had it found.

I dreamed about the box. The box had wings.

Finally, the second-to-last day I asked Emily. She was doing awkward back rolls and somersaults on the carpet in front of Tom Harris and Tad. They'd just come back from the Retrospective Exhibit of Family Trees, posted in the library in honor of Marion Werth's long service. Tad had expressed an interest in Emily's genes. I said, "Can I please ask you something?"

"Sure, what?" she said, stumbling up, rubbing her hands on the front of her thighs. "What?"

"You know that box I told you about that's somewhere here someplace. I'm really nervous because I need it and we're leaving. And I've had this detective for all this time now and we're at kind of a brick wall and whatever's been done before I really need to know about it. I need the box."

"Well, I'm sure they'd send it to you if they find it."

"No-oh," I kind of yelped. "It's here for sure and I've got to get it now. I can't just go back."

She looked at me with the keen still eye she had when she thought I was going crazy. "Dad?" she called through the house. "Dad!" She ran up the steps and I heard her nearing the distant sound of sifting that was Merl. When she bounded down again she said he was at the store and she was holding keys. "Well, let's go then."

"We don't have to. I mean, I can wait."

She just looked at me with that level eye again. We drove downtown. Emily had a special parking spot in the garage, one right next to the door of Briggs's. I sat in a chair outside his inner office while she talked to him. And then Pat came out and we took a walk through the store.

Pat had a way of acknowledging that this was serious by listening with his head down, almost parallel to the ground. His hands were clasped behind his back.

I'd explained again about the box and how badly I wanted—no, needed—it, and then he asked me, how is medical school going and cocked his head as if my answer were the one answer to my life.

I shrugged. "Okay. Not great, maybe. I've been a little preoccupied with this." I hated saying that. I knew the Briggses, people like that, expected me to do well. It was how they knew I was different from my mother.

He shook his head, wincing. We were on the escalator now down from the fifth floor to the fourth. "I always thought you'd be an architect. I thought we'd be hiring you to build a new Briggs's."

We'd always shared that when we saw each other, Doc Briggs and me. We'd talked about buildings. I'd shown him my drawings of towers and minarets.

"Ask Emily," I said. "She's the one in art history." Emily would have never done that.

"No, I know Emily. Emily's not a studier. Not that way."

I looked at him sideways but he was grinning in reverie, he was watching a memory of her moving through air and space.

"I always wanted to be an architect," I said.

He looked straight at me, the tic playing over his face. He seemed almost naked like that. "I remember John F. Kennedy Primary. I thought you were going to knock 'em all dead." That was a contest they'd had to design an elementary school in town and give it a name. Everyone had laughed at me but then my drawing had won and it was up on display in Briggs's. The school never got built, though, the budget was cut.

"Architecture is half an art, half a science," he said.

"Medicine too, I guess," I said.

"No, medicine is really just a blunter form of merchandising. What you're selling is time." He slid his hands into his pockets. "Let's get off here, I told Emily we'd stop by and see a ring she was looking at in Estate Jewelry. And I'll see to it, Mayan, that if that box is there we'll get it to you before you go."

"Thank you," I said. We walked through a forest of mannequins being moved. "Must be hard to be a dad, huh?"

He moved his shoulders a certain way, as if burrowing in. "Nothing like it. Before they're born, you want them to be like you. You want them to be sort of your type, the way you'd want a girl to be your type and if she was you might fall in love with her. Because you're scared. You want to love them but you don't know if you can. But it's stronger than that. You love them right away just the way they are. Whatever they are, that is your type, more than yourself is your type. And you'll see, your child will change who you can love in the world."

Emily was seated at a velvet-covered stool in front of a long glass case. A velvet black tray was out in front of her. She turned on the stool full of charm and asking, a tight string of triple pearls around her neck. "I saw this movie called *The Stranger*," she said. "And the girl had this dress that went up to here and pearls like this. I thought I'd get a video and give it to a dressmaker and . . ."

He was over her then, his hands on her neck.

I walked over to the window, behind a display of fur. It was okay. He'd heard me out and promised he'd find the box himself. Outside, snow had melted in patches and grass stood muddy and colorless. In the distance, down this hill and past another, you could see the red clay roofs and square steeples of the Belgian monastery and its vineyards. Everything looked different here than it did at my grandmother's house. There it was flat land as far as you could see, eventually the railroad yard and then the highway.

LATER, we were sitting on the living room carpet playing Monopoly. Tad acquired Marvin Gardens. "Boom, boom boom," he said, fists churning, "that's all three. A monopoly."

"The box?" I said.

Pat Briggs made a face that was like his wince, frozen. "Now? I've almost finished you gals off. Let me just nail Tad."

"I don't want to keep bugging people," I said.

I stopped trying. I let him win. Emily and I were out. It was him and Tad. Then just Tad.

"Okay." He sighed and got up. He'd get away with as much as he could, but finally, he'd do the fair thing. Emily tried to be like that, too. He went to a small drawer in the kitchen and got out a flashlight, he knew just where it was and I remembered, oh yeah, this really is his house. He pulled the string down from the ceiling in the hallway by the small bedrooms and climbed the steps to the attic.

I stood down below. "You sure it's in there? I saw a lot of boxes in the garage."

That was a stupid thing to say. Boxes were the main unit of filling in this house. There must have been a thousand in the basement, the garage was a solid cube. Merl Briggs sealed them squarely and labeled them in a neat, right-slanted script on all six sides. Pat's footsteps creaked the ceiling and a few minutes later he came down with the box labeled ADELE STEVENSON'S LEGAL PAPERS, as if he knew in the elaborate packing and storage and stuffing and mechanics of this house, with its deliveries and emissions, its trucks coming and going, its repairs, its scrubbings and supply drops, where the one box was buried in the attic with our name on it.

We went to the kitchen and set the box on the enamel table. He took a bread knife and cut through the metal-threaded tape. Then we bent over, Pat serious in his intent, glasses heavy on his face, like a drawn thing. His fingers went through the files one by one. The box, lidless, resembled an organized drawer of a file cabinet. Endless papers. He would lift out a piece of paper, read it and put it back. I just stood there. There wasn't much for me to do.

We went through my mother's divorce papers, I stared at my mother's signature on it, the tissue copy of my grandmother's will, marked Copy. For one breath moment in my life my mother was another story. I saw not one manila file with my father's name.

"Look at this," he said, handing me a paper. It was my birth certificate with an ink print of the whorls on the soles of my baby feet stamped in a marked square. He handed me a paper. I read it, we stacked it on the desk, in its manila file. I had decent hands. We had long digits. All of my family.

This took hours.

I heard the doorbell, activity, it all passed and we kept on.

We talked a little bit. We were back on our old subject of funerals. He was telling me about the new crematorium. "Four stories high," he said. "And they have little lockers, like a gym."

Then Emily slid in modeling the jacket she'd cut out from the magazine, the store tags still on the ends of the sleeves.

"It just came," she said, "Fed Ex. What do you think?"

He smiled a way that meant things that didn't have words.

"It makes me want to take a walk. You guys want to come?"

He bent his head down, demurring, and she tranced out, but he stretched up again for one last casting look which stopped everything for me and turned it all to salt.

Okay, let's get this over with, I was thinking. We went through every paper in the box and it was not there.

"Hmph," Pat said, tapping one thick envelope in his hands. He kept it from me a little longer than the rest. It was bills my father had run up in 1961, right before he left. All the Briggs invoices were marked "paid." They were kept together, inside the envelope with a rubber band. The items included two men's suits (size 44), six shirts, two dress shirts, mints from the delicacy section on the sixth floor, a hat, leather valise, talcum powder, thirty-seven dollars' worth of "sundries" in a category marked "men's toilet," a small radio, a dictionary, a driving scarf and pipe tobacco.

My grandmother had paid them all.

THERE WAS NOTHING to do then but eat. I didn't care anymore. I stopped weighing myself. Emily sluffed around in big socks and jeans mixing up one last batch of eggnog from scratch, whipping cream in a new copper bowl, beating egg whites until they winged like snow, passing the mugs out, grating nutmeg with a new grinder, special for this.

Later, we walked out on the main hill road and on one side of us were the crushed shapes of children's snow angels, their heads, the scraped wings and the mash of them getting up again after. I wasn't ready to go home tomorrow. Pat Briggs had told me a lawyer in Bay City had helped with the search, maybe he knew something. I had to see him. And Gish was in the hospital.

The box being wrong, which dead end would I call the last? At the end, I began to understand, there would always be a live chance that the address, the identity, the location of my father was a false lead, a bad tip, a dumb hope. I could fly somewhere, get maps and drive a rented car to an address and get out and still never meet him. Another city, another town, another shrine that was just a neighborhood where the dark green ordinary leaves had held my hope and were then forgotten.

Every time there was a setback, he grew.

I didn't even know the questions anymore. I had a memory of questions, but the answers now seemed apparent in their absence, unknowable. They were the kind of questions that bring a look of rue to the lips, a lift to the shoulders, a horizontal swing to the face.

"Where were you when we were here?

"Where were you when we suffered, the large and the small?

"Where were you when I had my life?"

And the answer is no answer and one I knew. When I was a child, when I started school, when I lost my key and stood locked out of the house, when I fell and cried, when I first saw the night, when I fell in love, when I was alone, the one we looked for and prayed to, and whispered over our hurt and bleeding skin to, and expected to hear us, wherever he was—was gone.

THAT NIGHT, Mai linn was playing saxophone in Detroit. Her roommate from music school was from Detroit, and she'd gotten them the gig. Emily and I flew up to hear her. Tad insisted. His treat. "No, it's no problem, I'll get the tickets, we'll have a car waiting for you, you can fly back the same night, boom boom boom." He punched the air. He didn't want to come to Detroit. He liked music with words.

Mai linn picked us up at the airport. She had a luxurious car, which was strange for her. She'd always had a VW bug she worked on herself. But this was an old white Falcon, with simple, stylish fixtures on the doors. Inside, everything was red and silver. It was a car a woman our age could have inherited from a careful grandmother, but this was not the case. Her roommate had bought it from an ad in the paper. A man in a UAW windbreaker had had the car propped on cinder blocks in his garage. She said the first few months, they'd kept the car perfect, like a museum. She'd polished the outside every week with kerosene. The man who'd sold it told her to do that. But by now, the leather was torn and worn cotton clothes tangled on the seats. "It feels more homey, anyway," she said and it did. The heat worked strong and right away. The car felt deeply comfortable. It was a consolation. I was big on consolation that night.

Mai linn had asked me what ever happened with that first detective.

"I should've paid him more. I don't think I gave him enough incentive. I'm too cheap."

"You are," Emily mumbled.

"What are you going to do when you find him?" Mai linn said. Emily was falling asleep in the backseat. Her eyes closed and her breath whined high and even.

The question made me blush. I really didn't know. "Meet him, I guess."

"Do you know, like, what you would say to him?"

"No," I said. I didn't. I looked down at my hands.

Then we were quiet for a while.

I watched Mai linn drive. I was glad to be going to hear her play. I

remembered how odd and convoluted Mai linn seemed the first time
I saw her. Another nun, not our own, had come into the classroom
and said we would be getting a new student from a faraway place who
was an orphan and she might look different than we did but we should
take pity on her and be good Christians. And then they brought her
in, already fitted out in one of our uniforms, but way too long. No
one hemmed it. I suppose they figured it would last that way. She was
short and so she sat across from me in the front row. She was so near
all day I saw her strangely. The way her ears came out seemed different and stiff like gills and her upper lip seemed an odd distance and
angle. There was something unnatural in her smoothness, coils of her
glasses seemed attached and almost alive.

With friends, sometimes you can know them for five or ten years
and all of a sudden see their beauty. And once you see it you know it
has always been there.

I used to believe there were beautiful and ugly faces. Now I don't,
really. There is young and old, there is clean, there is integrity.

But Mai linn still doesn't know her own face. It's a trick, what her
stepfather did. He molested her and all the while he made her be
ugly.

She still says now, she doesn't know what was worse. "Him or the
powdered milk. And that she kept a lock on the refrigerator. With her
kids, too, but you know she let them in if nobody was looking."

We were driving on a wide good Michigan highway, with quiet dark
hills close on one side of us, to the city where hardly anybody white
lived anymore. There were Arabs and blacks and Black Muslims.
W.D. Fard came from Arabia to Detroit as a traveling salesman and
established the Black Muslim Church.

The car had a long windshield, we could see stars. They pressed on
the dark glass sharply, and I knew they would fade by the time we
drove into the city. I leaned against the glass, wondering what I
looked like. I wasn't sure. I'd spent enough time staring at mirrors in
my life. Sometimes it seemed I was okay. Other times, not. I suppose
both were true. I was one of those people in the middle, like most of
us, not beautiful but not worth pity either. Two men had said they
were in love with me. But neither had lasted.

I leaned over the seat divider and looked down at Emily, whose eyes
had closed. I'd never been like her. Sometimes I thought I could have
been better looking if . . . if what? I hadn't fasted so much as a child?

I thought I grew funny because of it. If I'd washed my face in a more disciplined way. If I didn't have Egyptian hair?

The Briggses had taken Emily to a dermatologist when she was a child, just because she had white and fragile skin. Talk about end of the empire. From when she was eight years old on, Merl Briggs washed her face twice a day with special soaps and creams and they changed her pillowcase and gave her new towels every night. I remember her standing under her mother's diligent hands—she could never go outside without sunblock. She had gone to all kinds of doctors for everything. Once when they felt like her arches were falling they took her to a podiatrist and had arch braces made for inside all her shoes. And it had all worked.

In a line of a hundred women, Emily was likely to be picked as most beautiful by a hundred men. It was a fact of her life and had been for a long time now. It had been there, hard in her like a pit or a jewel, since she was a teenager. She had been recognized by the world, by everyone except my cousin Ben. He'd just shrugged. "She's okay," he said when I bugged him. Now, she was grown. She neither doubted nor exactly valued her beauty. But she needed it. She had had problems with men, too.

We were entering Detroit now, an elaborate labyrinth of old dark streets, cracked lights. I was thinking of the ways we measure a life: a person was healthy or ill, rich or poor, beautiful or plain, ugly, educated or not, the member of a majority group or suspected. But we didn't consider the age you were when your parents died. Or the years you lived. Time, too, could be a source of poverty or fortune. Most of us were loved, somehow. I measured things to myself, weighing luck, deciding each time that lives were equal, even despite everything. As a child I once wrote down, "Every life holds exactly forty-two thousand eight hundred and sixty-four minutes of happiness, no more, no less," on the inside cardboard cover of a spiral notebook. My mother had framed that penciled thing where she was. The notion pleased us. So we wouldn't miss out, after all.

My grandmother too had owned an aspect of beauty. Men stopped and stared after her, all her life.

Then Emily woke up and started talking about Tad. She always spoke of him like a difficult boss. "Tad's going crazy because we haven't screwed all week."

"Why haven't you?" Mai linn said.

"My periodical."

"So?"

"I don't know, he doesn't like to have sex when I have my period. A lot of people are like that. I think he's faint around blood. He told me once his mother wanted him to be a doctor, but he just couldn't. Physically. I mean, I'm not thrilled about it either. He's so clean, I'm always a little nervous in his apartment when I have my period. That I'll bleed on his sheets or something. Once I left a Tampax in his toilet and I didn't flush 'cause it was late at night and I didn't want to wake him, and I was trying not to sleep too soundly so I could get up and flush before he did and then I just remember hearing him in my sleep, get up and flush and then pee. But he never said anything about it. That was nice. He's a really superneat and clean person. He even brushes his teeth a lot. But I guess everyone's either too much one way or the other. And this is lucky. He picks up after me."

Mai linn and I didn't say anything for a minute.

"Oh, see that car there, that's Tad favorite car of all times."

"The red one?" I said.

"Mmhm, the red one."

"Doesn't it bother you that you spend so much more time and energy on his life, than he gives yours?" It was a mean thing I said, but a true one.

Emily's answer surprised me. "No. Because everybody's different." She didn't seem to have a flicker of embarrassment.

That made me laugh and crack the window. I looked back at her. Her hair was blowing over her eyebrows. I'd grown up so ashamed. I collected scraps of information about my father as if the discovery of this life were my great project. My grandmother had always scolded my curiosity. She waged a war against magic.

"And what does he care for you? Do you think he's wondering and thinking where you are and what you're doing right now? He could find you if he just picked up the telephone. And there you sit."

I could disobey my grandmother and not feel one needle of anger. She was only concerned for me. But she got me too late to coax me out of it with logic. I needed my father. He was a question planted in me, too young. Approaching him was a life's mission. And like all real missions it became daily and very slow.

"Do you have anything of your father's?" Emily all of a sudden asked. That was like her to remember the material.

Mai linn turned from the steering wheel. "Yeah, that'd be good, huh? Some shirts of his or something?"

"I didn't mean a shirt. I meant work he did or something. Or a watch or old jewelry from his family."

What's wrong with a shirt? I was thinking. But I just said no.

It had started to snow. Small dizzy particles trembled in every direction, up and in curved sideways trajectories, they seemed to mill more than fall.

"Want some music?" Mai linn knew these streets, we could have never found the place alone. She turned on the staticky radio and found a woman's voice like polished walnut, and for a moment I was just grateful to be there, circling the streets of this old city, part of the decrepitude and endurance and escape that fused to make jazz. The woman sang brokenly about rose petals on a staircase and in the snow I understood that a kind of lasting beauty could only come from accident or failure, that that was one of the axioms like gravity and the taste of the cigarette smoke in precipitation and then Mai linn slowed the car to a stop and we stepped out in the brick block of buildings with her torn envelope of address to find where she would play.

Mai linn was playing in a spotlight then, past the small rectangular desk that was the ticket booth, after two narrow flights of stairs. Inside, the light was right, deep yellow-orange, and on stage, she looked neat and studious in baggy charcoal pants, round boy's sneakers, a suit jacket, tie and suspenders, pigeon-toed, knee-bent, her hair clipped behind, glasses on, blowing like all anger and discovery. We sat in an old padded booth and ordered brown drinks. Even closing my eyes I saw the dizzy snow.

OUR LAST NIGHT, at Stevie's old house, Jane woke up and came out into the kitchen. Helen was in the bathroom. We'd all been sitting at the table, talking about looking for my father. I was telling everyone I loved, as if I were leaving on a long trip.

"You got a *detective*?" Jane shrieked. She had a loud amazed shrill voice. Already, she was so different from her mother. She was an enthusiast. "Is he really a detective? Wait a minute, Mo-om!"

The toilet flushed, they scuffled, Helen saying, wait, let me finish, Jane, and then they came back holding hands, double silence of concentration playing over their foreheads.

"You don't even know if he's dead or alive or if he has a red couch or a blue couch?" Jane said.

"No. I mean I'm not sure. I think he's alive."

"Atassi," Stevie told Jane. "That was her name."

"You could call yourself Mayan Atassi Stevenson," Helen said.

"See if you like the guy first," Jane said.

"Yeah. I don't know what he'll be like. I'm not expecting a swell guy necessarily. He's probably not a swell guy."

"But he might be, though, Mayan. There must be something of you in him, right? He might be anything."

"A swell guy, Mom? A swell guy if he left his daughter?"

"We don't know everything," Helen said.

"I have to meet him," the child said, "I just have to meet him."

"So what about you?" I tickled her and made her shriek louder in a star of points. "How's the third-grade boy scene? How's Trip?"

"We broke up. It was meaningless to go steady with Trip, what did it mean, we sat together on the bus and that's *nothing*!"

"Okay, so Trip's history, who's in."

"Well."

"Come on, out with it, is this a new commitment to second-grade spelling or what?"

"Well, he's a third-grader. Trevor. But I don't think he likes me. All the guys in third grade like me except one. And that's the one I like."

It was so common. Maybe it had nothing to do with him being gone.

I SAID GOOD-BYE at the windy airport. The Briggses stood together in new coats. Helen and Stevie and Jane were leaving too. "We're so glad you kids are all successful, doing so well in your lives," Mrs. Briggs called. I watched Emily, in her jacket, bounding up the tarmac. Tad ran after her with an armload of newspapers. I was supposed to be leaving too, but I decided to stay a little longer.

Even having the family I did, I was a snob. For all the Briggses' parties and decency, I couldn't help but prefer my own. I couldn't quite take any other family seriously.

. . .

I DROVE THROUGH A LANE OF TREES. They were plane trees, fisted, rare, trees I wouldn't have guessed possible in the Midwest. I knew from Stevie: there is not one continent without pine. And so many species have been mixed and transplanted from the last piratical century of expansion and conquest. Stevie had a Ph.D. in trees.

I was driving to see the lawyer Pat Briggs had mentioned. The lawyer was a man without children. I knew, everyone knew, that he and his wife had had a child who died years ago. The wife had taken the girl to the Twin Cities for treatment before she died and she stayed there for two years, after. Then she came back and that was all I'd ever heard about it. Jackson Fenwick was the richest lawyer in Bay City. He worked in a wooden office downtown, but this was his vacation and he'd asked me to drive out to his house. This was a district, forty miles south from where I'd lived, that I'd never seen. It was a neighborhood of big old houses that looked blinded and closed for long winters. At the end of his lane, you came to a plateau. A thicket of dry winter rosebushes still kept you from the approach to the house. I parked my grandmother's car and got out. From here you could see down the hill and many hills, ridged in the distance. This was a way hardly anybody in Wisconsin lived.

How could this man have accepted my grandmother's money?

A woman met me at the door. I'd expected a maid, from the movies, but it was Mrs. Fenwick and she had a kind, oval face, her hair just bunned back, some gray running in it. She was dressed all in suede, suede jeans and a suede shirt and suede loafers, and she moved noiselessly on the bare floors. She had many small teeth and an inwardly moving smile.

"Jackson's in the study, I'll bring you on out there," she said. A fire broke and whispered in the living room as we passed. The room admitted filtered, goldish light. I felt right away all that was wrong with the Briggses' house.

Jackson Fenwick sat, feet up, reading at a mahogany desk. From the opposite bookshelf came the low murmur of a football game on a small, cube-shaped television.

"Ouch, oh no, come on, get him down, get him, hold him, oh no." Jackson Fenwick turned the game off. "Have a seat," he said to me. He exhaled. "They're not on top today," he said. His wife slipped out, closing the wood door behind her. On one side, the wall opened to windows revealing an empty garden.

"You know, there is a box sitting around somewhere, in the Briggses' basement maybe, with those records" was the first thing Jackson Fenwick said.

I shook my head. "I don't think so. Pat and Merl tried, pretty thoroughly I think."

"Nothing?"

"No."

"Well, maybe it got thrown out somehow."

"I doubt it. They're not really a family that throws things out."

One knee bent and he caught it with his arms. "That's for sure true."

"Do you remember much?"

"I'm searching back a long ways here, you understand. I looked into it when the Briggses brought your grandma in and she asked me to find him in view of you. There were two colleges involved," he said. "And one was I think in Montana."

"When was this, do you remember?"

"Oh, 1970 maybe, '72. Remember I'm pulling this out of some cobwebs. And that was the last contact that anybody had had. Now I did have a name—and I believe it's somewhere in my notes in that box—of a guy who was probably as close to a friend as anybody your father ever had in the world. And I believe I talked to that guy—again I'm pulling a lot of stuff out of the hat—but I believe I actually talked to the guy."

"And did he have any idea where my father was?"

"Well, it wouldn't've surprised me. I got the feeling that he did but he wasn't going to tell me. I think he was pretty suspicious." I could understand somebody being suspicious of Jackson Fenwick. The way he talked. The guy was never just a guy but the best friend your father ever had. *In the world.* Maybe if I called, I was thinking. Or found the man, drove to where he lived, spent a day with him, took a walk. This friend—there were so many questions—

Just then, Mrs. Fenwick carried in a tray of tea with a plate of what smelled like warm gingerbread. She asked me if I wanted lemon or milk as she poured. Then she served us each the gingerbread, spooning whipped cream from a silver bowl so cold tiny beads of water formed on the outside.

"Mmph," Jackson Fenwick said. "Where'd you get this recipe, honey?"

I noticed her hands had spots like large freckles on the tops of them. This was something my mother worried about. She used lemon juice and the insides of vitamin E tablets to bleach them.

Her long neck bent, as if from the weight of her head, and she said, "Piro's?"

"In Chicago."

"Yes."

"You know what she does? We go somewhere and find something we really like, a superior pasta, or this, this was the best gingerbread I've ever had, she'll go the next morning to the kitchen and knock and have the chef show her how he does it."

Mrs. Fenwick stood a moment looking out the window to the still winter garden, her hands fallow on the front of her apron. Her profile was strong and settled. Then she turned back to us and smiled. She was a woman in whom even a smile contained elements of sadness.

"Beatrice doesn't like winter. Where she comes from, it doesn't get this cold." Outside, there were lemon trees, bare, and a large fig.

She closed the door behind her again and Jackson Fenwick said, hands basketed, "I am a lucky man."

I liked him kind of. I wanted him to like me. So I told him a little about my life. I was a way I thought he'd want a young woman to be. I told him that I was from here and that now I was in New York City in school to be a doctor. I told him I was pretty alone. I told him that I'd hired a detective and that he had checked credit and driving records and was now trying to do a search with immigration.

"I think your father traveled under a foreign passport," he volunteered.

"Did you ever come across a social security number?" I said.

"Your father used a number of aliases, if I recall," he said, almost as if I were to blame. "I think he had more than one social security number."

Aliases. For some reason that made me think of my father, benign, in prison. In the institutional mirror, a little black-and-white picture of himself, with a wavy border.

This guy wasn't at all charmed. None of what I said was working. He acted like I was responsible for being the unwanted kid of a man like my dad.

"Did Pat tell you, I don't know if Pat told you, but Marion Werth at the Racine Library unearthed something about him. See, your grandma had her on the case, too. She'd done some work on family trees, some such thing, but nothing like this before, I'm pretty sure of that. And Miss Werth dug up something pretty bad, I think. Something about getting some poor old ladies arrested. And when your grandmother heard about that, that was when we all stopped."

He looked at me while he said that as if I inherited all this.

"I see."

"In fact, you might try and get in touch with Marion Werth. She was in on all this. Maybe she's got that box."

"God, we don't know anything," I said. "He could even be in Egypt. See, it's weird that he's not turning up on any of these computer checks."

"By the way, I came to think there was a distinct possibility," Fenwick said, his hands straight now, the fingers touching only at their tips, "that he was dead."

The garden out the window looked still and old. A blue bird fluttered and beat its wings on the tilted birdbath pooled with brown water and old leaves. Somewhere a woman was cooking in the kitchen, using superior ingredients, reading handwritten recipes. This was nothing like love.

"Um, what made you think that?"

"Well, I had a feeling he might've conned the wrong people. He was mixed up with some Middle Eastern oil people. There was some educational program he was supposed to be putting together for them."

All of a sudden, I wanted to go.

Mrs. Fenwick came to the door to offer us more. "Mayan, anything? Jackson? Would you like your warm-up?"

"I sure would, honey," Jackson Fenwick said, swinging his legs off the desk and standing. I bolted up and streaked in an angle to the door. "Bye, thanks," I said, from a distance. I opened the heavy front door and let it drop back into its locks. Then I ran on the stone steps to my car.

I had heard once before that he'd taught in the West. My mother told me somebody had said so. That was years ago. And just this last week, in boredom, I'd paged through the architecture books in the Briggses' library and found a note I'd written two summers earlier on the inside cover. It said Idaho and the names of seven colleges, with the phone numbers of their personnel offices. I guess I'd kept it as a partial record, for when I would be more thorough later on. I never felt I'd checked a place completely. You couldn't do enough.

A light random snow began to fall and it stuck to the road like a thin soft veil of decoration just enough to make the wheels feel light, as if we were skating, about to take off. I'd call Marion Werth in California.

He might be dead.

I was not ready for him to be dead, even though I couldn't see him, even though I never heard him, even though I didn't know where he was.

I didn't believe I'd find him, not really. If I needed him I knew he'd never answer. I couldn't imagine his rescue, any salvation, except from myself and hard work and good habits and all the everyday things we all know, but I was not ready for him to be dead, forever, buried nowhere I could find and touch the ground, before I saw him and he recognized me as his child.

Father had become the name for a rock, a stark gray cliff in the Colorados, the echoing forever unanswered.

Still, he could not be dead.

My grandmother's heavy Oldsmobile flew over the narrow roads, sleek with snow. Briggses' house was empty when I got home, save Dorothy, who sat at the kitchen table with rubber boots on over her shoes, hands folded, work done, ready to be picked up to go home. I waited there with her, until the twin milky lights cornered in the room and she ran outside to her nephew's truck.

I lay belly down on Emily's bed, talking on her Princess phone. I tracked down Marion Werth in California. It didn't take too long. Four calls. Research, it occurred to me, was the same, whether you were searching out an old friend's phone number, a jacket seen in a magazine, or a doctor for the person nearest you.

I found Marion Werth in Fruitvale, California, picking up her phone after the second ring in the same lilt-upending voice she'd always had. "Hel-lowoh."

She thrilled hearing it was me calling from Wisconsin. I could see her in her house, sitting on a chair, her nails filed into curves, the discreet pink of a seashell's insides. Her talking voice had always had an upswing breathless quality. "Well you can imagine it didn't give us any pleasure to hurt people we loved or even to worry them but they seem to be settling down some now. My family. We've started some regular correspondence. Tell me, what does it look like right now?"

"What?"

"Racine," she said. "Is it snowing? Does it have that real winter smell?"

"Yeah, sort of. It's a windy day. Dark. Snowy. You know what that's like."

"Yes I do."

I thought of all the men on the way to my father. Marion Werth was from my own life. This was different.

She told me about the farm. Sort of midwestern, she said. It had a big porch they were painting blue. They'd already sent away for seeds of lilies of the valley, bleeding hearts, lilac bushes and gooseberries. The kitchen was huge and it had an old Wedgewood stove with a pancake griddle. They'd painted the kitchen walls apple green with white trim. She was sitting at a little table they'd found at a thrift store. It was very clean now. *Now,* she said. They'd had to get down together on their knees and scrub every tile in the kitchen and bathroom with toothbrushes and Ajax, and I could see them, their differences erased by the common midwestern horror of dirt, at unkempt oldness, lack of pride, sagging forgetfulness in a home. They'd painted the radiator a bright silver and found a piece of marble at a flea market to rest on top of that.

The farm was a small date farm, between Petaluma and Santa Rosa. They had dates, two cherry orchards and a field of artichokes. In summer, most farmers set up stands on the road tourists drove to the Napa Valley. Callie worked modernizing the farm all day and he'd enrolled in the agriculture school at Davis. She drove into Santa Rosa to the hat and glove shop. Tonight, Callie had found fresh cherries at ninety-nine cents a pound, "Can you imagine, Bing cherries in January?" so she'd made a pie, "In fact the pastry recipe your grandmother gave me once years ago with the cider vinegar in it. And no butter. It uses corn oil." I'd always liked the first sour bite of cherry pie. It sat right now cooling on the ledge, they'd go out and eat it soon and watch fireflies in the dark. They had eucalyptus trees in their backyard and date palms.

She sounded more for herself than she'd ever been. I was glad. It had been worth a call to hear that. I almost didn't want to ask her about the box.

But I couldn't not. I was that far in. I put the box and its questions in places they didn't belong. I was beyond etiquette.

But I didn't want her to think I was calling only about the box. There were too many people I'd lost like that. It was like a carousel. I didn't have time enough, it seemed, to just have friends. My years for play would come later. My mother had always promised me that. Too much of what I did had a point. And it wasn't even my own. I felt like I was chasing the world to find a grave. All this had been set for me by my parents.

So I just said it. "Marion, do you remember anything about a box of papers that were records of my grandmother's and Jackson Fenwick's?"

She paused a minute, thinking, I supposed. I just waited for her to tally up her memory and tell me she'd never seen the thing. But then she told me, of course she remembered the box, very well. When they'd driven out west they'd taken only her Volkswagen bug, they'd gone camping all of August in Glacier National Park so they'd traveled light, but that she'd put the box and other valuables, for safekeeping, in the basement at the convent.

"So you know about that. I wasn't sure, Ann, if they told you they were doing that."

"They didn't tell me. But, I finally found out. See, I'm looking for my dad myself now. I've hired a detective and all."

"Have you!" she said. "Oh my goodness." She sounded funny and I wondered if I'd offended her somehow, or if she dispproved.

"You know, we may just do that ourselves. Callie is adopted and he's always wanted to meet his real mother. Complicated lives we all have. Tell me what you find, won't you?"

"Maybe the nuns threw that box out," I said.

"Oh, heavens no. The nuns never throw anything out. They haven't lost a button since 1949 in the fire."

The nuns' fire in 1949—something we all knew about that was as big as the war in Racine, killing half a generation of teachers and nurses and more than thirty cats.

I KNOCKED EIGHT TIMES on the huge wood front door before a nun I didn't know whispered in long robes to admit me. She left me sitting on a bare bench in the hall. I'd asked to see Sister Mary Bede.

All our lives, nuns were a part of the inside clockwork of things.

When I went to their school they lived in the convent behind and when I came without a lunch, they made me a sandwich. They'd take me into the huge dry kitchen and get out bread from an ordinary breadbox, lunch meat. Even nuns, they were women.

In first and second grade, we had made altars in school. Little shrines we held on our laps on the bus. I made them secretly at home too. But all the things I wanted for my altar were lost, thrown away, because my mother was such a romantic. The ring, wedged in river sludge at the bottom of the river in New York City, a place I had never been then, the pictures lost in some shoe box in the attic.

Sister Mary Bede, in new eyeglasses, came down the hall, her face lit in amused pleasure. I was so glad to see her. I wanted to stand in the hallway and talk but then she told me it was suppertime there and she had to get back, so I followed the unsteady beam of her flashlight down the steps which she descended terribly slowly, jagged, with each step a hand grasp worthy of life on the old wood banister. I imagined all of their time was accounted for, the way they accounted for children's time when they taught. We scratched with light over one hundred boxes, old skis, big restaurant-sized food supplies, rickety bookshelves of Catechism readers until we finally hit the neat tied tarp covering Marion Werth's goods and we found mine, carefully labeled.

Sister Mary Bede probably knew what I was doing but she didn't ask anything. We went slowly back up the stairs and it was only at the door that she stalled me.

"I remember your class," she said, her old face hanging close to me, her eyes bright and the rest all gone. "I still have a picture." From the folds of her habit she withdrew a black-and-white picture of our class. I was in the front row, my hair pulled tightly back, my legs apart, my face with an expression of astonishment. We all looked like foreign children, it was that long ago. She was the second-grade nun and then, years later, she came to teach us Latin.

"Thank you, Sister." This was the woman who taught me how to write cursive. We had thick pencils and first for a long time we drew circles, then oblong loops, just to loosen our wrists for the new writing. She must have been middle-aged, then. Age was a way we never even thought about nuns. She filled the classroom ledge with jars of cocoons and wasp nests and the blue and speckled eggs of different birds.

"I'll say a novena for you," she said. "Whatever you find."

I was halfway down to the car when the door opened and she stood outside. "You know, your grandma's Gish slipped last night. She's under, she doesn't hear a thing anymore."

I'd been up to the hospital once since I'd been back. Gish's hand had been like the softest almost wet paper. She didn't recognize me. I'd paced the room by the windows, watching the traffic down on Van Buren Street.

"Maybe wait a little before you leave."

I nodded. I knew that from my grandmother when she got to be this age. You waited then for people to die. Your friends, their husbands. Death was a ceremony, a marker in the days.

I didn't drive back to Briggses'. I went to Boss's. He was still open. I had the box in my arms and I stuttered back and forth three times in the street changing my mind. My throat was sore and swelled up on the inside. It felt like the opening for air was the size of a dime.

I sat at the stool by the window. Bruce Nadel gave me a knife and I slit the box, opened the two flaps. It wasn't the box I'd expected. It was a new office-looking box but none of that mattered anymore now. What is real is real and there is nothing like it.

I took out the papers one at a time and held them. They were about my family, typewritten by someone I didn't know, someone prim and bored probably, sitting in an office. I read them and lay them down carefully, on a white scallop-edge place mat. This was a bible in which I was almost a character. There were names to follow, dates, addresses, places. Bruce Nadel behind the counter served me coffee which I swilled fast and too hot because I thought it might open my throat. His chili smelled burned, from the bottom of the pot, but I ate it anyway, stuffing it down my mouth, it tasted cardboard.

None of this mattered now. I had new names to call from the file, more recent than the detective found, fifteen years after Dorothy Widmer. I had a civil servant who worked for the Bureau of Vital Statistics in Madison. I had a man in Nevada, a whole college where my father taught in Montana. Now I felt I was hugely close. The whole known period of my life seemed about to be over.

I sat scribbling notes on the dry place mat.

I skipped over things I knew, racing to the end. The last page was a copy, paid for—the record of the check was there, too, Jackson Fenwick's letter enclosing the $7.50 duplicating fee—of my parents' marriage certificate. It said both their names, their addresses in Wisconsin. The dates of their birth, that they were white. I hadn't considered until just then that Arab was still white. He was listed as Egyptian, she as American. Leila was his mother's name. Then the rest was all official, the clerk's name, signatures from two witnesses who were called Thomas and Marjorie Miller. Where it said number of past marriages, the groom's side said none, the bride's side said none. Both their ages were twenty-four. It happened in Dane County, Wisconsin, on June 14, 1956.

For a certain kind of person, there is almost nothing more moving than the marriage certificate of their parents.

BRUCE NADEL HAD HIS APRON ON and the sound of his sweeping came near now. "Closed," he said, waving an arm, to a man in front trying the metal push bar on the door. He began to put all the stools except mine up on top of the counter so he could do the floor. He let me sit there, with my box, and he took a cream pie out of the refrigerated case. Only one piece was cut from it. It was banana. He just gave me the tin and a fork.

It seemed I sat there hours. Bruce Nadel swept the whole store, then washed the cases, ripped the tops off the newspapers and threw the rest away in big green plastic garbage bags, clearing the racks for the morning delivery. Then he took the garbage out back and came through to mop.

Why in a tobacco shop? This was the place where my mother first decided she wanted to give me away. Decisions had to be made someplace, no not made, because they were worked over many places, in time, but there was one place and a moment when they were realized and acknowledged and then it was as if they were written on the metal stools, in the old magazine racks themselves, on Bruce Nadel's high, pure forehead, Bruce Nadel who was still the same. I wondered where it was, earlier, that my father had known he was going to leave me. It could have been here too. Before he left Racine, he must have come to Boss's. Every man did.

Then Bruce Nadel was done and I was done, too. He took the pie tin, washed it out and dried it and then we both walked outside. He locked the heavy metal crunching locks in the door.

"Thank you," I said.

"Oh, was nothing. Nice to have the company. I s'pose a lot of things in your life came out in that store."

"Do you remember my father at all, Mr. Nadel?"

"I don't myself, no. But my brother's wife took a course from him over at Saint Norbert's. She said he told them if they were going to learn one thing in his course and no more, he'd be happy if he could just teach them to read the international page in the *New York Times* every day and really understand it, you know. And she learned that. She's read it every day now since. She made me first start carrying the daily. And that was, let's see, well you—must be over thirty years now."

"Did he come to the store?"

"I don't remember him myself but I s'pose he might have. Did he smoke, do you know?"

I shrugged. I didn't know.

GISH'S FUNERAL was at Shauer and Schumaker, run now by Jen's second son. I recognized a lot of people: the man who'd sold my cousins and me our childhood shoes and had given us a prize for every year's new pair of Keds, as if growing a size larger were a meritorious achievement, Sister Mary Bede, Bruce Nadel, all the girls' families, their sons and daughters and grandchildren, the owners of Coliseum Cinema. I recognized the Queen of Hearts and the Dunce, who both looked older out of their costumes.

I went around to every flower arrangement looking for the card that said Hans. Rene had died first, then Jen, then my grandmother. My grandmother had left Gish all the girls' correspondence from Hans in her will. My grandmother had gone second to last. So Gish had owned pictures of Hans and their worn card set, even though Gish hadn't been able to see anymore. The tablecloth was stitched with red and black clubs, hearts, spades and diamonds.

Later, I stood in the cemetery in my heels, snow seeding the ground. Danny Felchner leaned next to me holding my elbow.

"How did you know her?" I asked.

"Movies," he said. The cemetery ground seemed deep and forever absorbing. My car was parked at the edge of the trees and I'd said my good-byes already. I was leaving from here and not going home. I was going to drive today to Madison to talk to the first man whose name I'd found in the file. I had contacts in Madison, Reno, the state of Montana. I would drive. I had to get out. I never felt that. Usually I was housebound.

The detective was far away and I was not going back. I was closer.
I had a car. Maybe it had been a mistake ever to think anybody else
could find him. This was something that if it could be done, it would
be done by me and me alone.

"I'll come along," Danny whispered, his breath wet in my ear. He
looked at me with a long drill. "I need an adventure."

"No," I said.

"I can use it as a scouting trip. We can search and shop. I have a
credit card," he said, and he rummaged in his pocket and extracted
it, to show me, just the green plastic card all by itself.

Two young men dug the hard earth with awkward lurches, their
tails flapping in rebound to the ground's resistance, the shovel han-
dles vibrating. Gish had always been the very last.

DRIVING IN A CALM UNENDING SNOW, I was far away from any kind of
life. From here, it seemed my twenties hadn't been so different. I'd
had my college. I'd had my summer backpacking in Europe with a
boyfriend. I'd had breakups and long night conversations with Stevie
and Mai linn. But now I was stepping out of the parade. In New York,
school started tomorrow and I was already late for my job. I'd left
Racine too, with my suitcase of holiday clothes, my grandmother's
Oldsmobile and one credit card I wondered how long would last.

Still, away from it all, I felt I was living my one true life.

I had the map open on the seat next to me. I'd bought a Wisconsin
atlas from Boss's. I was driving to a J.D. Nash, who had signed eleven
letters in the documents I'd now read over again many times since
that first night in Boss's. J.D. Nash's penmanship had a backslant. I
hoped he was still alive. I figured I'd make it to Madison today and
from there, after—I didn't know, I hadn't let myself completely
think. It would depend. Everything depended now. I'd never lived
like this—so free and determined by outside things. I had a fate. I'd
tried too long to fight it. Now I would succumb. The last place anyone
seemed to have seen him, according to the found letters, was a tiny
point far in the Northwest. Ambrose, Montana, at a college called
Firth Adams. I'd found Ambrose in the library atlas. It was in mountains, near a slightly larger town named Galilee. I had the box sitting
on the floor of the passenger seat, the paper heart of the car. Half of
me whispered that I'd drive all the way there.

The sky seemed to be on my side. The afternoon luffed out timeless and silent in the soft fall of snow. I was the only car on this road, it was a two-lane highway, and driving was even and good. Occasionally, I passed a farmhouse far back in the curved banks of snow. The radio didn't work, but everything else ran perfectly, my cousin Hal used it and when he was away, Paddy Winkler would run the motor once a day standing still. Paddy couldn't get a license because he was blind. No cop would have ever come to our back road, but Paddy was a scrupulous person, like my grandmother. That was the cord of their friendship, a sympathy they found in so few people, really, around them in the world. Paddy would ride a tractor in the field, just for the fun of speed. "'S legal," he'd shout back at me, "nobody says I can't do it."

Many people seem conventional, but few truly are. My grandmother and Paddy were two such people. They would obey the rules always, even when no one, absolutely no one, was watching.

I was different. I learned morality and even manners, slowly, on a hard steep staircase.

I didn't want music now. I felt safe in the car, absolutely private. I thought about men. They seemed so far away. Jordan in New York seemed tinier now and more random than the dot labeled Ambrose on the map.

Little girls were supposed to go through stages of hating boys. But I never did. I thought of them too much. I always wanted something from one boy and even though the boys changed, I always wanted the same thing. And I never got it. I still hadn't.

The first boy in the world was my cousin Ben—and now he was dead.

Then came Carl Otter. In the class picture Sister Mary Bede showed me, he looked like the other seven-year-old boys, all wore the same crew cut, which made their heads look like certain pelts of fur. But he was the one I wanted it from then. He seemed to have a secret.

And he chose me, too. But it was different for him. I went over to his house after school. In his small backyard, he showed me how he hit the ball with a bat. The bat wobbled in his grip and he missed many times, scuttling down on the ground to retrieve the ball. He said his father was teaching him how every day, when he came home from work. I watched and felt the cross-armed impatience you get not just from wasting time but from wasting time when there is something important you should be doing. I was too pointed even then. Social life was already only a means. What I needed from him, this wasn't it. All the slow, average activities he found to amuse us I knew to be beside the point.

Even though we lived a long way apart, Mrs. Otter and my grandmother set arrangements for Carl and me to play. It didn't matter that he was a boy and I was a girl. Our friendship made something fragile, like the two wings of a moth, and these women respected it. Arrangements seemed ponderous. They worked them out over the telephone in advance, my grandmother shouting, Down Nine, can you hear me? Then you turn in at Guns Road, can you hear?

My grandmother drove into town to pick Carl and me up from school. Then, because I lived in the country, we used the best part of the day outside. I had butterfly nets and it was near summer, so we ran miles through the fields in pursuit of fragile color. We lifted the captured insects into jars, the lids of which my grandmother had punched holes in with a hammer and the end of a knife. She made us put grass in for them to eat. At night, she emptied them back into the sky. I found her standing on the porch holding the points of her elbows in her palms, the empty jars on the porch near her shoes. "There now," she said.

Carl came another day in winter and we made snowmen, large, wobbly globes that ceased to be spherical and took on the squarish shape of ballbearings. They became so big they touched our thighs and then they stopped where they were because we couldn't push them anymore. We ravaged the long front lawn. Behind us, we left the yard rutted with trails of snowballs. Jagged uneven tracks showed the frozen muddy earth. After three hours of our play, the yard looked like a white cake, eaten off and played with, left in messy pieces on the plate.

My grandmother never minded. She said, no, why should she, she was glad we had our fun. She was glad we could have some fun with just snow. But I wonder now if it was me and I lived in that quiet empty country, I'd want the snow to stay pure in its frozen steady waves, unbroken. I'd chase the children away.

Eventually, the car dwarfed in sunset, we watched Carl's mother drive up our road. My grandmother had coffee made for her and she wrapped warm molasses cookies in a bag for them to take along home. It was a kind of life none of us will ever know again.

Carl stamped his rubber boots on the porch while we said good-bye. My grandmother walked Mrs. Otter to her car so Carl and I would be private. We felt embarrassed standing where they could watch us. And it wasn't just them. The day with Carl was nice, but it wasn't . . . what? I'd wanted something out of it. Something permanent. I didn't know what it was. I thought I would recognize when I had it. And it would last. On the porch there, latching his boots, Carl said that he liked me and that I liked him. "Like" then meant something more hierarchical. But that was the end for him, all he needed. Then he was ready to run to his mother and go home. I wanted more and when I said, wait, and pulled his jacket sleeve, his eyebrows pushed closer together and he asked, what?

And that was the way it stayed.

The light passed out of Carl. Anyone watching would have thought that I was fickle and my grandmother sat me down and talked about the importance of keeping friends. But I hadn't changed my mind. All we ever did was play. I'd never liked that. I'd only endured it waiting for something else. And I finally understood that for days and years it would just be more of that slow toil. Whatever it was I needed, we never came close and the next boy rose into my attention. I saw the flicker of light behind in him.

I don't feel I missed too much in childhood. Play was just a taste I didn't have.

At Gish's funeral, I'd asked Sister Mary Bede about Carl Otter and she'd known where he was because his mother was active in the church. Carl Otter was stationed in Germany with the air force.

I stopped for gas. The station was red and small with one standing globe and the pumps, and the sky all around was deep with swirls of blue and white and a hint of gold, hidden like religion underneath. My one frail tie to my life now was through pay telephones, and Jordan screamed at me, "You better get back here, you were supposed to come home two days ago, I left flowers in your apartment—you didn't even lock your door—I was worried about you. School's already started and you flunked one class last semester. They're going to kick you out, Mayan. It's not worth it! You can find him later. But do this first." He was out of control, loud. But voices through plastic are always tiny and I hung up the phone. I was outside by a field of dry stubbled corn, dusted with snow. I thought of the flowers, dead by now, in my apartment. I stamped the cold blacktop and went back to the car with the hard steering wheel I could feel and my map out in front of me and I kept driving.

Those days in Wisconsin, when I was growing up, people worried about girls' bodies. My grandmother taught me, when I was too young to understand almost anything, that I should never take candy from a man in the park and never never let someone in a public bathroom touch me. It was always assumed boys would want to touch me. And this saying no was quite an alarming thing to explain, my grandmother's lips curled tense with purpose and her voice hardened. Because of course, generally, I was supposed to be nice.

But I was supposed to tell if a boy wanted to kiss, God forbid more than that. My grandmother needn't have worried.

I was the one who always brought up the subject.

I liked boys better than girls but they were small, too, fallible. The boys who, in the picture now, all looked old-fashioned with earnest foreheads and delicate hands, moved fluid with difference then. I had my favorites. But they stopped being favorites when I knew them and then they didn't seem enough. We played and did our homework, talked about our teachers. But they were no different. I wanted something big that would shake me through clothes like wind. I knew that was what my mother was waiting for, too. Even when she was married to an ordinary man who took out the garbage when she told him.

I grew up with women. Still there were men everywhere. But none of the ones I knew ever answered the mystery.

There was Paddy Winkler across the street. And the man who managed my grandmother's gas station. I knew the other fathers on our road. Pat Briggs talked to me about buildings and lent me picture books. I knew those men, and Ted the ice-skating pro and my boyfriends later, but they were not it. They were not it at all.

There was a time I thought they should have been. Once, not that long ago, I'd called Ted Stevenson. I'd tracked him down. He wasn't hard to find.

Then I called the orthodontist my mother had gone out with in Los Angeles, the man who had fixed my teeth. With both Ted Stevenson and the orthodontist, it was good, in a way, to recognize their voices. They seemed glad to hear from me too, our voices had something at the beginning of the conversation like, *there,* the last piece of the puzzle. I knew a lot of little things about them each, what they liked to eat in the morning, that Ted was a man whose mouth went a certain way, a person afraid to want too much for himself. He liked prime ribs medium rare, he wore turtlenecks, he cherished his car. He felt safest all alone in the basement office of the ice-skating rink. The orthodontist was a goofy man. I remembered his manicured hands, his wall-long aquariums, his rare fish and coolie loaches, which my mother overfed in the middle of the night and eventually killed, his trick lamps. He had lived a raucous indulgent life full of comfort. When I called him I found that, now, his children grown and living in other cities, he had moved back into the house on Arden Drive with his first wife, a woman my mother had never found pretty.

Still, after a while, those phone calls sputtered out. We hurried off the phone with promises to keep in touch and never did.

For the first moment, we rushed to the other to feel again and check what we had always known: we only lived near each other for a while in our lives, not because of us. That was all. There was never really anything there.

SOMETIMES when I was a child I saw a picture of a man on a billboard, or a man far away, someone I didn't know who looked a certain way.

ONCE, I SAT IN A FIELD, winding string for my kite around my hand and Chummy from across the street knelt to help me. Chummy's hands were big and dark from work. A man would be kind for a moment, bending down like a genuflection. Never for a long time. He would notice me, fix my kite and then forget. It was like that with orphans or half-orphans. People felt bad but they were busy. And you weren't theirs. They had their own worries. And there were kids worse off even on our own road.

For help anyway, your want had to show. After a while I tried to make that invisible. This was what made me seem hard. People said that. "You're a tough one such a one," they said, which meant they didn't have time. They decided I would take too much work. I was already too far gone.

You had to inspire people to save you. And they blamed you a little if you didn't.

And we weren't any better than the rest. After all my grandmother's admonishments about bathrooms in parks, we let Mai linn be sent to Hebron, the first girl Ben loved. Because her saxophone was too loud.

But that wasn't it anyway, kindness. No. Paddy Winkler was kind but old. His face seemed loose, eyes random, fluttery, uneven—he was not it.

I wanted power from a man, a different kind of power. People around me sure enough seemed capable. They could do things—but one at a time, piece by piece, manually. I wanted someone who could slip a hand into my chest without ripping skin, touch the center and bend that metal, transforming me. The nuns told my mother tests proved I was smart but not trying. Maybe I was bored? people asked. I shook my head no and meant it. And then I got in trouble.

The car skated over snow and farmyards split to both sides of the highway. A sign promised Madison in eighty-five miles. I began to consider where I'd sleep. I hadn't thought that far ahead.

In Racine, I wasn't the only one boy-crazy. All the popular girls were. And for the others it just came a year later. I had Emily over to my grandmother's house and we found hidden corners to have our private urgent conversations. We also played chess. Pat Briggs taught us to play. Emily never really took to it but he brought home a fancy ebony board and carved pieces from a buying trip to New York. "I know who Andy likes," Emily said. My breath hardened into something that felt like a wrapped candy just under my rib cage. Andy was the one then, for me, carrying the light.

"Who?"

"Emily," she pointed with a long finger to her own chest. She was probably right.

"And I know who else he likes," she said.

"Who?"

She pointed to me, with that same unpolished but filed nail.

The others all acted boy-crazy too but it meant more to me. For them it gave an afternoon's fun, for me it was hard serious. I thought of them all the time.

I was popular. Just be nice to everybody, my grandmother told me that when I started school—probably everybody's mother told them that then but by fifth grade they'd forgot. My being popular pleased my mother. Popularity was her goal in life, one she worked at too hard and too little. She won people fast and high, and then she'd do something bizarre and lose all she'd gained. Only the most loyal stayed loyal to her.

With my grandmother, it was all fine as long as it was girls. That she understood. But when boys started calling on the telephone, her mouth went lined. "What does he want with you?" she said.

I shrugged. I had the shrug that worked.

I was an advanced reader. Tests said so. I used this ability to read about sex in the small dusty section labeled psychology in the public library. Two architects in 1928 modeled our public library on the Parthenon, only smaller. "I like it better than the one over there," my grandmother said, after her first European tour. "Here they keep the pillars so nice and clean." I collected rocks at that time, and she'd brought me a little chip from the real Parthenon, labeled rock from the parthenon in her neat script.

Seldom used, except for Wednesday morning women's good-marriage-work reading group and Marion Werth's Family Tree Club, it really did smell dusty. I worked my way through psychology sitting on the floor, leaning against the old wall. I found little pamphlets on adolescence. I knew that word from my mother. Whenever she didn't like what I was doing, she'd sigh and say, "I can see you're going through adolescence." They were full of warning stories. One was called "Just a Friend." It was about two girls, you knew them, I mean you could have named them in any class—the Wanda and the Denise. Denise was friends with everyone. She didn't ever like boys specially, *for being boys,* everybody was *just a friend.* Wanda, on the other hand, Party Wanda, was always the first one to turn out the lights in someone's basement. Everything went along just like that for a little while, the book said, because the regular high school boys didn't know any more than Wanda did. But then, one night, Wanda got together with an *older boy.* It was dark, in a car, Party Wanda tried to stop him but by then it was too late. She got pregnant. Now who do you think has a greater chance for a healthy adult loving relationship with a man? the book asked at the end. Wanda or Denise?

It seemed dangerous but that kind of thrilled me. I didn't know what it was then, but I wanted to be taken like that, darkened out, overwhelmed.

I tried to talk my grandmother into letting me clean out the Polynesian room in the basement so I could throw a party there.

I was the one who always wanted to play Spin the Bottle and Truth-or-Dare.

The Briggses planned a boy-girl dance for Emily. That my grandmother understood. It was odd the things she liked and didn't like. Something appealed to her about the notion of a dance. She taught me even more steps and we practiced on the living room floor. I already knew but I never told her it wasn't going to be *that* kind of dancing. She became excited and concerned about sewing me a proper dress.

"Do you think it'll be long, floor-length?" She met me mouth-tight just inside the screen door when I came home from school one day. She'd driven downtown to Noble Fabric and Upholstery. She had swatches.

"I don't think so, Gramma. Not until I'm older."

I led Hughey Cartwright outside the Briggses' garage, by the Venus de Milo, saying I was too hot. He didn't get the idea so I put his hands around my neck and then he started breathing fast in little huffs and he kissed me. His lips were wet like worms.

I THOUGHT EVERYBODY else knew the thing I was looking for—they all had it and I just couldn't apprehend.

It was the secret no one told. The first time I thought I recognized a trail wasn't with anybody I expected. Not from school. It was with Stevie. He was just a boy from around home I'd known always. It was May and he worked after school and weekends picking strawberries for Grigg. It started in the old barn where we were just playing one day like we did a lot, after the truck brought him back from the fields. With a flashlight, we looked for kittens and mice babies in the hay. I lay on my belly, it was just my old clothes and my pants came too far up my leg. I would have never been seen in them at school. But my grandmother made me change out of my good things right when I came home. She didn't have enough to do all day. As soon as I took a thing off she'd start cleaning it and by suppertime, it'd be hanging back in my closet, ironed already. She didn't give me enough time to get dirty.

So I was crawling low with my hands and I felt something and then

I knew it was him, his mouth on my ankle. I started to shout, Stevie, don'—but then it felt good, a shot blooming. He crawled up on my jeans so his legs were over my legs, his front over my back.

"I'll show you something," he said. He lifted hair up off my neck. It was probably white under there. I felt a bite and then this prickly soft-rush. It felt under skin. He pulled up my shirt and did it on my stomach while I watched. He did something with his mouth, then lifted his face down so one eyelash brushed against my skin.

"Butterfly kiss," he said.

"Oh neat."

I moved other parts near him and I felt his knees on the back of my legs, his fingers pushing on my gummy skin like under wrists and the fine fluttery butterfly kisses. We moved in the hay and I started doing it too; it was like being under a gown, silk or something with threads or tentacles that moved all over you. He did it on my chest, my back, my neck all over, the backs of my legs, my face.

We were so remote, far from school or what we thought counted, it was just Stevie and me in the barn, nothing important. Except it was hard to stop.

Finally, we heard his mom on the porch calling him in for supper the way she did when she'd been calling for a while or when the dog was gone far away and he knelt, pulled his shirt back on and his sock up where I'd been on his ankle. He looked at me with those same eyelashes. "See you tomorrow?"

"Yeah, sure, probably. We're not doing anything. Like we ever do."

In his house, they always ate at five o'clock. His mom liked to have the dishes done and see a show that came on at six-thirty Central Standard time.

BUT THE NEXT DAY I walked home through Prebble Park and I had to stop and go to the bathroom. It was a bathroom with a lot of stalls and I left the door open a little, that was automatic by now, I'd been in there a hundred times in my life and I did my duty and then I stepped out of my stall and there was a guy there, an older guy.

He looked scary. His eyebrows met in the middle and he stared serious at me, without smiling, and said, "Take off your underpants."

I started doing what he said and when they were down, halfway at my knees and I had to start the awkward stepping out of them, I remembered I was supposed to say no and here I was doing what he said. He wore scuffed-up pointy black boots. They seemed enormous.

Now I had the panties off and in my hands and I looked up like for what to do next.

His lips were the color of the crayon named Magenta. "Give them to me."

But I didn't want to give him my underpants. "No," I said, but my voice was so small it was like a whimper or a mew.

"What," he said and then I didn't answer.

One hand clamped down on my shoulder and with the other he grabbed the panties and I pulled with him, I didn't want him to get my underpants and he let go my shoulder to grab them and I heard the *zup* of them ripping and then I just ran with my school uniform on and no underwear, up the hill under the water tower and out the park down Mason Lane, and then I finally tripped on a chestnut on the sidewalk and scraped my knee.

He wasn't anywhere. He hadn't followed. It was different to run without underwear and now it felt funny to be sitting down on my wool jumper and sucking the drops of blood from my knee with no panties on. In a way it felt good anyway, like running must feel if you're bald.

When I came to Grigg's fields, I saw Stevie bending and picking, legs far apart, in a line with other children. Every time he dropped a strawberry in the basket, he looked over his shoulder to find me and then he did. But I ran home into my house and up to my bedroom. I had to put on new underpants. I didn't want him to know. I was already used to secrets.

I opened my drawer, it creaked a little, it always did, and there they were, my pile of clean cotton underwear in soft Easter egg colors, pale blue, pale green, pale pink, bright white. My grandmother ironed my underwear. She ironed the shirts and panties flat and then once she folded them, she ironed the creases too. I put one on again and then I changed to my play clothes and went downstairs like the day was starting over again, this time normal, right.

"Well, hello," my grandmother said.

She had dough rolled for pie crust. I felt I had a million hours. I could loll around here in the kitchen and Stevie would still be waiting for me, bouncing a ball outside.

I never told Stevie or anyone. That was how alone I was. We all were.

It was Danny Felchner that day in the bathroom. I'd recognized something at the cemetery when he whispered in my ear, his voice went a certain way.

IN THE BARN, time dissolved. I didn't want it to stop and then once we did, it was over. There was never enough. Pleasure for me has always been that way. Like candy. Not lasting. It always seemed incidental to love.

My grandmother walked into the kitchen later where I sat scribbling my homework. I'd started a letter to my mother. My mother was away in California and Tuesday was my night to write to my mother. Sometimes in my bed I'd written letters to my father, but we had no address to send them.

"Mayan, say, when I took your clothes to wash, I couldn't find your underpants. I thought maybe they fell under the bed but I can't get down there, I started but ugh my knees are bad today. Would you just scoot up a minute when you're done and reach?" My grandmother's mouth went a certain four-pointed way. She hated to admit any infirmity.

My pencil stopped on the paper. She wanted doors bolted and windows barred, she always clicked the button that locked us into our car. I was always trying to prove we didn't have to be so careful.

"I lost them."

She frowned. "Well, how did that happen?"

I shrugged. My shrug didn't work that time. "In the park." Lying was hard then. I had to build, stick by stick.

"In the park," she repeated. She wasn't going to let me off. She adjusted her glasses on her eyes. She peered a way she never did. She was after something.

"They ripped. I climbed over a fence, I know I shouldn't have in my school clothes, I'm supposed to go around, but I just did and they ripped."

"So what did you do with them then?"

"I threw them out."

"Where? You didn't take them off right there, I hope, where everyone could see."

"I went into the bathroom and flushed them down the toilet."

"Well, next time you leave them on and come home. I could have easily mended such a rip like that. But you shouldn't be climbing fences, Mayan, you never know when a splinter just gets into your skin or those metal pieces stick up and they get rusty, you don't know all what's there, you could get infection. Tetanus. And Mayan, you know you should never flush a thing like that. Think of the poor plumber." Paddy Winkler had been a plumber and the life of their conversation was a mutual commiserating dismay and inexhaustible amazement at the objects people put into toilet pipes. He found them all and took them out—in their various states of decay. Because of Paddy Winkler, the house was full of Kleenex boxes. He contended that, due to harsh chemicals used in the production process, toilet paper should never touch the face.

"And he should know" was always her last word about that. Two of Paddy's grandchildren worked at the paper mill.

Later, she came back to talk to me. "Mayan, has your ma told you at all about menstruation?"

She hadn't but I already knew from books in the library. "Yes, Gramma."

"And you know all about that."

"Yes, Gramma."

"Well, good then."

There were certain things my grandmother wouldn't talk about. What she really meant was, you could just lose your virginity on such a fence and then what would your mother say? I could feel her resolving to watch out even more.

That night was the first time I noticed doing something I still do. I talked while I was warming into my bed, pulling the blankets around me, readying for sleep. I said, "Safety."

DRIVING ON THE EMPTY ROAD, I felt like calling Stevie and asking what went wrong. So I stopped at a gas station lot and dialed his number in Berkeley, but the phone just rang.

A little red sign in the shape of an arrow said Spring Green and I turned left. It was the middle of the afternoon. I hadn't planned this. But I'd always wanted to see Frank Lloyd Wright's school. I thought his grave was there too. No one I knew had ever been to it, living in

Wisconsin all those years. Pat Briggs had seen all the Chicago work and he'd heard Wright speak, but none of us had been here. This made the day feel more like a small vacation. I could take an hour for something that had nothing to do with my father. It was a curving farm road, low round hills on both sides. Farms, when they became visible, were set far away, napkined by neat, vast fields.

The farms looked rich and lush and large-siloed. I passed through a remote town, with its own main street, a restaurant and a clothing store that seemed to carry goods from a generation ago. Small hand-painted signs announced the Taliesen School. Because of the weather, a mixture of sleet and rain, fog billowed up from the ground and hung in creases of the hills and the building seemed to float like a kind of castle.

I took a tour, paying ten dollars to a woman with sensible shoes. With four others, I walked through the buildings. The main hexagonal room, with a grand fireplace, unused today when a fire would have warmed us, showed the erosion of years one would expect from wood and clay and stone. Water seeped in splits of the wood, the windows didn't hold tight. "Money," our guide whispered, and she shook her head every time we passed something cracked. "Dirty men," I remembered Merl saying.

Outside, I stood under an eave waiting for the rain to break so I could run across the gravel to my car. There was a bucket of workmanlike umbrellas, mud-spattered yellow canvas. I stole one. It could have looked like I was borrowing it to walk across to my car, then to drive it back; a person could've even believed I meant to use it then forgot, but it was not anything like that. When I took it I knew. I wanted to.

I stood in the rain under the umbrella at his grave, where his stone lurched, monumental and plain in this landscape. It was a large stone, ragged at the edges, a stone that could have been a plank upended, a bridge over a creek. Mamie's was only a marker in the ground, overgrown with moss and grass.

A man and a woman.

Later I found out, he wasn't even buried there. His body had been dug up and moved to Arizona by the later wife.

Driving back on that small road, I stopped on a bridge that had a little silver machine full of corn to feed ducks in the creek underneath. The ducks' feathers were ruffled from rain. A dime bought a handful and I threw the kernels, puckering the water's surface. The ducks darted and rushed, pecking their beaks underwater. I used the pay phone across the bridge. I felt like calling my old boyfriends and asking, Why didn't you fall in love with me? I called Paul first and got his machine. I asked him to write me a letter and explain. What a message to leave on a machine.

I kept on doing that on the road. I stopped at phone booths and little motels and called old boyfriends and asked, Why? Why did you stop? What's wrong with me?

That was my litany all across America. "This sounds crazy but I want to know."

I began to sense Madison. Dry cattails, some half frozen in the water, stood, stiffly guarding lakes. I wanted to stop and eat while it still seemed far enough away to be easy. I pulled up to a truckstop place and before I went in, I took the box out and locked it in the trunk. I picked a soft booth by the window and ordered eggs. Outside the window I could see the quiet snow.

"Have you called the medical school and told them you'll be late?" Timothy said, on the phone.

"No, not yet."

"You should do that."

"I'll just lie and say my mom's sick." I'd been using that excuse for years and it was always true.

"You don't have to give away that much. Tell them there's a personal matter keeping you in the Midwest."

THERE WERE certain things I knew my father wasn't. My father was not a pilot, for instance, or an elementary school teacher. It was like sunglasses, umbrellas and health insurance. Now I had all three.

WHEN MY MOTHER had gone away and left me with my grandmother, she called almost every week. She worried about my virginity. She saw it as some silk purse, all I had, about to be stolen.

"You've got to be careful with her now, Mom," she screamed to my grandmother on the phone.

"It's still here. It's not a sow's ear yet!" I yelled.

"Shht," my grandmother whispered. She too considered virginity no laughing matter.

My grandmother, though, studied dresses. She took an interest in my hairstyles. It took me a long time to understand. My mother, wherever she was, had ambitions for me. My grandmother recognized the years I was in from her own: this was courtship.

I got a hold of *The Joy of Sex*. The problem was I couldn't check it out of the library. I couldn't face Marion Werth and her polished pointed fingernails at the counter. And besides, there was nowhere I could hide it at home. So I read it every Tuesday and Thursday afternoon and tried to remember things. There were long sections about tricks from Asian prostitutes. I read the chapter about sleeping with a virgin. It was assumed the man was older and not. I remembered just what it said. I was ready.

But the boys weren't. They were all Catholics. That may have had something to do with it.

Even Stevie. Stevie climbed into my window at night. When his brick house sucked into the dark and returned to the landscape, he jumped out his low window and walked across the road, his head down and hands in his pockets.

My grandmother went to bed earlier and earlier. We both pretended I didn't notice. In our house, we'd both be in our pajamas right after supper, at seven-thirty, before the light left. I was the one who pulled closed the thick living room drapes. We both pretended that I'd stay up only a little longer to study. I watched my grandmother climb up the stairs with real keenness. She was getting too old to take care of me. She tried to hide her unsteadiness but I saw the lurch of her wrist on the banister.

She always reminded me to lock the doors. She felt bad that she was turning in first and that I would be up by myself. Every night, she meant to stay up later, but she was just too tired. Her body felt the mandatory order of dreams, already impinging. "Be sure and check the door" was the last thing she'd say.

She had already tried both doors twice. I changed from my pajamas back into my school clothes again. I hated being barefoot at eight o'clock. Bare feet on the carpet made me feel like a moist little kid. I couldn't have friends over, it would've been too weird and I couldn't really talk on the phone either, we just had one and it was in a corner of the kitchen, right under her bed. So I studied out of boredom and ate. I'd eat a cold pork chop left from dinner. I'd finish off the peach pie. I was always hungry those years.

And it was hours before Stevie would come. His family was young.

From the curtain I could see his father stretch in the small living room like a sulky lion. I'd be done with all my homework and whatever I was reading and more by the time Stevie shoved my window open. Sometimes I'd be asleep on top of my bedspread, not from exhaustion but the sheer boredom of waiting.

We'd mess around for a while and whenever I tried to bring us to it, he stopped, gasping. "No! I'm not gonna do that to you! You don't really want that! You'd be sorry. Just think you do now but you really don't. I'm not going to do that."

Stevie lasted years. Now I thought I really could have loved him if I wasn't always gone on other people. Still, there were his feet. Once, he came to visit me in California when I lived there with my mother. I was always bugged about his clothes and, I didn't know, his teeth. Underneath he was hard and straight and right. I knew that. But whatever we'd felt as children in the old barn, that was gone, completely gone.

I WAS APPROACHING the outskirts of Madison and I had to begin to think of things that were real. I had an address more than ten years old, who even knew if that was still good. People moved. In 1974 I lived on South Elm Drive with my mother. Nobody could have found me from that address anymore. And after that, I went to college and moved almost every year. I stopped at a gas station and called Madison information and asked the operator for the address too and sure enough, it was the same. Some people's lives were that way.

I asked the boy at the pumps for directions and he gave them to me, he knew the street, it was all coming out almost too easy. It was four-thirty, quarter to five, a home time of day.

I found myself hurrying back to the car, as if I had a real destination where people were waiting for me, setting a table.

HIGH SCHOOL had been the world. We had everything. I was only alive during my day there with the other kids. In California, I had no other life that I believed in.

I was okay in school but not that good. And it didn't mean much. I lived not for the classes but for the breaks between them, the ten minutes we had to get from one room to the next, and of course, for lunch, which was the height of the day. I always felt a pang when the one o'clock bell rang. Then there was nothing else until tomorrow.

The nuns in Wisconsin hadn't understood me and then the lay teachers in Beverly Hills didn't either. But only Sister Mary Bede who tried to teach us Latin in Racine had the nerve to say anything. She tried to warn me right before I moved away. The really popular kids, the nuns let go because they didn't make the grades. But I did sometimes. Sister Mary Bede read the grade on my paper and looked at me and shook her head.

"I'm afraid you're falling in with the wrong people," she told me.

"I don't think that will happen, Sister," I said.

"I pray for you every night," she said, reluctantly handing me back my test with the perfect score. "And for your poor grandmother. You've got a good head on your shoulders, it would be a shame to throw that away," she said.

"I won't throw that away, Sister." We both had our hands on the test paper. It lay on air between us. I grabbed it away too fast then, tugging it out from her dry fingers. I wanted to leave. Behind me I heard her sigh and the slow rusp of her sweeping, the broom across the linoleum classroom floor.

I had something new that day. One pant leg rolled up. I started that in Racine, when I got my district test back. The tests there were so easy. They didn't expect us to go to college. And they wanted to pass us, laying a hand on the tops of our heads, without having made us feel bad about ourselves. When I came to school that day with one pant leg rolled up, everyone stared. But since I was moving to California, they thought maybe I knew something. By two weeks later, the whole school, including older kids, rolled up one pant leg.

Just a few people took Latin in Beverly Hills High and the room was in the worst building, near the typing class. The teacher was a regular old woman who was fond of breaking out of grammar and telling us how each of her daughters had found her husband. For each one, it had been hard.

One thing I think would have been different if I'd been normal: school wouldn't have meant so much. The rest of my life I barely lived. All I cared about in my nights with my mother was that nobody from school would see us.

.   .   .

BACK AT HOME ONCE, at my grandmother's kitchen table, Paddy Winkler reached out and felt my face. "Tell me what she looks like now, Lil."

My grandmother had her back to us; she was fixing something at the stove. Paddy Winkler waited, hands politely folded on the table. He relished my grandmother's food. He had never had anybody to cook for him. In his little kitchen, he only heated beans and franks from a can. He couldn't see to cook. His fingers were dark with grease that didn't come off, the same way Chummy's were. My grandmother lifted up pieces of Czech coffeecake, rich and aromatic. Her hands were just manicured, in round ovals, a pale clear pink.

I sat at the end of the table, my feet playing on the metal bars under the chair.

"Here you go, Paddy, let me get you your coffee. Mayan, put out napkins, would you."

I gave Paddy his, you had to put a thing right into his hand. I'd been doing that all my life but now I was more conscious of touching. It felt kind of good. His fingers were rough as if you could feel all the lines that make a handprint raised up on his skin.

"I've been listening to movies on that TV Dickie and Stevie got me."

"What do you see?"

"Last night I got on that *Casablanca* again. Practically can remember it from the last time."

"Oh, you stay up late, Paddy, I can't stay up so late anymore. She does. This one does. But she studies. She's a very good student, she gets A's." She frowned like there was almost something wrong with that.

He reached out and felt my face again. "You didn't tell me yet what she looks like now."

"Ugh, be glad you can't see her, with all the makeup. She's a pretty girl underneath it, but out in California they all put on this charcoal, black around their eyes like raccoons. That I don't like."

It was strange the things she did and didn't like. She didn't like the makeup or the platform shoes I wore, but she liked anything I did to my hair. Little braids I made or dandelion chains, hippie things, reminded her of her own youth. "I think it's nice with the flowers, real real pretty," she'd say.

"You know, Mayan, the most beautiful women in the world don't wear makeup. Ingrid Bergman never wore makeup," Paddy said.

I gave my grandmother a look, like, what am I supposed to say to this guy, he's blind.

"Your grandmother don't wear makeup."

I skidded my chair back. "Well, I'm not the most beautiful woman in the world, okay, and I think I look better in makeup." I'd only started then, when I'd moved to California.

"Come back and sit down, why don't you, eat your coffeecake," my grandmother called. "To tell the truth, we don't care what you look like."

"S'all Greek to me," Paddy said and then spun in his wild laugh.

IN RACINE, we had had our own movie stars and they wore makeup too. They were girls three years older named Carrie, Corinna and Kim. Carrie eventually overtook the others because she got together with Enrico and they were one of those couples everybody watched. It was funny to think how we saw them separate for a year and watched them start to notice each other, like lines coming from two corners destined to intersect. Then they were the total couple.

Every girl in the school would have traded whatever boy she was going with for Enrico and every guy would have done the same for Carrie. You knew that. It was just something you lived with. And anyway, it wasn't about to happen.

She didn't let him take her for granted, even after. We all knew just when it happened, what day. It was their prom. Racine had all kinds of fancy dances even for young kids. It started with Cotillion. At the ninth-grade prom, Marion Werth and Eli Timber were still there as chaperones, her in a long colored dress and gloves that went up to her elbow.

We all watched Carrie and Enrico and the ninth-graders come to school different and hazy that day, the older kids. They took over the whole building with their happiness and their childhoods ending. Even nuns relented, studies flew out the windows into the air, I closed my eyes a minute and opened them and saw a swarm of numbers just over the sill like a moving haze of bees, we had every day left for learning, every hour every day all the next years and this was their only one prom.

Carrie stood calm and ripe, ready, nice to everyone in a way that didn't matter, seemed superfluous and thereby more kind. She inclined her head towards the nuns and that June day, even Sister Mary Bede felt charmed. The nuns with their other kind of faces looked with fondness at her too that day. They were letting her go ahead and go, and she and they both seemed to accept finally that it wasn't themselves, they each belonged to a system, a world system bigger and beyond their own powers to resist. In the end, the nuns didn't put much faith in willpower. For all their talk of phone books under laps and precautions, they themselves lived as women, with timid, curling nervousness, waiting to succumb.

Carrie had always been pretty; it wasn't only that. She owned something else that day. The color of her lips changed. It was a real red now, even in the daytime dullness without makeup. She'd put on weight and it went to all the right places the way it never would on any of us ever again. Her breasts turned up at the nipples like the stems of pears.

I was studying the way her brow went and how her ankles dipped and her thighs squared at the top. Everyone did that.

All the guys, the lay teachers and the priests too, and even Eli Timber, they all looked at her and you could see they were idly wishing they could do it, instead of Enrico. They noticed him with a new sharpness, almost like respect.

This was a warm Friday. The Monday after Enrico stood high, one of those guys: tall, thin-faced, incredibly long-necked, not serious. His red hair fell floppy in long tight curls, and his high beak-nosed face always roved open, ready for new interest.

You could imagine it: his high white butt, nose tipped up, eyes straight to her a plumb line, mouth pursed into something serious and small but only once. Enrico understood a hundred men and boys had looked at him and wished they could do what he was doing now. Naturally unsusceptible to solemnity or even the bands of concentration, still, numbers had not failed to impress him. And then too, she was his first girl, perfectly pretty. With her knees bent, her calves lay open on the bed, in the smooth curve of cut calla lilies.

Monday in school he was the same as ever but more, more with the guys, their laughter even easier and more free. She wore a gauzy dress and high sandals anyone else would have been sent home for, her hair pinned up on top of her head. You could see the whole shape of those legs through the dress. Stevie moved staring at her in the guidance office. She stood like a vase.

"Are you wearing a slip?" he asked.

"Yes, I am wearing a slip, Steven, and panties and a bra, too," she said.

I saw a priest and a teacher look right at her crotch, like a target, then away.

She still had her confidence, we saw that.

The last day of school, before I moved to California, I heard her in the bathroom, talking to Kim through the stalls.

"So he calls Thursday night and says, 'Hey, Cay, how 'bout Saturday?' I said, 'I'm very sorry, Rico, but I made other plans.' 'You did who-at?' he says. And I said, 'You didn't call and I made other plans.'"

I knew, even hearing her over the high bell sound of peeing, that she meant it. She wasn't going to change her other plans to see Enrico the way any of the rest of us would.

See, they had you after, because you didn't want to be a slut. After the once, they'd turned you into a girl sleeping with her boyfriend. That wasn't so bad. Some mothers would have died from heart attacks on cement floors, finding out, but for us, that wasn't so bad. It depended a lot on how you both looked, really.

But how could you leave him? What would you be then? A girl who'd slept with two of them? That was different.

Carrie was willing to hurl the risk.

Good for her, I thought, good for her.

"I always liked Enrico," I'd said to Eli Timber at the Briggses' Christmas party, "but I don't know if I respect him." By now Enrico already worked at the paper mill. For a while he'd been a salesman at Briggs's.

"I respect him," Eli Timber had said, "for being the first guy to get Carrie Hudson."

Carrie told me once, "You know how before you sleep with a guy, nothing works, you're always bumping into each other's foreheads, his arm's uncomfortable, you can never walk with your hands on each other, it's too awkward? Well, after you sleep together, everything fits."

But nothing turned out the way it seemed it would. Fifteen years later, Carrie was at home, working at Briggs's, bottom-heavy like a pear. Kim ran away to Chicago and became a fashion model in Japan. And when she came home, she paid for everyone, Eli Timber, Sister

Mary Bede, Carrie and Corinna. They all said she was real loose with money. They kept the clippings of her from the magazines. Nuns from other Wisconsin cities who'd never met Kim sent her cut-out picture to Sister Mary Bede.

MY GRANDMOTHER was always getting old. As if time were running out and nobody knew but us, a chestnut fallen on the sidewalk that she couldn't pick up anymore—I reached down to get it, my hand touching the stain on the cement, and when I rose our eyes met and we were in love for a moment the way anyone is in love, a man and a woman, a mother and a child. It was a kind of race. Could she stay standing long enough to deliver me, done, an adult? Or would she have to give me back to my mother? Even then, she'd lost her vigilance. She must have known something about Stevie. I expected her to stop me, but she didn't. She was tired. She climbed upstairs to go to bed at five after seven. It was more than tired. She was old. She didn't care so much anymore or she did care, but about different things, vastly different things than younger, headstrong parents. They had ego in their children, themselves planted over again like sex. My grandmother held something else altogether and what it was in her wasn't attached to me but by then to something high and vague as heaven.

All that time, I assumed, she was holding on to see me into college. We'd talked about college, the nuns and she and I in a conference room. This was during one of the times my mother was away without me. But my grandmother always seemed mild about college, veering into, We'll see. You never know, she'd say.

She would have rather delivered me to a husband. That would have let her rest.

FOLLOWING THE ROAD I was supposed to be on, I drifted into a windy, rising neighborhood of comfortable houses with shallow lawns and two-car garages. Lights began softening windows but there was still daylight too, a poignant winter blue. Finally I found the address and stopped the car. It was a stone house made with thin horizontal stones and a wooden garage door, shrubs lining the walkway. I stepped out slowly and straightened my skirt. I hadn't really thought that much about what I'd say to this man. The air smelled good, someone had a fire going. An open garage door across the street showed a boy mandering over a flat table of tools, his large, labile back. I remembered the luminous beauty of suburbs, the deep safety.

I walked up to the door thinking this was the same uncertainty I'd have when I neared the house that held my father, but it wasn't true, this was easier, and when I stood there hearing the doorbell ring through the house, what I felt was hot, real embarrassment.

Then I thought, what if nobody's home?

But a tall woman opened the door, a beagle beating against her leg, and she smiled, asking if she could help me. She was long-necked, long-faced, long-thighed, her hair pulled up and behind her in an oval bun.

"Is J.D. Nash here, please?"

"Sure, come on in. Jay," she called through the house, "you have a vis-itor." I followed her, her long feet canvassing the stone floor. Then the man emerged, blinking, fitting on a pair of thick plastic glasses.

He, too, was long-faced, long-legged and long-armed. And bald. One hand took the glasses down again and polished them on his shirt while the other arm was already out meeting me. He couldn't have guessed who I was yet. I knew he'd be nice. The sleeves of his shirt came down almost to the elbows.

"Do I know you?" He looked at me as if he were on the verge of recognition.

"No you don't. I'm Mayan Stevenson and, God—"

"Oh, I know who you are." He had a soft voice. I wondered if he was always like that.

"My grandmother got in touch with you a while ago."

"Yes." He nodded. His face was so long it seemed to be composed of two interlocking circular compartments. When he smiled, the bottom became rounder, cinching the middle.

"To find my father." This last thing seemed a confession.

He led me through a family room where two tall teenage boys lounged in stocking feet, long-faced, big-eared, blond. "Paula? I'll be in the office, this is Mayan Stevenson, Lillian August's granddaughter."

Now it seemed incredibly right that my grandmother had found this J.D. Nash. He was a civil servant. A blotter printed State of Wis-

consin Bureau of Vital Statistics covered his desktop and there was a
State of Wisconsin Municipal Authority paperweight, too. I suppose
that was just the place I'd expect Jackson Fenwick and my grandmother to dream up. It was the obvious place, the bureau you'd get
if you looked in the phone book for it. My grandmother had such
trust. If you were missing a person, you looked in the state of Wisconsin's lost and found. She had no idea what vanishing power she
was up against. He could disappear between the lines of an alpha-
betical listing, he could will himself invisible and remain forever.
I thought of my grandmother's weekly letters to me and to all her
relatives. She believed the systems worked the way they were supposed to.

"And my grandmother died now six years ago."

"Yes, I know that. I was sorry to read about it when we processed
it—you know, my department, Bureau of Vital Statistics, well, the
notice came in to me and of course, I recognized her name. I sent a
card, I don't know if it got there and you saw it, I'm assuming it did."
He said all this in a mumble with his long head near his chest.

"And now I'm looking for him." I tried to make a joke. "He's a
wily guy."

J.D. Nash smiled at me, bashful, as if I were really something. He
looked like a melon smiling, his forehead held the same slope.

"I thought you might call someday to do this. I'm glad you did"
was what he said.

This man had been waiting for me. Long before I knew he existed.
This was so good.

He bent over his desk drawer. "I'll have to look up the file. I can't
quite recall where I left things." His fingers raced over the file tops,
but he couldn't resist, even doing that, looking at me. I don't think
I'd ever felt that before: a stranger's fascination. I could have sat in
that chair, arms lax on the armrests, all night.

"We take in exchange students and we've had a number of them
from your father's part of the world," he said. "We had two engineering students and a medical student; last year we had a young
woman from India. We've got the two boys so when we talk to the
cultural group here we always ask for girls. And apparently we were
lucky to have her because they tell us everyone wants the girls."

So he was a man with sons and no daughter. He liked me. I was
secure in that already. There are the people who like you and the peo-

ple who don't, even if you work to make them. I knew I could get him to give me a back rub.

"Here. I do have all the correspondence. I think what I'll do is make you copies of this so we both have it." All of a sudden I was protected. I could have gone to sleep right then and there. I didn't panic anymore where I'd be tonight, food, anything. He said, "Now this goes back, oh, prettinear twenty years already. What do you say, why don't we just have some supper and then, after, we could walk to a copy shop that's open near campus and Xerox the papers for you then."

The line of men on the way to my father, they were all different, each one. They could have never been him. They were more like my stepfather or my mother's boyfriends, when both of us were sorry. I knew there was an underground trail of women who would eventually lead to him too. This guy liked me, though. He liked me easily after I'd tried so hard with the lawyer. I'd always had that—the some men who just liked me and the others I spent my life chasing.

And I felt he'd taken the search from me, like the box I'd been carrying. He could lift the weight and I'd follow. This J.D. Nash had some special interest in us. I didn't even wonder why. He was like all rectitude. I was just grateful.

He walked out of the door of his study, skating a little on the stones, calling "Paula," and I followed.

So there were homes like this really. I mean, you always kind of knew but then you think, no, everyone's life feels more or less the same from inside. Everybody has their forty-two thousand eight hundred and sixty-four minutes of happiness. But we sat around a plain wooden table, a modernish iron candle holder supporting candles with rich, wavering flames that smelled vaguely of warm honey. Dinner was like a restaurant. Paula Nash passed out a plate to each of us with a chicken portion, a sauce with some kind of liqueur and cherries and herbs and vegetables. Mashed potatoes. Green beans. Hot biscuits. It was just the four Nashes and me. The exchange student was at a lecture at the International House.

All of sudden, I felt sorry for the Briggses. I'd always guessed they didn't know how to live. But I'd thought that was just jealousy. Jay Nash was explaining who I was to the two boys and Paula chewed evenly, her forehead so high and rounded I thought, ballet, and then I bumped my elbow on the son next to me and realized I had someone on my left and I dropped my napkin and then, to make matters worse, knocked my knife down, too. When I was under the table retrieving, I saw Paula Nash's two feet, long and thin, the beating beagle held between them.

"So you're from New York?" One of the boys spoke when I popped up.

"Well, she's from Wisconsin, but she moved to New York. She lives there now."

"And do you like it there?" That son, across from me, wore glasses. I glanced at his brother on my left. Both boys were their parents' length, wand-touched, handsome. Their hair was corn-blond, their skin young and just fitting, their features rounded and tentative.

"Yeah, I do. I mean, it's a fun place to be young." They were looking at me for more and so I lied. "There's a lot to do. Lot of parties, and wonderful restaurants, museums." I was trying to remember things I'd read about in magazines.

"You're not scared or anything?"

"No. Oh no." I giggled. "Sometimes I even forget to lock my door."

At that Paula Nash looked at me sternly. It was hard for her to seem stern because her chin was rounded to her neck.

The conversation went on like that. I asked Paula if she worked. She did, she said, she was a nurse. Curtains over the long span of windows were almost floor-length, they left about three inches showing.

I sat back in my chair. So there were families like this in Wisconsin. Jay was telling me about his sons, that they liked to go ice fishing. He reached out and touched the smaller one, on the side of his neck below his ear. That was it—fathers. Those two boys charmed him without doing anything. But I did too. From being a girl.

Later Jay Nash and I sat in front of the fire. He'd made us a pot of coffee and lent me big hand-knit socks. He opened TV trays for us to write on. He had his glasses affixed again.

"I'm giving you both my numbers, my work number and my home number," he said, inscribing a clean manila file.

This helped me. I was used to things not working. I loved knowing where to find somebody. God, I thought, I am far away.

We'd already decided that I'd stay the night. In the morning, we would make copies of all the papers.

"So then you'll have the story from beginning to end," he said.

End, I thought, what end? There is no end.

"For example, I am not sure you know about the, as the attorney called it in one of his letters, the Cairo Caper. I notice that I'd written about that in detail, but then I decided not to send the letter. You're never certain whether you're telling people anything they want to hear or—"

"I want to hear everything."

"Well, I left it out. Later, I think I sent a summary of it all to your grandmother and so she in the end had it."

He handed me the file. "Now, this is the more detailed paragraph that I did not finally send to Fenwick, Stone and Arbinger."

I held the yellowed paper, marked with the State of Wisconsin Seal. "Apparently, events took a sad turn for Dr. Atassi after 1973. According to Firth Adams College, Dr. Atassi conducted an extension course tour of alumni and local citizens interested in Egyptology to the Middle East. The participants reported that Dr. Atassi was an amusing and informative guide through the Holy Land, the Pyramids and the Sahara. Several women particularly mentioned an enjoyable trip up the Nile. But apparently in Cairo, a group of women led by Dr. Atassi were cruelly deceived in a casino and were left stranded the next day when he disappeared. It was first suspected that he had run into foul play; however, it was later discovered that he went to Europe. He eventually made his way back to the United States and resigned from his position at Firth Adams College. He never returned for his papers or other possessions. A Firth Adams graduate later reported having seen him working as a maître d' at a restaurant in Southern California. Dr. Gunther did not know the name of the city or restaurant where he was reported to have been seen."

"That's a dead end," J.D. Nash said.

"Yeah, that sounds pretty dead end." We sat staring at the fire for a while. It was a clean stone fireplace, the flames leapt against the dull rock sides. I tried to think of my father in Cairo. On a camel. Casinos probably looked about the same anywhere. The line that got me was about him leaving his possessions behind at Firth Adams College. Maybe they were still there. A pipe, one of those felt desktop blotters with leather on either side. Maybe a cup for pencils and pens. I wanted it preserved, the whole office, so I could walk in and find the vertical-ribbed glass on the door, the brass peg, his jacket on it, a smell still in the sleeves. But of course, the things would be packed in standard boxes and stored somewhere. Probably thrown out.

I went slowly through the rest of the letters on the TV tray, thin tissue paper with raised typewriter marks, sometimes a hole where they dotted the *i*. Most of them seemed to be written by Mr. J.D. Nash to various members of the faculty at this Montana college. The answers to his letters all told one or another form of no. I finished them, closed the file. Montana.

"But," he said, "what I thought would be most helpful at this time, what we could do is check the indexes, the vital statistics indexes in likely states."

I guess he would think of that. Sometimes the world is wonderfully coherent, with a place for everyone. Officers of law and order, managers of vital statistics.

"Each state retains its own vital records," he told me, "and there's always an index to those vital records, a death index, a marriage index, a birth index. Do you know if the person you have hired explored any of these possibilities at all?"

"I don't think he did. What he did was he looked at DMVs and at credit—" At credit whats I didn't know.

"And he found nothing, huh?"

"No. Nothing of any use. I keep wondering if, do you think Firth Adams College would possibly give us the social security number?"

"Oh. Well, I bet he would. The man I spoke to there was a Dr. Gregory Geesie. He's there, in the file. He was, let's see, chairman of the International Relations Department at Firth Adams when your father left there in '73. It sounds like your father was marking time after that '73 debacle. You know, your father might've just been doing a fill-in job until he . . ."

Until he what, that was the question. "Yeah, it does sound like that, and it's been a while. So."

"But you know there's always the possibility that he did return to Egypt. On the other hand, given the life-style to which he had become accustomed, he probably didn't." He giggled a little.

We talked back and forth like old sisters chatting and speculating. Like my mother and her friend Lolly on the porch, going on about some man's absence.

How kind. How kind it was for him to take this up with me. He made it feel like it was our search, together. This was another person like Venise King I had to write or call if I ever found him. I could be bad like that. I never got in the habit of courtesies like thank-you notes. Emily sat me down and tried to instruct me at age twenty-two.

It was a funny thing, learning manners people expected from you as an adult. I was no one but my mother's child. And she had far too much rage in her to develop my steady good habits.

"I guess," I said, "given that he was in the US, it seems pretty steadily from '56 to '73, there's no particular reason we should think he's gone back to Egypt except that he's not showing up on any of these computer checks."

"Unless he took some a.k.a., you know, another name. If he were avoiding creditors, maybe."

"Yeah."

"That could be the case." He said that carefully, as if it could hurt me. That couldn't hurt me. I thought probably a lot worse. I turned to the side and through the dark window saw the moon, a yellow sickle moon. This was a good house.

"I tried calling information there in Alexandria, that's where he's from, and that was no easy feat. For one thing it's almost impossible even to just get an operator. And when they finally did get through was at three-thirty in the morning and I gave them the name, Atassi, and they said they had too many listed. They said there were a hundred Atassis."

"You know, I'm surprised I never met your father and mother because we were all students here at the University of Wisconsin at the same time, well, they were each a year older." The beagle moved between J.D. Nash's knees now. The beagle was long-faced too.

"It's a long time ago," I said. I wondered what made a man like J.D. Nash join me in this. I was more selfish. Still, good as he was, I would have rather had my father be my father. My parents were big, glamorous. My mother was popular in college. A Tridelt. She would never have gone out with someone like J.D. Nash. She should have, probably. "I wonder. Do you think I could talk to this Geesie."

"I don't see why not. You can identify yourself of course as his daughter. He was quite talkative when I spoke to him. Now he might be guarded for fear of offending because obviously that was a great—"

"Nightmare to them, sure."

"—blow to the college. Apparently they were just starting an International Relations School and that was—"

"I was thinking of driving out there tomorrow. I thought I could do more there, maybe find people who knew him."

He looked at me a way I'd seen before on faces. "You're going to drive from Madison to Montana?"

"Just 'cause it's been years since you asked them, who knows, maybe another student saw him someplace. Or some old friend. Or mistress. I mean, he might have even called them for a reference. I worked for the Wildlife Sanctuary in Racine once and there was a person who wasn't very good at all and left under bad circumstances. But still, three months later, somebody ended up calling us because the person had put our names down as references."

"When they leave under bad circumstances they still call."

"But I mean sometimes people are incredible, so who knows." I must have sounded pretty bad. I remembered all of a sudden, he just met me today.

But he kept looking at me from the side with a kind of awe.

I SLEPT PERFECTLY sealed in the guest couch Paula Nash made up for me. The beagle's tail beating low on the door woke me in the morning. After breakfast, I followed J.D. Nash's car to the Wisconsin Bureau of Vital Statistics, where we were the first ones there, standing at the Xerox machine, looking out at the lake, frozen blue. We both had mugs of coffee with the Wisconsin State Seal printed, and the badger, the state mascot, drawn.

"Well, what I was going to suggest last night was looking through indices in the most likely states," Jay Nash said. "Now, I would guess that California would be one likely state."

"It sounds like it, doesn't it, California and Nevada."

"What other states would you suggest?"

"Idaho and Montana, I guess. Maybe Washington. Oregon."

"I don't think we'd find him in the Midwest," he said, "he'd land on one coast or the other." It was odd hearing him say that. Mr. Wisconsin. He had on a Wisconsin tie clip. "I can contact my counterpart in each of those states. Each system differs, of course. The completeness of the indices varies from state to state. Some states have them in very poor condition and other states have them computerized so it's all over the map. If—what I think we should do—see if you think this makes sense—should we check the death indexes first?"

Something dropped a long way, then landed. "Sure."

"Because, I would suggest death and marriage. The only way a birth would show up is if he had a remarriage and had more children."

"Well, that's always possible."

"We could check them but in California, that's a big state, with immigrants from everywhere. That name probably exists in California."

"I bet it doesn't. I've done a lot of looking and it's never turned up. It's a really rare one."

"Except in Egypt." He giggled at his own joke, a hiccupy laugh. I liked him. "Okay, well, what I'll do then is start with California, although—they've had a recent change and I don't know the new person in California, Bill Shields worked there for years, it would have been easy with him, he probably would have done it as a favor, otherwise there could be a charge for looking into the files."

"I'm happy to pay for any of that."

The old copying machine huffed and churned, clanking like a homemade robot.

"Let me see what happens. I will find out the charges and I'll get in touch with you."

"But let's go ahead with it and I'll definitely be happy to pay, that's no problem. And let's do both death and marriage. I think the marriage isn't totally unlikely. The children does sound remote. But you never know."

"Let's now do the first two and if that fails then we can consider the third." The copied file was complete. He gave it to me. "Why don't we say we'll talk in three days, what is that, Wednesday."

He walked me down to the car and asked me if I knew the way out to the highway. I told him I did.

"Yes, you were in Madison too, weren't you? I always wondered why you didn't look me up."

I didn't say anything. I didn't want him to know that my grandmother had never told me he existed.

BEFORE LEAVING MADISON, I called my mother. I didn't know why. This was where she went to school too. She was the first one in all her family to make it to college. That was something. Sometimes I remembered a part of her life like that. I don't think I ever gave her enough credit. She'd met my father here. I missed my mother. I did.

"Oh, do me one favor," she cried on the phone, with a real fist of energy, like her old self. "Go to the student union and get a piece of black bottom pie."

My mother had always harped on that when I was here for a year and I never went. The famous black bottom pie.

"Mother, you were here in 1955. That's more than thirty years ago. They're not still going to have it."

"Yes they will!" Just that made me so sad. I slumped against the phone booth.

And then I did end up driving the Oldsmobile to the student union and it wasn't even a restaurant anymore, I know she pictured a wood-paneled restaurant. It was a cafeteria now, full of college kids from anywhere and a number of wide-faced farm kids, but I took a tray and went through the line and at the dessert spot I said, "Hi, this is crazy but my mother came to school here in 1955 and she told me I should come and get the black bottom pie and I'm sure you don't have it anymore, but I thought I'd check anyway and just—"

And then the pimpled boy handed me a white plate with a maroon border and a white and yellow piece of pie on it, a thin rim of chocolate, poppyseeds in the cream.

"Uh-huh. Black bottom pie. We still got it."

9

I DROVE IN A CLEAN morning spell and made good time. The signs rose clear and green, I felt grateful as they ticked by, reminding me I was still on the right road. The day opened light and spanning, low horizontal as if I could see everything, like objects on a table. Silos, barns, the occasional round trees. I touched the hard shelf of the dashboard with my right hand. The pale sun warmed a little and I was glad this car felt solid. My grandmother's cars always worked. She bought only Oldsmobiles, a new one every five years before they ever gave any trouble. This, her last, had under eight thousand miles.

Wisconsin ended. And the long Minnesota road widened in daylight. I stopped in Saint Cloud for gas and stood up, stretched on the square tar lot.

Down the block the stationary windows of small midwestern stores shined pearllike, waiting for the hour to open. A row of head dryers flipped back like broken bird necks at the front of the Chatterbox Beauty Shop, and a uniform store displayed the different colored plaid jumpers for Catholic school children. The door of the diner was already open. The man filling my gas had a stern Swedish face and blond cropped hair. No one here was going anywhere. Nothing was strange about their day. They could hold it before them, curved in their hand like a small crystal globe.

I DIDN'T LOSE MY VIRGINITY with who I should have right. Hardly anybody I knew did. And that morning in Saint Cloud it seemed to blame for everything and so nothing would be even and balanced until that was set right, like a coffee cup, fallen on its side.

I drove down the slow main street. People crowding the door of the diner looked middle-aged, wearing plaid jackets, hands hooked around the steaming white mugs.

It was hard to think about that even alone in a car in a place in Minnesota I'd never been before and probably never would be again. Hard to admit. My mother-cherished virginity, she was so sure I'd give away wrong. And I did, like an always present cheap childhood glittery bauble that cannot be found and values only after.

Nobody I knew lost their virginity with the one they should have right. And all of our grandmothers did it proper, in the slow and grand procession.

My mother had had one love before my father and I blamed her for him, kind of. She was always going wistful and saying she should have married him, no matter what her father said. His name was David Kale. " 'Course then," she'd say, sighing, ready to wind up and do something material in the world, like get in the car and see about dinner, "then I wouldn't have you."

Whenever she said that she usually followed with how glad she was to have me and nothing in the world would have been worth not having me and all kinds of life-and-death proclamations; still I never missed the level truth in her voice. She didn't know.

Emily still had her square of cotton panty, where she bled. She carried it in her purse during college even though she didn't speak to the guy. Frank, I think his name was. It was just on ski weekend once.

Mai linn just said, it doesn't matter. Bodies don't. What is first any-way? A number.

In science, there's a certain kind of confidence you either did or did not have. They called it hands. Whether you had good hands. In jazz, Mai linn said you wanted your horn to have legs. Poets were sup-posed to have an ear—a pitch-perfect ear. That part of you—the authority—didn't mean you had no doubts. It depended on whether there was a bottom. I had no bottom. Some part of me was ruined for love. I thought confidence with love came from knowing you were wanted on the earth. Could you be wanted by something other than your parents?

Talking about love, I never sounded right, like other people.

But I'd tried.

All the things I told no one, I said them in bed. That was love for me. Telling them the truth about my father. And I did it with every man I slept with. Night became my time for secrets, a cave we'd dig together that could go on and on, as long as we could last, all the way to China, where everything was foreign even street signs and even-tually words meant nothing and all we had was touch and murmuring sound.

I think I scared some of them shitless. I had two kinds of boy-friends. Jerks and the ones who helped me. The ones I thought I was really in love with and the ones who were really in love with me. I used to think that way: *really in love.* You either were or you weren't. I sat in ice cream shops or teahouses with my friends sucking a long time on straws discussing it.

When I was with Stevie I had a whole run of other crushes, one after the other. And when I was with Bud Edison, whom I loved but who never paid enough attention to me, I had other guys who helped me, day to day in my life. They gave me back rubs, they spent hours with me moving my grandmother's furniture around the tiny apart-ment like a puzzle. Everyone knew I wanted to find my father. That was something of mine always.

"Maybe the man doesn't want to be found," Paul said, when I called him from Saint Cloud. He was sitting at his Justice Department office with a mug of coffee. "You ought to leave the guy alone. He obviously wants nothing to do with you. The guy's got a right to live his life the way he wants to."

"He has a right to leave his children?" I said.

"You're over eighteen," he said.

He had always looked at me like I was a little less because I had a father like that and he blamed me for dwelling on it. He was the kind of man who believed in playing up your strengths.

It was an embarrassing thing to admit: my father left me. You knew the guy was going to see you a different way. It was something that happened to you. And a lot of the guys, I thought, would tend towards girls who were new—nothing had happened to them yet. I was someone left already. I wondered if that made me easier to leave again. A wrapped gift left behind on the conveyor belt. I'd begun to notice in the last year how many girls in the medical school wore pearls.

Even with the men who touched their daughters there was that: they were wanted. Mai linn yearned for the crystalline sugar garden of an unwatched childhood, a father with a clean lap, newspaper held, simple, interested in the daily meals. In a way, Mai linn and I had the opposite problem.

I lived out my childhood unwatched.

It was worse for Mai linn, though, telling guys in college. They're different, she said, but after none of them look at you the same.

We never wanted to be married too young, none of us, Emily, Mai linn or me. I always thought, twenty-seven. Now I was almost twenty-nine. Everything was late.

I was driving on an empty road. It was Sunday. Back in New York, weekend nights lit the sky with parties. This morning, people would be tangled asleep in couples, just beginning to blink awake. What did they do then? I thought they went out for brunch in the middle of the day, sank back into looseness from Bloody Marys and wandered the afternoon away in impending aimless sadness, the anticipation of separation and Monday morning.

But I was in the middle of the country sealed in a car and this was taking time. I was spending my youth trying to find him, and why? After, I'd still be alone.

I could find him and then I'd go back to my apartment broke and be behind in school and no better.

But I'd tried to forget about him and just live. I'd tried to do all the things I would have done if I were not waiting for anything at all. Sometimes when people asked, I said my father was dead.

Most of the years since I'd left my mother, I was looking for my father, but not like this. He was something I thought of, with fingers drumming the tabletop, eyes on the far horizon out the window. But I thought I could do that without disrupting the parade of my normal, sequential life. I talked about it in bed at night with men and in the daytime I did the regular things. I thought I could get by like that. I could find what I wanted, it felt like then, deep in the middle of the night, at that one first moment of entry, that was always new.

But that didn't last. That can't. Then in the late afternoons, I would wonder again where he was. I'd gather my backpack over my shoulder again and walk towards the evening of books.

I might have been losing my mind in that car or I might have been learning the things I needed to know for my life, I couldn't tell which, but hurtling in the straight line of that still landscape I feared as I always feared given wisdoms, could I keep them and hold them, or would they just streak the dark with their penmanship and fade before the word was through, like fireflies on a Wisconsin dusk, flickering, never captured, writing the story of the world but not on anything so stable as paper or stone but in time so that it was legible only through the decipherment of memory, which was always changing.

LONG FLAT PLAINS spanned out around me. The silos began, leaving blue, sharp-bladed shadows. They felt dangerous and important and I sped up each time, passing, until I couldn't see one anymore in my mirrors.

In college, I went for pilot types, strong and quiet, with sharp features so, my head on their chests, I heard heartbeats like underwater through leather jackets, and then owlish frail boys, who seemed they should be always lifting bell jars to examine specimens. Stevie Howard really was a pilot. He was in the air force three years before college. He slung his arm around me when we walked anywhere, those days, and his arm had weight.

Paul's eyebrows pressed together over me in bed. "You know what my father said once?" A terrible look passed on his face. "He said shiksas are for practice."

College was the first time I lived like everybody else. I ate the same food, lived in the same dorm, I had pretty much the same as all the others.

But I found too much beauty in mystery. This is not a way to happiness. The invisible always seemed more true to me than the people I'd always known.

Those years, after I slept with someone I always said, I love you. And once I'd said it once, I kept saying it, again and again, times when I really meant other things.

Like, *Where were you? Why don't you call?*

I sometimes stood before a mirror and bit my lip, thinking, if.

Enough people had loved me, for a while, or tried to. But I didn't want them. I made excuses. They seemed too small. I needed something else.

I'd tried and tried, for ten years now, at love. I'd tried the ones I thought I loved so much I didn't even know and I'd tried the ones who were there, who, every time I saw them again, I winced. I'd had enough boyfriends to know it was something in me. And now I'd stopped.

I remembered my father calling me once to the car. The house stood a long way from the road. This was still my grandmother's yard. He told me he would always be my father. No matter what. No one else could be that.

And nobody else ever was.

MY GRANDMOTHER LIVED like a regular respectable woman of Racine, but she never liked to get out of her everyday clothes. She hated the fancy in life. She made fun of it all, oh, yah, sure sure, I got all such stuff, I've got the purse and the belt, matching, oh yah sure, I can go with the best of them, sure. A religious woman, she felt odd in church, with the lace veil resting on her head, the gloves, the belt and purse. She had the unfussiness of a woman who had been beautiful all her life. And I supposed she liked that—you could see that in her cheeks sometimes. But she also felt ashamed of being noticed. She was so shy, a man whistling at her outside the hardware store made her feel wrong, like a stranger's touch would, as if they took something off of her.

IN MENOMONIE, when I'd stopped for coffee, I passed an old woman standing in front of a restaurant studying the menu on a wooden placard. It was a vaguely health-food place, pretty cheap. She held a square white patent leather purse in both hands in front of her. I knew she was pricing things, trying to decide if she should go in. She was an unassuming woman, curled in a little, wearing a cloth coat.

When she noticed me looking at her, she startled a little, like a bird. I turned away. She wavered a long time. I watched from a little ways off. Now, my grandmother would have never been like that. She always stood straighter, the light of beauty fell around her, like a ring of petals, and she had enough money for a meal all her life, without worrying. When I remembered that, it was a consolation. The woman I was watching was more like me.

It took years to understand that I was not the same as my grandmother or my mother, that we were each marked at birth, as with a fingerprint on our soul and our faces, and that our lives, close as they were once in that white house, would move in solitary ways.

I WAS VAIN ABOUT MY HANDS. I liked my hands. I knew I was not a woman who could just wear anything and not worry about it. My grandmother wore men's flannel shirts and an old plaid cap, she still looked herself, maybe more so, like a jewel set plainly.

I was always working at things. Stevie said once to me, "I love you because you try so hard."

But my hands—my hands I didn't have to do anything to. They were fine. I didn't wear rings or bracelets and when I saw them, the way your body surprises you in mirrored lobbies or small oblique car windows, they pleased me.

SOME OF THOSE MINNESOTA towns were rich. The road wound around a lake and wide old-fashioned mansions stood looking at themselves in the water, a history of all power and peace. It was too late to be rich myself. Even if I was, it wouldn't have been soon enough to save my mother's life for anything. I imagined her sitting in the place with tiered lawns, like Beverly Hills High School was, but quiet, a thousand times quieter. Her in a green long robe, a sad expression on her face, sorry, but glad to see me, infinitely kind. She would have a hairbrush on her lap.

"Comeer," she'd have said, "I want to brush out your hair."

I let myself wonder again what we would have been. This was weak: I'd lapsed into the soft reverie a hundred times. By now, my wishes like that were all for the past.

. . .

JUST OVER the Minnesota–North Dakota border, I pulled to the side of the road for a Dairy Queen. It was a small old stand, its roof shaped to resemble the curved tip of an ice cream cone. Red picnic tables, their paint peeling, ranged outside on the blacktop. Mostly, I supposed, for the summer. Still, the sun pressed midafternoon bright now and there was just a thin drape of snow on the plowed fields. I bought a butterscotch sundae and sat outside at one of the wooden tables. The air was cold but clean, with a sharp hook in it. The sundae tasted good. Even in a chain like Dairy Queen, quality varied a lot. It depended on who owned it, how clean they kept the machines, what grade ingredients they bought, how much they cared. You never knew which stands were good unless you lived there. There was a great one in Egg Harbor, Wisconsin.

This was a real one. You could taste the clean high-alcohol vanilla, the butterscotch, the nuts were fresh. I sat, studying the little yellow plastic cup while I ate. Then a giggle near me took my attention, the way a bird's call can sometimes interrupt even pure concentration.

The girl had a particularly long neck and a flat chest. Her shoulders sloped down. She had old-fashioned curly dirty-blond hair and a few pimples, regular bad-food pimples, on her forehead. On the East Coast or in California these would have been saladed and cleansered away, but here they just stayed, part of youth, like the late season flies on these picnic tables we shooed with our wrists but didn't even mind that much. Under the table, her socked ankle stretched long and thin beneath the end of her jeans. Then his hand reached her foot, peeled the shoe off, and placed it on his lap. He was big cheeked—an Indian—with solid arms. He had dark eyes and eyebrows that slanted up. His features fell even and simple. From across and under the table, they kept moving, touching in different ways. His butt left the bench a second and he leaned over to kiss her.

"Don," she said in a low, tomboyish call, because her wooden ice cream spoon had been knocked on the splintery table. Then he was back down and their hands toyed together. Now his foot roughed her thigh.

Oh. They were ten years younger, maybe more. In back of the small flimsy building a tractor started up with the hecking putt of its motor, we heard it jolt over the half-frozen fields. I finished my sundae still watching them, my spoon scraping out all the corners of the tiny yellow cup. Now they had long finished too but they still dallied there, toying together, the sky the palest blue, clouds high and calligraphic above us.

I got back in the car and there was nothing else on the highway. I just drove awhile. I was jealous, of their fun.

Just two kids raffing and fooling on a picnic table.

A dirt road led off the dull highway and I followed it, stopping the car at the edge of the woods. Snow had started again. I just waited awhile there. Close lines of snow fell around the car on all sides. Past the birches and pine, I watched a silent valley, trees and a mud-rutted road. It wasn't the world. I found the world beautiful, especially then. Snow fell in even stitches on the blue-green fir, the young white birches. I was just not right.

This was my only way of praying.

I tried to tell myself and remember: I had had my happiness too. My forty-two thousand eight hundred and sixty-four minutes of it. Some afternoons I'd felt all lined up right so the rest of life was in me and a part of me and I'd look at my hand and believe I was the same material, hair, skin, the cartilage of knees, gelatin of eyes, as the sky and the ground, the leaves stuttering with molecular press and collision, all of us built out of the color and substance, the paint pots of the periodic table, each a different weight, texture, feel, but still the same, endlessly breaking down and remixing. I believed that, sometimes.

The times like now when I drove to the end of a dirt road and sat holding the steering wheel, no one could see me and no one would ever have to know. I could bear it. I didn't mind that much. After, I would be in the world again, caught under the big net of light and thunder and snow with everybody else. I started backing out, blowing my nose. Driving towards Montana, the road climbing, I began to think maybe this was the wrong way to be. Twenty-eight and fixed on one thing. Still, I kept going. When you've wanted to find a person long enough and you are closer than you've ever been, you can't stop even if your faith changes. I would be better to finish, I knew that.

I began to count the things in the car, every time I stopped somewhere and got out. At gas stations where I filled up the Olds and used their bathroom and walked to the pay phone booth standing on the corner of the lot, I counted seven. The box. My purse. My earrings on each ear. The suitcase. Raincoat. My atlas. The umbrella I'd taken from Frank Lloyd Wright. And when I came back, from the phone booth or diner or gas station bathroom, I'd count again. I didn't mind anything, the whole trip, wasting time, if I wasn't losing any more of what I had. Every time that machine clacked over my credit card, I was losing.

I drove with the window open, a sharp cold dry snow taste in the air. The pale luffing winter sky going on as far as I could see, I started thinking what I'd do if I were a bride.

I knew all that Emily was accruing.

If I were a bride preparing myself for something sacred, I decided I'd start a long time in advance and give everything up. That would take a long time. I knew how I wanted to die and I guessed, as I thought about it, this would be the same. I would try to make up something to the people I'd disappointed, to the ones I hurt or left. I would give away my things, one by one, taking care to match them with the person. I would tell my secrets, one to each friend, until the compartment was empty. It would be a sort of confession. Years before she died, my grandmother starting giving away her things. "Just take it," she'd say, "I don't use it." But she never told her secrets.

Then I would make my days simple, eating little, drinking only water, keeping order among what I had, my few clothes clean and folded. I would own less and less. I would go to sleep every night early. I would give away more and more, write one letter each night before bed. Then I would begin to be ready. I would slip into the sheets, clean, with my hair brushed out. My bed would be solid and my sheets stiff. My stomach would be thin as a wafer. And I would wait like that a long time.

But sex in my life had never happened that way. That was a picture in a locket, an ancestor. I unlocked the door, shaking it, into the messy apartment, hoping the toilet's flushed, wishing I'd kicked things into closets, and I turn the light out while we undress because I'm wearing the bad underwear, ones pink from the wash. It's late, we smell the sharp grasping urgency of drinkers, the sheets feel gritty but warm, his skin is there, we begin and even unholy it is eternal, outside of time.

I PASSED TOWNS named Wing, Mott, Pillsbury, Fordville, Hamlet, Oberon, Warsaw, and Berlin. Every midwestern state has a Hague. I drove through Mechanicville, Kellogg, Witoka, Money Creek, Pilot, Lark, Carson, and Killdeer. I almost turned and followed the signs to Yucatan, North Dakota.

The only place I could ever picture was my grandmother's old house. I sat once with my grandmother and Paddy Winkler in the living room, each of us braced with TV tables. "Can I you get anything, Paddy?" my grandmother said, looking over to the television. We had it turned up, loud for him.

"Well, these waltzes don't do much for me, Lil. But those taps, them I like. I heard that Fred Astaire and Ginger Rogers on the TV the other night too."

She liked to watch dancing on TV. She followed the variety shows for the tap dancing. "Oooh, can he dance that little one. Listen to him go. That I like to see."

Can he ever dance—this was high conversation in Racine. My grandmother copied phrases she'd heard and repeated them. She applied herself diligently to learning the forms so she could put as little of herself into the world as possible.

"Can he ever!" Paddy replied.

It was easy to feel like a genius in Racine.

Just then a squadron of teenage girls tapped onto the stage of Ed Sullivan.

"Oh, lookit there, can you hear, Paddy? It's those little dark girls and can they ever dance. Even the real tiny ones. Lookit her go."

Outside on the porch my mother was sitting with her friend Lolly, both hugging their knees and looking out at the sky. They were talking about beauty and the habits of men.

Bud Edison said once, "I always really admire a white guy who can dance."

"Stevie can," I said, almost like an accusation. Bud Edison knew about Stevie the way we both knew about each other's loves before.

"I know what it is," I said and I did know just then, all of a sudden. "It's failure." Things like dance were compensation. It was the same thing with jazz. Stevie went on for years, during vacations, and then we started up in Madison. Once when we were still teenagers, Paddy Winkler called the police and reported him as a burglar. He lay under my bed while they prowled out around the edges of the house with their flashlights. The next night he came back.

After mass, my grandmother's car bobbed outside like a moored boat, always there, running, never late. I was the last one out. I always looked up once more as if he might be on the ceiling.

"Man, you haven't even seen me dance yet," Stevie said, curling a hip shove in the bathroom, before the shower. With him it was hard to describe. I knew his small vanities, the way you do. "He's a fixer-upper," I told my college friends, apologizing. He lived on people's couches. He'd just come back from the air force. He wasn't going to be enrolled until the next semester and he was much older than all the freshmen. But that wasn't really it. There was once we took a walk in a woods he knew. It was near dark and when we were inside the trees, a thunderstorm started and sheets of rain pounded with violence, echoing, and we had no clothes for it, nothing, we hugged our chests freezing, and he laughed softly, something mean to himself on the top of the voice, neck sloping down forward like a yoked animal, neither of us knew any way out and he was not surprised.

In the warm indoor pool of Cap Chief Motel at midnight in North Dakota, my arms and legs swam in the profound trust of being unseen.

I WAS STOPPED BY A SIGN, just a little green square on a weathered post by the side of the road saying, HEBRON, INCORPORATED, POPULATION 1,109. So it was here, it existed, this name I'd always known. I slowed the car and coasted in. My head turned back and forth, eyes greedy for the look of the place. It was ordinary, a flat blond brick elementary school with pipe-metal monkeybars in the playground. Oldish long cars stalled on the main street. Decent well-kept houses stood in a neat grid of tree-lined streets. It looked like a greatly distilled Racine.

I tried to imagine what it was for Mai linn arriving here, shipped through the agencies, papers all filled out. She might have pushed her cheek against the bus window, turned away from other passengers, she might have been crying. But, springing down, in her tennis shoes, she could have thought, this isn't so bad. Better than the orphanage in Racine where the cemetery ends, near the coal heaps and sulphur piles for the paper mill.

The downtown here was two tree-lined blocks. Standing with her duffel on the pavement, she might have even had a moment thinking, I lucked out.

When she'd moved into my aunt's house, she told me, she remembered the first time she woke up there alone. She was sick and everyone else had gone to church. She walked through the rooms and opened all the doors. She fisted the piano keys, just for noise in the empty house. She sat naked on the upholstered living room furniture eating a plum, letting the juice spill on her belly.

The Hebron family might have been standing in the parking lot where the bus halted, hands on their hips, waiting for her. They would have had her picture ahead of time, maybe the kids made a poster, WELCOME MAI LINN TO HEBRON.

In this flatness in winter, the sun fell a certain thin yellow on the sidewalk. These are not the things you say in letters, how you felt yourself alone stepping in your new Ladies-Auxiliary-of-Racine-bought white sneakers down the rubber-treaded bus steps onto the yellow blessed sidewalks under maples and elms, shoving your hands in your pockets, goofing a grin on your face, your new family watching, wanting them to like you but fighting the want at the same time because you feel dumb and bitter and far away. But you go with them down the main street and then you all pile in the station wagon, you in the front seat, the mother clambering big and awkward into the back for the first and last time ever, and then you see the house, a box-shaped brick house, pretty with a pointed roof and a big screened-in porch. You sit at the table that night and she serves coconut cake with lemon filling, a new one she cuts open in your honor. Mai linn wrote letters but you don't write those things. Most slow every minute things you don't ever say.

Then I saw the low rectangular ice cream store, Rudy's, and the parking lot in back where the Greyhound buses stopped. One yellow school bus was parked in its long slot. I stopped and went in. I ordered a grilled cheese sandwich and asked to use the telephone book. The kids behind the counter were teenagers, this was their after-school job and their movements had a slow play luster. Klicka, Kenneth, was listed in the book, 3939 Grove Street. I wanted to at least drive by the house. I could do that, anyway. And these kids could tell me where the junior high was. Bell Junior, I remembered it was called, from Alexander Graham Bell. I wanted to do more, though. I wanted to knock at the door and ask to talk to the father alone and say something to him, land him blame. But I couldn't do that without calling Mai linn.

I got so eager then I took the sandwich outside with me and held it in one hand in the phone booth on the corner. From in there, I could hear the slow drift of cars on the wide main street.

After two tries, I found her. The secretary of the music department went to get her from a practice room. "Guess where I am today?"

"Yesterday was Minnesota. You in Montana yet?"

"No. I'm in Hebron."

"You are?"

"Yup. I wish I had a camera. Maybe I'll go buy one."

"I could tell you where. The Camera Corner. Right next to the Jandrain's Music. There's one camera store and one music store. But you better be careful. We're never going to be able to pay your credit card bill. You know the total?"

"Unh-uh. But I'm only going to do this once. I don't care if I have to pay it off forever. I'm going to start at the bottom and get my life totally organized after. This is it."

I told her what I'd done in the last day and a half and I heard a small steady noise.

"I think you're running about thirteen hundred." She had a mathematical memory. It was all that was left of her genius for high school science.

"Listen, Mai linn, I called because I'm here and I kind of felt like going to their door and knocking."

She didn't say anything a minute. I could imagine her twirling the cord around her wrist. "What for?"

"Just to tell him it really happened. That he didn't get away with it. That you survived and are doing fine. Doing great."

"I don't want them to know where I am though."

"Listen, I probably shouldn't do it. It's just a whim. I'm sitting here at the ice cream parlor, outside, I mean, I'm eating a grilled cheese sandwich."

"Rudy's? You're outside Rudy's?"

"Yeah."

"On the corner of Main and Sullivan?"

"I guess."

"Hey, let me think about this."

"You don't have to. It's probably a dumb idea."

"Let me call you back in a few minutes. Give me your number."

I gave her the pay-phone number and then I sat in the booth finishing my food, the wash of slow life all around. One old woman with a scarf tied under her chin passed and looked at me sharply. A car slowed across the street and parked. A man got out and walked briskly into a store.

Then the phone rang. "I'm going to fly out and meet you. It'll take me pretty long probably, but just go to Dickinson and check into the Airport Ramada and I'll find you when I get there."

"What? No, I'm sorry I started this, but don't. You'll end up in the same shape I'm in. You have to stay and practice."

"But I want to. I'll only be a day. I'd like him to know that he thought he was doing something absolutely in darkness and he thought he was completely unwatched and I was just a kid, a yellow kid and I had no power and no recourse. He did the greedy thing to do that's always been done, he had more and he knew he could take what he wanted and not get punished. I know what he did. It's in me. I'll tell him I'm thinking of writing a letter to the superintendent of schools."

"Are you really thinking of that?"

"No. I don't want the hassle. But I'll scare him a little. I want him to know that someone is always watching. I want him to live like that from now on, looking over his shoulder."

And then I had the afternoon to wait. Dickinson was less than an hour's drive. I thought I'd just go and wait at the airport. But I wanted to be clean.

On the main street there was one old black brick building that said Deacon Hotel, but I didn't want to sleep in Hebron. I wound around until I found Bell Junior High, but it was locked, not a school anymore. I drove back to the elementary school I'd seen. The floors echoed and I found myself in a tiny bathroom, marked GIRLS, with tiny toilets, sinks that hit my thighs and a long rectilinear mirror. There was a bubbler just over knee high. I washed and combed my hair and put on something better. My shirt had a dried reddish stain where I'd spilled catsup. Things weren't lasting. I knelt down and drank from the little bubbler. The water was warm and nickel-tasting.

Outside of Dickinson, big handmade signs stood along the highway. SPORTS SHOW, STARK COUNTY ARENA.

And I passed the huge pale green domed building, the late-day sun glittering on the many cars quilting the tar lots. Then I thought, What the hell, and turned around. I parked, locked my six things in the trunk and walked across the long lot to the entry where I paid the five-dollar admission fee. I strolled up an improvised aisle where

International Harvester Tractors were displayed, gorgeously, next to power boats. I gave a dollar to the raffle for a catamaran. I stood in line with numerous children to catch trout in three huge tanks of water. The kids walked with the dead fish in plastic bags. I got almost to the front, and then I thought of the fish smell in my grandmother's car and ducked under the yellow cord that kept the line.

I just ambled up and down the aisles of equipment. Fishing poles, water skis, a fleet of nineteen orange-and-white snowmobiles. None of this would I ever use. I took a light interest in the colored flies, the oversized crop machinery. It was no more or less than most of the days of my life had become. I had veered off, out of the procession, and all of time had this quality of precarious lightness, subject to tilting over into another life altogether.

The airport told me that the first flight in would be at midnight and so I did what Mai linn had told me. I checked into the Ramada and left a key at the desk for her.

I slept dimly, rising up into the strange air, then sighing and slipping under again. Finally, I heard her key in the door.

"Should I get up?"

"No, I'll come to bed for a while."

I heard her unfastenings and droppings and the strange room felt more curved and round and I fell asleep with her weight so I could touch it with my right hand.

We got up late and took showers and dressed. I sat on the bed combing out the tangles in my hair. It was so nice to have a friend with me here.

She pulled up her jeans and tied on suede shoes. She always dressed like that but she stood staring down at herself with a crossed brow.

"You look fine."

"I was wondering if I should've brought a dress or something. I'd kind of like to prove I've gone up in the world."

I shook my head. I couldn't say why, but I knew that wasn't right.

We dallied in the hotel. We swam in the pool. We didn't want to get to the house before he was home from work.

Mai linn, all those years later, gave me directions to Hebron on a back road.

"Now I'm nervous," she said. We were still two blocks away but they were straight blocks and we could see ahead through the filtering chestnuts.

"God, I'm almost as scared about this as I would be meeting my father."

"He's not my father."

"I know."

"My father wouldn't have made you nervous. My father was sweet. A gentle guy."

Then when we parked the car and sat there a moment, I asked her if there was one thing she wanted from him that he could give her that would help her in her life. People had asked me that. And I didn't know.

She sat in the car, miserable, and said, "Tickling."

I just looked at her. She had to know I wouldn't get what that meant.

"When I came there I was ticklish and when I left, I wasn't anymore. That and a few other things. Little kinds of pain. Like you know, you've seen how I can touch my hands with matches."

I had seen Mai linn do that. It was a kind of trick. But that trick did not seem something he could take away and the tickling not something he had in him to give back.

Mai linn didn't want to come up to the door with me. She didn't want to see the mother or the sons. One was just a baby when she'd left. So she was going to wait in the trees behind the old junior high, a block and a half away. I had to get him there.

I didn't feel really odd until my heels creaked the wooden steps up to the door. The car glittered across the street. I stood there a minute smelling the fine edge of rot in the air, from melting snow. Then I knocked. A woman opened the door, wearing an apron, saying, "Hullo, what can I do for you?"

I told her my name and that I was a friend of Mai linn.

Her face endured two acrobat flips before she said, "Oh," and stuck out a slick wet hand for me to shake.

"Daddy, there's a friend here of that little Mai linn," she called into a room I couldn't see. I heard the mumbling underwater sounds of a television. "He'll be right out. I'm just frosting a cake," she told me. "Come follow me into the kitchen." I stood there while she emptied the contents of a box mix into a bowl, measured water and then stirred. She shook in a few drops of food coloring that came out a deep orange but then mixed to a thin pale yellow. So she used mix. The empty batter box still stood right on the table. And frosting is so easy, I was thinking. It's just powdered sugar and a little butter and milk. That was all.

"So where did you say you were from?" She wasn't old, only about fifty, and competent, making a routine social conversation the same way she armed the spoon in the bowl. Now she was spreading the pale yellow frosting on the cake. She did it nicely, swelled apostrophes of swirl, so by the end the whole cake would look even and professional.

"I'm from, uh, Boston, and I'm driving to Oregon. To see my dad." I didn't want them to know anything true. Not that she seemed so interested.

"That's nice."

Her cake finished now, she lowered a glass cover over it and immediately pulled open a drawer and counted out silverware. Then she began to set the table. "Well, you know, we haven't seen Mai linn for quite a while now. I'm surprised she even gave out our address because I don't get a thing from her, never a card on my birthday or the kids', or even a call on Christmas. Never a word."

There was nothing I could say to that.

She took a hot pan from the oven, her hand in a quilted glove. She cooked the way she no doubt did other things: with the proper equipment, updated regularly, and in perfect order. The pan held scalloped potatoes she set on a hot plate. From the refrigerator she took out parsley and chopped it, then sprinkled it over the dish. She was a woman unlikely to fault herself. Crouching down on the balls of her feet, she opened the broiler. Pork chops. They smelled good. She poked them with a fork, checking. Then she went into the other room, her hands on her hips, and called, "Daddy, come talk to that little Mai linn's friend because then we're going to eat in a few minutes. Scottie," she called up the stairs, one arm bracing the banister, her back arching, "supper! Get your hands washed now." A blast from a stereo jolted up in volume.

I bit my nail while she turned away. This wasn't working out right. They were going to eat and she'd set three places.

Then he came out from wherever he was. I tried so hard to look at him that everything went fast. He was not a large man. He wore narrow, stiff-looking slacks and a button-down shirt under a vest. The **vest** was mostly wool with two suede panels. His face seemed multifaceted like a cut stone, more than octagonal. "I haven't taken him out yet," he said.

"Oh, you better hurry. That's our dog, Moxie," she said. "Here Moxie. Here Moxie Moxie." She coaxed the dog from under a low table with her hands, squatting down on her heels.

He lifted the leash from a peg by the door and fastened it onto the collar. He seemed a man of small movements. I walked out with him, down the porch, then left on the sidewalk under bare, high elms. Good, this was the right way. At the end of the road we could see the playground, gold and empty in the still late-afternoon light. I couldn't see Mai linn but I knew she was there, in the small stand of trees. They were pine trees, not very tall. Beyond them you could see an old and peeling playground merry-go-round, the kind made of wood and piping that you ran to make it go on its own and then you jumped aboard and held on and rode round and round that centripetal whirl.

"So you know Mai linn," he said. He tapped a cigarette out of a pack from his vest pocket and lit it carefully. "She ran away from here," he said. "We never saw her again."

I kept looking at this man, a high school teacher. Band leader.

"Well, she's doing real well now. She's a musician. Getting her Ph.D."

"Is she really? Well, that I'm surprised by. She played that horn here too, but I thought she'd end up in trouble. She was kind of a troubled kid when she was here, always playing her horn all hours of the night, you couldn't stop her, my wife had to send away for special ear plugs."

The dog was rooting out a hole under a hickory tree, straining at his leash, then squatted in the compromised position every animal on the earth assumes, relieving himself, glancing back over his shoulder at us curiously.

" 'At's okay, Moxie, uza good dog," he said. When the dog finished and came trotting proudly back to our ankles, he turned again on the sidewalk, my heel hitting an old hickory nut, half eaten out by squirrels, its fibers and planes like the inside of a tiny skull. Oh no, not this way, I was thinking, but we were moving on, the park and its trees glittering in the last gilt light across the shallow street. We didn't say anything for a while and the corner where we'd turn again to go back to the house came closer and closer until finally I knew there was a chance nothing would happen. The house would come into vision and loom bigger and bigger and Mai linn would stay hidden in the trees and he would escape inside again without me having done anything.

"Well, give us her address and I'll drop her a card sometime. I'm glad she pulled herself up and made something of her life." He shook his head, dropping the cigarette and stamping it out with his shoe. "Like I said, I'm surprised." He shook his head again as if he still couldn't believe it.

"I know what you did," I said.

He didn't answer. His profile stayed forward as if I hadn't said anything. But then the dog saved the day, turning and straining towards the abandoned playground. We crossed the road and I wondered for a second if I really had said the words out loud, everything was so much like before. We still didn't say anything and the air was very quiet and the trees came closer and closer and my throat was closing and then we were there and nothing happened and I thought he would look at me and see through my skin to everything and I would be wrong.

He tapped another cigarette out of his pack and now cupped his hand around it, flicked the match away. He shook his wrist then and profiled the cloudy, darkening sky just the red tip alive, brighting the dusk. "I don't know what you're talking about," he finally said.

"Yeah you do." My voice was more level than I'd thought it would be, saying it, and behind him I saw a tire hanging on an old rope from a large oak tree and the strip of worn-away grass below it.

He looked at me sharp like it was easy not to believe me because I was a crazy person. I knew that gaze; I'd been caught in it with people aiming at my mother. And my mother had done it to me.

"Don't believe everything she tells you," he said. "She's a liar. I can't say we were sorry when she left."

I blushed. Mai linn did lie, I knew that, I could tell just when she did. She lied when she was bored and wanted to make something a little better, or when she was trying to get out of something. Or when she was really scared.

"But she didn't lie about this, though," I said.

Then Mai linn stepped out from behind the broad trunk of a tree and started walking towards us, her hands in her pockets. Her eyes were dark and her chin squared. She looked straight at him, without wavering.

The dog whimpered against his owner's leg. The man yanked the dog's leash up and looked down at it, deliberately, he patted the dog's head so we had to wait for him to finish and look up again.

Mai linn stopped a few feet away from him.

He raised himself up and looked at her and pulled at the dog's leash again. "Come a Moxie," and turned the dog away from the trees. He dropped his used cigarette, ground it down with his heel. Then, he looked sideways, as if it were nothing, and said, "What are you doing? Why didn't you tell me she was here?"

"I wanted to see you myself."

He shrugged, tapped out a cigarette from his breast pocket again, lit it, scut the match down. "Now you seen me."

They were at angles. He still wasn't facing her straight. She knew when to be silent.

"Listen, I don't know your friend, but talk to me after you've raised children and taken in foster kids who are messed up to begin with. I felt sorry for you. It wasn't your fault you were sneaky. You did what you had to do."

"But you could have been different. Instead of what you were."

The dog was rooting in the grass and then he snaked free of the man's hand and sniffed further, belly almost flat on the dirt.

And then all of a sudden they were alone. He didn't follow the dog, but moved an increment nearer her. Her head bent down like a flower too heavy for its stem. I was a third. Don't, I felt like saying, but they started walking away towards the old school. They stood almost like lovers, both their shoulders square and even. I didn't follow them, I thought I shouldn't, but I didn't want to let them out of sight either. I went a little ways and sat down next to the curb. The dog made a disagreeable snuffling sound near my knees.

They walked around the playground lot and then they started down the street towards the house. When he turned and called, the dog ran back, dragging its leash, grateful to be wanted. For a moment I felt an absurd jealousy.

Near the house they stood and waited for me. He was still smoking.

He shook his head, bent down and rubbed the dog. Then the wife appeared on the porch, another mixing bowl in her arm. "There you are. Your supper's ready. Scotty's sitting at the table."

"We're writing letters to people," I said in a plain voice.

He was already walking in, mumbling to the dog. He didn't even say good-bye.

The wife closed the door sealing him inside. She clearly saw Mai linn and closed the door anyway. It was easy to hate her the most of anyone.

We walked back to the car, like a home in the dark. Mai linn shook her head. "Let's get out of here."

SHE DROVE WITH ME as far as Williston.

We stopped at roadside stands and ate things we knew from childhood: French fries, wrinkled at their ends and translucent with dark grease, root beer floats, biscuits and roast beef sandwiches, even though Mai linn was most of the time a vegetarian.

"Mai linn, you know her homemade cakes are just mixes. Pillsbury. The cheapest kind of mix even," I said.

"Oh, I know, she always did that. I told you she used powdered milk."

After a while, Mai linn said, "You know, sex is the thing, though. I can never go through with it without some bad idea." She jabbed that out, eyes straight ahead, chin fair.

"What do you mean, bad?"

And she said, "No, really bad like one person having power over another or one of them a little kid." She snorted. "Wonder where that comes from."

I believed her absolutely and I knew what she meant because her first time with the artist in San Francisco, she'd told me she kept her eyes closed and it flickered back and forth between two ways, the one where she was a girl on an altar, sacrificed, laid on a clean white cloth, and the other, some ancient queen and him a servant, a boy just being used, meaningless, a pure mechanic instrument of pleasure.

"Remember your infection?" I said.

"Sure."

When Mai linn and the asshole artist started having regular sex, she got allergic. A rash spread all over, her nipples cracked with infection, oozing a yellow liquid, her eyes closed to slits, dry and red. She was going to Berkeley and the doctor at the student health center kept making Kevin June take away one thing at a time: his shaving cream, soap, deodorant, shampoo.

"He doesn't use shampoo," she'd told the doctor. "He just washes his hair with Ivory soap. He grew up kind of poor. He's proud of it. It's one of his things."

She bled for nine weeks. The doctor never found what it was. That was around the same time my periods pretty much stopped.

"You think we'll ever get normal with this?" She opened a window and was dragging her hand outside. The air was cold but the sky was wide and blue with dreamy wisps of cloud.

For me, what I imagined most of the nights, was a first time. A nice good way for it to have been. "I'm not even sure how unusual what we do is."

"It's not good."

"No."

"I mean it's not what you'd wish for for your kids."

"No. I've thought of that with Jane, like when she's old enough. I can imagine her with a guy, like that blond boy who lives next door to them now, and I can imagine them so she's not more and he's not more." They hated each other now and didn't even know how much they were friends.

"Yeah, but she's little. Who knows what'll happen to her."

"Hope nothing. At least it wasn't your parents. Your parents would have taken care of you if they'd lived."

"I know."

The day seemed to billow out into eternity. We went on like that in our consoling fugue. I thought of her ticklishness but I was afraid to say anything. I couldn't see how it would be any different.

"I saw this cartoon," Mai linn said. "At school the professors have cartoons on their doors and you can't believe some of the stuff they put up, but one was this couple in bed, and the guy looks up and says, 'Wait! For a minute there I couldn't think of who to think of.' And I thought that was really funny but then I thought this guy, he's a pianist, he has it up on his door, it was printed in some magazine, obviously other people thought it was funny too."

"Do you think Klicka's the reason you're gay? Because that would be something maybe, that didn't remind you of him."

She looked at me a way. "That was what he did, most of the time." She shook her head. "No."

We stopped at the Alpine Hunter, a supper club that had all the midwestern signs of fancy, for a real meal before her plane. We sat at a square table with paper place mats over a maroon cloth. Our waitress was a large woman bundled into her uniform and apron. She delivered us thick-faceted glasses full of ice water. The ice was crushed and as you held the heavy glass, it tinkled.

I turned the place mat upside down and started scribbling. Mai linn had gone off to find a phone and check the flight schedule.

"What would you like, Dolly?" the waitress said and I told her I was waiting for my friend.

"Sure enough," she said and swayed off. I liked to watch a woman gracefully manage a large pair of hips.

I drew buildings and a road with tumbleweed. Corners of a room with a fireplace. Mai linn slid back into her chair. "Eight o'clock," she said.

The waitress returned, bending near. "So where are you kids going?"

"How do you know we're going anywhere?" Mai linn said.

"Let's say I have powers." She smiled.

The restaurant was mostly empty, but a man a few tables away said, "Excuse me, miss, could we get some more sour cream?" and she reluctantly sashayed away, promising to return.

"Which means we don't look like we live in Williston, North Dakota," I said.

When she came back, we told her what we wanted. I wanted pork chops and Mai linn ordered a steak and mashed potatoes. For dessert we wanted two pieces of that white cake with yellow filling. I wanted vodka and Mai linn wanted gin.

"So you kids are on some kind of journey, I can tell, you're not just vacation gals."

"We're going to find our fathers," Mai linn said.

"You know, I can tell things about people," she said, "I knew I saw a journey around you two, I could see the color."

"So read our futures," I said. "Tell us what happens."

She shook her head, as if I'd laughed in church. "It's not so easy. I'll try later." She looked over her shoulder at the metal counter where two of her plates waited, steaming. She looked at us a moment putting one finger on each of her temples. Then she had to go and get her plates.

WE LOOKED AT EACH OTHER and laughed. We laughed with our mouths closed so it went deeper, shaking us inside. Everything now was a bonus and after. Mai linn pointed at the waitress's legs. She was wearing maroon bobby socks. This was hilarious and every time I looked the socks made me shake more. Just on a whim, this was really unlike me, I loomed up and bent over and stuck my fingers under Mai linn's arms and poked her ribs, and her mouth shot open and sound came out but it wasn't laughter at first it was a bottled explosive hacking almost like a choke, but it went on even as people around us looked and she ended up laughing in that desperate temporary gulping way you do when you're being tickled.

Our waitress delivered our meat. Double pats of butter were running generously over the top of the steak and each chop. I'd forgotten that they did that here. We hadn't eaten like this for years but we knew the only thing good to eat here would be meat.

I drank three vodkas.

At the end of our meal, the waitress sat down with us, propped her face on her fist and looked hard into our eyes.

"I can't really do this right when I'm working," she said. "I'm just doing this here because my old man walked out on me and I've got three little girls at home. But let's see you." She turned to me. "You have a long way ahead of you. I see restlessness. I really do. Whatever it is you're doing, you're not finished yet."

"Does she find her dad?" Mai linn said.

The waitress looked at me skeptically, as if she were appraising. "I don't see a man anywhere in your aura. Unless he's sort of way off to the left side."

"And what about me?" Mai linn said. "Do you see pain?"

The waitress stood up then with the strangest expression. "Yes I do. I do see pain," she said.

When we started laughing then, uncontrollably, another look came over her face. She thought we were laughing at her.

WHEN HER PLANE was in the air, I got back into the car and drove in my stockings until I was out of town. The sky rolled over my windshield, a light show of sunset, dense orange clouds, pink-bellied, higher purple wisps floating in a clear blue. When it seemed dark enough, I pulled over and changed into jeans. He was worse than I'd imagined, Kenneth Klicka. At first better—just smaller, no monster—but then worse, with no flicker of conscience, no curiosity or regret really, nothing at all.

I kept thinking of Emily. This week she was shopping for bridesmaids'shoes for Mai linn and me. The big dilemma was whether we should also be wearing hats. I hadn't told Mai linn about the letter from Interlochen. I pictured the envelope fatted with light, time stalled in it, a miniature Hebron, the sun-rained sidewalks, the short bubbler in the school, the perfect-looking cakes with yellow filling between the layers that when you bit into them were sweet with poison chemicals.

I KEPT DRIVING, drunk and a little crazy as the roads climbed and winded but I thought it was better this way because I wanted to get to Montana tonight, no more delays, I wanted to wake up tomorrow morning in that mountain valley where I would go over every inch and touch every tree and walk the same ground my father had. I'd look into each person's face with a question. And then I could go home and sleep. I yearned for my own bed, to start over again right.

My headlights fuzzed the dark and confused stars, making dense ghosts before me who then receded into the plain, insect-voiced bush of night. I rolled my window down and a sharp cold hooked in with the sounds. I counted the high small towns as I passed and the miles of highway between and sometimes I ran the middle of the road, crazy, swerving turns, almost missing, it seemed impossible I could drive so tired and dizzy but I did. The vodka lasted less like a drink than a drug and the night bent closer, the stars like mean stones, isolate, protecting their own beauty. I wanted to sleep but something in my heart kept racing, skidding back, and it was so desolate here I was afraid to just pull over to the side and lie down in the backseat. I was afraid of who would wake me and turn me over. The towns, when I passed them, stood dark and prim, miniature, the only other traffic an occasional truck rumbling by shaking the road so I clutched the steering wheel harder and tried not to change anything, to go straight until it was over, like a natural disaster. And then, finally, I saw signs and it was there, Ambrose, and I drove down into it, pieces of fog flying through the radiant mist of headlights, like freed veils loosened from a bound and beautiful face. Mountains loomed huge around the town, dark and hard. I passed a wood sign that said it, FIRTH ADAMS COLLEGE, so I backed up and drove through that gate and on a winding road that led past lawns and buildings. I kept driving slow, looking for any light. Names of my old loves came and numbered the dark buildings. Then I saw one bar of light. I drove to it, parked, necking over to scan the backseat, count, counting was hard, my vision doubled and blurred and I did it again, to check. Six. Six. Yes. I rolled up the window, got out, the cold wet air set my stomach to swirl and so it rose higher into my chest and I wavered, holding the car roof for settled balance. The stars above seemed to beat like something pulsing. Locking the car, I kept bending and trying, it was like fitting thread through a wavering needle, farsighted, and I tilted on the grass, still like driving the blind middle of the road, across and back the line, drunk and under the swelled night clouds and sharp stars and cliffs of the rocky great-shaped Northwest.

I pushed a huge wood door and behind a curtain, I saw angels, stuttering, sandaled, standing in light. They were men with men's feet, lines of hair on arches like veins in a leaf. I'd not believed in angels but that was because I hadn't understood that the feathered wings were floor-length. They hunched up from the shoulders, formed massive heavy plates and curved higher than the old men's heads. They swept down on the floor about eight inches past their heels. It must have been like dragging around a weighted train.

A woman lay belly-down on a table, it looked like they were plucking wings from her back, from the plug where they all grew from. She wore a leotard, and then I saw a huge trapeze swinging from the ceiling.

"Ware you?" someone called. I just watched and liked the air, splitting with peals of light and jewel, I leaned back against the rough door and let that wood take my weight. I was acclimating slowly to the light. In front, others rushed around, angels and kids in black clothes. The noise kept coming from different places and then all of a sudden, something opened and I understood these were people shouting at me. My hands found each other and worked and I spoke.

"I'm lost. I'm looking for Firth Adams College."

"Is Adams College. This is the Marsh Reed Theater but it's closed tonight. Rehearsal."

"Oh. A play?" No one answered me. "Do you know where I could find a hotel?"

"There's a Holiday Inn out on Nine."

"Where's Nine? I'm sorry, I'm not from here." One of the angels dragged up the stairs towards me, slowly, at each step pausing, his right hand on his right knee. I heard a thump and a whisper, the feathers sweeping the wood floor and his bare heels. "I'll show you," he said. Outside, he pointed a long arm. His sleeve filled with night wind.

I made it to the hotel, checked in, took the key, found its secret in the door and felt my heart hard like a desperate thing throwing itself against a wall on the cold, stiff sheets. Home, I kept saying, home. I thought of birds arrested in flight, small startled things and the strong mean impervious eagle and none could be both and none could be both.

IN THE MORNING, everything looked different. I moved in. I carried all six items from the car, hung up clothes, washed my hair. I set my brush on the ledge by the sink. I folded my underwear and bras in the little drawer, lining it first with a motel towel. Then I drove around the town. This was where my father had lived. It was a decent-sized mountain town. There was a movie theater, a newspaper office for the *Brown Mountain Times,* a flat six-store shopping mall. Like a small resort set in the mountains, but the landscape, the soaring rock, made even the downtown dwarf. I looked in the phone book twice, then three times for Atassi. Finally, at nine o'clock, I called the university and asked for Gregory Geesie. When they said he had retired, I panicked. What if he was dead?

I looked in the phone book and found him. I called, told him who I was and made an appointment to meet him at his house at two. He sounded willing but indifferent. If I'd said I wanted to come to do a survey on lawnmower owners, he would have complied in the same way.

I didn't know quite what to do until then. There was almost too much to begin. So instead I walked the main street like any tourist. I sat and drank cappuccino at the hippie coffee shop and bought a piece of carrot cake with cream cheese frosting. I remembered how we used to think carrot cake was health food. I put my hands on the place mat on either side of my cake. I looked at each bite on the fork before I ate it. This seemed all in the world that was mine and I was going to enjoy it. I tried to feel a little bit on vacation.

I knew the routine at medical school so well, every small thing I was missing. The coffee break, my midafternoon conversation, the way I got my short study-group partner to rub my shoulders while I closed my eyes. The funny thing was, I'd been there but I hadn't felt it enough. I only half heard and half believed, and I took even my back rubs with a shield on my skin. I'd not counted that for much because I always would have rather been away in the high altitude of my father. Well now I was and I felt kind of sick. I wasn't all here either.

I still had hours. I slipped on the sunglasses Danny Felchner and I had taken from Boss's. My hair looked thin. The sunglasses turned the town slightly blue. I felt like a sick person in glasses, not a glamorous one. Then I drove to the college and walked around. I found the administration building, a great Greek thing with columns and bas-reliefs, all vaguely blue. I followed signs to the Personnel Department door, lettering etched in gold on ribbed glass. It was only ten o'clock.

I canvassed the library, passing over young bent heads. Short new hairs wisped up in soft halos the way hair does when it's washed every day. When we were children in Wisconsin, hair was shampooed once a week. I felt like touching these heads with my palm and saying, rise now and go out and play. This toil won't matter so much later. Your A's will be only letters on paper. The intent scribbling all around me was steady, like faint music. It was one still vast room with an angle of light from high windows and old wooden tables. They were so young. I felt like the skull in a painting of lush fruit.

I missed home, but that wasn't anywhere. I needed regularity, the exile's substitute. It was Wednesday morning in the hospital and at medical school. People were working, holding wrists, counting blood beats. Classes had started. I almost wanted to go back, father or not. But I knew if I did this would rise up again and again.

The air glittered brightly and the mountains were white-hatted and forbidding. You could have had a life here. It was beautiful and all. But it wasn't my life. I was watching the library clock, indoors, when, at the age I was now, my parents themselves had moved out into the air brightly, gaily dressed, not a strand of guilt in their minds for their own parents or their child. They had danced. I could see my mother against this snow and sun in a calico swirl skirt and clackety heels.

I wanted clothes—dresses. All of a sudden I wanted pearls. I wanted to tip precariously over curbs on high heels with men on dates.

These seemed Halloween, raucous things.

I STOOD ON Gregory Geesie's porch at two o'clock like I was supposed to. I touched each of my earrings, the scarf. It was beginning to rain. I knocked on a rasping screen door, scrolled in fancy tin letters with the initials G.G.G. I wondered what his middle name was. Then I pushed the bell and set off three tripping bars of melody. I heard the shuffle of slippers.

"Who's there now?"

"Is Mr. Geesie in, please?"

"This is Dr. Geesie. Are you the one that called?'"

I said that I was and he opened the screen door a little the way you would to let in a dog. There was a tiny hall with one closet but I had no coat. Then, we were in a room full of foot rests, doilied tables, and cut-glass bowls. The nap of the rug was newly ruffed with a vacuum cleaner, all in one direction. Every cover seemed to be covered with something else. The carpet had area rugs over it, the sofa a throw, and the footstools were laid with crocheted lace. G.G. Geesie settled into a banked rocker, observing me. He was an old man, pale-skinned, in an old man's clothes. Another old man, this one much taller, stood eating raisins out of one hand. Three identically framed fuzzy pictures of the tropics hung over the couch.

"As I said on the phone, I'm actually John Atassi's daughter. And I haven't seen him, my family hasn't seen him for years."

"Well, I sure don't know where he is," Dr. Geesie said, rocking. "But this is Dr. Kemp. I asked him over because he knew your dad better than I ever did."

Dr. Kemp was tall, with a ponytail of very dull silver hair. He wore black jeans and cowboy boots and made a slight bow in my direction. "But now I don't know where you could find him either," Dr. Kemp drawled.

I settled into one end of the couch as Dr. Geesie rocked. Dr. Kemp paced in long strides back and forth over the small carpet. His head was level with a chandelier. He kept eating raisins from his hand. I heard the sound of a loud cuckoo clock. Dr. Kemp refilled his raisins from a cut-glass bowl on a doily. I counted the decanters of candy in this room—there were nine. I turned to Dr. Geesie and said I'd heard about him from Mr. Nash in Wisconsin.

"Mr. Who?" he said. His skin, particularly at the neck part that showed through his open collar, gathered in folds, the hair follicles raised like a plucked chicken.

"Mr. Nash?" Maybe I should have said Dr. Nash. "He talked to you a number of years ago, I think. He told me that you had known my father."

"Well, that's correct. But I don't remember any Nash. That very well could be though. Your dad and I were both in the Social Science Department. But I'm no longer at the university. Dr. Kemp either."

"I haven't seen my father for a long time. I'm basically trying to look for him just as a sort of family thing." I didn't want them to think I wanted money or anything.

"I have never heard a word," Dr. Geesie said. "I taught there several years after he left and so far as I know, nobody ever heard a word from him."

"Disappeared," Dr. Kemp said.

"Yeah, that was our experience of him too."

Dr. Kemp cleared his throat. "He stopped talking to everybody tied up in the university."

Dr. Geesie had a way of moving his tongue so a small click emerged, a sound on an insect register. "He never came back to his office! He left everything on his desk and just vanished."

So my father's office: it existed, like a preserved shack full of some stranger's daily things I always hoped to find every time I entered a woods and never did.

"Nobody ever saw him again."

"God, that's so strange," I said.

"Well, that's correct. It is strange. The custodians had to come in and box everything up. University had to pay to ship it all to him."

It was gone. At that moment, I'd have rather had the contents of those boxes than him. I would have given anything for an uninterrupted day in his office with his things. "I wonder if I could get the address they mailed it to?"

"Well, the person to contact there would be Dean Daniels. If anyone a-tall would know, the dean would. And if he doesn't know, let me tell you, no one knows."

"And what's his first name?"

That seemed to embarrass Dr. Geesie. His face wobbled and his eyes scratched frantically through the air. "Oh, gosh, my memory is terrible, do you remember, Dr. Kemp?"

"Don't think I ever knew."

"That's all right," I said.

"Well, he's Dean Daniels anyway. That's correct. He's university dean. What was his name? He was a strange fellow, your father, let me tell you."

"Really? I just knew him as a child." A glass bowl etched with robins was filled to the brim with candy wrapped in fancy colored foil. I wanted one. But it was across the room.

"Well, I hate to talk about your father as—"

"No, that's okay, I'm not expecting any hero."

"He was utterly"—his t's were hard, tongue pushing the back of front teeth with a sissing force, a sputtering, bittered firecracker—"charm-ing. When you met him. Utterly charming. He would particularly charm women. But he was basically conniving as all get out. When he wanted something like tenure or to be chair of the department, he would stack the decks."

"Oh? How?"

"Well, by ingratiating himself to the administration and playing one person off against another."

"Oh. That's not good." I said.

"Very Machiavellian. But he did it all under charm, you see. You'd meet him, he'd have a big smile, he was always impeccably dressed. Why, I'll bet you he was among the two or three best-dressed people at Firth Adams!"

That wouldn't have done it for my mother at all. She'd been one of the best-dressed people in the state of Wisconsin. And that hadn't been enough.

Dr. Kemp kept pretty quiet. He was still pacing, head down, eating raisins. I looked at the two men. All of a sudden, for some reason, I wondered if they had children. Dr. Kemp had no wedding band. Dr. Geesie did, with a starburst of some kind at the center.

He went on about my father's clothes. "Always just beautiful suits. Oh, and the silk ties, he had one tie with all different colored butterflies, I remember. He looked like a prince. Very very charming."

" 'Cause I remember even before that," I said. "The last time I saw him I was about twelve and he was even then sort of losing his hair and all." I tried to laugh a little. Both these men had hair.

"No, he didn't have much hair," Dr. Geesie conceded. "He had kind of a, you know, fringe. But I think his most attractive physical feature was his eyes. He had *most* attractive eyes."

It seemed odd that Dr. Geesie would mention clothes. Dr. Kemp wore a silver belt buckle. He had a certain style. He kept his hair back in a plain liver-colored rubber band. But Dr. Geesie had on a short-sleeved blue shirt, some kind of trousers, worn slippers with plaid inside. His hair had gone yellow, not white.

Then I began to think that maybe Dr. Geesie and Dr. Kemp weren't really friends, that Geesie had probably called Kemp just so he'd have proof of me for his old-man gossip and that was what Dr. Kemp kept silent over, his invitedness and dislike of Doctor Geesie. Now he was unwrapping the green foil for a chocolate in his big hands.

"Are you both married?"

"He is, I'm not," Dr. Kemp drawled.

"I am married." Dr. Geesie nodded.

"Did he seem settled in America at the point you knew him? Or do you think he might've gone back to Egypt?"

"Oh, no," Dr. Geesie said, "I got the impression that he was definitely ensconced here."

Dr. Kemp stopped. "'Course he might have been desperate enough to go back to Egypt. You know. Feeling that he no longer had a future here. But I think he liked the Western style of life. Pleasures of the flesh and whatnot. He liked to drink and do all these things. I think he has a feeling for the Middle East. I think he loves it dearly. But he didn't want to go back to a Muslim country where he'd have to live like a Mormon."

"Did he publish any papers?"

"Nothing that I know of," Dr. Geesie said. "But there was no great pressure. The idea was that Firth Adams was a teaching institution. We were supposed to be Top Teachers, see. Devote all our time to teaching students and advising students. Sort of the Williams College of the West."

The Williams of the West. Like East Lansing was the Training Ground for Harvard. The one-way analogy. Talk about unrequited. In the East, you didn't hear anyone from Williams or Harvard talking about them. It was the way poor relatives everywhere mentioned their rich affiliations much more frequently than the illustrious remembered them.

"Do either of you know anyone who might have been sort of close to him?"

"No. Because if he was close to anyone it was the women. Not the men," Dr. Geesie said. The underground of women again.

Dr. Kemp cleared his throat. "He knew a number of the Arab students. But I don't remember any faculty."

"That's correct," Dr. Geesie said.

I wanted to ask. But I felt like I knew already. They were both men without children.

"I would just hear, you know, that he had gone with people and even supposedly some secretary at the college, but I don't know who that was. And I made it a point not to ask questions. You never know when things'll get back."

"I think he did chase around." Dr. Kemp stood leaning against a wall now, peeling a tangerine. The tangerines were in a china bowl with the faint tracings of a dragon painted on it, mostly gone from washing. "I never knew any of them by name," he said.

"Right. Which is a pity," I said. "Do you have any recollection of him being married or anything?"

"Why sure," Dr. Kemp said, pacing again. "His wife's name was Sonia."

"Well, I knew too there was a woman he was calling his wife," Dr. Geesie said, "but of course I have no idea whether or not they really were married."

"Is she still here?"

"I don't know what happened to that. He was stepping out on her. He'd move out and be living in an apartment for a while and then he'd move back in again. And this went back and forth. I only heard about it through the grapevine. And as far as I know, she left here with him when he was fired."

"She had money," Dr. Kemp said in a straight low tone as if that underlined everything, which, I guess in a way, it did.

"Do you remember her maiden name?"

He shook his head. "I always knew her as Sonia Atassi. She was from the Reno area."

"But you know," Dr. Geesie said, "if we had the last name, you could probably track it down. You might get a Reno telephone directory. I would try, although he had an unlisted number here in Montana. You might also try Las Vegas and Palm Springs. Where're you from?"

"Oh, I live in New York. I'm in medical school." I wondered how long that would still be true.

"New York," Dr. Geesie said. "Couldn't get much further away."

Just then the cuckoo clock dinged two-thirty. A wooden carved goose revolved out with a girl following, all to a cranked merry-go-round tune.

"Why sure. Any major library should have telephone directories from around the country. I know the Missoula one does."

I said, "Actually I think I met his wife except I thought her name was Uta. Was she older than he was?"

"Could be. Maybe it was Uta, I don't know why I think it was Sonia," Dr. Kemp said. He stared down at me intently for the first time. "You were from the first marriage," he said.

"Yes." I'd never thought of it like that. For me it was the marriage, no matter what.

"I knew your mother. You see, I first met John when I taught for a semester at the University of Wisconsin."

"Oh. Wow. That's funny."

"How is she?"

"She's great. Fine." I didn't want any of these people near my mother. I always thought she was so fragile.

"I don't know if she'd remember me but give her my regards."

"I will," I said. "You know I met the second wife once. Once we flew out and we all went to Disneyland."

"He certainly *is* a man of mystery," Dr. Geesie said.

"Sure is," I said, thinking that old men and old women sound alike.

"Now, let's see. How you could find him," Dr. Geesie said. "I suspect he's probably in Nevada somewhere. But how you can find him down there in that maze, that I don't know. If he even kept his same name."

It's not the same name, I wanted to say, it's his name. His real name. But then I remembered it wasn't. His real name was Mohammed Abdul Atassi. "Do you think the school would give me his social security number? Then I could call the Social Security Department and see if they'd help."

"I have done that with genealogy," Dr. Geesie said. A genealogist. I should've known. "But the only success I've had is when someone is dead. And then they will take about a year and they'll phone you back personally and say, well, now you asked about such and such a person. And they'll tell you, well, that person died at such and such a place—"

"Huh."

"—at such and such a date," Dr. Geesie finished. "That they will do."

"He could be dead," I said. "I wouldn't know. He didn't have any children up here, did he?"

"No," Dr. Kemp said. "She had children. Grown."

"But not with him?"

"Not with him."

Dr. Geesie rushed in, "No, no, no. He wasn't the type that would want children."

"But he has one actually."

"Yes, and isn't it strange that he didn't try to keep in touch with you?" That seemed mean. Asking me to answer.

"Well, it's awful." What could I say.

"Yas I think that's, uh, unfortunate," Dr. Kemp said.

"Do you have children yourself?" I asked Dr. Geesie. The clock ticked one chime for the quarter hour.

"No," Dr. Geesie said. "My wife and I never did have children."

I looked to Dr. Kemp. "Me?" he said, a large hand on his chest, "I'm not married."

"Did he ever mention us?"

Dr. Geesie looked at Dr. Kemp. Dr. Kemp was now eating M&Ms.

"Why sure, I knew that you existed," he said. "But that's all."

I shook my head.

"Well, you know, if it hadn't been for his gambling." Dr. Geesie clicked his tongue again. "As I say, he was overly ambitious professionally but that's not unusual, there are a lot of people in academic life who are *that* way. His Achilles heel was his gambling. That's what got him in trouble in Cairo."

Now Dr. Kemp started. "We had an extension program for alumni and local people. It was a way the faculty could make a little extra money. By planning a trip somewhere. I did mine in Eastern Canada." I could see Dr. Kemp standing in a marsh like one arrow, his binoculars following a high triangle of geese. "John decided to take a group to the Middle East. He'd gone the year before to Seattle to see some mummies and they all loved that so a lot of the same ones signed up again. And he said he had a terrific program all organized. They were going to stop in New York at the UN and they were going to do something in Rome. Well none of that materialized, but still nobody was particularly concerned."

"It was mostly women, if I'm recalling correctly," Dr. Geesie said. "Dr. Atassi and fifteen or twenty women."

"Older ladies, you know, local people. A few of them even had an Egyptology club. They put together those replicas of Egyptian urns, you know, it was a little like paint-by-number. It was a pretty expensive trip. And so it was the banker's wife and her mother. That kind of person. And the first week or so, everything went pretty well. They took a boat up the Nile and they liked that. They saw the Pyramids."

"One woman passed out," Dr. Geesie said. "Kidney stones."

"Why sure, but he couldn't help that," Dr. Kemp said. "The way I heard it was everything went along pretty well until Cairo. They saw hieroglyphs and what-have-you. They saw some more mummies, I suppose. He got those old ladies up on camels. They all came home with their picture of that. And then one night, he took all the ladies out on the town. And that started all right too, they went to a fancy restaurant—"

"As fancy as they've got over there," Dr. Geesie interjected.

"And they ate in a big tent with an opening where they could see the moon and the stars. He was always good that way. With wines and food. But then he brought them to a casino. And I guess the first casino was all right. They walked around and saw everything. But the manager there wouldn't give them credit. So he rounded all the ladies up and took them to another casino."

Dr. Geesie was rocking again and shook his head. "A place they never should have been. Never ever."

"Yas. The second one was more down and out. A few of the ladies said later, they thought something was funny when they were following all these dark alleys. I don't know what he told them, maybe that they were all millionaire's wives, who knows, but he got them spread out over the casino, some were at blackjack, quite a few at roulette, one or two at the slot machines, and they gambled all night. I guess they liked it."

"Why, they lost almost thirty thousand dollars!" Dr. Geesie said.

"They just kept going. They thought it was some kind of big free party. He told them it was play money, the chips, and he'd paid some kind of admission fee for them all. They thought they were at a bingo game."

"He hooked them on it!" Dr. Geesie said.

"Of course he was playing blackjack."

"On their credit too!" Dr. Geesie said. "After he went through the tour money."

"He was upstairs at some kind of private table. Then, I suppose, it was closing time."

"Whatever closing time *is* in a casino over there," Dr. Geesie said.

"It must have been pretty late. The women got together with their coats and purses and all and the fellows running the casino weren't about to let them go. They wanted them to pay up. And of course this was all in Arabic. And then, the gals noticed, they can't find him anywhere. They said over there the police all wear white. They said at first when they came they thought they were doctors."

"Ended up in jail that night," Dr. Geesie said.

"And he just split?" I had to keep myself from laughing. I knew this was terrible, but it was kind of funny too.

"He just disappeared," Dr. Geesie said.

I asked. "What did they do, the old ladies?"

"Well, they wired home to their husbands! They had no money! No program!" Dr. Geesie nearly shouted. His hands were white gripping the arms of the chair. "Fortunately that one woman's husband was director of the bank here and he got right on a plane and went over and bailed them all out. Well, they wondered for several days where Atassi went and then they thought there was foul play and maybe he'd even been killed in Cairo. So this fellow from the bank got in touch with the US Embassy and the Embassy got in touch with the local police. They discovered that he had taken a plane for Athens, Greece. He'd gone from there to Rome and from Rome to Paris and from Paris to London and then to New York. First-class! And all this within a week after they'd left. And so here I was sitting in my office one day and a student came in and said, 'You know the strangest thing, I thought Dr. Atassi was in the Middle East but I saw him on the street in Missoula.' I said, 'Oh no, that's not possible,' and the student said, 'I tell you I saw the man with my own eyes,' and I said, 'Well that just couldn't be, he is in, he is in Egypt or in Lebanon somewhere.' Well, within a couple of days why the whole thing broke, of course, and the women called long distance to the university president, and said, 'We're stuck in Cairo and Dr. Atassi's disappeared.'"

He was still a doctor, even disappeared.

I missed medical school in a vague way, sitting in a room looking out at the rain. "So how did he explain himself?"

"Well, that he woke up one day with a lot of amnesia and the money was gone," Dr. Kemp said. "Nobody really believed him. They wanted him to go to a psychiatrist."

"Sounds like a good idea to me," I said.

"It got a lot of publicity," Dr. Geesie said. "The papers ate it up."

I tried to remember: call local newspaper for its archives.

"They had insurance, I think, to cover the money that was spent," Dr. Kemp said, "they didn't prosecute or anything of that sort. He just disappeared and, as far as I know, Uta went with him. Or Sonia. But I think it *was* Uta. Actually, she did leave him once while he was here. But she went back to him when his problems increased. She loved him a great deal." He said that with a gravity. I liked Dr. Kemp.

"If you only had her maiden name." Dr. Geesie made his clicking sound.

"But I really can't think back to anyone who was a close friend," Dr. Kemp said. "I've thought about him several times since. Actually, he hurt me in many ways."

"What?"

"Well, he conspired to get me kicked out of the chairmanship. He was very efficient and also a good teacher. But he had certain flaws in his personality. And one is gambling."

"Another is leaving his children."

"Yas, I feel the same way." Why couldn't this man have been my father? Anyone else would have been easier.

Dr. Geesie was sitting at the edge of his chair. "When he left, they published in the newspaper all the bills he'd run up! Why, he owed the dry cleaner alone more than eight hundred dollars! It turned out, he was borrowing money from the secretaries all that time. They never said anything about it until after he was gone and then of course it was too late."

"The more I think of it," Dr. Kemp said, "I'm sure the wife's name is Uta. I think the fatal flaw is the gambling, you know, it'd be like alcoholism or any number of others. He can't seem to resist it. It's one of the reasons I thought he had probably gravitated back to a gambling area. She might have even owned a hotel or a restaurant somewhere in Nevada. I seem to remember something about that."

"Do you remember the restaurant's name?"

"I think he even worked there one summer. Or maybe that's how they met. But the name, what was that? It might have been something like Donner Pass. Donner Lodge. We're not giving you much, but I suppose it's more than you had."

"Ut-terly charming," Dr. Geesie said again.

"I grew up with my mom. Which may have been lucky actually."

"Well, you'd have had a number of crises," Dr. Kemp said. "I don't know if they even have a Gamblers' Anonymous thing or not. But he also, I think, had delusions of grandeur. He always wanted to be more important than he was. The gambling thing was like buying lottery tickets. You think you're going to be rich tomorrow."

Dr. Geesie clicked again.

"I mean, I buy them, mind you," Dr. Kemp said. You knew that Dr. Geesie never had.

"But it sounds like he had money anyway from his wife. So what did he need more for?" He should have known how little we had. What we did. How we managed.

I watched Dr. Kemp unwrap and eat another chocolate. "You want one?" he said and then threw it across the room. It was blue foil. That set Dr. Geesie shoving himself up from the armrests and carrying the bowl of turtles around the room.

"I should have asked you already," he mumbled. "My wife usually—she's at birthday club."

"I'd like to know what's happened to John," Dr. Kemp said. "You know, he can sell himself and what he believes in. I don't know whether Uta has stuck with him. She loved him very much. And you know, put up with a lot."

"I hope she's still even alive to find," I said. "I remember her being pretty old."

"She might be in her sixties, I don't know," Dr. Kemp said.

"He'd be fifty-five now. I know 'cause that's how old my mom is and they're the same age." This seemed an increasingly fragile bit of romance.

" 'Course I'm seventy," Dr. Kemp said.

"I'm seventy-six!" Dr. Geesie said, like, *so there!*

God, I'd probably offended these guys, saying she was old enough to be dead. I tried to cover it. I said, "I bet she'd be about ninety now."

"No, she was younger than I was," Dr. Kemp said. "Well, she might be my age, I don't know. She had some wrinkles, I guess."

"Was she a nice person?"

"Yas."

"Was she smart and everything?"

"Why sure. And, as I say, she put up with a lot."

There was a racket at the front door, then a delicate stamping. "Well, hello." Dr. Geesie's wife took off plastic shoe covers and hung up her scarf. "I won't bother you," she said, tiptoeing through the room.

Dr. Geesie looked to Dr. Kemp. "Do you think she should check the Western Division of International Studies?"

"He doesn't seem like the joiner type," I said. It was like umbrellas and sunglasses. The medical insurance I might have been wrong on. The college probably gave him that.

"I'm sorry," Dr. Kemp said, "we can't tell you more."

"All these people from years ago, why would you remember?" I shrugged.

"You remember some, like Ted Bundy was a student of mine," he said.

"Oh, neat." I was winging it. I didn't know who Ted Bundy was. But the name sounded like some New England blazered politician. I talked too much. I talked too much all the time then. I just filled in the spaces.

"He was a very good student," Dr. Kemp said.

Mrs. Geesie came in and snapped the TV. "I'm just putting on the picture with no sound," she said. "Gregory, call me when you see my show."

"She has her show she watches every day," Dr. Geesie said. It seemed pretty soon time to go.

"Your mother may not remember me," Dr. Kemp said.

"She doesn't like the idea of me finding my father. So I probably won't tell her right away."

"Well I can understand why you'd like to find him. One likes to have some kind of contact. It doesn't have to be close. The way he treated you you probably wouldn't want to be close. But you'd still like to know. If you ever do find him, I'd like to hear."

"I will. I'll call you."

"John and I were good friends, I think he treated me shabbily but, you know, I still have some feelings about him. I don't have any bitterness."

"No. You don't sound like it." I stood up to go. On the TV were cut shots of bells in a cool place, a high tower. I wanted to hear them. All of a sudden, I wanted to hear music. Then a jewelry box opened somewhere else in the house and its vain cranked music sounded like an ice-cream truck.

"Well, he's either down on his luck or all of a sudden he made it big. I don't feel that he would be sort of in between."

"What'd you say your first name was?" Dr. Geesie asked me.

"Mayan."

"Mayan," Dr. Kemp said. "Why sure, I think I did hear him mention your name."

"Well, I don't know what else to tell you," Dr. Geesie said, "but there you've got some of the bad and some of the good. He was a charming fellow." He shoved himself up again and stood holding the bowl of M&Ms.

"I knew that a daughter existed, why sure," Dr. Kemp said. "Existed. That makes you sound like a statistic."

I was writing out my phone number on slips of paper. I asked them to call me collect if they ever heard anything. I kept stealing glances at the TV. It was still the high cold heavy metal bells.

"Oh, well," Dr. Kemp said. "I'm always broke."

"So definitely call collect then." Sometimes you crave music in a way that seems physical. This was in my chest.

"I have drug bills of two hundred dollars a month. And none of them are fun drugs."

"Do you have something wrong?"

"Oh, I have angina and diabetes. I've got the ball of wax."

At the screen door, I asked. "Oh, Dr. Geesie. What's your middle name?" George, I had decided.

Just then, the woman bent down in front of the TV, her heels rising out of her shoes. Bells spilled loudly and filled the room like a higher ceiling, a clean height.

"Graybner," He said. "Gregory Graybner Geesie. All my brothers and my father have the same initials. G.G.G."

I WAS THINKING of changing my name. It was just a little thing. I should have done it once when I changed schools. It would have been easy. I changed schools so many times. I didn't like to write my name. Mayan Amneh Stevenson. It was a kind of alias and not legal. But it was printed on my driver's license, all lines of credit. All my school records said this. My social security number was wrong, faked anyway, so I could work in Dean's Ice Cream Diner when I was thirteen. My mother shrugged at the time. "You'll just get your money a year earlier when you're old. You can be sixty-four. That'll be nice." Sometimes I took comfort in the big mess of this country. In not being found.

I was Mayan, a word you could finger like two beads on a chain. I had a chain with just two pearls. One of the times I'd seen my father when I was a child, we went to a restaurant that served oysters. You were guaranteed to get a pearl. We ate the whole plate of them and we didn't find a pearl, so they went to the back and got us two more oysters and this time they each had a pearl. We thought they had a special pail of them in back that they knew had pearls.

"But how could they know?" my mother said.

"X-rays," I said, a smart aleck.

They put them on an add-a-pearl-necklace right then, but I'd never gotten any more. Whenever we ate with my father, we ate better. We had whole meals of fancy food and dessert. We ate it all and never worried about our weight because we knew this would be just once and not always. It wouldn't last, it would go away and remind us that chances are only once, taste ephemeral, and life in this world, all its sweetness and rain, is nothing to count on continuing because it will, but only without us. Time is short, attachment expensive, but it was worth it for us to eat every time. It never tasted enough. We had such appetite. The thing I still love best about us, my mother and me, is that we wanted so.

I just started using the name Ann. It seemed pretty much the same thing. Amneh had always been my middle name, one I'd had to spell for a stair of teachers calling roll in elementary school. Somebody told me once that Amneh meant "wish" in Arabic. And that was all the truth in my name. I was almost a Jane, my mother said. But my father thought that was too American. Too short. "A Jane will grow up to have bangs," he apparently said. He allowed no name that could end up nicked, with a *y* or an *ie*. That eliminated Jennifer, Catherine and Rebecca. His family name we had lost, although it loosened a small waterfall of sounds: Atassi.

Stevenson was my stepfather's name. It wasn't even really his either. Ted had been adopted, back in upstate New York where he was from.

And Ted meant to adopt me as his child. I probably spoiled that. I couldn't decide if I wanted to or not. I wanted both at the same time, without my father ever knowing. It was up to me, my mother said, no one could help me, it was my decision, but I knew she wanted me to say yes to Ted. I tried to stall for time and it never happened anyway. My mother and Ted had their own problems and maybe they forgot. But before they honeymooned in upstate New York, my mother dressed in a suit and a square black hat with two feathers, colted up the cement stairs of the school board building and changed my name on the manila records. That was all she had to do. And when I was returned to my grandmother I was Ann Stevenson. Nothing legal had been done but it was official. And I was too young, it seemed, for any of the procedures to matter much. I guess most everybody in charge thought a mother could call her child whatever she pleased.

It had been more than twenty years since any of us saw Ted. That was longer ago than the last time I saw my father in California, although there was nothing comparable about the two men, and though I suppose I could have seen Ted, any time. Ted Stevenson was not a hard man to find.

The world of professional figure skating is not large. After us, Ted had moved to Milwaukee, remarried a younger woman and with her, he had five children, all boys. He lived, I believed, in Nebraska now, teaching figure skating, as he always had. I suspected he looked about the same too; he was a nice-looking man, thin-faced, not the sort to age. He once told me how he had toured with the Ice Capades through Cuba, before the revolution. Their crew went to small-town arenas and laid out the ice. In one remote province, he was the first man to introduce pictures. The people had seen cameras before, but Americans had come, taken, and never sent the prints. Or perhaps it was the mail down there, Ted said, maybe some sent them and they never arrived. Ted brought a Polaroid. He held the snapshot in his palm, looking from the shiny paper to the old man, tears coming from his face loosely as the picture developed. He was seeing a miracle, Ted told me.

"A science invention," I'd said. "Not a miracle."

"To them it was," Ted said.

"Not to me."

"Nothing is to you, Maya." He always called me Maya, like the Indians.

"That's right," I said. "I don't believe in Santa Claus either, in case you have any plans for a costume."

There was a father/daughter breakfast at my school once and I brought the slip home to my mother. She made arrangements with Ted. And then the day came and he was there looking serious and dutiful in a new white shirt and an ascot. None of the other fathers would be wearing ascots. Most of them worked at the paper mills or at the canning factory. I put on my regular shorts and got on my bike, ready to take off. My mother ran out to where I was, holding her bathrobe together, but you could see her slender naked body curved inside. "Go on in and change. Hurry," she said, "he took the day off from the rink and dressed up for this." His voice came from the door like a pulpit, "Let her be, Adele, it's up to her. Whatever she wants."

"I want to ride my bike," I said, my hands still on the handlebars. And I rode away.

A few years ago, I tracked Ted down. It took under an hour. I was working for the Wildlife Sanctuary and I was sitting alone at the little indoor desk that sold postcards and animal pins and ten-cent bags of dry corn to feed the ducks and geese. It was late afternoon. I liked it because you had to wear old clothes. I sat up on a stool. There was corn all over the ground. Once in a while I made long-distance calls from there. They never seemed to check. Certain things have always seemed socialistic. Books. Men's shirts. The phone.

Ted's wife answered. She was nice. She said how lucky it was that I'd called when he was home. But then when he got on the phone, we couldn't find much to say. He seemed slightly unhappy to hear from me. "Yeah, your mother," he said with a bad laugh. He had a rind of bitterness. I must have given him my address because his wife followed up our conversation with a photo Christmas card—the five boys in gray and green suede climbing shorts and green suspenders—and that was the end of that. On the bottom of the card, the wife had scribbled, "Ted is going to write you a letter." He never did.

I FINISHED my childhood without a father. I remember the consternation: I used to stand outside, my arms crossed, tennis shoes scraping the porch lip just for the feel of it, counting cars from the highway. It was still light out and my grandmother was asleep, already done for the day. This was the year before my mother and I left. I could see cars in the distance but from our porch I couldn't tell what make they were or if there was one person inside or two. I'd follow them to see if they'd turn at our off-ramp. They almost never did. I still believed my father would come back. But would he make it *in time*.

If you asked me if I thought he was alive, I would have said, yes, and I'd have meant it. Sometimes I wondered, would I ever just see him again in my life without my doing anything. If someone else, something, would arrange it. Now, I figured, if I found him, I would never know.

It is possible to believe and not to believe in someone's existence, equally, at the same time.

BUT FAR AWAY as my mother and I went, we both still kept Ted's name. In California, we tried to be that family for a while, proper, behind its screen door. It was like a raincoat. Stevenson. Sounding everything we were not: rich, old, respectable, standard, British. Not even legally mine.

In California, my mother bought things to make us seem like once we'd had more. Somewhere else, back in Wisconsin, where the new people here couldn't check. I'd come home from school once in the afternoon, during the rainy season, and a whole set of china was in the cupboards: plates, salad plates, cups, saucers, everything. The fragile china was shining, painted with blue and green peacocks, in the dull kitchen, on that dark afternoon.

My mother lifted one down to show me but we didn't eat on them. My mother focused her homemaking on kitchens. She didn't really know how to cook, but she could make a kitchen look beautiful. We had the plates and clear light-blue glasses and a yellow gingham tablecloth and curtains and by the sink, we had brushes made of rush twigs twined together, a deep yellow soap in the perfect shape of a moon.

Once a friend of mine came over after school, a true rich girl from the far north side. Calla lived in a mansion. This was a rainy day too. I never knew what would happen when I had a friend come over, but my mother was there that day and she was almost normal. She hovered near the kitchen, which seemed to me what she was supposed to do, to be a mother. In a while she came to my room and knocked and asked us if we wanted hot chocolate or tea and cookies. I loved her then. I don't know where she found the cookies. We hadn't had any cookies before. Then we sat in the kitchen with our tea and cookies, served, in honor of my friend, on the peacock china. Calla picked up the saucer and turned it over, and looked around the room in a distracted, enchanted way. That was one of those moments when I felt quiet because my mother was right. That was what she had intended.

Now, it seems to me wastefully funny: all the stunts and extravagant effort, the telephone wheedling after money, all to fool a dreamy thirteen-year-old girl on a rainy afternoon.

MY MOTHER SHRUGGED ONCE. "It's a great name," she said. "With Atassi, no one ever said it right. You always had to spell."

That was true. I was Mayan Atassi for seven years and I remembered saying "A-T-A-S-S-I" as if that were the name. I was Atassi with the nuns. On their simple elementary school rolls, that was my name. We had a white curved Volkswagen bug then, too, with plaid seat covers and the window on the passenger side wouldn't go all the way up. Both these circumstances, the oddness of our name and the cold wet from the window, formed snags I minded, but they were also ours and I would have never dreamed of changing them. I thought that was our car, we would have it forever. Once we ate creamed shrimp on toast in a restaurant downtown and when we came onto the street again, other cars had parked too close for us to get out. Our bug's name was Ginny. My mother pounded the front fender and said damnit and tears watered her face, but then she shrugged and sighed "Hokay," and pushed my neck with her hands, walking, until we stopped at the cab stand in front of Boss's Tobacco and Magazine Shop.

Later, I'd thought of changing my name back but there was the trouble of everyone else. I had been Stevenson for too long. A lot of my friends said they thought Stevenson was a better name. I felt the other but I wasn't sure. Plus about something like this, nobody else really cares. The world is busy.

But that was why I never liked parties. The first question was always, What is your name? Then, And where are you from? Both of those, for me had more than one answer. The truth was spiked and jagged and took too long for social conversation.

At least I was old enough now so people didn't ask right away, What does your father do? Children demand that of other children. When I met my college boyfriend's family, his little brother badgered me, "Come on, what does your dad do? He's a lawyer, right? Come on, tell us. I know it's either law or medicine."

It was neither law nor medicine, wherever he was. That much I did know.

"Gigolo," I said.

A thousand times people had said to me in my life, You don't know your father?

No, I'd answer. Or, well, some but not much.

And I lied. Once I told a man on a bus that I had six brothers and sisters and that my father was a baker and I played the violin. A lot of times I tried to tell the truth but making it sound more normal than it was. Well, we lived in different cities. I lived with my mom. He was a divorced dad. I didn't really know him that well.

Now, Atassi sounded to me like a shoe, I could draw it, a fancy slipper, tilting up at the toes. At the time, when it was my name, it seemed like a pair of thick squarish black eyeglasses that I always wore.

Ann Stevenson was like a name. But the name of someone else. I saw her in a boxy suit, bought this season or last, cautiously. I imagined Ann Stevenson as some young woman at a convention with a name tag on her upper left suit-jacket pocket. The suit was melon-colored or pale green. Dull blue. Maybe I had become a little this conventioneer.

I'd hated the name Mayan and liked it and gone around and around. Most of the time I didn't think of it. There are aspects of yourself you grow into with time, your nose, your face, your legs. You know them, finally, only as your own, the way you could never, except for a few flashing moments, love or hate your own body.

So many Americans were like me—changed. Look at the phone book. Anything foreign got ironed. Thousands of women sealed away their names for a husband's. And to their children, the old name was no big deal. They didn't think of it as her real name any more than they thought of their mother's childhood as her real life.

It happened to practically every woman in the world. I don't know what my problem was. It was common. All of this was. It didn't make me special. Still, I hadn't married Ted. I didn't love him.

I did love my father, though. However unrequited the feeling was.

I DROVE BACK TO THE HOTEL, drew the blinds and flopped on the made bed, belly down, chin to fabric so I smelled the old cotton and bleach, harshly clean. He wasn't anywhere when I was in high school, he was just here. Living a life. Breezing out in good suits to meet the high weather and his ambition. Dinners at so-and-so's to insure such and such a position. A gift for thus and such. Not thinking of me or my mother. Not ruining his life over us at all. Not even hampering it. He was just a man, nothing higher. And I was a fool. My grandmother had been right.

I had liked the old men, their fastidious distinctions, the way none of this moral business mattered to them anymore. They almost liked my father for his scandal, the way they once had for his clothes. A little color. Greed, ambition, all the vanities seemed milder to them now, themes like melodies with ends already known. But they were no relation. Neither of those men could have been my father.

After a little while on the bed, things began to be different. He'd never left his life to look for me.

I wanted to go home. I remembered coming out of a movie on an ordinary Tuesday afternoon and walking with Timothy to Tacita de Oro for café con leche and fried plantains. I craved rice and beans.

I called Mai linn. "Get this," I said. "Everybody I talk to here calls everybody else Doctor. They take the Ph.D. very seriously in the state of Montana. Even after my dad dumped these old ladies in a Cairo jail, he's still Dr. Atassi."

Mai linn told me, "One day last spring I was just walking, it must have been May or June, and there was this little ceremony going on in front of the bell tower. They were giving doctorates to four or five people. One was a woman, the rest were guys. And I just stood behind a tree and watched. And when they lifted the tassels around the woman's shoulders, that's what they do, I started crying. I couldn't believe it." Mai linn was two years away from her Ph.D.

It was still day. I had to get to work. I didn't feel like it much anymore. But I thought I better try and find Uta's maiden name. Maybe I'd call J.D. Nash and ask about the marriage records in Nevada. I'd go to the library here tonight and read through the local newspapers, then tomorrow, first thing in the morning, I'd hit all the administration buildings.

It was so strange to be doing this thing that nobody else wanted or valued, that nobody had asked for. The world didn't need it, it wasn't useful or even beautiful, but just this huge, year-wasting project in my life I hadn't even picked. My father's leaving just happened to me. It fell like a stone in the center of my childhood. We could either build everything around it or attempt to move it away or try to believe it didn't matter. I thought of Emory's toothpick structures, made up whole out of something as frail as a wish. That was more beautiful, surely.

This was built on shame, someone else's carelessness that we had shrined into our lives' cathedral. He'd tossed a cigarette butt down somewhere on the road and I'd taken that up and built a church around it.

I had to get out of that Holiday Inn room. I shoved up. I'd go to campus. This was the end.

It was my peculiarity to know things before they happened, not clairvoyance in any practical way, the kind of gift that involves policemen and German shepherds. My previsions were unreliable, some of the events did occur, some never materialized. That didn't matter. I had a nature given to anticipation and what I anticipated most were ends.

I felt things ending a long time before they did.

The night I knew I would get into medical school, I was at a party at Emily's house. Watching the moon and the rain in the lanterns, I went by myself out on Merl's stone terrace and felt the sorrow of being the one who would leave.

I knew when Providence for me was over, before my grandmother had a third stroke. It had to do with snow and not wanting to go to sleep.

New York was ending that way now, but with more regret because I had never really settled and lived there.

And I knew when it ended with my father. It was that afternoon, on the way back to Firth Adams College. I saw a sheer face of rock and a faint rainbow, already lopsided, mostly dissolved. I got out of the car and stood hands on hips and looked for a long time. The colors drained and then it was gone, just a play of old light on the cliffs and canyons like an expression that had left a face empty.

What was coming next?

It would not be what I'd wanted.

It would be something less, something I wouldn't recognize because I had not made him and he had not made me. Maybe we could learn to know each other slowly and something would build. But it would be something else, beside the point.

All my prayers, my years of prayers now were lost, spent, and I would have rather gathered them like coins in a hat than meet this man.

If I still wanted to believe, that would change too. It might not be possible.

It seemed, perhaps, through my own doing, I had made a grave mistake. Maybe it was better before, better to always believe, to live with an attitude of expectancy, a cocked still head, plumed like a bird.

That way you are always almost fully alive.

HE HAD JUST BEEN HERE, a man, chasing his own ends.

I stood with my hands on my hips absolutely alone. I started shouting to hear an answer and a long time later a pale echo circled back, but it was not my voice anymore, it had the hollowness of something big and expressionless, rock-dumb and empty, something from the huge identityless source and it was coming back, sound and motion, logarithm of language, my name, my old name over that mile of mountain.

Eventually it began to precipitate slightly, a fine close thread of sleet, not rain or snow, and there was a portion of rainbow just alighting there between the rock and the valley. I stood awhile holding my elbows.

Love a person, that is the answer to the world. Forget grandeur and sacrifice and ideal prayer. Just love a person.

And all that kept my work alive was the chance I might be wrong and still not find him.

I BOUGHT COFFEE at a cart and walked slowly in a diagonal, so as not to spill.

Sometimes I thought my mother's saying I was an overachiever had made me one. I was a person who couldn't quit. In a way, I was grateful.

It was after midnight in a library and there were six years of daily newspapers in two stacks on the floor: the read and the unread. I'd spent the day in a campus phone booth, the atlas open to Nevada on my thigh, calling county clerk's offices. J.D. Nash had checked the Bureau of Vital Statistics. Nevada had computerized in 1975 and only one Atassi showed up in the system. This was a Sahar Atassi marrying a Diane Thayer three years ago, when Sahar Atassi was twenty-seven. We scribbled with the birthdates and figured that the girl was then nineteen and born in Mountainview, California. For a moment, I thought he could be my brother, but then J.D. Nash told me that Sahar Atassi listed his father's name as Tarik.

"I know," he said. "I was thinking the same thing." They listed their home as San Jose. Then J.D. Nash told me that everything before 1975 in Nevada was still just paper records, files, and every county clerk's office kept their own. I volunteered to call the eleven counties. Seven took the rest of the afternoon and turned up nothing. Then I called San Jose information, idly, for Sahar Atassi. Nothing. I called Mountainview for those Thayers. I thought maybe I'd get her parents. Mountainview sounded rich to me, a certain way. I imagined high old trees, live oak, eucalyptus and pine, so the light came in plank-dense shafts and the air flecked green and gold. It was the kind of place you imagined going up hills and turning a corner and then seeing horses, huge and bright in the sun. I imagined the Thayers as riders, with yellow ruffled curtains in their ranch kitchen, formal dinners outside on their terrace. I saw Diane a tall cool blonde, sharp-featured, with big hands. A rider, a giver of summer lunches. No Thayers were listed in Mountainview. I could have ranged farther in the Bay Area, but that seemed a pretty remote tangent and I had to stop somewhere. That was the hardest part. Finding the place to stop.

I still had four more Nevada counties to go. I'd switched phone booths, to the one on the first floor, that had a view. My choices had narrowed to this. The counties got scratched off my list, mounting charges on my phone bill back home. Wouldn't they have gotten married where they lived? Dr. Kemp said Uta—or Sonia—was from Reno. But Reno was in Carson City, Clark County, and that county clerk said no.

Every county clerk I talked to was a woman and I told each one of them the truth. The tedium of their office jobs fell slowly like dust in their voices. I could see the old wooden files, the venetian blinds, the loud big fan, the boredom. My story brought a little silver; their files could change a life. Each one of them said no in a different way.

I thought I'd get lucky with the last county, Esmeralda, in Goldfield, Nevada. But that woman shuffled back to the phone slow and soft-voiced too. I heard the mix of paper on a desktop. "No, hon, I'm sorry, we've got nothing in that name. I went all the way back to '55."

Nights weren't so bad. It was two o'clock. The library hummed, quiet. Most everyone must have been home asleep. I stopped and started again. Stopped.

I was just staring at my hand.

DEAN DANIELS—Frank his name turned out to be—wouldn't talk. When he heard whose daughter I was, he told his secretary through the intercom that he had no information on the subject.

Then I went to the college president. His office was in an old, ivy-covered brick house. He sat behind an enormous desk in a high-ceilinged room, toying with a pencil. He wore a bow tie and suspenders. The suspenders encouraged me.

"I'm a daughter of Moham—John Atassi who taught for you, I understand, a long time ago."

"John Atassi," he said.

"Anyway, I'm looking for him and I haven't seen him since I was a very young girl and my mother and I are looking for him just, well, basically to meet my father . . ." I don't know why I blurted out my mother. It felt better to be two of us.

The pencil seemed purely balanced between his open palms. The sharpened tip hit the center of one, the pink eraser the center of the other.

"We haven't seen him for years. I was put in touch with Dr. G.G. Geesie, who told us about the fiasco you had with him. But I was really wondering if there was anything you could help me with, by way of finding him. If you knew any friends, Dr. Geesie said that he was a ladies' man, which he was I think in the old days, unfortunately with my mother, but I was just wondering if there might be some woman you'd know of in town I could call who might have some notion where he may be." I really talked too much.

He took the pencil and laid it on his blotter, parallel. "I . . . would . . . have . . . no . . . idea . . . whatsoever." He spit those words out hard like watermelon seeds.

NIGHT IN THE HOTEL WAS BAD. I left the library at two-thirty. I hadn't eaten. I began to see the numbers on my bills swarm off white pages like bees at my face and nothing different. I didn't need to eat tomorrow anyway, I was fat enough. If I ate one meal a day that would be better for everything, I decided. But sleep came hard, in bits. A strange light sided through the Holiday Inn drapes. My room was on the first floor and sometimes I heard pickup doors slamming in the parking lot and the walls trembled and I hugged my knees up under the covers.

Then the phone jolted my heart.

"Just come home," Jordan said. That loosened me to cry. "We can keep looking from here."

"I can't."

"Why?"

That started a new storm of it.

"How did you know I'm here?"

"I met up with your friend Emily. We were both going to your apartment, which I told you, you left unlocked. She was there to check your shoe size. She needs you to try on some dress. She called your friend in Philadelphia, too, to see where you were. Tell me, come on, just swallow and then tell me why you can't come home."

I stuffed knuckled sheet into my mouth. "Because it's not home."

"Aw." He laughed at that, his nervous high laugh. "That's a good reason. Well, we'll make it a home." I could see him shopping in a bright new furniture store, full of plastic receptacles and lamps.

"No, it's not that. I want to go to the personnel office tomorrow and ask about his records. And go visit his department. Those old guys said everybody there now is new but I'm right here, it's crazy not to check. Even if I could find an old address."

"So do that tomorrow and then get on a plane tomorrow night."

"I've got the car, Jordan."

"What?" This was the first real blade in his voice, as if I'd tricked him, showed some stranger in me he'd never seen. I'd heard this turn in other people's voices, but this was the first time in him.

"I've got the Olds, my grandmother's Oldsmobile. She left it to me when she died."

"Leave it there, we'll get it later." He said that without much conviction.

"I can't. Don't worry, it's not that bad. I'll just drive it back to Wisconsin and then fly home. Listen, I'm better than I sound." I could hear, he thought I'd gone really bad. He wouldn't even tell me anything about himself.

That afternoon, I'd run out from the library, needing something.

I thought something to eat. I bumped into a boy who was bending down to lock a bike and he looked up mad and then when he saw me his face changed. "Sorry," he said.

But really, I was still fine then, no worse.

TWO BIG MAPS hung on a bulletin board outside the personnel office. On one, colored pins marked the places Firth Adams students came from; on the other, the pins showed where they went. Someone now worked in Xian, China. A hometown pin was stuck in Racine. I wondered who could be here from home. I would've loved to have an old friend here now. I felt like a person at the end of life. But then I remembered, any student from Racine would be ten years younger.

I walked into the door stenciled PERSONNEL on a vertical ribbed glass panel.

"Yes, can I help you?" a young woman said.

"I'm here on a kind of delicate and bizarre personal matter." I leaned over the counter to whisper this.

The young woman took a step back. "Yes?"

"I'm looking for John Atassi, who was employed by you many many years ago, in '73, and left, I understand, in bad circumstances. But I'm actually his daughter and I haven't seen him since I was a young girl." I lifted my hand to my face and breathed against it, smelled. It was normal, just slightly warmed air. It didn't taste. Still she seemed as if my breath occupied physical space.

"'73. Mkay, then I don't know. He wouldn't be on this computer file. We only go back to 1980."

"Do you have any hard files before that?"

"We do keep records, but we don't update addresses once they leave and so . . ."

"Could you check them anyway. Whatever you had would be useful."

"Now, how exactly do you spell his name?"

I spelled it for her slowly.

"Okay. And the first name again was?"

"Was John."

"Did you want to wait while I see what we have in the basement or can I call you?"

"Oh, I'll wait."

"It's not . . . it may take a few minutes."

I sat in a chair, watching office life. She looked at me like I couldn't be helped. I sank further back into the chair. The room was still and full of small movement at the same time, like a pond. Young men and women with clipboards arrived and they were led to an inner office. They seemed lightly dressed, crisp. Every time the older woman came back out, she looked at me.

I smiled, arms on the armrests. I hadn't slept last night. Waiting was fine.

"Okay, I'm back," my girl finally said. "I checked with Rosabeth Larson, who is the personnel director. And she said that we cannot give out addresses or any identification codes of former employees. What we do do is if somebody wants to send us a letter that's already stamped, we will put the address on it and send it to that person. We can try that but the last thing that we have here is actually a letter that came to us from California in '76, so I don't even know if that would be current."

"You won't give me that letter? It's my father."

"I told you our policy."

"My father," I said. "Doesn't that give me any rights?"

She looked as if she was looking at me but she wasn't. She was spotting the wall to my left. Then she turned down and wrote something I couldn't see.

"I wonder if I might talk to Rosabeth—"

That took another wait in the chair.

"Rosabeth Larson, may I help you." She lowered an arm down for me to shake. She looked like women I knew in Wisconsin, that curled married hair, a plain good face, scuffed pumps.

"Hi, my name is Mayan Stevenson and I'm in medical school." I must have been far gone, I was gesturing. "Back on the East Coast," I said and then I laughed idiotically for no reason. "But I'm here—"

"Denise briefed me on your conversation," she said, folding her arms.

"Can I ask one thing?"

"Certainly."

"Are there any conditions in which, legally, one would be able to get—"

"You bet, if I had a subpoena. Certainly, I would be able to give out the information."

"I'll have to find out what the legal procedures are for things like that because—" I stood up. "Okay, I'll check into that."

"The only other thing that I could do is just send you anything that might be a matter of public information. Can I have your address, please?"

"Oh, I'm at the"—my hand was going again—"the Holiday Inn down here on Nine."

That got me a look, angled and steady. She shook my hand again, once, hard.

OUTSIDE THE PERSONNEL OFFICE, blue sheets of paper listed job vacancies. Administrative Assistant: 60–70 wpm, telephone work, filing.

The sky still showed the first wisps of light, my exhaustion now seemed clean and earned. It was just eight-thirty. I loped across the highway to the coffee shop. I already knew where things were here. The little things I had to do for comfort. It was a small campus and there was this one tin diner. Students and truck drivers had taken all the booths so I sat on a stool. I lifted my hand on the counter and I was surprised how red and thick my hand was, how ragged the coat sleeve. I fingered an end of my hair. Better wash, I thought.

I found a broken pencil in the bottom of my purse and wrote "Wynne: subpoena, passport" on a paper napkin. I had so many lists going. My pockets and purse were full of little scraps that my fingers balled while I talked to the administrators. I pushed the little balls under my fingernails until it hurt. But now, writing lists I'd lose and never read, it was morning still and I'd ordered breakfast: I'd decided to eat one meal a day, and it felt like I'd set up a little industry. I was following a chain of names. Sometimes for minutes I forgot the end. All I could think was the next name, like the next move in chess.

From the phone on the wall by the bathroom, I called the detective. It had been a long time. I was calm with him. I wanted his help more than I still believed in it.

"Hi. I've got a lot more information. In 1973, he was teaching in Montana at Firth Adams College."

"Yup."

"And the last address they have for him is from 1976, in California. Now here's the problem."

"Yabanow, wait a minute. You're going too fast. The last address

they have for him was in California? Was that an address I didn't
have?"

"Who never had?"

"Did I ever have that address?"

"Jim, you never got past, you know, '57."

"I didn't have that address. That what you're saying?"

"Right."

"Go ahead."

"The problem is they won't give it to me. Nor will they give me his
social security number. They can't. Legally. Because that's personal
information. They could if I had a subpoena."

"Yup."

"Is there any legal way to get a subpoena?"

"No, you have no court case."

"Oh, it has to be a court case?"

"Of course."

"Okay, that was my question."

"No court case. No subpoena power."

"Okay, so with confidential stuff like that there's just no getting it?"

"Of course there is. All you gotta do is give it to me in writing and
then I'll see if I can get it for you."

"Well, I was very honest with them, though. I went in and told
them I was his daughter."

"You went in where?" His voice wavered funny, as if he pulled the
phone six inches away from his head and looked at it.

"I'm here, in Montana."

"That was a big mistake."

"Well, maybe it is."

"Listen, I can tell ya the truth. It was a mistake. Not the way to do
it. Not when you deal with them. I can do better from here on the
phone. Gimme everything you got in writing and I'll see if I can get
it. It's gonna be harder now. I may or may not be able to succeed, but
send it over. And go home. You're makin' yourself crazy over this.
You're gettin' hysterical."

"She's—the woman I talked to's—gonna get me everything in the
file that's public information."

"Awright. But she has his social security number?"

"Well, yeah, he worked here, she must. And she's got to have insurance forms too. There's also, he was also married here."

"Now listen to me, hold on a minute, awright? What you gotta do is send me all that information. And then I'll handle it from here. You understand what I'm sayin'?"

"Yeah. Okay."

"Were any of those associations any help?" Once, he'd given me a list of American Arab associations. Those addresses came from a book he had, published in 1962.

"Unh-uh."

"None?"

"I mean, I've written to 'em all." This was simple. The second lie is always easier.

"Right. So get me all that information you got and then give me the names of the people that you spoke to. Because I'm gonna have to see if I can avoid 'em. If I can I probably can get that information. Now, I may not be able to. But with the social"—he sighed—"we certainly would be in better shape."

"I just— Tell me one thing. I mean, I don't understand why I couldn't get some sort of legal authorization, this is my father we're talking about."

"At this point in life you should really know that. I'll tell you why. A subpoena is issued by an attorney, awright? The attorney can issue the subpoena because he's an officer of the court by virtue of having become an attorney."

"Any attorney?"

"Any attorney. But listen to me. You're not listening because you're jumping way ahead and what you're thinking right now I can tell you is dead wrong. He has to get what they call an index number. In other words he files a suit. Only when you have a lawsuit and you put down the index number and what judge it's before, can you issue a subpoena."

"Oh."

"In other words, you can't issue a subpoena just to get the information. You have no court case, you have no right."

"Mmm."

"My God, everyone'd be issuing subpoenas to everyone. We cannot issue you any subpoenas."

"Even if—"

"No lawyer can issue you a subpoena."

"Hm."

"So you can forget about the subpoena. It's totally out."

An extremely heavy man pressed by me. He latched the bathroom door with a delicate metal hook. The diner walls were flimsy. I heard everything slowly as it happened.

"See, it's a small school and I don't think you're going to be able to get this stuff because this woman was efficient. I mean, nice but efficient. If we could only get this damn address from '76."

"Well, we're makin' progress, Mayan. None of these things're easy. It's very few of them come easy at all. You've just got to be patient and not get frustrated. You've got to use your head, be calm even though you're emotionally tied into this thing."

"I wonder if I keep calling this woman too."

"If you keep calling her *what*?"

"It just seems to me eventually they'd give us this information. Maybe not."

"Well, sometimes persistency pays off. If you do it the right way, and if you've got the right individual they bend a little. Did she give you your father's date of birth?"

"We have that."

"Yeah, but did she confirm it?"

"I didn't ask her to."

"See, that's one thing. Give her that date of birth. Maybe we're off or maybe he's using a different date of birth. I'd verify the date of birth, ask her, would you please just verify this date of birth. And then ask her again if she could get the social, which I doubt, or the medical. Anything. And let me know."

Just then the man emerged, buckling his belt again. He had snake-skin boots. He looked away from me too as if we'd had some intimacy.

"I didn't even ask for a social. I knew that was pushing my luck. But I'll see if I can get the medical."

"Awright, and then as long as you can, push your luck."

I went back and swiveled onto my stool at the counter where my coffee was cooling. I already knew I wouldn't send him anything in writing. I just wouldn't. Mail seemed too slow. For me now. For this time.

I'd vowed not to eat the night before and I hadn't. But it was nine-fifteen and now I was starving. The waitress slapped down my order: blueberry pancakes, steaming, the plate running with butter.

. . .

AFTER BREAKFAST, I bought a comb. On the counter by the cash register, there was a cardboard display of plain black combs and a glass bowl of nail clippers for sale. And I went to the bathroom and combed. The diner mirror was broken off on one corner, but the glass was clear, too clear. Ridges stayed in the hair from my comb. I looked at myself and thought, no wonder. A large red pimple had grown on the tip of my nose. I thought of driving back to the hotel and grooming, taking the day, but then some determination welled in me again and I decided, no I'd just keep going, it shouldn't matter what I looked like if I tried hard enough. I dragged across campus, my ankle hurt I didn't know why and then I endured Denise in personnel again. She looked at me the worst way. But still I sensed something decent in her, duty-bound proper. If you demanded, she'd do it. Dryly, her fingers flipping over the keys of her computer board or through the pages of her file defiantly, with a taut flex in them. But she would set her chin and do her duty. She was a girl who had been toilet-trained on time and adeptly, a girl who wore clean underwear to bed, a girl who would never pee in a lake or a pool.

She told me, she just told me, the name of the insurance my father had: Teal County Medical. So he did have insurance. Probably if I ever found him, he'd be wearing sunglasses and carrying a closed umbrella. Then I tried to pull a social security number out of her. She actually checked in her manila file. "We don't show one," she said.

"But could they have paid him without it?"

That tricked her. "Probably not," she said, head bent down so I could see the sheer discipline of her part, "that would be payroll anyway."

Then she confirmed his date of birth. That was something anyway, not just another name to call. I felt it when Jim Wynne told me the first time and even more now. It was something true and absolute.

And I walked out feeling, enough. I wanted something before more work. I knew I should go to payroll next but I just ambled. It was a cold bright day and wind seemed to curve around every surface, making the tree trunks and buildings shine. Students wore bright parkas and heavy boots that clunked on the snow, now streaked old white, gray and brown.

Then I saw the bike for sale. A cardboard sign was masking-taped to the handlebars of a thick-wheeled three-speed with a square wire basket on the front. "$15 or best offer" was scrawled at an angle up to the right corner, and a dorm number. I asked a girl who stepped back and pointed and I found the dormitory and climbed up four flights of stairs to the room. A boy answered, which surprised me because it was a girl's bike. I seemed to have roused him from sleep. He lifted the hem of his red shirt and rubbed his stomach, yawning. I knew, without touching anything, that his skin was warm.

I held out a ten and a five.

He squinted and his mouth flickered in an expression of incomplete understanding. "Ya wanna buy it?" he said. Now he was scratching that belly.

I nodded dumbly. I tried to smile.

"Well, hey. Cool," he said. "Waita minute." He took a pair of corduroy pants from the floor, and pulled a key from the pocket. "Here ya go."

I ran down the stairs, dragging one hand on the mud-streaked wall. The key worked and I wound the coiled chain in the metal basket. I wasn't really dressed for a bike; I had my old long coat that clung around my legs, I must have looked like a witch, tails flapping, but it was fun, speeding down the icy drive to the building that housed payroll, the hard chapping wind on my cheeks. I only rode a few minutes and then locked the bike in front of the building. I took care now because it was mine. Well at least I have that, I was thinking.

The payroll office was a dungeon in the back basement of the gym. A heavyish woman, wearing a tiny gold heart locket around her neck, stood behind the counter. We were separated by bars. She had short curled hair, tended hands and an eager expression about the lips. A cloud of smell came from her, deep irises.

"Hello, I just spoke to Rosabeth Larson. And I'm looking for, I don't know if you're going to have any information. I'm looking for someone who left in 1973."

"Uh-ha."

"Named Atassi, A-T-A-S-S-I. And the first name is John."

"Uh-ha."

"And I'm wondering if you have any records left."

"Yes, he was a professor here for a short time."

"He's actually my father."

"Oh."

When people didn't talk much, I talked more. "And I haven't seen him since I was a very young girl, before, way before he taught here. He left our family in sort of an unfortunate way, but now my mother and I are looking for him."

"Uh-ha. Well, we sure wouldn't have any way of knowing where he'd be at this time."

"No. That was a long time ago. I know." Her features were sharp and well-proportioned but the face itself seemed too large. Her eyes and nose and mouth seemed pressed together in the middle. I noticed her blouse was a delicate material, ruffled on the front, a floral that must have taken ironing. She prepared this morning before work, for what? Just for this? I looked around the basement office, the light falling in a slant from above. Yes for this. For work. For everyday. For nothing. "Although actually Rosabeth Larson had an address from 1976 which is—"

"Oh."

"Something."

"It's more recent than what we have."

"We were going to ask you if you by any chance had a social security number." It was just easier to say we.

"Well, she said I could verify it if you had it, but that uh, she'd rather I didn't give that out." She? Oh, they'd called. They were on to me. My fingers fiddled in the lining of my pockets. I felt fugitive, frayed. I looked sideways at the wall.

"Is there no way you can give it to me because I'm his daughter? I realize this—"

"Uh-ha. Well, I just talked to them over there and that's what they said." So that was it. Damn that clean Denise. Damn Rosabeth Larson.

"If I could get one?"

"I could verify it, uh-ha."

"Hmm. How could I do that! Well, I don't know what to say. I don't have one."

"Uh-ha."

"So I guess I'll have to just let that go."

"If he . . . would he be teaching at another institution, I wonder?" She was just lightly talking at the tops of things.

She had what I wanted in that dungeon. I kept feeling there was some way I could push her more. In New York, her little I'd-rather-not meant yes. With most women if they said I'd-rather-not, you could get it out of them. Anything but an absolute no was a yes and she hadn't given me anything absolute. So I just jabbered.

"I don't know, he's a kind of mystery to us. He left in a sort of bad way, apparently. From Montana, I mean from you here. And we don't know where he went next."

"Uh-ha."

"There's some sense that he might be in California."

"Oh, uh-ha."

"Um, he's Egyptian." I was fidgeting there in my bulky frayed coat, my fingers small and close like gnats.

"Uh-ha."

"And so he's a naturalized citizen and we've been trying to call, well, we've been trying to call information in Egypt."

"Oh. Uh-ha."

"You know for directory assistance. But that is really hard. Because there's about a million Atassis, such an unusual name here but there—"

"Well, I spose. Sure."

Her face moved in familiar expressions. She was sympathetic the way Marion Werth got at the library counter with cranks. Always pleasant on the surface, but she was very far inside. I looked at this woman. She had on white-pink lipstick, her nails were filed in ovals, her plump fingers carried rings. She seemed such an unlikely guard for the magic number.

I kept trying, though. Something would open her.

"So, we're not, we're not having terribly good luck." I laughed like a goon. "But we'll keep trying."

"Unless, I don't spose the dean's office would have anything on file?" She was like my grandmother without my grandmother's sadness, the deep lines of her complexion smoothed.

"I'll check. I don't know this offhand but would my father's social security number be connected in any way to my mother's?" This was a last ditch fling.

"No, no they're all separate. Unless she mistakenly took his and used it." Here she laughed in a can't-we-wives-be-naughty way.

"But she probably didn't. She's worked for years so I suppose she wouldn't have."

"Uh-ha."

"And if I can find any trace of a social security number to verify?"

"Surely."

"I'll come back. What's your name?"

"Well, my name is Josephine Lockhardt and I am payroll assistant."

I WALKED ALONG HITTING WALLS. Brick walls stone walls plaster. So she had it. Clearly she had it. Josephine fucking Lockhardt with the heart locket who was payroll assistant could open the old manila file and see the typed numbers, nine between two dashes, that meant nothing to her but would change my life and she wouldn't give them to me. I hated flowers. She was iron beneath those waves of ruffle. Hard ringing metal. I wanted to harm her. Really. And it was all her duty. Rules. She believed in them the way my grandmother did. As if they must have some reason, some higher good reason none of us could ever know in our earth-close life. Screw that. What could it possibly have been to her?

I stopped at an outside pay phone.

"It's Teal County Medical Insurance," I told Wynne. "That's located in Eileen, Montana. And the date of birth is May 21, 1931. That's what they had too so it must be right."

"That's confirmed then. I thought that coulda been wrong to tell ya the truth. Now we're going into a confirmed date of birth and we know his insurance carrier. We're makin' progress. You gotta remember, see you're talking to me different now, you're lightening up a little and that's the way you gotta be. You can't let them frustrate you."

"I know."

"We're up to '75, maybe '76. That's good. Here's what I want ya to do," he said. "Nothing. I don't want you to do anything further. Ya hear? Just write, do me a favor, will ya? I want you to write a very, it doesn't have to be any detailed thing, anything fancy, just write down what happened and the people you talked to and anything else so I have it in the file, awright?"

"She wanted to give me the social security number, the woman in payroll, it's just that they'd called before I got to her. From personnel."

"Awright, give me her name and I'll bypass her. You just leave it to me. It can't be done now, you've got to give it time. We'll see with the insurance company, maybe."

"Any news from the passport guy?"

"Not yet."

"I forgot to tell you. The woman from Reno he was married to here had money. She might have owned a hotel or restaurant in Reno. The problem is we don't know her last name."

"We're gettin' real close now."

"If we could get her name, I could probably call her kids."

"If she's a woman who owned hotels, you understand, we can work with that in itself."

"One more thing though. The restaurant's name was the Donner Lodge or something like that. And a guy here thought my father had worked there once. Now the question is, do you want to try and go the social security route with them?"

"Here's what you should do, see you're the daughter and also a female voice sometimes is better."

"But the last time you told me doing it myself was a big mistake."

"Here's what you do. Now. On this you're going to be direct." He thought acting could get him out of this. He was all contradiction and bluff. I already knew he was a charlatan. "Awright? Because this is different."

Why, I felt like saying.

"You're going to call up where he used to work. You're going to explain to them exactly who you are. You're gonna give them, you're going to tell them you're happy to give them your phone number, your address, all that. Say you've been searching for your dad, that you understand *he* had been looking for *you*. Understand what I'm saying? You don't think he'd even know where to reach you. Now there you gotta lie a little. You're a doctor, you'd been on a fellowship, whatever, you hadn't even been in the country. He'd been looking for you maybe some years ago and you're now trying, the last you heard he was here. And then put in some hearts and flowers. Very intense, you understand? Because, they just gotta have a social security number."

"Right."

"Do they know where he is now? As simple a question as that. Now remember one thing, the thing to do is, when you do these things, you've got to somehow get people to want to help you. That's not an easy task. But somehow, through a voice or a tone or something, you've got to make them want to help you, you understand? Use some charm.''

"Okay." Charm. I smarted a moment when I put down the phone. I touched the side of my neck the receiver touched. I was getting a rash there. I must not have charm, I smiled a grim way, because I sure couldn't get Wynne to want to help me much.

I STOOD THERE at that outside pay phone, glad to be told what to do. Even though I had no faith left in the detective. He was just talking too, off the top of himself. I was pretty far gone. I dialed and dialed. I called the Donner Lodge four times before I got through to owners, who had never heard the name Atassi. They bought the place ten, twelve years ago from people they said were named Gilbert.

I tried Gilbert. Maybe that was Uta. Information in Nevada gave a U.J. on Bradley Square in Sparks, another just U.

"Hello, I'm looking for Uta Gilbert? Hello?"

They hung up.

The plain U got a recorded message: "Hey there, you've reached the Goodtime Country Dancers. If you're trying to reach Linda or Ukiah, we can't come to the phone right now . . .''

So many different lives and I wasn't having any of them. Square dancing. My hair was blowing in the wind, stiff from the cold. I was half frozen, attached to the metal phone, following my father's bones. That was what I wanted from my youth: I wanted to bury him. And then go back to the colored circle by the mulberry bush, wet hands on both sides of mine, and join the game.

I called J.D. Nash in Wisconsin and he told me some good news and some bad. He'd found a marriage of my father's in Orange County, California, to a woman named Agnes Rilella, in 1965. But then he'd found their divorce in the same county, later that same year. I spent an hour and a half on the phone calling California information for Agnes Rilella, a name I liked. Nothing. And the absence of Rilellas from the face of the earth, as if marrying my father had kept her and all her relatives from ever listing their phone numbers again, made me almost believe in his power. But then there was Sahar Atassi, the twenty-seven-year-old engineer who married the much younger Miss Diane Thayer of Mountainview, three years ago. They might have had nothing to do with my father and they couldn't be found either.

I was so nervous and crazy I could hardly listen to Mai linn talk. I kept thinking of all the things I had to do. I heard a noise and then I saw it was my foot hitting the pole. Before we hung up there was the small clicking I'd come to associate with Mai linn's absorption. "Mayan? I think you're up to about twenty-eight hundred on the credit card."

"Don't tell me anymore," I said.

I tried the State Liquor Authority in Nevada. Then California. That was an idea from the owners of the Donner Lodge. They had been nice. I knew now what the detective meant when he said we. He meant me. I'd do it. I was crazy enough to stand outside for three hours at one phone booth just dialing, not letting go. I tried Nevada, California, nine states in all. Just one more, I promised. Each time I thought of my phone bill. I had no idea, I knew I was probably into the thousands. That made me shudder on the left.

There was a moment of hope in Oregon when a woman named June said, "I'll check," and I heard the whirring computer keys. But no go. Nothing in Oregon or anyplace.

Finally I couldn't dial. I stopped for a moment. The tip of my first finger hurt. I looked at the hand and it was bad. Blue-black and bal-looned out in a blood blister. I put down the phone gentle, into its holder. I felt my neck. I had a rash.

Then I started again. I made twenty-eight calls in all and on the twenty-ninth, a recorded voice came on and said my card number was not valid. I did it again, then called the operator and she said there was no mistake the number I was telling her had been stopped. So my card had given out. They knew.

I BIKED TO THE Social Science Department, my fingers off the handle-bars, but it was already locked. I went back to try Dean Daniels once more.

"Hiya," Sandy said. Sandy was his secretary. She knew me. "Frank told me that he's gone to Rotary and won't be back until tomorrow, but he said that if you called or came by again there's nothing that he could add to what President Fipps already talked to you about."

"Try again tomorrow," I said, tapping my pockets with chapped hands.

I wielded the bike in the thin mountain air, light on the handlebars, wobbly, thinking, actually the goddamn detective didn't do a fucking thing. I was really a fool to believe what people say.

It kept coming back at me like something bad, the dates, the calendar time. My father taught here in this bowl of mountains, he felt these cedars finger inside his chest, he politicked the department, he tied ties for faculty dinnering the years I went through high school. He wasn't everywhere and nowhere. He was just here in Montana. It was as if I'd believed he truly vanished and no longer walked on the earth. That was where my feelings had started. This was entirely different. Now I felt duped. If he was only here, he could have sent for me, he could have been a typical, exasperated, disorganized divorced dad, hapless, producing felt-lined long boxes with pearls for my birthday or Christmas. I could have flown on planes, been met at the airport by him and Uta. I wouldn't have liked Uta, I never would have, but she would have tried to be kind, tried more than he did. And my mother and I would have accepted. We would have been cooperative, if not buoyant. He could have called us too seldom on the telephone and we would have complained to our grandmother but never to him; and to every question he asked long distance, answered fine.

In a jolt, I backbreaked for a deer, stopping the bike with dragged feet. It was beautiful, the ragged lope, stiff and unevenly weighted, and it left a trail of new footprints in the snow. I was almost to the parking lot, ringed with woods. I could have ended up at college here. Without knowing. I could have come as a student and he would have stood at the front of the room as my teacher. A podium and behind it, shuffling through notes, him. Dad. Dressed as a college professor. That seemed preposterous, incredible.

Then my mother's voice stamped through me, laughing: you would have never gone to Firth Adams College. And it was true. I wouldn't have ended up here. I was always planning for somewhere better.

STILL IN MY LONG COAT, I biked past the theater. I stopped and pushed the big doors back. They were there again, all of them, still the lush full world. Two girls in sheets and head wreaths walked near the lip of the stage. Behind them a brown rabbit streaked across.

From a large old chandelier on the ceiling, ribbons of all colors trailed like a maypole. I just sat down, chin in hands, elbows on knees.

Someone settled in next to me, I felt the knees of their jeans against mine.

They picked up my hand that was stiff like a claw. They set it on their knee where a rip was so I felt the warm hard of skin. Knee. I still wasn't sure if this was boy or girl. I chanced a look. Boy. Good.

"Remember me?"

No, I told him.

"Remember heaven?" Just then a cymbal sounded somewhere and the shimmers hung in the air. "I'm the angel."

We were the same size. Our legs matched. Our shoulders leveled. The moon hung low like an ornament and the walls were painted an old orchard. This was almost romantic except for me. I was the same as before. My head itched. I was wrong all over. The shoelaces were unlaced and gray-wet trailing the ground. I had a scratch on one side of my ankle. A rash. I kept putting a finger there and then to my mouth tasting blood.

I said all my things and he listened. I talked and talked for a long time like filling up a bucket with tiny things.

"Mmhm," he kept saying as I talked too much.

Then he took my chin in his hand between two fingers and kissed me. I felt the rough of his cheeks, his lips fitting into mine. He slipped his tongue under my top lip crossing and recrossing the ridge there.

I must have sputtered and choked. I ended up hugging my knees, head down away from him. "I'm dirty," I said like it wasn't bad but I couldn't help it anymore.

I got up then and ran. I swooned out in the air again, dizzy with high pleasure. He had been the apparition. I thought of the trapeze swinging, empty on an empty stage.

I WENT BACK into personnel and started a polite conversation with Denise. But then pretty soon I was yelling. "It's not my fault this is my father. This could've happened to you—you could have been born me. You were just lucky, don't you see the difference? It's just one number—"

I was sobbing and yelling, pulling a piece of my hair out and an odd thing happened. I disappeared. I was truly invisible. The office took on an odd sound. A kind of intermediary quiet, like sand running. It was the sound of the world without me.

A wall clock hummed its slow patience. On the other side of the counter someone plucked the keys of an adding machine and then there was the ticker-tape whir of the strip calculations.

Denise stared down at the slow shuffle she was doing with the paper and cards. It was a day. Every person in the office was busy working slowly. I was not there. My spill of noise, my rash, people moved around me. Denise said a bright "Can I help you?" to a man at my left and they didn't see me or hear me, none of them. I was not there.

If I'd stayed a minute longer I might have never come out the same. That is the tearing, shrill way to madness.

But somehow I found my face in water in a many-sinked bathroom, the cool tick of it, one line streaking down my neck, clavicle, then breast.

Then outside, I was slower now, afraid. It was still daylight but I went back to the motel.

WHEN I OPENED MY DOOR at the Holiday Inn, Jordan was sitting on the bed, a bag between his knees.

He kept looking at me and looking. I remembered how I was and put my hand on my hair. There was nothing to do to help it anymore. I just stood there unevenly, hands by my sides. He was looking to see me really as I was and he was watching his love leave, like a person packing, it was gathering its things now and clamping the buckles and then with one long glance over the shoulder it was gone and he was only looking at me, raw, a girl he had slept with a couple times and come all this way for, to the far Northwest, because she was in some kind of crazy trouble that had nothing to do with him.

"I brought donuts," he said, holding up the bag. He said that with incredible sadness. I had told him about how nowhere but the West had decent donuts, how Stevie and I had become connoisseurs. Jordan remembered every little thing I said. This was a funeral for him. He lifted the lids off take-out coffees and extracted small white napkins from the bag. He looked pretty good even here. His shirt was wrinkleless and he wore a quilted orange down vest. His hiking boots were brown leather, worn in the right amount.

I reached in the donut bag and didn't even look. I guess I was hungry. He must have just gotten there. The bag was still warm and smelled like sugar. I pulled out a big one. "Nutmeg?"

"Cardamom. You were right. This is the kind of town that would have great donuts," he said. He and I lamented the lack of fine donuts in New York or California or anywhere we'd want to live. You had to be in Wisconsin, the Midwest, somewhere that didn't get many kinds of lettuce.

He lifted up my hand, very gently—more gently than he would've still in love with me, because then there was an element of rough fear—opening it on his palm. "You know I'm taking you home."

"I have a lot more to do here."

"Go look at yourself in the mirror." His voice was hard.

The donut was greasing my chin and nose tip and all around my mouth. "I wasn't expecting guests," I said, lifting the donut delicately like a wineglass. "Anyway, let me eat first."

"Eat. We have lots of time. And you need it. I got us two seats on a noon flight tomorrow." He crossed his arms over his head and slowly reclined, as if he were at the end of a sit-up. He landed softly on the pillow. I kept eating. He'd bought all different kinds. This one was chocolate glazed. "There's another coffee in the bag," he said, "milk instead of cream." Another thing he remembered.

I just kept eating. It was all quiet. I heard myself chewing, the unevenness. Jordan's eyes had closed and I was glad not to be watched while I ate. I ate the way a fox does. I held the food, tore at it, looking at nothing else, felt only the blood rising to my face. Then after the excitement of the first three, I looked around. He was a kind of man I couldn't bear; he was always listening. He remembered me. I was conscious about my table manners. In a little while he got up fast and darting in a way that reminded me of a mosquito. "I'm running a bath for you," he yelled over his shoulder. I was to the end of the bag anyway, the bottom now transparent with the gold shine of oiled wax paper. Walking away he had a swing to him. He walked like he knew he had a right to walk on the earth.

I kept eating methodically. I was finishing what I'd started. I looked at the eclair while I ate it, appreciating the cool custard filling. I was trying to remember when I'd last eaten. Breakfast and then breakfast the day before.

Then I gave in. I took clothes off, dropping them as I went across the floor, so by the time I met the steam of the bathroom, it was only a T-shirt. I stood in the tub water and he pulled it off as if I were a child.

"Mayan, you've lost about fifteen pounds."

"Good."

He put his fingers around my wrist. "Not good. Your bones show through. You're too thin, Mayan."

He bent over the bath, reaching the little plastic bottles the Holiday Inn provided.

What day was today, I was thinking. Oh no. Back in New York City, I'd had a hair appointment. All that was a different life. I'd missed my appointment with Shawn.

He sat on the closed toilet seat and I just sunk in warm water. It was good to weigh for a while in someone else's hands.

My one arm dangled out over the porcelain, I wanted to feel the cool. He picked it up, turned the wrist so it almost hurt and then stared at my palm again. I yanked it back and under the water. I had writing on that hand, my left. I'd scribbled a note to remind myself, "Gamblers Anonymous."

"I thought of that too," he said. "Actually, my father did." His father was a journalist and he'd always done well with the Anonymouses. He'd written articles about groups like that. He'd won some prize.

"You're ruining yourself."

I didn't say anything. What could I say?

"Well, now tell me," he said.

"What?"

"Start anywhere. Just blab."

"I'm nowhere. After all this. I've burned my life down to the ground. The detective has started treating me like an old lover." I looked at him. He was listening. We were talking, this time, like friends.

"He lies. He contradicts himself. Things he said were any day now, like checking passport records, two months ago, he doesn't even mention. One minute he's telling me he could have gotten the social security number from here if I hadn't gone and blown it and then I find another place in Nevada where my father worked and he tells me to go do the same thing again."

"Maybe we should give him some more. Throw money at him," Jordan said.

"My millions." I laughed in a bad way, with sharp points. "I'm scared. I am literally scared to know how in debt I really am, Jordan.

My phone bill. It's got to be over a thousand dollars. But anyway, I'm gonna pay the guy *more* when for this much he got us to 1957? I got us to 1976 and I'm supposed to pay him?"

"I know. But you're in this far already and now you've got some information. Maybe with what you know now he can really do something."

"I don't trust the guy anymore. Before Christmas he told me he had someone checking out the passport records. Any day now, he says. He's inconsistent. It goes on and on. Oh, and it was paramount that I find out if my father had any insurance. Then I did. And I got the name of the company. We'll see what he does with that."

He lost my track halfway through. I must have sounded cracked. I did.

"Are you crying?" he asked, after a while.

"I'm tired. How can you even see in this steam? There's so much still to do. There's old addresses I want to check, if I can go to places like the gas and electric company, all kinds of little things like that you wouldn't think of, they have records, maybe they'd tell me where he lived here and what was his forwarding address."

Jordan just sighed and squeezed my hand and I stayed in the water a long time, now and again saying more ideas of where to look. When I finally stood up, he covered me in towel.

"Go to bed now," he said.

"It's not even eight."

"You need it," he said. "I'll sit by you." I lay with my back to him under the covers. He sat on the bed, sheltering. "The thing about all these little leads and hints, Mayan, they'll never end. They'll go to infinity and you could spend the rest of your life. We've got to go."

"You go."

He sighed and I slept in and out and I heard him stand up and sigh again and stretch and move around the room. When I woke up more, he'd opened the curtains and the night was true and black with stars and he was sitting in a chair reading my little Hans Christian Andersen book I'd found in a box Gish had saved for me of things from my grandmother. It was a tiny book with my name written in it by my mother, signed, *Love, Mother and Dad.* That was how old it was. The book was covered in waxed paper, I knew by my grandmother, the edges folded perfectly, like an envelope.

"Look what I found," he said.

It was a piece of old wide-lined elementary school paper I'd written on and stuck in the book. It was a list:

Gills Rock

Ironwood

Escanaba

Flint

Madison

Chicago

Peshtigo

Janesville

Kewaunee

Those were places I'd taken field trips and looked up my father's name in the telephone book. I'd been keeping track. The farthest was Chicago. The rest were in Wisconsin and Michigan. I knew he probably was not there. But they were the only places I'd been to yet then. I'd meant to always keep track; if I kept track long enough . . . The pencil marks had faded and the penmanship was primitive, big, like drawings of animals.

If someone had told me then as a child that phone books came out new every year . . . I couldn't have borne it, the exhausting size of work ahead.

He stood up, wringing his hands. The room seemed all shadows, the one bureau a rounded known thing. "I'll stay and help you one day. Can we make that deal?"

Wind rattled the cheap metal window frame.

I waved him away.

"I wasn't going to tell you this right away, but Emily's coming tomorrow. She's flying in to Fargo."

"What's *Emily* going to do in Fargo?"

"She's coming with a dress she wants to have fitted on you. And she wanted to go to Fargo instead of here, she called all around to find the closest place to Montana that had a seamstress. Apparently you have to have a certain sort of seamstress to sew this kind of Italian silk she has."

I snorted. "No you don't."

"That's what she said. It's not as if I grew up around a lot of Italian silk. Anyway. And she and I both talked to Timothy. He thought that it was a good idea too."

"You shouldn't have done that. I'm fine. And I'm embarrassed now. Getting all my friends, everybody talking about me."

"She wanted to come, Mayan. I didn't make her."

Now we were yelling. We had hardly ever been like this.

"Anyway, Fargo's not—where is Fargo anyway? It's far."

"It's not so far. We'll get you on a plane or a train or a bus, I don't know, anything, and she'll meet you at the station. You'll forget this, have a good time, eat and drink a little, do whatever you do with a dressmaker."

"No! I don't want to. I'm here and I'm going to finish this."

He covered his face with his hands. "Okay, tell you what. You go and meet Emily and I'll stay here by myself and see what I can do."

"I've heard that before."

"Not from me you haven't."

"I'm not going to leave without my car anyway."

"I'll drive your car. I'll give back the rental and I'll drive all night to Fargo. All right?"

I didn't say anything for a minute or maybe more.

"Well, okay? Say something, Mayan."

EVEN TODAY I don't know why I said yes. It was probably only embarrassment. The idea of the three of them having conversations about me in concerned, attractive tones. It seemed the best way to stop it was to be there. I was someone who liked to keep the elements of my life apart. The idea that they'd found one another, Timothy and Emily and this guy Jordan, it made me shudder. And now they were focused on me in Ambrose, it seemed impossible to go on with my activities. I felt watched. There was not enough here to defend. My project had always been a project that depended on the dim light of worldly unconcern. It thrived in secret because there was nothing visible to show.

The Greyhound bus left at eleven.

I went once more to the president's office. He had on another bow tie and different suspenders. "I have neither seen nor heard of him in the intervening years," he said, this time.

I told him I just wanted to leave my name and number in case he ever did hear anything. I wrote it all out, neatly on a sheet of paper.

"Where is 212?" he asked.

"New York. I live in New York."

"I knew it was one: New York, Washington, D.C., or Los Angeles." This seemed to warm him some, it being New York. That was the most impressive thing I'd told him. That I lived in New York. "I use those numbers regularly," he said. That flimsy vanity made me almost like him.

"Oh, well great. Thank you, Dr. Fipps."

"And what is your first name?"

"It's Mayan Stevenson," I said. I didn't judge that he deserved an explanation.

We waited for the bus in back of the tin diner. I put my hand on the roof of the car. It was hard to leave the Olds. I had my six things counted and locked in the trunk. He promised not to open it. The bike was strapped now to the top.

I SLEPT THROUGH most of the ride and when I woke up, the bus was steeping through mountains and snow, brushing close to wide fir branches. It was too hard to look. I closed my eyes again and went to sleep tasting the collar of my coat. There was always a quarter-sized wet spot there, like a childhood winter, tasting your breath through the scarf.

The bus stopped for food breaks and you could walk down the small main streets of these western towns, but I just stayed in and pressed my head in the corner of the seat and slept.

Emily met me at the station in Fargo, which was next to the YMCA. Fargo was a regular city, noisy, and I was glad to see her. She had a rented red Ford parked out in front, where a line of men sat on benches half bent over. She moved the long stick shift with grace and deliberation. We drove through the old part of the city. Smoke blued out into the sky.

"I thought we could do this dress thing first," she said. She was following a crude map and gradually the streets became, not newer, but more high and polished. "Believe me, finding someone who knew how to sew around here wasn't easy. But her name is Alma and she's a Czech. Apparently very good. She used to do the costumes for the Kansas City Opera. Now she has her own store."

"Fashion in Fargo," I said.

"Don't laugh. You're close."

ALMA'S ATELIER the sign said in theatrical cream-colored cursive on maroon. The store was wedged between a furrier and a jeweler called LaVake, who seemed to also carry cut-glass and silver. The doorbell pealed a high operatic fall.

Then we were crushed into a small room, lushly carpeted with a little circular rise before full-length three-way mirrors. The mirrors worked as a sort of shrine. The carpeted foyer was a little soiled and jammed with fabric bolts and tiny marked cardboard boxes of thread and pins. The back room was fitted with fabric heads and millinery projects in various states of completion.

Emily opened a large box and extracted the dress. The seamstress bent in close, her head down and her bulbous gnarled hands up under the sheer fabric. It was a fine faint pink, evenly transparent.

"Is gorgeous," the dressmaker said, lifting the silver framed bifocals down from her heavy hair. "You need underneath something."

Emily had the underslip folded in tissue. It was the sheerest white cotton, plain, exactly the same straight box shape as the dress.

I hated dresses that showed my legs and especially my knees. I had horrible knees.

"So is for you?" the dressmaker said, running her gaze slowly over my contours a way I hated. "Go. Try it on."

I bunched the thing in my hands. The woman took it from me and laid it out over my arm. "Is fragile," she said.

"Where?" I wasn't going to take my clothes off just me while they both stood there.

She showed me to behind a curtain, a little corner with no mirror.

"With green shoes," I heard Emily saying, while I pulled my T-shirt over my head. "Light green but rich, you know what I mean? And a square heel. Very simple."

The dressmaker began to ask Emily about her dress and she started to describe it and then I came out with mine on, still in my sneakers and athletic socks. They stopped talking.

"Mayan, it's your size. I had it made your size."

"She too thin," the dressmaker said, head down, making tching noises even with pins in her mouth. "Got to eat. Eat while you're young and you can enjoy it. The men they don't like the skinny skinny women. They like skinny women. That's just the women think they do. And when you get older is bad, around the chest is all skin like a chicken, all gathered up like this, no good."

She was down on the carpet now, I felt her hair against my knees. She took pins from her mouth, setting the hem.

When she came to the back and shoulders Emily stopped her. "Don't make it as small as she is now," she said. "The wedding's still five weeks away. She'll gain. I'll make her."

WE WAITED IN A SODA SHOP, sipping seltzer. Emily ate a whole sundae in front of me, black and tan. She made them take it back the first time because they used cold caramel. She wanted hot fudge and hot caramel.

I didn't want anything. An hour and a half later, Alma came into the store, with the dress in a large cardboard box. She herself was wearing a mink coat and matching hat.

"I leave a little room," she said, pinching my hips. I was thin enough so the pinch hurt. It hurt a little just to sit.

Emily bent down writing her check. She always looked diligent when she signed credit card forms or wrote checks. She looked more intently serious then than any other time as if money were the most solemn duty in this life.

Jordan arrived in Fargo the next day, with the social security number.

"How did you get it?" I said, the first thing. I hadn't even said hello. This was the first time he'd truly impressed me.

His voice got sharp. "I don't want to talk about it now, okay?" he said. This was not like him. At the hotel, he was rushing us around, pushing our backs. "I want to put Emily on her plane and I want us to get going so we can dump this car back in Wisconsin and fly to New York tomorrow night. I have to get back to work and so do you."

"Okay, okay," I said. God. "I never said you had to come here."

"I know. But we're finished. So let's just go now."

This wasn't like him. And anyway, I had nothing to get back to. But we saw Emily onto her flight.

She stood at the gate looking a way she hardly ever did, the knees of her jeans bagging, her hair uneven. "You sure you shouldn't chuck the car or get a driveaway for it and come back home?"

They both looked at me. It was up to me.

"I'd take it myself," Jordan said.

"Nah," I said, looking at my shoes. "I want to do it."

She had just the box with the altered dress in it and her bright silver carry-on suitcase. Jordan carried her suitcase until they wouldn't let him anymore and then he bent down to kiss her.

Then we were in the car driving the straight black road through the flat landscape. It was late afternoon and already getting dark. Everything, all around, looked blue.

He stared straight ahead from the steering wheel. I just studied my hands and low small things out the window. It felt like he was ticking. If he didn't want to talk to me, he didn't have to.

"First thing," he finally said. "Emily is a good woman. I don't want to hear any more about that dress. She didn't come out here for the dress."

"Oh yeah."

"She loves you, Mayan. She was worried about you."

He stared at me then and the car swerved a little on the road, but there was no one else for miles, just a red-brown truck that looked toy, it was so far away.

"What are you trying to tell me, you're interested in her? I don't care. Be my guest. You think you can break up her and Tad, go ahead and try."

"I am not in the least interested in Emily and I never would be. Obviously. I'm saying this for you, Mayan."

I just looked out the window.

"And the way I got the number I don't want you to ever tell anyone. I mean it. No one."

I was interested all of a sudden.

"I went to see Rosabeth Larson. One look at that suit made me know there was no asking her. She wasn't going to break any rules. But there were all these girls in little Rosabeth Larson suits waiting in line with their little clipboards to take a typing test for the job of Ms. Larson's administrative assistant."

"Yeah," I said.

"Well, among many of my talents that you've overlooked, I type fast. Plus apparently Rosabeth Larson doesn't want a younger Rosabeth Larson working alongside her. She wanted me."

"You got the job."

"No, not exactly. Your ex-asshole boyfriend, no I'm sorry, your ex-boyfriend who is still an asshole, Bud Edison, he got the job."

I laughed. Then I looked at him with my head down.

"But seriously. I'm a lawyer, Mayan, and stealing documents like that, it's illegal, I could be disbarred for that. And then what would I do? My grandfathers come to my law school graduation to have me kicked out of the bar forever for impersonating a secretary in Montana? I don't want Emily or anyone else to find out about this. I mean, even if we don't know each other in a year, don't tell anyone."

"But what did you do?"

"Oh, she showed me around the whole place and then she went to lunch. They've got four filing cabinets. It didn't take too long."

"And then what?"

"And then I left."

"You just split?"

"I didn't leave a formal letter of resignation."

"Oh," I said. "Well, thanks." There really was no way to thank him. It was just numbers. All this for numbers.

We drove all night, taking turns, and we entered Wisconsin at dawn. He kept calling ahead for the plane schedules. He was so eager to get home. I wasn't. I felt a little insulted or something that he wanted this to be over so. The last plane out was at seven o'clock. I called Danny Felchner from Route 29 between Wausau and Shawano. He said he'd meet us at the Radisson. We could have a few drinks there, he'd take the car to my cousin's and first drop us at the airport across the highway.

And it all went just that way.

The Radisson across from the airport was new and redwood, with young Oneida kids in black jeans taking drink orders and carrying in luggage.

Danny had brought my cousin Hal along. I never hardly saw Hal anymore. Hal looked good; he was thin again and his hair now was light blond. His eyes came out stronger, their pale blue. He was one of the ones in Racine who weren't prospering. What he did for a living was travel to Wisconsin Catholic schools and lecture about drugs and how they'd gotten him in trouble. I kept staring at his hair.

"You been outside a lot?" I said finally.

"In summer I'm out in the sun, in winter it's Sun In," he said. He shrugged. "Works. Five or six women on the string, that's not bad, worth the price of peroxide."

Jordan gave him a look like, you heathen, but there was some awe in it too and appraisal, all while his lips stayed steady on his straw. Jordan was drinking diet Coke.

"You serious about any of them?"I said.

"See, the one I like is married to somebody else see. And she's a good Christian woman so she probably won't leave him. But I think she kind of likes me too."

Hal described the four others, just as Danny Felchner picked up my hand. One worked at Van Zieden Grieden, another at Fort Howard, one was a teacher and one a nurse. "In fact she was on the ward when Gramma was in, that last time."

I didn't remember any nurse. Apparently she was freckled, thin, light brownish hair. But I only got there the last two days.

"I remember her," Danny Felchner said.

I looked at him funny.

"I was there when your grandmother was in the hospital, the three or four days before."

"You never told me that."

"I really liked your grandmother." He said that as if it had not the slightest thing to do with me, and I guess it didn't.

"Yeah, this Wendy told me something I didn't even remember about that," Hal said. "She said when Gram was in the delirium—"

"I remember that," I said. I was getting almost competitive, everyone else with their memories of her dying. When I came up that time, she didn't even know me, any of us.

"She kept saying, 'Kids, have fun while you're young. Live while you're young.'"

Danny Felchner looked at me, his crooked smile. "That's true," he said. "I heard her."

I'd never known. I punched my cousin in the arm. "And look at what a good job we're doing."

"Live while you're young," Hal bellowed. Then he raised his drink. It was vodka and colorless.

10

I LANDED HOME if you could call it that. Bad. There was no real reason for me now to be anywhere. And New York was not a kind place to return to. It was busy and I didn't look good and I had nothing. The sky was a strange color so I didn't look up, and snow by the sides of the highway was old and pocked. I heard the steady roar of industry in the towered distance and closer, outside the taxi window, the equal bluff other random noise of a basketball on an empty playground. The school seemed vacant, abandoned. One black man, older than me, was dribbling.

It was February. School had started. I had to go to the administration and meet my preceptor and the dean. I wore the suit my mother had bought me a few years ago. I looked in the mirror a moment before I left and shook my head. I was never right.

We'd had a fight over this suit. I wore it to see her once in San Francisco, when Stevie got his Ph.D. Emily was along and Mai linn. My mother was going to take us to dinner in a fancy place. It was raining out and I came and met them all outside the restaurant with not just-washed hair, hair washed maybe the day before, and the wrong shoes. I had high heels in a plastic bag but I was wearing old sneakers because of the rain and so the pants folded over my shoe a little. My mother took one look at me and said, "Oh, Ann," her face a cringe. "Why do you do this to me? I just wanted to go out once and have it be nice."

"I'm wearing the suit you bought," I said.

"And it looks like nothing. Four-hundred-dollar suit and you look worse than the little secretaries in the valley."

I took off a sneaker right there, standing on one foot, and replaced the heel.

"Water ruins shoes, Mom."

"Oh, go ahead and ruin them then. Look at Emily, look at Mai linn, they look great. Just let me see you look nice once, give me that pleasure."

Mai linn and Emily and I went over the fight later, when my mother was alone in the hotel room, nursing her own hurts. Emily could see what my mother meant. "I know what she means too," Mai linn said. It was the hair. They thought she was right about the hair. Mai linn was always a little soft about everybody's mother.

Sitting on the other side of the dean's huge wooden desk, I was the accused in a tiny court. The heat clanged on stiffly. Outside the day was gray, dark already, though it was still morning. My preceptor and the dean both drank coffee. They were laughing at something I didn't know. They had ceramic mugs that looked like their own and they didn't offer anything. The dean made reference to my failed course last semester, my absence now. Then he closed the file and looked at me.

"What seems to be the problem?" He had a large hairless head, with small features crammed together in the center.

I looked down on my lap where I saw a stain. Ketchup. I started to make an expression but no words lifted out.

"Pardon?" my preceptor said. She crossed one leg over the other and I watched the dean's huge face follow it. Isabel Windsor. She was one of the women doctors who wore rings and many bracelets. My suit was all of a sudden dowdy. Her skirt was short and her legs draped long, ending in an undulating curve of foot.

"It's something personal," I said. They waited a minute for more but I kept still. I almost told them something about a boyfriend but I couldn't think of what fast enough. I didn't remember the words. Jilted? That sounded too old-fashioned, from my grandmother's life. Then too late, I remembered. Ditched.

I wasn't going to tell them about my father. That was too out there. And what could I really say? I'd driven around the West and spent about four thousand dollars, which was more than I had.

I almost used my mother again. But this time I didn't. I just sat and waited.

The dean heaved in his chair with disappointment. Then I understood they were still waiting and that the price of staying in was to tell them the truth. I could tell them I had been in the West and I'd hired a detective. I had this mission and that was where I was. That would have worked, especially if I had found him. Instead of what I did.

I'd done that all my life, told little stories about my family to get me out of trouble. Other people liked to laugh at us. We were always one of the families that made average people feel a little better about their lives.

"A lot more effort is in order." The dean's mouth frowned, increasing the mass and volume of white on his face. His nod was a commandment.

I obeyed. "Yes," I said.

"So you may begin again. But we're going to suspend you for a year. And we'll expect a major turnaround. You understand this is a warning."

"Yes."

"They're lining up outside the gates," he said. "We know it's a cage but they're dying to get in." At this he smiled and Isabel Windsor laughed, metal jingling. They liked that. At the doorway, I saw they were still sitting there, laughing. For them this was a routine day.

Outside, harming my shoes in the wet snow, I passed through the gate. I stopped before I turned and tried to find their window. The light was on. I saw the shape of his head, squarish, the top corners rounded, like a loaf. They would be laughing too the day they told me I was out forever.

I walked to the hospital where I used to work. I waited at the slow public elevator bank like everybody else, then went to my old ward. They'd filled my job. I stood and talked to two orderlies I knew at the nurses' station but then they got busy. I just waited there anyway, I didn't want to leave. But nobody really wanted to stand around and talk to me now. They had work, I was in the way. An old man stuttered out of Emory's room on a walker. That reminded me of my upstairs neighbor; I had to give him my cane. I hadn't seen him since I came back and there'd been no noises from his TV drifting down. All of a sudden I hoped he was still alive.

I'd left my door unlocked again. My suitcase was still where I'd first set it right in the middle of the room, open. I'd been back five days. I'd just been taking things as I needed them, one by one. My toothbrush was the only thing back where it belonged and I was out of toothpaste. I'd been using just water the last few days. Another thing. It made me feel kind of diseased. I'd taken the suit out this morning. Now I felt around the suitcase with my hand until I found the cane. I'd wrapped it in T-shirts. I saw how good it was all over again. I took it upstairs and knocked at my neighbor's door. My body settled with relief when I heard the slow shuffle inside, then the machinery of locks. I handed him the cane horizontally. By then it was a true gift because I really did want it myself.

"For you," I said.

"Where from?"

"Wisconsin," I said. "A church bazaar."

"Come, come," he said, and then I was seated and his hands worked in the closet making us tea. The apartment smelled like something but I couldn't say what. An old man antiseptic smell. The noise in the kitchen went on a long time, rattling and domestic clinks and I was glad because I didn't have to talk. There was nowhere I had to be today. Or tomorrow. I felt dizzy with time. My arms hung loose in their sockets. Then he came out with a tray and covered pale green tea mugs, very proper. A napkin for each of us on the tray. I took mine and opened the lid. The tea steamed up at me, jungly-smelling. It tasted like bark and grass. He sat across from me and for some time we blew on our tea, saying nothing. It was odd, this silence, but I liked it. I sipped the tea, blowing it cool enough to taste. The not talking swelled and stayed and went on much longer than I'd thought it could, and now I positively enjoyed it like you would breathing the first clean breaths of pine mountain air and by then there was no question of breaking it. My life with my grandmother had been like that—long pure silences.

Then it was done and I stood up to go. He shuffled with me to the door. "And how do you do with your collection? Your butterfly?"

I shrugged. "I haven't been doing much about it lately."

He stamped the cane on the floor. "But you must think of your own collection."

"It's still there," I said.

I ran down the flight of stairs into my apartment and undressed. From the one window it was already tender evening light. I folded the suit up on one chair in a little pile for the dry cleaners. I had about ten little piles all over the apartment of things to do that a busy normal person could've accomplished all in one annoying day, but I lay down on the couch in my slip, the suitcase still open on my floor, not about to do anything because I didn't have to.

When the phone rang I was glad. "Emily," I said, with more warmth around that name than I'd probably ever felt. I was grateful and I didn't know how to say it.

"The shower's moved again, I know, I know. But my dad thinks the old people can't handle the loft. So this is it, we're going to do it at the Sign of the Dove. They've got this big room upstairs."

"Fine. Next week still?"

"Yeah, Friday. Oh, God, you'll never guess who told me about that space? Your old friend Guy Edison."

I stood with my hand on the back of my grandmother's rocker, tight.

"I saw him in this bookstore downtown. Remember I told you about that great bookstore that was shaped in a triangle? Well, I met him there and I told him about the shower."

"And that's all?"

"Well, no. He took me to this great little Italian coffee shop and we had milk and cannoli. He sure knows a lot of places in New York."

"So you two are going to be friends?"

"Well, I felt like I had to invite him to the shower. He asked if it was co-ed."

Now I truly did falter. I slid to the floor and put the phone down. I dialed Bud Edison. I hadn't spoken to him for a long time but I knew his number. At his office, they told me he had a new extension. I lifted my shoe up off the floor next to me and wrote the number down on the sole.

"I need to see you," I said, when it was him. I knew a lot of time had passed but it was different for me, not being there. I'd carried him with me the way you would a picture of someone in a locket. It couldn't be the same for him. I'd known that. For him the normal clock was on.

He named a certain corner and said we'd just find a coffee shop nearby someplace. I got there first, on time, and when he came, we turned into a diner where the name was covered in scaffolding. I ordered coffee but it was hard to swallow. We sat across the booth from each other and my throat felt peculiar. I didn't know if I could talk. I knocked the white coffee cup so it spilled in its saucer and on the table. I wiped it with napkins. Then I saw on my suit sleeve, there was a stain too. Maybe chocolate. That ice cream in North Dakota. My breath felt thin, insubstantial. I took two gulps of the black coffee. I wanted the hot to sting my throat open so I could talk.

He took my hand over the tabletop, looked down and smiled as if at that. "So how are you, Mine." That used to be his nickname for me, from my name said fast.

"Bad." I choked that out.

He just rubbed my hand with his thumb and first finger. I closed my eyes. I wanted to stop right here. The end. This I could bear and forget. But he patted my hand and lifted his away and so I opened my eyes.

I finished my coffee, what wasn't spilled. Now I needed more. The first wash opened my throat a little, but right after it swelled up again. When a man did come and give us refills, I tried to say thank you but no words came out, only thin reeds of air. I swallowed more. Twice.

He lifted his hand and moved it with his wrists through one of those light expressions I always loved him for. His eyebrows rose an inch and then down again softly, without disturbing anything underneath.

"Don't do this," I said. "Please." I was begging but it wasn't the first time. And I wished I'd begged more in my life.

He shrugged.

Another bad wall toppled in me, all she could tell him. Emily knew all about me and my family and me looking for my father and what people had said about us. Things that maybe I didn't even know. That was mine. Now, sometime she would just tell him, starting, Oh you didn't know. They would maybe be in a walk-in closet, dressing, he would be buttoning cuffs. He might always think, now why didn't she just tell me that? It bothered me so much, this thought. He never knew my mother.

"Do you talk about me?"

His eyes swept a half circle. "No, I only saw her that once, at the bookstore."

"Thank you." It was a small thing but it meant something to me.

"Don't," he said, and his hands were all over my face with the napkin.

"She looks—"

"She looks like a party." His mouth went a certain way, part apology, part just oh well. "She's fun, that's all. It's not being done to hurt you." He took his wallet out of his back pocket. I searched in my pockets for a dollar, extracted one, wrinkled. "I got it," he said. "Come on. Let's go." His hand guided my back. We stood on the corner where we'd met.

That was the only instance I knew exactly as it was happening that I was seeing a person I'd loved for the last time.

I STOOD WAITING as the travel agent mumbled out the numbers of my credit card into the telephone. I was charging the ticket and figured if they put the charge through, if they didn't keep my card and say I was past my limit, I'd take it while I still could. He hung up the phone, everything normal, and started writing out the paper, and so there I was.

"When would you like to go?" he asked.

"Tomorrow?"

"You know you've got to have a visa."

"Yes." I'd sent away for one a long time ago and then when I came home from Montana it was just there in the mess of my mail, slotted like a prize. It was the only envelope that pertained to any future.

"Okay," he said. "That's twelve-thirty p.m., it's international so get to the airport an hour and a half early." He handed me the paper. I tried to take it but he didn't let go of his side. "I'm going to Bora Bora," he said, "South Pacific, four weeks from Tuesday. A lot nicer in February than Egypt. Half the price. I'll show you the seashells." He pulled out a colored spiral from his desk drawer.

"Not this time," I said.

I touched the ticket, feeling No! and the thrilling abandon of the first arc of downward motion, that lift in the chest when you hang in the air after diving—something will happen now. I'd always wanted to pledge myself to finding my father or else. My mother and I had lived like that. We'd dared life. But no one seemed to be watching. In the end when we thought something had to happen, something or we would die, the days went on their regular selves and the fountains rushed and foamed on Wilshire Boulevard and the shop owners came with keys, like every morning, opening their big glass doors. We didn't get rescued by any man, as we'd wanted, we just ended up calling my grandmother to wire us money again.

It was till ten in the morning and I had the ticket. I wanted to find some Arabs before I went. I knew there were supposed to be grocery stores that sold baklava in Brooklyn somewhere. I stopped at the place across from school that sold hummus and tabouli and shish kabob in pita. But the guys there turned out to be Israelis. Nice guys, though. I told them the whole thing and they gave me a falafel. My so-called relatives sure hadn't been any help. I'd called them both, oh, twenty thirty times since coming back. I was sure now they kept their machines on just to avoid me. Then I thought of the university. They'd have to have some kind of Arab Studies department.

I kept asking directions and going upstairs. Finally, on the third-floor corner, I found Near Eastern Studies. The department office door was wide open and the room was painted yellow. A woman in black jeans and a black turtleneck with a hood stood near a floor-to-ceiling wire cage which held a parrot. Inside the cage, which looked homemade, was a large driftwood branch where the parrot perched. The woman stood holding a finger in to the bird, the phone from one old wooden desk to her ear. In her left hand, she delicately lifted a cheeseburger. From the glint of jewel, I saw she was married.

"Hello," she said in a musical voice, putting down the phone. "My name is Rania." She was dark-skinned, wide-eyed with an extremely full, flower-shaped mouth. She sounded younger than she looked. She could have been anywhere in a decade.

"I'm Mayan Atassi." That was the first time I'd said that since before Ted Stevenson broke our names and then disappeared back into randomness. "I'm looking for someone Egyptian," I said.

Just then the parrot flapped its long wings and squawked. She laughed. "Egyptian. Let's see. Professor Nawafi is," she said, "but he's on leave in Paris this year."

"You're not?" I said.

"No, I'm from Lebanon," she said. Lebanon. I'd always been told that I was conceived there. In a resort town in the mountains. My whole life I'd heard of Beirut and how it was the Switzerland of the Middle East and long after 1970 my mother kept talking about Lebanon as a neutral country where everyone kept their money because they never took sides in any war.

"Do you know Arabic?"

"Yes, mmhm. Can I help you somehow?"

I began to explain.

My mother used to say she never wanted me to be alone with my dad. "He could have you on a plane to Egypt in fifteen minutes," she'd snap her fingers, "and they'd have you married off and swelled up pregnant at fourteen." She always said pregnant with a spit in her voice as if she almost liked the thought of them ruining me. "That's what they do to girls over there. Girls are nothing."

"What about . . . going to college?" I'd said.

"College, in Egypt?" she said. She burst out with a bad, bitter-rinded laugh. "Forget it."

I'd sort of wanted to go except for college. But I was afraid to be pregnant like that, young. When I was a little girl in Wisconsin she'd always told me I would go to college. "You'll go to Radcliffe," she said. "Don't you worry, when the time comes, you'll get in. I know people. You'll get in, you'll see." When she made promises like that, her eyes filled to the surface as if the part of her that wished crossed the part of her that lied and gave a certain kind of smiling face with tears, like a rainbow.

I hadn't thought about her saying those things in years but I'd believed her, in a way, until I saw Rania, in front of me, a beautiful statistic. A Lebanese woman my age, not pregnant, hovering over a handmade birdcage. She told me she was working in this office while going for her master's at night in educational psychology. She'd married an American, a doctor. I looked at her ring closely now. It was dark gold, the diamond capped on either side by bright blue-green gems cut in squares.

Her husband's parents had been foreign service. "He was my gym teacher," she said.

I could have gone to my father after all. Even if he had stolen me, I would have lived.

But he didn't want it enough. When my mother, holding the phone, her toe bobbing the whole weight of her shoe, said in a kind of tilting tease, "I'm not letting her alone with you," he must have just said okay.

He didn't fight.

On three sheets of paper, Rania wrote the Miramar address, my address in New York and a little paragraph I dictated saying who I was and that I was looking for my father whom I hadn't seen in years and his name.

I opened my wallet and slipped these three papers in the deepest part. They became treasures. Rania asked me if I would come back when I returned and tell her what happened.

I was halfway down the hall, a clean echoing hall of black tiles, and then I ran back. "Rania, do you know what the weather is like there?"

She stepped out from behind the desk. She was a plump-cheeked woman, big-breasted, wonderful-looking. "Nice. Perfect. Like your San Francisco."

I WAS A SECRET. I was on an airplane flying to Cairo drinking vodka and no one knew. I'd landed in London and switched planes. I'd packed in an hour. I had the same message on my answering machine I always had. It didn't say anything about being gone.

I'd called Stevie from the airport and he was sleeping and I kept talking until he sounded alive because I couldn't let him call me back later. He could probably hear them announcing planes around me, but I couldn't tell him. It was one of those weird talks where he was tired and muffled, and I didn't want to say what I should have said but I couldn't get off the phone either, so I just kept blabbing.

"What are you doing?"

"Well, I'm lying in bed here. Helen's in Chico. Visiting her grandmother. Um. What's up with you?"

"Oh, nothing. I mean the same."

"Yeah?"

"Yeah. I'm going away for a few days. Week maybe."

"Where?"

"Where? Uh, the Cape. I'm, in fact I'm at the airport now. I need some scenery, you know, the beach. I got hungry for a lobster. I should go to Egypt someday. Check out my roots." I laughed a little, but coming from me he knew that wasn't just funny.

"You haven't given up yet, have you?"

"I try to. I don't think I can."

"Well, hold off until they straighten things out over there. It's not a very safe place to visit right now. And it's waited this long, it can wait a little more."

That did it. Then I knew I wouldn't tell him. This was no finding-my-roots trip anyway. This was in and out. Go to Shahira Miramar Street, see if he was there, if the house was still standing, then come back. That was it. No scenery. I'd be home before anyone knew it and then I'd tell them.

Then they were announcing my plane. I counted on him not being able to hear the words. They said them first in English, then in Arabic. We had to get off the phone. I prolonged it, like a kiss.

"You know you've been a great friend always you know. I wish I'd been better when we were younger but I couldn't be closer to anyone now no matter what."

He had no idea why I was saying these things and I expected him to say *yeah, yeah* but instead he seemed to really like it, and sort of rise up, like a person when you're bending down to kiss him lifts up not only his head but his whole back and shoulders and stretches his neck to meet you.

Now on the plane I wished I'd told someone.

This plane was like any plane except that I kept ordering vodka. I ordered another one even before I emptied the first little bottle. I didn't want to be without. The belly of the plane shuddered under a cloud and so I saw nothing but white vapor and then it was all water, the blue a grayish dull color with ribs like I imagined on desert sand.

The vodka made the ride different, slower. Wings out the window rounded old-fashioned, plain nickel silver.

Here I was going to Egypt. That was my mother's worst threat always, he'll get you on a plane to over there in no time, he could put you on a plane in fifteen minutes and once they've got you there . . . The way she warned had a sock in it, a real menace. She felt a little shudder of pleasure imagining me ruined, had by them. What was that in her? She had all the other too, kindnesses, many-colored.

But I was a grown-up now and being pregnant didn't seem only shame. It appeared even beautiful, a common thing. It was strange outliving the life with my mother: I was forever discovering little things I believed and assumed that were not true. Pregnant was not always ruined. Anyway, I might never be able to get pregnant, I remembered, and that was because of me.

I knew nothing. An Egyptian father and no words except what I'd learned so far on the plane from my *Arabic at a Glance* phrase book.

There weren't many Arabs in America. Not a popular minority. On all the forms you filled out where it gave some kind of advantage to minorities, they listed about seven different kinds with little boxes for you to check, and Arab was never a box. I guess they considered it just white. Or other. Being Arab was not something you'd want to right away admit, like being a Cherokee or Czech.

Though this was a turn and even a fight against my mother, I was sitting in her seat, the one she always demanded on airplanes and arranged for me, when she flew me home alone from wherever she was so my grandmother at age sixty and seventy had to drive one hundred miles to fetch me in godforsaken places. My mother always picked the best seats the way someone would pick the best part of a chicken and reserve it. She insisted, we had to sit over the wing. And here I sat, the proud steel below me, cutting the air with its round blunt blade, the slow fire of gaskets under, and here in the murmur of the plane it was not quite like other regular planes either, some of the passengers were veiled and the stewardesses themselves spoke with accents and everything looked modern and semiprofessional but had the slight ragged edges of the third world, a better taste in the food, something older and scant and closer to the ground and real animals of the world.

I wondered what Egypt would be. I thought of patterns of sand on deserts, the skin of bare feet, veiled women stepping off camels, how their hands moved. It was supposed to be a modern international airport. I knew nothing. I didn't know if it would feel absolutely foreign or just like anyplace now.

It was something—this—that might stay whether I found him or not, this being Arab, half Arab, invisible in the world.

Not a popular minority. Not a popular name. Not a swell guy.

No good, I could hear Jordan saying and shaking his head. No good, Mayan.

Anyway, there I was on the plane, an American wearing heavy black-framed sunglasses with the *E* volume of the *Encyclopaedia Britannica* open on my lap, reading the history of Egypt. I was reading about the Pyramids. After this came the *I* volume for Islam.

I'd always been suspicious of ethnics. Especially those who, like me, didn't look it. I looked it a little, but not enough that I couldn't have been anything else. A Jew for instance, which to many Americans was like the absolute opposite. Indian maybe. Most darker Americans look like they could be a couple of things.

"I'm more Arab than you are X," I'd said a hundred times. That's how I used it. To prove the other person and I were, both of us, nothing. I had a perverse streak. I liked to topple people's pride.

"Shht, quiet," my grandmother would say.

I liked to call people on their lapsing moments of ethnic identification. I always felt surprised after, how touchy they were. I was quick to point out to friends that their great-great-uncles may have died in Stalin's camps, but they themselves only roasted marshmallows at summer camp. I wasn't nice. But I couldn't resist. I believed those veils were fake and I loved the tearing off of them. Now I wondered, Were everybody else's ideas this suspect or only mine? Now it seemed I'd just been jealous. If I couldn't have that, no one should.

My father hadn't taught me any Arabic. I knew more about Egypt from my mother than from him. Even when she was married to Ted and we lived in the house on Carriage Court, she would sometimes make kibbe with lamb and pine nuts. She was always looking for a good yogurt culture.

I read Egyptian history in the *E* volume. The American Civil War produced a boom in Egyptian long-staple cotton during the 1860s. A century later, in Wisconsin, all my mother's and her sister's monogrammed blouses, in pink-and-white and yellow-and-white pinstripes, were made from Egyptian cotton. See, she'd say, over the ironing board, showing me the fine sheen. Napoleon's wife opened the Suez Canal in 1869.

I thought my father was already here by the time of Nasser's coup in 1952, but I wasn't sure. He met my mother in 1953 during the burning of Cairo. I stopped for a moment and looked out the window at the loft white cloud thin as pulled cotton, and thought of the great cities that had been burned. The burning of Atlanta, the burning of Moscow and the burning of Cairo. Hiroshima. Dresden. Berlin. I would like to have been one of the architects of reconstruction. I'd read about a painter in Beirut who only painted the central market as it was before the Civil Wars. He talked about the Poles rushing into their own archives before the German occupation of Warsaw, to steal the city plans they would need to rebuild.

My mother was pregnant with me in Egypt when Nasser nationalized the Suez Canal. When I asked her why she flew home when she did, sometimes she said it was so I could have the very best medical care anywhere, in Wisconsin, and other times she pulled her top lip down and serious, as if how could anyone be so dumb to ask, and said, "Well, the Suez Canal Crisis." My grandmother said anyway she couldn't eat the food there.

My father had left us in 1961 as the United Arab Republic fell to ruin. The year of Israel's grand victory in the Six-Day War, my mother and I flew out to Los Angeles where my father and his new wife, Uta, took us to Disneyland for two days. We both had go-go boots then and white fishnet stockings. The summer of 1970, when Nasser died and Sadat became president, my mother and I took the biggest chance of our lives and drove to California in a Lincoln Continental we didn't own so I could become a child star on television. A year earlier Yasser Arafat was elected chairman of the PLO and a year later Assad took over Syria. In 1973, we lived in Beverly Hills and didn't even read the newspaper, so the Yom Kippur War was over before we even heard about it. My grandmother died in the same year that Israel invaded Lebanon.

My mother had always followed the career of Cleopatra. We knew that she made a bed of rose petals for herself and Mark Antony and that she bathed in milk. I once asked my mother why she didn't name me that, Cleopatra. She shrugged. "I guess I thought you were a boy," she said. We both believed that the greatest career a man could have on the earth was to be something royal or a genius or the president. For a woman, it was to be a beauty.

Most of the names in the encyclopedia meant little to me, except they sounded something like Atassi. I read once about a Palestinian terrorist named Abu Leila, which meant Father of Night, and I wondered if my father could have been like that. He could have gone back. Maybe he did. When I was a child, he told me once, "Mayan, if I'd stayed there, I'd be running the country now. I had everything there for me, a great career waiting. One of the best families. Connections, everything." That was before he left us in Wisconsin.

I gazed out the window again, into the gauzy nothing. The encyclopedia was all fact, things hard to picture. The Ottomans built three major railways and paved roads just before World War One. Tuberculosis is prevalent amongst the Bedouins in the desert and in city slums. The Suez Canal construction began by peasants using spikes and baskets, peasants who were drafted into service. Under "Culture," they listed the Egyptian National Library, Egyptian Museum, Institut d'Egypte. I read about Misr studios and Egyptian General Cinema Corporation. A radio program *Voice of the Arabs.* Under the other Arab countries all they could mention was that Jordan had had a resurgence of folk dancing in recent years and that in Damascus there was a waxwork museum.

I loved the names: Port Said, Port Wish, the Big Bitter Lakes, Small Bitter Lakes.

"Hardly a day passed during 1975 and 1976 without a battle somewhere in Lebanon." I was in college then, working for the food service. My father was already gone from Montana.

Islam means Surrender.

Vodka made me drifty. Outside the plane was battened in white. It swerved and bumped. I didn't trust enough to sleep. The metal seemed fragilely hinged.

Once in a school Christmas play I had to read a part from the Bible and I said Syria wrong, I said it like diarrhea. My mother and grandmother were both sitting in the audience and my mother winced.

"Why did you get that wrong? You know how to pronounce Syria, you've heard it all your life. Syria."

I shrugged to her but the reason was because Carl Otter, who was Joseph, had read first and he'd said it that way. That was the same year my mother wanted to forget about making me a costume to be Mary and just send me in a long white muslin caftan she had from Egypt. "For Mary?" my aunt accused. My grandmother and aunt had planned for me to be in royal blue velvet. "Well, that's what they wear over there," my mother said. "Might as well be realistic for once."

Even though this was all against my mother, the whole trip, I hadn't thought about her until now. Then I felt terrible then for not calling her. What if I died? She'd never know, she'd put together the few facts, geography, and make it all worse than it was. I was taking off on a lark, flying on money I didn't have, a baffling, staggered self-indulgent search that would benefit no one probably, not the poor, not the damaged, only me at best, and so far I was worse for it. But it was something I had to do, anyhow, the way people become addicted to an abiding pain. The way my grandmother, once she'd laid out the cards for solitaire, had to play the game out and finish.

MY COUSINS AND I had been taken to see *Lawrence of Arabia* when it came to Racine at the Coliseum Cinema. Tickets were sold in advance for the matinee and Gish, in a long dress with a stylish jacket, ushered us to front seats. During those years, Gish was still trying to meet someone. "Where better than the movies?" she'd say. We reserved those seats with our coats, then ran back to the lobby for popcorn and candy. We stared at the bigger-than-us posters.

"She's part whatever he is, isn't she?" Gish asked my grandmother. Gish had never had children and she didn't fully believe that we could understand English, being the size we were. When she spoke to us directly, she used the minimal vocabulary she used with her cat.

My grandmother shook her head, "Yah-sure, from the dad."

"Does she feel part from over there?"

"I don't know," my grandmother said, looking down at us. "Do you feel any of that, Egyptian?"

I shrugged. "No," I said.

"Well, watch and see if you think this fellow looks like your dad any. I think he's a real handsome fellow, this Sharif."

"And see I like the other one, the Englishman," my grandmother said.

"We're never the same," Gish said.

"Well, it's a good thing we're not."

We shared a big paper pail of buttered popcorn and an orange drink with crushed ice. Some other children had to be taken home, they cried of boredom. My grandmother and I sat, transfixed, the moment we saw Omar Sharif, and camels and the desert wind of fine sand. I knew it was supposed to pertain to me somehow, it seemed important and solemn, a glimpse behind a veil of something that was always there and I didn't know. It was my one-afternoon chance to see and judge whether it was good or bad, this being Arab.

Maybe my father did look like Omar Sharif. I couldn't really remember.

Years later, I saw *Funny Lady* in California with my mother and we both took Omar Sharif's side, against her.

We felt badly, later, when his career fell apart. "I even wonder if he's still alive," my mother said once. He was never in anything anymore.

Most of being Arab I learned from the movies. I taught myself what morality I own, brick by brick. There was no rule book bible to hand me. We were nothing. My parents thought everyone else in Wisconsin was old-fashioned. They slept late, tangled under huge white sheets, Sunday mornings while church bells pealed into our bare, wooden-floored apartment. I was allowed to eat oranges from the refrigerator.

And my grandmother never taught me how to think. I was someone else's child. What she did mostly was show me things. That was how she spent her life herself. Seeing, as she would say, what there was to see. Even the things she grew in her garden, half were wild like rhubarb. She cried easily, she paid attention to children, asked whether our shoes were too tight or whether our teeth hurt or whether we were warm enough at night or needed another quilt. My grandmother had several pairs of rubber boots and was always happy to give me one. But I never saw any thread of sex in her. Her husband was dead and buried before I was born.

Maybe that was what I was flying here for. For sex or the seed of that in me, darker confidences. All I remember of my parents together was that apartment—the billowing curtains, dirt scattered from a potted plant by the floor of their bed, the taste of citrus peel on my gums. I was coming here for legs and for feet bold and unashamed of themselves, the flurry of hands before faces near veils, the strike of gold in a nose, lashing a neck from an ear, that music I didn't yet understand. Something.

My mother was sick. She knew things but they were mixed in her, like bees or plaster letters of an alphabet strewn in drawers. She was not ordered enough to spread her apron over her lap and teach me. She owned a mouth of sex in her but it frightened me. I had seen it open in her too early in bad ways.

I went to the bathroom. Airplanes, like woods and I supposed the desert, made you aware what it was to be a woman and not a man. In woods, you hovered and crouched over a tangle of panties. There seemed something strong and proud about a man peeing in a ditch, singular, statuesque, unafraid. I rinsed my face. I looked bad. Sometimes I remembered what I was doing and I felt like a wan stretched girl, searching the world grimly for her father who kept eluding her, while he lounged somewhere, Persian, tasting, lips curled up petallike to receive some imagined sweetness, like a cloudberry.

Maybe by the time you find the person, they are beside the point. You're not even sure you still want to anymore.

When my father was a boy in Egypt, during World War II, local papers flubbed. "They stayed"—he smiled all knowing when he told me this—"too local." He told me these things at my grandmother's linoleum kitchen table before he left. "The only real news," he said, "came from London." But my father was the youngest son of a rich man and so, at age eleven, he owned his own transistor radio. Huna London, the announcer said, in important tones and my father said those two words, Huna London, on all the momentous occasions of his life.

Huna London, he remembered saying to his bride the day he married my mother. "Huna London," he whispered to her again the night of my birth.

"Can I get a transistor radio?" I asked him that evening at the table, but my mother told me hush. It was still light out there often, when we sat down for supper, just dusk on the tops of the fields.

There were three really good families in Alexandria, my father said. The Rifais, the Higazis and us. We are Atassis. Not only were we Atassis, but my grandfather was the richest of all. At one time, he owned more than half of Alexandria. He controlled the price of wheat in all of Egypt. "He'd get up in the morning and decide, ten, fifteen, eight, and that would be it," my father said, his hand high in the air, one finger pointing. "And he really did bury pots of gold under the ground, in the dirt, somewhere on his land." He told me that same night that we were descended from the great prophet Mohammed.

"You are Mohammed," I said.

They had all laughed at that.

And now I was flying to the Land of Atassis with a passport that called me Stevenson. I imagined a pale pink ribbed desert strewn with huge silk slippers with toes that curled and pointed up, light green, yellow, minty blue, faded red.

I wondered what my father had made of that poor kitchen table in Wisconsin, the plastic napkin holder, the plates given away free, one with each tankful at the gas station, the rumble of the highway at the edge of our land. I was used to being poor. I grew up there. I grew up a way I'd by now learned to call poor, though at the time we never believed ourselves that, only that the table was our table, the plates our plates, what we ate, our supper. And we knew the land was ours.

Now the notion of a rich grandfather didn't exactly thrill me. Once, when I was little, I talked to that grandfather through the black telephone in the corner of my grandmother's kitchen and he promised to send me a sheep. I didn't know how the sheep would arrive. In a crate? In a box? Would he have holes to breathe through and hay to sleep on and feathery grass for him to eat? Years peeled by and my sheep never arrived. I'd forget him for a while, but never completely. "Oh, lookit here, comere, Mayan," my grandmother called once, years later. I was curled over the kitchen table making my magnet, studying the library book already years out of date, but we didn't know that then. I got up and went to the living room where she stood by the window, holding the curtain. There was a full storm, snowflakes dense in every inch of air. We watched the tiny mail cart jetting through the snow like a motorboat and the small man in his cap, standing out for just a minute to snap open the jaws of our mailbox, stick the mail in and lift a mittened hand to my grandmother—and for all I knew to all the others on the street who spent the storm day at their windows just waiting for someone to appear on their lonely road. It seemed the people there owned endless time, time to wait and wait. It never occurred to me that my grandmother watched for the mail like that for any reason but the arrival of my sheep.

My father remembered sleeping among sheep on summer nights, his head on their sides, their hearts knocking close beneath the skin, their deep animal smell, the reverberations of their baaing, ten times, no, one hundred times stronger than a cat's, he said. He rode out into the desert on camels with his father and they slept on the sand in tents pitched by the Bedouins. For breakfast, they made him, the boss's son, his favorite food. A kind of thin fresh bread, cooked like a pancake on what looked like an upside-down Chinese wok. These they would spread with good rich camel butter and then sugar and then another layer of the same until it was high as a wedding cake and they'd cut you a wedge and you could see all the layers like rings inside a tree.

But that's probably all gone now, I thought. I doubted the Bedouins, whoever they were, did that anymore. Like the encyclopedia said, they probably lived in city slums, which was too bad for me. I'd always wanted to taste that bread.

Even at the time my father told me, I wanted to know more. "But dad, what is a Bedouin?" I asked, at the kitchen table.

"Shh," my mother said. She nodded with her chin. "Listen to him. Don't interrupt with your voice so loud. They're like Gypsies," she said.

I asked the question again louder, almost shrieking.

My father turned to me nice, as if it were the first time he noticed anything. My grandmother moved silently through all this, by the stove. When he was there, she hardly ever talked.

"Oh, sweetie, Bedouin is like a job description. They're nomads. They go from place to place on the desert, following sheep."

That was, of course, before he left. He leaned his face down close to me that night. "So remember your dad was a big shot in Egypt, Mayan," he whispered, flashing the smile he was, at least to me, famous for.

I had not seen my father for sixteen years, maybe seventeen. For some reason I went back and forth between those two numbers like rocking on heels, is it sixteen or seventeen, as if that would make some huge difference.

Childhood nights sleeping under a deep sky, rich with stars, his ear resting on the warm jiggle of a sheep's sheer belly, the moving mass, an occasional low tremolo sound, the sharp dark smell. Those were my father's nights. He had had time in his life. I had had my nights, too. I slept outside once with my cousin, biting the white ends of long weeds, the first time we admitted his family and all the families we knew were different from my mother. Later, I slept outside with Stevie Howard. I had my nights and days. Our whole family did— only they weren't together with each other, and the people we lived them with were ghosts now. We each kept our own memories privately.

A voice rippled over the public address system, first in fluid, lush-voweled Arabic, then in accented English, and finally in French, saying we must prepare for landing in Cairo and fasten seat belts.

I closed my eyes and did what I was told. The plane all of a sudden seemed old, the round of the wing a dull cleft silver, the plaid seats made long ago, and I felt again how no one knew I was here, no one, and if the worst happened now, I would have gone as my grandmother did leaving none of the ones I'd loved anything in my own handwriting. I didn't even have a will and I should have. I for sure had no money now, but I'd want certain people to have certain things. People like Emory, whom no one would remember.

The plane shuddered and fired and buckled like the last writhing moments of a birth. I squeezed the armrests of the seat and then we were there on the ground, still bouncing, the engine's roar louder, the wings outside beating up and down hard but all of a sudden we were slow and even, going forward on land. Planes seem the same everywhere but they aren't. This one had a smell like an animal, something alive.

I unbuckled the seat belt, took my backpack down from the overhead. This was the least I'd ever packed for any trip. I had just these clothes I was wearing, another white shirt and black pants, the two heavy books and my money. All the money I had left at all. This was not a trip or even a vacation, but a mission. Or an errand. I wanted to go to that one house in Alexandria, that was all, and then come home.

In the close line pressing out of the plane, a foreign smell rose up, like intensified paprika or cumin. We climbed down the silver metal staircase and onto a tarmac. The air tasted warm, with a thread of eucalyptus. In the distance, flat yellow and brown land ended with a line of cypress. The green of the palms seemed darker here, older, tinged with gold. They seemed to vibrate in the trembling air. And the sky was a different blue. It was light but not pale, a dense, sunshot blue, clear with a few far clouds. It was good.

I walked into the airport, plain signs etched in calligraphy, white on black. Hundreds of people moved on the ground. There were black veils, white veils like billowing curtains. Some veils went halfway down the back like nuns' habits, others were light little things, barely covering the face. Some women looked hidden and foreign and unrecognizable, but others wore it like an adornment, another accessory of fashion, the way the truly stylish use glasses—something to be accommodated and sighed over in the temporal glissening effort to be beautiful just now, here, on this modern, crossed, still man-run earth.

I put my pack down a second on the hard cement and just stood there. A scarved woman in white brushed by, her feet articulate in sandals. There were soldiers around, young boys in dusty black uniforms and cracked boots, carrying long guns. The cypress in the distance looked solemn and old. I knew, right away yes, this was a place. It was good. Outside the glass doors, chances smiled everywhere out of signs, many in English. I could see the desert on a two-day camel excursion, the Norman ruins, mosques. I could tour Cairo. The Pyramids. The Suez Canal. Antiquities. The Nile. One sign claimed Egypt owned four of the seven Wonders of the World. My pack leaning on my knee, I yearned for a moment to just go to the university. I imagined domed towers and minarets, Ottoman caliphs and formal Alhambra gardens all with the timeless lazy bookish peace of a university anywhere. That hurt to even think. All of a sudden, I missed home. Home for me was abstract, but it still existed. There was no house full of things anymore—there wasn't even room for me to stay in my mother's apartment. Home for a single person living in a city was different. It was two friends, my same pizza place, the faces at school and work. You were less independent really than a settled person in one house with a family, who could leave and go anywhere and with one phone call, get it all back.

For me, the real shrine of France was the living, café-noised, kid-ridden Sorbonne.

Still, this was different, this wasn't a foreign place to see like that. This was a place I was from. My mother told me I had been conceived in a resort hill town in Lebanon. And I had my mission or errand, whatever it was. The nineteen-hundred-dollar errand. I could bear to think that here. Here I could even bear it to be nothing. The way the air tasted and the sky went back and back, I could look at the good chance I was a fool and laugh. Maybe that was what Egypt was for: to give me back my sense of humor. That's what I would have if, at the end of all this search, I saw nothing. But how would I know it was the end?

Some kinds of confidence I did have. For example, backpacks. I believed I started leather backpacks. First I had had one and people stopped me on the street asking about it and now everywhere you looked, people had them, even here, by the counter, a woman in purdah.

I picked up mine and went to look for a driver, guidebook open in one hand, like any tourist. I didn't care how out of it I seemed. I was. And I wanted to make it to Alexandria tonight and get myself in a hotel there so I could find Shahira Miramar Street the first proper thing in the morning.

"Wel-comb in Egypt," a large man said.

Egypt, that first brass afternoon in spring, may have been the most stylish place I ever saw on the earth. Nobody had ever told me about the cars. The cars were old German and American cars from the 1950s and '60s, black and rounded. They honked, shined everywhere and I found a driver to Alexandria with my guidebook propped like a piece of music between two pronged fingers, a rabba lad aal budAlexandria. Alexandria was a long way—two guys turned me down before this one. He was handsome and young, with many teeth, and he had a dry grassy smell the closer I stood to him. We bargained a price in dollars, I had to get pounds still. He knew almost no English. He had a book. I sat in the back of the old Mercedes on deep leather seats made soft with time and watched out the rolled-down windows as we left Cairo in a circle like a maze and drove north into the horizon of cypress, eucalyptus and olive trees. It was good.

"I know no many words," he said.

I pointed to his head and said, "Head," then to his hair and said, "Hair."

"I know, I know," he said.

There was so much sky. All the ground and trees, people and even buildings rose about an inch and the rest was sky. It was February 24. I wanted to remember the day. I lay my head back on the seat and the smell of earth rolled over me. This wasn't desert like I'd expected. It was dirt, not light sand, but the vegetation was different, scarce and somber. Ragged trees moved slightly in what there was of wind, and they seemed to whine and creak, *we don't have to us what we once did.* There were date palm and eucalyptus, sycamore. Closer in, there were acacia, juniper, jacaranda and grass.

I felt looser in my clothes when I couldn't see Cairo behind us anymore. We were on an old road. The structures you saw in the distance here looked small, made of concrete and mud. A rich weedy taste came in from the air. I thought of my father and how, even though he was a boy who grew up here in this old, slow country, he'd moved in suits and silk ties all over the world, it sounded like. This was a place with its own smell where you'd take the city off and put your real clothes on, loose and cotton. The States, Italy and Paris and Greece on the way back from the Cairo Caper, and who knew where else how many times. And I'd traveled, too. I'd driven cross-country a lot of times, I had my college summer in Europe, all of us now, even my grandmother's friends in Racine had been around the world, but do we, any of us, love more?

Maybe that was the first mistake: leaving. I'd always followed the career of Yasir Arafat. I read an interview in *Playboy* magazine once where he was laughing and saying he almost came to America. "I was accepted into the University of Texas—I think it was the University of Texas," he said. "Anyways, I didn't go."

Seeing out the windows, shacks and stands of trees, camels became horses, familiar already, made one piece settle in place right like something lost from a puzzle. If this was Egypt, maybe that explained Wisconsin. His existence there. On the road ahead of us I saw a small wet lake and then a brown mountain, which disappeared when we came close. I'd been told about mirages, in school, when I learned the word, but I'd never seen one. This landscape made mirages. Maybe it took a desert, I thought, to produce them. Once in a while the driver turned to me and we'd try to talk but it was too hard so he'd fall back to his driving, which he did with an evenness and a happy hum that seemed odd and discordant as sitar music and with a vague smile meaning I didn't know what but which seemed to move through a sort of plot sequence and I'd rest back on the seat, thinking how I'd like to sleep with this boy just once just tonight in my hotel room and wondering if I could, how this worked and whether I should give him money and how if I did, this was so foreign no one would know. No one ever. The rest of my life no one would know.

I stared at the back of his neck. His hair was cut short there but it still curled. Right below where the hair ended were two lines of sweat, tiny drops balanced on the dark taut skin. I thought that moment how hard it was to be a man. Because this was all just in me. And the distance between imagining and placing a hand in the world on someone's skin—I didn't know how that happened. That seemed enormous. Even when there were two cultures and no language and you had the money.

But no. That wasn't good. Being bought with money could harm anyone. Whether he knew it or not. I shuddered then, thinking how much it attracted. There is a real temptation of, you are alone and you can get this and no one is watching from anywhere, no eyes, you are absolutely alone and you have some way to make this person yours. And no one will ever know. I could take what I wanted for American dollars and no one would see. Isn't that what Kenneth Klicka thought, I have her alone, she has nothing, no one, there is only this basement room and nothing else.

I tapped his shoulder—his skin through the cotton was warm—and pointed for him to stop at a market, a bazaar of some kind by the side of the road. It looked like a farm food stand anywhere in the country at home, except the trees were high date palms. I was hungry. He pulled over the Mercedes, its bulk calming smoothly on the dirt gravel pass. We got out. The canvas and tin-roofed tents shaded jars of oil, dates still on the branch, almonds, pine nuts, diamond-cut pastries in tin pans—running with honey and hazed by close thick black flies—pomegranates, olives; figs lay open and red, dusty purple on the outside. A thin man, dark-skinned with almost no hair on his legs and arms and head, sat cross-legged on a striped rug uneven on the ground. His eyes were mostly closed. A clear glass jar, like something you would buy jam in, sat full by his knee. I kept trying to get close enough to see. I browsed by a table with nothing recognizable on it: some kind of cheese in water, I thought. I saw then in his jar; it was a coiled snake, I couldn't tell dead or alive.

I wanted figs and dates and almonds and started to gather them, they had brown paper bags, but then my driver came up and with elaborate arm motions pointed to his chest establishing, I'll do this, without words, and the thin man's flat sunken mouth smiled a big smile like, I was caught, okay, she's an American, it's all game.

Walking back to the car with my bag of fruit, I heard a familiar monotonous sound. I walked across the sand and looked behind the tent. A rickety Ping-Pong table was set up on the ground and two boys were playing.

And then we were driving again, he conducting a long speech to me in Arabic, probably about how much money he'd saved me, and I murmured in ways that I hoped made it seem I understood. "Is no good for you, is better for you," was all I understood. His one arm sometimes lifted off the wheel articulate and graceful but I wished I could settle it back to driving and I ate the fresh dates, the skins crumbling like sugar and the fruit inside melting like honey. I could eat like this for a hundred years. In the backseat there was a long soft breeze and sun on the left side, so I took off my shoes and my long shirt and just lay down in my tank top and skirt, legs bare, feet on the leather, feeling it almost like another skin. I was sort of asleep but not really. The breeze played on my belly, my upper arms, the bones of my neck. It was good. The smell of the fruit in the footspace swelled up in shells of air.

A long time later he made some punctuating noise in the front and I sat up and in the distance we began to see Alexandria like a series of half staircases on a hill. This was the place my father grew up. It was early evening now, seven o'clock and not much light kept, and what was came oranging around the white buildings, at corners and window wells as he drove through the winding streets. The roads looked older than the Ottoman Empire, some of them, but still used, not kept for antique. There were geraniums in windows like Paris. Close up, the stone and plaster were crumbling and dirty. A lot of the houses had a clay pot on the roof, I wondered what for. Some of the buildings had a white sheen, with mosaic. The streets felt quieter than Cairo, neighborhoods lower, the old sun like a bucket full of water spilled on the bricks. This was a smaller city, I guessed, and it was supposed to be holy too, I knew that. Not just for me.

"Mumkin ahgiz ohda ghur-fa min hi-na?"

I tried to read to him from the guidebook but he didn't understand. Then I just gave up and moved to right behind his shoulder and showed him where it was printed in Arabic calligraphy, pointing with my fingernail while the car moved unevenly over the bricks. I wanted a hotel. He put his hand to his forehead thinking, I guess, and then exploded with the head-nod ecstasy of yes. He was so young. His shirt was striped, yellow and green. Just then I noticed a Band-Aid on his right arm, near the elbow, a Band-Aid printed with circus animals, the kind we always wanted as children. Is that what became of circus Band-Aids? The surplus shipped to the third world. That would be like American business.

Then we turned a corner and beyond us was the Mediterranean, blue and green and moving with unrest, like a sea of barking dogs. He drove me to an ugly hotel, modern and rundown, and he stopped the car. I said no, crossed my arms, and found the word for old in the guidebook. This set him wondering awhile and then he got it, and the next place was right: white and Persian-looking, with small cracks snaking down the towers. He just parked the Mercedes, pulled the keys out and came inside with me, carrying the pack. It seemed too hard to argue. He wanted to deal with the desk for me, so I stood next to him, holding out my credit card. The man behind the desk took it, produced a key and that was the end of it. An old cage elevator, with script I could never read, lyrical cursives strewn in fancy metal painted white, stopped at the ninth floor where the smell of old geraniums came profuse and dusty and breath-stopping almost, but I followed and he opened the door of my room and it was good.

French doors opened to a small terrace and a sunset fired outside. I looked in the bathroom, it was completely tiled, even the ceiling, so it seemed you could wash it out with a hose. The bed was plain and white, a small prayer rug waited in one corner. The carpet was a very faded red and dirty. Everywhere here's probably like that, I thought. I don't know why.

My driver put my backpack down and stood there.

I reached my wallet out of the pack and paid him the amount we agreed plus ten dollars.

He counted slowly, with complication, twice, then his face cleared and he handed me back ten one-dollar bills.

I shook my head no, pointed—for you, then I grabbed the phrase book and tried to find the words that meant "for the children." In the guidebook, it said you were supposed to say "for the children." He looked pretty young to have children and I couldn't find the damn phrase anyway, so I just pushed the money back in his hand and he started shaking his head no, and I put my hands behind my back meaning I won't take it and then he pushed my shoulders, gentle but a real push, the money held up in his hand between us, and for a minute we didn't know what was happening and then we were falling back, me first on the bed and then him.

I looked at his skin where it stretched and spread taut wings from his neck to his top chest bones and remembered he was young. Younger than twenty probably. All of a sudden I had to hear his name. I didn't want him to be Atassi. He could have been. My father might have come back. Then I remembered my father telling me around that old kitchen table, "If I went back, I'd be running the country." Well, he wasn't running the country. I read the newspapers. I knew those people's names. That's how much I still believed everything he'd said. He said so little to us, I kept every sentence saved. I could lift one up like a bracelet or strand of pearls from a box. As if any young man could be held responsible for grandiose dreams whispered to an infant daughter, when he was new in a country and still thought everything was possible.

But he could have come back. It was more than twenty years ago he'd said that. He was a very young man then.

I rolled over on my belly, reached down for the guidebook. My shoes fell off the side of the bed. He pulled me back by my ankle. I felt his fingers like a bracelet. I riffled through the pages. There it was, My name is _____. "Ismee Mayan Atassi," I said.

He pointed to his chest. "Me Ramadan el-Said. Me born during the Ramadan so my mother she call me that."

Okay. Fine. I lay back on the bed, the book dropped. This was good. We couldn't say a word and I'd stopped trying, but maybe because of that something else worked. I always talked too much in bed anyway I was thinking and I lay back and wished he would touch my neck for some reason I don't know why and I don't know if I've ever wanted that or thought that before, my neck, but he did, first with his fingers, hard so I felt my pulse flutter. I didn't know if it would be different or the same this far away with someone not in my same language or anything, a complete stranger, but I watched the fan in the ceiling slowly mark the room with carousel shadows and in a minute I was lifting my hips to shrug my skirt off and then we were both naked, he was dark and thin and not different really. I touched him and looked in his face, his cheeks seemed to spread wider apart and questions stood like cool statues in his eyes and I wanted him and started it and then it began. It went on a long time, well into first dark, it never really stopped. I'd turn over on my side and clutch some sheet around me and look out the windows at the clear stars and he'd be on my back with his hands and mouth and then something would feel like a shot, absolute and four-pointed but blooming pleasure and we'd begin again and it went on so long sometimes I'd forget and I'd feel I was the man, entering him and he seemed that way too, opened, split, eyes shallowing up like hungry fish on the surface, as if in the night we traded who owned the outside and the inside, who could penetrate and who could enclose. The stranger was in me and I wanted that. I guess I finally fell asleep. I heard water rushing then and he woke me. It was still dark. I dragged sheet behind me to the window where there was one loud star that almost hurt to look at like a too proud diamond, somebody else's, and then I wondered why he'd woken me so late or so early and then he pushed me to the bathroom where he'd run a deep tub with a flower floating on the top the whole thing smelling almond and he put me in it. Then I saw the blood. It wavered in the water like a frilly ribbon. I stepped out and saw him kneeling by the bed. The sheet was soaked red. I was bleeding. He started kissing the inside of my thighs, which were bloodstained like some all-directioned flower. I couldn't tell him how happy I was, with the guidebook, anything, there was no way to explain. Before I lost my period, like a stitch in knitting, I'd minded blood in a prissy way, hated the bother of it, worried about spotting. Now I could have tasted it. I felt like shouting. That was over, the long punishment for what I'd done to myself. I had my own full choices again. He was looking up at me now with different eyes, submissive. He knelt by the bed and capped my knees with his hands. He said words I didn't know.

Then he rampaged around the room. I found him squatting over the guidebook. He said in English, "I love you." He kept looking up at me in this slave way. Then I understood. The blood. He thought that meant virgin, that I'd given that to him. "No," I tried to tell him. "No." He picked me up then, an arm under the crook of my knees and one under my back. He took me to the tub again. He was carrying me like some fragile child. I had to clear this up. But there was no way. His brown eyes fixed. I slipped down into the water, and I heard him again in the other room. I heard him pull up his pants, the clink of keys and change. He stole out the door. I figured I'd never see him again and that was fine like a sealed perfect envelope. A tangerine peeled, every section intact. I got up out of the water to latch the door behind him, though. Then I went back to sleep, thrilling even in dream every time I felt the trickle of blood.

The next morning, the hills were still raw brown with a haze of purple on the surface. The ocean was a plain gray color. I felt proud because with the guidebook I ordered room service coffee and it came with a wet rose on the tableclothed tray. When I took a bath I remembered last night and pulled the petals which fell off easily because the flower was full and seedy. I sat with the coffee on the tiled rim of the tub. A line of blood ran jagged like the thinnest twig. This blood was going to be a problem. I went to the guidebook but there was nothing under Tampax. This was definitely the kind of thing you should bring with you to a place like this, but I hadn't had a real period for so long. I tried to think what my grandmother would have done. She wouldn't have liked it one bit, either. And I never was like her, the kind of woman who traveled prepared with things like safety pins and Handi Wipes. I called the desk and sat with the guidebook and finally sputtered "Tampax" in English and the man said, "Oh Tampax," and a few minutes later the elevator creaked and a boy appeared with a blue unopened box on a clothed tray with a new rose. I put on the white shirt, brushed on mascara. Then I left to get going.

His car was there, parked across the street, the sight hit me like a sling. I tiptoed up: he was asleep on the backseat. He looked pathetic. He was too big for the car, and he slept with one leg folded under him and his head bent against the window. I left him be and walked downhill to ask directions at a fruit stand. I waited my turn. The high citrus smell tickled my whole face and behind the man two towers hovered made of orange hulls and lemon hulls. When it was my turn, I showed the man my scrap of paper with the Miramar address and he pointed. I wanted to buy lemonade but then I remembered I still hadn't changed any money. So I started walking.

I passed a movie theater with calligraphy on the marquee. But the photographs by the ticket booth showed a huge Omar Sharif, older now, with salt-and-pepper hair. So his career hadn't fallen to ruins. He was just here.

This was the day. Morning was different here. The sun took its time and then alighted with weight.

The thing I hadn't expected in Egypt was the whirring of bicycles everywhere and they, like the cars, were all black and old. In the morning already and last night on the street, the wheels in the soft air made a constant running noise. It was not like insects but like butterflies, if butterflies had a noise. And at the edge of your hearing, you were always reminded by the tinny metallic dingings of little bells.

I heard birds as I climbed the winding street and I smelled myrtle and sage. There was also the distant hammer sound of construction. After a half hour outside I was used to camels. I'd stopped and felt one's black lips wet and soft, gumming my hand. Then all of a sudden, I felt something nudge my hip. It was the Mercedes. At first I was mad. I twisted my skirt to see if it made a mark. He sat at the wheel grinning, motioning me to get in. I didn't see what else I could do, so I got in the front seat, giving up my adventure already but glad anyway. I showed him the Miramar address.

He put a hand, softly, on my lower belly. I wriggled away.

But it was a good thing he found me. He studied a map and it took us fifteen minutes of turns on curving streets, in the opposite direction than I'd started.

Then we were there at the house. It still stood. A straggly tall eucalyptus waited in front. Ramadan handed me back the scrap of paper where the address was, written by the woman in the office with the parrot. Rania. I curled up out of the car. I almost didn't want to go. I knew before I started up the short walk that I would never forget. It was a wooden and concrete house, three floors with two balconies. Brownish-colored with some old rusty metal and stucco. The roof was red tile, Spanish looking. I saw a metal drainpipe like at home. The eucalyptus moved in wind above me. I wanted to get rid of the driver. Once I knocked on the door, I didn't know how long I would be. I didn't want anyone waiting for me.

I went back, banged on his window and motioned wildly, trying to say it could be a long time. He pointed to his chest, then to the floor of the car. I guess he meant he'd be here. I shrugged, tapping my watch. I spread out my hands wide. Eternity. He folded his arms and closed his eyes.

Fine. I didn't care. It was beyond me. I'd tried. The sky was a clear blue again with no clouds and I heard the drift of a slight wind in the eucalyptus leaves, a tired and very old sound. Patience, they seemed to whisper, patience. Summer is long, and peace. I straightened my skirt and walked to the door. My heart was beating like something flinging itself again against the wall of a room. There seemed to be no bell, so I knocked. Crude glass and metal pipes hung from the eave and worked as wind chimes. Nobody answered. The porch was cool, clay-tiled. I kept knocking. This was the end, I thought. I stood there at the door a long time. This was it.

There was a number printed on the door and I checked my slip of paper. Yes, this was right: 34. Outside the door was an old orange plastic chair and on the ground, the dish for a plant, filled with what looked like rainwater. Then I heard a window shove open in the house next door to the right, and a woman's hot, fast voice spilled through and I said, "Ismee Atassi. American," and in moments there was noise inside her building like feet on a staircase and a door whipped open and the woman stood there looking me over.

She crossed her arms firmly, like a known prayer, over her substantial chest, all the time saying words flying from branch to branch and the only ones I recognized came out "no America, no America," her head shaking. For a moment I thought she was trying to chase me away but then she was showing me into her house with her arms almost bowing, big loops of them hanging down like stretching dough from shoulder to elbow, then again from elbow to hand. She stood with her ample back to me, hands on hips, calling up the stairs and a little girl ran down, a round-limbed blue-eyed blonde. The woman said something to the child and the child gathered her skirts in both fists and started running. "No America," the large woman said again, this time bending in what was almost a curtsy. Now I got it; she meant she didn't speak English. She motioned me to sit and I did. She sat across from me and folded her hands on her lap and her feet one behind the other. I couldn't help notice her legs. Her calves were enormous, over that dainty gesture of the feet, patterns of black hair caught under nylon stockings. Then she sprang up—she was graceful and light on those feet—and she slowly lifted the lid off a green cut-glass bowl of some kind of candy. To be polite I took one. It was a date wrapped around nuts, rolled in sugar and ground pistachio. It was good. She slowly pantomimed drinking from a glass then lifted her eyebrows to ask if I wanted anything. I shook my head no, not wanting to get into the what-kind-of-beverage charade.

We sat politely in the still living room on fancy maroon velvet couches with gold tassels, our hands folded, looking different places in the room. She smiled at me every few moments. She was a large-featured woman and yet there was something delicate about her facial attentions, like a very fat woman balancing on tiny feet. Then, a long time later, the girl skidded in, calling back and forth in avid musical conversation with a boy who might have been her brother but didn't look like it. He stood before the woman, probably his grandmother, hands at his sides, chin tipped down awaiting orders. More fast pointed Arabic spewed. I rested with the ease of understanding absolutely nothing.

Then the boy turned so he was facing me and said, "I know little English."

"Oh, good," I said, too loudly. "Are you learning in school?"

"Yes," he said. "School."

"What is your name?" I said.

"My name is Nauras Awafti."

I stuck my hand out to shake. "My name is Mayan Atassi."

"Mayan. Yes. Is ver many here," the boy said.

The grandmother, who sat at the edge of her couch, head cocked, as if by listening with full and complete attention the translation would come to her by itself, finally became impatient and pulled the boy to her by the back of his shirt. He then turned and translated for her. She fired questions at him hard and fast. Then he swiveled back to me again and she smiled, all her teeth showing, some not white, her old plump hand lifting to wave at me.

"I am American," I said. "My mother is American, my father is from here. Egyptian. He grew up next door. My father is Mohammed Atassi and I came here to find him."

"Mohammed, ah yah," the old woman said, her head going up and down slowly as if, on a string far away, her mind was a kite searching high mountain grasses for something lost.

The boy translated.

"He left my mother years ago. I haven't seen my father—Mohammed—since I was twelve years old." Here I marked height in the air with my hand. "Around your age."

He turned and translated this to his grandmother, who kept rocking her head up and down, mouth closed, a sad expression like a slim nude woman on her face.

"I wonder if you, if your grandmother, knows where he is."

Here he grinned largely. "She no my grandmother," he said, as if this were a hilarious mistake. He giggled, translating to them. I hoped to hell she was not his mother, I kept looking at her, calculating. No, she couldn't have been. "She my grandmother sister," he shrieked. "My grandmother upstairs." He pointed to the ceiling.

The old woman grabbed his collar again sternly to get him back down to business.

He wheeled again towards me. "What?"

"Does she know where my father is?"

She shook her head so I knew my answer before he even translated. Then she spewed a long trailing scarf of words, all the while shaking her head. The nude woman in her face knelt down.

"You come all the way from America to find him?" the boy said.

"Yes," I said and she heard me too. She closed her eyes and kept shaking.

"He hasn't been there for a long time," she said, through him. "No thirty years. We never seen him again. She says he be somewhere in

America. But his father die. Next door here. And he not at funeral. We never seen him. And you have bad luck, because they live there next door. Tarik's wife and daughter. But they go for two month already to Americas."

America. I was astonished. "Where in America?" I said.

She shrugged.

"She says she don't know. But she think Californias."

I looked to my left a second. The little blond girl had been sitting the whole time in a big chair, her arms clutched to the armrests, her round legs ending in blunted sneakers, staring up at me, the American, rapt.

Then the boy said my father's mother was very old but still in the house next door and would I like to go and meet her.

I thought I'd heard the translation wrong. "Yes!" I said. "Yes!" My other grandmother.

Then the boy said his great-aunt would like to invite me to eat a meal with them first. She stood up, with her huge knees facing out, bent them, pliéing, lifting and spreading her arms to encompass the room. I recognized the woman's repertoire of gestures then. They belonged to a clown. A fat clown. I liked her very much, I appreciated her exaggerating courtesies, but I wanted to go. I tapped my watch and pointed at the house next door. I was sick of people, even Egyptians, even neighbors who saw my father once thirty years ago, and I didn't want more of strangers and kindness and dust. I had a grandmother locked in the house next door.

I still thought I might have misunderstood. But the old woman rose now, negotiating her weight around the furniture, swiveling, motioning me with a plump, fluid wrist to follow. The kids stood on either side of me, looking as if I were the strangest being they'd ever seen. We went through a mint-green kitchen that looked like any old-fashioned one at home and out the back door. The backyards went far. Three goats stood there facing us. There was a chicken coop too, with loud dirty white chickens. Behind the yard and a shed was a field, just weeds and nothing for a long time until you saw a stand of olive trees down the hill, and I knew my father must have grown up running there. From a eucalyptus tree in the backyard, an old tire hung and the lawn was worn smooth under in a grassless strip. If I could have proven he wasn't here, that would be different. Sometimes I wanted the world to be plain.

I could have stood and watched there forever, the way the sun hit

the backyard flat and orange, somehow level with the ground. But the
woman was entering the house's back screen door and I followed.
And then we were inside. First a cellar of some kind, full of vegetables
and fruits in clear jars, and cans with faded labels. Jars of honey and
vats of olive oil and sacks of grain. I understood now: everything was
magic to me here. It wasn't just food. This was the first room I came
to here. I picked up a jar of olives; they were put up that way still on
their branch. You could see the twig floating in the tea-brown liquid.

The woman stopped and tapped at a jar with something inside it
like yellow peanut butter. Her lips opened on her teeth in a large
expression urging for meaning. "Mohammed," she said, and moved
a hand on her ample belly.

The boy translated. "He like that. For meal. Want to eat. Every
day." I didn't know what it was.

Then we walked into a kitchen that looked like it had been remod-
eled twenty years ago, all in matching black and white checks. The
bottoms of the cupboards were scalloped. It looked clean and plain.
I liked the house. Then to get to the stairs, we passed through a living
room that was large and carpeted plush emerald green and had fancy
satin and velvet couches and chairs. Gold ropes stopped off certain
portions of the room. There was an old inlaid chess table and brass
trays; they looked Middle Eastern. But the mahogany console stand
holding an RCA color television could have been anywhere. There
were chrome-framed pictures on a shelf and I stopped to look. Several of the photographs seemed to have been taken at a wedding, the
bride a full, young, curly-haired girl who looked nothing like me, and
my father was not there. There were eight pictures of that same bride
sitting in her flower-decked throne and in each one she was wearing
a different dress. The old woman shook her head sadly, with raised
eyebrows. "Mohammed, no," she said.

We climbed upstairs, the children ahead. The woman ascended
slowly, holding the gold velvet rope that served as banister. On the
first landing, there seemed to be a family room, with another sofa and
chairs, a bookshelf, a standing globe and corridors leading to bedrooms. We started up the second stairs. Near the top, the woman
called the children back near us. She explained something to the
boy and he ran ahead, two steps at a time, arms scissoring with
purpose.

Then we entered the top room. A young woman with her hair held
back pressed by us out the door. She stood holding one elbow. She

was wearing a nurse's uniform with a long zipper. It was a wide, low-ceilinged pink-and-white room in the eaves. Outside, eucalyptus leaves fingered the windowpanes. The room was full of roses, their petals falling on tabletops, on the floor, on the lush satin bedspread from the night table. And there she was, rising from a chair with great effort, collapsing down again, an old woman with a very lined dark face, a mouth large as a harmonica, with many teeth and a puff of white hair. Her eyes were clear blue. She was large and short.

"Momo," she said, her whole face crumbling over the words. She hugged me and she smelled a way I hadn't ever known an old woman to smell, warmly sweet like caramel. After a while, we sat in white satin cushioned chairs and the boy translated between us. She had a clear sad look when she shook her head after the boy asked if she knew where her youngest son was. She had not heard from him for ten years, she said. Her eyebrows lifted and her large mouth formed a beautiful shape. She told the boy she had not seen him for almost twenty. Her hands lifted in front of her and I went close and knelt down so she could hold my face.

She told us that when my father was a boy, he always liked the animals. He was always out in the air with the animals. I asked if he had been smart. She shrugged herself up, frowning, then slowly nodded her head, like, I suppose so. Sure.

I moved to the small attic window. From there I could see the field and the goats. My father had run there, just a boy like any boy. There was a muddy pen. A sandbox. The woman from next door tilted her head and made a gesture that we should let the old woman rest.

I knelt to kiss her good-bye. We were walking out and the woman called us back in words I didn't recognize. She'd lifted herself up and got to a bureau. From the top drawer, open now, I saw a thousand things—threads, thimbles, scissors, papers, cards, scarves, veils, stockings, lipsticks, jewelry, but from one place she extracted a tiny photograph, about an inch square, black and white with a white ruffled edge, of my father.

She gave it to me and I closed my hand around it. I didn't let myself look at it really until later. In the cellar again, the woman from next door gave me the jar of what my father had liked. She pointed to the ceiling.

"From her. She wanted to you," the boy said.

.   .   .

BEFORE I LEFT I gave the boy the scrap of paper where the woman in the office with the parrot had written out my address. "So you can come visit me in America someday," I said.

"Enshahallah," he said. He copied it down in his house and ran back with it so I still had mine anyway.

I asked him what that word meant in Arabic. I'd heard it all around me.

"God willing," the boy said. "In Egypt no thing for sure. Everything enshahallah."

Then I asked him what my name meant.

"Is name like all other names, you know, but here is very common."

Oh. I'd always been told it meant light.

"I thought it meant light." I looked around at the sky.

"No, no. Nora means light."

"What about Amneh?" I thought it meant to wish.

"How you say. Believer."

I hoped all of a sudden that Ramadan was still outside in the car and that we could drive back to Cairo now and he would rub my back and that then I could fly home into the dawn. I just wanted to leave. This was enough. It was good but I needed to rest. I felt like a person who had thrown a diamond ring down off a bridge and watched it disappear into the dark water and now it was over, I'd lost the gamble, he'd eluded me this time forever and I wanted to go home. But I felt calm. I didn't care anymore. I'd had my Arab experience. It was too much for me all at once. And as I looked around me up at the tall slow trees with regret, I knew I'd be back here too, another time with different reasons.

The car was there and they walked slowly with me to it. I opened the front passenger door and the old woman rapped her knuckles on the window of the backseat and pointed.

I shrugged. " 'S okay."

Ramadan, who had just woken up, slumped over the steering wheel a way I hadn't seen him. He looked up from his dropped head like a yoked animal. The old woman kept rapping, she seemed upset. Ramadan then pointed to the back. I got out again and went in the back. I didn't get it or care, but I wanted to go. I rolled down the back window and looked for a moment at the house and the yard beyond, the three goats, their black heads, the shimmering yellow-green weeds of the plain field. It was as shabby as my grandmother's house, the land as old. I was sad for how many different lives there were to live and we only got once.

RAMADAN EXPLAINED WITH THE GUIDEBOOK. The word he pointed to was "rich" and he looked at me, nodding his head. He said the word, "rich," repeating to memorize. I kept shaking my head no. He persisted. The wind tore through the open windows. My mother had always told me we were royal. I laughed. 34 Shahira Miramar was a good house, but anywhere in the world, it wasn't royal. At one point we stopped I didn't know why. There was a small stand of trees by the side of the road, dusty olives. Ramadan got out and then I heard in the dry quiet that he was peeing. Below him was an old stone amphitheater. I came up behind him, toppled him, and we lay there an hour on the cool stone, laughing, toying, I hurt my back once on a eucalyptus button.

"Greco-Roman," he said, pointing to the stage below. It was a small, perfect tiered circle. It was easy to believe in the life there once.

"Arabs have everything, huh?"

"Me no Arab." He tapped his chest. "Egyptian. We have got Pyramids. We have got antiquities. History. This be in Germany, a whole room glass. Here—" He made a sound letting air out of his mouth.

When I put my underwear on again, the good ones, drops of blood trickled to the cotton, staining like a watercolor. I found the last scrap of paper from my wallet, where the woman in the office with the parrot had written that I was looking for my father, who might be here in Alexandria, and that I hadn't seen him for seventeen years. I gave it to Ramadan. He read it, it seemed to take a long time.

His face took on a new cast from underneath and then he lost the plot of his smile. His hands stayed on the wheel not playful anymore.

I showed him the word in the book that means airport. I made wing motions with my arms, pointed at myself—"Me, America."

We drove a long time keeping the silence and then we were there again in Cairo. On the way to the airport, he drove through a lush district of mansions on the Nile. They had the domed towers and minarets and columns and mosaics of mosques. They looked a thousand years old, older. These were the royalty of Egypt.

"Heliopolis," he said. He stopped before one mansion and pointed. "Omar Sharif."

At the airport, he came inside with me. I studied the English TV screen. There was a flight at eight o'clock tonight. It was only three. He took my hand and I followed him to a phone booth. He was carrying my pack again and it felt easy to let him. It was a regular modern phone booth. He lifted a book, paged through, found a spot and showed me. I remembered from his hand that Arabic scans from right to left.

His hand brailled over the whole page. "Atassi," he said. "Atassi. Atassi. Atassi."

I smiled and shook my head. It was too late for that now. I was finished with something. I wanted home. We spent time close in that phone booth, I sat on his lap, we decided with the watch. Back here at six-thirty for customs and security. Now, we'd eat. Eat, we could mime. I didn't want to close the book over the page of Atassis. He ripped it out, folded the paper up, and put it in my backpack, zipped the zipper. And then he drove me to a low neighborhood of two-story buildings, tenements, with children playing in the bare street. It was a small restaurant, underground, and we sat cross-legged on the floor. The tablecloths looked clean, many times washed. A short-stemmed pink rose leaned in a tin can on our table. Two of the petals, cleft in the center, had fallen to the cloth. The light from back and front of the room came in slanted and he ordered in Arabic and I sat low, against a pillow, and we looked at each other and sometimes smiled, sometimes not, but we stopped trying at all with words. And after time, the food began to come and make our clock. Olives and new cheese, then kibbe, then I think what was my father's layered pancake with different butter and burnt sugar. It tasted honey and deep caramel and rose water. I handed him a pencil and paper for the name. "Fatir," he drew and whispered it.

Then we used the guidebook. He pointed to his chest and showed me the word "poor." I smiled a little, embarrassed for him. He didn't have to ask me. I'd already decided to give him all the money I had and only save back twenty dollars for the bus into New York. He pointed to himself again, then made wing motions, then said, in an accent I'd never heard say the word "America." He pointed to me and I smiled. None of this seemed to matter. I gave him my address, he put it in the little bag he had around his neck where he kept money, clasping it shut again. He took my left hand and banded a cleft rose petal over my third finger. I knew before the book. "Marrying," he said. I got up to leave. He was so young, I was thinking.

It was still light when we walked outside again. I wanted to buy a souvenir, I didn't know what. There was still more than an hour. With the guidebook I showed him the word for bazaar and shrugged. We began walking and I followed him and then we were in a district of close streets and corners and brown buildings and smells of burning meat and then we rounded a corner and there was a square filled with market stands and around the sides were the neon-lit fronts of casinos.

He pulled me over to the edge of the square where there was a tiled drinking fountain and a man stood with a camera draped in black cloth and a camel tied to a palm. He seemed to be asking, did I want to have my picture taken with the camel? I thought of my father's old women and smiled. I wanted nothing like that from this trip.

We walked around the stands of the bazaar and I slowly became interested in things again. I wondered if all religions, all identity with a place or an origin or a culture that began late, began hokey. I wondered if Navaho doctors bought their children little tepees and tom-toms, but I felt a kind patience towards all that now because it was a start, I knew I would come back here again a different way, for longer. From a dusty market table, we picked out an everyday Turkish coffeepot, a little one. I wanted to open the jar of what it was my father had liked. When the woman had given it to me, I thought I'd save it for my father and give it to him as a present the first time I saw him, if I ever found him and we met again. But in this late afternoon light, sweet with dust and honey, I didn't want to wait. I'd waited and saved enough for him. The lid stuck. I gave it to Ramadan, he held it against his belly, straining, and again I thought, he's young, and then it was open. It was a rich distilled paste that tasted of almonds and honey. We ate it with our fingers, just walking through the market, past fabric bolts, animals, eating and licking our hands. We finished the whole jar. I turned my back for a moment and he bought me a dress and a small prayer rug. I was staring at a casino called the Las Vegas that had a wooden painted cutout of a bride and groom propped outside, the heads open circles for you to stand behind and have your picture taken. BE THE BRIDE, it said.

In the airport I bought a snowball paperweight with sand instead of snow, a scene with camels and tents in the desert. He paid for this. He'd paid for the coffeepot. He'd paid for dinner. He'd paid for the dress and rug and he'd try to pay for photographs of the two of us I didn't want. Then it was time to go. We passed a bar called the Ramadan Room, which was playing an orchestrated version of "Home of the Brave." At the gate where I had to go in and he had to stay, I tried to give him my money. I had two hundred and ten dollars cash, I wanted to give him all of it. He would take none. It got so I pushed the crinkled bills in his pockets. His mouth got hard, his chin made a clean line, he took it all, balled it, jamming it down in my pack. So I was the one after all who was paid.

At the metal bar going into the security gate, we drank a long kiss good-bye. His appellated, articulate hands moved around my face as if fashioning an imaginary veil there.

"Good-bye," I said. I knew in a way I could never explain but understood absolutely I would never see this soul again.

He said words I didn't understand but I made out Allah. Everything in his language had to do with God.

11

I STOOD IN FRONT OF THE MIRROR, in the middle of the day, and tried on the dress. It was white, a kind of cotton that comes from more than one third-world country and looks like it has already been washed. It fell in vague ruffles at my knees and on my shoulders. I felt foolish. It didn't look like me in it. My legs seemed wrong, under the dress, like two stiff, thin trees. I picked up my hair, fingered it. Too long. And the ends were split.

I came of age at a time when a dress was an almost quaint thing. I'd spent my childhood in dresses and school uniform jumpers, but then it was jeans every day. I'd never stopped wearing jeans. My grandmother sent me money for a dress every spring I was in college and I spent it, but never on a dress.

It was the middle of the day and I collapsed on the bed. A while later I pushed myself up with an arm and began to try. There was so much to do. It was hard to know where to start. So I called for a hair-cut appointment with Shawn, who had always made me look like a busy person you saw walking loosely on the street.

"Just one minute please," the girl said.

Someone else came on the line. "Shawn Timmelund is dead," she said.

"He's dead?"

"He died two weeks ago." All those cancellations. The time they'd said his elbow hurt. "Would you like an appointment with his assistant, Terry?"

I put down the phone.

ALL WEEKEND, I waited for something to happen. I thought I better not call people too much. I felt like having them hear my breath, but then I had nothing to say. I called Stevie and made him ask me questions but it seemed too much work to answer. I just mumbled yeses, mostly nos. I couldn't tell him much about Egypt. "Now you give up, Mayan," he said. "You've got to."

I had never quite been like this, how I was now, before. Or maybe I had, sometimes, and forgot because I wanted to. I was in bed. Depressed, round and round like a unthreaded screw in a socket. I couldn't read. My head hurt and I felt like, let somebody else do it.

And this seemed true. Of me. All the other times, when I'd been high and gay, marauding arm-in-arm with my friends down the streets, now that felt like I'd been trying, pretending. Making myself an imposter.

This seemed a completely flat, unemotional, almost sensible decision. It was too much work to live. I didn't want to. I have to try so hard, I reasoned, too hard. I was sick of being an overachiever. And my house was a mess full of little scraps of paper. Phone numbers and addresses, lists I couldn't throw out because I'd drawn on them. I had skyscrapers and swimming pools and fountains. Towers. Since I'd been to Egypt everything I drew had a place for water.

Somebody else would be born. They would have a life like mine, but a little more. One part of them, one shred, would survive less damaged. Preserved. And they could do it. Let them do it. They could build the towers, trace the viruses, find the cure. It didn't matter who did it. Only that it be done. It didn't have to have my name on it. I didn't even have my real name anyway.

The world could wait for them. It would have to. It was too hard for me. Not that I was doing much good, anyway.

The world couldn't wait, but it would. The world had been waiting for a long, long time. Those who have to wait have been waiting always, and they will wait some more.

Sometimes I sensed what I could have been otherwise, like a broken horse's dream of flying. I couldn't follow that, it was too long a thought. That was why I had always wanted a daughter. I kept feeling I could stand myself if I had a daughter who was better than me. Before, when I'd been dry and the doctors had told me they didn't know if I would have periods again or not, on the street, in line for movies, everywhere, I looked at girls, not boys, and thought, if I didn't shrink myself inside she could be my daughter someday and perfect. For what was still in me to have a chance again. It was hard to see what was erect in my spirit be laid down, while other people, heartier, but less of that, survived. And now that I finally could have children, I wouldn't, I was giving up. I hadn't eaten anything for almost a week. It seemed too much work to get up and buy food.

When they told me I was out for a year, Timothy said to me then, "You can't use everybody else's standards. A year off might be fine. When you look at what you've made out of what you've come from, you've done a lot." I felt then the way someone must feel when they're told for the first time, officially, they are retarded and they understand what they'd privately feared always can be seen from the outside.

My father had known me before he left. Perhaps he measured my qualities. Perhaps he stood over my small childhood bed and looked at my face; I was not the beauty he had wished.

But what were the allures—taste? Taste of wine, of the inside of mouths, the tart taste of sores, the feel of money, its usedness, Italian fabrics, reptile skins, leather, the casing feeling of vastly expensive clothes?

The lightness and forgetting of travel.

The thrill of adultery. Of gambling. Of throwing it all away—forever.

Of destroying the weak who know no better than to stare at your portrait like a faraway president and memorize your lost name.

I heard a rush of water from upstairs and thought, oh good, the old man was running a bath. The sound was powerful, voluminous, the force of water pushed through pipes. I liked the idea of the old man stepping into the bath, luxuriating. I could imagine him rubbing his small hands together, taking his little pleasure with a nervous relish.

My apartment seemed better and it was later in the day from the water. Falling Water. Waterfalls. I'd always wanted to go to see the Frank Lloyd Wright house in Pennsylvania and now I had time. Now I had nothing but time.

I dialed Bud Edison's number. Nobody answered. It was Saturday night.

I remembered Emory telling me, with the bad nickel taste in your mouth, the only thing to do like that is cry and sleep and wait. Tough it out.

I kept ricocheting back and forth between the numbers. 1971 to 1975 I went to high school. He was just in Montana. In 1973 I was fifteen, sitting by the garbage cans in the alley while my mother raged inside. He flew to Cairo. The Cairo Caper.

He was alive. He was not dead. Now I fully believed he existed.

I stayed in bed for two days. I didn't eat. It got worse. My mother called me and asked about her wedding dress. Was I wearing it? Because if I wasn't she would really like it back. It was hers after all, she said.

Her wedding dress? I would have loved to have her wedding dress.

"I never had it," I said.

"Yes you did, I gave it to you in college, I shouldn't have, I knew I shouldn't have."

"I wouldn't have thrown away your wedding dress!"

"Well yes you might have, it didn't look like a wedding dress. I had it shortened. I shouldn't have maybe. But it was like just a cocktail dress. Raw silk. It was two colors. A sort of pale silvery blue and off-whiteish."

Maybe I had lost it. I unplugged the phone. I didn't want to hear.

I knew whatever it was it wouldn't be enough because I wasn't. I believed the truth: I didn't have enough good in me. Not enough had been put in. And now, like my mother had said, I would always have to try so hard. Too hard.

I thought of different places I had wanted to see. Falling Water. Racine once more. Glacier National Park. The Grand Canyon. But I couldn't go anywhere. I couldn't go forward. I couldn't go back.

I stopped being afraid to die. The world was beautiful, so much I could not go outside. I knew the colors, spring, would hurt my eyes.

I wanted to leave it all be. I felt inside my grandmother's way finally, the wish to vanish, letting the animals go free.

I didn't want anyone to notice. On the old couch, I stayed home and pulled the covers up. The coward way. It was raining against the one window. This was glamorous rain. It gave a soft halo to the street-light. Even only that made me nostalgic. Two kids nudged on the side-walk below, both wearing black tight clothes and masks and I thought, good for them, let them, they can have it.

I was making lists; I scribbled in pencil on a bill envelope the names of all my friends.

Stevie

Mai linn

Timothy

Mom

Emily

Emory

Jordan

I laughed a bubble of a sound. Once, Edison would have been first. Now he wasn't even on it.

I had so much to do. I stood up to write more, but my wrist was incredibly light and I was already far away, everyone I knew in a pas-ture with long faces and ruffled edges, receding from me one by one.

That blurry shelling fade was the softness. But just then, in that state, the blanket held up to my neck, I thought of the way back. It was one word, slate blue, the shape of a key.

Food. I had to get out and buy food. Live while you're young, my grandmother said with her eyes already closed. I was still young, I remembered. Maybe it had something to do with finally believing he was alive. Maybe I thought we couldn't both be. Stay-ing awake was too hard. I hadn't eaten but I wasn't hungry. I knew I should go out and buy some food anyway but I was too tired. I slipped just a little once and then again. I counted my friends to my-self. I kept counting them naming their names. But then I dropped

Emory. I let them go one by one, like beads, unknotting, slipping from a string.

THE NEXT THING was sitting hard in a plastic hospital chair, egg bottomed, my hair a curtain over my face, a hand forcing me to drink a cup of something that dribbled down my chin. My lip fell loose and hanging.

The old man, my upstairs neighbor, stood there stomping his cane. He rapped loud on the floor, twice for emphasis.

"Drink it," he said. A firm nurse in white stockings held the cup to my mouth. "It's just high protein," she said. "You're a little weak. You fainted. You haven't been eating enough lately." This is where I was when it all sifted back into me.

"I telephone, but who?" the old man said, thumping my cane again on the linoleum. The linoleum was old and cracked and brown with age. The floor was consoling under these lights.

No one, I said. I didn't want to explain. He stamped his cane twice on the ground. Hard like he had no patience. Then I told him Timothy's and Emily's numbers. I wanted Mai linn but I was afraid to tell him a number that was long distance. It seemed to go on a long time that night, the bright lights like bullets of sun pressing down on my head so my hair felt limp and bad, the protein drink which tasted like chalk. Everyone handled me like a thing they didn't like. They were only professionally kind. The nurse held my chin and the back of my neck, hard, with rubber-gloved hands. "Come on, you have to finish before you can go home." I didn't blame her. I'd made myself this.

Then Emily was there. She clipped into the Emergency Room, wearing an orange skirt. She had a hard purse the shape of something we'd learned in geometry.

She put her hands on her hips, looked around. "So what happened?" she said.

"Nothing," I said. "I just didn't eat much."

The old man stamped his cane. "I come in with this for her collection." He held up a framed huge blue butterfly behind glass. The label read PAPILIO RUMANZOVIA. "I send away in catalog, rare butterfly, from China, and your door you left open. I find her there almost dead. She don't up."

"I'm fine," I said, "I was just tired. Jet lag. I just got back from a long trip. I was in Egypt."

"Where?" Emily said.

"Oh never mind."

"Egypt. Pfa," the old man said. "She look dead."

"Well let's get out of here," Emily said. "We'll start with breakfast."

I had to give the hospital my social security number and the name of my insurance, which I still had from school. Emily had her car and we offered the old man a ride home, but he just said "Pfa" again and walked off with his cane. We drove to my apartment for me to shower and change and then we were going to go eat. My apartment was open now, she could just see it. It was hardly my things anymore. I stripped and went into the shower and by the time I came out she'd sorted everything into three piles, the way you would anyone's, a stranger's. "Cleaners," she said. "We can stop on the way."

We went out and had French toast. And then she started to talk about money. She unclasped the maple-leaf clasp of her purse and started taking out bills. They lay curled on the table like dried leaves, each with a different tilt and crease and twist.

Sometimes I thought about money, how you know the feel of paper, you can separate it from the scraps of tickets and bank receipts in a purse flap or pocket with your hand, without even looking. And each country's money was different, on different paper. It was one of those deep habitual things we never think of knowing. That's probably the most patriotic thing about me. Knowing dollars by touch.

I knew I had to take Emily's money. I had to borrow from someone and start to straighten the piles out. But first I had to ask her about Bud Edison.

I asked the worst. "So are you . . . in love?"

The money lay there on the table, I was counting, it was over four hundred dollars.

She looked sideways, her profile majestic. Her head slanted down. "He's in London. Again." She shrugged. "It's in three weeks."

"I meant Edison."

"What? That was nothing. He just came to the shower. You know he is a jerk. He brought a negligee to the shower. It was embarrassing." She stopped for a second. "Is that why you didn't come? Because you didn't want to see him?"

"No. I was in Egypt."

"Oh."

I looked down at my food as if it were a duty. I took the money. I didn't deserve it. At least I had medical insurance still from school. That seemed as stolen now as the sunglasses from Boss's and Frank Lloyd Wright's umbrella. I didn't deserve anything right then. But I had those three things now and I was glad I had them. Most things in this world were undeserved. You had to believe that.

IT WAS A GOOD RUNNING DAY, blowy, melting, a vivid sky. It was spring now and I wanted to see the blossoms. I ran every day. The sky over the river was darkening though and I felt a little scared. But I wanted to see the pink-and-white trees because it was supposed to rain in the night and anyway I knew all things could be different tomorrow, so I ran. I saw the blue-gray clouds and the trees, mat light of the blossoms in the wind and I came home feeling, well at least I had that. I liked the increments of seasons, when I didn't miss a day. That made me feel I was living my life.

Really the attempt to find God was a selfish thing. Beauty was something you couldn't pass on or give away.

That evening I went up to the old man's apartment with a box of chocolates. He took it, looked down at the offering in his hands and did not invite me for tea.

"Thank you." I said.

"You a foolish girl." He shook his head as if to shoo me away. He started closing the door.

We stood there, the door open three inches.

"How did I look?" I asked. I'd wanted to know that. I still didn't think he had needed to take me to the hospital.

"You look ugly," he said, then shut the door.

So it was true.

SOME DAYS EMILY ran with me. She ran in all white like a tennis player. I sighed at the end of running, my body used for the day, spent but nothing else. In the pawing of our running shoes on the sidewalk, stretching, the question was there, neither of us saying it: so what are you going to do now?

WITH PERSIMMONS and cream from the farmer's market, I went to see Timothy. He still lived in the garage, but he'd moved his couch and his books to an empty storefront around the corner, a place with a sign on top that still showed the faded traces of lettering, spelling Cora's Cash Shop. I waited in a chair when I got there. His inner door was closed. A few minutes later, a woman with a baby sidled out, saying, "Thank you." Timothy saw other people now. On his desk were the standard forms from Welfare and Aid to Women with Dependent Children. He held office hours Wednesdays, when he wasn't at the Pleiades Palace.

"I'm damaged," I said, walking into the new room.

"What do you mean?" he said.

"In elementary school even, you don't know how much it meant to me, every A. I remember specific ones and then how it looked, the whole row. Getting into medical school was the happiest day of my life. You know who's running the world? In your field and in science and in every other field? People from good families. Not people like me. I was just barely keeping up and now I've thrown it all away."

"You took a risk."

"I thought I was doing it for love. I wanted love to work. More than anything, I wanted that to work. I had school but it wasn't enough. But now I've gone and ruined what I had. My mistake was trying to be cool and pretend I didn't care. I tried to be like other people. I didn't know my limits. Nobody gets everything."

"You did a brave thing. You wanted more than just school. People with lives like yours do succeed sometimes but they can't always connect with other people. But some people who had rough starts manage to do both. You're trying to do both."

"I could've made things different. I could have. I could have left California and gone home to live with my grandmother. I could've just gotten on a train home. My mother would've sent me. I was afraid my grandmother was too old. That she'd die. But if she'd died—she wouldn't have, she didn't die until later—but if she had the Briggses would've taken me."

I noticed his collection of prayer beads on the windowsill to the left of the aquarium. They were hanging over the window, all six of them, the nuns' beads made of waterlily seeds, the Franciscans' heavy

wooden beads, the Buddhist bone beads on a yellow cord and whatever the other three were.

"Yes, they probably would have."

"Emily isn't damaged."

"You wouldn't want to marry Tad."

"I know."

"You couldn't have left your mother then, when you were a child."

My head turned, lolling, looking around the room. I didn't really
know what to say right now.

"What do you think you've ruined?"

"Well, medical school, and I have no savings. No job. Now that I've
cut the string every bead'll fall on the floor and go in all directions
and scatter like marbles all over the place and I'll never be able to find
them again. I don't know if I even want to go back to medical school."

Timothy stood up and walked to his jacket, hanging on the doorknob. He took a Swiss army knife from the pocket. He always carried
that. He opened it to a small hinged metal scissors. He nodded
towards the beads hanging over the window. "Try it."

"No."

"Go ahead."

I took the scissors, felt the knife weigh in my hand. I walked to the
beads. "Which one?"

"Take your pick." I liked the bone beads but I picked the nuns', a
gift from one of Timothy's teachers. I didn't want to ruin any of these
looped beads. They were a perfect thing to collect; valueless; they had
been used so many times, touched, to pray on.

I cut the string and nothing happened. It snapped and became a
long line, not a circle, but intact.

"They're knotted," Timothy said. "Bring them here. We can tie
them again. Sometimes, in some ways, you're going to be behind
other people. You have to consider your start in life and what you've
done." I handed him the beads and he showed me the tiny knots. He
gave the ends back to me to tie. Our heads near each other, I saw
again how thick the lenses of his glasses were.

"Sometimes I think I don't really want to be a doctor. I picked that
because it was safe and I wanted to make money. Be a success. In
Montana, you should have heard, all the Ph.D.'s were calling each
other doctor. But I think if I were really free, if I'd had a different
life, I would've been an architect."

"You've never spoken of pursuing the really lucrative fields of medicine."

I shrugged. "Mmm, I don't know." I'd always thought I would be in family practice or maybe a child psychiatrist. "But it feels rich. Even if it isn't."

Then a kid with a boom box walked outside and for a long minute, we heard music.

It was organ music and gradual and then it was gone. For some reason, listening, I felt honored, like I was opening a gift. I felt like someone was telling me they loved me, one to one, me privately. And that is what heals. A person loving another person. In the same room or over time.

"Do you believe in God?" I said, suddenly.

I waited for Timothy to answer, thinking that if every person who heard the piece of music got something from it, that was the multiplication of the loaves. Music for everyone who needed it enough. Timothy still hadn't answered and he never did.

At the end I sat up cross-legged. I was concentrating on the string and the beads. Finally I slipped the tiny knot tight. I stood up and gave them back.

"You can keep them."

But I hung them back up on the window, with the others. You should never break up a collection. And you shouldn't give away a gift.

We used to eat whatever I brought together, in the kitchen of his house in the garage. I brought these persimmons for today. They were ripe and soft, translucent at the tips.

I WAS idle.

At the museum, I met Jordan on his lunch hour. We walked through a show of architectural drawings, contest entries from the Soviet Union, plans that had never been built. I caught him looking at me sideways, when I was studying a civic courthouse.

"What are you staring at," I said finally, wheeling around at him.

He looked down, shaking his head some more. "I don't know, you just look different to me. I don't know what it is. You didn't ever tell anybody what I did out there, did you?"

I shook my head.

"Can you even believe that was us?"

"You know I have a record," I said. I'd never told anyone. I didn't know why I was starting now.

"For what?" His voice got harder, I was used to that in him. It wasn't disloyal. He was prepared to take the worst and accept it. He was bracing himself.

"Parking tickets. I mean that's how it started." It was a bad time in my life, I'm not sure why. "It was right when I was leaving Wisconsin to come to medical school. And I had a lot of parking tickets. I hadn't paid them and they caught up with me. So I went in to the clerk, it's like a little bank where you pay, and I had the summons they'd sent me and where they wrote the total amount it was sort of blurry. I was at this counter, getting a check ready, and I just erased a zero. So instead of three-hundred-seventy dollars it was thirty-seven. And I went to the counter and paid the thirty-seven. And the clerk was normal. I left feeling like I got away with something. Then I get a worse summons, to criminal court. I had to delay coming to medical school for a week. I missed the orientation."

"I can't believe they booked you for that."

"Yeah, I had to get a lawyer and everything. I wrote a letter to the judge. They dismissed it, in the end, but the morning before court, I was sitting outside the room, the court was only this room, and there were three or four other people on the benches. Turns out they'd been bused there from jails. They were comparing jails, which ones didn't have toothbrushes, which ones never had toilet paper. I mean, it was scary. And then one of them looked at me and asked which place I was from. They completely believed I was one of them."

He put his arm around me. "Oh. Little you."

I shrugged him off. "So I could never be a lawyer. Which I don't want to be anyway."

"Sure you could. You have to be convicted of a felony to disqualify for the bar. You know, do something more like, what I did in Montana."

"I never want to be anything you could disqualify for. You know what I mean?"

"No. Plenty of people don't get into medical school."

"I'd have rather been something else anyway. Like this." I pointed to the hall of drawings. "You could have been a criminal and you could still do this if you were good enough."

"You were an architecture major weren't you?"

"City planning. Hey, don't tell anyone that, okay? I never told anybody. And it's weird because everyone around me, all these people I knew were doing other things, like that was when they had those blue boxes so you could charge your long-distance calls to big corporations? And I don't know, Emily stole a doctor's notepad to write herself notes when she wanted to change her flights around at the last minute. I think I felt worse because most of them were middle-class kids and they didn't really mean it. They wouldn't have done it alone. Or been ashamed to tell people. I did it because I really needed the money. I meant to."

"So did they."

"Not the same." I shrugged.

"I'm glad I know you," he said.

He had to get back to work then and I roamed through the museum. I reminded myself, it's two o'clock, eat lunch. After, I walked to Columbia and started wandering in the architecture building reading the bulletin boards, sort of standing there. Men darted in and out of offices. I saw notices for contests: one for a national monument, one for a lamp. I wrote them all down, the addresses, the specifications, the deadlines, dutifully, in the notebook I used to keep for finding my father.

At home I drew sketches for the contests, each one of them, and sent them off to the addresses. But when that was all done I went back to what I always did and even hated now, just because what else was there for me to do. I went back to finding him.

ALL INVESTIGATION is the same. You call a lot of different people. You ask questions, one leads to another, they form a chain. Science is like that. When I looked for a doctor for my grandmother, after the first stroke, it was the same way. Years later, I watched Emily Briggs sit cross-legged on the bare floor of her new apartment in New York, calling department stores all over America, trying to buy a dress she'd seen in a magazine because she believed it was the dress Isabel Archer wore on the day she discovered Europe. Texas had the dress but not her size.

And investigation was not all discovery. It was mostly not. It was mostly the mundane next ten things. Sending the three dollars for the copy from the county clerk's office. Calling back after somebody-you-don't-know's lunch. You woke up late no matter what time, and lists grew on paper in your own hand. Sometimes I forgot the end.

No one wanted to hear all the steps it took to find anything. But I'd never believed all this would work for him. Maybe all searches end the same. You are changed forever but not by what you were looking for.

I scribbled the name of the one more person to talk to, felt the scrap of an address, thrilled at an achieved phone number. That was a life. I kept promising myself just this one more thing, this was the last. Still, I was nagged by the thought of going back to Montana; in a way I knew I'd never be satisfied until I met every person who'd been touched by my father, every student who'd heard him lecture, any secretary or mailman who had a rub with his life. It felt like I'd never be able to sit still again. Any ending before the real ending was arbitrary.

I could not stop. Egypt hadn't done it.

I was becoming a crazy person. Stray. I let so many things go. Now I'd stopped even opening my bills.

I avoided people. I was so ashamed. This had gone on too long, farther than it should have and I knew better. Other women my age had obsessions with bad men. This was worse. I kept wanting to make the infinite end.

I was using the money from Emily just to live on. I paid a hundred on the credit card so they wouldn't close it yet and decided to keep the detective on for more. That was Timothy's idea.

"Yeah," Wynne said when he heard it was me on the phone. It had been that way for some time.

"Hiya. I was thinking, Jim, we should have a meeting and maybe I should pay you some more money. I'd like you to do some computer checks on the basis of what we've got now. I've got the social. But I need to get back to work and stay out of it."

"Well, there's a lot we can do, now we got the social. We made a lot a progress already. So when you wanna come in? What—you want to retain me for another thousand or so?"

"Eight hundred." I knew could borrow more.

"We can work with that, have to cut some corners, but it can be done."

It gave me some small pleasure to know that this was the one time

I could get him to meet me where I wanted. And I used that. I made a date for my place a week from tomorrow.

BUT I WAS CHEAP. Cheap enough that the idea of paying the detective more after what he'd done so far tugged at me. That's why our date was not until a week from tomorrow. I decided to do a little in the meantime. To be thorough. I am an overachiever. My mother was right.

I found the phone-book room in the New York Public Library. Thanks to Dr. Geesie. I'd probably touched a thousand phone books in America over the years, always looking for my name. But this was to make sure. Most of those were out of date by now anyway. A part of me warned: people who live unlisted don't all of a sudden list. I'd always been listed. I kept myself easy to find. This was plain work. I had little to no hope. I was just doing it. At some point, you had to be systematic.

I hadn't known there was such a thing as a phone-book room. It was a small room, high ceilinged, with a greenish overhead light casting down. Phone books from every city in every county in every state slouched on the old shelves. I started with Washington State. Nothing.

No one else was there. I shut the door quietly and lifted out the two cafés con leche from my backpack, opened the lids. I was not an obeyer like my grandmother. Today I needed this.

I went through Oregon. Nevada. Montana. Idaho. I found nothing but I didn't really expect to. This was almost—I didn't know—insurance. I moved to Arizona. No Uta Gilberts anywhere either. No Rilellas. Then California. In Oakland, California, I found an Atassi. A Farouk Atassi.

Then I was there.

I knocked over a coffee so I had to get out of that room fast. I cleaned it up the best I could with my T-shirt. I ran down the marble stairs to the wooden phone booths in the lobby.

It all went very quickly then. Farouk was this woman's husband. She sounded regular, nice. I said I was looking for John Atassi.

"He's an older guy, right? We haven't seen him in three, four years. We saw him in Mill Valley, Sausalito, something like that."

Three or four years.

"Um, he's my father."

She gave me her husband's number at work. He was more foreign-sounding. He said he was thirty-five and a structural engineer from Luxor. I asked him if he was going back there or if he'd settled here for good. I was trying to make conversation. He said yes, he wanted to move back at the end of the summer, it was fairer to the world that way.

I said yes, and thought how far from my father.

He said they'd seen my father a few years ago. My father, he said, managed a big Italian seafood restaurant in Mill Valley, but Farouk couldn't remember the restaurant's name. "And your mother is sick?" he said.

"Yes," I wavered, spinning. How did he know that?

"In Reno, she was sick, I remember."

Oh. "No, that's not my mother. That was his second wife." Reno death records, I scribbled down. Maybe Uta had died. Then, for a moment, I wished I could talk to Uta. Almost more than my father. I wished I could fly to Reno and find Uta somewhere in a junky desert spa, with huge metal immersion tanks littered around like a grave-yard, and take an afternoon talking to her through all these years. I had a feeling my father was going to be one of those people who is not there even when he was there. I wanted to talk to the people to the left and the right, the people around him, the way you can trace an ant's path by the ant itself or by the banks of sand on either side.

Farouk had a brother in New York. A doctor. He was my age. I couldn't stop hopping around the tiny phone booth in my socks when Farouk told me this. The brother's name was Ali and Farouk gave me his number. He told me Ali was gone, in Ohio, for the weekend and wouldn't be back until Monday. But I called that number about a hundred times before Monday.

This was so much so fast. All of a sudden these Atassis had seen him. Farouk was going to ask around, he said he'd call some other relatives in Florida.

"Atassis too?" I said.

"Yes, they are cousins. Amer Atassi and his brother."

He gave me both his numbers and his parents'. It made me feel so good when people gave me numbers. I knew I could find them again.

I didn't wait for Farouk to ask around. I called J.D. Nash in Wis-consin and whispered, "I think he's still alive." I asked him to check his death index in California. If he was there three years ago and didn't die . . .

I got a hold of Marion Werth early the next morning. Callie was already out at work. I could hear the light ssst of Marion filing her nails while we talked. Marion made the windows in the millinery and accessory shop. But she didn't go in until ten. I told her about what I found, in Mill Valley or Sausalito.

"Gracious," she said. "Right here. Wouldn't that be something."

I asked her to find me a detective out there. She would know what it took. It couldn't be much different than tracing family trees, only faster, because people gave them money to spend. They didn't have to wait for the mail.

"I'll go through the phone book and run over during my lunchtimes and meet each one." I heard her excitement building the way it had in Racine.

THE ONCE I did lock my apartment I goddamn lost the keys. As soon as I searched my pack and knew they weren't there, I figured out what had happened. I'd dropped them in. The only place they could have gone was an open manila envelope I'd had with papers I'd given to Emory. They were articles I'd Xeroxed for him on a drug and a used copy of Van Gogh's letters. My key ring had probably dropped in too.

It was late at night and so I just slid into a taxi. I rode all the way to Brooklyn, where Emory had moved. I knew the general area. But then when we got there, it was dark and scarce and not that many lights were on in the buildings. I told the driver everything and then I had to get out to look up the address. I stopped in a lit tiny supermarket, old, like from years ago, with sawdust on the floor and a Nehi Orange sign on the blank coolers, and asked to use the telephone book.

Guire, I remembered the landlord's name was. Guire.

There was nothing listed.

Then I wanted to stop at the phone booths and call information for a new listing.

I stopped at one and it was broken. I put a quarter in and nothing. I should have left but I didn't. I put another quarter in and then another. I stumbled back to the taxi driver and told him. The car moved silently in the dark to the next standing phone. I moved to go out, then I had to admit it. I had no quarter. He gave me one. This time the machine took my money again and flickered alive, but then nothing.

I had to go back and tell him that. He asked me, I had no idea where I was going?

It occurred to me then the man must think I'm crazy. Not all the telephones in Brooklyn could be broken.

We drifted in the dark streets around the school where Emory was supposed to work. But there were buildings and buildings and it could have been any. The driver had turned the meter off. I asked him to wait there and I would run into the school.

It was March and it was wet outside more than cold and the dry grass blew a little on the lawn. There was an old-fashioned door, painted brown, with nickel fittings and a push bar. The school was low and vast and covered with blond bricks. I rattled the door. It was locked. I ran on the grass, sinking in my heels past windows figured with dark cut-outs and a fringe of plants and jars on the wide sills. There was a central door leading off a sidewalk that went to a tall flag-pole. No one had taken the American flag down that night and it ripped and seared in the wind. I knocked on the door and I heard chains rattling and echoing. Still, I didn't see a light anywhere.

I kept on and finally I thought I heard footsteps. I quieted and waited them. Yes. It was something. I heard them behind the door, shuffling. Finally, a working of metal and chain and the door opened just a wedge inch and I saw eyes.

"Excuse me," I said, "I'm looking for Emory Sparn?"

The eyes registered nothing. Then the hand on the door moved and he showed himself. A small man with a huge plastic garbage bar-rel on wheels, the broom attached.

"Do you know him? The night janitor?"

The man made an expression, a shaking of his whole body, from the shoulders up, and his face and big ears jiggled and I knew he could not hear or did not understand or would not talk, he was through now, he pushed the door back shut and began to maneuver his cart around and I heard a sound issuing from him, a slight wheeze leaving like the stream of air from an open balloon, and I crossed the lawn, feeling the wet on the tops of my feet and slid back in the taxi and told him I gave up and we'd go back home.

I'd just call a locksmith. We rode slowly over the Brooklyn Bridge and I asked him about himself. He'd turned off the meter a long time ago. My mother had always made me know, when people do things for you, you owe it to them to at least ask about their life and to listen.

I asked him where he was from. He was foreign. He had some accent.

And he was from Jordan, he said. His whole family was still there. His wife, his four children. He had a young boy, thirteen months old. The rest were older, teenagers. So what was he doing here? I asked. He didn't tell me exactly. He said he was a doctor and a scholar. A scholar of what? I said. And he told me Islam. I told him my father was from Egypt and he was a Moslem too.

And what about you? What are you? he asked. Now he was looking back at me over the seat, peering.

"I'm nothing," I said. "Not really."

"Well you should read for yourself and decide. You should read the Koran and read the Bible and read the Torah. Read yourself and decide."

"My mother is just," I said, "you know, American."

He started to lecture me. I believed the guy was a scholar. He had an educated way about him.

"How often do you get back?" I said.

He paused before he answered. "Every three or four weeks," he said.

He said he was writing something, too. A small pamphlet. A book. He said his brother was the head of the Kuwait Shipping Company. He seemed to want me to get something from what he was saying.

Finally we returned where he'd found me to the front of where I lived and I gave him all the money I had. It was nineteen dollars, not enough.

"What is your name?" I said. "I'll write it down and watch for your book." I looked before he answered to where they had his name and his picture under plastic on the glove compartment.

"Forget about that," he said, "forget the name. Remember my face," and he held it for a moment, forward off his neck like a pert sunflower, in a strict expression as he would pose it perhaps for a newspaper photographer. "Remember this face. Someday you will know who I am."

. . .

THE WIND BRITTLED COLD when I stepped out. Ohmygod, I was thinking, he thinks he's the next Kahlil Gibran, but he wasn't really that way. I pulled my collar up and stood a moment, watching the car lights bob away in the dark. I still had so much to do. I had to call a locksmith and listen while they put me on hold and told me their minimum nighttime scandal rates. I had to wait on the bench in the lobby until they finally came and then plead with them to please take my check.

But I was excited again. He was maybe the truth. He could be someone important in the world and hidden. Remember my face, forget the name.

He was a terrorist, I decided. Maybe my father was too.

MY LAST DEAD END was more than a voice on a phone or paper records. Ali. Farouk Atassi's brother was finally home from Ohio.

It was Wednesday and I was all dressed up. My suit was delivered back perfect from Emily's dry cleaner. Putting my jacket on, I winced: I still hadn't talked to my mother. I hadn't gone to see her since her cancer. Now I didn't know when I would. I had no more money. I kept pushing her name down, not thinking of her. She could wait until after this was done. I buttoned the jacket, fitted the collar down. That morning, I'd received a letter with many stamps of animals, from Ramadan. He'd written "I love you" in big childish letters. There was more I couldn't understand.

Ali and I had a plan for dinner. His directions to his house turned out to be exactly correct except in miniature. His two miles went on forty minutes through the worst part of Brooklyn. Finally though, I walked up from the subway into innocent Queens.

He opened the door, thin-faced, and we climbed shag stairs to his apartment. He looked young, too thin, he still had pimples. He was nerdy, not like my father. Not like Ramadan. Not the Omar Sharif type, more like the foreign student in weird clothes, who you didn't know what nationality he was only different. The apartment seemed absolutely standard, a TV running on without sound. He offered me Turkish coffee and while he moved in the kitchen, making it, I touched the springy prongs of a brass tree on the table next to me.

Ali's English was halting, but under that lay a supple fluency. He told me about the hospital where he worked and showed me the pile of manila envelopes, all applications for a sub-specialty residency in pulmonary.

He really got going when I asked him about his visit to Ohio. It turned out he'd gone to see his fiancée. In 1986, in America, he was having an arranged engagement. But it turned out the marriage was off. He worked his hands together like old women in the Midwest used to on the laps of their aprons. "The Koran says, you marry for your family, love will come later. It will be hard for a Westerner to understand our ways. And you. Your father married Americans. But see, you. You haven't seen your father. You're looking for him. In a good Muslim family, this would never happen."

"A good anything family."

"But your father fell away from the religion. He married an American and—" He shrugged. "To us, family is the most important thing."

"Yeah, but don't you want her to be pretty?"

"Looks are not the most important thing to me."

"What about this girl in Ohio? What does she look like?"

"She is average. Not what you say gorgeous. Just average."

"How did you find her?"

"My family heard about her family and that she was a doctor and a good family, so my mother called them up."

"And then what?"

"They said, okay, we can have a meeting, she wasn't engaged or anything. So we went, my mother and father and brother, and visited Ohio."

"And?"

"What do you mean 'and'?"

"Then what happened."

"Well, we continued. I called her on the telephone and we talked and I visited twice. This was my second visit. But we learned we would not be able to get along, so we had to break it off."

"Why?"

"It was a question of values. I told you, it will be hard for a Westerner to understand."

"Oh, Ali. Try me."

"Well, in our religion what the parents say goes. So we talked about what would happen if there were disagreement between my mother and my wife. And she wants her life partner to be with her, she wants what she says to go. And I would have to go with my mother. So, it is not possible.''

"The old mother-in-law problem. Listen, Ali, tell me, if there were five young girls, all from good families, and your mother approved of all five. Say one is prettiest and you just have the most chemistry with her, wouldn't you want her?''

"Yes, sure, of course, if there are five, you pick the one with the most. But there are not five. Young women are hard to find here.''

It was late and I was beginning to give up on dinner. I was hungry but I still had the long subway ride home. I thought of what I had back in my refrigerator. I could get beans and rice at Tacita de Oro. I was trying to plan my meals now. I'd gained eight pounds. Ali moved in the kitchen, fixing another round of Turkish coffee.

"Ali," I called, "you know I think there's another cousin of ours in New York who's an engineer. Thirty years old. Aleya Azzam is her name." I didn't say that she didn't have time for me.

"Is she chemical engineering?''

"No, civil. Bridges and stuff." An Egyptian woman my age, not pregnant, hovering over a hinged-part model of a bridge. She'd become a figure for me. Her bridge would be so different from bridges Emory made with toothpicks and glue, little bits of broken glass and string, whatever he could find. Aleya's bridge would be built with money, connecting somewhere to somewhere else. Cars would run on it.

This time when he brought in the tiny coffee cups, very proper, on a tray, he also carried a red satin box of chocolates. "From my mother when she was here," he said. I took a couple out on a napkin to be polite. When he returned the tray to the kitchen, I snuck the chocolates into the bottom of my backpack so I wouldn't have to eat them. I didn't like to eat junk.

"She's very spunky," I called out.

"Oh, I should have to meet her.''

"I mean, you can't marry her, Ali, she's your cousin. But I think you'd like her.''

He blushed. "I didn't mean to marry her, I just meant—''

I waved him away. "I know.''

Then we started looking at his family pictures from Oakland. Farouk's wife, the young woman I talked to on the phone, wore full veil.

All the women did, and not the stylish veils. They looked ageless, sexless. No wonder looks weren't the most important thing.

I complimented him though on how nice they all seemed. I tried to see myself in these people's snapshots and I just couldn't. I pulled back my bangs from my forehead, which was what people always did, to show how Middle Eastern I looked. "Do you think I look Egyptian?"

"No," Ali said.

"Oh," I said. I'd always heard that I had an Egyptian face. "This part here." I'd seen it in Egypt. Hundreds of faces pear-shaped like mine, flat cheekbones, something oriental.

"Yes, but you're" here he relied on his hands to take in all of me, "your way of dress, everything, you are American. If you walked down the street in Cairo, people would look."

I smiled. They had. I remembered the neighbor's kids staring at me.

"Our girls are raised differently. They don't have boyfriends and so much experience as Westerners have. Have you had—" Here again he relied on his hands.

This was the first time I had ever been asked about my virginity by a stranger.

And so what did I do? I lied. "Well, I haven't had boyfriends, no. My career, it's very hard to get into medical school here. All my twenties, I've just worked and worked."

This pleased him. He gave me a look I can only describe as being like a slanted ray of light emanating from a dark bucket.

"Why did you say, about Azzam, that I could not marry her because she is a cousin?"

Oh, so that was it. "Because we don't do that here, blood relatives."

"In our religion, many people marry their cousins. Perfectly fine."

"What about genetic problems? Hapsburgs and all that. Chins."

"I am a doctor and I tell you, it's perfectly fine."

I didn't make a big deal out of it that I was a medical student too. And anyway, right then, I wasn't. It was time for me to go. I stood up, rubbing my skirt front. "So you don't know anything more about my father, like where he is or anything?"

"We only saw him that once with another cousin, Kareem, and then Kareem went back to Germany. But your father was running a big restaurant. I don't think he had such a good job. He fell away from the religion." Ali made an expression like a shrug with his mouth. "He married an American wife."

"Two," I said.

"His job, it was not such a good job. And he left your mother." He looked as if, what more was there to say.

"He's still my father," I said.

"Yes. But you see, in our religion, we don't live that way."

"In mine either," I said. Not that I had one, exactly.

I rifled quickly through his manila envelopes of pulmonary applications. I nixed Kansas, told him he'd hate Alabama, and pulled Boston, San Francisco, Chicago and Baltimore to the top.

"He's probably somewhere in California," he said.

I pulled Ramadan's letter out of my backpack. "Could you translate this?" I said.

He read a little and looked at me strangely, in a slant again. "You were in Egypt?"

I nodded.

He put the letter down. "Lower class. Uneducated. Your taxi driver fell in love with you." He laughed. "He wants to come over here and start a life, he says. Study. It's nothing. Throw it away. You're not in his class. You are like Princess Diana to him."

It was not like that. I had seen the house. I had to ask him for the letter back. He walked me to the subway station and waited until the train came. I knew he was already eyeing me to marry. I slipped into the car, waving—at least I didn't have to worry about him trying to kiss.

MARION WERTH CALLED ME THE NEXT NIGHT, saying, "Well, I think I found an agent for you. His name is Tom Carson and he used to be in the military and then with the FBI. I called seven or eight of his references and they all said they had good luck with him. I'll tell you what, see if you like this idea, I thought I'd work on it with the agent. And I thought if I learned from this and we found him, then after, we'd hire the same person and I'd help to find Callie's mother."

I decided then and there to send her the eight hundred dollars I'd borrowed to pay Jim Wynne, wrapped in tin foil.

J.D. Nash called me an hour later and told me there was no listing in the death index.

"So he's alive."

"Most likely," J.D. Nash said. "Most likely he is."

I started to go seriously crazy. Now I believed I would find him, and soon. I couldn't stay still. I didn't want to be inside. I just walked around on the street. I went into Tacita de Oro and slid onto a stool. I ordered one café con leche and drank it hot, fast, scalding.

Now, I decided, writing down my resolves on the napkin, I had to fire Wynne. There was more than one kind of man in the world. And I knew Marion. I trusted her. I understood her methods. They could be explained. I'd stopped trusting people who claimed to know more than they could tell me. In what I didn't understand being truer than what you could lay out on a table and see plain. Maybe I'd stopped believing in the invisible, even to find him.

From the pay phone outside Tacita de Oro, I dialed Jim Wynne's number. Then I hung up. This would be hard. But I made myself do it again. "Hi. It's me. Listen, I decided I need a detective in California."

"Awright," he said and hung up.

That was all it meant to him. I put down the phone and started walking. I didn't want to go home yet. It was spring already, almost warm. Now I began to doubt whether Wynne had done anything he said he had. If he'd really done a DMV check, why didn't he come up with the older Atassis in Oakland? Farouk must have had a license. Could he have lied about everything?

There was something shoddy about him always. His mystery was all there was to him. "I'm gonna find him. I'm getting close, I know I am." Yeah, right. He talked that way before he cashed my check. All confidence and then it's, oh yeah, you, what's new? He was what they meant with the old name, Confidence Man.

Still I had that one bauble from him, my father's birthdate, which was precious. I thought of it like one yellow emerald earring.

Marion Werth and this new man in California were completely different. Tom Carson was ex-FBI. Detectives were all either ex-cop, ex-psychologist, or ex-actor. I was learning a little about the trade. No more ex-actors for me.

Marion Werth and Tom Carson called me together Friday morning and said they'd like to do Department of Motor Vehicle and three credit checks in both Nevada and California.

"That'll cost $90," Marion said, after Tom laboriously explained the details. "I'm keeping a close eye on the budget."

I told them I thought Jim Wynne had already done DMV and credit.

"I'd rather go ahead and do it again ourselves, if you don't mind." This man sounded square-headed, crew-cutted, level.

If they found him he'd just be visible on the earth. They'd do it the old way, brick by brick by brick. There was no magic to them.

I couldn't let them do it alone though. By then I needed the work to shape my days.

I called the chambers of commerce in Mill Valley and Sausalito for the names of their big Italian restaurants. And their big seafood restaurants. I did it like a clerk. Black women were my salvation. I called all eleven places. Nothing. They'd never heard of him.

I hated this. I wanted to be done with this and young. I wanted to wriggle into short skirts and go.

I WAS EITHER ON THE PHONE or idle. I found myself dreaming of dresses and planning dinner parties. But never for now. For after.

MAYBE BY THE TIME you found a person, they were always beside the point. You don't need them so much anymore. What I needed most now was to find a way back to my life.

I called Marion Werth Thursday night. Just the routine checking-up-on-the-detective call. She was at the millinery store. I heard the friss of people in the background. "Mayan, I think we've found him. He's in Modesto. He works in a restaurant. I wanted to wait a day before I told you and let Tom do all the double-checks."

All I could do was ask for more. "Did you hear anything else about him?"

"Not really yet. He turned up with a California driver's license. It all cost seventy-five dollars."

I wanted to sue Jim Wynne. That was the first thing I thought.

He was there all along, the first place we checked. It was probably the laziness of one assistant, one of the contacts he'd talked to on the phone. Just a random typical sloppy error in the world which mattered to me and no one else. What if I'd believed Wynne and stopped?

One thing I knew, I didn't know many things now, but one thing I did know was that waiting would have never worked. My father had no plans to find me.

The infinite ended that day.

I MADE AIRPLANE RESERVATIONS. For tomorrow. And then I had nothing to do. For the first time, maybe ever.

I wandered through the rooms, rubbing my hands on my jeans. Everything seemed already done. In a flurry, I went outside to the small corner market and bought oranges and flowers, waxy anemones. I bought new milk for coffee. Then I rushed back and set the oranges on the table, the flowers in a pitcher. I began to dust.

My suitcase was packed. That took no time. Now that he was found, only in California, I didn't even think of buying a new suit. My ordinary clothes would do.

I was disappointed in more ways than I understood. That he could be found.

Disappearing was all you had to do to become somebody's god. And maybe being found was all it took to be mortal again.

I didn't want to go anywhere. I was discovering here. Later I dusted and cleaned the bathroom and the windowsill. I shoved open the window to the clear night air. I looked at small things randomly and for a long time. I opened my anatomy book and memorized two charts just for pleasure. The hand bones and the eye muscles. Wonder is a luxury of a certain emptiness of purpose. Wonder is the rest of the day after you find what you were looking for all your life.

On my desk, in the mess of papers where I had my father's tiny picture, was the engraved invitation, brown on white thick paper. Emily's wedding. It was in a week. I didn't even know if I'd be back.

I WENT OVER TO EMILY'S, but she only had a few minutes before she had to be somewhere. I zipped her up. Still, something lovely rose in the shape of her spine, it was straight like a tulip stem.

"Listen, Emily, I found him. And I'm going tomorrow to California. I think I'll be back for the wedding and even the dinner the night before, but I might not be. I don't know anything right now."

"My God, you found him. Where is he?"

"Modesto, California. He works in a restaurant."

"Shit." She sat down on her bed. "You're just going to fly out there? Have you called him yet?"

"Huh-uh. I'm not giving him the chance to get out of town."

"God, I'm jealous, kind of. I mean, what an adventure. Can I come?"

"You probably have every hour booked between now and next weekend."

"Yeah, I do," she said. "Three meals a day."

"How's all that going?"

"I saw my dad this afternoon and he told me, 'Honey, if I'm walking you down that aisle and you don't feel right, you go ahead and turn around and I'll walk you back out.'"

"After all that money?"

"Three hundred people. And the tent. I wanted it to look like a circus tent. And it does. It's white, with a hole in the top. So you can see the stars. Hey, I don't have to go to this dinner. Or you could come. I could lend you something to wear. Why don't you stay here tonight? Sleep over."

"Okay, I will."

"God, let me know from out there how it goes. I mean I completely understand if you can't make it back, but I don't even want to go through with it if you and Mai linn aren't there. That's the best part, you guys in those dresses. I wanted them to be like flowers. I think you'd wear it again after. I know everybody says that about bridesmaids' dresses, but these I think you really would. And you need something like that."

Yeah, right.

I called the detective from Emily's phone while she was finishing in the bathroom.

"How's New York?" Tom Carson asked. He said Marion had left to drive home. She and this man I'd never met had found my father, whom I'd been looking for all my life.

"Good," I said. "I don't know, I guess kind of cold tonight. I bought the ticket for tomorrow morning."

He told me that we had a work address and a work phone number. The place was called The Lighthouse. Its address was 808 Third Street in Modesto. Emily passed me a lipstick liner. I wrote on the back of a receipt. They were all over, in her house.

"Do we know for sure he's still there?"

"Yes. I'll tell you what I did. I called and asked about making reservations. And I said, well what time does the kitchen serve until? They said they usually close at eight but what time did I want?"

"That's kind of strange for a restaurant." It sounded shady to me.

"Yes it is. So then after the reservation chat for a few minutes I said, is John Atassi still there? And they said, oh sure. We could, if you want, get a home address but that'll cost you about another sixty."

"Let's do that. And see if we can find out anything more about the restaurant too. Sounds like a front, closing at eight o'clock."

Nothing would have surprised me.

I CALLED HIM again an hour later.

The address was 970 Fifth Street. "That's as of last June," he said.

"Sounds near Third Street."

"Yes it is. Oh, and the restaurant is a nice restaurant. I wanted to tell you we do have an office in Modesto too, so if you run into any trouble, they'll try to help you out. And you have Marion's number. She says she'll stay by the phone all day."

I sat on the windowsill and waited for Emily to come home. You could see stars and the church across the street and the stores' awnings on the ground floors, the upstairs lighted windows. New York looked tranquil and small that night. I wanted to come back here already. Maybe by the time you find somebody, they are beside the point.

THEN I WAS DRIVING a rocket-silver car to Modesto. It was the first time I didn't just rent the cheapest. I flew to Oakland, slept on Stevie and Helen's little futon on the clean floor. I slept open on my back and woke easily, dark fir branches tapping the high windows, a new blue-and-white streaked sky. Stevie was still asleep, but Helen and Jane were up with me. Helen was taking corn muffins out of the oven. A wind came in from the back door, we heard the turning of leaves and pine needles shifting on the porch floor. Their life seemed simple. Helen's kimono smelled of laundry soap. Her feet were straight and bare, the linoleum floor clean. Jane sat with her lunch box open, putting in things her mother handed her, one thing at a time.

Then I was driving, first through sleeping Berkeley, then east on

580. I pressed the computerized radio search button and sang along to every AM hit from my life I could catch the end of. Stevie was always telling me how many people died changing stations on the radio. He told me that once from his car phone, on the way to the Sierras. Then when the land spread out clear past Livermore, I turned the radio off and rolled the window down and remembered this wasn't just any day I wanted to use up and forget. This was a day that would have to make a difference.

So then I watched the sky. I tried to remember things for a while. This was spectacular land anyway. The hills were navy shale and hard in the distance, pure slate, what you'd call mountains in the Midwest. And closer, it was only rolling hills, dry-colored, haylike, with fields and trees and pastures mixed together. The land, though, took up only a small portion, a thin strip on the bottom of what you saw because the sky that day was all things, light and dark, dull and sun-shot, full of clouds and windy dashes.

I was remarking to myself to try and remember that it was a clear blowy day, the way you always thought of dumb, simple things like the weather on days like births or deaths or weddings because everything is too big and too small at the same time, and just when I'd wished I could write it down so I'd remember for sure, something broke gently and it was raining around me.

Every time I let myself think too long I started crying, not over anything particular. I was just crying and the rain kept coming over all the slick metal and glass of this warm car. You could control the heat by pressing buttons with pictures on them to blow on your ankles or warm your seat or rush to the back of your neck. I controlled the heat.

Then the road carved into the hills and on the banks of the low rises, cherry trees lurched like a misshapen exercise class half bent down in the old orchard. And the funny thing was that some of these crooked windy trees, glazed slick with rain, bandaged by gray-blue fog, some of them were in blossom, some not yet, and some trees blossomed only in a patch as if a hand had touched one part and made it glow. The way these trees had spaced themselves, twisted and deformed by weather, rain dulling everything, the dark clouds and the shadowing light made the rare blossoms seem almost miracle, a smile on a damaged child.

I skidded the car to a stop. On the slope, there was a red picnic table in the dull light. Under cherry blossoms. That was it. I had dreamed of that before. And all of a sudden, I stepped out and the air was a billow of cool expansion. This had been it, what I was driving half the country to see. And now I had seen it.

From Mantica, a smell of manure came from the open windows, heavy like meat. Beyond a long field, there were shanties and farm buildings. When he was doing research for his Ph.D., Stevie had come this way, to study a particular tree disease in the Sierra. There was a lab station in Blodgett. What if I'd come along and we'd gone into his restaurant knowing nothing? That wasn't even a question anymore.

For me, this reunion cost time and money and life and work.

Or maybe I didn't believe enough. Maybe if I'd waited longer. But my father was born in 1931. He would be fifty-five. How much longer could I wait?

By the time I heard on Thursday, certain things were obvious, a flat bottom in my stomach. I came right away. But it wasn't jump on a plane. I haggled with the travel agent, complained about the price. I felt grim about it all.

"Should I bring something good?" I'd asked Emily. "Or just jeans." I kind of wanted to go in just my regular stuff.

"Bring one thing so you can dress up if you need to. You don't want to be thinking about clothes." She went to her closet, chose an older dress, a loose print that was long. She knew I liked long. "Take this."

"Not the suit?"

"No."

I did as I was told.

So many dead ends had stopped me still before, numerous enough I couldn't count: times at phone booths, me standing alone at a gas station in a new state, somewhere in the West spelling A-T-A-S-S-I to an operator with a slow accent. There was always no listing, more than a thousand times, a thousand places, some twice probably, more. And the absence of Gilberts and Rilellas from the face of the earth, as if marrying my father had kept women and all their relatives from ever listing themselves in phone books again.

Now I was entering Modesto, a valley city, with its own curving concrete freeway ramps like a child's game. I picked one and ended up on a long tree-banked street leading to downtown. That turned out to be good. Gridded cities were easy and the numbered streets followed in order. In ten minutes I was driving past The Lighthouse, a stucco building that looked like anywhere else. His house was close by, but the one-way streets stalled me. Then, there it was. It was across the street from a regular-looking park, just flat grass, a chain-link fence all around and a dirt baseball diamond. It was a duplex on a street of duplexes. His was pale brown. It looked closed up, the blinds drawn.

I WASN'T READY THOUGH. Not yet. I wasn't clean.

I drove around looking for a hotel. I went towards what I thought was charm in the distance and turned out to be a decrepit Elks Lodge. Old in the East meant good, in the West it was something else. I checked into a motel, unpacked and made coffee on a little hot plate they had in all the rooms. This was good. I was an adult and I could handle a motel. I showered, washed my hair.

Before I'd come it was this big question whether or not to call him. I didn't want him to have a chance to say no. I figured if he didn't want to talk to me, I'd get more from having him tell me that with a face than I would from just having him say no and hanging up on the phone. "I don't want to ask him," I'd told Mai linn. "I want to just be there."

But now that I was here I worried about manners. Maybe he was busy at certain times. Out the window Modesto didn't seem to move, except the top ferns of palm in the light wind. There seemed no need for all this. Out the window a couple walked by, arms curled around each other's backs in one s.

I called the restaurant number. It rang and rang. Nine times. Eleven. I hadn't planned what I'd do if he was there.

I tried again. Sixteen.

I called the hotel's front desk and asked how to make local calls. Yes. I was doing it right.

I steadied myself, pulled the towel up further on my chest. I poured another cup of coffee, then I called information, checked the number.

I didn't panic. I dressed and walked out to the motel lobby. I told the girl there I wanted a reservation at a place called The Lighthouse.

"They're not answering, now," she said, after a few moments. "I'm so sorry, would you like me to give you their number?"

"Do you know if they're open?"

"I guess they can't be open if they're not answering."

"You don't sound sure. Is there anyone here who would know for sure?" I looked around. The office was small and empty.

"I'm pretty sure they're not open today if they're not answering the phone now. Otherwise they'd be there already serving lunch."

"Do you know if they're open tomorrow?" Each word was a tooth. Tomorrow was Sunday. My rage hardened dense as a block. Not again.

"No, I doubt it. If they're closed today they're probably closed tomorrow too."

"Thanks," I said. A little bell hung on the lobby door tinkled behind me as I left.

There was nothing to do. I'd have to go to the house. I tried to think what if no one was there. I felt that trickle almost like a relief; I knew how to make a day in a strange city. Outside the motel a stray piece of paper ticked, blowing on the gutter. I'd find a coffee house, write letters, I'd see a movie while it was still light out.

Then I'd planned such a safe easy day for myself, full of consolations, I almost wanted that.

I blow-dried my hair. I put on makeup, mascara and eyeliner. When I searched for the lipstick, I found Ali's chocolate hardened like goo at the bottom of my pack. A white shirt, jeans, the earrings. The shoes with the ghost of Edison's phone number. As I walked outside, I thought of my soles sanding against the pavement, wearing the numbers of his location all away.

Then I went. I parked in front of the duplex.

I turned the motor off. I knew now as I looked at the blind face of the town house, this could be another dead end. Another false tip, a mistake, another place he wasn't. I promised myself, this would be my last dead end. I'd give up. I had to get back. I had to so bad.

First I moved my stuff to the trunk. I had my backpack with Timothy's camera in it. I took his picture out from where I'd saved it and looked at it in my palm. In the little picture, he looked about my age, proud-seeming, well-dressed, not exactly handsome. In a sharp double-breasted suit. I put it away again. Whatever society there was in America didn't work the way my mother and dad thought it should, from looks. Education was the great leveler and opportunity, if you wanted that. It wasn't, as my mom thought, a matter of clothes.

Then I had a hard time fitting the key into the lock, I wobbled on my heels. I thought, my father could be at his upstairs window wondering who the crazy woman was ministering to her car door. At least, I had the consolation, he'd never in a million stars guess me.

I saw the door. A screen door and then a wood door. I didn't see a nameplate or anything but I pushed the doorbell and I heard it work inside and then a little dog was barking madly, I don't know how I knew it was a little dog, bellow size I guess, hurling itself against the door.

"Oh, only the dog's home," I thought, letting myself down, and then the door opened. There was the wire mesh netting of the screen door, the dog, turning flat against it, head to tail, a terrier, long-haired, messy, a man in a maroon bathrobe, barefoot, pajamaed, I only recognized at the shoulders was my father.

"What do you want?" he said, his eyebrows sharp in a V.

He looked at me a full moment and I knew him, the curled lip, the chin tilting the whole face like a bowl. His eyes ran back and forth over me and got nothing. He didn't smile. He seemed foreign then. His face was thinner now, a smooth vertical. He'd lost hair down the center and grown beautiful.

"I'm looking for John Atassi," I said. "And that's you, isn't it?"

I wondered for a moment if I would have to prove who I was and I thought of the shoes he once promised me he would get me in Beirut when he left and I smiled because of course I couldn't put on the slipper and lift my leg up to show because it wouldn't fit, I had grown, time had come in and changed the ending and I was not the same anymore. My mother still had a basket with a half-knit sweater for the tiny child I was.

He said "Yes," and the face was nude like an old sad clown's, full of mime, and I told him, because he did not know, "I am your daughter," and then everything turned different, he was jumping and yelling, he pulled me in waltzing, crying over my hand. I knew he would never remember the shoes from Beirut, he'd forgotten years ago, maybe even while he was saying the words of the promise, like the disappearing ink of fireflies on a Wisconsin night sky.

I was in and he was only a man.

12

"YOU KNOW, HONEY, you should of called," he said after the tears were over, wiped delicately from his face with his own hand, holding a colored tissue Uta delivered to him. "We almost went away for the weekend. We were going to drive up to the mountains."

Uta tched. "Yes, we were planning on it."

"Isn't it lucky, Uta, we didn't go. Yah, it's really fortunate. We could have just been gone."

The day I met my father was the way Stevie described his own wedding, long and hot and rich with food. Stevie was always asking everyone else what his wedding was like, as if he wasn't there. I was in a daze. All around me was light and heat and noise and lots of champagne.

And there is no one I can ever ask.

His house was ordinary, nothing. Walking through the little entry hall, I immediately revised everything. He had standard furniture. It could have been rented but it wasn't new enough.

Uta was still there, in nylons and slippers, carrying a Kleenex box over to him. She offered me one too, but only after.

Uta: nobody thinks their parents could do better than each other. Few people ever have such positive proof. Four-foot-eleven, brittle, she had odd points of hair where sideburns would be, a style Liza Minnelli adopted briefly in the late '60s.

We settled ourselves down in the furniture and Uta brought a pot of coffee.

His eyes were red from crying but we'd stopped.

"Your father is a great man," Uta said to me.

Oh really, why? I felt like saying, what has he done? From what I hear he's not been so dandy to you.

"He's just a wonderful, wonderful man. I've seen him go through so many things. I really admire him."

I kept stealing shy looks at him and he was just there. I couldn't tell if he looked like me or not. His skin was whiter than I'd thought. Ramadan had been better looking.

Like any strangers, we talked about geography. Modesto, Stockton, Yosemite, the immediate area. I said I liked Berkeley. I said that I was there last summer, visiting Stevie, my childhood friend.

"Well, how come you waited till now then?" my father said. "Why did you take so long?"

"How come I waited till now?" I hit his shoulder a way I thought was playful. This was how I'd seen people do it. "You're hard to find. I'm not that hard to find. Maybe I am. I don't know."

"Your mom's still listed in Los Angeles?" he asked idly. The answer to that was yes. She was.

"You wanted to play the cello, didn't you?" Uta asked out of the blue.

"I played drums for a while, when I was a kid."

"No, I think it was the cello," she said. "Well, did you ever do it?" She said that as if it were some accusation. "Where was she born?" she asked him instead of me.

"She was born in Bay City, Wisconsin."

"But wasn't Adele pregnant in Egypt?"

"Yah, we lived in Luxor. I was working for a Saudi petroleum company. We had a brand-new place but she just didn't like it. She didn't like the food. Didn't like the style of life. She just was unhappy. But you were born here, in Bay City July 2, '58, see yah. Yah." He had a foreigner's voice. Then he lapsed, looking out into the small patio. "Midafternoon."

"You find out all kinds of things now maybe, huh?" Uta volunteered. "Did you ever know your birthday?"

"Sure she knows her birthday."

"Birthtime, I mean."

"No, I don't think so. I have a birth certificate but I don't think it has a time on it," I said. "And your birthday is May 21, 1931, right?" His birthday was the same day as Yasir Arafat's, even though Arafat's was in 1929. In my wilder moments I'd let myself think they were the same person.

He shrugged. "I don't have a birthday. Isn't that funny. But you know in those days, Mayan, in Egypt, they didn't have a doctor come and deliver a baby. They had a kind of traveling midwife, an itinerant. And I was the youngest of four children and one day I asked my mother when I was born and she couldn't remember. Can you imagine that? She just didn't know. They didn't keep track of those things the same way they do here. And so next time the woman came around, we asked her and she didn't remember either so when I came to school here, to Columbia University, I just made it up."

SO THE ONE FACT I had from Jim Wynne didn't even turn out to be true.

I ASKED HIM ABOUT MY BIRTH. I told him that my mother had always said I was in an incubator. "No," he said, shaking his head. "It was a normal birth. 'Huna London,' I said, 'Sheesh, Huna London.'" Then he just broke out and cried. "You know there's not a day that went by when I didn't think of you. And now when I'm getting older I thought what would happen if I died. You wouldn't even know. I wouldn't know how to find you."

I cried a lot too and let him hold my hand in his. My hand was always wet from his tears. I noticed, though, that his hands weren't mine either. They were small hands, boxy. I recognized my mother more and more in my own body.

I didn't think it exactly then, but I wasn't so hard to find. And why wasn't he going to find me until he was dying? But he spoke well, in a way that didn't suggest questions.

Uta was up and down a lot, getting him things. He took no more notice of her than you would a small, tail-beating, somewhat fragile and always beckoning dog. In fact they had such a dog. I'd made them put the dog upstairs because I was allergic. Every once in a while the dog would scratch and whimper and Uta would say, "Aw, he's lonely for his daddy. He loves his daddy so much."

"I SEEM TO REMEMBER something about your father promising me a sheep."

"That right?"

"Could that have been?"

"Well, you never met him, Mayan. When we were over there, you weren't born yet."

"And then you, we, lived for a little bit in Michigan." For years I'd had a red toy truck from East Lansing.

"Was Adele with you the whole time in Michigan?" Uta asked him.

"Yes, we broke up in Michigan," he said. "I had made the mistake of inviting some Egyptian immigrants who lived in the Ann Arbor area to my house for dinner. And you know these people had never been to Egypt. So we're talking, they knew Adele and I had been there and they wanted to get some first-hand information. Our impressions.

"What I'm going to say is not very nice about your mother but she was young and we were unhappy. But she, she knocked things down, she told them the most miserable things, how dirty the people were, how dusty, how pessimistic. And these people, you know, they didn't want to hear that."

"They wanted to go there," Uta said, trying to follow along.

"Sure, they want to go there! It's their whole life, their homeland, I mean they want to hear some nice things about it."

I smiled. They were probably second generation like me, or third. Egypt was never my whole life.

"Well, didn't you speak in Arabic, sweetheart, and tell them what it is really like?" That was Uta.

"They didn't speak Arabic. They were immigrants, you know. So after that I remember I took my suitcase and got the car and that's the last I saw of Adele, I mean, we saw each other again but that was really it. And the next day I resigned, took a train to Chicago and got on a plane and went back home. I was going to go and I wasn't going to come back to this country ever."

Well that's a good father, I was thinking.

"WOULD YOU LIKE a glass of champagne to celebrate our reunion," he said. It was not much after noon, but this was less a question than a statement and he returned with a wash towel and the opened bottle and poured a glass for each of us.

His stories were never an explanation really. Uta made a few attempts. When she came in and joined us again with napkins for the champagne, she said how hard my mother had made it for him.

"Oh, she was terrible, she made him feel so bad, Mayan. I remember she'd call him and tell him he could see you and then she'd call back and call it all off. Many times I know she hurt his feelings bad."

"She's crazy," I said. She was.

"He wanted to see you but . . ." She just bent her neck down and shook her head.

"Is she still crazy? She always was," he said, his head rising. He had a flat smile, buoyant. "She was a great girl, beautiful, very intelligent, everything, but always a little crazy. But you shouldn't talk bad about her, Mayan, because she is the one who really raised you."

What did he mean, really. She is the only one who raised me at all.

He just patted my hand, sometimes looking at the low ceiling. "The daughter I never had."

And whose fault is that, I want to say now, remembering. Whose fault was that?

At the time, though, it was a romance. The day was like a river trip on slow brown water, the banks always changing, water the same. I didn't have to do anything. Everything made sense before he said it and I'd forgiven him already. I kept looking at him and he was beautiful. Everything was easy that day. Love was perfect. Roses, champagne, our hands fit. The day went on. It was long and unfolding. We talked and stopped talking and everything he said was right.

I was quiet, still. I didn't have to do anything.

HE SIGHED and looked at his hand. He picked up his champagne glass and held it up in front of him a level moment, then took a sip. His face closed on the taste, severe a moment.

"This is very good champagne," he said. "Drink some, darling."

"Mmm, very very good," Uta churned her slippered legs, which didn't reach the ground.

"And then, and then, I couldn't do anything to Mayan, you see," my father said.

"That's what you told me, sweetheart." That whole day, Uta really only talked to him.

"I couldn't hold her, I couldn't pick her up."

"That she wouldn't let you."

"No. I couldn't do anything."

"She wouldn't let him kiss her. Kiss you."

"That's not good," I said, but all I could think was how Uta was. What a rah rah.

"I couldn't do anything, you see. If the baby cried and I went to pick it up, that was all wrong. She wouldn't let me change you. She wouldn't let me touch you. You would cry and I'd go to pick you up and she'd say, Let her cry. She should cry. She read all these books, see. And I thought, if I can't touch my own baby, then fuck it. Anything I would do was the wrong thing to do. So we got in fights over it. From the beginning. From the day you were born. That's the way it was. Everything had to be her way and she had a whole philosophy about child-rearing and so on and I was a dummy."

"And believe me she wasn't so good."

"She was pretty good. Because after all she raised you. She did it. Not me. She and your grandmother. From the little bits and pieces I gather, your grandmother really raised you."

"Is that your mother?" Uta shrilled.

"No no, that's her grandmother."

Now Uta addressed me. "His mother's sister lived in Cairo and we visited her. And his mother was there too. That's how I met her."

My mother had always told me my father left because I cried. She'd always said it was because I cried and he said, let her cry, he wanted to go out and go dancing. But she wouldn't let me cry. I would never know what was true.

THE DAY WAS BORING in the way most important, unrepeatable days are. Funerals, weddings and the ceremonies surrounding birth when no one is sure what to do. None of us was at our normal work.

After a while he stood up. "I suppose I better get dressed so you can see your father looking a little better than just a couch potato." He still had his foreigner's accent.

And they went upstairs to dress. I relished the time alone. I stood up and explored. It was a small kitchen, a small living and dining room. They had the latest video equipment. Everything else seemed about five years old. There were no pictures or anything personal that I found. There were no books. Upstairs I heard Uta cooing at the dog. Its tail beat hard through the floor.

There was a wedding that day at The Lighthouse, which was why, it turned out, it was closed, and there was much discussion of how long he would have to go in. He decided he'd work for a few hours and then after we would have dinner. It took a long time for him to get us a reservation. That seemed much on his mind—getting us the very best place. "It's Saturday night," he kept saying, as if we were defeated already, as if I should have given him a week's notice to get reservations.

"His restaurant is the best in town," Uta offered, looking at him. "They get married there even."

"I guess so," I said.

"And the receptions. Wedding receptions and so forth," she said.

The restaurant he really wanted was booked. He was a single-activity man. When he was talking on the phone he was talking on the phone, not like my mother, or me for that matter, who were always dancing, mimicking, pacing, tapping, fidgeting, carrying on primarily with each other, the one present there with us in the room.

He asked if he could speak to the owner. But the owner wasn't there. Then he made a bid to whomever he was talking, saying he was John Atassi from The Lighthouse and his daughter was here and it was a special night and could they possibly get us in. "No," he repeated the other man's word. "All right. I understand."

I remembered my mother slipping the waiter two rolled-up twenty-dollar bills so we could get in to see Barbra Streisand at the Sands Casino in Las Vegas. My mother and I—we would never take no so easily.

He looked at Uta and shrugged. "If they're booked they're booked," he said. He said it again later when we were walking up the gravel, my heels sinking, to the restaurant he'd chosen second, as he was explaining the hierarchy of restaurants in Modesto. "But," he shrugged, "when they're booked they're booked."

"WERE YOU IN CHICAGO for a while?" Uta asked me.

"No."

"Somebody told us sometime or other that you were in Chicago and in some kind of television work or radio work . . ." That seemed to be all. Somebody told them that and that was it.

"No I've been in New York doing graduate work, well medical school."

"That right?" he said.

"Following in your dad's footsteps, huh?" Uta said.

"My mother went to graduate school too."

"Do you go full-time to graduate school? Daytime?" he said.

"Yeah," I said. "You can't really do medical school at night. They don't have it."

"That right?" he said. "You didn't want to go on and get a Ph.D.?"

"No," I said. "The only other thing I really was interested in is architecture. And you don't need a doctorate for that either."

"New York," Uta said. "Well there's always something to do there, that's for sure."

"It's the most cosmopolitan city in the world, really," he said.

It was determined that the dog needed to go out. Uta went up to get it on its leash. He rose and stretched, offering me the last glass of champagne. I refused and he poured it for himself. "What time is it now?" he said, walking to the clock. "Two o'clock."

When Uta descended with the dog she asked how I got there. "Did you come on 580?"

"Yes, I came on 580, it was very easy."

"You could have flown into here."

"I don't think there's a direct flight," I said.

"Well honey, your dream came true," she said, lingering at the door.

"I'll show you something," I said to him. I took the chain out of my pocket. I'd brought it along but I hadn't decided until just this minute that I would tell them. "You gave me an add-a-pearl necklace when I was very little. So right before when I left on the plane I found it to bring along."

He took it in his hands, examining it under the lamp.

"She has the long fingers like you, honey," Uta said.

"No, I have my mother's hands," I said.

He handed the chain back to me and I put it away. "The daughter I never had," he said again, looking into his champagne. "Yah."

"Now you have her, honey," Uta said.

"Yeah, you've got to give me your phone number now," I said. "Masters of the unlisted, you two."

Uta said, "We've always been unlisted."

"I think I'm going to get unlisted too, actually," I said. I was just talking.

"It's kind of nice. For a while there we didn't have it and you get so many calls that you don't care about. This way you talk to who you want to call."

Uh-huh, I was thinking, hearing her. Yup. "I'm sorry to just surprise you like this," I said. This was absurd. I heard myself and hated it.

"Well that's okay, that was nice," Uta said. This woman will cure me of just talking to fill the space, I understood. I heard myself like her. "I don't think you ever could have done anything more delightful for John."

"I'm still in shock," he said. "The most gorgeous surprise. Really it was a shock. For about a fraction of a second, you know, you looked familiar. But I couldn't trust my eyes."

"You have a dad you can be very proud of."

"What, you're trying to do a sales job on the poor girl?"

"No, honey, but she doesn't, she hasn't had a chance to know you before. He's really something else."

"Well, I'm making some progress now. I had some very—"

"He was a rascal for a while there."

"I was a bum."

"No, you weren't a bum. You were mixed up. You made a few mistakes in life but we all do, you know. We've had a good life, haven't we, honey?"

He didn't answer. He looked down into his champagne and swirled the glass.

I WENT BACK TO MY MOTEL while he went to his restaurant to tend the wedding. There was some talk of Uta giving me a tour of the city but for once I said what I wanted, that I was tired.

"We'll do that tomorrow, darling," he said. "You'll stay with us a couple days."

I felt caught in lights. "I can't," I said. "I have to get back tomorrow night." My mouth went rigid, strange.

I didn't know how much more I was up for. I was exhausted, truly drained. I fell on the made motel bed with clean gladness. They'd wanted me to get my stuff and check out and stay with them. I'd used the dog as my excuse. There were so many people I was supposed to call. Venise King. Marion Werth. Emily. But I was tired. Purely, simply tired.

Now I was really ready to go home. I wanted to be there and start again. I knew I would think of this later. Maybe I would understand more then. I had so much to do home again, just to begin. I was out of school, out of a job and out of money. People had given up on me.

The phone rang and I jolted. "Hello, Mayan, this is your dad."

Somehow him calling us that. I was bolt up in the bed. It felt strange, him calling me. "I told them to go to hell, they can manage the damn wedding by themselves. No really, it's fine, I've got a good staff, everything's under control, so we can come early and we can go and get a drink."

I said okay, I'd be ready in fifteen minutes, even though I wanted the long hump of afternoon to sleep.

I WAS WAITING IN THE LOBBY. I didn't want them in my room, I felt funny even just getting into their car like that. I really didn't know him.

The restaurant was small-town fancy, even though Modesto wasn't that small. It was in a three-story Victorian house, with excess atmosphere. Orchids at our table. A framed poster-art reproduction on the wall. Leather-bound books on glass shelves, backlit.

During dinner we talked about food.

"I think the best restaurant in town is yours," Uta said.

"I have a good chef," he conceded. "See, the others can't afford him. I stole him away from San Francisco."

"The way he makes that salmon is, umph." She shuddered in exactly the way I'd seen poodles shake, after immersion.

We'd already had champagne. Now we were drinking white wine from enormous long-stemmed goblets.

"We had quite an Arabic dinner last week," Uta said.

"Do you like Arabic food, Mayan?" he said.

I shrugged. "I eat a lot of dates."

It took them a long time to ask me how I found them. And the truth was, by then I didn't feel like talking about it. It seemed too long and not that interesting. But they asked so I told them I'd had a detective. I said, too, that I'd talked to Dr. Geesie and Dr. Kemp in Montana.

"Oh, Duke Kemp. How is he? I should call him. He's a nice guy."

"Yah, he said if I ever found you I should ask you to call, he said he'd love to talk to you."

"I should give him a call," he said, "yah," in an attenuated way that made me know he never would. It was like my shoes from Beirut.

"I think he's alone, he has no kids. He's sick too, he said."

"He's gay, I think, Duke Kemp. Uta, did you hear, she saw Duke Kemp. Yah I'm pretty sure he's gay."

I told them the little incidentals. I told my father about the woman in Madison from the alumni association.

"Dorothy Widmer?" he said. "No. I don't remember that."

And then I said that I'd checked marriage records. I said that I'd found his marriage record to a woman called Rilella, but that then I couldn't find any Rilellas anywhere under the sun.

"That's not your name, is it, Uta?"

"No, no, she's Wells. She's Uta Wells."

"Of course I'm Uta Atassi now, but I was Uta Wells, yes."

"What was that with Rilella?"

"I don't know. I've never heard of it."

"But it was definitely you. Because it had my mom listed as the previous marriage."

"I don't know, Mayan, it must be a mistake. Because I never heard of that name."

That was that. He looked clear ahead, lifted his fish to his mouth, tasted.

"The lamb is very good," Uta said.

I stuck with marriage. I told them the only Atassi in the California records was a Sahar Atassi, who was my age or a little younger, and married to a Diane Thayer. "I even wondered if you'd had more kids and he was my brother, but he listed his father as Tarik." I poked him in the ribs, trying to be playful. So this is how you do it, I thought as I went along. This is how it works.

"Oh, you found Sagi! That's my nephew. Sure. I was at his wedding," he said, tapping his chest. "I was his witness. Uta, when we get home, we have to call the nephews. They will be so happy for me."

"Oh, yes they will, John," Uta said. "That's where we were last weekend, down at Sagi's and they made the most delicious Arabic meal."

I could have sent away for that license and it would've had my father's name on it. I smarted. But still, it wouldn't have been easy to find him from that. It really wouldn't have. I'd tried to track this Sagi and his wife, Diane Thayer. I hadn't found anything on them.

"You know, Mayan, one of the nicest things that's happened to me in the last years is my sister's sons have come from Egypt. My brother-in-law came before he died and we got very close then at the end. And now his sons are here and I've helped them out, you know, with jobs and all, and we see each other pretty often, every other month or so.

The oldest one is a doctor down in Santa Barbara and the others are there this weekend because their mother is over from Egypt with the little sister. They're trying to arrange a marriage for her with a guy in Kansas City. But I think that's off now. But we'll call them. Wait till we get home. We'll call them."

I didn't tell them I'd been in Egypt. I don't know why. I just didn't want to. They seemed too normal. As if it were the most average thing in the world that we would be sitting there eating this fancy dinner with too many flavors on one thing and I would be telling them I'd combed every period of their lives and walked places they had lived and met people they knew and they just smiled and chewed and said, oh, how is he. I should call him. Yah, yah, my father said, gazing into his wine before tasting, as if what I was telling him made him think more of that time in his life with Duke Kemp or at Sagi's wedding than it did of me finding him, spending hours in telephone booths, any of that. None of his questions was about me or my search. None of them at all. It was as if I'd happened to meet Duke Kemp at a dinner party that I was going to go to anyway.

I asked him, just blandly, if he'd been back to the Middle East. "Sure, sure I've been back a number of times, but I haven't been there since 1975. Uta was there. I got Uta up on a camel. She's got the picture of herself on the hump."

He paid for dinner and I fumbled and offered to contribute, fool that I am.

WHEN HE GOT BACK to his town house, all he could think of was calling his nephews. He was a long time talking in Arabic. "Would you like to say hello to your cousins, honey?" he said, handing me the phone.

They sounded much more foreign than he did, and we only talked a minute. There was nothing to say. They said how much they wanted to meet me. "Me too," I said right away. I told Sagi about finding his marriage license but that he wasn't at that address anymore.

"I know," he said, "we moved. But if you would have written me a letter I would have gotten it." That stunned me. I put down the phone.

"I'll bet they all drive up," he said, hitting his knee.

Uta yawned. "So Uta, darling, why don't you go to bed and I'm going to make a pot of coffee and have a long talk with my daughter."

She didn't want to go. She minced while he plugged in the coffee maker and took out the can of coffee from the refrigerator. She stalled halfway up the stairs. "Don't be too long, honey," she said, "because you know how I can't sleep without you there in your spot."

He brought the pot of coffee to a TV tray in the living room. He drank coffee black. I had to ask for milk.

"Now I am going to tell you the good, the bad and the ugly," he said. It became clear after a few hours of conversation that he was a man whose only intellectual activity for years had been reading the daily newspaper. "I am telling you because you are my daughter and I love you and because I really always loved you even though I did not know you and you didn't know me."

I wanted to stay awake and hear but I was sleepy. My mind was like one small animal, alert but frightened, in a corner of a huge cave. It was trying to see out of the large darkness to the light, straining.

"I thought if I died, you would not know." His eyes wetted again. I felt moved by the sight of his sad, heavy-lidded eyes, but I also felt nagged by something I couldn't quite identify. Perhaps it was the way he presented his emotions, the angle of their focus. He was so certain he was going to be the one to die.

He seemed to assume my sturdy, unimperiled existence somewhere else, and only wondered if I would be there to mourn his passing. And with my mother, our lives hadn't been so safe.

"I thought that if I died, you would not know." He repeated this as if it were the most profound thing in the world. And I suppose it was, for him. But if anything else happened I wouldn't know either. And what would his dying mean if I hadn't ever really known him? What about if I died?

"Are your parents alive?" I asked him although I already knew the answer. I knew he hadn't even gone to his father's funeral.

"No, not my father. But I saw him before he died. I spent time with him. In 1961."

"What was that like?"

"It was a very structured relationship, very businesslike. My brother-in-law, Tarik, he was forty years old and he would go and kiss my father's hand every morning and put it on his forehead."

"What was your mother like?"

"I never liked my mother. She was a troublemaker. An opportunist. But she was a survivor. She had to do what she had to do to survive. My father was not an easy man to be married to. He might have slapped her. She had no rights. When you married a man like that over there you're stuck. Two or three times he beat her. It was civilized slavery, really. He had three daughters and one son and we were chattel. He owned us.

"But I still love my dad. I don't know why. I still dream about him years after he died. Basically he was a giver. As harsh as he was. When the holy Ramadan came on, he took us out to get everybody new suits and new shoes. Whatever. And he didn't care about any of that for himself. Shoes or clothes. But he was a stubborn guy.

"Before Nasser took over, Mayan, he was a multi-multi-millionaire. We had all kinds of land, buildings. And he had all his money in the banks. And in the late fifties when I was studying at the American University in Beirut and I saw what was happening, I tried to tell him, get it out, move it to Switzerland, and he said, No, they wouldn't dare do that.

"And in 1961, two-thirds of it was gone. They left us some buildings. A little land. But one day he was worth fifteen, twenty millon, the next day half a million. It was tragic. It killed him. A year later he died."

I shrugged. I could hardly pity them. I grew up poor. And two thirds of fifteen million gone was not half a million. But it never would have been my money anyway.

"Didn't Nasser make life better for the peasants, though?"

"Yes, he did, and I am in agreement with what he did. I don't think it is fair for one guy to own the destinies of all these peasants. As a child my father would take me to the village. He was like God. He would inspect their work. If he didn't like it, he'd slap them, he'd beat the shit out of them. And they'd be on their knees begging, Oh master, tomorrow I'll do better. At the same time, he worked all his life. But I was happy when Nasser took over the land and all. When I was young I spent too much."

Not on me, I was thinking. Not on us. We were living on very little, my mom and I.

"I went to the American University in Beirut. And I always was fascinated by America, American things. So after I graduated I came to study at Columbia University. I lived at 116th, I forget what the cross street was, I rented a room from an English professor. And I worked part-time at a store on Madison Avenue called Countess Mara. They sold ties."

The ties. The Uncle was right. I pinched the inside of my hand to remember to ask him about the Uncle.

"I wrapped the packages for Christmas. And for Christmas, they gave each employee a turkey. And I took mine home and gave it to the English professor's wife. And she was just delighted and said, 'Well, come back on Christmas day and I'll cook it for dinner.'

"And the day of Christmas eve, they closed the store early in the afternoon and had a party for the salespeople and the wrappers and the administrative staff. And they had a very elegant party and I saw trays of red glasses and trays of white glasses. And this was my first year from Egypt and I was very innocent. I didn't drink, I was a virgin, everything. So first I tried the white glass but that was too sour for me. And then I tried the red glass and that was sweet and I thought, okay, that's for me. They were Martinis and Manhattans. And all I know is that a couple hours later, I was the life of the party. I was telling stories and people were laughing. And I don't know how, a couple hours after that I managed to get to the subway. And this was during the Korean War, I remember because a GI in uniform helped me. He must have seen that I was drunk and he asked me where I was going and he told me he'd tell me when I should get off.

"And I got to my room where I lived and I went to sleep and when I woke up it was the day after Christmas. I missed the whole Christmas and the turkey altogether. And to this day, I won't touch a Manhattan. Just the taste of it makes me sick. To this day."

I said, "I met Salimiddin when I was trying to find you."

"That right? Is he still there? He must be pretty old by now."

"Yeah, he was, I think."

"That right? He helped me a little when I first came to New York. He would take me to good restaurants and whatever club was the hot place then and show me where to go and how to order. You know, I didn't know anything about Western life."

We were still for a moment. "He never made ambassador and that was his dream. He wanted to attend parties at the White House and rub shoulders with the Kennedys and date those women. He was a second secretary but he didn't live like a second secretary. He always had a Porsche and the most stylish clothes, always a girl on each arm. I don't think he did much work. And he didn't do what you have to do to make people like him. Even when my cousin Mahmoud was Minister of Foreign Affairs, Salimiddin came to me and said, Now is my moment, please ask Mahmoud. And I went to Mahmoud and asked him on my behalf, but even Mahmoud wouldn't do it. Those were the days when the ministry was made of families, you know. They needed an Atassi to put up for the minister. So Mahmoud got it.

"I almost married Salimiddin's sister. She even wrote and asked him. He said, he's crazy but if you want to, okay, go ahead. But she was unattractive. She was short and her face was ugly. Yah. Salimiddin is very smart and all but he's a little stiff. He gave the worst talk when I brought him to Madison. And I warned him, I said, Salimiddin, you've got to bring them in, you've got to say something to get the audience interested. I'd been building him up as a delegate, here he was second secretary or something."

"What was his subject?"

"Trusteeship in these small African countries. And he went on with the most academic, dry talk you can ever imagine for over an hour.

"But that is when I met your mom. I was president of the International Club and she came that night to hear Salimiddin speak. I met her afterward, at the reception. She was a gorgeous girl full of energy, full of life. I was madly in love with her."

"I kept pestering him to find you. He was going to the Middle East and he was supposed to check around there, but he never called me back. And I called him a few times." Like seventy.

"He could have found me."

"Why didn't he, you think?"

He shrugged. "Salimiddin thinks of Salimiddin."

"So then what?"

"Well, then I guess I got married to your mom and the rest you know. You were conceived, Mayan, in Lebanon. In Ehamendown. A tiny summer resort in the mountains. And about a month later when she found out she was pregnant she raised hell. She really didn't want to have a baby. She was turned off on sex, period. She was afraid she was gonna get another baby. She didn't want a large family.

"But when you arrived, she was happy and then she went crazy. The world didn't matter anymore. Nothing else mattered. But there was no discussion of having any more children."

"But you went back to Egypt then with my mom?" I knew that already. My mother had talked about Egypt as "over there," and she retained a relish for certain elements of the diet. In Wisconsin, she drove twenty miles to a woman from Armenia who cultured her own yogurt.

"I was going to make my career there. I should have. I should have really made my life there, with the connections I had, from a big family, you know, and with my education. If I'd have stayed I'd be running the country now. I really could have, with my connections."

"Why didn't you then?"

"Well, your mother didn't like it." He shrugged. "I don't know why really, she just wouldn't have it. And you know, my father was still alive then and she was always a gorgeous girl and my father just adored her and he set us up in a brand-new apartment and he told me, whatever she desires she should have. But still she wasn't happy. My cousin Mahmoud had married a German wife and she was a very elegant lady, very refined. And I asked her if she wouldn't go over and talk to Adele every afternoon and she did and they became friends but that still didn't do it. And then too she didn't learn the language. When people talk and you don't know what they're saying, you know, you think they're talking about you. I remember one day, we were with my sisters and they were all talking and giggling and Adele said to me, they're talking about me. I said, no they're not, of course not, Adele, and she said, yes they are, they're laughing at me. And then, right there, she said to me, you're lying, and she slapped me. For your wife to slap you in front of your three sisters, they think you're not a man. You know that's the way they think there. So we left. But I'll tell you, Mayan, the day after we left, they sent a car for me, they went to where we were living, my brother said, and sent a car to take me to Cairo and make me the Minister of Finance. That's the way they did it. They just sent a car. I heard that and it was like many airplanes going up and down inside myself. It would have been a different life for me, ha? Yah. But I had a wife here in Wisconsin and she was about to have a baby."

We are all endlessly telling the explanations of why we are not more. At a certain age, this begins. And for my mother and my father, the explanation was still, after all these years, the other's name.

"I should have stayed," he said. "Yah."

I asked him if he'd ever given a talk at Saint Norbert's, the college in Bay City. I knew he had. I'd heard about that talk all my life.

"Oh, sure. And Mayan, they asked me for three lectures and I gave the first one and they said after that, that's it, there wouldn't be any more. They thought I was a Marxist. Well, that's a Jesuit college. Can you imagine? Me a Marxist?"

I shook my head sadly. No, I really couldn't.

"I said, I am from an aristocratic family in Egypt. I am a capitalist by nature. I was ten years ahead of my time. I only gave one of the three lectures. And I'm telling you, Mayan, it was my finest hour."

It must have been, I was thinking.

"I said, we have to see Red China. I was twenty years ahead of my time. I was advocating the recognition of Red China."

"But was that after Michigan? Because I remember you living with us at my grandmother's, but you said you left in Michigan."

"Well later on I came back to visit you and I don't know, I guess we tried it again. We had some chemistry, your mom and I. But she was crazy."

"So after you and my mom broke up, why didn't you go back and stay in Egypt?"

"I don't know really. I should have probably. But I would have had to go into the army. I would've been an officer because I had an advanced degree. But the old families had a hard time in the army when the socialists came in. One of the Higazi boys got badly beaten up. They say, you're a Higazi, well I'll show you."

Then Uta was on the staircase in a child's nightgown, holding the banister, looking only at him. "Honey, don't be much longer because I can't sleep without you." She hung there waiting for an answer.

"Uta darling, go to sleep now, I am having a talk with my daughter. I'll be up later but go to sleep."

"I'll try again, but I don't think I can sleep without you there."

It was hard not to blame her for everything. But she was old. And when we'd gone to Disneyland, years ago, she had been kind. She'd tried, more than he did, to make us seem like a father and daughter.

"Take the dog, Uta. And try. Go on and try."

She thumped back up.

He looked at where she was a moment, poured us each another cup of coffee. "I haven't touched her for twenty years," he said. "You know you asked me at dinner about Rilella and I couldn't say because Uta doesn't know. But that was me. I was married to her for two weeks. She was a dealer in Las Vegas and it turned out she was married to somebody else already." He shrugged.

The long story seemed to be gambling, but there wasn't much he would tell. "It really ruined my life in a lot of ways, Mayan. Someday I'd like to go to a psychiatrist and find out what made me do it. I quit playing two years ago because I looked and saw I was getting old and I could end up with nothing. Alone, you know. I had to start preparing a little for the future. I haven't been back once, to Reno or any of those places."

"What was your game?" I said.

"Twenty-one," he answered instantly, just like that. "The most I won was twenty thousand dollars. That was in London. The most I lost, I think, was ten. In the game of twenty-one, there are two problems," he said. He peered at me with the most severity I'd seen.

"One is greed. The other is if I am on a winning streak, I should bet big and know when to take a chance."

"Don't the big casinos like in Atlantic City and Vegas cheat?" I said.

"They don't have to cheat, honey."

They don't have to cheat. That's what some people say about God. That He doesn't have to intervene at all, that all the cards work out, like a long game of solitaire with a full deck.

"The majority of people who gamble, gamble small. And they all lose. And even the big winners. I was in Monte Carlo once and I saw one of the young Saudi princes win fifty thousand dollars. And the owner of the casino sent a case of the best champagne to his room on ice. So I said to the owner, the guy just cleaned you out and you're sending him champagne? And he said, oh, it'll be back, that money's just out with him on loan. On a high-interest loan."

"You should run a casino, you know about it all." I spent my life cheerleading behind these two small adults, You could do this, Mom, sure you could, why don't you, you still have time. They had both failed themselves. Neither could ever make the world work the way I already had and I gave it all up to find him.

"Yah, but it takes a lot of money. I might like to teach again someday. That I may just look into one of these days. Some small college. I really threw away my career, Mayan, because I had a position I really loved I was chairman of the department at Firth Adams College, in Montana. And my career was just going up and up. They gave me tenure, they made me chairman, I'd probably be University president by now if I'd stayed. And I really threw it away. I took a group to the Middle East one Christmas, I'm telling you now, the worst thing I ever did, and I went to a casino one night and I don't know I kept going and going, I had lost some of the group's money so I had to keep playing to get it back. I never did and I was so ashamed I left. So Uta came and of course we paid all the money back. See that's one reason I could never leave her. She is a good person, Mayan, and she helped me when I needed help for all those years. And now that she's dependent on me, I could never leave her."

I was nodding off, so we went to the garage and got into the car. He had a banana-yellow Cadillac, about seven years old. "One thing that has been very fortunate for me in the last six years is I have met a lovely woman in Sacramento, Elizabeth. I'd like you to meet her, Mayan. We see each other, oh, twice a week, sometimes more. And that has given me the real connection that I never have with Uta. The chemistry, you know, the inner . . . we just click."

"Does she mind you still being married?"

"Well, she's young. She's just a little older than you are. She wants to do lot of things before she gets married. She wants to travel, lot of things, before she ties herself down."

"How old is Uta?"

"She is eighty."

He parked in front of my hotel and we just sat there for a moment. I looked up. There were amazing stars. I turned and asked, a whim, "Do you practice Islam at all?"

"No, not really. Not when I'm here. I like to think I believe in God and so on."

We said goodnight and I went to my room, locked the door. I slept like a stone.

THE NEXT MORNING I didn't want to be there anymore. I wanted to be done and go home. I had the shrill headache you get from eating too much chocolate and you know you won't be okay again until the next day. It was half past eight and already hot. I heard a wind outside, moving eucalyptus buttons and hard unfertilized dates on the pavement. At nine o'clock exactly the phone rang and it was him.

"You won't believe it, honey. Didn't I tell you the cousins would drive up? Well they're all here and my sister Amina and my niece from Egypt. They rented a Pontiac and drove all night. So come on over as soon as you can, Mayan, and we'll go out for brunch."

It seemed so much was going on and nothing was about what I'd waited for him for. Now I couldn't say anymore what that was.

. . .

EMILY CALLED.

"How'd you know I was here?"

"There aren't that many motels in Modesto. I'm calling from Briggs's. The buyers asked the people they knew there and they all said it was either the Hyatt or something called the East West. I knew you wouldn't be at the Hyatt."

"You're in Racine?"

"Yeah, I came home to see about the tent and all."

"Well, I'll be there. I'm getting out of here tonight."

"You don't have to. I mean it's off."

"What do you mean?"

"Oh, I don't know, I just decided, I'm pretty young and there's a lot of things I should do. No big deal."

"You called off the wedding?"

"Mmhm."

"But how's Tad taking it?"

"You know, like you'd expect. Not good."

"What about all the people who are coming?"

"Well, my father had the direct mail department go through the list and call them all. Except you. I'm calling you."

"God, Emily, what happened?"

"Not any one thing. I don't know. I was walking along the river. I'd had lunch on the top of the store with Dad and so we were walking, feeding the pigeons with a roll from lunch. I was saying how I was glad I was his daughter because he and I were really more the same than Mom in a lot of ways. And he looked at me and said, no, we really weren't because Mom picked him and he said I never would have fallen in love with him. At first I said, of course I would've and he just said, not like he was mad or anything or even hurt, he just said, no, he knew me, and I wouldn't have. Do you think I would have?"

The guys Emily fell for were always the same. They were handsome, careless boys, all with a kind of smile that granted favors and dispensations.

"Well, maybe not," I said.

"I don't know, I just decided you were the smart one after all this time. All these parties I've gone to and all I've done for men these years, and what do I have for it?"

"What do I have? Less than nothing."

"But you found your father."

"Yeah. I found him. I did."

I FASTENED ON MY WATCH as I was leaving the motel. I checked out. I could drive back to San Francisco, I promised myself, in eight hours. This I just had to get through. And why? Because they expected it. He did.

When I walked into their duplex it was full of people, and I let myself stand still and answer questions. It was easy once I decided to give up all control.

There were five Egyptian young men, all more foreign-looking than my father, none of whom spoke much English. Then there was their mother, a heavy, graceful woman in several sweaters, and their sister, who was eighteen, ample, pretty in a way with many moles, and neither of them spoke any English.

And there was Diane Thayer. The day was worth it because of Diane. She was large the way some people are large, only on top, as if the bottom half of her body had been squeezed. Her hair was long, a dry limp mouse color, and her face was patched with pimples. She sure wasn't the horse girl I'd imagined.

"Youse people cut it out," she said. "Talk in English."

All day there was a lot of food. First we drove to the Hyatt Hotel and ate from an enormous buffet. A man stood in a little enclave of heated aluminum plates making omelettes to order. There were piles of fruit, bowls of salads, trays of eggs Benedict, hams, bacon, prosciutto. There were two whole long tables of desserts. There was pasta. There were cooked entrées, chickens, hot vegetables. I stuffed myself even though I couldn't taste anything. My throat hurt and I kept eating. He sat in the middle of the long table, with me on his left, Uta on his right. He kept filling my champagne. He talked raucously in Arabic so Uta had to say, "John remember, Mayan can't understand you when you're speaking in Arabic either."

"I keep remembering you as Momo," I said. That was what my mother called him.

"His name is John now," Uta said.

"That's my name too," he said.

"Honey, don't you remember? We agreed. His name here in this country is John. We call him John."

Fuzil, the lightest of my cousins, kept staring at me. Now he asked me, "We thought you were a TV broadcaster. Or radio. There was supposed to be an Atassi doing that in Ohio, I think."

"But she isn't Atassi, is she?" Uta said. "Do you go by the name of—"

"No. Mayan Stevenson."

He put his head down. No one said anything. That passed.

"But you are part of the Atassi clan now," Sahar said with flourish, "and you will attend our next Atassi summit!"

There were loud jokes and toasts. More champagne. The aged, large Egyptian mother sat, lifting embroidery from her lap and working serenely, not understanding a word of the English looping past and participating as seldomly in the Arabic, only once in a while reaching a hand over the top of her daughter's glass. Her eyes had a calm, straight quality of timelessness, as if she would sit in her sweaters and embroider wherever she was, wherever her energetic children carried her and put her, but in her vision there would always be the shimmering deep patch of field I'd seen in her backyard in Egypt.

They were spirited boys, lovely, full of an immigrant's uproar and victory, a buoyant charm. Nora, the eighteen-year-old girl, kept smiling generously. But the truth was, I didn't care anymore. Now that I'd found him, I couldn't have cared less about Egyptian cousins.

It was an indolent day. It had to do I think with the weather. After brunch we went to a place that had steps going down to the river. The boys and my father helped the women down, as they stepped cautiously in their fragile shoes. We sat at tables by the river and then there was more champagne. I lapsed in boredom and felt the sun on my skin, I turned my face towards the easy pleasures. The day after getting what you wanted. The vague twitter of birds shimmering aloft in color.

"Here you go," my father said, handing me a tinfoil and cellophane bouquet of four grocery store roses. We were standing by my car saying good-bye. I had both his phone numbers now.

I had recognized him and he did not know me, his only child.

13

BUT THAT DAY—that—didn't last.

It hangs there, discreet, a gem crystal, but it's one day in with all the other days of my life.

Over time he was still a man who had left his family and not tried to find us. I learned that people cannot be more or better than their lives. For one day they can. But everyday matters more. Love is only as good as days.

I think of my grandmother now more than I think of him. "She saved you from a lot worse," Timothy said once.

At first it seemed amazing. So he was a restaurant maître d' living in Modesto. All the time he was just there. A month or so after I came back, Emily was over once and the phone rang and I picked it up and said, "Oh, hi Dad." And just Emily's face.

He was only a man with his own troubles who didn't manage to keep track of his wife and child. After all those years, I was wrong about him. He was only a man.

LATER, IN LITTLE BITS, I tried to get from him what I needed.

You know what I want to ask you sometime and I'm afraid to ask you this because I think you'll think I'm mad which I'm not—but sometime you have to like, write me a letter or tell me or something why you . . . got out of touch with me.

Yah.

'Cause I think it's a—I don't mean to make you feel badly, I really don't, just—I think it causes me problems in my life.

Okay.

Not with you, really, but with men almost—

Sure, sure.

I kind of want to know why just so I can know—

Sure. I will.

And I'm not mad!

I know.

It's not that, it's just one of those things I kind of need to know.

I think really, I will write it down but in a, you know, in a brief summary, it had nothing to do with my love for you, Mayan. You know what it is—I was totally irresponsible, you know, I was a spoiled little—

Why is that? Because you were from a rich family?

I was selfish. I was brought up without a sense of—that, you know, you, in this life, you really have to really fend for yourself and you have to care and you have to do these things. So I was torn between feeling, here I am, I have a daughter that I really loved but at the same time I'm saying, gee I want to enjoy life for myself, I want to be selfish.

What was the selfish part? What was fun for you at that age? That was probably about my age now.

Oh, a lot of things. I mean, you know, I did a lot of traveling, I did this, I did that.

Girls? Gambling?

Sure, combination of both. But I'll write it down. I'll put some of my feelings down on paper in some detail for you. I understand. I will. The old question is when you get to a certain age, you say I wish I could turn the clock back. But you can't you know. Anyhow. Your mom was a spoiled brat too. We both were. Though we came from different cultures, different backgrounds. They weren't so rich. But she was spoiled. We both were selfish. We had some bad habits, some artificial goals and artificial values.

What did you want in life then?

Huh?

What did you want from your lives?

Oh, lots of things I guess but, I don't know. I think the objectives are unrealistic, lots of dreams, you know. Your mom wanted to get a Ph.D. and she wanted to conquer the world with her education and this and that. And I wanted to get my Ph.D. and do other things, you know.

(I'd discovered one reason I'd have never in a hundred years guessed I wanted my father: to quiz him about her, what she was like when she was young. He was already far less mysterious. Her glitter and distance remained a solid crown.)

I always thought she wanted high society and fancy parties and dresses more.

I don't know. I think she probably wanted both.

But she was really serious about her education at one point?

Sure. Oh sure.

Because she's not like that so much now.

High society now probably.

No, she's sort of like semi-spiritual.

Well, spirituality will help.

In her thirties, she wanted beautiful dresses.

Maybe that's why you take the opposite extreme, huh? My feeling was, maybe you're rebelling against that.

Actually I've been buying clothes lately, too.

I WAS. Even though I was supposed to be learning architecture and proving myself all at once. I won one of those competitions I'd sent off sketches for when I flunked out of school. A tiny commission. Still, it was six months' rent. But I wanted other things too now. Things to the right and the left. Some days all I wanted to do was buy dresses.

I WANTED PEARLS. I wanted something from my father.

I don't know which came first.

I was different now, greedy to catch up all at once. All the things to the right or the left of the straight road, the silly things I never picked up, the glittery things I'd had no time for.

I'd started dreaming of dresses. A perfect black pleated aerodynamically impossible party dress.

And pink luminous pearls, with green and blue echos.

IN THE YEAR since we met he'd sent me two presents. The first was for my birthday and he called several times before it arrived; he was nervous about its value. It was a thick gold-chain necklace. I'd noticed that all my Eygptian cousins wore gold chains around their necks. I studied it under the kitchen light. It was marked 18K in tiny letters. By Christmas it was a bracelet, interlocking links, some shiny, some frosted gold. This was gold plate.

I didn't get the bracelet until late. I went to Racine for Christmas. When I got home I waited two weeks and then wrote a note. He called irate, because I hadn't acknowledged receipt of his gift.

"Did you get my note?" I asked him.

"No. I never got a thing from you," he said.

Timothy said it probably made him feel better, that he had something to be mad about.

But we seemed to get over that. And in one of our regular conversations I determined to ask for pearls. But once he was on the phone it wasn't easy. He was mild but the way he talked didn't open many nets for questions.

"Not too bad, not too bad," he said. "Put a beautiful tree in yesterday. What kind, oh, it's just a tree, I don't know."

"Like a pine or deciduous? Does it have leaves?"

"Yah, sure it has leaves."

He asked how things were with my boyfriend. This was a guy I'd had three dates with. His voice had a nervous quality when he asked that, as if my condition were fragile. He made me feel like I was old, twenty-nine, and not that pretty. So if this guy left, that was it.

But I tried to be jaunty. "Well, he's kind of short but other than that he's cute."

"Sometimes you have to make some adjustment, some compromise. You'd like to wait for everything but then everything might not come along, Mayan. I guess the most important thing really, is if there's something that clicks inside then you know there's something that's going on. But if you're feeling cold like a fish then you can't force yourself to like him."

"But with Uta you didn't have it really."

"No, not really."

"And you had it with my mom and lookit how that worked out."

"Sure, sure that's true."

"What would happen if you ever met my mom again? Do you think you guys would fight?"

"I honestly don't know. I don't think so. I don't see any reason to do that. I don't know. I don't have that answer either, you know. Crazy life, huh. All kinds of tough questions. Tough questions, yah."

"You probably aren't friends with many people from that time in your life and she isn't either. So those are years that maybe no one else remembers but you two—like your college years."

"Sure. That's probably true."

"How are you feeling?"

"Healthwise? I went to see the doctor day before yesterday and he says I have to give them a five–six day journal of my eating habits." He always had a certain delicacy talking about his own condition. He seemed to visit doctors a lot. "When you were talking about that other subject, there was somebody standing here so I couldn't discuss it freely with you. It's an interesting question, though. I don't know. It tingles something inside you know."

"I bet."

"Well it does."

"Dad, do you have any things from your family, like jewelry or anything, because all these girls in America have pearls from their families, like pearls their fathers gave their mothers or their grandfathers gave their mothers or something."

"I don't know, I'll check. There's a few suitcases I have. I haven't even opened them. But I'll check. I'm going to work on it. And if we don't find something, we'll fake it. I'm going to fake it."

MOST OF OUR CONVERSATIONS now ended up with me talking about my mom. What was she like then. I wanted him to give her something: money, her life back.

I wanted him to have to send her a monthly check. I hadn't found a way yet, to ask.

MAI LINN AND EMILY were intrigued by the pearls. It was us again, sitting in a triangle, but this time in a New York restaurant with our elbows on the table.

"But of course you'll ask for more," Mai linn said.

"What do you mean?" I said. "I'm going to try and pick them out here and somehow suggest to him what I want." I looked at Emily.

"We'll go to Chanel this afternoon." Emily had been giving me the full range of choices. The large South Sea pearls were in the ten thousands, that I knew was further than I could push him. Anyway, I wanted him to give the big money to my mom. But Emily said for the price of good small pearls you could get Chanel, which weren't real, but I should see because they were beautiful anyway.

I looked at Mai linn kind of guiltily. I hadn't really wanted her to know I was following Emily through all these stores.

"I've priced them anyway," I said.

"How much are they?" Mai linn asked.

"Well, they start at about five hundred."

"But you don't want those. They're too small," Emily said. "They look like a child's pearls."

"The ones I want are a thousand. I think he'll do that."

"He should," Mai linn said. "But then what?"

Emily said, "You mean she'll ask for more and more?"

"The fight will come," Mai linn said.

I nodded. "And maybe I want that."

"So you're kind of upping the ante. Testing his limit. But whatever it is, I don't think you'll be satisfied. Pearls aren't going to make up for it."

"But I still want pearls. I think I'd just like to have some."

My friends' fathers gave them to their wives. Or my friends got them at graduation. One mother I knew bought her daughter pearls on an installment plan, paying on time every month. I never wanted such things in Wisconsin. I had them. In abundance. My grandmother's house was full of mysteries, you opened a drawer and it was there, the big colored chalk, pearls, a little dish of hand-cut nails. None of it was real, but it didn't matter. It was real enough for us.

But I didn't just want pearls. I wanted them to be hard for him to afford.

And if we don't find something, we'll fake it. I'll fake it.

EVENTUALLY, we pushed up from the café table and went outside. Mai linn said, "So Emily, whatever happened to Boom-boom-boom?"

Emily shrugged. "He doesn't talk to me anymore. He sent a bonded messenger to pick up his ring."

"And what about your little lawyer?" she asked me.

"He's around. We're friends."

"He's a nice guy. I don't know why you didn't go for him."

I shrugged. I didn't know either. You never really know.

These are the beauty years for me, I was thinking. The best was probably over, or else it was right now. I'd written my mother and asked her if I could have one of her old suits.

She'd called me up on the telephone, furious. "You're just take, take, take," she said. "That's all I have to wear, do you think I ever get anything new! I wear things five years, ten years old to work every day." She was still yelling when I set down the phone.

There was nothing else I was waiting for and I was behind. I made Emily take me shopping and give me lessons.

And she was a happy tour guide. That day she led us to a small store with large communal dressing rooms. We took blouses and jeans and slacks and jackets and dresses and skirts into the room and all started trying them on.

I never wore skirts. I couldn't because of my legs.

Emily said, "Both of you I think would look really good in this. Let me go see if there's another one."

We each slipped on the matching skirts. They were a black fabric, short, well over our knees. Mai linn looked right, the way a person is supposed to. My knees looked loose, like a fried egg on top of bone.

"No," I said. I unzipped it and I was stepping out, it was around my ankles.

"Put it on again." Emily pulled it up, zipped, ran her hands over my hips and down the outside of my legs, smoothing the fabric.

"My legs, I can't. They're too short."

Mai linn pushed her calf up next to mine. "They're exactly the same," she said, and in the mirror, they were.

We left with our shopping bags. I was spending all the money I had in the bank. But after my grandmother's money, other money was easy to spend. Then we went to the library so I could show them old typefaces I found. I was looking at typefaces for the inscription on my fountain.

I STARTED TO WORRY that he'd get my pearls at Macy's. The other jewelry he'd sent me had come from there. I wanted nice ones, good quality.

I was going to see him around my birthday. I wanted to pick out the pearls myself.

I don't know which came first.

I wasn't that direct about it. It had been a year, a little more. We'd talked on the phone but I hadn't seen my father, since that first time. I was going to be in California anyway so we planned a trip in the wine country, for two days.

It wasn't until then that I remembered all the things I'd saved for him. Well, I'd taken that little add-a-pearl chain to show him, the two pearls like tiny baby teeth. But there were pictures of my childhood. All my altars and shrines. I threw them out, but then I took my favorite, made of butterfly wings and my baby teeth, back from the garbage. I wanted to keep it for myself. I'd saved the roses he'd bought me from the grocery store a year ago and they were dead and dry now. He'd given me pictures of himself.

Of my mother and me in our life?

He never asked.

I called him to say, don't get anything for me for my birthday, I wanted us to go shopping together.

STEVIE HOWARD DROVE ME at seven in the morning to the place I was going to meet my father.

"Why is it," he said on the way, "that women, basically law-abiding women, want to steal men's clothes?"

I thought of Mai linn. When Mai linn first left Racine and moved to North Dakota, she used to sleep with Ben's shirt. I had sweaters and too-long-footed socks from old boyfriends. Eventually, I threw the stuff away. It made you feel safe for a while but they didn't really fit. Later, when you had to go out into the world on your own again, they didn't work at all.

"Remember how I used to wish I had a shirt or an old sweater of my father's?"

"You could get one now, huh?"

"I don't want one now. Now I want pearls."

WE MET MY FATHER at a café in Berkeley. We all had coffee and then I threw my backpack in the trunk of my father's Cadillac. Before we left, my father invited Stevie to join us the next night in San Francisco for dinner. Driving at fifty miles an hour towards the Napa Valley, he asked me if I'd ever been there before. I lied and said no but I had gone there once with my mother.

My father was wearing new green and gray suede hiking boots. He had a map with instructions to a place we could hike. "I am prepared," he said, showing me the canteens of water. "People all told me that hiking would be an enjoyable way to spend some hours."

Fine with me. I'd hiked for years in college and I knew Napa was pretty flat. I didn't need anything but the stuff I was wearing.

He had a tape of Arabic music he slipped in the car's stereo. It sounded like the kind of thing you heard in Greek restaurants.

"This is Om Kulthum. She's the Frank Sinatra of the Arab World."

"Where is she from?"

"Cairo."

"What's her name again?"

"Om Kulthum. That means, technically, Mother of Kulthum. See when you have a son you take the name of your oldest son. So my father's real name was Azziz but he went by the name of Abu Moham-med. But you'd never say, Abu Mayan, in the Arab world. Call it sex-ist, call it what you want."

Then I remembered something I'd learned from Ramadan. The word "tarboosh." It meant a tall hat, a fez. And my father when I was little used to play a game where he lay on the floor and pushed me up in the air on the bottoms of his feet. I always thought he was saying Kaboosh, just a sound, but maybe I was high up like a hat. I asked him.

"I don't know." He shrugged. "I don't remember. Could have been."

"I HAVE BEEN THINKING about your wedding," he said. His bottom lip curled open in concentration. I suppose to him I was pretty old.

I tried to divert him by asking about Egyptian weddings.

"Oh, well, I don't know what they're like now, honey, I suppose they're just about like here now."

"But when you were growing up?"

"Oh, well, when I was growing up, the traditional Arabic wedding was in the home of the bride. And first of all it was only women."

"No men? What about the groom?"

"He comes later. But it starts out all women. See, the women of the family have been cooking for days and days preparing the food and the cakes and the sweets and so on and they throw an enormous feast. And the bride sits in her dress on her little throne and they eat. They dance a little. If they're rich, they may even hire a eunuch to dance in the middle. And this is all non-alcoholic, remember."

In his house in Alexandria, there were wedding pictures of a girl on a fancy throne.

"And then, after a little while, the bride will go into the house and she will change clothes into her next outfit and she'll keep doing that all night. To get married in Egypt, the girl has to have nine or ten dresses and not only the dress but the whole thing. You know the shoes and stockings and accessories. And if it's a wealthy family like mine, they would go—"

"Paris."

"Well I suppose now they'd go to Paris but then we would all go and shop in Beirut. Beirut, Lebanon."

I remembered the pictures of the girl in the different dresses.

"So they'd have music and the meal. She'd go and change, and then she'd stay on her throne. And the women eat and drink, just soft drinks, and dance. Then the groom will come a little before midnight and he takes her to the bedroom. They leave them alone for a while. And then after an hour, I don't know, two hours, the mother of the bride will go in and she'll come back out and bring—this sounds barbaric but it is that way—she brings out the bloody hankie and they all dance around it. And then the marriage is consummated. If there's no blood there's trouble. My brother-in-law Tarik was kind of a timid guy and he was in there with Amina until ten in the morning."

"Do people ever fake it?"

"Oh, you mean like kill a chicken and use that. I have heard of it, but I've never known it to happen, personally. The mothers there watch their daughters pretty carefully. It's part of the mother's pride, that her daughter is perfect and untouched."

Now I looked at the road and let it go awhile. There was nothing I could really say to that. We passed one town, then another. It was hot but the air-conditioning was on. It was an old enough car so that all the controls seemed plastic, not old enough to get better with age. I snuck a look at him sideways.

He was wearing hiking clothes, brand new. Shorts, shirt, the suede boots. He had carefully fitted sunglasses over his ears.

"If you open the glove compartment, Mayan, you'll see some pictures I brought for you."

They were of himself, young. He was standing with a group of other students, all Egyptian. A microphone stood in the picture for no apparent reason. I'd take that suit in the picture, I was thinking. It was double-breasted, long, you could tell it was a great suit even now. Almost all of the girls in the picture, one hair-back studious type, two heavy girls, one stray-haired, a voluptuary, were glancing at him.

"Nice suit," I said. "When was this?"

"At the American University in Beirut. I used to go to Beirut and spend a fortune on suits. I'd buy all Italian, all French suits, and just charge it to my dad. I'd spend eight hundred, a thousand dollars on a suit. Now I spend two hundred. And it makes no difference to me. It doesn't matter to me anymore."

Yeah, good for you, I was thinking, you had your turn. He had his turn, but when would be mine? And when my mother's? When are most people's turns but in heaven or in their dreams or in their chests, the first hard run of childhood.

"Now I fly coach and it makes no difference to me. We used to fly around the world first class and never think about it." On Uta's money, I was pretty sure. Or on the tour groups'.

When he talked like that I wanted to kill him. There was no guilt. He didn't look at me nervous or hide it or anything as if what he was saying could have any effect on me. My mother and I, most of those years, were living in Los Angeles, on thirteen thousand dollars.

He spoke as if he were speaking to a stranger, which I guess he was, not to a person he owed anything. Maybe enormous guilt—like that for killing life or the giving away of children—is impossible to bear or maybe it doesn't exist. The people who feel and live great amounts of guilt are the only faintly guilty. Those who have never been strong enough to do anything.

"See, if my father had put his money in the banks. You know, Mayan, he kept gold coins hidden in pots under the ground, can you believe that?"

"Yeah," I said. The last time he'd told me it was in banks.

"But if he hadn't," he laughed, "we'd all be a lot better off, financially."

I doubted I would be.

"When they nationalized everything, it destroyed him."

"I grew up poor, Dad," I said. I allowed myself some truth. "Those people should be lined up and shot."

"Honey, he was your grandfather."

"I never met him."

"I know that, Mayan."

Compared to us, my mother and me, he was so mild.

IF MY MOTHER hadn't been crazy, I was thinking, I don't know if I could have kept believing.

But my mother lied. She still lies all the time, she is a person altogether without spine or erectness. She bent to anyone's will and so I would look to the sky and believe it was possible, it was just scarcely possible, that he could be good and have a reason.

I tried to give him reasons. All my life I collected them. The man who told me that in India parents were too busy to raise children because they were building the New India.

But I doubted my father was making the New Egypt. Those people's names were in the paper.

So, I'd thought, maybe the PLO. He wasn't Palestinian, but still. Maybe he was somehow underground. I had a picture of Yasir Arafat glued to the cover of a gray notebook I used in college. I'd study his face in the dotted newsprint photograph and see it one way and then another.

That day on our hike, I asked him about the PLO. The hike was unideal. It was hot. And this was no national park. We followed the elaborate directions to a kind of camp, where we had to pay a thirty-year-old hippie twenty dollars to walk on his trails. And if there were trails we never found them. We went along a path that petered out on the banks of a stream, and we gave up, and followed a rutted road up the side of a small hill. The woods were not cleared to any views.

"Well, in 1952 I got my B.A. from the American University in Beirut and George Habash was there too. You know, George Habash is the head of the more intellectual branch of the PLO. That same year he got his M.D. And he was already starting what would become the PLO. He had a reading study group once a week and he tried to recruit me. I went one or two times. Once I remember the subject of discussion was Mao Tse-tung. I don't remember what the material was the other time."

"So did you ever think of hitching up with them?"

"Who me?"

WE COULDN'T HAVE HIKED a mile when he said he was tired and we better turn around. I gave him a look like, work on it. This was nothing like Yosemite or Glacier. You don't really appreciate a national forest until you saw this.

"You see, the PLO really lost its thunder when Israel surrounded them in Lebanon, when was that, '79, '80—"

That was 1982. Summer, I was thinking. We were walking through the heat and falling dry pine needles in the ramparts of orange light.

"And they had the choice of staying and having their heads cut off or leaving. So they fled. That's when Arafat went to Tripoli, Habash went to Damascus. Now, according to leftist doctrine they should've fought until they dropped. If they had stayed and fought to the end, their cause would have been eternal. As it was . . ."

You should talk, I was thinking. And anyway, nothing is eternal, not even the best of what I want to be. Not even the works of better men and women than you and me, not even the lines of their generation. All species are doomed to extinction and who will ever know what we did in the world? Who will uncode the symbols? And will the archeologists of the new world look for us with such blunt instruments as me looking for my father in the telephone book? And does it matter that we will not be found? Not our souls, what was essential. What we loved. Does it matter that all that is beautiful is lost? Not if we die together looking into each other's eyes and are buried in a common grave.

I shoved my hands in my pockets. It seemed then that eternity was an old-fashioned idea of youth, with a nineteenth-century charm like ruffled lace collars and the things of exploration, globes and compasses, a relic of the time of expansion and exploration and colonialism and the last vestigial belief in heroes.

His small hiking boots marched up and down in the soft needles as his arms conducted through the air. He was finding this enjoyable, I could tell, a talk about politics with his daughter, on a long walk in the woods. I don't think my father really had many people to talk to.

I was thinking of how Yasir meant easy. He had been born Mohammed too, both of them named after the prophet. Now they called him Al-Khityar, the old man.

"I WAS JUST to a wedding yesterday, the daughter of a man I used to work for. It was on a boat."

We began to compare weddings. The wedding on the boat was too much. So was Emily's. I mean it would have been. We agreed on that. We had that in common.

"If you got married in California, I could do a gorgeous wedding for a hundred, hundred-fifty, I know just what I'd do." His fingers were precise, calligraphic, his thumb and first finger touching, his lower lip stern. "We start with some light hors d'oeuvres and cocktails."

"Sushi, maybe," I interjected.

"Sushi would be ideal and a few other hors d'oeuvres to be passed around, you know, while people drink. And we'll have a very simple meal. What they do most of the time is they have too much and then they don't pay attention to the quality. We could either start with a cold smoked salmon or a pasta."

"Pasta would be good. We could even have pasta for the main dish."

"No, we would start with a pasta and a beautiful wine, I know what we'll get, a Far Niente. But people want a entrée, a meat or a fish."

I was getting carried away. This guy was planning my wedding and he didn't even know what I ate.

"Fish," I said.

"All right. Fish. Salmon. We serve that with wild rice and asparagus and then we follow that with a green salad of garden lettuces, we'll get a gorgeous salad with nasturtiums and wild leaves, everything. And then just champagne with the cake. And that's it."

"You know, you can't get such good lettuces and stuff on the East Coast like you get here." It was true. Every salad in California was a masterpiece of rare weeds.

"We'll ship it over. Sure. We'll box it up, I know who to get it from and we'll send it overnight Federal Express."

"I don't know where we'd have it in New York."

"See the place itself is going to be expensive there. But if you had it in California, you could have more people. I have a budget for a hundred, maybe a hundred-twenty-five."

I was stopped again. He was telling me how many people I could have at my wedding. I didn't even really have a boyfriend.

"There's a problem, though. What about my mother?"

"What about her?"

"Well, don't you think she's gonna want to be involved?"

"Involved how? Either she does it or I do it. And if I do it, I do it."

"That can't be. I'm her only daughter and if I get married, she's going to be a part of it, I don't know, with the flowers or something, she's good at all that."

"Sure, she can do the flowers then."

"I don't know how that would be, with both of you there in the same room." I thought it was possible that she would kill him.

He shrugged, hands in his pockets. We were descending now to the gravel parking lot. "I don't see why it would be any problem. We both just shake hands and agree to put aside our differences that day to celebrate your wedding." He was right, in a way, I knew. But wasn't it always easier for the one who left lightly to say that, to decide, years later, that politeness was possible?

Clearly this was preying on his mind. In the car, going to the hotel where we were going to change for dinner, he offered to write my mother a letter. But what is that? He's never, I'm sure, been short of soft words. I wanted to get him to promise, this weekend, some kind of reparation to her. A monthly check. What he should have sent, years ago.

I sighed. "My mom's not well anyway," I said. "Who knows, if I had a wedding, if she could even come."

He smiled. His shoulders dropped easily. "Maybe that will solve the whole problem."

I looked at him.

WE HAD ROOMS next to each other in a large hotel. I sprawled out right away on the bed. This was hard. I wasn't getting what I had come here for. Every time the talk verged on something really interesting from the past, he veered away from it.

He knocked on my door.

He was holding a gift box wrapped in bright green with a white ribbon. Oh no, I thought. It was a cube of about fourteen inches. It couldn't be pearls.

"I thought you could use it," he said. "I don't know, I just saw it and thought, you know, you might like it."

It was a crystal clock.

It reminded me of a place I hadn't remembered for years, a place my mother stopped on her way driving to work in Wisconsin, called O'Malleys. It was a gas station and a little store. Inside, every ledge, every surface was covered with little shiny things.

"Thank you. It's nice."

"Do you like it really? Because tell me if you don't and I can take it back."

"No, I like it."

And then he left me alone for an hour before dinner.

.   .   .

I SUGGESTED ONE PLACE I'd heard about but he'd already picked a restaurant in a vineyard. "We will be their guests," he said. I knew from the way he said that he meant the money.

He was obviously excited about the restaurant. It was a pretty place. They served us champagne outside in a garden before we went in.

And he was at home here, at his best. "Never order the chef's special," he told me. "That's a one-shot deal, what they're trying to move out of the kitchen. The real stuff is on the other side, on the regular menu."

I was already pretty drunk.

We were seated at right angles to each other. My father was ordering for both of us, patiently asking the tall, remarkably formal waiter questions about the menu. I lifted my feet up onto the chair. I was wearing formal black shoes, high heeled, arched like a swan's neck. My feet looked like a girl's hands, waiting tentatively, groomed, on something velvet.

There were a thousand graces I had not known about before. They were not less than medicine or architecture, only they did not last. They were perishable.

"We are going to indulge ourselves," my father was telling the waiter, "with a bottle of Grigich Hill 1982 chardonnay."

"Very well, sir," the waiter said with an obsequious nod. I wondered if the waiter knew we weren't supposed to be paying.

My father began talking about my wedding again. "Wouldn't it be something to have the wedding and the reception here. Gorgeous."

I sighed. "At least I hadn't gotten Emily's present yet," I said. "I never know what to get."

He shrugged. "I just give, like that wedding day before yesterday, I just put a hundred-dollar bill in a card."

The restaurant was quiet, each table lit with a febrile candle in a glass bowl. The walls were windows to the garden and tiered hills of grapevines. It was a dignified crowd, at ripe middle age, the men in suits, the women in deep gem-colored clothes, their hair as neatly in place as the fitted feathers of birds. Two ladies, I saw, from their reflections in the long window, were wearing hats.

We ate and drank and he told stories about his love affair with the woman named Elizabeth. "She would like to meet you," he said.

"Invite her tomorrow night."

"Oh, she'd love to come," he said.

I was very drunk. I went to the bathroom and tottered on the carpet in my heels. The air was soft and dark, blunting movement. As I stood for a moment, looking over the tables, the people's movements, the men's in black and white and the women's lush color, seemed undulant, aquatic. In the bathroom, I touched my hand to the wall and turned off the light, and let my head hang between my knees. I put water on my face.

The food was so good.

Later, when the tall waiter brought the bill, my father had to say, "Excuse me, but there has been some misunderstanding. I spoke to Judith Nelson in the publicity office and she invited us here as her guests." He gave the waiter his card.

"Of course," the dour man said. "I'm sorry for the confusion."

After he'd gone, my father said, "He's first rate. Absolutely first rate. If I ever start a restaurant I'd come here and hire him. I would."

He left the waiter a hundred-dollar tip.

I COULD BARELY OPEN my room lock with the key. I locked it again on the inside as soon as I shut the door. He was in the suite on the left.

The next morning I slept late. I decided to do better today with my questions. This was the last day. And I didn't want to have too many more vacations like this. Chatting, talking about how great he was. Hearing about him and his mistress.

We were planning to tour a vineyard and then drive through Marin County back to San Francisco. The vineyard was like an office. We were the only people there who weren't at their job. They asked us to wait awhile and look around at their pictures on the wall. Then they poured us tastes of wine. I refused to touch any. I'd had too much to drink the night before.

And then in the car to Marin, I started asking.

I wondered if he had ever stood in a drugstore by the tall racks of flowered greeting cards and remembered me. And if he did think of me, what stopped his hand, what stalled the mail, tricked the telephone into silence. It was going to be too easy to blame Uta. She was easy enough to blame. But if she could tilt him, then the weight of a feather could, the stray beautiful seeds of a dandelion weed.

"Dad, all these women you had affairs with, like Elizabeth and

Rilella, did they ever ask you if you had children? And what did you say?"

"I told them I had a daughter."

"And when they asked, did that make you think of me and think of calling me? And since you didn't, what stopped you?"

"I didn't think of it in that way. I knew you existed. I knew you were somewhere in California."

In Sausalito we stopped for lunch. I wasn't hungry, but we sat by the windows onto the serene bay, where colored sailboats with neat white sails lolled on the evenly ridged water.

"Why were you unlisted?"

He shrugged. "Why be listed?"

I could shrug too. "Maybe because your kid might have tried to call you."

"You have every right to be mad at me and your mother, Mayan," he said. "More at me." He sounded tired, impatient. But that wasn't enough. To me then that was nothing.

"You don't seem to want to talk about any of this."

"I can't take this kind of confrontation. I need time to reflect."

"Well, I've been reflecting twenty-nine years. I know what I want to know. You must have wondered about me too. So did you?"

"I wanted to close that door, forget about it."

"Did you think you'd see me again?"

"Yes."

"Would you have done anything to find me?"

"Yes."

"When?"

"I don't know. But I would have."

"Now? In twenty more years?"

"I can't answer that."

"You know, we have a problem, Dad, because I have these questions and as nice as it is to go to restaurants and everything, this has really got to come first."

"I don't think whatever I'm going to tell you, you'll find excusable."

"Why is that?"

"Because you are preconditioned."

"By who?"

"By your mother."

"And whose fault is that?"

"Why did you find me?" Now he was angry, as if why would I care to find him if I didn't want to join his shrunken lame chorus telling him again and again that he was still, despite all evidence on the earth, a great man.

"I wanted to hear your side."

"And now I—" He faltered with his hands.

"You don't have a side."

"No. I have a side, but as I said before, you are preconditioned."

"Do you think it's that I'm preconditioned or that your actions are inexcusable?"

"Maybe a little of both."

He was bored with this, tired of me. This was not what he had wanted to have a daughter for.

We sat in silence and chewed our fruit.

"I knew your mother was a difficult person, but I never thought that she would not be a good mother with you. She didn't let me touch you or hold you or change you. She was obsessed with you. Fine, I thought, you want it you can have it."

We were walking back to the car. "Dad, I've been thinking, I like the clock, but you don't really know my taste and that's okay, there's no reason why you would, but what I'd really like more from you is something to wear, like jewelry."

"All right, that's fine, darling, I'd rather exchange it than you just take it and throw it out."

IN SAN FRANCISCO, we drove right to the restaurant we were going to eat in that night. He had the whole two days planned in terms of restaurants. He had already called his mistress and invited her. He picked the table he wanted and tipped the waitress some amount I couldn't see so she would make sure we got that table. Probably a hundred dollars.

I was hoping he would just take the clock back with him home and return it later, on his own, and that we could go right to Tiffany's and look at pearls, but we left the car at the restaurant and took a taxi to Macy's.

Returning the glass clock took a long time. We had to go up to the housewares department, a long expanse of china and cutlery. Finally, they gave him back cash. The clock had cost a hundred dollars.

"Well where do you want to go now?" he said to me.

"I'd like to look at pearls," I said. "Let's try Tiffany's."

He snorted. "There's no Tiffany in San Francisco. The only Tiffany is in New York."

"No, they have one here. I'm pretty sure they do." I was absolutely sure and in fact I had their address in my pocket, but we made a show of asking a man behind the counter. He told us it was three blocks away.

We rode the escalator back down to the main floor and then walked past the long glass cases of costume jewelry.

"And you don't want to look here for pearls?"

"No. I don't trust Macy's with pearls."

He said nothing but just followed me. I didn't care anymore. I was after one thing. I walked with an uphill hiking energy. He was falling behind in his suede boots. The sky above us was one of movement, clouds in procession to the sea. It was a city of Asians, but Asians who looked and were American. The gates of Chinatown waited on top of the hill we were climbing. The glass doors of Tiffany's reflected the loft afternoon sky.

I found the pearl counter and he loitered behind, hands in pockets. I asked a woman about pearls. She looked at us and didn't even take them out of the case. I asked what the smallest ones started at, for the string that went just around the neck.

"They start at nine hundred," she said, "and they're very good quality pearls." I stood looking at them inside the case, set into a wall. They hung them in a cache, there must have been forty strands of them.

He shuffled behind, bored, like someone's little brother, brought along with his mother and sisters to stores that held no interest for him.

Finally we went out.

On the sidewalk I said, "So Dad, do you have a price limit for this birthday present?"

"I'll give you five hundred dollars. You do what you want with it."

I dragged him to a dress store. I didn't even know what I was doing anymore. But the afternoon was round ahead of us and this was a store Emily had said was the best in San Francisco. It was all new designers she'd said. French. Japanese. SoHo-ish, she'd said.

Here he lurked around too. I would pull a jacket out from the metal rack and just study it. They were having a sale. Right away, I found a dress I'd seen in New York with Emily. It was beautiful, six hundred dollars, marked down from more. I'd never spent anything near this much on clothes, but right away I knew I wanted it. But I kept looking, just to browse.

"Look at that woman's shoes," my father said pointing. "They're like the old shoes my grandmother wore, back in Egypt."

"Yeah, those are in fashion nowdays. Everybody wears those."

"I can't believe you think those are all right."

I tried on a hat. "I like this," I said. He picked up a price tag and hissed through his teeth. "Two hundred dollars for this! You're crazy. I wouldn't pay fifteen cents for this."

I shrugged. I moved towards the jewelry. These were handmade, wilder things.

"I can't believe the stuff in this store and what they're asking." He sidled up and whispered in my ear. "This is ugly." I cannot describe his voice then. It was explosive, almost obscene. "Your mother always had elegant taste in dress and clothes and I would have thought you might've inherited it, but I see you didn't. You like all this stuff that is ugly."

I knew then, he was saying things I would not forget.

When I tried on the dress I liked, he conceded that it was almost elegant. He said I should try and bargain with the saleswoman. But I wouldn't. He gave me five hundred dollars cash and I charged the extra hundred on my credit card.

The woman said I wouldn't have to pay sales tax, if she sent it to me in New York.

"But don't you want to wear it tonight, Mayan?" he said. He wanted to show his mistress that he'd bought me something. Or invested in the purchase.

We finally settled: We said I would wear the dress that night, and then I'd bring it back and the woman would ship it to me at home. She didn't charge me the tax. Of course this was a lie. I was leaving the next morning. Stevie Howard was taking me to the airport.

Outside, with the sky still high and almost foreign, banners of wind cornering up from the small ratchety streets, the paper bag with the dress knocking lightly against my thigh, I said, "I hope she doesn't do anything when I don't bring it back."

"No, it was understood. That was her way of making it clear."

I wasn't so sure. And it was easy for him to dismiss it. His money was cash. They had my credit-card number.

And in fact, about a month later, I received a call in New York from the store.

WE STILL HAD HOURS before dinner and there was really nothing to do. We walked around, tending towards the restaurant. He wanted to find a coffee shop or a bar but this was the financial district and everything was closed. We kept walking aimlessly, with no more to say.

"You should just be lucky you weren't around all these years. That's a lot of what being a father is, is buying dresses."

"I guess so, huh?"

I had the feeling we'd both already made final decisions about each other.

We settled on a little outdoor bench and I left him there and went across the street to the phone booth. I called Jordan in New York.

"Just remember," he said. "*You* found *him.*"

"You helped."

We talked a long time and I watched him, a solitary figure, sitting with his legs crossed by a fountain.

Later we went to the restaurant where we each took our dinner clothes into the bathrooms and changed there. I couldn't resist pointing out the one waitress's shoes. She was a pretty girl, no more than nineteen.

"Well that I can see," he said, "because she's working and it's for comfort. There's a practical reason."

Then his mistress walked in and I saw right away, not that she looked like my mother, only taller, but that she was wearing large, generous pearls.

14

EVERY TIME HE CALLED, I asked him about the letter he said he'd send. I was pretty relentless. I just need to know, I kept saying.

Finally, five months later, it came.

Dear Mayan,

Who me?

That's what I really want to write to you, darling. With all your questions. When I was a child in Alexandria growing up, I was the youngest of four, and I remember that feeling, when my mother came into the room or my older sisters or my teachers in school. Who me? I wanted to hide in the well or behind coats in the closet, I'm thinking they got the wrong guy.

All I can say in answer to your question is, It had nothing to do with you. It had nothing to do with you at all. I haven't been all I wanted in my life. You get to a certain age, you want to turn the clock back and you can't.

I try and sit down and write you a letter about my life, but the funny thing is too, Mayan, I don't remember much from the time I came here. Hardly anything at all. I remember Egypt and my childhood much more clearly.

I think, really, I never felt at home here. The men when they get together and talk and make jokes, I never laugh at the same things. With American men. When my brother-in-law came over before he died and now with the nephews, we laugh at the same things.

You asked me about your name. You know, Mayan, I come from a family a thousand years old in Egypt and when I came to this country I got a job in that tie shop and they gave me a new name. First of all you weren't allowed ever to tell a customer your last name. You were supposed to be just John of Countess Mara. Or Mike. They called me Mike. And after a while I got used to it. It was like having a good costume at a costume ball.

But your name was always Atassi. A name is something you give your children. Maybe the most important thing. You had no right to change it, Mayan. Your mother was wrong to do that.

You know I was named after the great prophet, and our clan, the Atassis, was supposed to be descended from him. I don't know if I believe that or not. But we are an old family, it's not like these Saudis or these Kuwaitis you see now who are really two generations away from a tent. My family, Mayan, was a big family, nothing like here. It was eight hundred, nine hundred people. Imagine like the Mafia but all legitimate, all highly placed in the government.

I still remember the house I was born in. It was built around a courtyard, so we had sun in the daytime and then stars. Any hour of the day or night we heard water from the fountain. This was in my grandparents' village outside Alexandria.

You said you're sorry you can't buy your mother a house. Well, darling, don't feel too bad because that's just the way it is here. No one owns property but the real millionaires, in America. We rent too. They give me this condominium as part of my compensation for my work at the restaurant.

While my father was still alive, that was different. My father was really a patriarch and he built a virtual empire in his lifetime. When I was growing up, he owned many villages and about a thousand families, who worked the land. He planted a variety of food crops, but after the war it was all cotton. That's what really made him rich.

My father was the tallest man most people had ever seen. You know, Egypt is not like here—it doesn't grow those giants. Arabs are small-boned generally, delicate. But my father was 6'6" and he stood perfectly straight, his spine erect even on a camel or a horse.

I think it helped him in his business. People looked up to him and trusted him. And they were afraid of him too. I don't think the people who work for me feel frightened. They tell me their problems and their dreams.

We didn't see our father much at home. He spent most of his time working. He woke up at dawn, rode his horse out to his villages. In the late afternoon he'd ride back, change into western clothes to do whatever business he had to conduct.

He was always good with numbers. He'd sit in his office with a cup of Turkish coffee and an abacus, and we weren't supposed to disturb him. That was when he was supposed to be making us our millions. He was an extraordinarily healthy person who never smoked or drank. And never, I believe, did he have relations with women.

Even when we got a Ford with a chauffeur, he still used his horse every day. The hours out in the desert, between his villages, were his happiness. Later, he went on the haj and he was always devout, but I think his real religion was out in the desert, horseback. He was never sick, never once saw a doctor, and he died in his sleep at the age of eighty-six.

So you come from some good genes for a long life.

My mother married him at age fourteen. He was a brilliant man, a bargainer, an opportunist. Their marriage was brokered by the elders, who kept an eye on "the blood" and still wanted Atassi brides for all the sons.

My mother was a different kind of person. She was very social. She had a high voice and the sound of her laughter annoyed him. She spent most of her energy watching three daughters and looking for husbands for them.

I always felt sorry for my sisters. They were intelligent and attractive, but their destinies were settled before they were born. They couldn't go away to university the way I could, and most of their lives at home were very limited, very watched. This was like jail. They could never go out and taste life on their own. Marriage was their only way out.

My oldest sister, Amina, married her first cousin who lived next door. Zohra married an Atassi from Cairo, who was feeble-minded. She didn't want him, but it was not her choice. Cleopatra, the youngest of the sisters, was always my favorite. She and I grew up together. Cleopatra had everything. She was beautiful, tall, smart, gracious. She loved people, was a kind person. If she had been born here, she could have been anything. But there she was married to a bureaucrat, a relative—older, conventional, boring.

It's like another life, really. Here I do my job, I get up at around nine or ten, I go to the restaurant, check on the morning shopping the sous chef did, I supervise his preparations for lunch. Then I work out at the gym for a few hours. I lift the weights. I'm working on my aerobics for our hiking next time. I'm just a guy working in a restaurant, trying to keep the food coming out looking like something and to avoid the bad cholesterol myself.

I'm going to give you a gorgeous wedding when the time comes. I know just how to do it. It's my business. I've given nine hundred, maybe a thousand weddings.

So you do your part now and find the guy.

You asked about money for your mother. I can't help you with that, darling. It wouldn't be fair to Uta. I have to think of her and of my own retirement. But Adele's probably not so bad off. I wouldn't worry about her so much. She's probably all right.

I can't do a lot of what you ask me. You're my daughter and I always loved you but I can't tell you much more than that. I can't stand all this confrontation.

Now if we were still in Egypt, everything would be different. I could give you whatever you want. You want a house for your mother. Sure, okay, no problem. If I'd have stayed I'd be running the country now. I really could have, with my connections, my family.

I'm telling you Mayan—I was the John F. Kennedy of Egypt.

Epilogue

IT'S OUT OF THE SKY.

What happened next is hard to explain because I became a different person.

Nothing begins absolutely in one instant. Beginnings renew themselves again and again, and what we remember as the beginning—helping the blind man—might only have been the first moment we understood what had already happened to us. But an ending can be instant and absolute, as small as the last match blown out by a breath.

The year I was twenty-eight I found my father. I hadn't seen him since I was a child, in grammar school. I did not know that he was alive.

And this was the end of many things.

For a long time before, I'd tried to figure out silly things. I had problems with my boyfriends and I knew that was somehow because of my father. In college, my boyfriend and I fought all the time. He blamed me and it was probably my fault. Once, it got so bad, we walked around the block again and again and when we came to his door, he wouldn't let me in. I fought to force his arms. Later, I felt terrible and wrote him a letter. I said I thought it was because my father had left on a Tuesday.

"Leave your father out of this," he said.

THERE ARE CERTAIN mysteries that should never be solved. Because they cannot be, they can only seem to be.

I don't know, honey, he said, his lip lifting a little and eyes crossed in consternation. I really don't know myself.

Why you are unwanted: that is the only question. In the end, you understand, that is always the question you came here to ask, you crossed the globe for, spent years of your life, and at the same time as you see his face hearing those words in your voice, you understand too, like something falling, that this is the one question no one can ever answer you.

They will talk. There is so much around the thing. Ruining castles, gardens, cities, work in a restaurant where all the night long fountains spoke the sound of hands running through coin.

But there is no answer. Never. You recognize what he tells you for what it is: the truth. He does not know. At that moment, you understand every time you have been lied to and every time a man told you this truth.

Once, in exasperation, Stevie broke out about Bud Edison. "He's not in love with you, no matter what he's saying, he's not in love. That's not the way somebody acts when they're in love."

I understood now, that is true.

"WHAT ANSWERS DO YOU WANT?" Stevie said. "What would make you happy?"

Something that sounded true, I said. But that wasn't it only. He wants to step in now. He has visions of walking me down the aisle at my wedding. You'd think I'd want that. I think when I dreamed of having a father, I wanted that. I wanted to just sort of have a father. As if you could just have a father.

I've got a life and he's in it. I think I feel the same things other girls with fathers feel, but in miniature. If you would have told me two years before I found him that you're going to find your father and he's going to want to spend a week with you on vacation, and you can only find two and a half days for him, I would have said, no way, any time my father would have for me I'd love.

MAYBE YOU'RE BETTER OFF, my grandmother said.

WHEN I FIRST RETURNED home it was spring. I took my bike out in the warm night and rode and rode. My tires were soft and wobbly from the winter inside. And air at the closed gas station was free. The wind, when it touched through my clothes, was still warm.

I was beginning at love. More than ever, I felt behind.

Was this or not? It was more fragile than the mission I'd thought was love. It hovered, on and around like a moth to a blossom, never exactly still. There's a certain way you feel in a nightgown with just panties on underneath, walking in the breeze. The tree leaves were ferny, light green and delicate against the sky.

Love can stun you still, I knew, but it was not that kind of bond. This was more fallen, of the earth, full of practicalities and chatter.

I began to see the underworld of night. Everyone else was there too, my friends, in the walls and corners.

But it is always a surrender.

I WOULD ALWAYS WONDER, how to love. And sometimes I felt, So this is it. This afternoon. We are sunburned from the beach and so it hurts to touch many places and the whole car smells of oil and crumbs, we are in the back seat, him behind me. My head on his chest, my knees bent up against the door. He had an arm around my front, the way you do, a kind of ornament of protection. His skin was a dark olive, changed from the sun to something redder, gold, and his hairs all over it, were black. He had, even a dark-skinned man, seven spaced freckles, and then over the bone by his wrist, the raised pink incline of a bite. His veins were pronounced beneath the skin running into his hands that I used to think too small but which were right now, strong, and the light caught the fingernail of his thumb as light does on fingernails so they shine, not shiny but mat light, the gleam of clouds with a moon behind.

I thought, we are still young. There is one minute left and then we will be dead.

Mai linn was in the front, driving, with her roommate. The car kept moving, we were near home, full of chores and obligations and whines of all kinds. There might be a message on the phone from my father. But I did not know him. His name would go on the list with the others. And now there is no more time.

The problem with forgiveness is there is never enough time.

I'LL NEVER REGRET finding him.

I had to find him to stop waiting. And as long as you look for them, you're looking in the wrong place.

MY MOTHER AND I only talked on the phone now. One day, she called
and left a message on my machine. "I'm calling because I'm moving
and I want to give you the post office–box number. I don't know
where I'm moving yet. Maybe in my car." With an accusing cry, she
hung up. The next time we talked, she was all optimism. "I'm going
on a trip all over the country," she told me. "I've saved up seventy
thousand dollars and I'm going to visit Tallahassee, and an island off
of Seattle, Washington, and Petoskey, Michigan, all these places I
have friends."

I mailed her letters, one every week. I was too old now to write letters I wouldn't send.

Finding him has once again left my mother and me alone. A thousand times in my life I have pictured her death. And now it is in a
different way. A hospital room lit with floods. We laugh. We are altogether there.

He gave us ourselves back in real light.

Does anyone ever love a person again the way they loved their
mother?

SOMETIMES I THOUGHT that anyone who can do it will and that the
only point is to get started as soon as possible because time, all our
time, is running out, and the depth of love is only known at the end,
from the other side of life.

I WAS FLYING AROUND the kitchen making a pie. I could do that. The
air had the soft polleny quality of fine white flour dust. I was rolling.
I'd rummaged through my pockets for all the dollars and bought the
expensive kind of champagne I knew. This was my way of apology.
I'd done something wrong and I was trying to make up.

Emily sat cross-legged, watching me, brushing her hair. Jordan was
over too. I was teaching him how to bake.

"Do you think it'll work?"

"It's look-what-you-get-when-I-hurt-you," Jordan said. "But you
get the pleasure of knowing you can hurt him. The profound pleasure. The exquisite pleasure."

It was true. I had plenty of energy for the makeup. My mother made up to me all my life. We had no rules. My mother meant to. It was like a lover exactly. The same way a child folds their arms and their lover reaches in and takes them apart, opens the limbs up to the world again.

Sometimes I was dumb in love.

I'm GLAD I FOUND HIM. I'll never regret that. But I know nothing I ever do in my life will be that hard again.

Light a match.

Blow it out.

It's hard to remember, after the end. This all happened very recently. Perhaps I will understand it better later.

I needed to stop looking. I'd lost time. I wanted other things in the world now.

Now I just thought of it less. Everyone had secrets. Everyone owned shame. While I was wincing over *What does your father do?*, Emory suffered from *Where'd you go to college?*, a question I inflicted, I suppose, as many times as the next person.

WHEN PEOPLE ASK ME, I say right away I'm half Arab.

"Which half?" people ask.

"Father."

I RAN INTO BUD EDISON at a party. I was talking about something and I said, my father. "Your father? You found your father?"

"Oh, yeah," I said. "I guess you knew me before all that, before I was looking for him. You knew me when my family was still almost normal."

"First, there was no before you started looking for your father. And second, normal, you and your mother normal? It was a fucking opera, Mayan."

I shrugged.

"Where'd you find him?"

"Modesto, California."

"What's he doing?"

"Running a restaurant."

"Middle Eastern?"

I smiled. He sent me a new menu a few months back, all excited because he'd added an Egyptian dish. It was tabouli. "No," I said. "Just a restaurant."

I received three more letters in Arabic from Ramadan that I never answered. Finally, at Christmas, I got a card in English. "I wish to see you again as soon as its posible did you Remember me who was help you for to buy carpet."

I HAD A LIST OF PEOPLE TO THANK. Venise King, Duke Kemp, Marion Werth, Timothy. More. Everyone wrote back but the old man upstairs. He started playing his television loud again. I moved out a year later and started a new life in building. But that whole time, he never spoke to me again. I guess some things, involving strangers, are too much to forgive.

"Remember how hard you looked?" Mai linn asked.

I do remember. But I'm still looking, just not there. I used to think, before I found him, that the sun or the moon had to be my father. And now I'm kind of back to that.

I still haven't found what I'm looking for. But I am more like anybody else.

Acknowledgments

I would like to thank the Guggenheim Foundation, the Whiting Prize, the Hodder Fellowship at Princeton University, Leon Botstein and the Bard Center Fellowship at Bard College, Yaddo and the MacDowell Colony, for support, both material and moral, during the writing of this book.

Many of my old friends read drafts of *The Lost Father* and contributed their committed attention and belief. I'm grateful especially to Robert Cohen, Jonathan Dee, my editor Gary Fisketjon, John D. Gray, Allan Gurganus, Peter Smith, Laura Truffaut, my agent Amanda Urban, Marie Behan, and Steve Wong. And I'd like to thank my husband, for everything.

A NOTE ON THE TYPE

This book was set in a version of a typeface called Baskerville. The face itself is a facsimile reproduction of types cast from molds made for John Baskerville (1706–1775) from his designs. Baskerville's original face was one of the forerunners of the type style known to printers as "modern face"—a "modern" of the period A.D. 1800.

Composed by University Graphics, Inc.,
Atlantic Highlands, New Jersey
Printed and bound by R. R. Donnelley & Sons,
Harrisonburg, Virginia
Designed by Virginia Tan